VOLUMES 3 & 4

WHAT MIGHT HAVE BEEN

WHAT MIGHT HAVE BEEN

VOLUMES 3 & 4

ALTERNATE WARS
ALTERNATE AMERICAS

EDITED BY
Gregory Benford &
Martin H. Greenberg

SPECTRA™

BANTAM BOOKS
NEW YORK • TORONTO • LONDON • SYDNEY • AUCKLAND

CONTENTS

Volume 3   ALTERNATE WARS   1
Volume 4   ALTERNATE AMERICAS   237

VOLUME 3

ALTERNATE WARS

CONTENTS

INTRODUCTION   5
Gregory Benford

AND WILD FOR TO HOLD   9
Nancy Kress

TUNDRA MOSS   50
F. M. Busby

WHEN FREE MEN SHALL STAND   70
Poul Anderson

ARMS AND THE WOMAN   95
James Morrow

READY FOR THE FATHERLAND   113
Harry Turtledove

THE TOMB   128
Jack McDevitt

TURPENTINE   143
Barry N. Malzberg

GODDARD'S PEOPLE   155
Allen Steele

MANASSAS, AGAIN   176
Gregory Benford

THE NUMBER OF THE SAND   190
George Zebrowski

IF LEE HAD NOT WON THE BATTLE
   OF GETTYSBURG   201
The Right Honourable Winston S.
   Churchill, M.P.
OVER THERE   215
Mike Resnick

INTRODUCTION

No matter how good a story might be, no one will continue reading it if a fistfight breaks out in the same room.

Conflict focuses the mind wonderfully. When we consider the possible variations of history, war looms as the obvious mechanism for decisive change.

I personally feel that inventions and scientific progress are the most effective ways of changing the world, and the most lasting, but they are usually not very dramatic. And one can usually argue that if Watt, say, had not invented the steam engine, somebody else would have done so rather soon after. (An interesting countercase is paper, invented once by a Chinese monk and never independently reinvented. The secret was eventually stolen by Arabs, who tortured the secret out of a Chinese papermaker.) Wars, on the other hand, often yield unique, quirky results. The fate of an entire society can hinge on a single line of infantry. Those who proclaim that wars never settle anything should ask the inhabitants of Carthage for their opinion, or perhaps the adherents of Nazi Germany.

To be sure, many conflicts do not prove truly decisive. The problem of Germany's role in modern Europe was settled by the Second World War, not by the First; or arguably, by the Cold War that followed. But World War I did disrupt the deep foundations of European society, beginning its erosion of influence—which may prove to be the deeper issue, historically.

Wars do often afford us a clear look at interesting questions. Poul Anderson's classic short story "Delenda Est" shows us a world where Carthage defeated Rome; often his Time Patrol has to patch up conflicts gone (from our point of view) awry. In science fiction, alternative outcomes for World War II and the American Civil War top the list of most-studied events. (We earlier collected the notable Axis-triumph short stories in *Hitler Victorious*.) Like most science fiction, this view of history expresses an American outlook.

Probably the best novel that treats alternative wars is Ward Moore's *Bring the Jubilee*, which recalls life in the twenty-six states after Lee won at Gettysburg. It portrays a defeated, backwater North and a rigid South. Things have generally gone badly abroad, for the world missed the revolutionary impact of the United States. This allowed Moore to use a utopian-didactic mode, commenting indirectly on the crucial role of the War of Secession in our country, and of the United States in the world. To my taste it is immensely satisfying, packed with detail, precise in its ideas and plotting, rich in feeling for its era. The best World War II alternative novel is probably Brad Linaweaver's *Moon of Ice*, in which the Nazis do get the atomic bomb.

In assembling this collection of original studies of alternative wars, we have tried to span a wide range of outcomes. World War II gets the expected attention in "Tundra Moss," "Goddard's People," and "Ready for the Fatherland," which differ markedly in viewpoint and ambience. "Arms and the Woman" and "The Number of the Sand" consider ancient conflicts, each with an interesting, fresh spin.

Each author takes a different tack. Indeed, "The Number of the Sand" explicitly shows us the infinite possibilities implied by the Everett model of quantum mechanics, in which every physical event yields a spectrum of outcomes—with an entire alternative universe to suit.

Nancy Kress reflects on just what war means to us, and what the power to "correct" the past would mean, in a strong story, "And Wild for to Hold." It forms an interesting counterpoint with the fevered remembrance (for he was there) of Barry N. Malzberg for the greatest year of domestic violence in our time: 1968. An American propensity for foreign engagements, and their often unanticipated effect on us, appear as well in "Over There." Some alternatives, no matter how gaudy, may not add up to much.

I could scarcely neglect what my grandmother called the War of Northern Aggression. My own story here uses a vastly different context for a civil war that might have resulted from a Roman Empire that survived well through the 1200s. I argue that in many ways we would have advanced farther technologically, and it would have been a better world—though not one without uncomfortable resonances with our own. The Civil War was a breakdown of our greatest skill: compromise. We will need it again.

"The Tomb" considers the outcome if events in the closing acts of Roman history had gone differently—and makes a poignant point about the fate of historians as well. The breakup of empires and the fall of great nations are not always bad news, however. Poul Anderson portrays in evocative prose how the fresh, young United States would have fared if it had been faced with a far more powerful France, one that did not sell off the Louisiana Territory for quick cash and thereafter leave the distant revolutionaries alone. He reflects an opinion many have of the United States—that we have been not so much wily, savvy, and brave but instead, just plain lucky.

Bring the Jubilee was not the first study of an alternative American Civil War. For the most intriguing precursor to it, I have reached far back into 1931, when a politician many considered permanently finished as a major figure was struggling along, ignored in Parliament, making ends meet with his pen. He wrote histories, current commentary, and just about any odd free-lance piece he could. The diligent J. C. Squire commissioned a short essay from this back-bench figure for *If It Had Happened Otherwise: Lapses into Imaginary History*. (A curious word choice; I find historical speculations do not make anything "lapse" but rather illuminate.) The rest, as they say, is history.

Squire produced a remarkable book of rather scholarly essays by such noted literary figures as Belloc, Chesterton, and Harold Nicholson. It remains the classic essay collection of its kind. My favorite of them all is the piece that concludes this volume. World War I dominated the minds of many in 1931, and this vision of a Southern victory at Gettysburg performs the unusual feat of projecting a better world than our real one. I personally do not find the argument quite compelling, but it is fun, well done, and worth considering. It expresses a wish that a decade later animated history itself, at the hands of its author.

That is the purpose of such fiction, whether couched in overt drama or in the pseudofactual essay style. War is inevitably a calamity for some. Pondering its true impact is the obligation of all.

GREGORY BENFORD

AND WILD FOR TO HOLD

Nancy Kress

The demon came to her first in the long gallery at Hever Castle. She had gone there to watch Henry ride away, magnificent on his huge charger, the horse's legs barely visible through the summer dust raised by the king's entourage. But Henry himself was visible. He rose in his stirrups to half-turn his gaze back to the manor house, searching its sun-glazed windows to see if she watched. The spurned lover, riding off, watching over his shoulder the effect he himself made. She knew just how his eyes would look, small blue eyes under the curling red-gold hair. Mournful. Shrewd. Undeterred.

Anne Boleyn was not moved. Let him ride. She had not wanted him at Hever in the first place.

As she turned from the gallery window, a glint of light in the far corner caught her eye, and there for the first time was the demon.

It was made all of light, which did not surprise her. Was not Satan himself called Lucifer? The light was square, a perfectly square box such as no light had ever been before. Anne crossed herself and stepped forward. The box of light brightened, then winked out.

Anne stood perfectly still. She was not afraid; very little made her afraid. But nonetheless she crossed herself again and uttered a prayer. It would be unfortunate if a demon took up residence at Hever. Demons could be dangerous.

Like kings.

Lambert half-turned from her console toward Culhane, working across the room. "Culhane—they said she was a witch."

"Yes? So?" Culhane said. "In the 1500s they said any powerful woman was a witch."

"No, it was more. They said it *before* she became powerful." Culhane didn't answer. After a moment Lambert said quietly, "The Rahvoli equations keep flagging her."

Culhane grew very still. Finally he said, "Let me see."

He crossed the bare, small room to Lambert's console. She steadied the picture on the central square. At the moment the console appeared in this location as a series of interlocking squares mounting from floor to ceiling. Some of the squares were solid real-time alloys; some were holo simulations; some were not there at all, neither in space nor time, although they appeared to be. The project focus square, which *was* there, said:

TIME RESCUE PROJECT
UNITED FEDERATION OF UPPER SLIB, EARTH
FOCUS: ANNE BOLEYN
        HEVER CASTLE, KENT ENGLAND, EUROPE
        1525: 645:89:3
CHURCH OF THE HOLY HOSTAGE TEMPORARY
PERMIT #4592

In the time-jump square was framed a young girl, dark hair just visible below her coif, her hand arrested at her long, slender neck in the act of signing the cross.

Lambert said, as if to herself, "She considered herself a good Catholic."

Culhane stared at the image. His head had been freshly shaved, in honor of his promotion to project head. He wore, Lambert thought, his new importance as if it were a fragile implant, liable to be rejected. She found that touching.

Lambert said, "The Rahvoli probability is .798. She's a definite key."

Culhane sucked in his cheeks. The dye on them had barely dried. He said, "So is the other. I think we should talk to Brill."

The serving women had finally left. The priests had left, the doctors, the courtiers, the nurses, taking with them the baby. Even Henry had left, gone . . . where? To play cards with Harry Norris? To his latest mistress? Never mind—they had all at last left her alone.

A girl.

Anne rolled over in her bed and pounded her fists on the pillow. A girl. Not a prince, not the son that England needed, that *she* needed . . . a girl. And Henry growing colder every day, she could feel it, he no longer desired her, no longer loved her. He would bed with her—oh, that, most certainly, if it would get him his boy, but her power was going. Was gone. The power she had hated, despised, but had used nonetheless because it was there and Henry should feel it, as he had made her feel his power over and over again . . . her power was going. She was queen of England, but her power was slipping away like the Thames at ebb tide, and she just as helpless to stop it as to stop the tide itself. The only thing that could have preserved her power was a son. And she had borne a girl. Strong, lusty, with Henry's own red, curling hair . . . but a girl.

Anne rolled over on her back, painfully. Elizabeth was already a month old, but everything in Anne hurt. She had contracted white-leg, so much less dreaded than childbed fever but still weakening, and for the whole month had not left her bedchamber. Servants and ladies and musicians came and went, while Anne lay feverish, trying to plan. . . . Henry had as yet made no move. He had even seemed to take the baby's sex well: "She seems a lusty wench. I pray God will send her a brother in the same good shape." But Anne knew. She always knew. She had known when Henry's eye first fell upon her. Had known to a shade the exact intensity of his longing during the nine years she had kept him waiting: nine years of celibacy, of denial. She had known the exact moment when that hard mind behind the small blue eyes had decided: *It is worth it. I will divorce Katherine and make her queen.* Anne had known before he did when he decided it had all been a mistake. The price for making her queen had been too high. She was not worth it. Unless she gave him a son.

And if she did not . . .

In the darkness Anne squeezed her eyes shut. This was but an attack of childbed vapors; it signified nothing. She was never afraid, not she. This was only a night terror, and when she opened her eyes it would pass, because it must. She must go on fighting, must get herself heavy with a son, must safeguard her crown. And her daughter. There was no one else to do it for her, and there was no way out.

When she opened her eyes a demon, shaped like a square of light, glowed in the corner of the curtained bedchamber.

Lambert dipped her head respectfully as the high priest passed.

She was tall and wore no external augments. Eyes, arms, ears, shaved head, legs under the gray-green ceremonial robe—all were her own, as required by the charter of the Church of the Holy Hostage. Lambert had heard a rumor that before her election to high priest she had had brilliant, violet-augmented eyes and gamma-strength arms, but on her election had had both removed and the originals restored. The free representative of all the hostages in the solar system could not walk around enjoying high-maintenance augments. Hostages could, of course, but the person in charge of their spiritual and material welfare must appear human to any hostage she chose to visit. A four-handed spacer held in a free-fall chamber on Mars must find the high priest as human as did a genetically altered flier of Ipsu being held hostage by the New Trien Republic. The only way to do that was to forego external augments.

Internals, of course, were a different thing.

Beside the high priest walked the director of the Time Research Institute, Toshio Brill. No ban on externals for *him*: Brill wore gold-plated sensors in his shaved black head, a display Lambert found slightly ostentatious. Also puzzling: Brill was not ordinarily a flamboyant man. Perhaps he was differentiating himself from Her Holiness. Behind Brill his project heads, including Culhane, stood silent, not speaking unless spoken to. Culhane looked nervous: He was ambitious, Lambert knew. She sometimes wondered why she was not.

"So far I am impressed," the high priest said. "Impeccable hostage conditions on the material side."

Brill murmured, "Of course, the spiritual is difficult. The three hostages are so different from each other, and even for culture specialists and historians . . . the hostages arrive here very upset."

"As would you or I," the high priest said, not smiling, "in similar circumstances."

"Yes, Your Holiness."

"And now you wish to add a fourth hostage, from a fourth time stream."

"Yes."

The high priest looked slowly around at the main console; Lambert noticed that she looked right past the time-jump square itself. Not trained in peripheral vision techniques. But she looked a long time at the stasis square. They all did; outsiders were unduly fascinated by the idea that the whole building existed between time streams. Or maybe Her Holiness merely objected to the fact that the Time Research Institute, like some larger but hardly richer institutions, was exempt from the all-world taxation that supported the Church. Real-estate outside time was also outside taxation.

The high priest said, "I cannot give permission for such a political disruption without understanding fully every possible detail. Tell me again."

Lambert hid a grin. The high priest did not need to hear it again. She knew the whole argument, had pored over it for days, most likely, with her advisers. And she would agree; why wouldn't she? It could only add to her power. Brill knew that. He was being asked to explain only to show that the high priest could force him to do it, again and again, until she—not he—decided the explanation was sufficient and the Church of the Holy Hostage issued a permanent hostage permit to hold one Anne Boleyn, of England Time Delta, for the altruistic purpose of preventing a demonstrable, Class One war.

Brill showed no outward recognition that he was being humbled. "Your Holiness, this woman is a fulcrum. The Rahvoli equations, developed in the last century by—"

"I know the Rahvoli equations," the high priest said. And smiled sweetly.

"Then Your Holiness knows that any person identified by the equations as a fulcrum is directly responsible for the course of history. Even if he or she seems powerless in local time. Mistress Boleyn was the second wife of Henry the Eighth of England. In order to marry her, he divorced his first wife, Katherine of Aragon, and in order to do that, he took all of England out of the Catholic Church. Protestantism was—"

"And what again was that?" Her Holiness said, and even Culhane glanced sideways at Lambert, appalled. The high priest was playing. With a *research director*. Lambert hid her smile. Did Culhane know that high seriousness opened one to the charge of pomposity? Probably not.

"Protestantism was another branch of 'Christianity,'" the director said patiently. So far, by refusing to be provoked, he was winning. "It was warlike, as was Catholicism. In 1642 various branches of Protestantism were contending for political power within England, as was a Catholic faction. King Charles was Catholic, in fact. Contention led to civil war. Thousands of people died fighting, starved to death, were hung as traitors, were tortured as betrayers..."

Lambert saw Her Holiness wince. She must hear this all the time, Lambert thought. What else was her office for? Yet the wince looked genuine.

Brill pressed his point. "Children were reduced to eating rats to survive. In Cornwall, rebels' hands and feet were cut off, gibbets were erected in market squares and men hung on them alive, and—"

"Enough," the high priest said. "This is why the Church exists. To promote the holy hostages that prevent war."

"And that is what we wish to do," Brill said swiftly, "in other time streams, now that our own has been brought to peace. In Stream Delta, which has only reached the sixteenth century—Your Holiness knows that each stream progresses at a different relative rate—"

The high priest made a gesture of impatience.

"—the woman Anne Boleyn is the fulcrum. If she can be taken hostage after the birth of her daughter Elizabeth, who will act throughout a very long reign to preserve peace, and before Henry declares the Act of Supremacy that opens the door to religious divisiveness in England, we can prevent great loss of life. The Rahvoli equations show a 79.8% probability that history will be changed in the direction of greater peace, right up through the following two centuries. Religious wars often—"

"There are other, bloodier religious wars to prevent than the English civil war."

"True, Your Holiness," the director said humbly. At least it looked like humility to Lambert. "But ours is a young science. Identifying other time streams, focusing on one, identifying historical fulcra—it is such a new science. We do what we can, in the name of peace."

Everyone in the room looked pious. Lambert hid a smile. In the name of peace—and of prestigious scientific research, attended by rich financial support and richer academic reputations.

"And it is peace we seek," Brill pressed, "as much as the Church itself does. With a permanent permit to take Anne Boleyn hostage, we can save countless lives in this other time stream, just as the Church preserves peace in our own."

The high priest played with the sleeve of her robe. Lambert could not see her face. But when she looked up, she was smiling.

"I'll recommend to the All-World Forum that your hostage permit be granted, Director. I will return in two months to make an official check on the holy hostage."

Brill, Lambert saw, didn't quite stop himself in time from frowning. "Two months? But with the entire solar system of hostages to supervise—"

"Two months, Director," Her Holiness said. "The week before the All-World Forum convenes to vote on revenue and taxation."

"I—"

"Now I would like to inspect the three holy hostages you already hold for the altruistic prevention of war."

Later, Culhane said to Lambert, "He did not explain it very well. It could have been made so much more urgent . . . it *is* urgent. Those bodies rotting in Cornwall . . ." He shuddered.

Lambert looked at him. "You care. You genuinely do."

He looked back at her in astonishment. "And you don't? You must, to work on this project!"

"I care," Lambert said. "But not like that."

"Like what?"

She tried to clarify it for him, for herself. "The bodies rotting . . . I see them. But it's not our own history—"

"What does that matter? They're still human!"

He was so earnest. Intensity burned on him like skin tinglers. Did Culhane even use skin tinglers? Lambert wondered. Fellow researchers spoke of him as an ascetic, giving all his energy, all his time to the project. A woman in his domicile had told Lambert he even lived chaste, doing a voluntary celibacy mission for the entire length of his research grant. Lambert had never met anyone who actually did that. It was intriguing.

She said, "Are you thinking of the priesthood once the project is over, Culhane?"

He flushed. Color mounted from the dyed cheeks, light blue since he had been promoted to project head, to pink on the fine skin of his shaved temples.

"I'm thinking of it."

"And doing a celibacy mission now?"

"Yes. Why?" His tone was belligerent: A celibacy mission was slightly old-fashioned. Lambert studied his body: tall, well-made, strong. Augments? Muscular, maybe. He had beautiful muscles.

"No reason," she said, bending back to her console until she heard him walk away.

The demon advanced. Anne, lying feeble on her curtained bed, tried to call out. But her voice would not come, and who would hear her anyway? The bedclothes were thick, muffling sound; her ladies would all have retired for the night, alone or otherwise; the guards would be drinking the ale Henry had provided all of London to celebrate Elizabeth's christening. And Henry... he was not beside her. She had failed him of his son.

"Be gone," she said weakly to the demon. It moved closer.

They had called her a witch. Because of her little sixth finger, because of the dog named Urian, because she had kept Henry under her spell so long without bedding him. But if I were really a witch, she thought, I could send this demon away. More: I could hold Henry, could keep him from watching that whey-faced Jane Seymour, could keep him in my bed. . . . She was not a witch.

Therefore, it followed that there was nothing she could do about this demon. If it was come for her, it was come. If Satan, Master of Lies, was decided to have her, to punish her for taking the husband of another woman, and for... How much could demons know?

"This was all none of my wishing," she said aloud to the demon. "I wanted to marry someone else." The demon continued to advance.

Very well, then, let it take her. She would not scream. She never had—she prided herself on it. Not when they had told her she could not marry Harry Percy. Not when she had been sent home from the court, peremptorily and without explanation. Not when she had discovered the explanation: Henry wished to have her out of London so he could bed his latest mistress away from Katherine's eyes. She had not screamed when a crowd of whores had burst into the palace where she was supping, demanding Nan Bullen, who they said was one of them. She had escaped across the Thames in a barge, and not a cry had escaped her lips. They had admired her for her courage: Wyatt, Norris, Weston, Henry himself. She would not scream now.

The box of light grew larger as it approached. She had just time to say to it, "I have been God's faithful and true servant, and my husband, the king's," before it was upon her.

"The place where a war starts," Lambert said to the faces assembled below her in the Hall of Time, "is long before the first missile, or the first bullet, or the first spear."

She looked down at the faces. It was part of her responsibility as an intern researcher to teach a class of young, some of whom would become historians. The class was always taught in the Hall of Time. The expense was enormous: keeping the hall in stasis for nearly an hour, bringing the students in through the force field, activating all the squares at once. Her lecture would be replayed for them later, when they could pay attention to it. Lambert did not blame them for barely glancing at her now. Why should they? The walls of the circular room, which were only there in a virtual sense, were lined with squares that were not really there at all. The squares showed actual, local-time scenes from wars that had been there, were there now, somewhere, in someone's reality.

Men died writhing in the mud, arrows through intestines and neck and groin, at Agincourt.

Women lay flung across the bloody bodies of their children at Cawnpore.

In the hot sun the flies crawled thick upon the split faces of the heroes of Marathon.

Figures staggered, their faces burned off, away from Hiroshima.

Breathing bodies, their perfect faces untouched and their brains turned to mush by spekaline, sat in orderly rows under the ripped dome on Io-One.

Only one face turned toward Lambert, jerked as if on a string, a boy with wide violet eyes brimming with anguish. Lambert obligingly started again.

"The place where a war starts is long before the first missile, or the first bullet, or the first spear. There are always many forces causing a war: economic, political, religious, cultural. Nonetheless, it is the great historical discovery of our time that if you trace each of these back—through the records, through the eyewitness accounts, through the entire burden of data only Rahvoli equations can handle—you come to a fulcrum. A single event or act or person. It is like a decision tree with a thousand thousand generations of decisions: Somewhere there was one first yes/no. The place where the war started and where it could have been prevented.

"The great surprise of time rescue work has been how often that place was female.

"Men fought wars, when there were wars. Men controlled the gold and the weapons and the tariffs and sea rights and religions that have caused wars, and the men controlled the bodies of other men who did the actual fighting. But men are men. They acted at the fulcrum of history, but often what tipped their actions one way or another was what they loved. A woman. A child. She became the passive, powerless weight he chose to lift, and the balance tipped. She, not he, is the branching place, where the decision tree splits and the war begins."

The boy with the violet eyes was still watching her. Lambert stayed silent until he turned to watch the squares—which was the reason he had been brought here. Then she watched him. Anguished, passionate, able to feel what war meant—he might be a good candidate for the time rescue team when his preliminary studies were done. He reminded her a little of Culhane.

Who right now, as project head, was interviewing the new hostage, not lecturing to children.

Lambert stifled her jealousy. It was unworthy. And shortsighted: She remembered what this glimpse of human misery had meant to her three years ago, when she was an historian candidate. She had had nightmares for weeks. She had thought the event was pivotal to her life, a dividing point past which she would never be the same person again. How could she? She had been shown the depths to which humanity, without the Church of the Holy Hostage and the All-World Concordance, could descend. Burning eye sockets, mutilated genitals, a general who stood on a hill and said, "How I love to see the arms and legs fly!" It had been shattering. She had been shattered, as the orientation intended she should be.

The boy with the violet eyes was crying. Lambert wanted to step down from the platform and go to him. She wanted to put her arms around him and hold his head against her shoulder... but was that because of compassion, or was that because of his violet eyes?

She said silently to him, without leaving the podium, *you will be all*

right. Human beings are not as mutable as you think. When this is over,
nothing permanent about you will have changed at all.

Anne opened her eyes. Satan leaned over her.

His head was shaved, and he wore strange garb of an ugly blue-green.
His cheeks were stained with dye. In one ear metal glittered and swung.
Anne crossed herself.

"Hello," Satan said, and the voice was not human.

She struggled to sit up; if this be damnation, she would not lie prone
for it. Her heart hammered in her throat. But the act of sitting brought
the Prince of Darkness into focus, and her eyes widened. He looked like
a man. Painted, made ugly, hung around with metal boxes that could be
tools of evil—but a man.

"My name is Culhane."

A man. And she had faced men. Bishops, nobles, Chancellor Wolsey.
She had outfaced Henry, Prince of England and France, Defender of the
Faith.

"Don't be frightened, Mistress Boleyn. I will explain to you where
you are and how you came to be here."

She saw now that the voice came not from his mouth, although his
mouth moved, but from the box hung around his neck. How could that
be? Was there then a demon in the box? But then she realized
something else, something real to hold on to.

"Do not call me Mistress Boleyn. Address me as Your Grace. I am the
queen."

The something that moved behind his eyes convinced her, finally, that
he was a mortal man. She was used to reading men's eyes. But why
should this one look at her like that? With pity? With admiration?

She struggled to stand, rising off the low pallet. It was carved of good
English oak. The room was paneled in dark wood and hung with
tapestries of embroidered wool. Small-paned windows shed brilliant
light over carved chairs, table, chest. On the table rested a writing desk
and a lute. Reassured, Anne pushed down the heavy cloth of her
nightshift and rose.

The man, seated on a low stool, rose, too. He was taller than
Henry—she had never seen a man taller than Henry—and superbly
muscled. A soldier? Fright fluttered again, and she put her hand to her
throat. This man, watching her—watching her *throat*. Was he then an
executioner? Was she under arrest, drugged and brought by some secret
method into the Tower of London? Had someone brought evidence
against her? Or was Henry that disappointed that she had not borne a
son that he was eager to supplant her already?

As steadily as she could, Anne walked to the window.

The Tower Bridge did not lie beyond in the sunshine. Nor the river, nor the gabled roofs of Greenwich Palace. Instead there was a sort of yard, with huge beasts of metal growling softly. On the grass naked young men and women jumped up and down, waving their arms, running in place and smiling and sweating as if they did not know either that they were uncovered or crazed.

Anne took firm hold of the windowsill. It was slippery in her hands, and she saw that it was not wood at all but some material made to resemble wood. She closed her eyes, then opened them. She was a queen. She had fought hard to become a queen, defending a virtue nobody believed she still had, against a man who claimed that to destroy that virtue was love. She had won, making the crown the price of her virtue. She had conquered a king, brought down a chancellor of England, outfaced a pope. She would not show fear to this executioner in this place of the damned, whatever it was.

She turned from the window, her head high. "Please begin your explanation, Master..."

"Culhane."

"Master Culhane. We are eager to hear what you have to say. And we do not like waiting."

She swept aside her long nightdress as if it were court dress and seated herself in the not-wooden chair carved like a throne.

"I am a hostage," Anne repeated. "In a time that has not yet happened."

From beside the window, Lambert watched. She was fascinated. Anne Boleyn had, according to Culhane's report, listened in silence to the entire explanation of the time rescue, that explanation so carefully crafted and revised a dozen times to fit what the sixteenth-century mind could understand of the twenty-second. Queen Anne had not become hysterical. She had not cried, nor fainted, nor professed disbelief. She had asked no questions. When Culhane had finished, she had requested, calmly and with staggering dignity, to see the ruler of this place, with his ministers. Toshio Brill, watching on monitor because the wisdom was that at first new hostages would find it easier to deal with one consistent researcher, had hastily summoned Lambert and two others. They had all dressed in the floor-length robes used for grand academic ceremonies and never else. And they had marched solemnly into the ersatz sixteenth-century room, bowing their heads.

Only their heads. No curtsies. Anne Boleyn was going to learn that no one curtsied anymore.

Covertly Lambert studied her, their fourth time hostage, so different from the other three. She had not risen from her chair, but even seated she was astonishingly tiny. Thin, delicate bones, great dark eyes, masses of silky black hair loose on her white nightdress. She was not pretty by the standards of this century; she had not even been counted pretty by the standards of her own. But she was compelling. Lambert had to give her that.

"And I am prisoner here," Anne Boleyn said. Lambert turned up her translator; the words were just familiar, but the accent so strange she could not catch them without electronic help.

"Not prisoner," the director said. "Hostage."

"Lord Brill, if I cannot leave, then I am a prisoner. Let us not mince words. I cannot leave this castle?"

"You cannot."

"Please address me as 'Your Grace.' Is there to be a ransom?"

"No, Your Grace. But because of your presence here thousands of men will live who would have otherwise died."

With a shock, Lambert saw Anne shrug; the deaths of thousands of men evidently did not interest her. It was true, then. They really were moral barbarians, even the women. The students should see this. That small shrug said more than all the battles viewed in squares. Lambert felt her sympathy for the abducted woman lessen, a physical sensation like the emptying of a bladder, and was relieved to feel it. It meant she, Lambert, still had her own moral sense.

"How long must I stay here?"

"For life, Your Grace," Brill said bluntly.

Anne made no reaction; her control was aweing.

"And how long will that be, Lord Brill?"

"No person knows the length of his or her life, Your Grace."

"But if you can read the future, as you claim, you must know what the length of mine would have been."

Lambert thought: We must not underestimate her. This hostage is not like the last one.

Brill said, with the same bluntness that honored Anne's comprehension—did she realize that?—"If we had not brought you here, you would have died May nineteenth, 1536."

"How?"

"It does not matter. You are no longer part of that future, and so now events there will—"

"*How?*"

Brill didn't answer.

Anne Boleyn rose and walked to the window, absurdly small, Lambert thought, in the trailing nightdress. Over her shoulder she said, "Is this castle in England?"

"No," Brill said. Lambert saw him exchange glances with Culhane.

"In France?"

"It is not in any place on Earth," Brill said, "although it can be entered from three places on Earth. It is outside of time."

She could not possibly have understood, but she said nothing, only went on staring out the window. Over her shoulder Lambert saw the exercise court, empty now, and the antimatter power generators. Two technicians crawled over them with a robot monitor. What did Anne Boleyn make of them?

"God alone knows if I had merited death," Anne said. Lambert saw Culhane start.

Brill stepped forward. "Your Grace—"

"Leave me now," she said without turning.

They did. Of course she would be monitored constantly—everything from brain scans to the output of her bowels. Although she would never know this. But if suicide was in that life-defying mind, it would not be possible. If Her Holiness ever learned of the suicide of a time hostage . . . Lambert's last glimpse before the door closed was of Anne Boleyn's back, still by the window, straight as a spear as she gazed out at antimatter power generators in a building in permanent stasis.

"Culhane, meeting in ten minutes," Brill said. Lambert guessed the time lapse was to let the director change into working clothes. Toshio Brill had come away from the interview with Anne Boleyn somehow diminished. He even looked shorter, although shouldn't her small stature have instead augmented his?

Culhane stood still in the corridor outside Anne's locked room (would she try the door?). His face was turned away from Lambert's. She said, "Culhane . . . You jumped a moment in there. When she said God alone knew if she had merited death."

"It was what she said at her trial," Culhane said. "When the verdict was announced. Almost the exact words."

He still had not moved so much as a muscle of that magnificent body. Lambert said, probing, "You found her impressive, then. Despite her scrawniness, and beyond the undeniable pathos of her situation."

He looked at her then, his eyes blazing: Culhane, the research engine. "I found her magnificent."

She never smiled. That was one of the things she knew they remarked upon among themselves: She had overheard them in the walled garden. *Anne Boleyn never smiles.* Alone, they did not call her Queen Anne, or

Her Grace, or even the Marquis of Rochford, the title Henry had conferred upon her, the only female peeress in her own right in all of England. No, they called her Anne Boleyn, as if the marriage to Henry had never happened, as if she had never borne Elizabeth. And they said she never smiled.

What cause was there to smile, in this place that was neither life nor death?

Anne stitched deftly at a piece of amber velvet. She was not badly treated. They had given her a servant, cloth to make dresses—she had always been clever with a needle, and the skill had not deserted her when she could afford to order any dresses she chose. They had given her books, the writing Latin but the pictures curiously flat, with no raised ink or painting. They let her go into any unlocked room in the castle, out to the gardens, into the yards. She was a holy hostage.

When the amber velvet gown was finished, she put it on. They let her have a mirror. A lute. Writing paper and quills. Whatever she asked for, as generous as Henry had been in the early days of his passion, when he had divided her from her love Harry Percy and had kept her loving hostage to his own fancy.

Cages came in many sizes. Many shapes. And, if what Master Culhane and the Lady Mary Lambert said was true, in many times.

"I am not a lady," Lady Lambert had protested. She needn't have bothered. Of course she was not a lady—she was a commoner, like the others, and so perverted was this place that the woman sounded insulted to be called a lady. Lambert did not like her, Anne knew, although she had not yet found out why. The woman was unsexed, like all of them, working on her books and machines all day, exercising naked with men who thus no more looked at their bodies than they would those of fellow soldiers in the roughest camp. So it pleased Anne to call Lambert a lady when she did not want to be one, as Anne was now so many things she had never wanted to be. "Anne Boleyn." Who never smiled.

"I will create you a Lady," she said to Lambert. "I confer on you the rank of baroness. Who will gainsay me? I am the queen, and in this place there is no king."

And Mary Lambert had stared at her with the unsexed bad manners of a common drab.

Anne knotted her thread and cut it with silver scissors. The gown was finished. She slipped it over her head and struggled with the buttons in the back, rather than call the stupid girl who was her servant. The girl could not even dress hair. Anne smoothed her hair herself, then looked critically at her reflection in the fine mirror they had brought her.

For a woman a month and a half from childbed, she looked strong. They had put medicines in her food, they said. Her complexion, that creamy dark skin that seldom varied in color, was well set off by the amber velvet. She had often worn amber, or tawny. Her hair, loose since she had no headdress and did not know how to make one, streamed over her shoulders. Her hands, long and slim despite the tiny extra finger, carried a rose brought to her by Master Culhane. She toyed with the rose to show off the beautiful hands, and lifted her head high.

She was going to have an audience with Her Holiness, a female pope. And she had a request to make.

"She will ask, Your Holiness, to be told the future. Her future, the one Anne Boleyn experienced in her own time stream, after the point we took her hostage to ours. And the future of England." Brill's face had darkened; Lambert could see that he hated this. To forewarn his political rival that a hostage would complain about her treatment. A *hostage*, that person turned sacred object through the sacrifice of personal freedom to global peace. When Tullio Amaden Koyushi had been hostage from Mars Three to the Republic of China, he had told the Church official in charge of his case that he was not being allowed sufficient exercise. The resulting intersystem furor had lost the Republic of China two trade contracts, both important. There was no other way to maintain the necessary reverence for the hostage political system. The Church of the Holy Hostage was powerful because it must be, if the solar system was to stay at peace. Brill knew that.

So did Her Holiness.

She wore full state robes today, gorgeous with hundreds of tiny mirrors sent to her by the grateful across all worlds. Her head was newly shaved. Perfect, synthetic jewels glittered in her ears. Listening to Brill's apology-in-advance, Her Holiness smiled. Lambert saw the smile, and even across the room she felt Brill's polite, concealed frustration.

"Then if this is so," Her Holiness said, "why cannot Lady Anne Boleyn be told her future? Hers and England's?"

Lambert knew that the high priest already knew the answer. She wanted to make Brill say it.

Brill said, "It is not thought wise, Your Holiness. If you remember, we did that once before."

"Ah, yes, your last hostage. I will see her, too, of course, on this visit. Has Queen Helen's condition improved?"

"No," Brill said shortly.

"And no therapeutic brain drugs or electronic treatments have helped? She still is insane from the shock of finding herself with us?"

"Nothing has helped."

"You understand how reluctant I was to let you proceed with another time rescue at all," Her Holiness said, and even Lambert stifled a gasp. The high priest did not make those determinations; only the All-World Forum could authorize or disallow a hostage-taking—across space *or* time. The Church of the Holy Hostage was responsible only for the inspection and continuation of permits granted by the Forum. For the high priest to claim political power she did not possess...

The director's eyes gleamed angrily. But before he could reply, the door opened and Culhane escorted in Anne Boleyn.

Lambert pressed her lips together tightly. The woman had sewn herself a gown, a sweeping, ridiculous confection of amber velvet so tight at the breasts and waist she must hardly be able to breathe. How had women conducted their lives in such trappings? The dress narrowed her waist to nearly nothing; above the square neckline her collarbones were delicate as a bird's. Culhane hovered beside her, huge and protective. Anne walked straight to the high priest, knelt, and raised her face.

She was looking for a ring to kiss.

Lambert didn't bother to hide her smile. A high priest wore no jewelry except earrings, ever. The pompous little hostage had made a social error, no doubt significant in her own time.

Anne smiled up at Her Holiness, the first time anyone had seen her smile at all. It changed her face, lighting it with mischief, lending luster to the great dark eyes. A phrase came to Lambert, penned by the poet Thomas Wyatt to describe his cousin Anne: *And wild for to hold, though I seem tame.*

Anne said, in that sprightly yet aloof manner that Lambert was coming to associate with her, "It seems, Your Holiness, that we have reached for what is not there. But the lack is ours, not yours, and we hope it will not be repeated in the request we come to make of you."

Direct. Graceful, even through the translator and despite the ludicrous imperial plural. Lambert glanced at Culhane, who was gazing down at Anne as at a rare and fragile flower. How could he? That skinny body, without muscle tone let alone augments, that plain face, the mole on her neck.... This was not the sixteenth century. Culhane was a fool.

As Thomas Wyatt had been. And Sir Harry Percy. And Henry, king of England. All caught not by beauty but by that strange elusive charm.

Her Holiness laughed. "Stand up, Your Grace. We don't kneel to officials here." *Your Grace.* The high priest always addressed hostages by the honorifics of their own state, but in this case it could only impede Anne's adjustment.

And what do I care about her adjustment? Lambert jeered at herself. Nothing. What I care about is Culhane's infatuation, and only because he rejected me first. Rejection, it seemed, was a great whetter of appetite—in any century.

Anne rose. Her Holiness said, "I'm going to ask you some questions, Your Grace. You are free to answer any way you wish. My function is to ensure that you are well treated and that the noble science of the prevention of war, which has made you a holy hostage, is also well served. Do you understand?"

"We do."

"Have you received everything you need for your material comfort?"

"Yes," Anne said.

"Have you received everything you've requested for your mental comfort? Books, objects of any description, company?"

"No," Anne said. Lambert saw Brill stiffen.

Her Holiness said, "No?"

"It is necessary for the comfort of our mind—and for our material comfort as well—to understand our situation as fully as possible. Any rational creature requires such understanding to reach ease of mind."

Brill said, "You have been told everything related to your situation. What you ask is to know about situations that now, because you are here, will never happen."

"Situations that *have* happened, Lord Brill, else no one could know of them. You could not."

"In *your* time stream they will not happen," Brill said. Lambert could hear the suppressed anger in his voice and wondered if the high priest could. Anne Boleyn couldn't know how serious it was to be charged by Her Holiness with a breach of hostage treatment. If Brill was ambitious— and why wouldn't he be?—such charges could hurt his future.

Anne said swiftly, "Our time is now your time. You have made it so. The situation was none of our choosing. And if your time is now ours, then surely we are entitled to the knowledge that accompanies our time." She looked at the high priest. "For the comfort of our mind."

Brill said, "Your Holiness—"

"No, Queen Anne is correct. Her argument is valid. You will designate a qualified researcher to answer any questions she has—any at all—about the life she might have had, or the course of events England took when the queen did not become a sacred hostage."

Brill nodded stiffly.

"Good-bye, Your Grace," Her Holiness said. "I shall return in two weeks to inspect your situation again."

Two weeks? The high priest was not due for another inspection for six months. Lambert glanced at Culhane to see his reaction to this blatant political fault-hunting, but he was gazing at the floor, to which Anne Boleyn had sunk in another of her embarrassing curtsies, the amber velvet of her skirts spread around her like gold.

They sent a commoner to explain her life to her, and the life she had lost. A commoner. And he had as well the nerve to be besotted with her. Anne always knew. She tolerated such fellows, like that upstart musician Smeaton, when they were useful to her. If this Master Culhane dared to make any sort of declaration, he would receive the same sort of snub Smeaton once had. Inferior persons should not look to be spoken to as noblemen.

He sat on a straight-backed chair in her tower room, looking humble enough, while Anne sat in the great carved chair with her hands tightly folded to keep them from shaking.

"Tell me how I came to die in 1536." God's blood! Had ever before there been such a sentence uttered?

Culhane said, "You were beheaded. Found guilty of treason." He stopped and flushed.

She knew, then. In a queen, there was one cause for a charge of treason. "He charged me with adultery. To remove me, so he could marry again."

"Yes."

"To Jane Seymour."

"Yes."

"Had I first given him a son?"

"No," Culhane said.

"Did Jane Seymour give him a son?"

"Yes. Edward the Sixth. But he died at sixteen, a few years after Henry."

There was vindication in that, but not enough to stem the sick feeling in her gut. Treason. And no son. . . . There must have been more than desire for the Seymour bitch. Henry must have hated her. Adultery. . .

"With whom?"

Again the oaf flushed. "With five men, Your Grace. Everyone knew the charges were false, created merely to excuse his own cuckoldry—even your enemies admitted such."

"Who were they?"

"Sir Henry Norris. Sir Francis Weston. William Brereton. Mark Smeaton. And... and your brother George."

For a moment she thought she would be sick. Each name fell like a blow, the last like the ax itself. George. Her beloved brother, so talented at music, so high-spirited and witty... Harry Norris, the king's friend. Weston and Brereton, young and lighthearted but always, to her, respectful and careful... and Mark Smeaton, the oaf made courtier because he could play the virginals.

The long, beautiful hands clutched the sides of the chair. But the moment passed, and she could say with dignity, "They denied the charges?"

"Smeaton confessed, but he was tortured into it. The others denied the charges completely. Harry Norris offered to defend your honor in single combat."

Yes, that was like Harry: so old-fashioned, so principled. She said, "They all died." It was not a question: If she had died for treason, they would have, too. And not alone; no one died alone. "Who else?"

Culhane said, "Maybe we should wait for the rest of this, Your—"

"Who else? My father?"

"No. Sir Thomas More, John Fisher—"

"More? For my..." She could not say *adultery*.

"Because he would not swear to the Oath of Supremacy, which made the king and not the pope head of the church in England. That act opened the door to religious dissension in England."

"It did not. The heretics were already strong in England. History cannot fault that to me!"

"Not as strong as they would become," Culhane said almost apologetically. "Queen Mary was known as Bloody Mary for burning heretics who used the Act of Supremacy to break from Rome— Your Grace! Are you all right... Anne?"

"Do not touch me," she said. Queen Mary. Then her own daughter Elizabeth had been disinherited, or killed.... Had Henry become so warped that he would kill a child? His own child? Unless he had come to believe...

She whispered, "Elizabeth?"

Comprehension flooded his eye. "Oh. No, Anne! No! Mary ruled first, as the elder, but when she died heirless, Elizabeth was only twenty-five. Elizabeth became the greatest ruler England had ever known! She ruled for forty-four years, and under her England became a great power."

The greatest ruler. Her baby Elizabeth. Anne could feel her hands unknotting on the ugly artificial chair. Henry had not repudiated Elizabeth, nor had her killed. She had become the greatest ruler England had ever known.

Culhane said, "This is why we thought it best not to tell you all this."

She said coldly, "I will be the judge of that."

"I'm sorry." He sat stiffly, hands dangling awkwardly between his knees. He looked like a plowman, like that oaf Smeaton.... She remembered what Henry had done, and rage returned.

"I stood accused. With five men... with George. And the charges were false." Something in his face changed. Anne faced him steadily. "Unless... were they false, Master Culhane? You who know so much of history. Does history say..." She could not finish. To beg for history's judgment from a man like this... no humiliation had ever been greater. Not even the Spanish ambassador, referring to her as "the concubine," had ever humiliated her so.

Culhane said carefully, "History is silent on the subject, Your Grace. What your conduct was... would have been... is known only to you."

"As it should be. It was... would have been... mine," she said viciously, mocking his tones perfectly. He looked at her like a wounded puppy, like that lout Smeaton when she had snubbed him. "Tell me this, Master Culhane. You have changed history as it would have been, you tell me. Will my daughter Elizabeth still become the greatest ruler England has ever seen—in *my* 'time stream'? Or will that be altered, too, by your quest for peace at any cost?"

"We don't know. I explained to you... We can only watch your time stream now as it unfolds. It had only reached October 1533, which is why after analyzing our own history we—"

"You have explained all that. It will be sixty years from now before you know if my daughter will still be great. Or if you have changed that as well by abducting me and ruining my life."

"Abducting! You were going to be killed! Accused, beheaded—"

"And you have prevented that." She rose, in a greater fury than ever she had been with Henry, with Wolsey, with anyone. "You have also robbed me of my remaining three years as surely as Henry would have robbed me of my old age. And you have mayhap robbed my daughter as well, as Henry sought to do with his Seymour-get prince. So what is the difference between you, Master Culhane, that you are a saint and Henry a villain? He held me in the Tower until my soul could be commended to God; you hold me here in this castle you say I can never leave where time does not exist, and mayhap God neither. Who has done me the worse injury? Henry gave me the crown. You—all you and my Lord Brill have given me is a living death, and then given my daughter's crown a danger and uncertainty that without you she would not have known! Who has done to Elizabeth and me the worse turn? And in the name of preventing war! You have made war upon *me*! Get out, get out!"

"Your—"

"Get out! I never want to see you again! If I am in hell, let there be one less demon!"

Lambert slipped from her monitor to run down the corridor. Culhane flew from the room; behind him the sound of something heavy struck the door. Culhane slumped against it, his face pasty around his cheek dye. Lambert could almost find it in herself to pity him. Almost.

She said softly, "I told you so."

"She's like a wild thing."

"You knew she could be. It's documented enough, Culhane. I've put a suicide watch on her."

"Yes. Good. I . . . she was like a wild thing."

Lambert peered at him. "You still want her! After that!"

That sobered him; he straightened and looked at her coldly. "She is a holy hostage, Lambert."

"I remember that. Do you?"

"Don't insult me, intern."

He moved angrily away; she caught his sleeve. "Culhane—don't be angry. I only meant that the sixteenth century was so different from our own, but—"

"Do you think I don't know that? I was doing historical research while you were learning to read, Lambert. Don't instruct me."

He stalked off. Lambert bit down hard on her own fury and stared at Anne Boleyn's closed door. No sound came from behind it. To the soundless door she finished her sentence: "—but some traps don't change."

The door didn't answer. Lambert shrugged. It had nothing to do with her. She didn't care what happened to Anne Boleyn, in this century or that other one. Or to Culhane, either. Why should she? There were other men. She was no Henry VIII, to bring down her world for passion. What was the good of being a time researcher if you could not even learn from times past?

She leaned thoughtfully against the door, trying to remember the name of the beautiful boy in her orientation lecture, the one with the violet eyes.

She was still there, thinking, when Toshio Brill called a staff meeting to announce, his voice stiff with anger, that Her Holiness of the Church of the Holy Hostage had filed a motion with the All-World Forum that

the Time Research Institute, because of the essentially reverent nature
of the time rescue program, be removed from administration by the
Forum and placed instead under the direct control of the Church.

She had to think. It was important to think, as she had thought
through her denial of Henry's ardor, and her actions when that ardor
waned. Thought was all.

She could not return to her London, to Elizabeth. They had told her
that. But did she know beyond doubt that it was true?

Anne left her apartments. At the top of the stairs she usually took to
the garden, she instead turned and opened another door. It opened
easily. She walked along a different corridor. Apparently even now no
one was going to stop her.

And if they did, what could they do to her? They did not use the
scaffold or the rack; she had determined this from talking to that oaf
Culhane and that huge ungainly woman, Lady Mary Lambert. They did
not believe in violence, in punishment, in death. (How could you not
believe in death? Even they must one day die.) The most they could do
to her was shut her up in her rooms, and there the female pope would
come to see she was well treated.

Essentially they were powerless.

The corridor was lined with doors, most set with small windows. She
peered in: rooms with desks and machines, rooms without desks and
machines, rooms with people seated around a table talking, kitchens,
still rooms. No one stopped her. At the end of the corridor she came to a
room without a window and tried the door. It was locked, but as she
stood there, her hand still on the knob, the door opened from within.

"Lady Anne! Oh!"

Could no one in this accursed place get her name right? The woman
who stood there was clearly a servant, although she wore the same ugly
gray-green tunic as everyone else. Perhaps, like Lady Mary, she was
really an apprentice. She was of no interest, but behind her was the last
thing Anne expected to see in this place: a child.

She pushed past the servant and entered the room. It was a little boy,
his dress strange but clearly a uniform of some sort. He had dark eyes,
curling dark hair, a bright smile. How old? Perhaps four. There was an
air about him that was unmistakable; she would have wagered her life
this child was royal.

"Who are you, little one?"

He answered her with an outpouring of a language she did not know.
The servant scrambled to some device on the wall; in a moment
Culhane stood before her.

"You said you didn't want to see me, Your Grace. But I was closest to answer Kiti's summons . . ."

Anne looked at him. It seemed to her that she looked clear through him, to all that he was: Desire, and pride of his pitiful strange learning, and smugness of his holy mission that had brought her life to wreck. Hers, and perhaps Elizabeth's as well. She saw Culhane's conviction, shared by Lord Director Brill and even by such as Lady Mary, that what they did was right because they did it. She knew that look well: It had been Cardinal Wolsey's, Henry's right-hand man and chancellor of England, the man who had advised Henry to separate Anne from Harry Percy. And advised Henry against marrying her. Until she, Anne Boleyn, upstart Tom Boleyn's powerless daughter, had turned Henry against Wolsey and had the cardinal brought to trial. She.

In that minute she made her decision.

"I was wrong, Master Culhane. I spoke in anger. Forgive me." She smiled and held out her hand, and she had the satisfaction of watching Culhane turn color.

How old was he? Not in his first youth. But neither had Henry.

He said, "Of course, Your Grace. Kiti said you talked to the Tsarevitch."

She made a face, still smiling at him. She had often mocked Henry thus. Even Harry Percy, so long ago, a lifetime ago . . . No. Two lifetimes ago. "The what?"

"The Tsarevitch." He indicated the child.

Was the dye on his face permanent, or would it wash off?

She said, not asking, "He is another time hostage. He, too, in his small person, prevents a war."

Culhane nodded, clearly unsure of her mood. Anne looked wonderingly at the child, then winningly at Culhane. "I would have you tell me about him. What language does he speak? Who is he?"

"Russian. He is—was—the future emperor. He suffers from a terrible disease: You called it the bleeding sickness. Because his mother, the empress, was so driven with worry over him, she fell under the influence of a holy man who led her to make some disastrous decisions while she was acting for her husband, the emperor, who was away at war."

Anne said, "And the bad decisions brought about another war."

"They made more bloody than necessary a major rebellion."

"You prevent rebellions as well as wars? Rebellions against a monarchy?"

"Yes, it—history did not go in the direction of monarchies."

That made little sense. How could history go other than in the direction of those who were divinely anointed, those who held the power? Royalty won. In the end, they always won.

But there could be many casualties before the end.

She said, with that combination of liquid dark gaze and aloof body that had so intrigued Henry—and Norris, and Wyatt, and even presumptuous Smeaton, God damn his soul—"I find I wish to know more about this child and his country's history. Will you tell me?"

"Yes," Culhane said. She caught the nature of his smile: relieved, still uncertain how far he had been forgiven, eager to find out. Familiar, all so familiar.

She was careful not to let her body touch his as they passed through the doorway. But she went first, so he could catch the smell of her hair.

"Master Culhane—you are listed on the demon machine as 'M. Culhane.'"

"The . . . oh, the computer. I didn't know you ever looked at one."

"I did. Through a window."

"It's not a demon, Your Grace."

She let the words pass; what did she care what it was? But his tone told her something. He liked reassuring her. In this world where women did the same work as men and where female bodies were to be seen uncovered in the exercise yard so often that even turning your head to look must become a bore, this oaf nonetheless liked reassuring her.

She said, "What does the 'M' mean?"

He smiled. "Michael. Why?"

As the door closed, the captive royal child began to wail.

Anne smiled, too. "An idle fancy. I wondered if it stood for Mark."

"What argument has the church filed with the All-World Forum?" a senior researcher asked.

Brill said irritably, as it were an answer, "Where is Mahjoub?"

Lambert spoke up promptly. "He is with Helen of Troy, Director, and the doctor. The queen had another seizure last night." Enzio Mahjoub was the unfortunate project head for their last time rescue.

Brill ran his hand over the back of his neck. His skull needed shaving, and his cheek dye was sloppily applied. He said, "Then we will begin without Mahjoub. The argument of Her Holiness is that the primary function of this institute is no longer pure time research but practical application, and that the primary practical application is time rescue. As such, we exist to take hostages, and thus should come under the direct control of the Church of the Holy Hostage. Her secondary argument is that the time hostages are not receiving treatment up to intersystem standards as specified by the All-World Accord of 2154."

Lambert's eyes darted around the room. Cassia Kohambu, project head for the institute's greatest success, sat up straight, looking outraged. "Our hostages are—on what are these charges allegedly based?"

Brill said, "No formal charges as yet. Instead, she has requested an investigation. She claims we have hundreds of potential hostages pinpointed by the Rahvoli equations, and the ones we have chosen do not meet standards for either internal psychic stability or benefit accrued to the hostages themselves, as specified in the All-World Accord. We have chosen to please ourselves, with flagrant disregard for the welfare of the hostages."

"Flagrant disregard!" It was Culhane, already on his feet. Beneath the face dye his cheeks flamed. Lambert eyed him carefully. "How can Her Holiness charge flagrant disregard when without us the Tsarevitch Alexis would have been in constant pain from hemophiliac episodes, Queen Helen would have been abducted and raped, Herr Hitler blown up in an underground bunker, and Queen Anne Boleyn beheaded!"

Brill said bluntly, "Because the Tsarevitch cries constantly for his mother, the Lady Helen is mad, and Mistress Boleyn tells the church she has been made war upon!"

Well, Lambert thought, that still left Herr Hitler. She was just as appalled as anyone at Her Holiness's charges, but Culhane had clearly violated both good manners and good sense. Brill never appreciated being upstaged.

Brill continued, "An investigative committee from the All-World Forum will arrive here next month. It will be small: Delegates Soshiru, Vlakhav, and Tullio. In three days the institute staff will meet again at oh-seven hundred, and by that time I want each project group to have prepared an argument in favor of the hostage you hold. Use the prepermit justifications, including all the mathematical models, but go far beyond that in documenting benefits to the hostages themselves since they arrived here. Are there any questions?"

Only one, Lambert thought. She stood. "Director—were the three delegates who will investigate us chosen by the All-World Forum or requested by Her Holiness? To whom do they already owe their allegiance?"

Brill looked annoyed. He said austerely, "I think we can rely upon the All-World delegates to file a fair report, Intern Lambert," and Lambert lowered her eyes. Evidently she still had much to learn. The question should not have been asked aloud.

Would Mistress Boleyn have known that?

Anne took the hand of the little boy. "Come, Alexis," she said. "We walk now."

The prince looked up at her. How handsome he was, with his thick, curling hair and beautiful eyes almost as dark as her own. If she had given Henry such a child . . . She pushed the thought away. She spoke to Alexis in her rudimentary Russian, without using the translator box hung like a peculiarly ugly pendant around her neck. He answered with a stream of words she couldn't follow and she waited for the box to translate.

"Why should we walk? I like it here in the garden."

"The garden is very beautiful," Anne agreed. "But I have something interesting to show you."

Alexis trotted beside her obediently then. It had not been hard to win his trust—had no one here ever passed time with children? Wash off the scary cheek paint, play for him songs on the lute—an instrument he could understand, not like the terrifying sounds coming without musicians from yet another box—learn a few phrases of his language. She had always been good at languages.

Anne led the child through the far gate of the walled garden, into the yard. Machinery hummed; naked men and women "exercised" together on the grass. Alexis watched them curiously, but Anne ignored them. Servants. Her long, full skirts, tawny silk, trailed on the ground.

At the far end of the yard she started down the short path to that other gate, the one that ended at nothing.

Queen Isabella of Spain, Henry had told Anne once, had sent an expedition of sailors to circumnavigate the globe. They were supposed to find a faster way to India. They had not done so, but neither had they fallen off the edge of the world, which many had prophesied for them. Anne had not shown much interest in the story, because Isabella had, after all, been Katherine's mother. The edge of the world.

The gate ended with a wall of nothing. Nothing to see, or smell, or taste—Anne had tried. To the touch the wall was solid enough, and faintly tingly. A "force field," Culhane said. Out of time as we experience it; out of space. The gate, one of three, led to a place called Upper Slib, in what had once been Egypt.

Anne lifted Alexis. He was heavier than even a month ago; since she had been attending him every day he had begun to eat better, play more, cease crying for his mother. Except at night. "Look, Alexis, a gate. Touch it."

The little boy did, then drew back his hand at the tingling. Anne laughed, and after a moment Alexis laughed, too.

The alarms sounded.

"Why, Your Grace?" Culhane said. "Why again?"

"I wished to see if the gate was unlocked," Anne said coolly. "We

both wished to see." This was a lie. She knew it. Did he? Not yet
perhaps.

"I told you, Your Grace, it is not a gate that can be left locked or
unlocked, as you understand the terms. It must be activated by the
stasis square."

"Then do so; the prince and I wish for an outing."

Culhane's eyes darkened; each time he was in more anguish. And
each time, he came running. However much he might wish to avoid her,
commanding his henchmen to talk to her most of the time, he must
come when there was an emergency because he was her gaoler, appointed
by Lord Brill. So much had Anne discovered in a month of careful trials.
He said now, "I told you, Your Grace, you can't move past the force
field, no more than I could move into your palace at Greenwich. In the
time stream beyond that gate—*my* time stream—you don't exist. The
second you crossed the force field you'd disintegrate into nothingness."

Nothingness again. To Alexis she said sadly in Russian, "He will never
let us out. Never, never."

The child began to cry. Anne held him closer, looking reproachfully at
Culhane, who was shifting toward anger. She caught him just before the
shift was complete, befuddling him with unlooked-for wistfulness: "It is
just that there is so little we can do here, in this time we do not belong.
You can understand that, can you not, Master Culhane? Would it not be
the same for you, in my court of England?"

Emotions warred on his face. Anne put her free hand gently on his
arm. He looked down: the long, slim fingers with their delicate tendons,
the tawny silk against his drab uniform. He choked out, "Anything in my
power, anything within the rules, Your Grace . . ."

She had not yet gotten him to blurt out "Anne," as he had the day
she'd thrown a candlestick after him at the door.

She removed her hand, shifted the sobbing child against her neck,
spoke so softly he could not hear her.

He leaned forward, toward her. "What did you say, Your Grace?"

"Would you come again tonight to accompany my lute on your guitar?
For Alexis and me?"

Culhane stepped back. His eyes looked trapped.

"Please, Master Culhane?"

Culhane nodded.

Lambert stared at the monitor. It showed the hospital suite, barred
windows and low white pallets, where Helen of Troy was housed. The
queen sat quiescent on the floor, as she usually did, except for the brief
and terrifying periods when she erupted, shrieking and tearing at her

incredible hair. There had never been a single coherent word in the eruptions, not since the first moment they had told Helen where she was, and why. Or maybe that fragile mind, already quivering under the strain of her affair with Paris, had snapped too completely even to hear them. Helen, Lambert thought, was no Anne Boleyn.

Anne sat close to the mad Greek queen, her silk skirts overlapping Helen's white tunic, her slender body leaning so far forward that her hair, too, mingled with Helen's, straight black waterfall with masses of springing black curls. Before she could stop herself, Lambert had run her hand over her own shaved head.

What was Mistress Anne trying to say to Helen? The words were too low for the microphones to pick up, and the double curtain of hair hid Anne's lips. Yet Lambert was as certain as death that Anne was talking. And Helen, quiescent—was she nonetheless hearing? What could it matter if she were, words in a tongue that from her point of view would not exist for another two millennia?

Yet the Boleyn woman visited her every day, right after she left the Tsarevitch. How good was Anne, from a time almost as barbaric as Helen's own, at nonverbal coercion of the crazed?

Culhane entered, glanced at the monitor, and winced.

Lambert said levelly, "You're a fool, Culhane."

He didn't answer.

"You go whenever she summons. You—"

He suddenly strode across the room, two strides at a time. Grabbing Lambert, he pulled her from her chair and yanked her to her feet. For an astonished moment she thought he was actually going to hit her—researchers *hitting* each other. She tensed to slug him back. But abruptly he dropped her, giving a little shove so that she tumbled gracelessly back into her chair.

"You feel like a fat stone."

Lambert stared at him. Indifferently he activated his own console and began work. Something rose in her, so cold the vertebrae of her back felt fused in ice. Stiffly she rose from the chair, left the room, and walked along the corridor.

A fat stone. Heavy, stolid yet doughy, the flesh yielding like a slug or a maggot. Bulky, without grace, without beauty, almost without individuality, as stones were all alike. A fat stone.

Anne Boleyn was just leaving Helen's chamber. In the corridor, back to the monitor, Lambert faced her. Her voice was low like a subterranean growl. "Leave him alone."

Anne looked at her coolly. She did not ask whom Lambert meant.

"Don't you know you are watched every minute? That you can't so much as use your chamberpot without being taped? How do you ever expect to get him to your bed? Or to do anything with poor Helen?"

Anne's eyes widened. She said loudly, "Even when I use the chamberpot? Watched? Have I not even the privacy of the beasts in the field?"

Lambert clenched her fists. Anne was acting. Someone had already told her, or she had guessed, about the surveillance. Lambert could see that she was acting—but not *why*. A part of her mind noted coolly that she had never wanted to kill anyone before. So this, finally, was what it felt like, all those emotions she had researched throughout time: fury and jealousy and the desire to destroy. The emotions that started wars.

Anne cried, even more loudly, "I had been better had you never told me!" and rushed toward her own apartments.

Lambert walked slowly back to her work area, a fat stone.

Anne lay on the grass between the two massive power generators. It was a poor excuse for grass; although green enough, it had no smell. No dew formed on it, not even at night. Culhane had explained that it was bred to withstand disease, and that no dew formed because the air had little moisture. He explained, too, that the night was as man-bred as the grass; there was no natural night here. Henry would have been highly interested in such things; she was not. But she had listened carefully, as she listened to everything Michael said.

She lay completely still, waiting. Eventually the head of a researcher thrust around the corner of the towering machinery: a purposeful thrust. "Your Grace? What are you doing?"

Anne did not answer. Getting to her feet, she walked back toward the castle. The place between the generators was no good: The woman had already known where Anne was.

The three delegates from the All-World Forum arrived at the Time Research Institute looking apprehensive. Lambert could understand this; for those who had never left their own time-space continuum, it probably seemed significant to step through a force field to a place that did not exist in any accepted sense of the word. The delegates looked at the ground, and inspected the facilities, and asked the same kinds of questions visitors always asked, before they settled down actually to investigate anything.

They were given an hour's overview of the time rescue program, presented by the director himself. Lambert, who had not helped write this, listened to the careful sentiments about the prevention of war, the nobility of hostages, the deep understanding the Time Research Institute held of the All-World Accord of 2154, the altruistic extension of the

Holy Mission of Peace into other time streams. Brill then moved on to
discuss the four time hostages, dwelling heavily on the first. In the four
years since Herr Hitler had become a hostage, the National Socialist
Party had all but collapsed in Germany. President Paul von Hindenburg
had died on schedule, and the new moderate chancellors were slowly
bringing order to Germany. The economy was still very bad and unrest
was widespread, but no one was arresting Jews or Gypsies or homosexu-
als or Jehovah's Witnesses or... Lambert stopped listening. The delegates knew all this. The entire solar system knew all this. Hitler had
been a tremendous popular success as a hostage, the reason the Institute
had obtained permits for the next three. Herr Hitler was kept in his
locked suite, where he spent his time reading power-fantasy novels
whose authors had not been born when the bunker under Berlin was
detonated.

"Very impressive, Director," Goro Soshiru said. He was small, thin,
elongated, a typical free-fall spacer, with a sharp mind and a reputation
for incorruptibility. "May we now talk to the hostages, one at a time?"

"Without any monitors. That is our instruction," said Anna Vlakhav.
She was the senior member of the investigative team, a sleek, gray-
haired Chinese who refused all augments. Her left hand, Lambert
noticed, trembled constantly. She belonged to the All-World Forum's
Inner Council and had once been a hostage herself for three years.

"Please," Soren Tullio said with a smile. He was young, handsome,
very wealthy. Disposable, added by the Forum to fill out the committee,
with few recorded views of his own. Insomuch as they existed, however,
they were not tinged with any bias toward the Church. Her Holiness
had not succeeded in naming the members of the investigative
committee—if indeed she had tried.

"Certainly," Brill said. "We've set aside the private conference room
for your use. As specified by the Church, it is a sanctuary: There are no
monitors of any kind. I would recommend, however, that you allow the
bodyguard to remain with Herr Hitler, although, of course, you will
make up your own minds."

Delegate Vlakhav said, "The bodyguard may stay. Herr Hitler is not
our concern here."

Surprise, Lambert thought. Guess who is?

The delegates kept Hitler only ten minutes, the catatonic Helen only
three. They said the queen did not speak. They talked to the little
Tsarevitch a half hour. They kept Anne Boleyn in the sanctuary/
conference room four hours and twenty-three minutes.

She came out calm, blank-faced, and proceeded to her own apartments. Behind her the three delegates were tight-lipped and silent.

Anna Vlakhav, the former hostage, said to Toshio Brill, "We have no comment at this time. You will be informed."

Brill's eyes narrowed. He said nothing.

The next day, Director Toshio Brill was subpoenaed to appear before the All-World Forum on the gravest of all charges: mistreating holy hostages detained to keep peace. The tribunal would consist of the full Inner Council of the All-World Forum. Since Director Brill had the right to confront those who accused him, the investigation would be held at the Time Research Institute.

How? Lambert wondered. They would not take her unsupported word. How had the woman done it?

She said to Culhane, "The delegates evidently make no distinction between political hostages on our own world, and time hostages snatched from shadowy parallel ones."

"Why should they?" coldly said Culhane. The idealist. And where had it brought him?

Lambert was assigned that night to monitor the Tsarevitch, who was asleep in his crib. She sat in her office, her screen turned to Anne Boleyn's chambers, watching her play on the lute and sing softly to herself the songs written for her by Henry VIII when his passion was new and fresh six hundred years before.

Anne sat embroidering a sleeve cover of cinnamon velvet. In strands of black silk she worked intertwined H and A: Henry and Anne. Let their spying machines make of that what they would.

The door opened and, without permission, Culhane entered. He stood by her chair and looked down into her face. "Why, Anne? Why?"

She laughed. He had finally called her by her Christian name. Now, when it could not possibly matter.

When he saw that she would not answer, his manner grew formal. "A lawyer has been assigned to you. He arrives tomorrow."

A lawyer. Thomas Cromwell had been a lawyer, and Sir Thomas More. Dead, both of them, at Henry's hand. So had Master Culhane told her, and yet he still believed that protection was afforded by the law.

"The lawyer will review all the monitor records. What you did, what you said, every minute."

She smiled at him mockingly. "Why tell me this now?"

"It is your right to know."

"And you are concerned with rights. Almost as much as with death." She knotted the end of her thread and cut it. "How is it that you command so many machines and yet do not command the knowledge that every man must die?"

"We know that," Culhane said evenly. His desire for her had at last been killed; she could feel its absence, like an empty well. The use of her name had been but the last drop of living water. "But we try to prevent death when we can."

"Ah, but you can't. 'Prevent death'—as if it were a fever. You can only postpone it, Master Culhane, and you never even ask if that is worth doing."

"I only came to tell you about the lawyer," Culhane said stiffly. "Good night, Mistress Boleyn."

"Good night, Michael," she said, and started to laugh. She was still laughing when the door closed behind him.

The Hall of Time, designed to hold three hundred, was packed.

Lambert remembered the day she had given the orientation lecture to the history candidates, among them what's-his-name of the violet eyes. Twenty young people huddled together against horror in the middle of squares, virtual and simulated but not really present. Today the squares were absent and the middle of the floor was empty, while all four sides were lined ten-deep with All-World Inner Council members on high polished benches, archbishops and lamas and shamans of the Church of the Holy Hostage, and reporters from every major newsgrid in the solar system. Her Holiness the high priest sat among her followers, pretending she wanted to be inconspicuous. Toshio Brill sat in a chair alone, facing the current premier of the All-World Council, Dagar Krenya of Mars.

Anne Boleyn was led to a seat. She walked with her head high, her long black skirts sweeping the floor.

Lambert remembered that she had worn black to her trial for treason, in 1536.

"This investigation will begin," Premier Krenya said. He wore his hair to his shoulders; fashions must have changed again on Mars. Lambert looked at the shaved heads of her colleagues, at the long, loose black hair of Anne Boleyn. To Culhane, seated beside her, she whispered, "We'll be growing our hair again soon." He looked at her as if she were crazy.

It *was* a kind of crazy, to live everything twice: once in research, once in the flesh. Did it seem so to Anne Boleyn? Lambert knew her frivolity was misplaced, and she thought of the frivolity of Anne in the Tower, awaiting execution: "They will have no trouble finding a name for me. I shall be Queen Anne Lackhead." At the memory, Lambert's hatred burst out fresh. She had the memory, and now Anne never would. But in bequeathing it forward in time to Lambert, the memory had become secondhand. That was Anne Boleyn's real crime, for which she would never be tried: She had made this whole proceeding, so important to Lambert and Brill and Culhane, a mere reenactment. Prescripted. Secondhand. She had robbed them of their own, unused time.

Krenya said, "The charges are as follows: That the Time Research Institute has mistreated the holy hostage Anne Boleyn, held hostage against war. Three counts of mistreatment are under consideration this day: First, that researchers willfully increased a hostage's mental anguish by dwelling on the pain of those left behind by the hostage's confinement, and on those aspects of confinement that cause emotional unease. Second, that researchers failed to choose a hostage who would truly prevent war. Third, that researchers willfully used a hostage for sexual gratification."

Lambert felt herself go very still. Beside her, Culhane rose to his feet, then sat down again slowly, his face rigid. Was it possible he had . . . No. He had been infatuated, but not to the extent of throwing away his career. He was not Henry, any more than Lambert had been over him.

The spectators buzzed, an uneven sound like malfunctioning equipment. Krenya rapped for order. "Director Brill: How do you answer these charges?"

"False, Premier. Every one."

"Then let us hear the evidence against the Institute."

Anne Boleyn was called. She took the chair in which Brill had been sitting. *"She made an entry as though she were going to a great triumph and sat down with elegance"* . . . But that was the other time, the first time. Lambert groped for Culhane's hand. It felt limp.

"Mistress Boleyn," Krenya said—he had evidently not been told that she insisted on being addressed as a queen, and the omission gave Lambert a mean pleasure—"in what ways was your anguish willfully increased by researchers at this Institute?"

Anne held out her hand. To Lambert's astonishment, her lawyer put into it a lute. At an official All-World Forum investigation—a *lute*. Anne began to play, the tune high and plaintive. Her unbound black hair fell forward; her slight body made a poignant contrast to the torment in the words:

> Defiled is my name, full sore,
> Through cruel spite and false report,
> That I may say forever more,
> Farewell to joy, *adieu* comfort.

> Oh, death, rock me asleep,
> Bring on my quiet rest,
> Let pass my very guiltless ghost
> Out of my careful breast.

Ring out the doleful knell,
Let its sound my death tell,
For I must die,
There is no remedy,
For now I die!

The last notes faded. Anne looked directly at Krenya. "I wrote that, my Lords, in my other life. Master Culhane of this place played it for me, along with death songs written by my... my brother..."

"Mistress Boleyn..."

"No, I recover myself. George's death tune was hard for me to hear, my Lords. Accused and condemned because of me, who always loved him well."

Krenya said to the lawyer whose staff had spent a month reviewing every moment of monitor records, "Culhane made her listen to these?"

"Yes," the lawyer said. Beside Lambert, Culhane sat unmoving.

"Go on," Krenya said to Anne.

"He told me that I was made to suffer watching the men accused with me die. How I was led to a window overlooking the block, how my brother George kneeled, putting his head on the block, how the ax was raised..." She stopped, shuddering. A murmur ran over the room. It sounded like cruelty, Lambert thought. But whose?

"Worst of all, my Lords," Anne said, "was that I was told I had bastardized my own child. I chose to sign a paper declaring no valid marriage had ever existed because I had been precontracted to Sir Henry Percy, so my daughter Elizabeth was illegitimate and thus barred from her throne. I was taunted with the fact that I had done this, ruining the prospects of my own child. He said it over and over, Master Culhane did..."

Krenya said to the lawyer, "Is this in the visuals?"

"Yes."

Krenya turned back to Anne. "But Mistress Boleyn—these are things that because of your time rescue did *not* happen. Will not happen in your time stream. How can they thus increase your anguish for relatives left behind?"

Anne stood. She took one step forward, then stopped. Her voice was low and passionate. "My good Lord—do you not understand? It is because you took me here that these things did not happen. Left to my own time, I *would have been responsible for them all.* For my brother's death, for the other four brave men, for my daughter's bastardization, for the torment in my own music... I have escaped them only because of *you*. To tell me them in such detail, not the mere provision of facts that I myself requested but agonizing detail of mind and heart—is to tell me that I alone, in my own character, am evil, giving pain to those I love most. And that in this time stream you have brought me to, I *did* these things, felt them, feel them still. You have made me guilty of them. My Lord Premier, have you ever been a hostage yourself? Do you know, or can you imagine, the torment that comes from imagining the grief of those who love you? And to know you have caused this grief, not merely loss but death, blood, the pain of disinheritance—that you have caused it, and are now being told of the anguish you cause? Told over and over? In words, in song even—can you imagine what that feels like to one such as I, who cannot return at will and comfort those hurt by my actions?"

The room was silent. Who, Lambert wondered, had told Anne Boleyn that Premier Krenya had once served as a holy hostage?

"Forgive me, my Lords," Anne said dully, "I forget myself."

"Your testimony may take whatever form you choose," Krenya said, and it seemed to Lambert that there were shades and depths in his voice.

The questioning continued. A researcher, said Anne, had taunted her with being spied on even at her chamberpot—Lambert leaned slowly forward—which had made Anne cry out, "It had been better had you never told me!" Since then, modesty had made her reluctant even to answer nature, "so that there is every hour a most wretched twisting and churning in my bowels."

Asked why she thought the Institute had chosen the wrong hostage, Anne said she had been told so by my Lord Brill. The room exploded into sound, and Krenya rapped for quiet. "That visual now, please." On a square created in the center of the room, the visuals replayed on three sides:

"My Lord Brill . . . was there no other person you could take but I to prevent this war you say is a hundred years off? This civil war in England?"

"The mathematics identified you as the best hostage, Your Grace."

"The best? Best for what, my Lord? If you had taken Henry himself, then he could not have issued the Act of Supremacy. His supposed death would have served the purpose as well as mine."

"Yes. But for Henry the Eighth to disappear from history while his heir is but a month old . . . we did not know if that might not have started a civil war in itself. Between the factions supporting Elizabeth and those for Queen Katherine, who was still alive."

"What did your mathematical learning tell you?"

"That it probably would not," Brill said.

"And yet choosing me instead of Henry left him free to behead yet another wife, as you yourself have told me, my cousin Catherine Howard!"

Brill shifted on his chair. *"That is true, Your Grace."*

"Then why not Henry instead of me?"

"I'm afraid Your Grace does not have sufficient grasp of the science of probabilities for me to explain, Your Grace."

Anne was silent. *Finally she said, "I think that the probability is that you would find it easier to deal with a deposed woman than with Henry of England, whom no man can withstand in either a passion or a temper."*

Brill did not answer. The visual rolled—ten seconds, fifteen—and he did not answer.

"Mr. Premier," Brill said in a choked voice, "Mr. Premier—"

"You will have time to address these issues soon, Mr. Director," Krenya said. "Mistress Boleyn, this third charge—sexual abuse . . ."

The term had not existed in the sixteenth century, thought Lambert. Yet Anne understood it. She said, "I was frightened, my Lord, by the strangeness of this place. I was afraid for my life. I didn't know then that a woman may refuse those in power, may—"

"That is why sexual contact with hostages is universally forbidden," Krenya said. "Tell us what you think happened."

Not what *did* happen—what you *think* happened. Lambert took heart.

Anne said, "Master Culhane bade me meet him at a place . . . it is a small alcove beside a short flight of stairs near the kitchens. . . . He bade me meet him there at night. Frightened, I went."

"Visuals," Krenya said in a tight voice.

The virtual square reappeared. Anne, in the same white nightdress in which she had been taken hostage, crept from her chamber, along the corridor, her body heat registering in infrared. Down the stairs, around to the kitchens, into the cubbyhole formed by the flight of steps, themselves oddly angled as if they had been added, or altered, after the main structure was built, after the monitoring system installed. . . . Anne dropped to her knees and crept forward beside the isolated stairs. And disappeared.

Lambert gasped. A time hostage was under constant surveillance. That was a basic condition of their permit; there was no way the Boleyn bitch could escape constant monitoring. But she had.

"Master Culhane was already there," Anne said in a dull voice. "He . . . he used me ill there."

The room was awash with sound. Krenya said over it, "Mistress

Boleyn—there is no visual evidence that Master Culhane was there. He has sworn he was not. Can you offer any proof that he met you there? Anything at all?"

"Yes. Two arguments, my Lord. First: How would I know there were not spying devices in but this one hidden alcove? I did not design this castle; it is not mine."

Krenya's face showed nothing. "And the other argument?"

"I am pregnant with Master Culhane's child."

Pandemonium. Krenya rapped for order. When it was finally restored, he said to Brill, "Did you know of this?"

"No, I . . . it was a hostage's right by the Accord to refuse intrusive medical treatment. . . . She has been healthy."

"Mistress Boleyn, you will be examined by a doctor immediately."

She nodded assent. Watching her, Lambert knew it was true. Anne Boleyn was pregnant, and had defeated herself thereby. But she did not know it yet.

Lambert fingered the knowledge, seeing it as a tangible thing, cold as steel.

"How do we know," Krenya said, "that you were not pregnant before you were taken hostage?"

"It was but a month after my daughter Elizabeth's birth, and I had the white-leg. Ask one of your experts if a woman would bed a man then. Ask a woman expert in the women of my time. Ask Lady Mary Lambert."

Heads in the room turned. Ask whom? Krenya said, "Ask whom?" An aide leaned toward him and whispered something. He said, "We will have her put on the witness list."

Anne said, "I carry Michael Culhane's child. I, who could not carry a prince for the king."

Krenya said, almost powerlessly, "That last has nothing to do with this investigation, Mistress Boleyn."

She only looked at him.

They called Brill to testify, and he threw up clouds of probability equations that did nothing to clarify the choice of Anne over Henry as holy hostage. Was the woman right? Had there been a staff meeting to choose between the candidates identified by the Rahvoli applications, and had someone said of two very close candidates, "We should think about the effect on the Institute as well as on history. . ."? Had someone been developing a master theory based on a percentage of women influencing history? Had someone had an infatuation with the period, and chosen by that what should be altered? Lambert would never know. She was an intern.

Had been an intern.

Culhane was called. He denied seducing Anne Boleyn. The songs on the lute, the descriptions of her brother's death, the bastardization of Elizabeth—all done to convince her that what she had been saved from was worse than where she had been saved to. Culhane felt so much that he made a poor witness, stumbling over his words, protesting too much.

Lambert was called. As neutrally as possible she said, "Yes, Mr. Premier, historical accounts show that Queen Anne was taken with white-leg after Elizabeth's birth. It is a childbed illness. The legs swell up and ache painfully. It can last from a few weeks to months. We don't know how long it lasted—would have lasted—for Mistress Boleyn."

"And would a woman with this disease be inclined to sexual activity?"

"'Inclined'—no."

"Thank you, Researcher Lambert."

Lambert returned to her seat. The committee next looked at visuals, hours of visuals—Culhane, flushed and tender, making a fool of himself with Anne. Anne with the little Tsarevitch, an exile trying to comfort a child torn from his mother. Helen of Troy, mad and pathetic. Brill, telling newsgrids around the solar system that the time rescue program, savior of countless lives, was run strictly in conformance with the All-World Accord of 2154. And all the time, through all the visuals, Lambert waited for what was known to everyone in that room except Anne Boleyn: She could not pull off in this century what she might have in Henry's. The paternity of a child could be genotyped in the womb.

Who? Mark Smeaton, after all? Another miscarriage from Henry, precipitately gotten and unrecorded by history? Thomas Wyatt, her most faithful cousin and cavalier?

After the committee had satisfied itself that it had heard enough, everyone but Forum delegates was dismissed. Anne, Lambert saw, was led away by a doctor. Lambert smiled to herself. It was already over. The Boleyn bitch was defeated.

The All-World Forum investigative committee deliberated for less than a day. Then it issued a statement: The child carried by holy hostage Anne Boleyn had not been sired by Researcher Michael Culhane. Its genotypes matched no one's at the Institute for Time Research. The Institute, however, was guilty of two counts of hostage mistreatment. The Institute's charter as an independent, tax-exempt organization was revoked. Toshio Brill was released from his position, as were Project Head Michael Culhane and intern Mary Lambert. The Institute stewardship was reassigned to the Church of the Holy Hostage under the direct care of Her Holiness the high priest.

Lambert slipped through the outside door to the walled garden. It was dusk. On a seat at the far end a figure sat, skirts spread wide, a darker shape against the dark wall. As Lambert approached, Anne looked up without surprise.

"Culhane's gone. I leave tomorrow. Neither of us will ever work in time research again."

Anne went on gazing upward. Those great dark eyes, that slim neck, so vulnerable. . . . Lambert clasped her hands together hard.

"*Why?*" Lambert said. "Why do it all again? Last time use a king to bring down the power of the church, this time use a church to—before, at least you gained a crown. Why do it here, when you gain nothing?"

"You could have taken Henry. He deserved it; I did not."

"But we didn't take Henry!" Lambert shouted. "So why?"

Anne did not answer. She put out one hand to point behind her. Her sleeve fell away, and Lambert saw clearly the small sixth finger that had marked her as a witch. A tech came running across the half-lit garden. "Researcher Lambert—"

"What is it?"

"They want you inside. Everybody. The queen—the other one, Helen—she's killed herself."

The garden blurred, straightened. "How?"

"Stabbed with a silver sewing scissors hidden in her tunic. It was so quick, the researchers saw it on the monitor but couldn't get there in time."

"Tell them I'm coming."

Lambert looked at Anne Boleyn. "You did this."

Anne laughed. *This lady*, wrote the Tower constable, *hath much joy in death*. Anne said, "Lady Mary—every birth is a sentence of death. Your age has forgotten that."

"Helen didn't need to die yet. And the Time Research Institute didn't need to be dismantled—it *will* be dismantled. Completely. But somewhere, sometime, you will be punished for this. I'll see to that!"

"Punished, Lady Mary? And mayhap beheaded?"

Lambert looked at Anne: the magnificent black eyes, the sixth finger, the slim neck. Lambert said slowly, "You want your own death. As you had it before."

"What else did you leave me?" Anne Boleyn said. "Except the power to live the life that is mine?"

"You will never get it. We don't kill here!"

Anne smiled. "Then how will you 'punish' me—'sometime, somehow'?"

Lambert didn't answer. She walked back across the walled garden, toward the looming walls gray in the dusk, toward the chamber where lay the other dead queen.

TUNDRA MOSS

F. M. Busby

Until the Alaska Communication System sent him here to live in a Quonset hut on Amchitka Island, PFC Buster Morgan hadn't known weather that was all sideways. Nor slogged through mud over his ankles while gusting wind dried the surface and blew dust in his eyes.

Tonight it was blowing sixty, maybe sixty-five. Over seventy made it hard to walk; you had to lean into it. And it could shift in no time, slap you flat in the mud.

When God made the Aleutians he couldn't have been sober.

Squinting against cold, slashing rain, Buster kept his dim light on one edge of the boardwalk. Losing track of that edge could put you in deep mud. He had the walks' layout down pat; just by flashlight, he couldn't have told where he was.

The boardwalks, connecting huts throughout the area, were planks laid crosswise over paired phone poles. Long as you didn't get blown off, you could get anywhere you wanted.

Where Buster wanted was the messhall, for a snack before graveyard shift and a sandwich to take along. The cooks were good about leaving stuff out special for the hootowl crew.

He'd had a good day's sleep. At shift's end that morning, after breakfast the sun showed. So he and Scooter in crypto and Silent Yokum the shift chief and teletype operator Chmielevski—Shemmy, who missed women even more than most—hiked down the moss-cushioned ravine to the Bering shore. Under the bluff lay no real beach; jagged rocks cluttered the narrow strip of sand.

This stretch was so bad that the cable ship had landed the Adak and Attu teletype cables at the next cove west, below a bowl-shaped valley. Buster had been there with Sergeant Thorne, to open the steel-covered cable hut and unseal the terminal boxes for the quarterly landline tests.

Learning that chore was why Buster was brought along. And to carry some of the bulkier gear.

Today the four walked only to the creek mouth at the near cove. Shemmy said he hoped there'd be a sea otter again, floating with food laid out on its chest, eating each piece from its front paws. Then rolling over and over, fast, to wash off.

Or the time one spooked a seabird bobbing offshore. It shot up from the water, missing by maybe a foot as the bird fled, then lay and rolled. Just for fun, the otter did that.

No such fun this day. Scooter pointed to a whale spout, but nothing else was happening. Buster turned to the dirt bluff. With the wind strong behind him he ran straight at it, then on *up*, sixty degrees or better, the wind holding him.

Almost at the top he remembered *you can't trust the wind!* He doubled forward, grabbed tundra grass and clambered, hands and feet both. He'd barely topped the bluff when it went dead calm.

"It all depends, George," the president said. "If Stalin allows us the refueling bases, we can go ahead with the northern prong of the offensive. If he doesn't . . ." Roosevelt shrugged.

"Yes, sir." General Marshall knew the problem. Doolittle's one-way raid, striking four cities although Tokyo got all the news play, had been worth it in morale. But for a real campaign, men and planes were too valuable to be used only once. And from the Aleutians, bombers couldn't reach Japan and return. Without the use of Siberian bases, no northern offensive could succeed.

FDR hadn't chosen to run the war this way. Along with Churchill, he had wanted a Europe First policy. But a mild stroke kept him from delivering his "day of infamy" speech in person. Public and congressional pressure, then, insisted that the country's major effort go toward avenging Pearl Harbor.

It wasn't only Stalin, Marshall thought, who kept the president worried. MacArthur's obsession with the Philippines made him hard to manage. The man was a strategic genius; his concept of island-hopping, bypassing strong-points, left major southern Pacific Jap forces dying on the vine. But he *would* keep pushing for a premature Philippine assault, Damn it.

Roosevelt sighed; the general looked at him more closely. Always tired these days; perhaps that was why he catered too much, in the general's opinion, to "Uncle Joe."

Marshall didn't trust the Old Bolshevik. But for an effective Aleutian thrust, Stalin's cooperation was vital.

* * *

From the headland, the hootowl shift quartet trudged back up toward the ACS area, staying clear of the central sag in the ravine's deep moss cover. Thin spots weren't always obvious; you could fall through. Up nearer the ridge, Scooter led the way with bouncing steps off springy humps of moss. "Beautyrest..."

Coming slantwise against the wind, the Navy PBY was over them before they heard it. Barely a hundred feet up, the big flying boat was drifting sideways more than not. Eerie.

Wind or no wind, the four reached the messhall in time to have lunch, then went to their Quonset—filled with ten men's clutter, and like every hut in the area, smelling of stove oil. Graveyard did take it out of you; Buster folded early and didn't get up for dinner. What woke him, not long before time to relieve Thorne on duty, was somebody screeching on the radio.

It was the Late Mystery. Buster remembered one about an armed maniac stalking the island with a killer wolf. Late at night Weevil Hawkins had *believed* it, holed up in the messhall with his carbine, and damn near shot Buster Morgan at the door.

Tonight's sounded good, but Buster had to go. He pulled up his parka hood, went through the little storm porch and stepped outside. To struggle a hundred yards through sideways rain.

On the messhall porch he stomped mud off his feet. Here on The Rock all windows were covered; there'd been no Jap planes over for several months, but still you kept blackout. So until he opened the inner door, Buster couldn't know who was inside.

Nobody was. Weevil had been rotated Stateside, anyway.

If you want to stay out of drafts, stay out of Russia.

Sure thing, thought M/Sgt. Hardeman, but that's where they sent me. The embassy building in Moskva was old; heating wasn't its strong point. Especially in this anteroom, where he sat with half a pot of chilling coffee, waiting for word from Ambassador Harriman and wishing he'd never heard of the U.S. Diplomatic Corps.

The trouble was, they heard of him first. So here he sat, he and his crypto clearance, in Moskva. Drinking vodka off-duty instead of bourbon, and each day sweating against a Dear John letter from Eloise, whom he hadn't married for her patience.

The coffee wasn't fit to drink. Hardeman propped his chin on one hand and closed his eyes. The ambassador's secretary didn't catch him asleep, though; the man's shoes squeaked.

"Here." The paper Hardeman was handed carried several lines of number groups. "Send this to CINCCOM, for the president, via SHAEF

for Eisenhower's records. On each leg, return copy will be required for
validation. Repeat transmission until good copy is confirmed; sender will
then authorize further relay."

"Yes, sir." The sheet was marked Operational Priority and Send In
Clear. Looking at the string of six-digit numbers, Hardeman grinned.
Book code: each number group denoted a page, line, and word within
the line. Since no one but originator and recipient knew *which* book,
anyone else would play bloody hell trying to decode the apparently
simple cipher. Including Ike.

Well, that was Franklin Roosevelt for you.

Hardeman took the message down to Comcenter. This time of night
the radioteletype to Britain was fairly solid. But it still took one rerun to
confirm correct copy.

Being alone in the messhall always felt strange. Buster fast-fried a
slice of meat and made a couple of potato patties; while they sizzled he
fixed a sandwich for later. After eating and washing up, he filled his
canteen. This building, with a shower and washroom on the far end, had
the only running water in the ACS area. It came from a tundra lake; one
washing turned white cloth khaki. And to keep the big water bugs out of
your mouth, you drank from the canteen with your teeth closed.

Time to go.

Lieutenant Akaji disliked having to reprove subordinates; he wished,
heartily, that his small raiding force did not include Private Miyake.

In the matter of obeying orders, Miyake simply did not try. Back from
reconnaissance with Corporal Yamagiwa and Privates Suyama and Arimura,
Akaji found the impromptu shelter warm, its driftwood fire banked.
Perhaps two hours, it had burned.

Which meant that Miyake had lit fire as soon as he was left alone.
Even though, in these latitudes at this time of year, for hours enough
twilight lingered to show smoke against sky. Let alone the smell of it,
should Americans walk nearby, above.

The man had no excuse. Here at the bottom of the ravine, roofed by
decades' growth of tundra moss, no wind came; padded clothing gave
warmth enough. But Miyake was an obdurate man.

He had almost cost their lives, let alone the mission, even before they
reached Amchitka's shore. Perhaps halfway between the submarine and the
looming headland, the inflated raft pitching in harsh swells, Miyake inexpli-
cably stood. In saving him from immersion they came close to capsizing.

And as all had been told, life expectancy in Arctic waters was less than
twenty minutes, padding or no.

Akaji felt his spirit sink. A sacrifice mission should be a glorious venture. If only this man were assigned elsewhere! Or, Akaji's demon whispered, he *had* fallen into the sea...

Miyake was of some use; now he heated rations and sake. As they ate, Akaji reviewed matters. It was their second night ashore. During the first they collapsed and hid the liferaft, then sought shelter. Tundra moss bridges clefts and smooths contours; it was Corporal Yamagiwa who espied, where the headland's bluff met the ravine's mouth, an overhang of moss which could be undercut to provide entrance.

Through the underlying tangle of dead moss and roots, with much effort the five made a tunnel up along the ravine's bottom, nearly forty yards to a place where the banks widened. Here they chopped and pushed and flattened vegetable debris to open a cave: barely five feet wide and four high, but nearly eight lengthwise. And with good, fresh water running down the center.

Overhead lay several feet of solid, untouched growth. Except for the one ragged hole, not wholly clear but thinned enough to allow the escape of smoke.

They lay less than a half mile from the nearest American huts. But if caution were adhered to—if Miyake would heed restraint—the enemy might as well seek them on Paramushiru!

And tonight's reconnaissance had found for Akaji the Americans' communication lifeline. He did not know why it must be interrupted at this time, only that he had been ordered to do so.

How to disable it was the question. Bullets had not worked. The exposed part of the steel box, roughly the size of a small trunk, was possibly the lesser portion; pushing and prying could not budge it. And when, deeming it safe, Akaji directed Yamagiwa to fire at the box's padlock, the rifle bullets ricocheted without effect.

In the area between box and shoreline, where water cut a gash down the bank, it was young, eager Suyama who discovered several feet of exposed cable. Handlamp taped to emit only a slim pencil of light, Lieutenant Akaji inspected the find.

A large, heavy cable: its outer sheath, under tattered wrappings of tarred jute, consisted of almost a dozen spiraled steel finger-thick wires. Like the padlock, it withstood rifle fire. The final attempt splattered lead against Arimura's helmet; an inch lower would have taken his eye.

Sipping the last of his cooling sake, Akaji sighed. Next and soon he would lead two of his men to the rolling tundra above and reconnoiter the nearby American unit. To find targets for ingenious sabotage, the more effective if unsuspected as such.

He would take Suyama and Arimura, leaving Corporal Yamagiwa to ensure Miyake's behavior.

From the messhall it was maybe eighty yards to Operations. Two huts sat side by side, dug into the hillside at the rear. Entering the longer one Buster went past the locked crypto room and the desks—captain's, chief op's, and unit clerk's—to the teletype shop, where he hung up his parka.

The shorter Quonset alongside was all Operations; at its rear a covered hallway connected the two.

The hallway leaked some.

Entering Ops from the back, Buster saw the Adak and Attu cable gear to his right, across from the teletype machines for Post HQ, Navy, Air Command and Navy Weather, all idle this time of night. In between sat the cable amplifiers and power bays, the trick chief's desk, and the oil stove. The Quonset's walls, brown fiberboard, showed drab under a single row of fluorescents.

Buster glowered at the stove. It sat where you couldn't run an oil line; fuel had to be carried by hand. And Smitty, the chief op, had laid it on his maintenance crew to keep it filled.

It was a chore Buster didn't appreciate: running oil from a stand-mounted barrel into the can, wind blowing much of it onto his pants. One night he'd stood, looking across to the blinking red lights of Baker Strip, the bomber runway, and caught himself thinking it was a *town* over there. Really crazy. . .

He found Thorne feeding reversals into the Adak cable apex and adjusting the artificial line's external resistor boxes to reduce the imbalance kicks, drawn in ink on moving paper ribbon.

Two-way cable circuits used a double Wheatstone bridge; each end sent into an apex and received *across* it, balancing the cable against a heat-stabilized artificial line. To read the tiny incoming pips through the much greater sent signal, that balance was crucial. The slightest change of sea temperature, or a chip of oxidation growing in a soldered splice, could throw it off.

This part, Buster knew. The rest, signal shaping and all, building the received twitches into enough of a square wave to fool a teletype machine: those things left him stumped.

Luckily for him, once the shaping was set up it stayed put.

The Aleutian cable ran eight such legs end to end: Whittier–Kodiak–Cold Bay–Dutch Harbor–Umnak–Atka–Adak–Amchitka–Attu. Then a simpler rig on to Shemya. Whittier connected to Alaska Command near Anchorage via Alaska Railroad lines and ACS local loops.

There was no way *anyone* could tap submarine cable.

With Adak down, perforated tape from Attu was piling up; tape *to* Attu, it looked like, had all gone out. Nothing clacked but the Attu reperf and monitor printer; Silent Yokum and Frank Chmielevski, tonight's operators, sat with coffee, nodded hello, and looked bored. Scooter must be in the crypto room, working. Or maybe taking a nap. Morgan grinned; security had its uses.

He walked over to Thorne, who had been to cable school and knew his business; the man looked around, saying, "I've got most of it; you should have it up to traffic pretty soon."

"Sure. Have yourself some sack time." Thorne left. Buster checked the resistor dial readings against the last log entry. Thorne had changed the head-end balance appreciably and was working down the cable. Careful not to throw a big surge and maybe break the thin glass siphon pen, Buster fiddled.

Thorne was right; in a few minutes Buster flattened the two remaining peaks to mere wiggles. He ran the reversals up to signal speed. No bad spots, so he patched the circuit back to normal and sent QUICK BROWN FOX tape. From Adak, Buster's old drinking buddy Slim Barger responded with his own test tape. Solid both ways; they put the circuit back to message traffic.

Looking at his useless info copy of Harriman's latest to Marshall, Dwight Eisenhower frowned. Book code again. Maybe what Moscow said to Washington *was* none of his business—and compared to Marshall and MacArthur, certainly he was the new boy in school. Still, when Averill talked over his head to George so obviously, he felt slighted.

Eisenhower shrugged. Sooner or later, Mac would take the Japs' measure. Then the European Theater of Operations would get the attention it merited. And he with it.

With Adak restored, Buster went across to the shop. He was adjusting relays when Silent Yokum the trick chief came to tell him the oil had run out. Always on graveyard! Buster shucked on his parka, picked up the five-gallon can and went outside.

The wind was beating seventy; Morgan walked crouched. Up the slope to the oil dump and over to the rack. He held the can to the tap and pushed the handle, but no oil came.

The damn barrel was empty!

He rolled it off and went for a full one. But by himself he couldn't get one free without bringing down the whole stack.

He went back inside. Silent Yokum being a sergeant and all, Buster braced Chmielevski. "Shemmy? I need some help."

Shemmy wasn't Frank's pet nickname, but it beat some he'd had. You take what comes. He got his parka and followed Morgan.

It seemed to him he was running in bad luck. Like going to shower with the shampoo his folks sent him and pouring almost half before he smelled it for bourbon. Which ran fifty bucks a fifth off the merchant marine, a month's pay for a buck private.

Or the day he put gas in the stove instead of oil, and lucky somebody smelled the difference before he lit it. That's when Smitty put the job onto Maintenance.

Isolated duty wasn't good for Frank. Except for the nurses and Red Cross girls you saw sitting in the officers' section at Post Theater, there weren't any *women*. Not any. None.

He wasn't a gash hound like the guys said. He *liked* girls, and they could tell he did; that's why he'd always scored so steady. He really missed it; the Rock was driving him bughouse.

One of these days, though, he'd get lucky. . . .

After he helped get the barrel loose, he waited while Morgan ran oil. Then they went back in and got the stove filled.

Lying in mud under a truck, Lieutenant Akaji watched the Americans wrestle an oil drum onto a rack, fill a container, and return to their pair of hemicylindrical huts.

Leading the way Akaji had brought Suyama and Arimura up to this area of scattered huts. Most would be sleeping quarters. One leaked smells of food; at its farther end a pipe led down to a fairsized tundra lake. Wading out to plug the pipe's open end with moss, Arimura returned giggling. No great act of sabotage—yet in their peril here, good for the men's morale.

So vulnerable, these Americans! Given a platoon, automatic weapons, and explosives other than mere grenades, Akaji could destroy this unit, material *and* personnel, and be quickly safe to ground. But with only four enlisted men, it could not be.

Reconnaissance photos marked this area as the communications unit Akaji must cripple. But how? Run from hut to hut, hurling grenades and leaving havoc? The comm center itself, almost certainly the paired huts the soldiers had reentered? But known damage was the most easily countered, and soonest repaired.

No. The submarine cable, the circuit that could not be intercepted, was the vital link. It must be broken. And in a fashion as near to untraceable as could be managed.

So that the Americans would not know where to begin.

When the code clerk Denison brought Ambassador Harriman's message, George Marshall sighed with relief. Roosevelt waved for him to do the decoding. "Tell me the gist."

"Yes, sir." It didn't take long. "Averill reports that our use of Siberian bases for refueling is approved, effective now."

FDR's palm smote the desk. "Good work! Denison, code my order of this date to Alaska Command: General Buckner at Fort Richardson. Via the secure submarine cable circuit from Anchorage, he is to alert our bomber groups on Amchitka and Shemya to commence Operation Downdraft in—let me see—ten days."

Alarmed, Marshall cleared his throat. "That's awfully short notice, sir, for the necessary coordination with Mac."

But Roosevelt had the bit in his teeth. "They can do it. And so can we. By Jove, we'll have to."

Crossing the rocky stretch below the cable hut, Lobo Tex Riggins felt goosebumps. Daylight was only a promise, but in the wet muck, below the wash gully where several feet of cable lay uncovered, he spotted tracks. And not of familiar design.

Well, this was the kind of thing he was paid to do, and two years in the Alaska Scouts had made him good at it. They called him Lobo for the way he made time over rough terrain, and how he worked when he got there. Like those hideout Japs on Attu.

The sky was lightening; on the cable armor wires he saw shiny marks. "Bullets. Softnose." U.S. troops didn't carry softnose much. And the shoe tracks—he looked some more—still weren't quite right.

None of this said it *couldn't* be some dogface with wore-out shoes and a grudge. But didn't say it was, either.

Lobo went up to the cable hut. Not your usual shed, like the big one at Attu with the stove in it. Here, some fruitcake put a grenade to one of those, so the Signal Corps set up a steel box—torchwelded together on the spot—half-buried, with rocks in the bottom to hold it down. And except for the washout he'd just been looking at, cables and landlines were buried, too.

He peered closer. On the hut's padlock, more lead smears. He frowned. Could be some dumb GI kid, shooting things up just 'cause they were handy; there's always a lot of that.

If it wasn't . . . Lobo shrugged. Heading east, the tracked mud petered

out among the rocks. So follow the shoreline around to the docks at
Constantine Harbor. Either he'd catch up to somebody or he wouldn't.
He'd report this, do a stakeout. If there was real trouble, another
Scout or two could help. Malemute Red was tied up on Norton Sound,
but Afognak Pete was savvy. If Pete was out of the stockade yet. For now
Lobo had four-five miles to go before he got back to HQ, for his first hot
breakfast in over a week.

Major Spencer had his ass in a sling. CINCCOM's message, off the
Ketchikan cable, was the hottest item to hit Fort Rich since the
go-ahead to take Attu. But General Simon Bolivar Buckner was up at
Fairbanks on a "morale inspection." And the Alaska RR lines were out: a
landslide near McKinley Park.

These orders detailed coordination with MacArthur's CINPAC; if they
didn't arrive on time, the whole operation was cold soup. The general
was needed here at Anchorage sooner than now—and there was no
secure way to tell him so.

Spencer considered forwarding the message in Buckner's name. But if
he guessed wrong, he'd always be a major. Or maybe less.

Pooped, Buster was glad when his relief showed up. He signed off the
log and was on his way out when Captain Rodgers, the Officer-in-
Charge, sent him to pick up a message from Post HQ. Couldn't wait a
half hour for the circuit to open. . . .

Outside in unexpected sunshine he took a shortcut around and up the
hillside, above the lake where ACS got its brown water. At HQ he ran
into a lot of routine GI crap he wasn't used to. Working around the
clock, ACS didn't have time for that stuff.

Back to Ops he dropped the sealed envelope into the slot alongside
the crypto room door. Too tired to bother with breakfast, he went
straight to his hut—watching an approaching storm wall cut visibility off
solid, while to his other side, forty miles away gleamed the snowy peaks
of Semisopochnoi.

If you don't like the weather, wait a minute.

He ate half a Snickers bar, went to bed, and was halfway to sleep
when Scooter came in. "Hey, you know the rumor, there's an Alaska
Scout on duty here, patrolling the beaches? That message you brought
was the post commander asking for two more."

With coded stuff, Scooter was sometimes like a little kid.

General Buckner returned to Fort Richardson a day early; Major
Spencer met him in a jeep. Thirty minutes later Buckner's directive was

on its encrypted way. To ACS and to Whittier, then through Arctic depths to Aleutian HQ at Adak.

As the teletype clattered, Buckner stood over its operator. "I like that cable. The one circuit they can't intercept."

Sadly, Akaji considered the exquisite silver penknife, a parting gift from his wife Mayu. Of items available, only its blade was both thin and sturdy enough for the job at hand.

In dim slit of light from his handlamp, Akaji set the tip between two thick steel wires. With Arimura's handaxe he tapped until the blade penetrated. In fear it might miss the central conductor, Akaji held breath.

But his next blow brought a thin blue flash; jolting shock threw him headlong in the mud. Slowly he rose, unable to keep his voice steady as he said, "I believe that is far enough."

Now he struck sidewise; the impaling blade snapped. Akaji hammered its broken end farther, drawing momentary sparks as he drove it flush. Finding his ruined pen-knife was not easy; for long moments he held it, thinking of Mayu who had given it. Then abruptly, swallowing regret, he threw it high and far, to make a tiny splash in Arctic seas.

"Come, Arimura. It is time we foxes scurried to cover."

With the detachment's field phones all on one big party line, the one over Shemmy's bunk rang so much that Buster was used to it. Not until Scooter leaned over and shook him did he come awake. "Adak's gone *all* to hell. Thorne says grab a bite and get your ass in gear."

Sitting up, fumbling his clothes together, Buster got out of the sack. Thorne wasn't a man to panic; if he said jump, he had a reason. "Okay, Scoot; tell him I'm on the way."

Outside, rain came in spurts, like somebody throwing it a bucket at a time. The wind was having itself a clambake. Up the path, the outhouse had tipped over again, half its guy wires torn loose. So far it hadn't ever got away completely.

Right now he'd use the Officers'. It was closer, anyway.

Lobo Tex meant to get on stakeout earlier, but he loved poker and purely hated to leave a winning streak. Close on midnight, he neared the cable landing. Wind was gusting loud, but he quiet-walked anyway because he was in the habit.

Off toward the beach he heard something, a hammering noise, so he took out his handpiece and moved quicker. Nobody there, though; he wiped the gun dry as he could and reholstered it.

Also he had, shoulder-slung, a cased Springfield ought-three. But that one was for daylight and distance.

At the steel hut and where the cable lay unburied, he found no kind of trail to chase. Last time he'd been here, though, tracks had headed east. Lobo followed the shoreline that way.

In the messhall Buster fried and ate some eggs, filled his canteen, and fixed two sandwiches to go. Then, outside and heading for Operations, again he bucked the hellacious wind.

Coming into Ops he found Captain Rodgers chewing on Thorne. "That garbled radio message is clear on one point: we're to expect an Urgent by cable. An *Urgent*. And you say the Adak cable's out. Nothing more. Sergeant, what the hell is wrong?"

When Thorne's dark skin went pale he looked almost greenish. He said, "I don't know yet, sir. I need some time to find out."

Shaking his head, the OIC stalked off toward the other hut. Buster came up. "Thorne? What's it doing?"

"Balance went to hell; trying to check it I broke the pen."

Buster hadn't ever seen Thorne this way. He said, "Go eat something, lemme take a look." Giving the sarge orders? Well, maybe it needed doing, just now. . . .

Thorne parka'd up and went out. Buster took a deep breath. The captain hadn't given Thorne any chance to think. He didn't believe PFCs *could* think, so likely he'd leave Buster alone.

To break a pen, either Thorne screwed up or the cable itself was shot. Thorne didn't screw up much. Buster rigged the test set. Conductor Resistance, normally about twelve hundred, was down around forty. Pretty much like the quarterly test, with the landline shorted at the cable hut. This one he couldn't blame on Adak.

"What d'you mean, the message isn't going out?" Standing over Slim Barger, Major Poulsen glowered. "The tape's moving, isn't it? And the meters—" he gestured toward the cable amplifier cabinet "—they're all wiggling the way they always do. So how do you know. . . ?"

The trouble with Adak duty in the ACS was having the Area Commander on your back. Slim stayed patient. "Sir, you see that needle *there*?" Signal input, sitting solid on zero. "Amchitka isn't giving us any signal. None at all, sir."

"That doesn't prove they're not reading ours! It could be any simple trouble. Just because—"

"One of two things, sir. Power failure there, or the cable's out. Either way, they're not receiving. And power—it shouldn't take this long to come up on emergency."

"But if it's the cable..." Poulsen looked worried.

"Our balance is good; any trouble, it's their end."

The major's evident relief didn't last long. "But we've *got* to get that message through. The general said, expressly..."

Breaking off, Poulsen scowled. "How's the radioteletype?"

"Running test both ways, sir. Garbling badly here. That on-off RTTY signal isn't much good when the aurora kicks up."

"Can't use it for an Urgent, anyway." The major cracked his knuckles. "What else could we try?"

Major Knowitall was *asking*? Barger thought. Adak and Amchitka both had frequency-shift RTTY to Seattle. "If you had authorization, sir..." And Slim told him the rest of it.

Poulsen nodded. "I'll tell the general. And if *he* suggests it..." Then, "Stay on that cable problem. And keep me advised."

He stalked out, leaving Barger to face a dead receive meter. The test set told him that the only voltage on the cable was earth currents, and that the Amchitka end had to be shorted.

Back to sending test tape. Into an unmistakably dead end.

Captain Rodgers glared. "You're sure the line's shorted?"

Buster Morgan nodded. "Yes, Captain. The reading's solid."

Hands clenched behind his back, Rodgers took two paces away, pivoted, and returned. "Where's Thorne?"

"The messhall, sir. Shall I go get him?"

"No. Start putting gear together. Anything you can use to repair a damaged cable."

"I'm not a splicer, sir." And neither was Thorne. The nearest one Buster knew of was Absher, if he was still on Adak.

"You can cut and patch, rig something to get the signal through. Make sure you have—" he spread his arms "—hell, you know what you need. Get to it."

Starting to walk away, he turned again. "When Thorne gets back, I'll run you two down in the jeep."

"Down?" Down that steep tundra valley? "I don't think—"

"*I'll* do the thinking. And I'll set you down there in one piece. Though God knows how we'll get the jeep back up."

"The message reached Adak, Mr. President," said George Marshall. "Buckner confirms that much. But no farther."

"Does he know what the difficulty is?"

"The secure circuit. Adak has no contact with Amchitka."

Roosevelt grimaced. "And Mac's primed to move on schedule. Fully depending on the Aleutian thrust to split enemy response."

Marshall never said I told you so; now was no time to begin. "General MacArthur's risks are not much worsened, sir. It is our plan of surprise, our one-two punch, that I hate to lose."

"For want of a nail..."

"Or likely a tenpenny fuse on a Godforsaken windblown rock."

But Roosevelt was off on a new scent. "What of Eisenhower's proposal to expand daylight bombing? In particular, certain installations on the Baltic coast, almost due north of Berlin."

Marshall racked his brain. "That would be Peenemünde." Silver leaves to four stars, in as many years, was quite a rise. Sometimes, Marshall thought, Ike got too big for his breeches.

Rounding the headland, Lobo Tex scanned the creek-mouth area. Not much to see, but it felt wrong. The kind of tingle he'd had once when a rattler didn't rattle but he heard it anyway.

The creek was easy wading, but past it he lost the feeling. Something behind, he should have stopped to look at.

The creek, yeah. Lobo dipped fingers into icy water, brought them up to smell. He couldn't put a name to it, but something wasn't what you'd expect. And the way the terrain lay, no GI area drained into here.

It took him a time longer to find the hole in the bank.

Buster hadn't pegged the captain for a cowboy driver, but once the jeep turned downhill, Katy bar the door. The topheavy vehicle slithered, speeding up no matter what Rodgers did. The slitted-down headlights showed only moss that all looked alike.

Flat and grating, Rodgers cursed. Brakes sent the jeep skidding wild; the man had to gun hard to straighten out.

Buster hung on with all four paws; beside him, Thorne had better be doing the same. At this rate they'd all wind up in the drink! But Rodgers swung the jeep at an angle, then the other way, half-broadside to get more resistance, like skiers in the newsreels. Tricky as hell; jeeps tip over too easy. If this thing rolled, the homemade cab would crunch like an egg crate.

Now the captain yelled: a highpitched ki-yippy like a rodeo hand. Why, the crazy bastard was *enjoying* this!

A trick of the lights showed the final dropoff all too near. Rodgers cramped the wheel and slammed brakes; the jeep spun end for end and Rodgers floored it. In four-wheel drive the cleated tires threw moss like a cat in a sandbox.

Less than five yards from the edge, they stopped.

"All right, men. Hand me some of that gear. Let's get out there and fix the sonofabitch."

Great—if they had any idea where the trouble was. . . .

The cable hut sat unharmed except for bullet smears; the fault had to be down at the beach. Glad that the dark hid how scared he felt, Buster picked his way down the bank.

Akaji brooded. The Americans' secure circuit was disabled, yes, but repairable. If within three days he could render it useless, he could signal the submarine for rendezvous.

Such thoughts led nowhere; he had not the means. He and the others must remain here, inflicting such damage as might be devised, so long as their lives endured.

They would move westward, to unpopulated, less perilous terrain. And there create a more secure shelter from which to mount further incursions.

They would, at times, need to raid the Americans' food supplies. That need would serve as continued tactical training.

Preparing for sleep, Akaji was pleased; he had achieved greater serenity than his predicament could possibly warrant.

Lobo Tex paused. The mouth of the hole showed some spade marks but didn't tell him whose. Last time out he'd noticed a moonshine still was gone from East Cape; could've moved to here. So Lobo Tex had in mind, this didn't *have* to be Japs.

Most likely was, though; he didn't smell any mash. So did he feel like crawling up that hole all by himself?

Not right away. Anybody in there, be most apt to come out at night. At the cable landing he'd heard noises, but not since; if they'd holed up again, his best bet was wait here and watch.

He checked inside, a few feet; didn't find any traps or alarms, and backed out again. To set up one of his own. Nothing fancy, just a half dozen rocks placed where somebody coming out would knock a few off to hit the boulder straight below.

Loud enough to wake him up. Locating himself for a good clear shot at somebody outlined against nothing but sky, Lobo Tex crawled into his fartsack to catch some sleep.

Thorne spotted the uncovered stretch of cable, but it was the captain who found the little shard of metal wedged between two armor wires. "Somebody spiked this thing, men. Now then—how do we fix it?" As rain came in bursts.

Thorne had worked with a splicer, rigging the new cable hut. Now the sergeant said, "We'll have to cut some armor wires—four at least. Pull that thing out, melt rubber to seal the Anhydrex insulation. If the conductor's damaged . . ."

He took a deep, shuddering breath. "We should make a full splice, but even if I knew how, there isn't time." He spread his hands. "Over the Anhydrex is steel tape. All right, I cut so it overlaps when I lay it back, and lash on extra armor. But—"

"You'll do fine," said Rodgers. "How do we cut the armor?"

The hacksaw blade wore out fast; they had only one spare. Rodgers sent Morgan for some more, and for a head start ran the jeep as far as it would go, up the least steep part of the slope.

When it stalled, Buster jumped out. "Thanks!" He saw the jeep was making it back down okay, so he leaned into the spraying wind and began to climb. Once up on the level he just kept trudging, until finally he reached the Detachment area.

He was hungry again, but that would have to wait.

Chmielevski always knew he'd get lucky sometime, and his night off, tonight, sure looked like it. Red Cross girls *never* had to do with anyone but officers. Yet after the movie he'd been trudging back up from Post Theater to the Detachment area, and this redhead girl Clarice Dawson, driving a jeep all alone, gave him a lift. And then a drink of whiskey. Back home it would have been pretty bad whiskey, but here on The Rock there wasn't any such thing.

They'd stopped near the edge of the ACS area, off the road but not out of sight. With the engine on idle: low battery.

They got to talking, like old times back home. Shemmy just had to try and kiss her, he couldn't help it, and now here they went hand in hand down the tundra slope. Him carrying her sleeping bag. Well, he knew he had to get lucky *some*time. . . .

Silent Yokum and Scooter were in Ops. Buster said, "Somebody spiked the cable; I need saw blades and some stuff."

In the shop he found the blades, and wire to lash across the armor break. To avoid more talk, he went straight out the front.

His shortest route lay across the area, out the headland. He was past the Motor Pool when off the road a little he saw a jeep, motor idling. Then down the ravine he heard rifle fire.

Somebody yelled, ". . . *shot* me, dammit!"

And a woman screamed.

* * *

Awake in seconds, Lobo Tex got himself out of the bag and set to placing those sounds. Upslope, and not all that far. But part came from the *hole*; somebody in there was shooting out.

Which way to do this? Whoever was being shot at was topside, so going up the tunnel might surprise somebody.

Lobo uncased both guns and slung the rifle so he could get at it. Moving his alarm rocks aside he slid into the hole.

Scratchy, compacted moss roots dug him from both sides. Jap tunnel, all right. GIs, they'd make it bigger.

The confined blast of gunfire jarred Akaji awake, dazed. Fumbling brought his light to hand; it showed Miyake crouched awkwardly, aiming his rifle up the smokehole "Hold!" But Miyake, deliberately ignoring him, fired again.

Akaji repeated the command; Miyake did not lower his weapon. Dimly Akaji discerned the other three, frozen in lack of purpose.

The mission—! For *any* chance of success—Akaji drew his pistol. With little regret, he shot Miyake through the head.

"Gather your equipment," he said. "We must leave here."

Amid sudden silence, he heard rustlings from the tunnel.

Buster found himself in the jeep, heading down to where the noise was. This wasn't steep like the next valley, but squinting at patches of dim light he felt the jeep teeter and knew he was too near the treacherous center; he pulled to the right a little.

Ahead he saw a man on the ground and a woman trying to pull him up. Double-clutching the jeep down to compound, Buster got it stopped. Another shot sounded; he jumped and hit the dirt.

The man yelled, "They're down the hole! I stepped in it and fell; sonofabitch shot me from below." Buster knew the voice: Shemmy's. But who was the woman?

And what to *do*? Wait a minute—the gas can, flat against the jeep's side. He tore at its web belting; the can came free. He scrambled past the two and slid to rest alongside the hole.

"What—?" No time to answer. Buster took the cap off and tipped the can flat; gas poured out, down the hole. Then with a convulsive shove he sent the can after its contents.

He was reaching for a matchbook to light and throw down, when the explosion pelted him with moss.

Akaji smelled the gasoline; when he felt it spatter on him, he realized the source. "Leave everything! We must escape!"

To one side he glimpsed movement; Yamagiwa's rifle lifted.

But he was the *dependable* one! "No!"

Too late. Yamagiwa fired. The flash created inferno.

A few yards into the tunnel, Lobo Tex had no warning; the *Whoom!*, the heat and impact, stunned and half-strangled him. All he could do—fighting not to pass out *or* breathe more of the searing fumes—was wriggle backward to open air.

Even before he could quit coughing he had his Springfield ready. Any half-fried Jap did come out, wouldn't get far.

From the hole, flame popped and whistled.

"Godamighty!" Shemmy rose to one knee. "Clarice honey. I never would've thought . . ." Then, "Hey Buster! Wha'd you do?"

The woman's voice came calmer than she had any right to. "You have to help me. His leg—"

Buster took Shemmy's other arm, which held some bulky object. "Come on; maybe I can get the jeep up out of here."

Once they were in, Buster turned uphill and gunned ahead. When the engine began to lug he slacked off, letting the slope eat momentum. And reached the edge of the road. Barely.

"*Left* now." Her tone made it an order, but Buster stopped. Voice higher, she said, "The hospital, for heaven's sake!"

"Hospital?" Shemmy sounded plaintive. "What's the rush?"

Buster asked, "How much you bleeding?"

"Not a lot. Hey, I can even walk."

Buster nodded. "All right. Ma'am, it's only about fifty yards to Ops. Call Post Hospital; they'll send a wagon."

Bringing the woman along, Shemmy climbed down. She didn't like it. "Are you both insane? This man's been *shot*."

What Shemmy had under his arm was a sleeping bag. He said, "Can't it wait?" Maybe it could, maybe not, but Buster couldn't.

"I have things they need at the cable hut. *Now*. Okay?"

In a hurry to get there, he didn't wait for an answer.

If Rodgers could move a jeep down and not wreck it, Buster figured he could too. He was more than halfway when he saw he was wrong. The jeep broke loose; he could barely keep it aimed downhill, let alone slow it. As dim-lit patches of moss flashed by, he wished he'd unmasked his lights and the hell with orders.

Skidding, he saw the ACS jeep square in his path. *Hellfire!* He swung the wheel and hit brakes, but slammed into it broadside.

Grazing the cable hut, the captain's jeep went off the drop.

Breathing hard, Buster picked up what he'd brought, climbed out, and walked over to the edge. "Thorne? Captain Rodgers?"

The captain's voice had an edge to it. "Jesus Christ, Morgan! What took you so long?"

"Yes, Mr. President; *very* satisfactory." The Aleutian raids were beginning to help tip the balance. In Marshall's opinion, the Pacific War was now embarked on its final phase.

If MacArthur could be kept in check. Toward that end, the general had a thought. "Sir? About Mac; a suggestion?"

The cigarette holder waved. "Yes, of course."

"Well sir, supposing that *if* he stays strictly in line, he will be given full command of the eventual occupation of Japan?"

The famous Roosevelt chuckle. "Capital. Oh, capital!"

Tired or not, George Marshall never went to bed without checking his briefing room digest. Tonight's was not designed to help him get a good night's rest.

Eisenhower reported that fighter pilots escorting daylight bombers had observed, emanating from a ship lying well north of Peenemünde in the Baltic Sea, a phenomenal explosion. It had thrown a blinding glare across more miles than Marshall cared to believe, and a glowing toroidal cloud into the stratosphere.

Marshall called Oak Ridge. "How soon can you test?" The answer made him set the phone down harder than he intended. Hitler was at least a year ahead of the Manhattan Project.

Evaluation time. With the Aleutian offensive in support of MacArthur's southern push, Japan was a matter of months.

But Europe was going to be a bitch.

Author's Note

The specific depictions of Franklin D. Roosevelt, George C. Marshall, Dwight D. Eisenhower, and Simon Bolivar Buckner, plus attribution of various offstage activities to Douglas MacArthur, Malemute Red, and Averill Harriman, are fictitious. As are the other characters in this story.

The ACS Aleutian cable, however, did move a great lot of secure message traffic.

WHEN FREE MEN SHALL STAND

Poul Anderson

Clouds hid that dawn, prolonging night toward endlessness. A wind arose. At first it went sultry as the air had lain, then slowly cooled, strengthened, loudened. River smells mingled with those of town, of smoke, kitchens, warehouses, wastes, horses and their droppings, men and their sweat. A few early, heavy raindrops fell down the wind; thunder grumbled afar.

Blind where they waited, troopers shifted in their saddles, muttered among each other, passed forbidden flasks from hand to hand. Hoofs stamped on pavement, bits jingled, leather creaked. Here and there a cigar or a pipe made a flickery red star. They should have had real stars above them, to pale before an honest morning. Instead, rue de Bourgogne hemmed them in darkness, which a few gleams from shuttered windows only seemed to deepen, and doors were barred against them.

They were bold men in the Appomattox Horse, Indian fighters, their oldest bearing scars and memories of the First French War; they had been at the forefront of the assault that cleared the way into New Orleans; but James Payne could well-nigh feel the morale draining from them. He sensed it in himself. So did his mount. It became a mute contest to hold the both of them steady.

"Sir," he heard at his elbow, "ain't they never goin'a start? Must be past six by now."

"Shut up, Sergeant," Payne snapped.

"Yes, sir. Sorry, sir." Hollis was a dependable man. That he had spoken at all was a bad sign.

"First light sooner by canal," said Hog Eye on the lieutenant's left. Fewer walls to shut it out, a shimmer on the water, maybe the coal glow of enemy campfires.

Payne's mind flew homeward—sunrise silvering the woods along the

Blue Ridge; Harpers Ferry, where the rivers meet and the rapids run white, Mary Elizabeth Dodge and words spoken in a rose garden . . .

Guns crashed him back. Did he hear bugles and shouts? Suddenly the wind was full of brimstone. "Jesus Christ!" Hollis yelled. "They're goin'!" The whole platoon cried aloud.

"Hold tight," Payne ordered.

How had daybreak so sneaked and pounced? All at once he picked shadows from the murk, gleam off carbines and drawn sabers, then shapes, ornate grilles edging balconies, then colors, blue tunics and caps, sky still dark and formless but ever more mercury glints of rain. His pulse thuttered, his head felt curiously light. When he spoke, he heard the voice as a stranger's. "Have y'all forgotten? We move when Lee has the Frenchies' full attention. Remind our boys. Pass the word along."

Those in earshot nodded and obeyed. A shiver went through the ranks, as far down the street as they filled it. Firmness followed. Good men, thought the remote calm part of Payne's awareness. Not yet blooded to this kind of warfare, where gallantry isn't enough; but ready to learn it.

Have I learned it? Me, twenty-five years old, no, young? Awful young to die. Lord Jesus, into Thy hands I give myself. Forgive me my trespasses. Don't let me be afraid. Watch over Mother and everybody. Please. Amen.

Flame lifted above roofs and exploded on high. A rocket. The signal. "We're off, Sergeant," Payne said.

He touched spurs to his horse. Traveler nickered and broke into a ringing trot, left on rue d'Orleans, on toward the rampart. The gate there swung wide. As he went between its blockhouses, he glimpsed a cannoneer, who waved. The Stars and Stripes flapped wildly from a staff. Thunder rolled more and more often, louder now than the racket of combat.

The new defenses beyond were all too near, hastily thrown together when the fresh enemy troops appeared, barely sufficient to repel three assaults. Payne rode among fascines and gabions—trenches were no good in this swampland—into the open.

Glancing battleward, he saw only smoke and confusion through the hardening rain. If everything went as it ought to, Captain Lee's sortie had drawn the Imperials toward it, for he led the main squadron, and this might well be the start of an effort to break out. It wasn't, of course. The besiegers were too many, too well armed and well established. The maneuver was simply a massive feint, which was to end in withdrawal back into town—cover for the real mission, which belonged to Payne's enlarged platoon.

Or so the plan read. The lieutenant felt a grimace in his mouth. He wasn't a West Point man, but his officers in the reserve corps at William and Mary had been, and high among their maxims stood: "The first casualty of any battle will probably be your battle plan."

No matter. His duty was plain. The troop was deploying as it emerged, forming a blunt wedge for him to lead, to drive.

"Yonder," said he whom they called Hog Eye, and pointed. Payne's gaze followed the buckskin-clad arm over two miles or more. At the end of blurred vision he made out a house half wrecked, and a vague bulk that might be his target.

Must be. Hog Eye would know. The Cherokee had led the scouts who first warned that the foe were dragging a monster gun into position. ("Barged across the river, upstream of here," General Houston had concluded. "They can't bombard from that side; the town's shore batteries command it. But landward they'll have the range of us, and knock our works down in two–three days, I reckon. Less'n we can discourage 'em. Y'all game?")

"Bugler, sound the advance. Trot."

"Sir." The notes soared.

Water splatted dirty, hock-high. You couldn't make better speed through this mud, not unless you wanted to wear your horses out. Crécy, Agincourt. Save their strength for the final charge. But how nightmare-slowly you rocked forward. A row of cypress, bearded and gloomy; ruts alongside a rail fence; the house growing clearer ahead, its forlorn chimney, the cannon on a carriage that could have borne stones for a pyramid, its mule train, men in formation, rifles, muskets, whatever they had, flash, flash, flash, an Imperial standard sodden above them, nearly as mired as they. . . .

"Full charge." Payne drew his revolver.

Spurs, muscles astrain between thighs, thud and splash, *crack-craçk* and *bee*-buzz, somewhere a scream, Hollis's saddle vacant, but now in at them, onto them, ride them down!

A man fired at Payne, missed, raised his bayonet, and braced himself. His face gaped through the rain, a boy's face, the barest dark fuzz on its olive skin, Spanish, most of the Imperial force hereabouts was actually Spanish, not French or Creole, don't plunge against that point. The revolver bucked in Payne's grip. The boy's face erupted, dissolved, splashed. He fell, and Payne felt hoofs break ribs.

The Americans were among them, firearms emptied, sabers free. Some of the enemy drew wicked broad knives and tried to hamstring

the beasts that ramped above. Payne spied Hog Eye in action. The
Indian didn't whoop or anything; he worked, silent, wielding his blade
as methodically as though it were a scythe. Otherwise the melee was a
whirling fever-dream.

Which broke.

Payne stared around him. Surviving hostiles were in panic flight,
every direction. Wind hooted, rain hissed, like silence's voice. The
thunder seemed far away, too. Louder were moans and screams off the
ground, from men who maybe knew why they had been torn and horses
that did not. The horses threshed horribly. Whenever lightning leaped,
puddles sheened muddy red.

Payne realized he had been an engine, a harvester. He changed it into
another kind of machine, a chess automaton such as he'd read about.
Hollis was down, but Martin rode in that place. "Sergeant, put this
artillery out of commission," Payne directed.

"Sir!" Teeth gleamed in glee. Martin brought his gasping mount
around and barked orders. His gang already knew what to do. A spike
was insufficient; besides, this turned out to be one of the new percussion-
fired pieces. Cram the damned thing full of its own powder from breech
to muzzle, cut the carriage till the mouth was in the earth, lay a fuse,
touch a match, and skedaddle.

Payne rode about, seeing to the care, of his wounded, the recovery of
his dead. Losses weren't as bad as they might have been. Where was
Hog Eye? Off on his own, no doubt. No matter what unit you attached
them to, Houston's redskins gave strict heed to none but the Raven.
How did the diversionary skirmish go? No telling. There was only the
remote coughing of it, overridden whenever the thunder sounded.

Abruptly, freakishly, the rain paused. From the saddle Payne saw over
miles of grass and marsh, from the Mississippi and the steeples of New
Orleans clustered behind its walls, to the glimmer on Lake Pontchartrain.
He saw soldiers, toys at their distance, quick-step by hundreds from the
misty edge of sight. Cavalry covered their flanks, and fieldpieces trun-
dled after. A little nearer, Lee's squadron was disengaging to retreat.

The Imperials had reinforcements to call on, closer than we knew
about, Payne understood. More than we guessed they might. Newly
ferried down from St. Louis or wherever? They've got the whole rest of
this continent for a hinterland. Fingers closed around his heart.

The rain returned, heavier.

Hog Eye appeared through it, reined in, and sketched a salute. "We
cut off," he stated impassively. "Never make it back inside before they in
our way."

"They'd surround us," Payne's tongue added. "We've got to head north, fast."

"No supplies."

"We'll requisition what we can, and otherwise cinch our belts tight." Why did he explain? To make it clear to himself, so he could make it clear to his noncoms? Or because this scout would eventually, if they lived, report directly to Houston? "First we'll complete our task, demolish the gun. Then—reinforcements of our own ought to be bound here, you know. We got a message off before the Impies cut our telegraph. But looks like they'll meet still more strength than we reckoned when we called for help. They need a warnin'."

Maps unrolled in his mind: the narrow approaches to New Orleans between sea, lakes, and river; the military railhead at Natchez, doubtless enemy-occupied but tracks reaching east from it, a strand of the web that Andrew Jackson had decreed be spun across the States; yes, surely any relief expedition would come along it. Your job, son, is to pull what's left of your command out of this hole and take it thataways.

Payne straightened. Weariness dragged at his shoulders. It was a luxury neither he nor his men could afford. Martin was busy, but Corporal Bradford sat close at hand. Payne issued his orders.

For a moment lightning whitened the Cathedral of St. Louis against a heaven where every raindrop speared incandescent. The sight blinked away amid monstrous thunder, and again candle-flame reflections curtained off most of the world beyond the glass. Though a grandfather clock declared that the sun had risen, the room continued to need its chandelier.

The chandelier was crystal, suited to a chamber as gracious as everything else within the Cabildo. Government house, church, Presbytère, and several mansions nearby had seemed very European to Houston. They looked across rue de Chartres to the Place d'Armes and barracks, then onward to the markets, the waterfront, and the great brown river, like aristocrats, yet not without a part in the common life. Besides, here were the living links to Paris, Madrid, Rome, London. New Orleans wasn't really a frontier settlement. Much of the land beyond might still be thinly peopled or wild, north to the Arctic Ocean or west to the Pacific; but white men had dwelt here for more than a hundred years, and in Mexico, Havana, Rio, Buenos Aires, Lima for some three hundred; and all of them acknowledged the same Emperor.

That was a thought to daunt an American. He must not let it.

"Difficult, waiting, no?" said Gaston Lamoureux at his back.

Samuel Houston, major general, Army of the United States, turned from the window. "It is that," he sighed. "A lot easier leadin' boys out than sendin' them. Leastways, if you've got any kind of spirit or, or conscience."

"Unsuitable for you, 'owever."

"Too old, you mean? Shucks, I'm only—what is it?—fifty-six." Houston forced a smile. "Don't need spectacles except to read and write, nor a cane or anything else."

"I t'ink not of age," Lamoureux replied. His English, while accented, was fluent; he had been long in Dublin before they transferred him to the New World, where he regularly dealt with Americans. It was one reason Houston was glad to have him on hand. Houston's French lessons had been few and in the far past, and until now he'd had scant practice. Service in the last big war hadn't counted. He'd just fought then. Cherokee had remained his useful foreign language.

"Se time 'as gone w'en 'igh commanders rode in se van,"Lamoureux went on. "You should put be'ind you all sose years of yours among se Indians."

"I know!" Houston strode from the window. This place was a cage, carpet, portraits, bookshelf with bust of Napoleon I enlaureled, delicate chairs, mahogany table, escritoire at which Lamoureux perched, all hemming him in.

But it was a refuge as well. He must needs stay in the building he had made his headquarters, at least till word came about the foray. Finally he could endure the staff room no longer, silences punctuated by banalities, sense of putting on a show for an audience who expected it but had other things on their minds, same as he did. He'd given his officers an excuse and sought here, where he allowed Lamoureux to continue the historical researches that beguiled his retirement. As usual, the puckered little man was awake betimes, happy to shove codices and documents aside for some talk.

Houston stopped at the table, fumbled in his breast pocket, drew out a cigar, reached for the silver box of matches. He shouldn't smoke so early in the day, on an empty belly. He should go open the door and tell the orderly who waited outside to bring coffee. And maybe beignets; the siege hadn't yet closed all bakeries and patisseries. No, damn it, he wanted what fire he could get, between his jaws if not his hands.

He glowered at Lamoureux. "I'm not ignorant, whatever you think," he said.

The Frenchman looked straight back at him, countenance creasing multitudinously as he smiled without many teeth behind the lips. Light glistened on bald liver-spotted head and gold-framed lenses. "Certainly not. I meant simply sat time never flows upstream. You will understand.

You are in fact a man of se most complex, my general, farmer, explorer, schoolmaster, Indian friend and agent, politician, soldier; and I 'ave 'eard you cite ce *Iliad* in as natural a fashion as a man might quote from yesterday's newspaper. If you are no Pericles, you are at least a Lysander."

"Uh, thanks," said Houston, pleased despite himself. "Though I'm not quite that ruthless, I hope. And I reckon I wouldn't have burned Athens, either." He grinned. "Time hasn't diminished *you* any, sir, not where it comes to long-windedness." A jape felt good.

Lamoureux chuckled like parchment rustling. "It is se proper function of a diplomat."

I suppose, Houston thought. Did you welcome your assignment to New Orleans? Small use any more for diplomacy in Europe, after the Concord of Vienna, was there? But here, well, all right, Louisiana's gone back from Spanish to direct French rule, the king of Mexico's as much a puppet as the king of Spain or the queen of England, and so on and so forth—but here you've had us to deal with.

A match scratted in Houston's fingers. He brought it to the tobacco and drew deep. Harshness eased his heart. "Diplomat," he said slowly. In conversation, too, was relief. "The art of gettin' along with people."

Lamoureux shrugged. "As a means to an end. Alsough one does not admit sat in public."

Lightning glared anew; thunder boomed. Houston found a chair and sat down, mostly because it seemed impolite to keep looming over the other and he didn't want to give offense. He wanted company, somebody to save him from fretting about the action that the storm veiled from him. "You've sure been pleasant to me."

"You treat me kindly."

"I've no cause not to, sir. But how do you really feel? We are at war, your country and mine."

Lamoureux's tone gentled, as if in compassion. "I 'ave no personal animosity. Wars 'appen. Naturally, patriotism requires I pray for your speedy defeat, but you, my general, are a chivalrous opponent. Yes, I may call you 'umane."

"Not much bloodshed when we took this town, no. But not much resistance."

Lamoureux's calm cracked in a scowl. "You 'ave our Governor Antonio López de Santa Ana to sank for sat, I believe." He rolled the name out with sarcastic sonorousness.

Houston couldn't forbear to laugh. "Sure, we knew about him. His leadership was part of our strategy. Too bad he escaped, hey?"

"Indeed too bad. I pity sem in Mexico, and selfishly wish we do not get 'im back. But *hélas*, 'e 'as—you say?—connections."

"We'll spare you that."

Lamoureux donned the mask of scholarly detachment. "Of course, you want to keep New Orleans and control se mout' of se Mississippi. Se Emperor cannot permit you."

Houston turned serious. "Why not, really? We'd pay well. We'd make concessions. It'd be a good peace; ought to last."

Again, quite briefly, Lamoureux frowned. "It is painful to say, but you should know permanent peace between our nations is impossible. We can only 'ope to stay friends person by person, as 'uman beings."

"Why's it impossible? I've heard Frenchmen call us the heirs of the English, and I don't believe a word of it. We threw them off us way back in '76. Besides, you've settled with them yourselves. Why keep old grudges?"

"We fought sem for 'alf a t'ousand years. We would be fools to let you take seir place. It is not a matter of 'atred, I swear. Many of us like you Americans, yes, we admire you for your courage and energy."

Houston inclined his head. "And I remember reading how Tom Jefferson said every civilized man has two mother countries, his own and France."

"You are gracious, my general. But I speak about policy, necessity. Se *pervenche*—se, se periwinkle?—it 'as lovely flowers. But a prudent gardener will not let it grow freely. Else it soon overruns se 'ole garden."

"Well, sure, our population's growin' pretty fast, but if that's all you mean—"

"A single part of my intention. Sere are many sings to make sis conflict ineluctable. May I speak frankly?"

Houston rolled smoke over his tongue and streamed it forth. "Go ahead. I don't care for pussyfootin'."

"W'y did you not accept your defeat gracefully after se last war and abide by se quite generous terms we granted? A spirit of revenge? 'Ope to gain back w'at you lost, and more? I sink only in part. I sink you fear, far down inside your souls, sat if you do not eat se Empire, it will piece by piece eat you. And so you 'ave acted to become se predator before you become se prey."

"Come *on*, now! This war has perfectly plain causes."

"Oh, your President Polk, 'e was shrewd. I admire 'is timing. A debated succession in Paris w'ile se sepoys mutiny in India and rebellion erupts in Sout' America—yes, a well-chosen year to increase se provocations beyond w'at we could tolerate."

Houston flushed. "I ought to resent that," he snapped.

"Please do not be angry. You said I could express my honest opinion. My friend, se very presence of se United States subverts us. Our

German colonists in Louisiana, our British in Canada, our Spanish and Portuguese everyw'ere else, sey see you independent and grow restless. Se Russians in seir Nort'western possession, sey, too, remember because of you 'ow once seir Tsar was not anosser lackey but lord of 'is own empire. And your illegals in our fur trade, sey were also inevitable. But you deliberately send agents out, stirring up revolt. You wink at piracy. Your forcing se wild Sauk and Winnebago tribes across our border, sat was only w'at you call se last straw."

"Well, if your government had been more willin' to negotiate—"

"Let us not deal in excuses. I am not angry, me. Sis is all in se nature of nations." Lamoureux paused. "And we Europeans, we are accustomed to taking se long view. We can let you wait for our full attention. Meanw'ile, pardon me, but it seems you cannot 'old New Orleans. I beg you surrender it before sere is more useless killing. I can speak for you to my colleagues. Santa Ana is fled. Se French aut'orities 'o are left, sey still listen a little to an old man's words. I sink we could arrange you march out wit' full honors, if you do it soon."

Houston stiffened. "I'm not a sailor," he snapped, "but I'll quote John Paul Jones anyway: 'I have just begun to fight.'" A loud rap sounded on the door. "Come in!"

An ensign stepped through and saluted. He was young, white-cheeked, shaken. "Sir," he blurted, "they need you back in the staff room. The Virginians are returnin'. They, they report new hostile troops, a swarm of 'em—"

Houston was already out the door.

The enemy did not give pursuit. Maybe no one saw Payne's retreat through the driving rain. Maybe no one thought it worth the trouble and risk, when the noose was being drawn tighter around the city and it was unsure what American forces might be where to the north. Payne didn't know or much care. He was content to offer thanks, and ride.

The next days were nevertheless hellish. He didn't head straight east for U.S. territory; yon bridge was surely well guarded, with French at both ends of it. Instead he took his band northeast cross-country, fording the Bogue Chitto, till he came on the road along the Pearl River and followed that north. It was broad, graveled, well graded, a military highway in both the Empire and the Republic. The stream provided water. But there was no food for men, and mainly snatched grass for horses. Once beyond the marshlands, territory higher and drier, they passed plenty of farms and villages. However, crops weren't ripe, and they dared not stop to forage. The best they could grab was an occasional pig or some chickens, which didn't go far whenever they took a few hours' rest. Otherwise they must struggle on, while inhabitants stared after them in sullen resentment.

Struggle it was, ever more, as hunger and exhaustion whittled on them. Three of the wounded developed fever and died, to be buried in shallow graves with a hasty prayer. Soon half a dozen others could go no longer. Payne left them in the churches nearest to where they gave out, hoping the priests would keep the people from lynching them. Because this took time, and he must do it for each, talking to that man, taking whispered messages for folks at home, it hurt still worse than it had hurt to leave the wholly incapacitated behind on the battlefield alongside the dead. Officers might expect good treatment and eventual parole; enlisted prisoners' chances of surviving malnourishment and sickness in the stockades were poor.

The platoon must keep moving, though. It was God's mercy that they weren't attacked. To be sure, when Houston came down through here, he captured and burned every outpost on his way, widely to right and left. Maybe the garrisons hadn't yet been replaced. Maybe the Imperials figured it was smarter for the time being just to keep patrols about, on the watch for any new invasion—for the Americans had cut their telegraph lines, and when they got their first reinforcements, they cut those the Americans had strung. Be that as it may, if a detachment spied Payne's starvelings and sent after assistance, that would be that.

The border was ghostly. When word came that war had been declared, the French struck at once out of New Orleans, unexpectedly hard. They reduced Fort Burr to ruin before they withdrew. Now their Fort Lafitte was likewise charred timbers, ashes, and bones among broken things.

Few Americans had ventured to settle hereabouts, when the exact line between the Grand Duchy of Louisiana and the state of Mississippi remained in dispute and was, in fact, one occasion of this war. Greenwood brooded on either side of the road, heavy with shadows and earth odors. A squirrel ran up a tree, a cardinal winged by in vivid scarlet, a mockingbird trilled—somehow they sharpened desolation. Payne's troop stumbled onward.

Then on the fourth evening of their journey—or the fifth? He could not immediately remember—Hog Eye glided out of some brush. The scout alone had seemed immune to misery and, sparing his mount, ranged around afoot, Indian-style. He drew nigh the lieutenant's stirrup and said, impassivity yielding to a broad grin, "Hurry now. Your soldiers. Short ride."

A cheer of sorts muttered along the lines as the news passed back. The animals themselves seemed to smell relief. Their heads lifted, and when the forest stopped, they broke into a trot. Hoofs thumped, metal jingled. By God, Payne thought, we'll meet them like Virginians.

Road and river wound on through a plantation. Sun-beams from the west reached long across pastures where livestock grazed, fields of sprouting corn and cotton, shade trees around the big house. At this hour the slaves must be done hoeing and back in their cabins. South-bound with Houston, Payne had wondered whether so big a property so near the frontier wasn't tempting Fate. Well, he'd decided, the owner of such a spread could afford enough armed guards to put up a resistance till help came from Pearl Bridge Station.

That had been Payne's goal, the Army post where the military railroad crossed this river on its way to the Mississippi. Natchez was likely in French hands, but he felt sure the enemy hadn't made it much farther east. He'd report in and stand by for whatever orders came over the wire. Probably they'd be to feed his men up and wait till the reinforcements arrived, then join them.

But yonder the regiments were! So they'd already reached Pearl Bridge, made it the place where they got off the trains, and started toward New Orleans. For a hysterically funny moment Payne speculated on how Massa felt about his rescuers, bivouacked in choice meadows that would be trampled clay tomorrow morning.

Never mind. "Bugler," Payne croaked, "I want 'dress lines' and a smart advance. Scout"—to Hog Eye—"back in your saddle and ride on my left." He didn't quite know why he said that, unless it was because the Cherokee, not in uniform but in leather and oddments, was neater and cleaner than anybody else, and was Sam Houston's man.

Fires smoked, tents stood taut, sentries paced across acres. Horses seemed a lot fewer than mules, field guns about as many as supply wagons. Mostly infantry and artillery, passed through Payne's mind. Cavalry was auxiliary and minor. Crossing a ridge, from the crest he caught an overview of the camp. It was laid out as a grid, with mathematical precision. Vague memories stirred, Latin classes, Roman *castra*. Were the cannon on the perimeter placed equally exactly? He was too tired and hungry to be certain.

A squad of riders galloped to meet him. Their uniforms were a darker blue than his. The corporal in charge saluted crisply. "Where are you from, please, sir?" he asked. His accent twanged flat.

Payne identified himself, his command, and their point of departure. The corporal whistled. "Quite a ways, sir. Uh, we're the Fifth and Seventh Illinois, the Third Michigan, and the Wisconsin Rangers."

Wonder drove fatigue from Payne's attention. "Michigan, Wisconsin? Shouldn't you be holdin' the Canada line?"

"No need, sir. Not that we hear much in the ranks, but I do know the Yankees have got Maine back and are moving in on Quebec. Maybe they've taken it by now; maybe Montreal, too. The Canucks got enough to keep 'em busy." The corporal broke off. "Beg pardon, sir. Not for me to talk about." He was quite young. "If the lieutenant please, let's proceed. Our officers will get you quartered fast, I bet."

Maine is ours! Gladness jumped in Payne. The next peace treaty, by God, we won't cede it again. And we'll kick all the goddamn Pierres out, too.

Exhilaration sank as he rode into a section where the tents sheltered Negroes. Negroes, armed, a few bearing stripes on their sleeves—he'd been aware of such units but never expected to see any in these parts. Better keep his mouth shut, though. He must admit they were as clean and orderly as the whites. In truth, the entire camp, thousands of men, hummed and clicked quietly. Also around their fires, they sat alert, and sprang up to salute when they saw the bars on his shoulders. It was more like a military academy than any army in the field.

A Southern army, that is, he realized.

Heartiness waited at the end of his ride, in the person of a large blond captain named Bergmann, who bade him welcome and bawled orders in a German accent. Payne was quickly seated on a folding stool, a tin cup of coffee in one hand and a sandwich in the other. His platoon was dispersed among surrounding groups—"Ve vill assemble dem in de morning, Lieutenant"—except for Hog Eye. "Johansen, you take de Inchun ofer to de niggers and tell Sergeant Grant to zee to him." Payne paid slight heed. How good to shed responsibility for a while and rest, rest, rest. Warmth crept into the corners of him. He nodded. . . .

Bergmann shook him awake. "Kvick! De general vants you should report. Aftervard vill be a cot and zix nice hours sleep for you. First ve clean you a liddle, ha?"

Payne blinked. "Wouldn't the general understand how come I'm dirty?"

"Yah, yah, but you vant to be like a pig? Ve are zoldiers here, boy. Got hot vater, zoap, sponch, and den clean clothes vot fit maybe not too bad. Ve vash and repair your own outfit later."

Scrubbing himself, Payne regained some life. Nor did it hurt that the uniform lent him was Ranger. Everybody knew what those boys had done in the Indian wars.

Bergmann guided him to the commander's tent, chatting at drumfire rate. He was among the Germans who'd emigrated after King Joseph hanged the signers of the Heidelberg Manifesto and put down the uprising that resulted. Soon he was altogether devoted to his adopted country. It had given him a farm, presently a family and a vote. The stiff service requirements of Illinois—cadet corps; three full years after leaving school; then three months' active duty annually, till the war made it full-time again—were to him less a task than a joy, a second occupation more interesting than his cows and corn. "Europeans, bah! Ve vip dem back to deir kennels and teach dem respect for men, by damn!"

"You've got tough opposition ahead," Payne warned. "I think, from what I've seen, you'll be pretty heavily outnumbered."

Bergmann spat. "Numbers? Dey don't know how to fight no more dan packs of dogs. Ve seen action against dem already in Minnesota. I don't t'ink does greaser troops here giff us any more trouble dan de frogs did."

"M-m, I hope you haven't left the North unguarded."

"No, no. We is just vat de high command can spare."

Payne mustered nerve. "Is that how come you got niggers along?"

Bergman blinked. "Vot you got against darkies? Dey do serfice same like us. Ve don't haff slafes in de Nort'."

"I know. But, well, sir, not meanin' any offense or anything, but I don't believe it's wise bringin' them south. The sight could give ours ideas. I'd hate havin' to make examples, the way they had to in 'Bama a few years ago."

"You got dem kviet, dough, did you not?" It was hard to tell by the yellow sunset glow whether Bergmann's face reddened. His tone chilled. "You should not talk, boy. I saw dat Inchun vit' you. I hear you Sudderners got whole corps of Inchuns. *Dat* is de great mistake. Vere I come from, ve know does murdering saffages too vell."

Payne swallowed. "Sorry, sir. I told you I didn't mean any offense." Let the newcomers argue with Sam Houston, if they dared.

Bergmann eased. "All right, all right. Not to vorry much, so long as vite men keep strongest, ha? Maybe better first ve vorry about all dose Jews coming in."

"Well, true, we are gettin' quite a few of them in our seaboard cities. Not like among the Yankees, not yet..."

But then they had reached the big tent. Lanterns inside filled it with dull light, unrestful shadows, and oil smells.

Major General Stephen Watts Kearny sat behind a table, maps spread before him, taking notes. From time to time he lifted a briar pipe from a bowl and took a puff. Nonetheless his appearance, his manner, the whole iron-gray being of him made Payne, bathed or no, feel like a boy caught in truancy. Lieutenant and captain snapped salutes. Kearny returned the gesture and indicated two campstools. "At ease," he said.

"Be seated, gentlemen." Despite long service elsewhere, a trace of the Northeast lingered in his voice.

Payne and Bergmann made haste to obey. "I gather you've quite a story to tell us," the general continued. "We're happy for all the information we can get. Well done, Lieutenant."

He's human, Payne thought. He don't act easy like old Sam, but he's no martinet; and you better not bungle with Houston, either. "Thank you, sir."

"Speak. Proceed chronologically if you can."

Payne commenced. Kearny interrupted after a minute: "It isn't clear to me how that first lot of fresh Imperials arrived right after you took New Orleans, and bottled you up. No proper account came through."

"No, sir, I reckon not. I hear tell our dispatcher was still sendin' when they showed, and barely got away."

"Do you happen to know?"

"We officers of the Appomattox Horse were told, sir. You see, we were to make a sortie against a siege gun the enemy was bringin' to bear. General Houston reckoned somethin' like this might happen, some of us be forced north. Not that he knew more troops were on their way, but it could've happened somehow. In that case, we might as well try carryin' the news. I don't s'pose any of his couriers made it to Pearl Bridge?"

"Evidently not. You were lucky; you men. Of course, mine wouldn't have heard anything while they were crammed in the troop trains, but when we arrived, no further word was waiting for me."

A vision passed before Payne, wires and rails spread across a fourth of the continent, electrical halloos racing north and east—surely to end in the head of the supreme commander, old Winfield Scott—and then the decision, the orders, and locomotives fired up a thousand miles away, men and animals embarking, guns and munitions and stores loaded— how fast it had gone, after all. They were sharp enough in the South, but you would not have seen that kind of machine efficiency there. And the lonesome whistles through the night, the prairie miles falling behind— yes, his countrymen had built strongly on the foundations that President Jackson laid.

"Well, what did go wrong?" Kearny demanded.

"The way I was told, sir, while our main army made straight for New Orleans, a couple of regiments swung down into West Florida and ripped out the rail lines, figurin' then the Imperials couldn't get troops from there to Louisiana till we were settled in too firmly for them."

Kearny nodded. "That's obvious. Westward, the Empire hasn't got much this side of the Rio Grande, and the Comanches and Mexican guerrillas keep it occupied. Go on."

"Well, sir, what I heard—it was learned from prisoners, I reckon—was that the French had a lot of ships at Cuba that we didn't know about. Navy, fixin' to move against ours. And there's a cable between Havana and St. Augustine. So the steamers that they had amongst them went to Florida, took on the Spanish units, and carried them across the Gulf to Lake Borgne. Caught us by surprise, they did, and drove us back into the city."

Kearny tugged his neat beard. "I thought that was how it might have been."

"And now, sir, they've fetched still more. I don't know where from. Northwards, I'd guess. But anyhow, I saw 'em comin', just when my platoon was out there disablin' that cannon. They'll have numbers now to bar those narrow strips of land around Lake Pontchartrain—"

Kearny chopped the words off. "Leave strategy and tactics to your superiors, Lieutenant. What I want you to do is think back, think hard, ransack your memory."

His questions flew like musket balls, probing into the chaos that had been action, striking after facts, estimates, possibilities. When at length he said, "Enough," Payne barely checked himself from collapsing off his stool.

"You've been helpful," Kearny finished. "I daresay I can get more out of you after you've rested, and in any event you can point out things on our line of march. Captain, I want Lieutenant Payne reporting to me again in the morning, right after breakfast. Make all necessary arrangements for him and his men. Dismissed." His glance went back to the maps.

The two rose, saluted, left.

Dusk was thickening into night. Stars glimmered through warm air and a haze of smoke. Lanterns glowered on poles, bobbed in hands. Banked fires smoldered ruddy. Some distance off, in a space left vacant, one still burned high. Payne couldn't see it clearly, for men surrounded it—several hundred, maybe, and more in the lanes between tents. Amid and above them, upheld on a pole, a steel cross gave back the flickery light. A hymn began, deep voices, a swinging, tramping chant that sent ghost fingers up and down his backbone.

In the blood the Lord did shed for us we take our cleansing bath,
That His holy spirit lead us on the straight and thorny path
Till the nations of unrighteousness have felt His mighty wrath.
We march to victory.
   Glory, glory, hallelujah,
   Glory, glory, hallelujah,

Glory, glory, hallelujah,
We march to victory!

Day squatted surly on the world. Clouds seemed only to cast more heat downward. Air lay waterlogged into silence, except for the whine of innumerable mosquitoes. Houston felt sorry when his inspection along the shore side was over. He breathed a little easier there and saw a huge river vista instead of walls everywhere around him.

Of course, he'd also judged it necessary, or at least smart, to make the tour once again. Thus far the batteries, booms, and torpedoes he'd captured were interdicting enemy vessels. He had a growing notion, though, that a fleet was bound over the gulf to force a passage. It would account for the low level of French activity since they lost their big gun. Ordinarily a siege was not a matter of sitting still. Fights raged around the whole neighborhood, till they got into the city and then might well go on street by street, day after day. But if aid from the sea was expected, why not wait for it and meanwhile let hunger and eventually sickness do their sappers' work?

Or did the Imperials simply mean to starve the Americans out? That ought to spare much destruction and shouldn't take awfully long. Since this was a keystone place, he had found both civil and military store-houses full. However, when their stock must be doled out to the population as well as the army, it went fast, no matter how meagerly. Houston had been tempted to expel the inhabitants. But that would be barbarous—and, he admitted, lose him their hostage value.

Besides, he didn't think the French enjoyed keeping so many troops staked here. They were needed elsewhere, to defend Florida and the upstream marches, in due course to join a counteroffensive. Yet they didn't appear to be preparing to storm New Orleans. Therefore, he figured, they probably expected their navy units would be along soon.

As he left the inner emplacement on the west side, several of his bodyguard went down the stairs first. The others came right behind him and promptly fanned out. They were a wild sight, those Shawnees, Cherokees, and Chickasaws, like a tomahawk thrown into a crystal bowl. He could have put them in uniform—most of their kind wore civilized clothes at home—but in skins, feathers, and paint they overawed the city and kept things peaceful. He didn't want snipers potting at him, nor want to shoot people who got out of hand. You couldn't really blame such folks, could you?

He strode on along the wharf. A few men lounged on the decks of four idled ships. The rest must be ashore passing the time in sailor wise—no dearth of loose women, nor rum very scarce. Sentries faced to and fro, sunlight reflected harsh off bayonets. Fishing boats and oar-powered trawlers were out under the protection of the cannon, taking what they could to sell at fancy prices. Well, it helped. Otherwise the scene was almost deserted, eerily quiet.

No, wait. A familiar small figure stood by an unused cleat, stoop-shouldered, hands behind back, staring across the water. Impulsively, Houston moved toward him and halted. "Howdy, sir," he greeted. His Indians formed a semicircle and poised alert.

The Frenchman blinked at him and said an automatic *"Bon jour"* before adding, with a parched laugh, "Pardon, please. I forgot w'ere I am. I was 'alf a century and an ocean away."

"Left your books for a while, eh?" Why not a few minutes' conversation before the return to grimness?

Lamoureux shrugged. "One feels need for some sky now and sen. Even old men do. Or per'aps especially old men. We 'ave not much time for it any more." His look strayed again to the great slow current. "Also, 'ere is se sense of 'istory I search for and do not find in most philosophers."

"History? Isn't all this country kind of new and rough?"

"It is of Europe—as are you, my friend, w'esser you like it or not." Lamoureux's voice dropped so low that he became hard to make out. "But w'at I have in mind is more old and deep san sat—older san se Pyramids, and it will remain long after sey are crumbled to dust. Se flowing, se onwardness. Fate, if you wish to use sat word. Causality, se serene working out of nature's law among us as among se planets—sat is w'at se river teaches."

"I see."

"Sere is comfort in knowing we are in se stream of time, a tiny part, nossing sat makes any difference, but still a part of se Oneness."

"You've said as much before." Houston shook his head. "And I don't buy it. We've got free will. We can and we do help decide how things will go. Why, blind accident does; and we can cope with it, too."

Lamoureux smiled. "Se 'istory of your nation predisposes you to believe sat, but—"

"Sure. Shouldn't it? King George thought he could keep our fathers under his heel. The whole world did. But they learned different, because free men chose to take arms."

"I sink we French 'ad somesing to do wis se outcome. And as I was about to say, you must agree sat once se Empire was victorious in Europe, se changes in your own society sat followed were inevitable."

"Well, required, some of them."

"And se rest, sey were logical corollaries."

"No, not really. When President Jackson called for a second Constitutional Convention, most of us delegates just meant to strengthen the government so we could defend ourselves better—"

"But 'e made pressure and forced you to adopt more radical provisions."

"He had his reasons, whether or not men like me were happy with them." The talk had gone down a trail Houston didn't care for. He tried a diversion. "Besides, look, I spoke of sheer accident playin' a role. If Jackson hadn't died in office in his fourth term, his Uniform Military Service amendment would've passed, sure. But he did and it didn't."

"It will, or somesing similar, unless se Empire reduces you to se status of Britain."

"Ah, ha! You say 'unless.' You mean it's not fated."

"In 'indsight, 'istorians will see sat w'atever does 'appen was certain to 'appen, just as I see today sat we stand 'ere, you and I, because se French and Spanish fleets broke se British off Cape Trafalgar."

Houston had often heard that battle called one of the decisive ones—without mastery of the seas, England was doomed, long though it took to wear her down—but he was vague on details. Anyhow, he naturally felt that what happened on land was always more important. "They couldn't have done it if they hadn't spent years first, building up their naval strength," he argued. "Somebody had to make that decision."

"True," Lamoureux conceded. "Matters are less simple san I pretend. Many factors work togesser, and it is seldom clear to us 'ow sey do. My sense of inevitability is more intuitive san scientific, I grant you. Neverseless, 'ere on se bank of sis mighty river, I *feel* se current of time."

Still he looked outward. "In fact, before you came, my soughts, sey 'ad wandered up sat stream, 'alf a century. For, do you see, I was reminded of *la Manche*—se English Channel, agleam on a winter day outside Boulogne."

"Not much like, I'd say."

Lamoureux shivered. His tone had gone remote; it was if he spoke to himself, foreign language or no. "Yes, it was a cold light. 'Ow cold. Our ships in se 'arbor, sey were many, many, masts and spars a leafless forest. We men, we sat or stood or paced in an upstairs room of ce *hôtel de ville*, a warm room wis fire and candles, drapes and carpet, clear glass for us to see t'rough from 'igh above, as if we were gods. Yet I 'ave never felt a sight was more forbidding san sose steely waters under sat leaden sky. I rejoiced in my 'eart w'en I learned we would not cross sem. And I was young sen, wis flame in me." He sighed. "We were all young. Se Emperor 'imself, 'e was only—'e was not quite t'irty years of age. Se 'ole world was young, for us."

"The Emperor?" asked Houston, startled. "The first Napoleon? You met him?"

Lamoureux returned to heat and silence and tarry smells. "Oh, 'e was not Emperor sen. We 'ad still our name of a republic, and Bonaparte, 'e was not even First Consul so far. 'E 'ad se title of General of se Army of England, for an attack across se Channel was being prepared. But in se reality, after 'is victories, 'e was as powerful in France as any osser man. I stood in 'is awe—in awe of 'im. Everybody did."

"What were you doin' there, if I may ask?"

"I was merely a clerk, a...a secretary on se staff of se foreign minister, Prince Talleyrand-Périgord. 'E 'ad many assistants more important by far. But because I was nobody, and 'ad shown I could keep confidences, and sis matter must be discussed in deepest secrecy, it was me 'e chose to take to Boulogne to record for 'im. And so I was sere w'en 'e, and General Berthier, and Napoleon's brosser Lucien, and Napoleon 'imself weighed se grand decision."

"And figured they'd better not try to invade England," Houston knew.

"Correct. Se fleet was not yet strong enough; se risk was too large. But if sis plan was canceled, somesing else must be done. Else sey would seem weak, and soon lose control."

Houston nodded. "Ridin' a wild stallion, they were, hm?"

"A tiger, Prince Talleyrand said. I sink, besides, 'e argued against attacking England because 'e 'ad friends sere, and interests. 'E was utterly corrupt—but intelligent—yes, I know well w'y at last se Emperor sent 'im to end 'is days on St. 'Elena. Sere in Boulogne, 'e 'ad proposed striking into Egypt, to cut se British off from India. And Napoleon, 'e took fire at sat idea. Audacious as Alexander marching east, fame immortal, oh, sis Sout'land sun does not so blaze so bright as sat little dark man in sose winter days! I could not stand before 'im; se splendor of se vision swept me away into itself. But of course I did not matter. I was less san se lowliest *moustache* in 'is army."

"Lucien, 'owever, Lucien could resist 's is brosser 'o 'e 'ad tumbled wis in sat poor 'ouse in Corsica. And Berthier 'ad talked Lucien over. 'E was a brave man, too, Berthier, none more valiant, but 'e 'ad a different idea, not so magical but more...systematic? 'E persuaded Lucien to 'elp 'im persuade Talleyrand and Napoleon.

"To go to Egypt, sey said, would be to court disaster. If se English 'o were scouring se Mediterranean, if sey found our ships, we could lose everysing we sent on sat expedition. Let us for now stay in Europe. *Les allemands*—se Germans might be well subdued; but Italy was only newly conquered and restless. We should secure it beyond any possibility of revolt, Berthier said. And sen we should go into Spain and

Portugal—Talleyrand could easily invent reasons—and over se straits to Tangier. So would we shut se Mediterranean to se English, reduce seir fleet sere in detail, and build more ships for ourselves at our leisure. . . . But you know sis, for it is w'at 'appened.

"Me, I remember hours of dispute in sat room in Boulogne. Se short winter day drew to a close. Servants brought food sat se men barely bit at. And I, I 'ung in a corner, my writing board on my knees, t'rowing down quill after quill as I wore sem out, never seeing w'at sey scrawled, so lost was I in se spectacle—'ow 'e 'o stood colossal at Campo Formio and decreed, 'e now stormed and shouted and, yes, sulked—sen suddenly se first fire went out, but ce new fire caught 'old, and '*Oui*,' 'e said, oh, 'ow softly, '*comme Charlemagne*'—but sis time we do not wisdraw across Roncesvalles!"

Lamoureux stopped short, gulped for air, hugged himself, old blood turned cold within the Louisiana heat. Someday, Houston thought, will I be like that, harkin' back to when my Indians called me their Raven? Please, God, no.

He started to lay a hand on the other man's shoulder, though he wasn't sure what to say. A sudden thud of gunfire afar saved him.

Ahead, eastward, shone Lake Pontchartrain and the highest spires of New Orleans. On the left, Lake Maurepas snuggled close to the vast sheet of water; on the right ran the Mississippi. Between them reached some ten miles of mostly open ground, flat, boggy, intensely green with grasses, reeds, stands of cypress and gum, cottonwoods bordering the highway along the river. Aside from hunters, humans had made little use of it until, here and in the narrow strip between the lakes, the Imperials set their defenses against assault from outside.

Payne shifted in the saddle, restless as his mount. "Sir, if you'll just let me and my boys lead your horse . . ." It wasn't that he was stupid-eager, it was that he had come to feel he must show these stolid Northerners what Virginians were worth.

"How fast d'you expect to charge over this mud?" Kearny snapped.

"We'd come on the road and those drained shoulders, sir, hit their left and roll them up."

Kearny shook his head. "A Southern thing to do. The last of the Celtic war bands, your state militias. No."

"Sir—"

"Shut up." Kearny lifted telescope to eye.

Without a hill beneath him he could see little, and most of it already lost in smoke. Artillery dueled, flash and roar down the opposing lines, blunt earth-quivers where round shot struck, fountains where canister burst to spray horseflesh and manflesh. Americans had stood off attack after attack while Kearny's crews worked their guns into position. Now the infantry simply stood.

A shell exploded nearby. Three men became red remnants. Others dragged wounded comrades and their own hurts back to the rear. A mule stayed behind, threshing in a tangle of guts. Its screams were hideously womanish.

Kearny lowered the telescope. His face showed nothing beneath the weathered and grimed skin, but Payne thought the lips within the beard had whitened the least bit. "Poor lads," he said low. "Well, ours can take this better than those spigs can."

I don't see how any human beings can much longer, Payne thought. Not Hog Eye, for one. "I find my chief," the Indian had said, appearing out of dawn-dusk to pluck the lieutenant's sleeve; and with the same suddenness, he was gone. But it wasn't fair to call him a coward. This just wasn't his style of fighting. He'd make his secret way to the city and Houston.

Anyhow, he'd taken enough foul words on the march south, whenever he came forth among whites; and he couldn't have felt at home among the blacks, either. Some of his people kept slaves, too.

For his part, Payne had mostly ridden near Kearny, and learned he'd damn well better have an instant and accurate answer to every question flung at him. This general didn't tiptoe forward. His men double-timed the whole distance. Water, gumbo, skirmishers on their flanks hardly slowed them at all. And still they arrived ready for combat. Payne liked to believe his scraps of information had helped, ever so little.

A new din grabbed at him. Incredibly, his mind had wandered. He stood in his stirrups to peer north. A moment's breeze scattered sulfury smoke clouds and he saw, yes, a blue swarm—ants at their distance, but myrmidons, sparks where metal threw back sunlight, and—did he only imagine?—a gnat's-wing dance of colors, American colors.

He whooped. "They did it, sir! By God, they did it!"

"I expected they would," Kearny answered.

—expected that the fourth of his forces that he detached, foot alone, rifles and naked steel, would storm the earthworks and cannon and troops between the lakes, overwhelm them in an hour's slaughter, pass through without heavy loss, and take the rest of the enemy from behind.

Confusion crawled over the green and the wet yonder. The Imperials had seen what was bound for them and were trying wildly to regroup and meet it. Kearny spoke to the officer on his right, who saluted and cantered off. More came, received their orders, and departed.

"Sir—" Payne begged.

"Not yet," the general denied him. "Wait a while. I don't hold with sending men to useless death." A brief grin. "It's worse than a crime, it's a blunder."

Bugles rang. Drums rolled. In rank upon rank, the Americans who had been waiting advanced.

Fire darted among them. They fell and they fell. Each time, the one behind stepped up to take that place, and the jog trot never slackened. On horseback though he was, Payne felt the mass of them beat through the ground into his bones. When at last they had passed, the litter bearers followed, coolly gathering those wounded who lived. Payne's mind flew ahead, into a soldier he never knew; a young fellow; a boy maybe, French, Spanish, Creole, Cajun, mestizo, whatever, who crouched against some turfs and watched the blue host move in on him. Roses by moonlight, a snatch of song, or his mother's hands tucking him into his crib once. . . .

The tide reached the barriers and burst over them. An Imperial standard toppled, white and gold down into the muck underfoot.

Payne shuddered with horror and glory. "Sir, that, that's magnificent!"

"It's proper training, discipline, supply, and leadership," Kearny said. Almost wearily: "Very well, a cavalry charge may serve some useful purpose at this stage. Major Cleland's been urging it himself. Report to him."

"Sir!" Payne was off.

Of the hour that came after, he kept no clear memories. They whirled, they hewed, they bled, sometimes they shrieked. During that span he was cool enough, aware and in control, too busy for fear or fury. Men dropped, right, left, behind, shot as they rode or pitched from the saddle when their horses crumpled and toppled. There was no exact moment when they penetrated the foe, just more and more alien uniforms, saberwork, pressing at a crowd that split and then enclosed him, poor Traveler finally sinking with scarlet a-spurt from three different cuts, but Payne found his feet and lashed about, but the blade had gone so heavy, moved so slowly—and then, and then the new uproar, blue trampling gray aside, and somehow he was in Hog Eye's arms. . . .

Recollection began making sense again about sundown. Cleland had taken charge of their survivors. An orderly found Payne at an offside spot, slumped on the ground, resting, emptily staring into empty air. His wounds, miraculously minor, were bandaged and didn't hurt too much. Exhaustion deadened that sort of thing some.

The orderly said that General Houston would like to see him if the lieutenant felt up to it.

Certainly the lieutenant did! A measure of excitement in him, Payne limped after the man.

The western sky turned the waters as luminous a gold as itself. The soldiers had herded prisoners together under guard, fixed hospital tents for their badly hurt, made bivouac. They'd begun collecting the dead of both sides. That job wouldn't be finished today, though. Payne wondered about burial. It wasn't very good practice in these parts. But how can you build tombs for so many before they rot?

Nor was this a pleasant ground to camp on; and with fuel low, fires were sparse, food cold. Tomorrow they'd have better quarters, in and about the city. Tonight must be endured. Nonetheless, Payne went between serried arrays and saw men cleaning their outfits as best they were able. He didn't suppose the camp of those who had come from New Orleans was anything like so neat.

A tent with a plank floor had been raised for Kearny. The floor extended a ways beyond it. He stood on this, under open heaven, with Houston. The light made gilt of the gray in their hair. Their cigars waxed and waned, small red demon stars. A hush had fallen, camp noises the merest undertone, so that Payne heard their voices clearly as he approached.

"Gallant youngster," Houston was saying. "I want to promote him on the spot, right this evenin'. It'll do his men good, too, after all they been through."

"Whatever's left of them," Kearny replied. "I'm sorry now I let them go. They did screen my horse, which did loosen up that flank of the enemy, but the results weren't worth the cost."

"You can't reckon such things just by countin'. A regiment lives by its battle honors. That's why we sallied to help you today, whatever your opinion of the move.'

"And whatever the consequences when the French steam up the river." Kearny sighed. "Well, I guess we can cope with them regardless."

"And go on from here." Excitement throbbed in Houston's throat. "We can take all Texas, I swear."

Payne halted at the deck and stood unnoticed, diffident.

"Given sufficient and adequate troops," Kearny said.

Houston stiffened. "The South has plenty, suh."

Kearny turned to face him head on. "Sir, no offense. Your men are brave. Their leaders are often brilliant. And . . . I do understand what it means, names on regimental flags, the names of fields where, win or lose, men fought well. Forgive me if I said the wrong thing. It's been a long day, hasn't it?"

Not altogether mollified, Houston replied quietly. "I'd still like to know just what you meant."

Kearny drew breath. "Why, simply this. We, the United States of America, have the Empire to cope with. The end of these hostilities, the next peace treaty, won't buy us more than time to make ready—time equally available to them. We can't go on relying on professional cadres, volunteers, and whatever higgledy-piggledy lot of service requirements the various states have enacted. The Jackson Constitution needs further work. The Northwestern militia are our best from the standpoint of organization and preparedness, but I admit they are not good enough either. We need a stricter code. Start boys drilling when they start school. Give men longer active duty hitches each year. Provide for the quick-mobilization not only of units but also of industry and the press. And we need these laws the same for all Americans."

"I don't know as how I like that," Houston said slowly.

Kearny's tone went low. "I can't say with all my heart that I do. But look at what happened today."

"Yes, I'll grant you that," Houston said. "Your regiments were... Cromwell's Ironsides reborn."

No, thought Payne, somewhere in his weariness and exaltation. His glance went beyond the tent, on into the ranked shelters and ordered guns bulking across this land. No, they weren't, they aren't any such thing. They are the future.

ARMS AND THE WOMAN

James Morrow

"**W**hat did you do in the war, Mommy?"

The last long shadow has slipped from the sundial's face hours ago, melting into the hot Egyptian night. My children should be asleep. Instead they're bouncing on their straw pallets, stalling for time.

"It's late," I reply. "Nine o'clock already."

"Please," the twins implore me in a single voice.

"You have school tomorrow."

"You haven't told us a story all week," insists Damon, the whiner.

"The war is such a *great* story," explains Daphne, the wheedler.

"Kaptah's mother tells *him* a story every night," whines Damon.

"Tell us about the war," wheedles Daphne, "and we'll clean the whole cottage tomorrow top to bottom."

I realize I'm going to give in—not because I enjoy spoiling my children (though I do) or because the story itself will consume less time than further negotiations (though it will) but because I actually want the twins to hear this particular tale. It has a point. I've told it before, of course, a dozen times perhaps, but I'm still not sure they get it.

I snatch up the egg-timer and invert it on the nightstand, the tiny grains of sand spilling into the lower chamber like seeds from a farmer's palm. "Be ready for bed in three minutes," I warn my children, "or no story."

They scurry off, frantically brushing their teeth and slipping on their flaxen nightshirts. Silently I glide about the cottage, dusting the lamps and curtaining the moon, until only one candle lights the twins' room, like the campfire of some small, pathetic army, an army of mice or scarab beetles.

"So you want to know what I did in the war," I intone, singsong, as my children climb into their respective beds.

"Oh, yes," says Damon, pulling up his fleecy coverlet.

"You bet," says Daphne, fluffing her goose-feather pillow.

"Once upon a time," I begin, "I lived as both princess and prisoner in the great city of Troy." Even in this feeble light, I'm struck with how handsome Damon is, how beautiful Daphne. "Every evening, I would sit in my boudoir, looking into my polished bronze mirror..."

Helen of Troy, princess and prisoner, sits in her boudoir, looking into her polished bronze mirror and scanning her world-class face for symptoms of age—for wrinkles, wattles, pouches, crow's feet, and the crenelated corpses of hairs. She feels like crying, and not just because these past ten years in Ilium are starting to show. She's sick of the whole sordid arrangement, sick of being cooped up in this overheated acropolis like a pet cockatoo. Whispers haunt the citadel. The servants are gossiping, even her own handmaids. The whore of Hisarlik, they call her. The slut from Sparta. The Lakedaimon lay.

Then there's Paris. Sure, she's madly in love with him, sure, they have great sex, but can't they ever *talk*?

Sighing, Helen trolls her hairdo with her long, lean, exquisitely manicured fingers. A silver strand lies amid the folds like a predatory snake. Slowly she winds the offending filament around her index finger, then gives it a sudden tug. "Ouch," she cries, more from despair than pain. There are times when Helen feels like tearing all her lovely tresses out, every last lock, not simply these graying threads. If I have to spend one more pointless day in Hisarlik, she tells herself, I'll go mad.

Every morning, she and Paris enact the same depressing ritual. She escorts him to the Skaian Gate, hands him his spear and his lunch bucket, and with a quick tepid kiss sends him off to work. Paris's job is killing people. At sundown he arrives home grubby with blood and redolent of funeral pyres, his spear wrapped in bits of drying viscera. There's a war going on out there; Paris won't tell her anything more. "Who are we fighting?" she asks each evening as they lie together in bed. "Don't you worry your pretty little head about it," he replies, slipping on a sheep-gut condom, the brand with the plumed and helmeted soldier on the box.

Until this year, Paris wanted her to walk Troy's high walls each morning, waving encouragement to the troops, blowing them kisses as they marched off to battle. "Your face inspires them," he would insist. "An airy kiss from you is worth a thousand nights of passion with a nymph." But in recent months Paris's priorities have changed. As soon as they say good-bye, Helen is supposed to retire to the citadel, speaking with no one, not even a brief coffee klatch with one of Paris's forty-nine sisters-in-law. She's expected to spend her whole day weaving rugs, carding flax, and being beautiful. It is not a life.

Can the gods help? Helen is skeptical, but anything is worth a try. Tomorrow, she resolves, she will go to the temple of Apollo and beg him to relieve her boredom, perhaps buttressing her appeal with an offering—a ram, a bull, whatever—though an offering strikes her as rather like a deal, and Helen is sick of deals. Her husband—pseudohusband, nonhusband—made a deal. She keeps thinking of the Apple of Discord, and what Aphrodite might have done with it after bribing Paris. Did she drop it in her fruit bowl... put it on her mantel... impale it on her crown? Why did she take the damn thing seriously? Why did any of them take it seriously? Hi, I'm the fairest goddess in the universe—see, it says so right here on my apple.

Damn—another gray hair, another weed in the garden of her pulchritude. She reaches toward the villain—and stops. Why bother? These hairs are like the hydra's heads, endless, cancerous, and besides, it's high time Paris realized there's a mind under that coiffure.

Whereupon Paris comes in, sweating and snorting. His helmet is awry; his spear is gory; his greaves are sticky with other men's flesh.

"Hard day, dear?"

"Don't ask." Her nonhusband unfastens his breastplate. "Pour us some wine. Looking in the speculum, were you? Good."

Helen sets the mirror down, uncorks the bottle, and fills two bejeweled goblets with Château Samothrace.

"Today I heard about some techniques you might try," says Paris. "Ways for a woman to retain her beauty."

"You mean—you *talk* on the battlefield?"

"During the lulls."

"I wish you'd talk to *me*."

"Wax," says Paris, lifting the goblet to his lips. "Wax is the thing." His heavy jowls undulate as he drinks. Their affair, Helen will admit, still gives her a kick. In the past ten years, her lover has moved beyond the surpassing prettiness of an Adonis into something equally appealing, an authoritative, no-frills sexuality suggestive of an aging matinee idol. "Take some melted wax and work it into the lines in your brow—presto, they're gone."

"I *like* my lines," Helen insists with a quick but audible snort.

"When mixed with ox blood, the dark silt from the River Minyeios is indelible, they say. You can dye your silver hairs back to auburn. A Grecian formula." Paris sips his wine. "As for these redundant ounces on your thighs, well, dear, we both know there's no cure like exercise."

"Look who's talking," Helen snaps. "*Your* skin is no bowl of cream.

Your head is no garden of sargasso. As for your stomach, it's a safe bet that Paris of Troy can walk through the rain without getting his buckle wet."

The prince finishes his wine and sighs. "Where's the girl I married? You used to care about your looks."

"The girl you married," Helen replies pointedly, "is not your wife."

"Well, yes, of course not. Technically, you're still *his*."

"I want a wedding." Helen takes a gluttonous swallow of Samothrace and sets the goblet on the mirror. "You could go to my husband," she suggests. "You could present yourself to high-minded Menelaus and try to talk things out." Reflected in the mirror's wobbly face, the goblet grows weird, twisted, as if seen through a drunkard's eyes. "Hey, listen, I'll bet he's found another maid by now—he's something of a catch, after all. So maybe you actually did him a favor. Maybe he isn't even mad."

"He's mad," Paris insists. "The man is angry."

"How do you know?"

"I know."

Heedless of her royal station, Helen consumes the remainder of her wine with the crude insouciance of a galley slave. "I want a baby," she says.

"What?"

"You know: a baby. *Baby*: a highly young person. My goal, dear Paris, is to be pregnant."

"Fatherhood is for losers." Paris chucks his spear onto the bed. Striking the mattress, the oaken shaft disappears into the soft down. "Go easy on the *vino*, love. Alcohol is awfully fattening."

"Don't you understand? I'm losing my mind. A pregnancy would give me a sense of purpose."

"Any idiot can sire a child. It takes a hero to defend a citadel."

"Have you found someone else, Paris? Is that it? Someone younger and thinner?"

"Don't be foolish. Throughout the whole of time, in days gone by and eras yet to come, no man will love a woman as much as Paris loves Helen."

"I'll bet the plains of Ilium are crawling with camp followers. They must swoon over you."

"Don't you worry your pretty little head about it," says Paris, unwrapping a plumed-soldier condom.

If he ever says that to me again, Helen vows as they tumble drunkenly into bed, I'll scream so loud the walls of Troy will fall.

The slaughter is not going well, and Paris is depressed. By his best reckoning, he's dispatched only fifteen Achaians to the house of Hades this morning: strong-greaved Machaon, iron-muscled Euchenor, ax-wielding Deichos, a dozen more—fifteen noble warriors sent to the dark depths, fifteen breathless bodies left to nourish the dogs and ravens. It is not enough.

All along the front, Priam's army is giving ground without a fight. Their morale is low, their *esprit* spent. They haven't seen Helen in a year, and they don't much feel like fighting anymore.

With a deep Aeolian sigh, the prince seats himself atop his pile of confiscated armor and begins his lunch break.

Does he have a choice? Must he continue keeping her in the shadows? Yes, by Poseidon's trident—yes. Exhibiting Helen as she looks now would just make matters worse. Once upon a time, her face launched a thousand ships. Today it couldn't get a Theban fishing schooner out of dry dock. Let the troops catch only a glimpse of her wrinkles, let them but glance at her aging hair, and they'll start deserting like rats leaving a foundering trireme.

He's polishing off a peach—since delivering his famous verdict and awarding Aphrodite her prize, Paris no longer cares for apples—when two of the finest horses in Hisarlik, Aithon and Xanthos, gallop up pulling his brother's war chariot. He expects to see Hector holding the reins, but no: the driver, he notes with a sharp pang of surprise, is Helen.

"Helen? What are *you* doing here?"

Brandishing a cowhide whip, his lover jumps down. "You won't tell me what this war is about," she gasps, panting inside her armor, "so I'm investigating on my own. I just came from the swift-flowing Menderes, where your enemies are preparing to launch a cavalry charge against the camp of Epistrophos."

"Go back to the citadel, Helen. Go back to Pergamos."

"Paris, this army you're battling—they're *Greeks*. Idomeneus, Diomedes, Sthenelos, Euryalos, Odysseus—I *know* these men. Know them? By Pan's flute, I've *dated* half of them. You'll never guess who's about to lead that cavalry charge."

Paris takes a stab. "Agamemnon?"

"Agamemnon!" Sweat leaks from beneath Helen's helmet like blood from a scalp wound. "My own brother-in-law! Next you'll be telling me Menelaus himself has taken the field against Troy!"

Paris coughs and says, "Menelaus himself has taken the field against Troy."

"He's here?" wails Helen, thumping her breastplate. "My husband is *here*?"

"Correct."

"What's going on, Paris? For what purpose have the men of horse-pasturing Argos come all the way to Ilium?"

The prince bounces his peach pit off Helen's breast-plate. Angrily he fishes for epithets. Mule-minded Helen, he calls her beneath his breath. Leather-skinned Lakedaimon, runs his internal invective. He feels beaten and bettered, trapped and tethered. "Very well, sweetheart, very well..." Helen of the iron will, the hard ass, the bronze bottom. "They've come for *you*, love."

"What?"

"For you."

"Me? What are you talking about?"

"They want to steal you back." As Paris speaks, Helen's waning beauty seems to drop another notch. Her face darkens with some unfathomable mix of anger, hurt, and confusion. "They're pledged to it. King Tyndareus made your suitors swear they'd be loyal to whomever you selected as husband."

"*Me?*" Helen leaps into the chariot. "You're fighting an entire, stupid, disgusting war for *me?*"

"Well, not for you per se. For honor, for glory, for arete. Now hurry off to Pergamos—that's an order."

"I'm hurrying off, dear"—she raises her whip—"but not to Pergamos. On, Aithon!" She snaps the lash. "On, Xanthos!"

"Then where?"

Instead of answering, Paris's lover speeds away, leaving him to devour her dust.

Dizzy with outrage, trembling with remorse, Helen charges across the plains of Ilium. On all sides, an astonishing drama plays itself out, a spectacle of shattered senses and violated flesh: soldiers with eyes gouged out, tongues cut loose, limbs hacked off, bellies ripped open; soldiers, as it were, giving birth to their own bowels—all because of her. She weeps openly, profusely, the large gemlike tears running down her wrinkled cheeks and striking her breast-plate. The agonies of Prometheus are a picnic compared to the weight of her guilt, the Pillars of Herakles are feathers when balanced against the crushing tonnage of her conscience.

Honor, glory, arete: I'm missing something, Helen realizes as she surveys the carnage. The essence eludes me.

She reaches the thick and stinking Lisgar Marsh and reins up before a foot soldier sitting in the mud, a young Myrmidon with what she assumes are a particularly honorable spear hole in his breastplate and a singularly glorious lack of a right hand.

"Can you tell me where I might find your king?" she asks.

"By Hera's eyes, you're easy to look at," gasps the soldier as, arete in full bloom, he binds his bleeding stump with linen.

"I need to find Menelaus."

"Try the harbor," he says, gesturing with his wound. The bandaged stump drips like a leaky faucet. "His ship is the *Arkadia*."

Helen thanks the soldier and aims her horses toward the wine-dark sea.

"Are you Helen's mother, by any chance?" he calls as she races off. "What a face you've got!"

Twenty minutes later, reeling with thirst and smelling of horse sweat, Helen pulls within view of the crashing waves. In the harbor beyond, a thousand strong-hulled ships lie at anchor, their masts jutting into the sky like a forest of denuded trees. All along the beach, Helen's countrymen are raising a stout wooden wall, evidently fearful that, if the line is ever pushed back this far, the Trojans will not hesitate to burn the fleet. The briny air rings with the Achaians' axes—with the thud and crunch of acacias being felled, palisades being whittled, stockade posts sharpened, breastworks shaped, a cacophony muffling the flutter of the sails and the growl of the surf.

Helen starts along the wharf, soon spotting the *Arkadia*, a stout pentekontor with half a hundred oars bristling from her sides like the quills of a hedgehog. No sooner has she crossed the gangplank when she comes upon her husband, older now striated by wrinkles, but still unquestionably he. Plumed like a peacock, Menelaus stands atop the forecastle, speaking with a burly construction brigade, tutoring them in the proper placement of the impalement stakes. A handsome man, she decides, much like the warrior on the condom boxes. She can see why she picked him over Sthenelos, Euryalos, and her other beaus.

As the workers set off to plant their spiky groves, Helen saunters up behind Menelaus and taps him on the shoulder.

"Hi," she says.

He was always a wan fellow, but now his face loses whatever small quantity of blood it once possessed. "Helen?" he says, gasping and blinking like a man who's just been doused with a bucket of slop. "Is that *you*?"

"Right."

"You've, er... aged."

"You too, sweetheart."

He pulls off his plumed helmet, stomps his foot on the forecastle, and says, angrily, "You ran out on me."

"Yes. Quite so."

"Trollop."

"Perhaps." Helen adjusts her greaves. "I could claim I was bewitched by laughter-loving Aphrodite, but that would be a lie. The fact is, Paris knocked me silly. I'm crazy about him. Sorry." She runs her desiccated tongue along her parched lips. "Have you got anything to drink?"

Dipping a hollow gourd into his private cistern, Menelaus offers her a pint of fresh water. "So what brings you here?" he asks.

Helen receives the ladle. Setting her boots wide apart, she steadies herself against the roll of the incoming tide and takes a greedy gulp. At last she says, "I wish to give myself up."

"What?"

"I want to go home with you."

"You mean—you think our marriage deserves another chance?"

"No, I think all those infantrymen out there deserve to live. If this war is really being fought to retrieve me, then consider the job done." Tossing the ladle aside, Helen holds out her hands, palms turned upward as if she's testing for raindrops. "I'm yours, hubby. Manacle my wrists, chain my feet together, throw me in the brig."

Against all odds, defying all *logos*, Menelaus's face, loses more blood. "I don't think that's a very good idea," he says.

"Huh? What do you mean?"

"This siege, Helen—there's more to it than you suppose."

"Don't jerk me around, lord of all Lakedaimon, asshole. It's time to call it quits."

The Spartan king stares straight at her chest, a habit she's always found annoying. "Put on a bit of weight, eh, darling?"

"Don't change the subject." She lunges toward Menelaus's scabbard as if to goose him, but instead draws out his sword. "I'm deadly serious: if Helen of Troy is not permitted to live with herself"—she pantomimes the act of self-slaughter—"then she will die with herself."

"Tell you what," says her husband, taking his weapon back. "Tomorrow morning, first thing, I'll go to my brother and ask him to arrange a truce with your father-in-law."

"He's not my father-in-law. There was never a wedding."

"Whatever. The point is, your offer has merit, but it must be discussed. We shall all meet face-to-face, Trojans and Achaians, and talk the matter over. As for now, you'd best return to your lover."

"I'm warning you—I shall abide no more blood on my hands, none but my own."

"Of course, dear. Now please go back to the citadel."

At least he listened, Helen muses as she crosses the weatherworn

deck of the *Arkadia*. At least he didn't tell me not to worry my pretty
little head about it.

"Here comes the dull part," says whiny-tongued Damon.
"The scene with all the talking," adds smart-mouthed Daphne.
"Can you cut it a bit?" my son asks.
"Hush," I say, smoothing out Damon's coverlet. "No interruptions," I
insist. I slip Daphne's cornhusk doll under her arm. "When you have
your own children, you can tell the tale however you like. As for now,
listen carefully. You might learn something."

By the burbling, tumbling waters of the River Simois, beneath the
glowing orange avatar of the moon goddess Artemis, ten aristocrats are
gathered around a vast oaken table in the purple tent of Ilium's high
command, all of them bursting with opinions on how best to deal with
this Helen situation, this peace problem, this Trojan hostage crisis.
White as a crane, a banner of truce flaps above the heads of the two
kings, Priam from the high city, Agamemnon from the long ships. Each
side has sent its best and/or brightest. For the Trojans: brainy Panthoos,
mighty Paris, invincible Hector, and Hiketaon the scion of Ares. For the
Achaian cause: Ajax the berserker; Nestor the mentor, Menelaus the
cuckold, and wily, smiling Odysseus. Of all those invited, only quarrel-
some Achilles, sulking in his tent, has declined to appear.

Panthoos rises, rubs his foam-white beard, and sets his scepter on the
table. "Royal captains, gifted seers," the old Trojan begins, "I believe
you will concur when I say that, since this siege was laid, we have not
faced a challenge of such magnitude. Make no mistake: Helen means to
take our war away from us, and she means to do so immediately."

Gusts of dismay waft through the tent like a wind from the underworld.
"We can't quit now," groans Hector, wincing fiercely.
"We're just getting up to speed," wails Hiketaon, grimacing greatly.
Agamemnon steps down from his throne, carrying his scepter like a
spear. "I have a question for Prince Paris," he says. "What does your
mistress's willingness to return to Argos say about the present state of
your relationship?"

Paris strokes his great jowls and says, "As you might surmise, great
King, my feelings for Helen are predicated on requitement."
"So you won't keep her in Pergamos by force?"
"If she doesn't want me, then I don't want her."
At which point slug-witted Ajax raises his hand. "Er, excuse me. I'm a
bit confused. If Helen is ours for the asking, then why must we continue
the war?"

A sirocco of astonishment arises among the heroes.

"Why?" gasps Panthoos. "*Why*? Because this is *Troy*, that's why. Because we're kicking off Western Civilization here, that's why. The longer we can keep this affair going, the longer we can sustain such an ambiguous enterprise, the more valuable and significant it becomes."

Slow-synapsed Ajax says, "Huh?"

Nestor has but to clear his throat and every eye is upon him. "What our adversary is saying—may I interpret, wise Panthoos?" He turns to his Trojan counterpart, bows deferentially, and, receiving a nod of assent, speaks to Ajax. "Panthoos means that, if this particular pretext for war—restoring a woman to her rightful owner—can be made to seem reasonable, then *any* pretext for war can be made to seem reasonable." The mentor shifts his fevered stare from Ajax to the entire assembly. "By rising to this rare and precious occasion, we shall pave the way for wars of religion, wars of manifest destiny—any equivocal cause you care to name." Once again his gaze alights on Ajax. "Understand, sir? This is the war to inaugurate war itself. This is the war to make the world safe for war!"

Ajax frowns so vigorously his visor falls down. "All I know is, we came for Helen and we got her. Mission accomplished." Turning to Agamemnon, the berserker lifts the visor from his eyes. "So if it's all the same to you, Majesty, I'd like to go home before I get killed."

"O, Ajax, Ajax, Ajax," moans Hector, pulling an arrow from his quiver and using it to scratch his back. "Where is your aesthetic sense? Have you no appreciation of war for war's sake? The plains of Ilium are roiling with glory, sir. You could cut the arete with a knife. Never have there been such valiant eviscerations, such venerable dismemberments, such—"

"I don't get it," says the berserker. "I just don't get it."

Whereupon Menelaus slams his wine goblet on the table with a resounding thunk. "We have not gathered in Priam's tent so that Ajax might learn politics," he says impatiently. "We have gathered so that we might best dispose of my wife."

"True, true," says Hector.

"So what are we going to do, gentlemen?" asks Menelaus. "Lock her up?"

"Good idea," says Hiketaon.

"Well, yes," says Agamemnon, slumping back onto his throne. "Except that, when the war finally ends, my troops will demand to see her. Might they not wonder why so much suffering and sacrifice was spent on a goddess gone to seed?" He turns to Paris and says, "Prince, you should not have let this happen."

"Let *what* happen?" asks Paris.

"I heard she has wrinkles," says Agamemnon.

"I heard she got fat," says Nestor.

"What have you been feeding her?" asks Menelaus. "Bonbons?"

"She's a *person*," protests Paris, "she's not a marble statue. You can hardly blame *me* . . ."

At which juncture King Priam raises his scepter and, as if to wound Gaea herself, rams it into the dirt.

"Noble lords, I hate to say this, but the threat is more immediate than you might suppose. In the early years of the siege, the sight of fair Helen walking the ramparts did wonders for my army's morale. Now that she's no longer fit for public display, well . . ."

"Yes?" says Agamemnon, steeling himself for the worst.

"Well, I simply don't know how much longer Troy can hold up its end of the war. If things don't improve, we may have to capitulate by next winter."

Gasps of horror blow across the table, rattling the tent flaps and ruffling the aristocrats' capes.

But now, for the first time, clever, canny Odysseus addresses the council, and the winds of discontent grow still. "Our course is obvious," he says. "Our destiny is clear," he asserts. "We must put Helen—the old Helen, the pristine Helen—back on the walls."

"The old Helen?" says Hiketaon. "The pristine Helen? Are you not talking fantasy, resourceful Odysseus? Are you not singing a myth?"

The lord of all Ithaca strolls the length of Priam's tent, massaging his silky beard. "It will require some wisdom from Pallas Athena, some technology from Hephaestus, but I believe the project is possible."

"Excuse me," says Paris. "*What* project is possible?"

"Refurbishing your little harlot," says Odysseus. "Making the dear, sweet strumpet shine like new."

Back and forth, to and fro, Helen moves through her boudoir, wearing a ragged path of *angst* into the carpet. An hour passes. Then two. Why are they taking so long?

What most gnaws at her, the thought that feasts on her entrails, is the possibility that, should the council not accept her surrender, she will have to raise the stakes. And how might she accomplish the deed? By what means might she book passage on Charon's one-way ferry? Something from her lover's arsenal, most likely—a sword, spear, dagger, or death-dripping arrow. O, please, my lord Apollo, she prays to the city's prime protector, don't let it come to that.

At sunset Paris enters the room, his pace leaden, his jowls dragging his mouth into a grimace. For the first time ever, Helen observes tears in her lover's eyes.

"It is finished," he moans, doffing his plumed helmet. "Peace has come. At dawn you must go to the long ships. Menelaus will bear you back to Sparta, where you will once again live as mother to his children, friend to his concubines, and emissary to his bed."

Relief pours out of Helen in a deep, orgasmic rush, but the pleasure is short-lived. She loves this man, flaws and all, flab and the rest. "I shall miss you, dearest Paris," she tells him. "Your bold abduction of me remains the peak experience of my life."

"I agreed to the treaty only because Menelaus believes you might otherwise kill yourself. You're a surprising woman, Helen. Sometimes I think I hardly know you."

"Hush, my darling," she says, gently laying her palm across his mouth. "No more words."

Slowly they unclothe each other, methodically unlocking the doors to bliss, the straps and sashes, the snaps and catches, and thus begins their final, epic night together.

"I'm sorry I've been so judgmental," says Paris.

"I accept your apology," says Helen.

"You are so beautiful," he tells her. "So impossibly beautiful..."

As dawn's rosy fingers stretch across the Trojan sky, Hector's faithful driver, Eniopeus the son of horse-loving Thebaios, steers his sturdy war chariot along the banks of the Menderes, bearing Helen to the Achaian stronghold. They reach the *Arkadia* just as the sun is cresting, so their arrival in the harbor becomes a flaming parade, a show of sparks and gold, as if they ride upon the burning wheels of Hyperion himself.

Helen starts along the dock, moving past the platoons of squawking gulls adrift on the early morning breeze. Menelaus comes forward to greet her, accompanied by a man for whom Helen has always harbored a vague dislike—broad-chested, black-bearded Teukros, illegitimate son of Telemon.

"The tide is ripe," says her husband. "You and Teukros must board forthwith. You will find him a lively traveling companion. He knows a hundred fables and plays the harp."

"Can't *you* take me home?"

Menelaus squeezes his wife's hand and, raising it to his lips, plants a gentle kiss. "I must see to the loading of my ships," he explains, "the disposition of my battalions—a full week's job, I'd guess."

"Surely you can leave that to Agamemnon."

"Give me seven days, Helen. In seven days I'll be home, and we can begin picking up the pieces."

"We're losing the tide," says Teukros, anxiously intertwining his fingers.

Do I trust my husband? wonders Helen as she strides up the *Arkadia*'s gangplank. Does he really mean to lift the siege?

All during their slow voyage out of the harbor, Helen is haunted. Nebulous fears, nagging doubts, and odd presentiments swarm through her brain like Harpies. She beseeches her beloved Apollo to speak with her, calm her, assure her all is well, but the only sounds reaching her ears are the creaking of the oars and the windy, watery voice of the Hellespont.

By the time the *Arkadia* finds the open sea, Helen has resolved to jump overboard and swim back to Troy.

"And then Teukros tried to kill you," says Daphne.

"He came at you with his sword," adds Damon.

This is the twins' favorite part, the moment of grue and gore. Eyes flashing, voice climbing to a melodramatic pitch, I tell them how before I could put my escape plan into action, Teukros began chasing me around the *Arkadia*, slashing his Janus-faced blade. I tell them how I got the upper hand, tripping the bastard as he was about to run me through.

"You stabbed him with his own sword, didn't you, Mommy?" asks Damon.

"I had no choice. You understand that, don't you?"

"And then his guts spilled, huh?" asks Daphne.

"Agamemnon had ordered Teukros to kill me," I explain. "I was ruining everything."

"They spilled out all over the deck, right?" asks Damon.

"Yes, dear, they certainly did. I'm quite convinced Paris wasn't part of the plot, or Menelaus either. Your mother falls for fools, not homicidal maniacs."

"What color were they?" asks Damon.

"Color?"

"His guts."

"Red, mostly with daubs of purple and black."

"Neat."

I tell the twins of my long, arduous swim through the strait.

I tell them how I crossed Ilium's war-torn fields, dodging arrows and eluding patrols.

I tell how I waited by the Skaian Gate until a farmer arrived with a cartload of provender for the besieged city... how I sneaked inside the walls, secluded amid stalks of wheat . . . how I went to Pergamos, hid myself in the temple of Apollo, and breathlessly waited for dawn.

Dawn comes up, binding the eastern clouds in crimson girdles. Helen leaves the citadel, tiptoes to the wall, and mounts the hundred granite steps to the battlements. She is not sure of her next move. She has some vague hope of addressing the infantrymen as they assemble at the gate. Her arguments have failed to impress the generals, but perhaps she can touch the heart of the common soldier.

It is at this ambiguous point in her fortunes that Helen runs into herself.

She blinks—once, twice. She swallows a sphere of air. Yes, it is she, herself, marching along the parapets. Herself? No, not exactly: an idealized rendition of herself, the Helen of ten years ago, svelte and smooth.

As the troops march through the portal and head toward the plain, the strange incarnation calls down to them.

"Onward, men!" it shouts, raising a creamy-white arm. "Fight for me!" Its movements are deliberate and jerky, as if sunbaked Troy has been magically transplanted to some frigid clime. "I'm worth it!"

The soldiers turn, look up. "We'll fight for you, Helen!" a bowman calls toward the parapets.

"We love you!" a sword-wielder shouts.

Awkwardly, the incarnation waves. Creakily, it blows an arid kiss. "Onward, men! Fight for me! I'm worth it!"

"You're beautiful, Helen!" a spear-thrower cries.

Helen strides up to her doppelgänger and, seizing the left shoulder, pivots the creature toward her.

"Onward, men!" it tells Helen. "Fight for me! I'm worth it!"

"You're beautiful," the spear-thrower continues, "and so is your mother!"

The eyes, Helen is not surprised to discover, are glass. The limbs are fashioned from wood, the head from marble, the teeth from ivory, the lips from wax, the tresses from the fleece of a darkling ram. Helen does not know for certain what forces power this creature, what magic moves its tongue, but she surmises that the genius of Athena is at work here, the witchery of ox-eyed Hera. Chop the creature open, she senses, and out will pour a thousand cogs and pistons from Hephaestus's fiery workshop.

Helen wastes no time. She hugs the creature, lifts it off its feet. Heavy, but not so heavy as to dampen her resolve.

"Onward, men!" it screams as Helen throws it over her shoulder. "Fight for me! I'm worth it!"

And so it comes to pass that, on a hot, sweaty, Asia Minor morning, fair Helen turns the tables on history, gleefully abducting herself from the lofty stone city of Troy.

Paris is pulling a poisoned arrow from his quiver, intent on shooting a dollop of hemlock into the breast of an Achaian captain, when his brother's chariot charges by.

Paris nocks the arrow. He glances at the chariot.

He aims.

Glances again.

Fires. Misses.

Helen.

Helen? *Helen*, by Apollo's lyre, his Helen—no, two Helens, the true and the false, side by side, the true guiding the horses into the thick of the fight, her wooden twin staring dreamily into space. Paris is not sure which woman he is more astonished to see.

"Soldiers of Troy!" cries the fleshly Helen. "Heroes of Argos! Behold how your leaders seek to dupe you! You are fighting for a fraud, a swindle, a thing of gears and glass!"

A stillness envelops the battlefield. The men are stunned, not so much by the ravings of the charioteer as by the face of her companion, so pure and perfect despite the leather thong sealing her jaw shut. It is a face to sheath a thousand swords, a face to lower a thousand spears, a face to unnock a thousand arrows.

Which is exactly what now happens. A thousand swords: sheathed. A thousand spears: lowered. A thousand arrows: unnocked.

The soldiers crowd around the chariot, pawing at the ersatz Helen. They touch the wooden arms, caress the marble brow, stroke the ivory teeth, pat the waxen lips, squeeze the woolly hair, rub the glass eyes.

"See what I mean?" cries the true Helen. "Your kings are diddling you . . ."

Paris can't help it: he's proud of her, by Hermes's wings. He's puffing up with admiration. This woman has nerve, this woman has arete, this woman has chutzpah.

This woman, Paris realizes as a fat, warm tear of nostalgia rolls down his cheek, is going to end the war.

"The end," I say.

"And then what happened?" Damon asks.

"Nothing. *Finis*. Go, to sleep."

"You can't fool us," says Daphne. "All *sorts* of things happened after that. You went to live on the island of Lesbos."

"Not immediately," I note. "I wandered the world for seven years, having many fine and fabulous adventures. Good night."

"And then you went to Lesbos," Daphne insists.

"And then *we* came into the world," Damon asserts.

"True," I say. The twins are always interested in how they came into the world. They never tire of hearing about it.

"The women of Lesbos import over a thousand liters of frozen semen annually," Damon explains to Daphne.

"From Thrace," Daphne explains to Damon.

"In exchange for olives."

"A thriving trade."

"Right, honey," I say. "Bedtime."

"And so you got pregnant," says Daphne.

"And had us," says Damon.

"And brought us to Egypt." Daphne tugs at my sleeve as if operating a bell rope. "I came out first, didn't I?" she says. "I'm the *oldest*."

"Yes, dear."

"Is that why I'm smarter than Damon?"

"You're both equally smart. I'm going to blow out the candle now."

Daphne hugs her cornhusk doll and says, "Did you really end the war?"

"The treaty was signed the day after I fled from Troy. Of course, peace didn't bring the dead back to life, but at least Troy was never sacked and burned. Now go to sleep—both of you."

Damon says, "Not before we've . . ."

"What?"

"You know."

"All right," I say. "One look. One, quick peek, and then you're off to the land of Morpheus."

I saunter over to the closet and, drawing back the linen curtain, reveal my stalwart twin standing upright amid Daphne's dresses and Damon's robes. She smiles through the gloom. She's a tireless smiler, this woman.

"Hi, Aunt Helen!" says Damon as I throw the bronze toggle protruding from the nape of my sister's neck.

She waves to my children and says, "Onward, men! Fight for me!"

"You bet, Aunt Helen!" says Daphne.

"I'm worth it!" says my sister.

"You sure are!" says Damon.

"Onward, men! Fight for me! I'm worth it!"

I switch her off and close the curtain. Tucking in the twins, I give each a big soupy kiss on the cheek. "Love you, Daphne. Love you, Damon."

I start to douse the candle—stop. As long as it's on my mind, I should get the chore done. Returning to the closet, I push the curtain aside, lift the penknife from my robe, and pry open the blade. And then, as the Egyptian night grows moist and thick, I carefully etch yet another wrinkle across my sister's brow right beneath her salt-and-pepper bangs.

It's important, after all, to keep up appearances.

READY FOR THE FATHERLAND

Harry Turtledove

19 February 1943—Zaporozhye, German-occupied USSR

Field Marshal Erich von Manstein looked up from the map table. Was that the distant rumble of Soviet artillery? No, he decided after a moment. The Russians were in Sinelnikovo today, yes, but Sinelnikovo was still fifty-five kilometers north of his headquarters. Of course, there were no German troops to speak of between there and here, but that would not matter—if he could make Hitler listen to him.

Hitler, however, was not listening. He was talking. He always talked more than he listened—if he'd listened just once, Manstein thought, the Sixth Army might have gotten out of Stalingrad, in which case the Russians would not be anywhere near Sinelnikovo. They'd come more than six hundred kilometers since November.

"No, not one more step back!" Hitler shouted. The Führer had shouted that when the Russians broke through around Stalingrad, too. Couldn't he remember from one month to the next what worked and what didn't? Behind him, Generals Jodl and Keitel nodded like the brainless puppets they were.

Manstein glanced over at Field Marshal von Kleist. Kleist was a real soldier; surely he would tell the Führer what had to be said. But Kleist just stood there. Against the Russians, he was fearless. Hitler, though, Hitler made him afraid.

On my shoulders, Manstein thought. Why, ever since Stalingrad, has everything—everything save gratitude—landed on my shoulders? Had it not been for him, the whole German southern front in Russia would have come crashing down. Without false modesty, he knew that. Sometimes— not nearly often enough—Hitler glimpsed it, too.

One more try at talking sense into the Führer then. Manstein bent over the map, pointed. "We need to let the Soviets advance, sir. Soon, soon they will overextend themselves. Then we strike."

"No, damn it, damn you! Move on Kharkov now, I tell you!"

S.S. Panzer Division Totenkopf, the force with which he wanted Kharkov recaptured, was stuck in the mud outside Poltava, a hundred fifty kilometers away. Manstein said as much. He'd been saying it, over and over for the past forty-eight hours. Calmly, rationally, he tried once more: "I am sorry, my Führer, but we simply lack the resources to carry out the attack as you desire. A little more patience, a little more caution, and we may yet achieve satisfactory results. Move too soon and we run the risk of—"

"I did not fly to this godforsaken Russian excuse for a factory town to listen to the whining of your cowardly Jewish heart, Field Marshal." Hitler invested the proud title with withering scorn. "And from now on you will keep your gross, disgusting Jewish nose out of strategic planning and simply obey. Do you understand me?"

Manstein's right hand went to the organ Hitler had mentioned. It was indeed of impressive proportions and impressively hooked. But to bring it up, to insult it, in what should have been a serious council of war was—insane was the word Manstein found. As insane as most of the decisions Hitler had made, most of the orders he had given, ever since he'd taken all power into his own hands at the end of 1941, and especially since things began to go wrong at Stalingrad.

Insane . . . Of itself, Manstein's hand slid down from his nose to the holster that held his Walther P-38 pistol. Of itself, it unsnapped the holster flap. And of itself, it raised the pistol and fired three shots into Adolf Hitler's chest. Wearing a look of horrified disbelief, the Führer crumpled to the floor.

Generals Jodl and Keitel looked almost as appalled as Hitler had. So did Field Marshal von Kleist, but he recovered faster. He snatched out his own pistol, covered Hitler's toadies.

Manstein still felt as if he were moving in a dream, but even in a dream he was a General Staff-taught officer, trained to deduce what needed doing. "Excellent, Paul," he said. "First we must dispose of the carrion there, then devise a story to account for it in suitably heroic style."

Kleist nodded. "Very good. And then—"

"And then . . ." Manstein cocked his head. Yes, by God, he did hear Russian artillery. "This campaign has been botched beyond belief. Given the present state of affairs, I see no reasonable hope of our winning the war against the Russians. Do you agree?"

Kleist nodded again.

"Very good," Manstein said. *"In that case, let us make certain we do not lose it...."*

27 July 1979—Rijeka, Independent State of Croatia

The little fishing boat putt-putted its way toward the harbor. The man who called himself Giorgio Ferrero already wore a black wool fisherman's cap. He used his hand to shield his eyes further. Seen through the clear Adriatic air, the rugged Croatian coastline seemed almost unnaturally sharp, as if he were wearing a new pair of spectacles that were a little too strong.

"Pretty country," Ferrero said. He spoke Italian with the accent of Ancona.

So did Pietro Bevacqua, to whom he'd addressed the remark: "That it is." Bevacqua and Ferrero were both medium-sized, medium-dark men who would not have seemed out of place anywhere in the Mediterranean. Around a big pipe full of vile Italian tobacco, Bevacqua added, "No matter how pretty, though, me, I wish I were back home." He took both hands off the boat's wheel to show by gesture just how much he wished that.

Ferrero chuckled. He went up to the bow. Bevacqua guided the boat to a pier. Ferrero sprang up onto the dock, rope in hand. He tied the boat fast. Before he could finish, a pair of Croatian customs men were heading his way.

Their neatly creased khaki uniforms, high-crowned caps, gleaming jackboots, and businesslike assault rifles all bespoke their nation's German alliance. The faces under those caps, long, lined, dark, with the deep-set eyes of icons, were older than anything Germany dreamed of. "Show me your papers," one of them said.

"Here you are, sir." Ferrero's Croatian was halting, accented, but understandable. He dug the documents out of the back pocket of his baggy wool pants.

The customs man studied them, passed them to his comrade. "You are from the Social Republic, eh?" the second man said. He grinned nastily. "Not from Sicily?"

Ferrero crossed himself. "Mother of God, no!" he exclaimed in Italian. Sicily was a British puppet regime; admitting one came from there was as good as admitting one was a spy. One did not want to admit to spying, not in Croatia. The Ustashi had a reputation for savagery that even the Gestapo envied. Ferrero went on, in Croatian again, "From Ancona, like you see. Got a load of eels on ice to sell here, my partner and I."

"Ah." Both customs men looked interested. The one with the nasty grin said, "Maybe our wives will buy some for pies, if they get to market."

"Take some now" Ferrero urged. If he hadn't urged it, the eels would not have got to market. He knew that. The pair of fifty-dinar notes folded in with his papers had disappeared now, too. The Croatian fascists were only cheap imitations of their German prototypes, who would have cost much more to bribe.

Once they had the eels in a couple of sacks, the customs men gave only a cursory glance at Bevacqua's papers (though they did not fail to pocket his pair of fifty-dinar notes, either) and at the rest of the ship's cargo. They plied rubber stamps with vigor and then strode back down the dock, obviously well pleased with themselves.

The fishermen followed them. The fish market was, sensibly, close to the wharves. Another uniformed official demanded papers before he let Ferrero and Bevacqua by. The sight of tbe customs men's stamps impressed him enough that he didn't even have to be paid off.

"Eels!" Ferrero shouted in his bad but loud Croatian. "Eels from Italian waters! Eels!" A crowd soon formed around him. Eels went one way, dinars another. While Ferrero cried the wares and took money, Bevacqua kept trotting back and forth between market and boat, always bringing more eels.

A beefy man pushed his way to the front of the crowd. He bought three hundred dinars' worth of eels, shoving a fat wad of bills into Ferrero's hand. "For my restaurant," he explained. "You wouldn't happen to have any squid, would you?"

Ferrero shook his head. "We sell those at home. Not many like them here."

"Too bad. I serve calamari when I can." The beefy man slung his sack of eels over his shoulder, elbowed himself away from Ferrero as rudely as he'd approached. Ferrero rubbed his chin, stuck the three hundred dinars in a pocket different from the one he used for the rest of the money he was making.

The eels went fast. Anything new for sale went fast in Rijeka; Croatia had never been a fortunate country. By the time all the fish were gone from the hold of the little boat, Ferrero and Bevacqua had made three times as much as they would have by selling them in Ancona.

"We'll have to make many more trips here," Bevacqua said enthusiastically, back in the fishing boat's cramped cabin. "We'll get rich."

"Sounds good to me," Ferrero said. He took out the wad of bills the fellow from the restaurant had given him. Stern and unsmiling, the face of Ante Pavelic, the first Croatian *Poglavnik*, glared at him from every twenty-dinar note he peeled off. Pavelic hadn't invented fascism, but he'd done even more unpleasant things with it than the Germans, and his successors weren't any nicer than he had been.

In the middle of the notes was a scrap of paper. On it was scrawled a note, in English: *The Church of Our Lady of Lourdes. Tomorrow 1700.* George Smith passed it to Peter Drinkwater, who read it, nodded, and tore it into very small pieces.

Still speaking Italian, Drinkwater said, "We ought to give thanks to Our Lady for blessing us with such a fine catch. Maybe she will reward us with another one."

"She has a fine church here, I've heard," Smith answered in the same tongue. The odds the customs men had planted ears aboard the boat were small, but neither of them believed in taking chances. The Germans made the best and most compact ears in the world, and shared them freely with their allies.

"May Our Lady let us catch the fish we seek," Drinkwater said piously. He crossed himself. Smith automatically followed suit, as any real fisherman would have. If he ever wanted to see Sicily—or England— again, he had to *be* a real fisherman, not just act like one.

Of course, Smith thought, if he'd really wanted to work toward living to a ripe old age, he would have been a carpenter like his father instead of going into Military Intelligence. But even a carpenter's career would have been no guarantee of collecting a pension, not with fascist Germany, the Soviet Union, the U.S.A., and Britain all ready to throw sunbombs about like cricket balls. He sighed. No one was safe in today's world— his own danger was merely a little more obvious than most.

Not counting Serbian slave laborers (and one oughtn't to have counted them, as they seldom lasted long), Rijeka held about 150,000 people. The older part of the city was a mixture of medieval and Austro-Hungarian architecture; the city hall, a masterpiece of gingerbread, would not have looked out of place in old Vienna. The newer buildings, as was true from the Atlantic to the fascist half of the Ukraine, were in the style critics in free countries sneered at as Albert Speer Gothic: huge colonnades and great vertical masses, all intended to show the individual what an ant he was when set against the immense power of the state.

And in case the individual was too dense to note such symbolism, less subtle clues were available: an Ustashi roadblock, where the secret police hauled drivers out of their Volkswagens and Fiats to check their papers; three or four German Luftwaffe troops, probably from the antiaircraft missile base in the hills above town, strolling along as if they owned the pavement. By the way the Croats scrambled out of their path, the locals were not inclined to argue possession of it.

Smith watched the Luftwaffe men out of the corner of his eye till they rounded a corner and disappeared. "Doesn't seem fair, somehow," he murmured in Italian to Drinkwater. Out in the open like this, he could be reasonably sure no one was listening to him.

"What's that?" Drinkwater murmured back in the same language. Neither of them would risk the distinctive sound patterns of English, not here.

"If this poor, bloody world held any justice at all, the last war would have knocked out either the Nazis or the bloody Reds," Smith answered. "Dealing with one set of devils would be bad enough; dealing with both sets, the way we have the last thirty-odd years, and it's a miracle we haven't all gone up in flames."

"We still have the chance," Drinkwater reminded him. "Remember Tokyo and Vladivostok." A freighter from Russian-occupied Hokkaido had blown up in American-occupied Tokyo harbor in the early 1950s, and killed a couple of hundred thousand people. Three days later, courtesy of the U.S. Air Force, the Russian port also suddenly ceased to be.

"Fuuny how it was Manstein who mediated," Smith admitted. "Of course, Stalin's dying when he did helped a bit, too, eh?"

"Just a bit," Drinkwater said with a small chuckle. "Manstein would sooner have thrown bombs at the Russians himself, I expect, if he could have arranged for them not to throw any back."

Both Englishmen shut up as they entered the square in front of the cathedral of Our Lady. Like the Spanish fascists, the Croatians were ostentatiously pious, invoking God's dominion over their citizens as well as that of the equally holy state. Any of the men and women heading for the Gothic cathedral ahead might have belonged to the Ustashi; it approached mathematical certainty that some of them did.

The exterior of the church reminded Smith of a layer cake, with courses of red brick alternating with snowy marble. A frieze of angels and a statue of the Virgin surmounted the door to the upper church. As Smith climbed the ornate stairway toward that door, he took off his cap. Beside him, Drinkwater followed suit. Above the door, golden letters spelled out ZA DOM SPREMNI—Ready for the Fatherland—the slogan of fascist Croatia.

Though Our Lady of Lourdes was of course a Catholic church, the angels on the ceiling overhead were long and thin, as if they sprang from the imagination of a Serbian Orthodox icon-painter. Smith tried to wipe that thought from his mind as he walked down the long hall toward the altar: even thinking of Serbs was dangerous here. The Croats dominated Serbia these days as ruthlessly as the Germans held Poland.

The pews of dark, polished wood, the brilliant stained glass, and the statue of the Virgin behind the altar were familiarly Catholic, and helped Smith forget what he needed to forget and remember what he needed to remember: that he was nothing but a fisherman, thanking the Lord for his fine catch. He took out a cheap plastic rosary and began telling the beads.

The large church was far from crowded. A few pews away from Smith and Drinkwater, a couple of Croatian soldiers in khaki prayed. An old man knelt in front of them; off to one side, a Luftwaffe lieutenant, more interested in architecture than spirituality, photographed a column's acanthus capital. And an old woman with a broom and dustpan moved with arthritic slowness down each empty length of pew sweeping up dust and scraps of paper.

The sweeper came up on Smith and Drinkwater. Obviously a creature of routine, she would have gone right through them had they not moved aside to let her by. "Thank you, thank you," she wheezed, not caring whether she broke the flow of their devotions. A few minutes later, she bothered the pair of soldiers.

Smith looked down to the floor. At first he thought the sweeper simply incompetent, to go right past a fair-sized piece of paper. Then he realized that piece hadn't been there before the old woman went by. He worked his beads harder, slid down into a genuflection. When he went back up into the pew; the paper was in his pocket.

He and Drinkwater prayed for another hour or so, then went back to their fishing boat. On the way Drinkwater said, "Nothing's simple, is it?"

"Did you expect it to be? This is Croatia, after all," Smith answered. "The fellow who bought our eels likely hasn't the slightest idea where the real meeting will be. It's the God's truth he's better off not knowing, that's for certain."

"Too right there," Drinkwater agreed. "And besides, if we were under suspicion, the Ustashi likely would have come down on us in church. This way we run another set of risks for—" He broke off. Some names one did not say, not in Rijeka, not even if no one was close by to hear, not even in the middle of a sentence spoken in Italian.

Back at the boat, the two Englishmen went on volubly—and still in Italian—about how lovely the church of Our Lady of Lourdes had been; no telling who might be listening. As they talked, Smith pulled the paper from the church out of his pocket. The message was short and to the point: *Trsat Castle, the mausoleum, night after tomorrow, 2200.*

The mausoleum? Bloody melodrama, Smith thought. He passed the note to Drinkwater. His companion's eyebrows rose as he read it. Then he nodded and ripped the paper to bits.

Both men went out on deck. Trsat Castle, or what was left of it after long years of neglect, loomed over Rijeka from the hills outside of town. By its looks, it was likelier to shelter vampires than the Serbian agent they were supposed to meet there. It was also unpleasantly close to the Luftwaffe base whose missiles protected the local factory district.

But the Serb had made his way across Croatia—no easy trick, that, not in a country where *Show me your papers* was as common a greeting as *How are you today?*—to contact British military intelligence. "Wouldn't do to let the side down," Smith said softly.

"No, I suppose not," Drinkwater agreed, understanding him without difficulty. Then, of themselves, his eyes went back to Trsat Castle. His face was not one to show much of what he was feeling, but he seemed less than delighted at the turn the mission had taken. A moment later, his words confirmed that: "But this once, don't you wish we could?"

Smith contrived to look carefree as he and Drinkwater hauled a wicker basket through the streets of Rijeka. The necks of several bottles of wine protruded from the basket. When he came up to a checkpoint, Smith took out a bottle and thrust it in a policeman's face. "Here, you enjoy," he said in his Italian-flavored Croatian.

"I am working," the policeman answered, genuine regret in his voice. The men at the previous checkpoint hadn't let that stop them. But this fellow, like them, gave the fishermen's papers only a cursory glance and inspected their basket not at all. That was as well, for a Sten gun lurked in the straw under the bottles of wine.

Two more checkpoints and Smith and Drinkwater were up into the hills. The road became a dirt path. The Englishmen went off into a narrow meadow by the side of that path, took out a bottle, and passed it back and forth. Another bottle replaced it, and then a third. No distant watcher, assuming any such were about, could have noticed very little wine actually got drunk. After a while, the Englishmen lay down on the grass as if asleep.

Maybe Peter Drinkwater really did doze. Smith never asked him afterwards. He stayed awake the whole time himself. Through his eyelashes, he watched the meadow fade from green to gray to black. Day birds stopped singing. In a tree not far away, an owl hooted quietly, as if surprised to find itself awake. Smith would not have been surprised to hear the howl of a wolf—or, considering where he was, a werewolf. Still moving as if asleep, Smith shifted to where he could see the glowing dial of his wristwatch: 2030, he saw. It was full dark. He sat up, dug in the basket, took out the tin tommy gun, and clicked in a magazine. "Time to get moving," he said, relishing the feel of English on his tongue.

"Right you are." Drinkwater also sat, then rose and stretched. "Well, let's be off." Up ahead—and the operative word was *up*—Trsat Castle loomed, a deeper blackness against the dark, moonless sky. It was less than two kilometers ahead, but two kilometers in rough country in the dark was nothing to sneeze at. Sweating and bruised and covered with brambles, Smith and Drinkwater got to the ruins just at the appointed hour.

Smith looked up and up at the gray stone towers. "In England, or any civilized country, come to that, a place like this would draw tourists by the bloody busload, you know?"

"But here it doesn't serve the state, so they didn't bother keeping it up," Drinkwater said, following his thought. He ran a sleeve over his forehead. "Well, no law to say we can't take advantage of their stupidity."

The way into the castle courtyard was open. Whatever gates had once let visitors in and out were gone, victims of some long-ago cannon. Inside . . . inside, George Smith stopped in his tracks and started laughing. Imagining the sort of mausoleum that would belong to a ruined Balkan castle, he had visualized something somber and Byzantine, with tiled domes and icons and the ghosts of monks.

What he found was very different: a neoclassical Doric temple, with marble columns and entablature gleaming whitely in the starlight. He climbed a few low, broad steps, stood, and waited. Drinkwater came up beside him. In the judicious tones of an amateur archaeologist, he said, "I am of the opinion that this is not part of the original architectural plan."

"Doesn't seem so, does it?" Smith agreed. "It—"

In the inky shadows behind the colonnade, something stirred. Smith raised the muzzle of the Sten gun. A thin laugh came from the darkness. A voice followed: "I have had a bead on you since you came inside. But you must be my Englishmen, both because you are here at the time I set and because you chatter over the building. To the Ustashi, this would never occur."

Smith jumped at the scratch of a match. The brief flare of light that followed showed him a heavy-set man of about fifty, with a deeply lined face, bushy eyebrows, and a pirate's mustache. "I am Bogdan," the man said in Croatian, though no doubt he thought of his tongue as Serbian. He took a deep drag on his cigarette; its red glow dimly showed his features once more. "I am the man you have come to see."

"If you are Bogdan, you will want to buy our eels," Drinkwater said in Italian.

"Eels make me sick to my stomach," Bogdan answered in the same language. He laughed that thin laugh again, the laugh of a man who found few things really funny. "Now that the passwords are out of the way, to business. I can use this tongue, or German, or Russian, or even my own. My English, I fear, is poor, for which I apologize. I have had little time for formal education."

That Smith believed. Like Poland, like the German Ukraine, Serbia remained a military occupation zone, with its people given hardly more consideration than cattle: perhaps less than cattle, for cattle were not hunted for the sport of it. Along with his Italian, Smith spoke fluent German and passable Russian, but he said, "This will do well enough. Tell us how it is with you, Bogdan."

The partisan leader drew on his cigarette again, making his face briefly reappear. Then he shifted the smoke to the side of his mouth and spat between two columns. "That is how it goes for me, Englishman. That is how it goes for all Serbia. How are we to keep up the fight for freedom if we have no weapons?"

"You are having trouble getting supplies from the Soviets?" Drinkwater asked, his voice bland. Like most of the Balkans' antifascists, Bogdan and his crew looked to Moscow for help before London or Washington. That he was here now—that the partisans had requested this meeting— was a measure of his distress.

He made a noise deep in his throat. "Moscow has betrayed us again. It is their habit; it has been their habit since '43."

"Stalin betrayed us then, too," Smith answered. "If the Russians hadn't made their separate peace with Germany that summer, the invasion of Italy wouldn't have been driven back into the sea, and Rommel wouldn't have had the men to crush the Anglo-American lodgment in France." Smith shook his head—so much treachery since then, on all sides. He went on, "Tell us how it is in Serbia these days."

"You have what I need?" Bogdan demanded.

"Back at the boat," Drinkwater said. "Grenades, cordite, blasting caps..."

Bogdan's deep voice took on a purring note it had not held before. "Then we shall give the Germans and the Croat pigs who are their lackeys something new to think on when next they seek to play their games with us in our valleys. Let one of their columns come onto a bridge—and then let the bridge come down! I do not believe in hell, but I shall watch them burn here on earth, and make myself content with that. Have you also rockets to shoot their autogiros out of the air?"

Smith spread his hands regretfully. "No. Now that we are in contact with you, though, we may be able to manage a shipment—"

"It would be to your advantage if you did," Bogdan said earnestly. "The Croats and Germans use Serbia as a live-fire training ground for their men, you know. They are better soldiers for having trained in actual combat. And that our people are slaughtered—who cares what happens to backwoods Balkan peasants, eh? Who speaks for us?"

"The democracies speak for you," Smith said.

"Yes—to themselves." Bogdan's scorn was plain to hear. "Oh, they mention it to Berlin and Zagreb, but what are words? Wind! And all the while they go on trading with the men who seek to murder my nation. Listen, Englishmen, and I shall tell you how it is . . ."

The partisan leader did not really care whether Smith and Drinkwater listened. He talked, letting out the poison that had for so long festered inside him. His picture of Serbia reminded Smith of a fox's-eye view of a hunt. The Englishman marveled that the guerrilla movement still lived, close to two generations after the Wehrmacht rolled down on what had been Yugoslavia. Only the rugged terrain of the interior and the indomitable ferocity of the people there kept resistance aflame.

"The Germans are better at war than the cursed Croats," Bogdan said. "They are hard to trap, hard to trick. Even their raw troops, the ones who learn against us, have that combination of discipline and initiative which makes Germans generally so dangerous."

Smith nodded. Even with Manstein's leadership, fighting the Russians to a standstill had been a colossal achievement. Skirmishes along the borders of fascist Europe—and in such hunting preserves as Serbia— had let the German army keep its edge since the big war ended.

Bogdan went on, "When they catch us, they kill us. When we catch them we kill them. This is as it should be." He spoke with such matter-of-factness that Smith had no doubt he meant exactly what he said. He had lived with war for so long, it seemed the normal state of affairs to him.

Then the partisan's voice changed. "The Germans are wolves. The Croats, their army and the stinking Ustashi, are jackals. They rape, they torture, they burn our Orthodox priests' beards, they kill a man for having on his person anything written in the Cyrillic script, and in so doing they seek to turn us Serbs into their own foul kind." Religion and alphabet divided Croats and Serbs, who spoke what was in essence the same language.

"Not only that, they are cowards." By his tone, Bogdan could have spoken no harsher condemnation. "They come into a village only if they have a regiment at their backs, and either flee or massacre if anyone resists them. We could hurt them far worse than we do, but when they are truly stung, they run and hide behind the Germans' skirts."

"I gather you are coming to the point where that does not matter to you," Smith said.

"You gather rightly," Bogdan said. "Sometimes a man must hit back, come what may afterward. To strike a blow at the fascists, I am willing to ally with the West. I would ally with Satan, did he offer himself as my comrade." So much for his disbelief, Smith thought.

"Churchill once said that if Germans invaded hell, he would say a good word for the devil," Drinkwater observed.

"If the Germans invaded hell, Satan would need help because they are dangerous. If the Croats invaded hell, he would have trouble telling *them* from his demons."

Smith laughed dryly, then returned to business: "How shall we convey to you our various, ah, pyrotechnics?"

"The fellow who bought your eels will pay you a visit tomorrow. He has a Fiat, and has also a permit for travel to the edge of Serbia: One of his cousins owns an establishment in Belgrade. The cousin, that swine, is not one of us, but he gives our man the excuse he needs for taking his motorcar where we need it to go."

"Very good. You seem to have thought of everything." Smith turned away. "We shall await your man tomorrow."

"Don't go yet, my friends." Agile as a chamois, Bogdan clattered down the steep steps of the mausoleum. He carried a Soviet automatic rifle on his back and held a squat bottle in his hands. "I have here slivovitz. Let us drink to the death of fascists." He yanked the cork out of the bottle with a loud pop. "*Zhiveli!*"

The harsh plum brandy burned its way down Smith's throat like jellied gasoline. Coughing, he passed the bottle to Drinkwater, who took a cautious swig and gave it back to Bogdan. The partisan leader tilted it almost to the vertical. Smith marveled at the temper of his gullet, which had to be made of something like stainless steel to withstand the potent brew.

At last, Bogdan lowered the slivovitz bottle. "Ahh!" he said, wiping his mouth on his sleeve. "That is very fine. I—"

Without warning, a portable searchlight blazed into the courtyard from the open gateway into Trsat Castle. Smith froze, his eyes filling with tears at the sudden transformation from night to brighter than midday. An amplified voice roared, "Halt! Stand where you are! You are the prisoners of the Independent State of Croatia!"

Bogdan bellowed like a bull. "No fucking Croat will take me!" He grabbed for his rifle. Before the motion was well begun, a burst of fire cut him down. Smith and Drinkwater threw themselves flat, their hands over their heads.

Something hot and wet splashed Smith's cheek. He rubbed the palm of his hand over it. In the actinic glare of the searchlight, Bogdan's blood looked black. The partisan leader was still alive. Shrieks alternated with bubbling moans as he writhed on the ground, trying to hold his guts inside his belly.

Jackboots rattled in the courtyard as men from the Ustashi, including a medic with a Red Cross armband, dashed in from the darkness. The medic grabbed Bogdan, stuck a plasma line in his arm. Bogdan did his best to tear it out again. A couple of ordinary troopers kept him from succeeding. "We'll patch you up so you can sing for us," one of them growled. His voice changed to gloating anticipation: "Then we'll take you apart again, one centimeter at a time."

A rifle muzzle pressed against Smith's forehead. His eyes crossed as they looked down the barrel of the gun. "Up on your feet, spy," said the Ustashi man holding it. He had 7.92 millimeters of potent persuasion. Smith obeyed at once.

An Ustashi major strode into the brilliant hole the searchlight had cut in the darkness. He marched up to Smith and Drinkwater, who had also been ordered to his feet. Smith could have shaved on the creases in his uniform, and used his belt buckle as a mirror for the job. The perfect outfit served only to make him more acutely aware of how grubby he was himself.

The major studied him. The fellow had a face out of a fascist training film: hard, stern, handsome, ready to obey any order without question or even thought, not a gram of surplus fat anywhere. An interrogator with a face like his could make a prisoner afraid just by looking at him, and instilling fear was half an interrogator's battle.

"You are the Englishmen?" the major demanded. He spoke English himself, with a better public-school accent than Smith could boast. Smith glanced toward Drinkwater. Warily, they both nodded.

Like a robot's, the major's arm shot up and out in a perfect fascist salute. "The Fatherland thanks you for your help in capturing this enemy of the state and of the true faith," he declared.

On the ground, Bogdan's groans changed tone as he realized he had been betrayed. Smith shrugged. He had a fatherland, too—London told him what to do, and he did it. He said, "You'd best let us get out of the harbor before dawn, so none of Bogdan's people can be sure we had anything to do with this."

"It shall be as you say," the major agreed, though he sounded indifferent as to whether Smith and Drinkwater gave themselves away to

Bogdan's organization. He probably *was* indifferent; Croatia and England loved each other no better than Croatia and the Communists. This time, it had suited them to work together. Next time, they might try to kill each other. They all knew it.

Smith sighed. "It's a rum world, and that's a fact."

The Ustashi major nodded. "So it is. Surely God did not intend us to cooperate with such degenerates as you. One day, though, we shall have a true reckoning. *Za dom Spremni!*"

Fucking looney, Smith thought. If the major read that in his eyes, too bad. Croatia could not afford an incident with England, not when her German overlords were dickering with London over North Sea petroleum rights.

The trip down to Rijeka from Trsat Castle was worse than the one up from the city. The Englishmen dared not show a light, not unless they wanted to attract secret policemen who knew nothing of their arrangement with the Ustashi major and who would start shooting before they got the chance to find out. Of course, they ran the same risk on (Smith devoutly hoped) a smaller scale traveling in the dark.

Traveling in the dark down a steep hillside also brought other risks. After Peter Drinkwater fell for the third time, he got up swearing: "God damn the Russians for mucking about in Turkey, and in Iraq, and in Persia. If they weren't trying to bugger the oil wells there, you and I wouldn't have to deal with the likes of the bloody Ustashi—and we'd not have to feel we needed a bath afterwards."

"No, we'd be dealing with the NKVD instead, selling out Ukrainian nationalists to Moscow," Smith answered. "Would you feel any cleaner after that?"

"Not bloody likely," Drinkwater answered at once. "It's a rum world, all right." He stumbled again, but caught himself. The path was nearly level now. Rijeka lay not far ahead.

THE TOMB

Jack McDevitt

The city lay bone white beneath the moon. Leaves rattled through courtyards and piled up against shattered walls. Solitary columns stood against the sky. The streets were narrow and filled with rubble.

The wind off the Atlantic carried the smell of the tide. It sucked at the forest, which had long since overwhelmed the city's defenses and crept into its forums and market-places. A surge of oak and pine in the north had washed over a hill and crashed into sacred environs anchored by a temple and a tomb.

The temple was a relatively modest structure, projecting from the side of the hill. It was, in fact, almost diminutive, but a perceptive visitor would have recognized both Roman piety and Greek genius in its pantheonic lines. The roof was gone, and the circular walls had disappeared within the tangle of trees and brambles.

The front of the building, save for a single collapsed pillar, remained intact. A marble colonnade, still noble in appearance, looked out across a broad plaza. Carved lions slumbered on pedestals, and stone figures with blank eyes and missing limbs kept watch over the city.

Twelve marble steps descended from the temple into the plaza. They were as wide as the building itself, precisely chiseled, rounded, almost sensual. The marble was heavily worn.

One would have needed several minutes to walk across the plaza. Public buildings, in varying states of disintegration, bordered the great square. They stood dark and cold through the long evenings, but when the light was right, it was possible to imagine them as they had been when the city was alive.

The eastern side, opposite the temple, opened onto a fountain and a long pool. Both were dry and full of dust. Weary strollers, had there been any, would have found stone benches placed strategically for their use.

The tomb stood beyond the fountain on a direct line with the temple. It was an irregular octagon, constructed of tapered stone blocks, laid with military simplicity. The structure was gouged and scorched as high as a man on horseback might reach. If ever the tomb had borne a name, it lay now among the chunks of stone scattered at its base.

The tomb itself lay open. There was no evidence that a slab had ever sealed the gaping shaft. But it must have been so.

A device that resembled a sword had been cut into marble above the entrance. In keeping perhaps with the spirit of the architecture, it, too, was plain: The hilt, the blade, and the cross guard were all rectangular and square-edged.

The vault rose into a circular, open cupola. Two stone feet stood atop the structure, placed wide in what could only have been a heroic stance. One limb was broken off at the ankle, the other at the lower part of the shin.

On a tranquil night, one might easily apprehend the tread of divine sandals.

Three horsemen, not yet quite full-grown, descended from the low hills in the northwest. In the sullen wind, they could smell the age of the place.

They wore animal skins and carried iron weapons. Little more than boys, they had hard blue eyes and rode with an alertness that betrayed a sense of a hostile world. The tallest of the three drew back on his reins and stopped. The others fell in on either side. "What's wrong, Kam?" asked the rider on the left, his eyes darting nervously across the ruins.

"Nothing, Ronik..." Kam rose slightly off his mount's haunches and looked intently toward the city. His voice had an edge. "I thought I saw something moving."

The night carried the first bite of winter. Falon, on Kam's right, closed his vest against the chill, briefly fingering a talisman, a goat's horn once worn by his grandfather and blessed against demons. His mount snorted uncertainly. "I do not see anything," he said.

The three riders listened for sounds in the night.

"Where?" asked Ronik. He was broad-shouldered, given to quick passions. He was the only one of the three who had killed. "Where did you see it?"

"Near the temple." Kam pointed. They were still high enough to see over the city's fortifications.

"No one would go there," said Ronik.

The words hung on the night air. No *man*, thought Falon. But he said nothing.

"*We* are going there," said Kam. He was trying very hard to sound indifferent.

Falon stroked his horse's neck. Its name was Carik and his father had given it to him before riding off on a raid from which he had never returned. "It might have been best," he said, "if we had not bragged quite so loudly. Better first to have done the deed, stayed the night, and then spoken of it."

Kam delivered an elaborate shrug: "Why? You're not afraid, are you, Falon?"

Falon started forward again. "My father always believed this city to be Ziu's birthplace. And that"—he looked toward the temple—"his altar."

They were following an ancient roadway. It had once been paved but was little more than a track now, grassed over, occasional stones jutting from the bed. Ahead, it drove straight on to the front gate of the city.

"Maybe we should not do this," said Ronik.

Kam tried to laugh. It came out sounding strained.

Falon gazed across the ruins. It was hard to imagine laughter within those walls, or children being born. Or cavalry gathering. The place felt, somehow, as though it had *always* been like this. "I wonder," he said, "if the city was indeed built by gods?"

"If *you* are afraid," said Kam, "you may return home. Ronik and I will think no less of you." He made no effort to keep the mockery out of his voice.

Falon restrained his anger. "I fear no man," he said. "But it *is* impious to tread on the works of the gods."

They were advancing at a walking rate. Kam did not answer, but he showed no inclination to assume his customary position in the lead. "What use," he asked, after a moment, "would Ziu have for fortifications?"

This was not the only ruined city known to the Kortagenians: Kosh-on-the-Ridge, and Eskulis near Deep Forest, Kalikat and Agonda, the twin ports at Pirapet, and three more along the southern coast. They were called after the lands in which they were found; no one knew how their builders had named them. But there were tales about this one, which was always referred to simply as "The City." Some thought it had no name because, of all the ancient walled settlements, it was the oldest. Others thought it a concession to divine origin.

"If not the home of gods," said Ronik, "maybe *devils*."

There were stories: passersby attacked by phantoms, dragged within the walls, and seen no more. Black wings lifting on dark winds and children vanishing from nearby encampments. Demonic lights, it was said, sometimes reflected off low clouds, and wild cries echoed in the night. Makanda, most pious of the Kortagenians, refused to ride within sight of the city after dark, and would have been thunderstruck had he known their intentions.

They rode slowly forward, speaking in whispers. Past occasional mounds. Past solitary oaks. The wind stiffened and raced across the plain. And they came at last to the city gate.

The wall had collapsed completely at this point, and the entrance was enmeshed in a thick patch of forest. Trees and thickets crowded together, disrupting the road and blocking entry.

They paused under a clutch of pines. Kam advanced, drew his sword, and hacked at branches and brush.

"It does not want us," said Ronik.

Falon stayed back, well away from Kam's blade, which swung with purpose but not caution. When the way was clear and the city lay open, and Kam had sheathed his weapon, he advanced.

The streets were dark and still.

"If it would make either of you feel better," Kam said, "we need not sleep in the plaza."

The horses seemed uneasy.

"I don't think we should go in there at all," said Ronik. His eyes had narrowed, and his features, usually aggressive and energetic, were wary. Falon realized he was frightened. But less adept than his companions at concealment.

Kam's mount took a step forward, a step back. "What do *you* think, Falon?"

The road opened out into a broad avenue. It was covered with grass, lined by crumbling walls and broken courtyards. "We have said we will stay the night," said Falon, speaking softly to prevent the wind from taking his words into the city. "I do not see that we have a choice."

Inside, somewhere amid the dark streets, a dry branch broke. It was a sharp report, loud, hard, like the snapping of a bone. And as quickly gone.

"Something *is* in there," said Ronik, backing away.

Kam, who had started to dismount, froze with one leg clear of the horse's haunches. Without speaking, he lowered it again and tightened his grip on the reins.

"Ziu may be warning us," said Ronik.

Kam threw him a look that could have withered an arm.

Ronik returned the glare. Kam was oldest of the three, and the others usually acceded to his judgment, but Falon suspected that, if it came to a fight, Ronik would prove the more capable. And perhaps the less likely to flee.

"Probably a wolf," said Falon, not at all convinced that it was. Wolves, after all, did not snap branches.

"I am not going in." Ronik dropped his eyes. "It would be wrong to do so."

Kam came erect. "There's a *light*," he whispered.

Falon saw it. A red glow, flickering on the underside of the trees. In the plaza. "A fire," he said.

A shudder worked its way through his belly. He damned himself and fought it down.

"It's near the *tomb*." Kam turned his horse, started back through the trees. Ronik moved to follow, paused, and clasped Falon's shoulder to pull him along.

Falon tried to ignore his own rising panic. "Are we children to be frightened off because someone has built a fire on a cool night?"

"We don't know *what* it might be." Kam's tone had grown harsh. Angry. His customary arrogance had drained completely. "I suggest we wait until daylight. And then see who it is."

Falon could not resist: "Now who is afraid?"

"You know me better," said Kam. "But it is not prudent to fight at night." He turned his mount, and started out.

Ronik was tugging at Falon. "Let's go," he said. "We can retire to a safe distance, in the hills. Stay there tonight, and return to camp tomorrow. No one will ever know."

"We would have to lie," said Falon. "They will ask."

"Let them *ask*. If anyone says I am afraid—" Kam gripped his sword hilt fiercely—"I will kill him."

Falon shook free of Ronik's hand. Ronik sighed, began to back out through the copse, and encountered some difficulty getting his wide shoulders through the twisted branches. He kept his face toward the city, several times jerking his arm toward Falon in a frustrated effort to persuade him to follow.

The forest smelled of pine and dead leaves and old wood.

Kam's voice, impatient: "Hurry..." As if he saw something coming.

Falon was about to comply when Ronik—good, decent Ronik, who had been his friend all his life—spoke the words that pinned him within the city: "Come with us, Falon. It is no disgrace to fear the gods."

And someone else replied with Falon's voice: "No. Carik and I will stay."

"Ziu does not wish it. His will is clear."

"Ziu is a warrior. He is not vindictive. I do not believe he will harm me. I will stay the night. Come for me in the dawn."

"Damn you." Kam's mount, visible through the hole they had cut in the forest, moved first one way, then another. "Farewell, then. We will return in the morning. I hope you will still be here." And they wheeled their horses' and fled, one swiftly, the other with reluctance, out along the paved road.

The wind moved through the trees.

Have no fear. I will not betray you.

The red glow of the fire faded and went out. Falon made no effort to track its source.

He rode deliberately into the city. Down the center of the avenue. Past rows of shattered walls and occasional open squares. Past enormous broken buildings. The hoofs were loud in the night.

He stopped in a wide intersection, gathered his courage, and dismounted. The city lay silent and vast about him.

He spoke to Carik, rubbed his muzzle, and continued on foot, leading the horse. The temple came into view, standing serenely on a mild slope.

His heart hammered, and he debated whether it would not be prudent after all to join Kam and Ronik. And the answer to that was clearly *yes*. Yet he knew that if he ran now, fled beyond the gate, he would in the end have to come back.

Leaves swirled behind him, and Falon glanced fretfully over his shoulder.

Something about the temple stirred him. Some emotion to which he could not put a name fluttered deep in his soul. He walked to the next intersection and looked again. Ghostly illumination filled the building.

Carik moved closer to him.

It was *moonlight*. Nothing more: a trick of the night.

The temple looks complete, but the roof is off. The moon shines directly inside.

He decided against sleeping in the plaza. Better to camp out of the way. Just in case.

He found a running spring and a stout wall on the east side of the avenue. Anything coming toward him from the direction of the tomb would have to cross that broad space.

Falon removed Carik's saddle, loosened the bit, and hobbled the animal. He set out some grain, and sat down himself to a meal of nuts and dried beef. Afterward he rubbed Carik down and took a final look around. Satisfied that he was alone, he used saddle and animal skins to make a bed, placed his weapons at hand, and tried to sleep.

*   *   *

The moon sank behind the wall. Shamed by his own fears, Falon withdrew into the skins and listened for sounds in the city.

Afterward he was never sure whether he had actually slept. But suddenly, deep in the night, he was acutely, vividly awake: The smell of grass was strong, insects buzzed, the wind stirred. A few paces away, Carik shook himself.

There had been a sound out there that didn't belong: a footstep, perhaps. Or a falling rock. He glanced at the horse, which stood unconcerned. Good: It could see over the wall, and if something were approaching, Carik would sound a warning.

Beneath the skins, Falon pressed his hand against the goat's horn to assure himself it was still there. His fingers closed on his sword.

Somewhere, far off, he heard the clink of metal. Barely discernible, a whisper in the wind.

The horse heard it, too. Carik turned his head toward the temple.

Falon got to his feet and looked out across the ruins.

A deeper darkness had fallen over the thoroughfares and courtyards. The temple, no longer backlit by the moon, stood cold and silent.

The sound came again, this time different: a rock colliding with a hard surface. Bounding along. _

He was thoroughly awake now, and a few gray streaks had appeared in the east. Dawn was yet far away, but he could retreat, leave the city and its secrets, and still claim truthfully to have stayed the night. And who could blame him?

A light flickered in the plaza.

He couldn't see it directly, but shadows moved across the face of the temple.

Falon shivered.

"Wait," he said to Carik, and slipped over the wall.

Rubble and cold starlight.

He crept through the dark streets, crossed an intersection, passed silently through a series of courtyards, and moved in behind a screen of trees that looked out over the square.

A lantern had been set on the ground before the tomb. In its yellow light, a robed figure crouched like an animal on hands and knees.

It seemed compounded of night and wind and a sense of things long dead.

Its face was hidden within the folds of a hood.

Falon froze. The creature was digging in the dirt with its fingers. Abruptly it stopped, grunted, looked at something in its hand. Held it near the lantern. Flipped the object into the dark. Falon listened to it crash out toward the middle of the plaza and recognized one of the sounds he'd heard.

He *saw* the source of the other: The area was thoroughly dug up. Piles of earth were heaped everywhere, and an iron spade leaned against a tree.

Falon surveyed the plaza, noted sparks from a banked campfire behind a wall to the north. The figure in the robe seemed to be alone.

It repeated the process, picking up a second object, a stone, turning it several different ways, holding it under the lantern. This time it murmured its satisfaction and got clumsily to its feet. Light penetrated the folds of the hood: It *was* human. A man.

A portion of ground had been cleared, and filled with individual rocks. The figure hunched over them, rearranged them, added the one he held. Lifted it again, placed it elsewhere. Said something Falon couldn't make out. But he understood the pleasure in the voice.

Falon wished he were close enough to see better. It appeared that the man was assembling pieces of statuary. One of the pieces looked like an arm.

With a sudden swirl of robes, the figure raised his lantern as if he knew he was not alone, straightened with an obvious effort, picked up a stick he had laid by, and started toward Falon. He went only a few steps, however, before he stopped, poked at the ground with the stick, and fell again to his knees.

He scrabbled in the tall grass, grumbling and muttering in a strange tongue, thrusting the light forward, and throwing rocks about in a frightful manner. The creature gasped and wheezed throughout this frenetic exercise.

Falon released the breath he had not realized he was holding, touched the goat's horn with the tips of his fingers, and stepped out of the shadows.

The hooded man should have seen him, since the young warrior stood directly in his line of vision. But he did not, and continued rather to poke and prod in the weeds.

Falon closed to within a sword's thrust. "Who are you?" he asked.

The man, startled, finally aware he had a visitor, looked up. "Hello." With considerable effort he got to his feet, wiped clay and dust from his robe, and raised his hand in greeting.

Falon did not return the gesture. "I am Falon the Kortagenian," he said, appraising threat potential and dismissing it. He saw neither arms nor skill.

"And I am Edward the Chronicler." Edward stood so that the light from the lantern played across his features. He looked simultaneously cheerful and wary. His eyes drifted across Falon's blade, which he had not bothered to draw.

"And what sort of chronicle do you compose," asked Falon, "that you dare the spirits of this place?"

Edward seemed to relax somewhat. "If you are really interested," he said, "it is indeed the spirits I pursue. For if they live anywhere on the earth, it is surely here." He swept up the lamp and held it so he could read Falon's face. "A boy," he said. "Are you alone, child?"

The man was short and quite stout. His head was immense, too large even for the corpulent body that supported it. He had a tiny nose, and his eyes were sunk deep in flesh. A series of chins hid his throat altogether from view. His voice suggested he was accustomed to receiving deference.

"I am no child," said Falon, "as you will discover to your sorrow should you fail to show due respect."

"Ah." Edward bowed. "Indeed I shall. Yes: You may rely on that, friend Falon."

"Edward that pursues spirits: What is your clan?"

The dark eyes fastened on him from within the mounds of flesh. "I am late of Lausanne. More recently of Brighton. He collapsed onto a bench, drew back his hood. The man would have been approximately the age of his father. But he was a different sort. This one had never ridden hard. "What," he continued with good humor, "brings you to this poor ruin in the dead of night, Falon?"

"I was passing and saw lights." Yes: That sounded fearless. Let the stranger know he was dealing with a man who took no stock in demons and devils.

"Well," offered Edward in the manner of one who was taking charge, "I am grateful for the company."

Falon nodded. "No doubt." He glanced surreptitiously at the tomb, at the open vault. The passageway into the interior was dark and quiet. "Your accent is strange."

"I am Briton by birth."

Falon had met others from the misty land. He found them gloomy, pretentious, overbearing. It seemed to him that they rarely spoke their minds. "Why are you here?"

Edward sighed. "I would put a name to one of the spirits. And answer a question." He picked up a leather bag. "Can I offer you something to eat?"

"No. I have no need." Falon looked past him, at the temple. "What is the question?"

Edward's eyes locked on him. There was something in them that was unsettling. Something ancient and weary that seemed kin with the city itself. "Falon, do you know who built this place?"

"No. Some of our elders think it has *always* been here."

"Not a very enlightening reply. It was constructed ages ago by a race whom we now remember only dimly. If at all." He turned a sharp eye on Falon.

Falon was too interested to take offense. "And who were they, this forgotten race?" The man spoke with authority, and Falon was accustomed to taking others at their word. Skepticism was not in his nature.

The Briton took a long breath. "They were called Romans," he said.

Falon ran the name across his lips. "I have never heard of them."

Edward nodded. Branches creaked, the flame in the lantern wobbled. "The world," he said, "is full of their temples and cities. The hand that carved *this* tomb created others very much like it across the Alps, in the valley of the Tigris, among the pyramids. They built an immense civilization, Falon. Bridges, temples, viaducts. Roads to tie it together. A system of laws. They gave peace and stability to much of the world." His dark eyes seemed to have fastened on the temple. "But today the Romans and their name are dust, blown across the forests and plains."

Too many words for Falon to follow. He thought of a confederacy of clans that was now attempting to impose its will on the Kortagenians. He supposed the chronicler had something similar in mind, although no one *he* knew had ever shown an inclination toward city-building. "What happened to them, Edward the Chronicler?"

"*That* is the question I have pursued all my days. To discover what force can initiate the decline and cause the collapse of such power."

"Only the gods," said Falon. "These Romans must have offended Woden grievously, that he would destroy even the memory of their accomplishments."

Edward's gaze seemed unsettled. It touched Falon, the tomb, a point somewhere among the stars. "They were forgotten," he said at length, "because they failed to create an institution, independent from the state, that could carry their memory forward."

Falon nodded, not understanding, but not wishing to betray his ignorance.

"A society of scholars, perhaps, might have done it. An academy. A foundation. Possibly even a religious group—"

Falon shrugged it all away, into the night. "What spirit," he asked, "would you name?"

Edward looked toward the stones with which he'd been working. "The occupant of the tomb."

A supernatural chill ran through Falon. He hesitated to reply, not sure of his voice. "Then you are indeed late," he said finally, pleased with his boldness.

The Briton was smiling. Falon saw that several pieces of a human figure had been assembled. The arm was almost complete. There was part of a leg, a shoulder, a trunk, a shield. The leg broke off at the shin. The shield was emblazoned with the same sword device that marked the front of the vault.

"No," he said. "I think not."

Something moved in the trees.

"Then who is he?"

Edward joined his hands within his sleeves to warm them. "A matchless commander, the hero who might have prevented the general disaster. Dead now these fourteen hundred years, more or less; the chronicles are sometimes inexact." He straightened his robe, adjusted it across his shoulders. "Does the name Maxentius mean anything to you?"

"No," said Falon.

"He was a tyrant who controlled the Roman capital when this city was young. A vicious, licentious, incompetent coward." Edward's voice shook with indignation. "Under his sway, no man's dignity was safe, nor any woman's honor. Wives and daughters were dragged before him and abused. Those who protested were put to death. The people were enslaved. The soldiers were the only order of men whom he appeared to respect. He filled Rome and Italy with armed troops, connived at their assaults against the common people, encouraged them to plunder and massacre. He was, I suspect, a symbol of all that went wrong with the Empire."

Falon's hand fell to his weapon. "I would gladly have ridden against such a monster," he said.

The Briton nodded. "There was one who did. His name was Constantine, and I have no doubt he would have welcomed you to his cause."

Falon felt a surge of pride.

"Constantine appears to have recognized that the empire, which was fragmented in his time, was disintegrating. But he laid plans how it might be preserved. Or, if it were already too late, and collapse could not be prevented, he considered how the essence of its greatness might be passed on." Edward stood unmoving against the night. "Had he been able to seize power from Maxentius, things might have been different."

"He failed in the effort?"

"He was a reluctant crusader, Falon. And he marched against Maxentius only when the tyrant threatened to invade *his* domains."

"I cannot approve of such timidity," said Falon.

Edward smiled. "I would be disappointed if you did. But Constantine wished to conserve the peace and welfare of his realm."

"And where was his realm?"

"Britain," he said. "And here."

"But I do not understand." Falon grasped Edward's shoulder, turned him that he could look into his face. "If this Constantine was a commander of great ability, as you have said, how did it happen that he did not prevail?"

"Heroes do not win all engagements," Edward said slowly. "Maxentius sent army after army against him. Constantine swept them away. Most of the Italian cities between the Alps and the Po not only acknowledged his power but also embraced his cause. And at last he appeared before Rome itself. The seat of the tyrant." Edward paused. They were exposed out here, and the wind cut through Falon's thin vest. The Briton stopped his narrative and stared up at him. "Are you cold?" he asked.

"No. Please go on."

"Maxentius had by far the larger army. He also had armored cavalry, a type of opponent that *you*, Falon, will never see. Fortunately. But he chose not to rely on military force alone." Without another word and without explanation, he walked into the shadows. Moments later he returned with a woven garment and held it out to the young warrior.

Falon pulled it over his shoulders. "Thank you."

Edward resumed his seat. "There was, across the Tiber, a float bridge that connected the city with the plain. This was the Milvian Bridge. Maxentius directed his engineers to weaken it. Then he rode out of his capital to engage the invader.

"Constantine was waiting, and the armies fell quickly to battle. For much of the afternoon the conflict raged back and forth, and the issue was uncertain. It was one more of a series of calamitous events that sucked the lifeblood of the Empire. However that may be, Constantine's troops pressed forward, and gradually the tyrant gave way."

"Now," urged Falon, "strike the chief."

"Yes," said Edward. "One might almost think you were there. And he did: He rallied his personal guard and led them against that part of the line in which he could see the tyrant's colors. The banners wavered at the onslaught, and the shock of the charge broke the Roman line. The defenders panicked. But Maxentius, with his picked men, retreated across the fateful bridge. Unmindful of caution, Constantine pursued, bleeding from a dozen wounds.

"And in that terrible moment, when his great enemy had reached the center of the bridge, the tyrant gave the signal, and the span was hurled into the Tiber."

"The coward," said Falon with a snarl. And then, philosophically, "Valor is not always sufficient to the day. Constantine need not be ashamed."

"No. Certainly not."

"And did there arise a hero to avenge him?"

"Yes. But that is another story, for the avenger lacked political wisdom, and soon after his success the empire's lights dimmed and went out. Then the world fell into a night that has had no dawn."

"But what connection has the tale with this vault? Is the tomb indeed empty?"

Edward arranged his robe, draped it over his knees. He held out the lantern to Falon. "Perhaps you would care to look?"

"No." He drew away. "It is quite all right."

The Briton rose. "You should assure yourself. Please. Follow me."

They entered the passageway, Edward leading with his lantern, stepping over mulch and earth and weeds. It was narrow, the ceiling was low, and the rock walls were cracked. Falon had to duck his head.

It sloped at a modest angle and ended in a small chamber. The chamber was bare, devoid of furniture or marking save for a marble shelf laid against the inner wall. "There were rumors," said Edward, "that Constantine survived. One account, of which I have a copy, maintained that he was taken half-drowned from the Tiber and returned to a friendly but unnamed city. The story holds that he lived in this city one year. Other sources say three. It's difficult to recover the details. All agree that he hoped to lead another army against Maxentius but that he never fully recovered. And when he died..." Edward shrugged. "I've looked for many years, seeking the truth of the event."

"And how would you know the truth?"

"Easily," he said. "Find his tomb." He kicked away dead leaves and dirt and pointed toward scratches on the stone floor. "Here is where his sarcophagus once stood. There, on the shelf, they placed his armor."

"Then this *is* his tomb?"

"Oh, yes, I am quite satisfied on that score. Yes: Unquestionably he was interred here. And a great deal more, I fear."

Falon wondered how he could possibly know such things.

"While he lived, he talked of building a second Rome, in the East." Edward's voice was filled with regret. "Something to survive."

The smoke thrown up by the lantern was already growing thick.

Edward lapsed into silence. He coughed, tried to wave away the noxious cloud.

Falon's eyes had begun to water. "Let's finish this outside," he said.

"What?"

"Outside." He seized Edward's elbow and steered him back up into the starlight. The air was cold and tasted good. Falon took it gratefully into his lungs. "How do you *know*?" he asked. "How can you be sure it's *his* tomb? It is not marked."

"Oh, yes, it *is*. Look behind you." He pointed at the statue, which lay partly assembled. "Look on the shield."

A burst of wind pulled at his garment.

Edward held the lantern close. In its flickering light, Falon saw only the curious sword. It was identical to the blade on the vault.

"I do not know the sign," he said.

"It was *his* device."

Falon pressed his fingers against it. "Can you be so certain? There are many who use weapon devices."

"This is *not* a weapon," said Edward. "It was a symbol sometimes used by an obscure religious cult. For many centuries, in fact, a mark of shame. Said to have magic properties. It's called a cross."

Falon fingered his talisman. The sense of the horn's power was reassuring. "The mark is strange to me."

"Only Constantine ever used it."

"You said something else was buried in there with him."

Edward picked up his bag. "An old man's idle dream, perhaps. I wonder whether everything we might have been does not lie inside this vault."

Brilliant Sirius was framed within the cupola atop the tomb. "It's getting colder," he said after a moment. "I suggest we retire to my camp and restart the fire."

TURPENTINE

Barry N. Malzberg

The sociologist was defiant all the way to Kirk's office, but when he saw the scene, when he got what you could call a sociological perspective of the ordnance, his mood changed right quick. What is this? he said. What the fuck is this? Trust a sociologist to toss a *fuck* in when he is talking to the troops. That's what they teach them in the schools now, get down, get right, be *relevant*, talk out of that hip side of your mouth. Saying *fuck* puts everybody at his or her ease, like the sociologist and you, you are on the same side of the party, fighting the *e*stablishment. Except we don't really go along with that shit anymore, there is our side and there is the rest of them and the line is not to be crossed by sociologists, white sociologists from the University of Chicago with a Ph.D. in population, as the catalog we had researched put it. Give us the plans, Richard said, just give us the plans. We know you have them.

The sociologist stared, little guy, maybe five and a half feet, still gripping the satchel he had snatched when we grabbed him from his office. What are you talking about? he said. He took in the scene pretty good; we could see him making sociological calculations behind that forehead of his. I should have gotten out of here, he said. That was my mistake. When the going was good, I should have got. We had trashed Kirk's office pretty good by then, although nothing as to what the press was going to say later. I could figure out what the press would say. By the time the Rosenthals were through with us, they would have the dung piled feet deep; as they say would be talking about the jism on the carpets instead of into the Barnard girls, where it had been properly aimed. But there was no way to put off that kind of crap; as Richard said, you took your shot and you aimed it and the rest of it was establishment blues, that was all. The plans, he said again. The underground reactor, the tunnels, the way in. We know you have them. They were planted in your office a month ago when the stuff started getting serious. I want them now.

The sociologist stared at Richard. You're crazy, he said. You've got to be crazy. What are you talking about, nuclear reactors, tunnels? That's for the Department of Physics, not for me. I'm in the soft sciences.

You in soft sciences, mother, Richard said, going into his deep Panther act. Maybe I should explain that we were a mixed crowd—heavily mixed, as they say, boys and girls, black and white—but Richard in shades and full regalia had asked for the whole show and we had fallen back against the walls. If there was one thing he knew, Richard had said, it was how to put the screws to a white sociologist. Watch me jive, he had said, lean back and learn how we're going to deal with the rest of these mothers from the point of revolution *on*. We had laughed then but it didn't seem so funny now, Richard himself being carried away a bit with the shades and the chain act. But we were deep in by then and no arguing it. You *real* soft, Richard said. Let me explain to you, he said, coming up to the sociologist and giving him the finger in the gut, one, two, three, the rhythm boys. Back when things started moving around here about a month ago, foxy old Administration whose very offices you will note we now *occ*upy thought that it would be best to get the plans, the secret plans for the underground tunnels out of the head offices and to some place relatively innocent. *Inno-cent* you get that, you understand the frame? We're just trying to be helpful and refresh your memory.

I don't know what's going on here, the sociologist said. Believe me, you have me at a loss. I am willing to help, but I never heard of anything like this. You have me at a loss, I told you, I want—

You see my friend Ronald X here? Richard said. Ronald X is my security consultant, my comrade-in-arms, you dig? He is a desperate man.

That is right, I said, I am a desperate man.

He comes from a greatly deprived background, Richard said. You know all about cultural deprivation, they give out Ph.D.'s in that subject. Your guy Alinsky in Chicago, he runs seminars on the streets about people like my friend Ronald X. There is *capital funding* from the government to study the deprivations in the head of this desperate man over here.

The sociologist stared at Richard as if he had never seen anyone like him before. Possibly this is true. It is possible that Richard was a new experience for the sociologist, just as he had been for me back in those times when we were sharing backgrounds down at the Union. You can see what a desperate man he is from the look in his eyes, Richard said.

He is from CCNY, which makes him even more frantic because he does not have that fine education and potentially prestigious degree behind him. He is just your basic nigger, Ronald X, and he is very angry.

I want your help, I said, I want you to find me the plans. That is a simple request and then I will not be so desperate. I will leap over my cultural background and be as solid and reasonable as you. But right now I am strictly speaking not civilized.

The sociologist seemed tormented, or perhaps the word was abstract. These shades of meaning are more for Richard than me. Clear to us, though, *no* part of Chicago population studies seemed to have prepared him for this, or at least he had not taken the course. That had been an elective, dealing with mad up-against-the-wall niggers in the president's office at 2:00 A.M. with about twenty-five hundred police ringing the campus and the place going crazy. Maybe if he went back to school for some postpostgraduate work he would remember to take that course next time. But right now he was flat out of luck. That out-of-luck expression seemed to filter through all of his hard little features and then he said, I still don't know what the deal is. But I'll go back with you and look through desk drawers. I don't care.

That is a righteous cooperative attitude, Richard said, we can praise that motherfucking attitude. Richard always leaves the *g* on when he uses the big word. He says that it makes them more terrified, proper grammatical perspective in a brute scheme, something like a doctor explaining the logistics of testicular cords just before he cuts your balls off. Brings it all home. We'll just send you on your way then, Richard said, and soon you'll be back.

I stayed behind to help you, the sociologist said. I didn't want to run out of the buildings, I wanted to show solidarity.

Well, you showing it, Richard said. Ain't he showing it, Ronald? Let's go.

I take the sociologist by the arm in a deep Muslim squeeze and propel him through the door. Some of the brothers separate themselves from the wall and follow us, but this is our party and I know it. Richard has left it all up to me, this part, and I would say I were proud if I did not have so much else on my concentrated and busy mind.

They got reactors, Richard had said to me a few hours earlier, while we were working the plan, this just after we had crashed through into Kirk's office and sent them running. We're going to get hold of them. We're going to get the nukes.

It's a dumb plan, Jonathan said. Look at me. Listen to me. We can't get at reactors.

They got a motherfucking atomic pile under this place, Richard said. Everybody knows that. Had it for years. You can feel the little heat, the explosions bouncing through the grass when you cut across the quad. Once I was taking a leak in the physics building, I could feel *atomic heat* pass through my generous organ.

I didn't say they weren't there, Jonathan said. Everyone knows it, all right. But messing with nukes is high-caliber business. They get wild, we get hold of atomic shit.

Your trouble, Richard said, you a gentle-ass white guy from the suburbs of *Mahopac* or somewhere, you're interested in symbolic gestures, in *radicalization*, in heavy rioting in dress gear. Both me and Ronald, though, we got a different background, we got a somewhat different grasp of the situation. We're here, we're going to take it all the way.

This is not the answer, Jonathan said. He took out a handkerchief, shook it, removed his glasses, began to wipe them. We're doing just what we should. We got the buildings clear, we got the campus secure. The campus is ours tonight. They're afraid to come in, and we can get out anytime we want. Now we press the nonnegotiable demands.

You white boys amuse me, Richard said. He took the glasses from Richard's hand, gave them a few strokes with his fingers. You think this is display, you with your nonnegotiable demands, your symbolic gestures, your *liberating* the president's office. You're full of shit, that's what you are. You're playing and they're playing. But we're not, that's the whole difference. Ronald and I, we're in this for keeps. Wake up in the morning, you can go back to Mahopac. Wake up in the morning, Ronald and I are still black. He's humping for dollars at CCNY, I'm kissing ass down here in the department of stripes and ribbons, but they put the lights on and we're niggers. So we're serious. We got to be serious, that's our condition.

So what are you going to do? Jonathan said. You're going to hold up the university, that's it? You're going to go nuclear on them? That's heavy shit, heavy water down there, you fuck around with it, you'll blow all of us up.

I got techniques, Richard said, I got plans. Me and my ringleader, Ronald, we got big plans. We get access to the atomics, they're not going to be so quick to rush in.

Jonathan put the glasses back on his nose. He looked like what he was going to become, a professor of literature, the glasses flashing clean bright white light now. In that angle I could see Richard's point, finally, and the answer that went through me was as clean as the light. That's about it, I said, the man has just about put it right.

They're not coming in anyway, Jonathan said. They're ringing the buildings but they're not going anywhere. I tell you, it's a triumph, we got them paralyzed. We're getting our story out to the press and they're listening.

You white fool, Richard said, you think they're listening? They're just holding off, letting the little boys and girls play. Three days from now, they can't tear-gas us out, they'll come in with grenades and clean out the place. You're in a playpen, boy, you don't understand anything. But it's a lot more serious for us and that's the fucking truth. The confab is over. Split. We're going to get us a sociologist and some directions.

Jonathan looked at me. Can't you understand? he said. If we go for the reactor, that's a whole different gig. That changes the rules on them and they'll come in and kill us.

You never understood, did you? I said. I grabbed him by neat handfuls of his shirt, pulled him toward me. We not interested in symbolic gestures, I said, we not interested in little white boys' and girls' game, playing around in the toilets, making the nursery school mad. We are in this for *keeps* now and you just opened the door to that. You let us in, you wanted a collaboration, you wanted a multiracial movement, you wanted a national protest—well, that's what you got. And now it's time to stand aside and let the men work this out.

Jonathan looked at me and then away, stared at Richard. The stare was a good preparation for what we would see from the sociologist a little bit later. I can't believe it, he said, you *are* serious. You really think that this is going to work.

We don't care if it works, Richard said, it's just something we do, dig? We go all the way. You want multiracial, you got it. You want up against the wall, this is it. We not talking about humping in the president's chair, leaving Kirk a little white stuff on the walls. We talking about power, about possession. So that's it. You understand the situation?

He surely do, I said to Richard. He surely does. I do not think that it is necessary to discuss it with the stud anymore.

Oh one more thing, Richard said. You staying with us, you understand?

Of course I'm staying with you, Jonathan said. I wouldn't—

You think you sneak out of the building about 4:00 A.M., you turn to white in the morning sun and go back to Mahopac, you got it wrong. You in it all the way, just like us. We got fifteen bloods with carbines and serious intentions, you change your mind on that.

He's not changing his mind, I said. His mind is visibly unchanged.

Richard laughed. I did some laughing, too. Then we went back into the main room and announced that there would be a continuation of the plan, there being no need to tell the boys and girls in the outer echelon anything more at this point, and then we went hunting for a sociology professor. Jonathan had been very good at getting hold of the secret plans and administration fallback positions. We had to give him credit for that. Before our little disagreement, so thoroughly resolved, Jonathan had been a real worker for the cause. Of course, he had had a different name for it.

In the concrete it was just Richard and me, looking at the dials, watching the dials do their little dance, hearing the thunder of the machines, smelling all of those compressors and atom splitters and heavy isotopic remedies. The sociologist had come across like a hooker, and the plans had been airtight. Everything was exactly where it was supposed to be, us and the place together. Now, Richard said, adjusting his weapon and rubbing his hands, now we show them some *real* nonnegotiable demands. Nonnegotiable isn't a slip of paper and four little white girls screaming and shaking their tits. Nonnegotiable is here it is baby or we blow up Riverside Park and the West End tavern and the place where Kirk's asshole sits, too. How about that? He giggled, higher-pitched than I've ever heard him. Can a CCNY guy dig it? he said.

I can dig it, I said. I can dig a lot. It is heavy business.

I think we can do this, Richard said. I got five, six guys with heavy-tech brains and good mechanical aptitudes, I think they can really twist those dials and make this thing work. I thought it was a wild chance when we started, yes. Wild; I know it, he said, I thought Jonathan was crazy. But now it's not so wild. I think it can work.

What can work? I said. Anything?

Anything at all. We'll put a few demands, we'll test them out. For openers, Richard said, I want New York City.

What's that? I said.

Oh, not all of it, he said. They can keep Harlem. They can even keep Brownsville and Bed-Stuy, they so crazy for it. But they can hand me Park Avenue and Seventy-ninth and the stock exchange and we'll go on from here. He gave me a gleaming smile. That's what I think.

Looking at Richard, it occurred to me—and not for the first time—that the boy was really crazy, that he was as crazy as the sociologist and maybe Jonathan thought he was. But that didn't make him any less lovable, only a hell of a lot more dangerous, I thought. We better rejoin the troops, I said. The troops be getting anxious soon.

Oh, we rejoin, Richard said. We rejoin and then we reup. How would you like Arpels? Me, I'm going to take Tiffany's. We're going to shake things up a little in this city. You know why? he said.

Because we are desperate men, I said. Because we are the underclass, we are the natives right out of Congoland and we got nothing to lose.

That's right, Richard said. Oh, you is a righteous lad, all right.

The white boys and girls aren't going to take that too much to heart, I said.

No, they ain't, Richard said. But they let us in, didn't they? You invite the piper, you buy the meal.

The rumbling goes on and on as we draft our statement and then it is time to get back to the troops. But only for a while, I think. We have our battle plan now. We have our heads toward the situation. Soon enough, maybe, there will be no need for the troops. When they go through the stuff left in Kirk's office, maybe they don't necessarily find our names and pedigrees after all. It depends. It is, as they say, a fluid situation. It is closing in on the end of the sixties and everything is not as it was here in walrusland.

The first communiqué meets silence and the second communiqué gets only a beat from whoever is on the phone at the other end. The third communiqué, however, setting a midnight deadline, does get some response. We'll get back to you, they say. They do not believe it. Obviously they do not believe it. We have to begin reading off some coordinates and serial numbers on isotope containers before the tone of the responses changes.

I think they believe us now, Richard said. I do believe that they believe we got nukes here and we are ready like the boys in Vietnam to die. I think midnight will see some interesting responses.

We have asked them to withdraw all of their troops by midnight and also to issue a statement of capitulation. Otherwise the first reactor goes off. We have guarantees that this can be done although, of course, one can never be sure. The phone, dead for so long, is suddenly lively. They plead for more time, time to work things out. We read them a few more serial numbers. A senior physicist from the State Department, or that is what he says he is, gets on the line and we have to convince him, too. After a while he goes away.

The sociology professor is crashed out on the floor, a couple of ladies around him, rubbing his shoulders. We tell him that we will not necessarily identify him as the collaborator but he will have to stay with us for a while. We will, however, make it as easy and pleasant for him as possible. The white girls are cooperative, as is so often the case with white girls and white men, also black men now that you asked.

We sit and pass the time, Richard and I sharing some old stories. Our backgrounds may be different, me with my gentle middle-class thing and he on the harder rock, but they are also quite similar. We are both niggers, after all. They plead for another twelve hours' extension and Richard gets on the horn this time and tells them this is the commander and they can fuck themselves. Two hours, that is it; 2:00 A.M. and their troops and dogs are off the campus or the first reactor goes on-line. We will talk about Tiffany's later. They say they will get back to us.

Jonathan comes in from the back room, where we have stashed him. After three hours' sleep we would expect him to be more reasonable or at least less wired, but this is not the case. He is more frantic than ever.

I've been thinking this through, he said. Been talking to a few people.

That's good, Richard said. Talk is always good. High communication, that was your original demand, right?

We have to pull back, Jonathan said, this isn't going to work. It won't work with these odds.

It's working fine, Richard says. Don't you think so, Ronald? I shrug. Working okay by me, I say.

This guy, Jonathan said, this LBJ. He just pulled out, you understand? The war did him in, *he* did him in. All he wanted in the world was to be the king and they took it away from him and worst of all he had to sink the knife in himself, you dig that?

I dig that fine, Richard says, it is a satisfying source of pleasure. It is an inspiration. It sends us on our way.

So this guy lost everything, Jonathan says, Old LBJ, he doesn't care anymore, don't you see? The worst that can happen has happened. He won't be president.

Still got the Hump, Richard says. He giggled. The Hump will keep the chair mighty warm, also his mouth, don't you agree?

You don't get it at all, Jonathan says, you really don't get it. He grabs Richard's wrists. You are dealing with a guy who has already lost everything. He has nothing more to lose, not the Hump, not anything. He doesn't care, you're pushing him over the edge. He is leaning over, half-trying to bring Richard up.

Let go of my wrists, white man, Richard says very quietly. Just release your grip.

Damn it, Jonathan says, I worked this out. I may be white but I'm not stupid. You're dealing with a guy who has already lost everything, you're putting him in a box now, don't you see?

See? Richard says. I see everything. I am far-ranging. You are still grasping my wrists. You let them go within the next ten seconds or you see who will lose everything and how.

He hates New York, Jonathan says, letting him go, crouching beside us. He thinks that everything that beat him came out of New York anyway. Now he's got the enemy at home, waving nukes. You know what that means?

I know what it means, I say. It means that we are finally making an impression.

We're making an impression, Jonathan says, we're making a *big* impression. He's going to hit us, that's what's going to happen. He'll send in the Strategic Air Command.

Oh, white boy, Richard says, you have a fertile mind and heart. The Strategic Air Command. He chuckles. You don't understand who has who by the balls here, he says. You don't understand the situation.

I understand the situation, Jonathan says, we are in heavy shit. We are in the heaviest shit. We are dealing with a crazy man by being crazy. You know what happens then?

I don't know, Richard says, help me.

He's just looking for an excuse, Jonathan says. You've given him all the excuse he needs. You've brought Vietnam home.

Time he got to Vietnam, Richard says. Time for sure.

And he's got the provocation now. He'll use the bomb.

Richard says, Jonathan, you losing your cool. Nuke out a bunch of college kids with a reactor? Shit, what you talking about? We can't do *nothing* with that machine, that little bitty old separator. That's the word from the Chemistry Department. We can rattle the bones, Richard says, but we can't pull no action.

LBJ doesn't know that, Jonathan says. LBJ's no nuclear scientist.

Neither are we, Richard says. He's figured that out already. But he's got poor public relations.

You don't get it, Jonathan says. He doesn't know about bitty old separators and radioactivity. Doesn't *care*, either. For him, we've turned into Viet Cong. He thinks he's got the Viet Cong right here at home and he's going to trash us out, that's what I think.

Talk to the Chemistry Department, Richard says. Examine their *isotopes*, see what they got to say.

LBJ has freaked out, Jonathan says. He's over the line. He doesn't care what we can do, he's got the excuse. I'm telling you, we better back off.

Richard takes Jonathan by the wrist, hauls himself up, gives him a push. *You* back off, he says. You back off all your life, in the morning you're still white. It's a game for you and now the stakes are a little too high. But you can't get out. He points to the sociology professor, the professor hiding between four tits over on the carpet, the little coeds stroking his hair.

You and he are black as us tonight, he says. You going to stay through the end, see this through one time.

We'll see it through, Jonathan says. You fool, there's nowhere to hide. There's no place to go, you think it's any safer on Thirty-fifth Street or up in Inwood than it is right here? We can't get out anywhere, none of us. We're cooked to a circumference of four hundred and fifty miles. Because we're the enemy and now he's got the rationalization he needs.

It's throwdown time, Richard says. That honky, he's not going to throw it down, that's all.

You'll see, Jonathan says. He walks out the open door. It feels as if we have been shouting, but for all the notice our conversation takes, we might have been whispering. Or maybe all the troops, the sociology professor and his companions, they, too, are simply asleep. It is deep night, and in the extinguished spaces now I can barely see Richard.

White boy, Richard says. Establishment bitch. Just another one all the time.

What if he's right? I say.

What's that?

I said, What if he's right? What if LBJ doesn't give a shit anymore? What if he just hits us with everything he has? Jonathan's right, he's a dead man anyway. He's out of office. How long is he going to live?

You're as crazy as the rest of them, Richard says. Me, I'm going to get a little sleep, be alert at 2:00 A.M. Need my beautify sleep for some serious negotiating.

He could be right, he says. You just know it.

You, too, Ronald? Richard says. His eyes are round, maybe amused, hard to tell in the dark. You going to go establishment on me, too?

I'm not going anywhere.

That's good. Because it's too late, Richard says, you get that? It's just too goddamned late and we're going to see it through now. We got the plan and the plan is going to work right through to the end and that's the end of the plan. He rambles off toward the couch. Crash me back in half an hour, he says. Stand the sentry. Play watch.

I get up, follow him partway across the room, then lean against the wall to brace myself, feeling unsteady. There is a sudden shift and uneasiness in the room. I can hear the sound of distant humming.

It would happen so fast, I say to Richard, we wouldn't even know it had happened.

He says nothing.

I have read about these things, I say. It is like a head-on automobile crash. If you know it's happened, it hasn't happened. It's so fast you are dead before you know it.

I am already asleep, Richard says, I am finding my righteous moments.

In the dark, I lean against the wall. The professor is muttering something. Maybe other things are going on outside; the lawn seems suddenly close against me and I can smell the stink of the occupiers.

And then there is an amazing light, the light of Calvary.

I see the light; I know it is happening.

Which means then according to Richard that if I see it going on it isn't going on, except it is.

It is and it *is*.

And the screaming, and the fire...

GODDARD'S PEOPLE

Allen Steele

A morning in wartime: May 24, 1944, 5:15 A.M. PST. Day is barely breaking over the California coastline; for the crew of the B-24 Liberator *Hollywood Babe*, it's the fifth hour of their mission. The bomber has been holding a stationary position since midnight over the ocean southeast of the Baja Peninsula, flying in narrow circles at twenty-five thousand feet. Their classified mission has been simple: Watch the skies. The vigil is about to end.

Gazing through the cockpit windows, the captain notices a thin white vapor trail zipping across the dark purple sky. Many miles above and due west of his plane's position, the streak is hopelessly out of *Hollywood Babe*'s range, even if the bomber was ordered to intercept the incoming object. Becoming alert, he glances over his shoulder at the civilian in the jump seat behind him.

"Sir, is that what you're looking for?" the captain asks.

The civilian, an agent of the Office of Strategic Services, quickly leans forward and stares at the streak. "Son of a bitch," he murmurs under his breath. For a moment he can't believe what he's seeing. Only yesterday he had been telling someone that MI-6 must be getting shell-shocked, because now they were sending science fiction yarns to the OSS. But, incredible or not, this was exactly what the OSS man had been told to watch for.

He turns to the radio man in the narrow compartment behind the cockpit. "Sergeant, alert White Sands now!" he yells over the throb of the B-24's engines. "It's on its way!"

Many miles away, warning Klaxons howl at a top-secret U.S. Army facility in the New Mexico desert. Around a spotlighted launch pad, technicians and engineers scurry away from the single-stage, seventy-five-foot winged silver rocket poised on the pad. Cold white oxygen fumes venting from the base of the rocket billow around the steel launch tower. The gantry is towed back along railroad tracks by a locomotive, and fuel trucks race away to a safe distance where the ground crew and several soldiers wait, their eyes fixed on the pad.

In a concrete blockhouse four hundred yards from the launch pad, more than a dozen men are monitoring the launch. Among them, nine civilian scientists are hunched over control panels, anxiously watching hundreds of dials and meters as they murmur instructions to each other. In the middle of the blockhouse a frail, scholarly man peers through a periscope at the launch pad as the countdown reaches the final sixty seconds.

For more than two years, these ten men have worked toward this moment; now in the last minute, most of them are scared half to death. If the launch is unsuccessful, there will be no second chance. If the rocket blows up, as so many other rockets have before it, the Navy pilot inside the machine will die. But far worse than that, New York City, thousands of miles to the east, will suffer a devastating attack. An eighty-ton incendiary bomb will drop into the middle of Manhattan, and there will be nothing in heaven or on earth to stop it. If the launch is successful, it will be the crowning achievement of American technology; if it fails, it may be the beginning of the end for free society. The stakes are that high.

"Ten . . . nine . . . eight . . ." an Army officer recites tonelessly. Staring through the periscope, Robert Hutchings Goddard absently wipes his sweaty palms against the rubber grips and silently begins to pray. . . .

Forty-seven years ago, in the early morning hours of a summer day in World War II, a huge rocket called the A-9—the *Amerika Bomber*—hurtled down a horizontal track in Germany and climbed to the highest altitude ever achieved, 156 miles above the earth. Horst Reinhart, a young Luftwaffe lieutenant, became the first man in space. One hour and thirty-six minutes later, the rocket christened the *Lucky Linda* blasted off from New Mexico, and U.S. Navy pilot Rudy "Skid" Sloman's triumphant howl was picked up by ham radio operators across the continent as the United States became the world's second spacefaring nation.

This much is well known; what has been largely lost to history, though, is the leading role played by a mild, stoop-shouldered physics professor from Worcester. Not because of neglect—Robert H. Goddard's place in the annals of spaceflight as the father of American rocketry has been assured—but because of enduring cold war suspicions. In the years since his death in 1945, facts about his private life, particularly during the Second World War, have remained hidden, mainly because of national security interests. Goddard was known to have had a vague "consultant" role in Project Blue Horizon, but little more has been discovered by Goddard's biographers. The official story is that Goddard spent the war teaching at Clark University in Worcester, Massachusetts. Not much else is in the public record.

Yet if that part of Robert Goddard's biography is opaque, even less is known about the top-secret research group that was once code-named Team 390. Each year, on the anniversary of *Lucky Linda*'s flight, the seven survivors of the American rocket team gather at a sportsman's lodge in New Hampshire, on the shore of Lake Monomonock. Once again, in the lodge's den, the secret tale is told. As the seven old men speak, more than a few times their eyes wander to the framed photo of Goddard that hangs above the mantel.

They are all that remain of Team 390, but they rarely call themselves by that name. Now as then, they are known among themselves simply as Goddard's people.

The affair began on the morning of January 19, 1942, when OSS agent William Casey (later to become the Director of Central Intelligence during the Reagan Administration) arrived in Washington, D.C., from London on a U.S. Army DC-3. An attaché case handcuffed to his wrist contained a top-secret Nazi document that British MI-6 agents had discovered on the island of Peenemünde. By noon, the document— code-named Black Umbrella, unofficially known as the "Sänger Report" —was on the desk of President Franklin D. Roosevelt.

The United States had been directly involved in World War II for only six weeks when the Sänger report was unearthed. Isolationism had crumbled after the Japanese attack on Pearl Harbor, and fear was running high in the country that North America itself was the next target of the Axis powers; in Washington itself, antiaircraft guns and air-raid sirens were already being erected on city rooftops. Black Umbrella could not have arrived at a better time to have been taken seriously.

Peenemünde is on an island off the coast of Germany in the Baltic Sea. Once the site of a seldom-visited fishing village, during the war the island had become the location of secret Nazi rocket research for the German Army. Germans had been vigorously developing liquid-fuel rockets even before Adolf Hitler had become chancellor, and the Nazis had incorporated rocket research into their war plans, recruiting a team of civilian rocket scientists, with Wernher von Braun as its chief scientist. British Intelligence had known that Peenemünde was the site of secret rocket experiments; a large missile called the A-4 was alleged to be in the final phases of R&D. "Silver" and "Gold," two MI-6 agents working undercover in Peenemünde as janitors, had been monitoring the continuing development of the A-4 rocket, later to be known by the Allies as the V-2.

However, in recent months more puzzling things had been happening in Peenemünde. Something new was being developed in a warehouse that was kept locked and guarded at all times; rumors around the base had it that an even more ambitious weapon than the A-4 was being built by von Braun's rocket team. High Command officers such as Hermann Göring, Rudolf Hess, and Heinrich Himmler had been regularly visiting Peenemünde, spending long hours in the warehouse. Yet Silver and Gold had no idea of what was going on, except that it was even more top-secret than the A-4 project.

Finally, the two agents had a stroke of luck. For a few precious, unguarded moments, a four-hundred-page document stamped "State Secret" had been carelessly left out on von Braun's desk by his personal secretary. Without reading the report, Silver had used a miniature camera to photograph as many pages as possible. The team then managed to smuggle the microfilm out of Germany, not knowing what information it contained except that it was part of a report that should have been kept under lock and key. The microfilm made its way to Whitehall in London, where MI-6 intelligence analysts had translated the contents. Horrified by what was found in the report, they rushed the transcript to Washington.

Black Umbrella was a detailed proposal by Dr. Eugen Sänger, an Austrian rocket scientist employed at the Hermann Göring Institute, the Luftwaffe's research center. Sänger had proposed construction of a one-man, winged rocket plane, an "antipodal bomber" capable not only of orbital flight but also of flying around the world to attack the United States. The rocket plane—nicknamed the *Amerika Bomber* by Sänger— was to be almost a hundred feet long, weigh a hundred tons, and be propelled by a liquid-fuel rocket engine. Carrying an eighty-ton bomb load, it was to be launched on a rocket-propelled sled that would race down a two-mile track to a sharp incline. The rocket plane would disengage from the sled at the end of the track and, now accelerating at 1,640 feet per second, would climb under its own power to suborbital altitude.

Using the earth's rotation for a "slingshot" effect, the *Amerika Bomber* would make a series of dives and climbs along the top of the atmosphere, skipping like a rock on the surface of a pond as it orbited the earth. The skips would not only help preserve fuel but also keep the rocket plane far above the range of conventional aircraft. In this way the bomber could fly over Europe, Asia, and the Pacific Ocean to the United States. Two of its atmospheric skips could carry it across the continent and, after diving to an altitude of forty miles above the East

Coast, the ship could drop an eighty-ton bomb on New York City. The *Amerika Bomber* then could fly across the Atlantic back to Germany, landing like an airplane on a conventional airstrip.

It would be obviously a tremendous effort by the Nazis to develop and successfully launch the Sänger bomber; New York was not a military target, either. But the sheer terror of the scheme—the vision of a Nazi rocket plane diving from space to drop an eighty-ton incendiary bomb on Times Square—would be worth its value in propaganda alone. And if a squadron of antipodal bombers were built, as Sänger suggested, Germany would be in control of the highest of high grounds: outer space.

There was little doubt in the White House that the Nazis could pull off Black Umbrella. According to British intelligence, German civilians had been actively engaged in sophisticated rocket research since the 1920s under the aegis of the Verin für Raumschiffarht, commonly referred to as the German Rocket Society. Almost immediately after Adolf Hitler became chancellor, the Gestapo had seized all journals and records of the German Rocket Society, and the German Army had scooped up almost all members of the VfR, including Hermann Oberth, von Braun's mentor. It was also known that the German Army was diverting enormous amounts of men and matériel to Peenemünde, although it was also suspected that the Nazis had another, more secret missile base somewhere else, deep within the German borders.

According to declassified White House minutes of the meeting, President Roosevelt turned to OSS director William "Wild Bill" Donovan after hearing the report on the Sänger project. "So, Bill, who's in charge of *our* rocket program?" he asked.

"We don't have a rocket program, Mr. President," Donovan replied.

"All right," Roosevelt said calmly, "then who is the leading rocket expert in America?"

"I don't know if there is one," Donovan said.

"Yes, there is," answered the president. "Somewhere out there, there's got to be someone who knows as much about these things as von Braun. Find him. He's now the most important man in the country."

The man they found was Robert H. Goddard, and he didn't feel like the most important man in the country. He was only a brilliant scientist who had long since become fed up with being called a crackpot.

Goddard had been obsessed with rockets since reading H.G. Wells's *The War of the Worlds* as a youngster. Born in Worcester, Massachusetts, in 1882, Goddard had pursued his obsession throughout his life; he earned his bachelor's degree in engineering from Worcester Polytechnic Institute and shortly thereafter became a professor of physics at

Clark University. Goddard's secret dream was to build a rocket capable of landing men on Mars. It was a wild idea that would drive the scientist throughout his life, and also earn him as much trouble as encountered by predecessors such as Galileo Galilei and Percival Lowell.

In January 1920 the Smithsonian Institution, one of Goddard's sources of funding for his early rocket research, published a sixty-nine-page monograph written by him. Titled "A Method of Reaching Extreme Altitudes," it mainly described how liquid-fuel rockets (themselves still only a theoretical possibility) could replace sounding balloons for exploring the upper atmosphere. The paper was mostly comprised of equations and tables and thus would have escaped the notice of the general public had it not been for brief speculation at its end of how such rockets, perhaps someday in the future, could be used to reach the moon. Goddard wrote that a rocket could crash-land on earth's satellite and explode a load of magnesium powder that would be visible to astronomers on Earth.

Compared to Goddard's real objectives of manned space exploration, this was a rather modest proposal, but the press didn't see it that way. Newspapers reported Goddard's speculation with little accuracy and less respect. He was either scoffed at from such pinnacles as *The New York Times* (which claimed that rocket propulsion was impossible in outer space because there was no air for rockets to push against) or treated as wild-eyed fantasy by papers such as the local *Worcester Telegram* (whose headlines speculated that passenger rockets carrying tourists into space would be possible within a decade). Few newspapers took Goddard seriously; for the most part he was regarded as a crazy college egghead.

Goddard, a shy and soft-spoken person, was appalled by the press attention and embarrassed by the ridicule. He henceforth took his research underground, particularly his experiments with rocket design and his efforts to launch a liquid-fuel rocket. Although he continued to devise means of sending rockets into space—including his own design for a rocket plane—he carefully hid his notebooks in his laboratory file cabinet, in a folder ironically marked "Gunpowder Experiments." There were no reporters present in the hilltop farm field in nearby Auburn, Massachusetts, on the cold morning of March 16, 1926, when Goddard successfully fired the world's first liquid-fuel rocket.

By 1942, though, Robert Goddard was no longer in Worcester. Following the explosion of one of his rockets, the Auburn town council outlawed all types of "fireworks" within city limits. Following a brief series of experiments at the U.S. Army's Camp Devens in nearby Ashby, Goddard went on a sabbatical from Clark University in 1931 and moved his residence and rockets to Roswell, New Mexico. There were a couple of contributing reasons for the move besides the unacceptability of rocketry in Massachusetts. Throughout his life, the professor had battled tuberculosis, which the damp New England climate scarcely helped, and the arid southwestern desert also was a better site for rocket tests. In this sense, rural New Mexico was a fair trade for urban Massachusetts. He broke the sound barrier with a rocket in 1936, and by 1942 Goddard rockets were reaching record altitudes and achieving greater sophistication. Although largely unpublicized, his rocket experiments were on a par with the A-series rockets being developed in Nazi Germany. Few people knew about the feats that Goddard rockets were performing over the New Mexico high desert.

Yet Goddard's fortunes had also suffered, largely because of the bad press he had already endured. Although he continued to receive grants from the Guggenheim Foundation and from one of his admirers, Charles A. Lindbergh, the Smithsonian Institution had stopped funding his research. And though he had already developed solid-fuel ordnance such as the bazooka for the U.S. Army, the war department had expressed no interest in his liquid-fuel rocket research. Obscurity had become a double-edged sword for Goddard: He had found the solitude he craved, yet he was struggling to finance his experiments.

All that changed on the morning of January 29, 1942, when two civilians from the OSS and an officer from the U.S. Army General Staff, Colonel Omar Bliss, found Robert Goddard in the assembly shed at Goddard's ranch with an assistant, working on another high-altitude rocket. The rocket scientist greeted his unexpected visitors with courteous surprise; he dismissed his assistant and sat down on a bench outside the shed to hear what they had to say.

Bliss, now living in retirement on Sanibel Island, Florida, remembers the meeting he had with Goddard. "He was completely shocked, horrified," Bliss says. "He told us that he had kept up with German research during the '30s and knew that they were making progress with their rockets, but he had no idea that their work had come this far. We asked if Sänger's plan was possible and he thought about it a minute, then told us that if they had the resources and a little luck, yes, they could make it work. He knew that von Braun and Oberth were working for the Nazis, and he had no doubts that they and others had the knowledge to develop the *Amerika Bomber*."

The men from Washington asked Goddard if he had any ideas how to prevent New York from being blitzed from space; Goddard indicated that he had a few notions. "Then we asked him if he would help us," Bliss recalls. "I was afraid that he would refuse. People had treated him so unfairly before, after all. But he at once nodded his head, yes, he would do whatever was necessary to stop the Nazis."

The space race had begun.

Robert Goddard's role in what would become known as Project Blue Horizon, however, was not played in New Mexico. For various reasons, the War Department returned the professor to his hometown. Although *Lucky Linda* would be launched from the White Sands Test Range less than a hundred miles from Goddard's ranch, Washington decided that the best place for Blue Horizon's brain trust was in Massachusetts.

The Department of War wanted to keep Goddard within arm's reach, and Massachusetts is closer to Washington, D.C., than New Mexico is. Yet it was also decided not to take unnecessary risks. Goddard was reputed to tinker with his rockets personally while they were on the launch pad. This fact was known by Dr. Vannevar Bush, President Roosevelt's science adviser, who gave orders for "the professor" to be kept away from the rockets themselves. In hindsight, this was good logic. Over the next two years of the crash program there were in White Sands many spectacular explosions, one of which claimed the lives of two technicians. It would have been disastrous if Goddard himself had been killed during one of these accidents.

There was some resistance by the War Department to having Project Blue Horizon in Worcester, however. Another top-secret military R&D program was already under way in Massachusetts: the radar-defense project being developed in Cambridge at MIT's so-called "radiation laboratory." It was felt by many in the Pentagon that having two secret projects working so near to each other would be risky. Goddard was not eager to return to Worcester, either. It had become difficult for him to endure the New England climate, and he especially chafed at not being able to witness each rocket test. Bush argued, however, that neither Clark University nor MIT were high-profile enough (at the time) to attract Nazi spies; having Blue Horizon camouflaged by a college campus, like MIT's "Rad Lab," made perfect sense.

The White House won out over the Pentagon, and Goddard went along with his relocation orders. Esther Goddard, always protective of her husband's health, naturally returned to Worcester with Robert. They moved back into their former residence, where Goddard had been born, and readjusted to life in New England's second-largest city.

To build the security cover for Blue Horizon, the FBI coerced Clark University's directors into reinstating Goddard's status as an active faculty member. It was arranged that Goddard's only real academic work load was to teach a freshman class in introductory physics. In the university's academic calendar for the semesters in 1942 through 1943, though, there was a listing for an advanced-level class, "Physics 390," whose instructor was "to be announced." But even senior physics students at Clark found it impossible to enroll in the class; it was always filled at registration time.

Goddard's "graduate students" in Physics 390 were a group of nine young men enlisted from the American Rocket Society, unrepentant rocket buffs and farsighted engineers with whom Goddard had corresponded over the years. Goddard had quickly handpicked his group from memory; the War Department and the FBI had contacted each person individually, requesting their volunteer help. None refused, though the Selective Service Administration had to issue draft deferrals for four members. The FBI moved them all to Worcester and managed to get them quietly isolated in a three-decker on Birch Street near the campus.

Team 390 (as they were code-named by the FBI) were strangers even among themselves. Almost all were from different parts of the country. Only two members, Lloyd Kapman and Harry Bell, both from St. Louis, had met before, and although Taylor Brickell and Henry Morse were known to each other from the letters page of *Astounding Science Fiction*, of which they were both devoted readers, they had never met face to face. The youngest, Roy Cahill, had just passed his eighteenth birthday; the oldest, Hamilton "Ham" Ballou, was in his midthirties and was forced to shave off his mustache to make him appear younger.

And there were other problems. J. Jackson Jackson was the only black member of the team, which tended to make him stand out on the mostly white Clark University campus (his odd name earned him the nickname "Jack Cube"). Michael Ferris had briefly been a member of the American Communist Party during his undergraduate days, which meant that he had undergone intensive scrutiny by the FBI and nearly been refused on the grounds of his past political activity before he had agreed to sign a binding pledge of loyalty to the United States. And Gerard "Gerry" Mander had to be sprung from a county workhouse in Roanoke, Virginia: A rocket he had been developing had misfired, spun-out across two miles of tobacco field, and crashed into a Baptist preacher's house.

Once they were together, though, Blue Horizon's R&D task force immediately hit it off together. "We spoke the same language," recalls Gerry Mander, who now lives in Boston and who was then the team's "wildcat" engineer. "Rockets were our specialty, and putting something above the atmosphere was a dream we all shared. I mean, I was a young snot from backwoods Virginia, so sharing a room with a colored man like Jack Cube, at least at the time, seemed more unlikely than putting a guy in orbit. But Jack talked engineering, so we had that much in common, and in a couple of days I didn't even care."

"We were all a bunch of rocket buffs," says Mike Ferris, the team's chemistry expert, "and the War Department had given us *carte blanche* to put a man in space." He laughs. "Man, we were like little kids thrown the key to the toy store!"

Team 390 had little doubt about what was needed. The only device capable of intercepting the Sänger bomber was another spacecraft, and the only reliable navigation system was a human pilot. Since the 1920s, Robert Goddard had written, in his "gunpowder experiments" notebooks, rough designs for a rocket plane, along with notes for gyroscopic guidance systems and other plans that turned out to be useful for the team. Studies at the California Institute of Technology had also suggested that a single-stage rocket plane could be sent into space on a suborbital trajectory, with the ship gliding back through the atmosphere like a sailplane.

The team postulated that a spaceplane, launched by a liquid-fuel engine and ascending at a forty-five-degree angle, could function as a one-man space fighter capable of intercepting the *Amerika Bomber*. Upon studying the Sänger report, Team 390 further realized that the bomber would be most vulnerable during the ascent phases of its flight. At these points the ship was slowest and least maneuverable, a sitting duck for another spacecraft's ordnance. So if the U.S. ship was launched from New Mexico just as the German ship was flying over the Pacific coast, it could intercept the *Amerika Bomber* before it reached New York City and shoot it down with ordinary solid-fuel rockets.

"We came up with it in one night over beer and pretzels in the Bancroft Hotel bar," says Henry Morse, the team's electrical engineer who now lives in Winchester, New Hampshire. "Bob wasn't with us that night, but we had gone through his notebooks and read all that stuff he had thought up, so it was mainly a matter of putting it together. We knew we didn't need a very sophisticated ship, nothing like a space shuttle today. Of course, we didn't have time to make anything like a space shuttle. Just something quick and dirty."

"Quick and dirty" soon became buzzwords for Goddard's people. The team took the plan to Goddard the following morning, during their "class" in Goddard's lab at the university. By the end of the day, following many hours of arguing, scribbling notes on the chalkboard, and flooding the trash can with wadded-up notes, Team 390 and Goddard settled on the plan. The professor was amused that his "grad students" had come up with the scheme in a barroom. "If Mrs. Goddard will let me out of the house, I'd like to be in on the next session," he told Morse.

* * *

The FBI, though, was not amused when they discovered that Team 390 had been discussing rockets in a downtown Worcester bar. There was always the chance of Nazi spies. The FBI was especially sensitive, given the proximity to the MIT Rad Lab only forty miles away. Team 390 was ordered to stay out of the Bancroft, and J. Edgar Hoover assigned special escorts for Goddard and his team. The team thought the FBI was overreacting.

"It was a pain, of course," Roy Cahill recalls. "We couldn't visit the men's room without having a G-man escorting us. They were almost parked all night outside Bob's house and our place on Birch Street. Esther couldn't stand it at first, but she changed her mind after the City Hall thing."

By early 1943, the V-2 missiles were perfected and the first rockets launched against targets in Great Britain. The Allies had been flying air raids upon V-2 launch sites in occupied northern France, and finally against Peenemünde itself. During one of the early reconnaissance missions over France, Ham Ballou—temporarily brought over to England to gather much-needed intelligence on the V-2 rockets—flew over the Normandy coastline in the backseat of a P-38J Lightning, snapping pictures as the pilot dodged antiaircraft flak. Ballou returned to Worcester with little that was immediately useful to Team 390, but for a while he was able to claim that he was the only person among Goddard's people who had come under enemy fire—until Goddard himself almost caught a bullet.

Following a devastating Allied air raid on Peenemünde, the German High Command covertly transferred the principal R&D of the *Amerika Bomber* 250 miles inland, to Nordhausen, where the base of a mountain had been hollowed out into vast caverns by prisoners from the nearby Dora concentration camp. This was the secret Nazi rocket facility that MI-6 had been unable to locate. Many of the same European Jews who built the Nordhausen site were later sacrificed, over the objections of von Braun and Oberth, in grotesque experiments that tested human endurance to high-altitude conditions.

Little of this mattered to SS commandant Heinrich Himmler. Now that the Luftwaffe had taken over the A-9 project from the German Army, he was more concerned with the fact, surmised through briefings with von Braun, that the German rocket team's work had been largely inspired by Goddard's research; he suspected that the United States might be embarked on a secret rocket program of its own. Although Gestapo agents in America had not found any evidence of a U.S. space initiative, Himmler decided not to take chances. In March 1943 he ordered the assassination of the only known American rocketry expert: Robert Hutchings Goddard.

For all his brilliance, Goddard was also absent-minded about the mundane tasks of life; he could forget to fold his umbrella when he walked in from the rain. On March 30, 1943, the Worcester city clerk's office sent the professor a letter informing him that he had not paid his city taxes. Goddard received the letter while working in his lab. Both irritated and alarmed, he put on his coat and immediately bustled out to catch the Main South trolley downtown. He left so quickly that his FBI escort, who was relieving himself in the men's room, missed the professor's departure.

But the Nazi Gestapo agent who had been watching Goddard for a week and waiting for such a break, didn't miss the opportunity. Following Goddard from his post on the Clark campus, the assassin also took the downtown trolley, getting off at the same stop in front of City Hall. As Goddard marched into the building, the Nazi slipped his silenced Luger Parabellum from his trench-coat pocket and followed the scientist inside.

At the same moment, Worcester police officer Clay Reilly was walking downstairs from the second floor of City Hall when he spotted a trench-coated man, carrying a gun, closing in on another man, who was walking toward the tax assessor's office. The second man was unaware that he was being pursued, but Reilly immediately sized up the situation.

"I didn't think twice," Reilly, now retired from the force, says in retrospect. "I pulled my pistol and shouted for the guy to freeze. He decided to mess with me instead."

Reilly was a crack shot on the WPD firing range; his skill didn't fail him then. The Gestapo agent turned and aimed at Reilly, but the officer nailed the assassin with one shot to the heart before the Nazi could squeeze his trigger. Goddard himself fled from City Hall, where he was spirited away by his FBI escort, who had just arrived in his car.

No identification was found on the body of the man Patrolman Reilly had shot. The *Worcester Telegram* reported the story the next day under the front-page headline "Mystery Killer Shot in City Hall." No one knew that he had been trying to kill Goddard; Reilly didn't recognize the scientist, and Goddard had not remained at the scene. Clay Reilly was promoted to sergeant for his quick thinking, but it wasn't until long after the war that the policeman was informed of the identity of the man he had shot or the person whose life he had saved, nor the fact that J. Edgar Hoover himself had insisted on his promotion.

* * *

"Everything changed for us after that," says Henry Morse. "I guess we were sort of looking at Blue Horizon like it was a kid's adventure. Y'know, the Rocket Boys go to the Moon. But Bob's close call sobered us up."

The incident also sobered up the White House. On the insistence of Vannevar Bush, the FBI hastily sought a new base of operations in New England for Team 390. Within a week of the attempted assassination, a new locale for Project Blue Horizon was found: the Monomonock Gun & Rod Club, which had been closed since the beginning of the war. The lodge was in the tiny farm community of Rindge, due north of Worcester just across the New Hampshire state line, close enough to Worcester to allow the rocket team to relocate there quickly. Because the club was accessible by a single, unmarked dirt road only, it had the isolation the FBI believed was necessary to keep Team 390 hidden from the world.

The FBI purchased the property, and in the dead of night on April 6, 1943, all the rocket team's files and models were loaded into a truck. As far as Clark University's collegiate community was concerned, Dr. Goddard had taken an abrupt leave of absence due to health reasons, and nobody on campus seemed to notice the sudden departure of the small, insular group of grad students from Physics 390.

The Monomonock Gun & Rod Club was set in seven acres of New Hampshire forest on the northwestern side of Lake Monomonock. The club consisted mainly of a two-story whitewashed lodge that dated back to the turn of the century; it had a handsome front porch that overlooked the serene main channel of the lake, a couple of Spartan rooms on the upper floor that contained a dozen old-style iron beds, and a single outhouse beyond the back door. Mail from relatives was still sent to Worcester and forwarded once a week to New Hampshire; except for Esther Goddard, none of the families of the rocket team was made aware of the fact that their sons and husbands were now in New Hampshire.

The former sportsmen's club was a far cry from the comforts of Clark University; most of the rocket team were unused to roughing it in the woods. Mice had taken up occupancy in the kitchen next to the long dining room, and the only sources of heat were a fireplace in the den and a potbellied stove on the second floor. One of the first orders of business was to knock down the hornet nests in upper bedrooms and under the porch eaves. "The first week we were there, we almost went on strike," says Gerry Mander with a laugh. "If we hadn't been in a race against time, we might have told Bush and Hoover and all the rest to stick it until they found us some decent accommodations. As it was, though, we knew we had little choice."

Yet there was another major problem in the relocation. In New Mexico, the engineering team at White Sands was building unmanned prototype rockets based on the plans sent by Goddard's team, firing the rockets as soon as they could be made. The major hurdle was in producing a reliable engine for the spaceplane, now dubbed the "X-1." It had to be able to lift 65,500 pounds to orbit, yet most of the prototypes exploded, sometimes on the launch pad. For each small success, there were dozens of setbacks. There had been several pad explosions already, and in the latest failure a couple of technicians had been killed when the liquid-hydrogen tank ruptured during pressurization.

"Part of the problem was that the team wasn't in New Mexico to oversee the final stages of each test," Morse says. "We were expected to build rockets without getting our hands dirty, and you simply can't compartmentalize a project like that. What it came down to, finally, was that we had to have a testbed in New Hampshire, whether Van Bush liked it or not."

It took Robert Goddard several weeks of lobbying to convince Vannevar Bush that some of the hands-on research had to be done by his people. Once Bush finally caved in, though, the next task was to locate an appropriate location for the construction of the new prototype. A giant rocket engine is difficult to conceal; it could not be constructed on a workbench in a former sportsmen's club.

One of the prime military contractors in Massachusetts was the Wyman-Gordon Company of Worcester, which was making aircraft forgings for the Army in its Madison Street factory. Upon meeting with Wyman-Gordon's president in Washington, D.C., Vannevar Bush managed to finagle the company into renting out a vacant warehouse on the factory grounds. Final assembly of Team 390's new prototype engine—referred to as "Big Bertha"—would be made in Warehouse Seven, from parts made across the country and secretly shipped to Wyman-Gordon. Big Bertha's aluminum outer casing was cast at Wyman-Gordon as well, although only a few select people at Wyman-Gordon knew exactly what it was.

Secrecy was paramount. Only a handful of Wyman-Gordon workers were involved in the construction of Big Bertha; all had survived extensive background checks by the FBI, and what they were told was on a strict "need to know" basis. The FBI put counterspies to work in the factory to guard against Nazi infiltrators, and work on Big Bertha was done only after midnight, when the least number of people were at the plant. When necessary, the Team 390 members were brought down from New Hampshire to the plant to supervise the engine's construction, making at least three transfers to different vehicles en route, with the final vehicle usually being a phony Coca-Cola delivery van owned by the FBI.

It was a little more difficult to find a suitable site for test-firing Big Bertha; Wyman-Gordon's plant was in the middle of a residential neighborhood. This time, though, the rocket team didn't leave it to the FBI; Henry Morse and Roy Cahill borrowed Esther Goddard's car and spent several days driving around southern New Hampshire trying to find a place for the test-firing. After only a few days, they finally located a dairy farm in nearby Jaffrey, New Hampshire.

Jaffrey had a freight line that ran straight up from Worcester, and the farm was only two miles from the siding. Its owner, Marion Hartnell, was a World War I veteran who just had lost his only son in the fighting in France. He had no love for the Nazis, and once he was approached by Goddard himself, he eagerly volunteered to let the team use his barn for the test-firing of Big Bertha. "We told Mr. Hartnell that there was a possibility that our rocket might blow up and take his barn with it," Cahill recalls. "The old duffer didn't bat an eyelash. 'So long as you can promise me you'll shoot that rocket of yours right up Hitler's wazoo,' that was his response. He even turned down our offer of rent."

On the night of November 24, 1943—Thanksgiving Eve, almost exactly six months before the launch of *Lucky Linda*—Big Bertha was loaded onto a flatcar at the Wyman-Gordon rail siding. A special freight train took it due north across the state line to Jaffrey, where after midnight on Thanksgiving Day the massive rocket engine was carefully off-loaded onto a flatbed truck, which in turn drove it to the Hartnell farm. An Army Corps of Engineers team from Fort Devens in Ashby, Massachusetts, spent the rest of the morning anchoring the prototype engine onto the concrete horizontal testbed that had been built in the barn. Shortly before noon, Goddard and his scientists began making preparations for the test while the townspeople of Jaffrey unwittingly enjoyed their Thanksgiving meals. Team 390 waited until exactly 10:00 P.M.; then Robert Goddard threw the ignition switch on the control board outside the barn.

"I think everybody was standing a hundred feet away from the barn door when we lit the candle," Mander recalls. "When it went, I almost wet my pants. I thought we were going to blow up the whole damn farm."

Big Bertha didn't explode, though; the engine produced sixty tons of thrust for the requisite ninety seconds. "When it was over," Morse says, "Bob turned to us, let out his breath, and said, 'Gentlemen, we've got a success. Now let's go have that Thanksgiving dinner.' I swear, the old man was ready to cry."

The next night, Big Bertha was taken back to the Jaffrey railhead, loaded on another flatcar, and began its long journey across America to

New Mexico. The first big hurdle of Blue Horizon had been jumped. Yet, despite the place he had earned in history, farmer Hartnell never told anyone about the Thanksgiving rocket test that had been made on his farm. He died in 1957 still maintaining secrecy, leaving the new owners of his farm puzzled at the strange concrete cradle that rested inside his barn.

The final months of Project Blue Horizon were a race against time. MI-6 and the OSS knew that the Nazis were in the final stages of building the *Amerika Bomber*, but the location of work was still unknown, and the Nazis' rate of progress was uncertain. "Silver" and "Gold" had long since been pulled out of Peenemünde, so the Allies were now blind as to what the Nazis were doing. Reconnaissance flights by the Allies over Germany had failed to locate the two-mile launch track that Sänger had specified in the Black Umbrella document. Unknown to MI-6, it had been built near Nordhausen by the Dora concentration camp prisoners and camouflaged with nets. The Luftwaffe's scientists were coming steadily closer to fulfilling their primary objective; within the secret caverns of Nordhausen, the sleek antipodal rocket plane was gradually taking shape and form.

Nonetheless, there was talk within the White House and the Pentagon that the Black Umbrella report had been a red herring. There had already been one similar instance, earlier in the war, when the Nazis had been suspected of developing an atomic weapon. In response, the War Department had begun a crash program to develop its own atomic bomb. This program, based in rural Tennessee and code-named the Manhattan Project, had been unsuccessfully struggling to develop an atomic bomb when a Danish physicist, Niels Bohr, managed to escape to the West with the reliable news that the Nazis were nowhere close to attaining controlled nuclear fission, let alone perfecting an atomic bomb.

Although minimal atomic research was secretly continued at the Brookhaven National Laboratory on Long Island, the Manhattan Project had been scrapped, mainly to fund Project Blue Horizon. Now, however, some people within the Pentagon were saying that Sänger's antipodal bomber was another chimera and that vital American resources were being wasted. On their side in the White House was Vice President Harry S Truman, who had begun referring to the American rocket program as "Project Buck Rogers." Yet Vannevar Bush persisted; unlike the atomic bomb scare, there was no proof that the Nazis were *not* developing the *Amerika Bomber*. Roosevelt pragmatically followed his advice, and Project Blue Horizon was not canceled.

"Not knowing what the Germans were doing was the scary part," Roy

Cahill recalls, "so all we could do was work like bastards. We stopped thinking about it in terms of the glory of putting the first American in space. Now we only wanted to get someone up there without killing him."

Through the early part of 1944, Team 390 rarely left its makeshift laboratory at the former sportsmen's club. The ten scientists were constantly in the lodge's dining room, pulling twenty-hour days in its efforts to design the rest of the X-1. The FBI bodyguards had taken to cooking their meals for them, and the long table in the middle of the room was buried beneath books, slide rules, and teetering mounds of paper. Big Bertha had only been one component that had to be designed from scratch; life-support, avionics, telemetry and guidance systems, even the pilot's vacuum suit still had to be developed. As the long New Hampshire winter set in, the days became shorter and the nights colder; tempers became frayed. More than once, members of the team went outside to settle their disputes with their fists. The only instance of relaxation any of the team's survivors remember was the December morning after a nor'easter dropped seven inches of snow on them; they dropped work and had a spontaneous snowball fight on Lake Monomonock's frozen surface.

"Bob was the one who really suffered," Henry Morse remembers. "His health had never been good, and the overwork, plus the hard winter we had that year, started ganging up on him. Esther used to come up from Worcester to make sure he didn't overexert himself, that he rested once a day, but he started ignoring her advice after a while. None of us was sleeping or eating well. We were frightened to death that the very next day we would hear that the *Amerika Bomber* had firebombed New York. It was that much of a race."

Piece by piece, the X-1 was assembled in New Mexico from the specifications laid down by Team 390. Unlike Big Bertha, some vital components such as the inertial guidance system were installed virtually without testing. There was simply not enough time to run everything through the wringer. The White Sands engineers knew that they were working from sheer faith. If Goddard's people were crucially wrong in any one of thousands of areas, the spacecraft they were building would become a death trap for its pilot.

"How in the hell did we get a man into space?" After many years, Morse shakes his head. "Because we were scared of what would happen if we failed."

In the end, it was a photo finish. Both the *Amerika Bomber* and the X-1 were finished and brought to their respective launch pads in the same week. Goddard and his team left New Hampshire for White Sands on May 15 to oversee the final launch, whenever it occurred. It was now a matter of waiting for the Germans to launch the *Amerika Bomber*.

The denouement is well recorded in the history books. The vigil at White Sands ended early on the morning of May 24, 1944, when high-altitude recon planes and ground-based radar spotted the *Amerika Bomber* over the Pacific Ocean. Within twenty minutes the X-1—christened the *Lucky Linda* by its pilot after his wife—was successfully launched. Skid Sloman piloted the X-1 through a harrowing ascent and intercepted the A-9 in space above the Gulf of Mexico—during its final ascent skip before the dive that would have taken it over New York. Sloman destroyed the *Amerika Bomber* with a solid-fuel missile launched from the X-1's port wing. He then successfully guided his ship through atmospheric reentry to touchdown in Lakehurst, New Jersey.

With the landing of the *Lucky Linda*, Project Blue Horizon was no longer top secret. Once the X-1's mission was announced to the American public by Edward R. Murrow on CBS Radio, it became one of the most celebrated events of World War II. The destruction of the *Amerika Bomber* was also one of the final nails in the Nazi coffin. So many resources had been poured into the project that the rest of the German war machine suffered. Sänger's squadron of antipodal bombers was never built, and within a year Germany surrendered to the Allies. The *Lucky Linda* flew again in August 1945, modified to drop a massive incendiary bomb on Hiroshima, Japan. Japan surrendered a few days later, and World War II ended with the dawn of the space age.

Yet the story doesn't end there.

Because the technology that had produced the *Lucky Linda* was considered vital to national security, the OSS clamped the lid on the history of the spaceplane's development. The story that was fed to the press was that the ship had been entirely designed and built in New Mexico. The OSS felt it was necessary to hide the role that Robert Goddard and Team 390 had played.

In the long run, the OSS was correct. When the Third Reich fell, the Russian White Army rolled into Germany and took Nordhausen, capturing many of the German rocket scientists. Josef Stalin was interested in the *Amerika Bomber* and sought the expertise that had produced the spaceplane. Unknown to either the Americans or the Germans, the Soviet Union's Gas Dynamics Laboratory had been secretly working on its own rockets under the leadership of Fridrikh Tsander and Sergei Korolov. The Soviet rocket program had stalled during Russia's long "patriotic war," however, and Stalin wanted to regain the lead in astronautics. But von Braun, Oberth, and other German rocket scien-

tists escaped the Russians and surrendered to American forces; eventually they came to the United States under Operation Paperclip and
became the core of the American space program.

The lead was short-lived; in March 1949 the USSR put its own
manned spacecraft into orbit. Shortly thereafter, Brookhaven physicists
announced the sustenance of nuclear fission, demonstrated by the
explosion of an atomic bomb in the Nevada desert. This was followed, in
less than a year, by the detonation of a Soviet atomic bomb in Siberia.
The new Cold War between the two superpowers moved into the
heavens; for the next twenty-five years, until the passage of the United
Nations Space Treaty in 1974, which outlawed nukesats, no person on
Earth could ever feel safe again.

Nobel laureate Richard Feynman accurately assayed the situation in
his memoirs, *Get Serious, Mr Feynman:* "It was bad enough that the
United States and USSR shared the capability to launch satellites into
orbit; now they both had atomic bombs to put in the satellites. In a more
sane world, it would have been bombs without rockets, or rockets
without bombs—but, God help us, not both at once!"

Because the United States was now competing with the Soviet Union
for dominance in space, the American rocket team lived under oaths of
secrecy for more than forty years, forbidden to discuss publicly what
they had done in Worcester and Rindge. Robert Goddard himself died
on August 10, 1945, the day after the firebombing of Hiroshima. Esther
Goddard remained silent about her husband's involvement with Blue
Horizon until her death in 1982.

Other members of Team 390 passed away over the years with their
lips sealed, yet almost all remained involved in the American space
program. J. Jackson Jackson became the presidential science adviser
during Robert Kennedy's administration, and Hamilton Ballou was the
chief administrator of NASA during the time of the first lunar landing.
Ham and Jack Cube are both dead now, but each May 24, the seven
remaining members of Team 390 make their way to Rindge. Sometimes
they are accompanied by children or grandchildren; in the last forty-
seven years, seldom have any of the former teammates missed this
anniversary. The Monomonock Gun & Rod Club belongs to them now, a
gift from their grateful country.

They spend the day getting the club in shape for the summer—or,
rather, telling the kids what to do, now that the youngest founding
member is in his midsixties. The old men sit together in rocking chairs
on the front porch, drinking beer, kidding each other that FBI agents
are watching them from the woods. When the chores are done, they and
their families have dinner together, sitting alongside each other on

benches at the long oak table in the lodge's dining room where they once scrawled notes and bickered. This is always a festive occasion, punctuated by laughter and dirty jokes. Another tradition is seeing who can get raunchiest, within certain unspoken limits. Their wives roll their eyes in disgust and the kids make faces, but none of the seven men give a rotten damn what they think.

After dinner, as the wives and young people tend to the cleanup, the old men retire to the lodge's main room; Henry and Roy and Mike, Lloyd and Harry, Gerry and Taylor settle into chairs around the field-stone fireplace, cigars and drinks in hand, their feet warmed by the fire. After a while, they begin to talk. As the wives and children and grandchildren gradually filter into the room, while the sun sets beyond the lake and the crickets and bullfrogs strike up the nocturnal orchestra, seven friends once again tell their secret tale.

On occasion they look at the framed photo of Robert Goddard that hangs above the mantel. At other times, though, their eyes wander to another, smaller picture that hangs beside it, a shot familiar to nearly every person in the civilized world: the space-suited figure of Neil Armstrong, the first American to set foot on Mars during the joint U.S.-Soviet expedition in 1976, opening an urn and scattering Goddard's cremated ashes across the landing site at the Utopia Planitia.

(The author extends his appreciation to Dorothy Mosakowski, Michael Warshaw, and Joe Thompson for their assistance.)

MANASSAS, AGAIN

Gregory Benford

There were worse things than getting swept up in the first battle of the first war in over a century, but Bradley could not right away think of any.

They had been out on a lark, really. Bradley got his buddy Paul to go along, flying low over the hills to watch the grand formations of men and machines. Bradley knew how to keep below the radar screens, sometimes skimming along so close to the treetops that branches snapped on their understruts. They had come in before dawn, using Bradley's dad's luxury, ultraquiet cruiser—over the broad fields, using the sunrise to blind the optical sensors below.

It had been enormously exciting. The gleaming columns, the acrid smoke of ruin, the distant muffled coughs of combat.

Then somebody shot them down.

Not a full, square hit, luckily. Bradley had gotten them over two ranges of hills, lurching through shot-racked air. Then they came down heavily, air bags saving the two boys.

They had no choice but to go along with the team that picked them out of their wreckage. Dexter, a big, swarthy man, seemed to be in charge. He said, "We got word a bunch of mechs are comin' along this road. You stick with us, you can help out."

Bradley said irritably, "Why should we? I want to—"

"Cause it's not safe round here, kid," Dexter said. "You joyriding rich kids, maybe you'll learn something about that today."

Dexter grinned, showing two missing teeth, and waved the rest of his company to keep moving into the slanting early-morning glow.

Nobody had any food and Bradley was pretty sure they would not have shared it out if they had. The fighting over the ridge to the west

had disrupted whatever supply lines there were into this open, once
agricultural land.

They reached the crossroads by midmorning and right away knocked
out a servant mech by mistake. It saw them come hiking over the hill
through the thick oaks and started chuffing away, moving as fast as it
could. It was an R class, shiny and chromed.

A woman who carried one of the long rods over her shoulder whipped
the rod down and sighted along it and a loud boom startled Bradley. The
R mech went down. "First one of the day," the woman named Angel
said.

"Musta been a scout," Dexter said.

"For what?" Bradley asked, shocked as they walked down the slope
toward the mech in air still cool and moist from the dawn.

Paul said tentatively, "The mech withdrawal?"

Dexter nodded. "Mechs're on their way through here. Bet they're
scared plenty."

They saw the R mech had a small hole punched through it right in the
servo controls near the back. "Not bad shootin'," a man said to Angel.

"I *tole* you these'd work," Angel said proudly. "I sighted mine in fresh
this mornin'. It helps."

Bradley realized suddenly that the various machined rods these dozen
people carried were all weapons, fabrications turned out of factories
exclusively human-run. *Killing tools*, he thought in blank surprise. *Like
the old days. You see them in dramas and stuff, but they've been illegal
for a century.*

"Maybe this mech was just plain scared," Bradley said. "It's got
software for that."

"We sent out a beeper warning," Dexter said, slapping the pack on his
back. "Goes out of this li'l rig here. Any mech wants no trouble, all they
got to do is come up on us slow and then lie down so we can have a look
at their programming cubes."

"Disable it?"

"Sure. How else we going to be sure?"

"This one ran clear as anything," Angel said, reloading her rifle.

"Maybe it didn't understand," Bradley said. The R models were deft,
subtle, terrific at social graces.

"It knew, all right," Angel said, popping the mech's central port open
and pulling out its ID cube. "Look, it's from Sanfran."

"What's it doing all the way out here, then, if it's not a rebel?" a black
man named Nelson asked.

"Yeah," Dexter said. "Enter it as reb." He handed Bradley a wrist comm. "We're keepin' track careful now. You'll be busy just takin' down score today, kid."

"Rebel, uh, I see," Bradley said, tapping into the comm. It was reassuring to do something simple while he straightened out his feelings.

"You bet," Nelson said, excitement lacing his voice. "Look at it. Fancy mech, smarter than most of them, tryin' to save itself. It's been runnin' away from our people. They just broke up a big mech force west of here."

"I never could afford one of these chrome jobs," Angel said. "They knew that, too. I had one of these classy R numbers meanmouth me in the market, try to grab a can of soybean stew." She laughed sarcastically. "That was when there was a few scraps left on the shelves."

"Elegant thing, wasn't it?" Nelson kicked the mech, which rolled farther downhill.

"You messed it up pretty well," Bradley said.

Dexter said, "Roll it down into that hollow so nobody can see it from the road." He gestured at Paul. "You go with the other party. Hey, Mercer!"

A tall man ambled over from where he had been carefully trying to pick the spines off a prickly pear growing in a gully. Everybody was hungry. Dexter said to him, "Go down across the road and set up shot. Take this kid—Paul's your name, right?—he'll help with the gruntwork. We'll catch 'em in a crossfire here."

Mercer went off with Paul. Bradley helped get the dead mech going and with Angel rolled it into the gully. Its flailing arms dug fresh wet gouges in the spring grass. The exposed mud exhaled moist scents. They threw manzanita brush over the shiny carcass to be sure, and by that time Dexter had deployed his people.

They were setting up what looked like traps of some kind well away from the blacktop crossroads. Bradley saw that this was to keep the crossroads from looking damaged or clogged. They wanted the mechs to come in fast and keep going.

As he worked he heard rolling bass notes, like the mumbles of a giant, come from the horizon. He could see that both the roads leading to the crossroads could carry mechs away from the distant battles. Dexter was everywhere, barking orders, Bradley noted with respect.

The adults talked excitedly to each other about what the mechs would make of it, how easy they were to fool about real-world stuff, and even threw in some insider mech slang—codes and acronyms that meant very little to mechs, really, but had gotten into the pop culture as hip new stuff. Bradley smiled at this. It gave him a moment of feeling superior to cover his uneasiness.

It was a crisp spring morning now that the sun had beamed up over the far hill at their backs. The perfect time for fresh growth, but the fields beyond had no plowing or signs of cultivation. Mechs should be there, laying in crops. Instead they were off over the rumpled ridgeline, clashing with the main body of humans and, Bradley hoped secretly, getting their asses kicked. Though mechs had no asses, he reminded himself.

Dexter and Bradley laid down behind a hummock halfway up the hill. Dexter was talking into his hushmike headset, face jumping with anticipation and concern. Bradley savored the rich scents of the sweet new grass and thought idly about eating some of it.

Dexter looked out over the setup his team was building and said, "Y'know, maybe we're too close, but I figure you can't be in too close as long as you have the firepower. These weapons, we need close, real close. Easier to hit them when they're moving fast but then it's easier for them to hit you, too."

Bradley saw that the man was more edgy here than he had been with his team. Nobody had done anything like this within living memory. Not in the civilized world, anyway.

"Got to be sure we can back out of this if it gets too hot," Dexter went on.

Bradley liked Dexter's no-nonsense scowl. "How did you learn how to fight?"

Dexter looked surprised. "Hobby of mine. Studied the great Roman campaigns in Africa."

"They used ambushes a lot?"

"Sometimes. Of course, after Sygnius of Albion invented the steam-driven machine gun, well sir, then the Romans could dictate terms to any tribes that gave them trouble." Dexter squinted at him. "You study history, kid?"

"I'm Bradley, sir. My parents don't let me read about battles very much. They're always saying we've gotten beyond that."

"Yeah, that Universal Peace Church, right?"

"Yessir. They say—"

"That stuff's fine for people. Mechs, they're different."

"Different how?"

Dexter sucked on his teeth, peering down the road. "Not human. Fair game."

"Think they'll be hard to beat?"

Dexter grinned. "We're programmed for this by a couple million years of evolution. They been around half a century."

"Since 1800? I thought we'd always had mechs."

"Geez, kids never know any history."

"Well, sir, I know all the big things, like the dates of American secession from the Empire, and the Imperial ban on weapons like the ones you've got here, and how—"

"Dates aren't history, son. They're just numbers. What's it matter when we finally got out from under the Romans? Bunch of lilly-livers, they were. 'Peace Empire'—contradiction in terms, kid. Though the way the 3D pumps you kids full of crap, not even allowin' any war shows or anything, except for prettified pussy historicals, no wonder you don't know which end of a gun does the business."

This seemed unfair to Bradley but he could see Dexter wasn't the kind of man he had known, so he shut up. *Fair game?* What did that mean? A fair game was where everybody enjoyed it and had a chance to win.

Maybe the world wasn't as simple as he had thought. There was something funny and tingly about the air here, a crackling that made his skin jump, his nerves strum.

Angel came back and lay beside them, wheezing, lugging a heavy contraption with tripod legs they had just assembled.

Nelson was downslope, cradling his rifle. He arranged the tripod and lifted onto it a big array of cylinders and dark, brushed-steel sliding parts unlike anything Bradley had ever seen. Sweating, Nelson stuck a long, curved clip into all this freshly made metal and worked the clacking mechanism. Nelson smiled, looking pleased at the way the parts slid easily.

Bradley was trying to figure out what all the various weapons did when he heard something coming fast down the road. He looked back along the snaky black line that came around the far hills and saw a big shape flitting among the ash trees.

It was an open-topped hauler filled with copper-jacketed mechs. They looked like factory hands packed like gleaming eggs in a carton.

Dexter talked into his hushmike and pointed toward three chalk-white stones set up by the road as aiming markers. The hauler came racing through the crossroads and plunged up the straight section of the road in front of Bradley. The grade increased here so they would slow as they passed the stones.

Bradley realized they had no way of knowing what the mechs were doing there, not for sure, and then he forgot that as a pulse-quickening sensation coursed through him. Dexter beside him looked like a cat that knows he has a canary stashed somewhere and can go sink his teeth into it any time he likes.

When the hauler reached the marker stones Angel opened fire. The sound was louder than anything Bradley had ever heard and his first reaction was to bury his face in the grass. When he looked up the hauler was slewing across the road and then it hit the ditch and rolled.

The coppery mechs in the back flew out in slow motion. Most just smacked into the grass and lay still. The hauler thumped solidly and stopped rolling. A few of the factory mechs got up and tried to get behind the hauler, maybe thinking that the rifle fire was only from Angel, but then the party from across the road opened up and the mechs pitched forward into the ditch and did not move. Then there was quiet in the little valley. Bradley could hear the hauler's engine still humming with electric energy and then some internal override cut in and it whined into silence.

"I hit that hauler square in the command dome, you see that?" Angel said loudly.

Bradley hadn't seen it but he said, "Yes ma'am, right."

Dexter said, "Try for that every time. Saves ammo if we don't have to shoot every one of them."

Nelson called up the slope, "Those're factory mechs, they look like Es and Fs, they're pretty heavy-built."

Angel nodded, grinning. "Easier just to slam 'em into that ditch."

Dexter didn't hear this as he spoke into his hushmike next to Bradley. "Myron, you guys get them off the road. Use those power-override keys and make them walk themselves into that place where the gully runs down into the stream. Tell 'em to jump right in the water."

"What about the hauler?" Bradley asked, and then was surprised at his own boldness.

Dexter frowned a moment. "The next batch, they'll think we hit it from the air. There was plenty of that yesterday to the west."

"I didn't see any of our planes today," Bradley said.

"We lost some. Rest are grounded because some mechs started to catch on just about sunset. They knocked three of our guys right out of the sky. Mechs won't know that, though. They'll figure it's like yesterday and that hauler was just unlucky." Dexter smiled and checked his own rifle, which he had not fired.

"I'll go help them," Bradley said, starting to get up.

"No; we only got so many of those keys. The guys know how to use 'em. You watch the road."

"But I'd like to—"

"Shut up," Dexter said in a way that was casual and yet was not.

Bradley used his pocket binoculars to study the road. The morning heat sent ripples climbing up from the valley floor and he was not sure at first that he saw true movement several kilometers away and then he was. Dexter alerted the others and there was a mad scramble to get the mechs out of sight.

They were dead, really, but the humans could access their power reserves and make them roll down the road on their wheels and treads and then jounce down the gully and pitch into the stream. Bradley could hear laughter as the team across the road watched the mechs splash into the brown water. Some shorted out and started flailing their arms and rotors around, comic imitations of humans swimming. That lasted only a few seconds and then they sank like the rest.

Nelson came running back up the hill, carrying on his back a long tube. "Here's that launcher you wanted. Rensink, he didn't look too happy to let go of it."

Dexter stood and looked down the road with his own binoculars. "Leave it here. We got higher elevation than Rensink."

Dexter took the steel tube, which looked to Bradley exactly like the telescopes he and his friends used to study the sky. Tentatively Bradley said, "If you're not going to use that rifle, uh, sir, I'd . . ."

Dexter grinned. "You want in, right?"

"Well, yes, I thought that since you're—"

"Sure. Here. Clip goes like this," he demonstrated, "you hold it so, sight along that notch. I machined that so I know it's good. We had to learn a whole lot of old-timey craft to make these things."

Bradley felt the heft and import of the piece and tentatively practiced sighting down at the road. He touched the trigger with the caution of a virgin lover. If he simply pulled on the cool bit of metal a hole would— well, might—appear in the carapace of fleeing mech. A mech they would not have to deal with again in the chaos to come. It was a simple way to think about the whole complex issue. Something in Bradley liked that simplicity.

The mechs still had not arrived but Bradley could see them well enough through the binoculars now to know why. They were riding on self-powered inventions of their own, modified forms of the getarounds mechs sometimes used on streets. These were three-wheeled and made of shiny brass.

They were going slowly, probably running out of energy. As he watched one deployed a solar panel on its back to catch the rising sun and then the others did but this did not speed them up any. They did not look like the elegant social mechs he usually saw zipping on the bike paths, bound on some errand. They were just N- or P-class mechs who had rigged up some wheels.

They came pedaling into the crossroads, using their arms. The one in front saw the hauler on its side and knew something was wrong right

away and started pumping hard. Nelson shot at him then even though
Dexter had said nothing. He hit the lead mech and it went end over
end, arms caught up in its own drive chain. Angel could not resist and
she took out the next three with a burst. Then the others came in with a
chorus of rattling shots and loud bangs, no weapon sounding like the
other, and in the noise Bradley squeezed and felt the butt of the rifle
kick him.

He had been aiming at one of the mechs at the rear of the little
column and when he looked next the mech was down, sliding across the
road with sparks jetting behind it, metal ripping across asphalt.

"Stop! Stop shooting!" Dexter called, and in the sudden silence
Bradley could hear the mechs clattering to a halt, clanging and squealing
and thumping into the ditch.

"Get them off the road—quick!" Dexter called. He waved Bradley
down the hill and the boy ran to see the damage. As he dashed toward
them the mechs seemed to be undamaged except for some dents but
then up close each showed a few holes. He had time to glance at Paul,
who was red-faced, breathing hard, his eyes veiled. There was no time
to talk.

The men and women from across the road got most of the mechs
started up again on override keys but one had suffered some sort of
internal explosion and the back was blown off. Bradley helped three
men tilt it up enough to roll off the gentle rounded asphalt, and once
they got it going it rolled and slid into a copse of eucalyptus. They threw
branches over it. Bradley looked for the one he had shot at but it was
impossible to tell which that was now.

He felt a prickly anticipation, a thickening of the air. The fragrances of
trees and grass cut into his nostrils, vivid and sharp. They ran back up
the slope. Bradley found the rifle he now thought of as his and sprawled
down with it in the grass, getting down behind a hummock near Dexter.

Bradley lay there just breathing and looking at the rifle, which
seemed to be made of a lot of complicated parts. Dexter tossed him
three clips and a box of coppersheathed ammunition. The box promised
that they were armor-piercing. Bradley fumbled a little learning how to
load the clips but then moved quickly, sliding the rounds in with a
secure click as he heard the distant growl of a tracked vehicle.

It was coming closer along the other road. The crossroads looked
pretty clear, no obvious signs of the ambush.

The Mercer team had laid two mines in the road. They had a
chameleon surface and within a minute were indistinguishable from the
asphalt. Bradley could tell where they were because they were lined up

with the white marker stones and from up here were smoother than the asphalt.

He wondered if the mechs could sense that. Their sensorium was better than human in some ways, worse in others. He realized that he had never thought very much about the interior life of a mech, any more than he could truly delve into the inner world of animals. But in principle mechs *were* knowable. Their entire perspective could be digitized and examined minutely.

The clatter and roar of the approach blotted this from his mind. "Activate!" Dexter shouted, his tight voice giving away some of his own excitement.

A big tracked vehicle came flitting through the trees that lined the black road, flickering like a video-game target. There were mechs perched all over it, hitching rides, and many more of them packed its rear platform. When Bradley looked back at the road nearby the mines jumped out at him like a spider on a lace tablecloth. The entire valley vibrated and sparkled with intense, sensory light. Smells coiled up his nostrils, the cool sheen of the rifle spoke to him through his hands.

The mech driver would surely see the mines, stop, and back away, he thought. And the mechs aboard would jump off and some of them would attack the humans, rolling down the road and shooting the lasers they had adapted from industrial purposes. Bradley had heard about mechs that could override their safety commands and fight.

He tightened his grip on his rifle. He was dimly aware of Dexter sighting along his tube-shaped weapon and of Angel muttering to herself as she waited.

"If they were like us they'd stop, first sign of trouble they see," Dexter muttered, probably to himself, but Bradley could hear. "Then they'd deploy fighter mechs on both sides of the road and they'd sweep us, outflank."

"Think they will?" Bradley asked wonderingly.

"Naw. They don't have what we do."

"What . . . what's that?" Bradley knew the wide range of special abilities mechs possessed.

"Balls."

The mechs perched atop the tracked vehicle were looking forward down the road and holding on tight against the rough swerves as they rounded curves.

Then one of them saw the mines and jerked a servo arm toward them. Some mechs sitting near the front began sending warning wails, and the track car slammed on its brakes and slewed across the road. It stopped at the lip of the ditch and made a heavy, grinding noise and began backing up.

Three mechs jumped off its front. Bradley brought his sights down onto one of them and the air splintered with a huge rolling blast that made him flinch and forget about everything else.

The gunmetal hood of the transport seemed to dissolve into a blue cloud. The tailgate of the tracker flew backward with a sharp *whap*.

The air became a fine array of tumbling dots as debris spewed up like a dark fountain and then showered down all across the hillside. Thunks and whacks told of big mech parts hitting nearby. Bradley tucked his head into the grass. He yelped as something nicked his knee and something else tumbled over him and was gone. Pebbles thumped his back.

When Bradley looked up he expected to see nothing but small scraps left on the road. His ears roared with the memory of the sound and he wondered if he would be deaf. But through the smoke he saw several mechs lurching away from the disemboweled transport. There were five of them bunched closely together.

He brought his rifle up and shot very swiftly at the lead mech. It went down and he shot the next object and the next, seeing only the moving forms and the swirling blur of action.

Angel was firing and Nelson too, sharp bangs so regular and fast Bradley thought of the clack of a stick held by a boy as he ran by a picket fence—and in a few seconds there were no more Mechs standing on the road.

But there were two in the ditch. Gray smoke billowed everywhere.

Bradley saw a mech moving just as a quick rod of light leaped from it, cutting through the smoke. He heard Angel yelp and swear. She held up her hand and it was bloody.

Another instantaneous rod of light stood for a second in the air and missed her and then a third struck her weapon. It flew to pieces with a loud bang. Bradley aimed at the mech and kept firing until he saw it and the second one sprawl across the ditch and stop moving.

A compressed silence returned to the valley. The transport was burning but beyond its snaps and pops he could see nothing moving on the road.

Angel was moaning with her wound and Nelson took care of her, pulling out a first-aid kit as he ran over. When they saw that her wound was manageable, Dexter and Bradley walked slowly down to the road. Dexter said, "Bet that's the last big party. We'll get strays now, no problems."

Bradley's legs felt like logs thudding into the earth as he walked. He waved to Paul, who was already on the road, but he did not feel like talking to anybody. The air was crisp and layered with so many scents, he felt them sliding in and out of his lungs like separate flavors in an ice cream sundae.

"Hey!" Mercer called from the transport cab. "They got food in here!"

Everyone riveted attention on the cab. Mercer pitched out cartons of dry food, some cans, a case of soft drinks.

"Somethin', huh?—mechs carryin' food," Angel said wonderingly. For several minutes they ate and drank and then Paul called, "There's a boy here."

They found Paul standing over a boy who was half-concealed by a fallen mech. Bradley saw that the group of mechs had been shielding this boy when they were cut down. "Still alive," Paul said, "barely."

"The food was for him," Mercer said.

Bradley bent down. Paul cradled the boy but it was clear from the drawn, white face and masses of blood down the front, some fresh red and most brown, drying, that there was not much hope. They had no way to get him to cryopreservation. Thin lips opened, trembled, and the boy said, "Bad . . . Mommy . . . hurt . . . "

Dexter said, "This ID says he's under mech care."

"How come?" Angel asked.

"Says he's mentally deficient. These're medical care mechs." Dexter pushed one of the mech carcasses and it rolled, showing H-caste insignia.

"Damn, how'd they get mixed in with these reb mechs?" Nelson asked irritably, the way people do when they are looking for something or someone to blame.

"Accident," Dexter said simply. "Confusion. Prob'ly thought they were doing the best thing, getting their charge away from the fighting."

"Damn," Nelson said again. Then his lips moved but nothing came out.

Bradley knelt down and brushed some flies away from the boy's face. He gave the boy some water but the eyes were far away and the lips just spit the water out. Angel was trying to find the wound and stop the bleeding but she had a drawn, waxy look.

"Damn war," Nelson said. "Mechs, they're to blame for this."

Bradley took a self-heating cup of broth from Paul and gave a little to the boy. The face was no more than fifteen and the eyes gazed abstractedly up into a cloudless sky. Bradley watched a butterfly land on the boy's arm. It fluttered its wings in the slanting yellow-gold sunlight and tasted the drying brown blood. Bradley wondered distantly if butterflies ate blood. Then the boy choked and the butterfly flapped away on a breeze, and when Bradley looked back the boy was dead.

They stood for a long moment around the body. The road was a chaos of ripped mech carapaces and tangled innards and the wreck of the exploded transport. Nobody was going to run into an ambush here anymore today and nobody made a move to clear the road.

"Y'know, these med-care mechs, they're pretty smart," Paul said. "They just made the wrong decision."

"Smarter than the boy, probably," Bradley said. The boy was not much younger than Bradley, but in the eyes there had been just an emptiness. "He was human, though."

The grand opening elation he had felt all morning slowly began to seep out of Bradley. "Hell of a note, huh?" he said to no one in particular. Others were doing that, just saying things to the breeze as they slowly dispersed and started to make order out of the shambles.

The snap and sparkle of the air were still with him, though. He had never felt so alive in his life. Suddenly he saw the soft, encased, abstract world he had inhabited since birth as an enclave, a preserve—a trap. The whole of human society had been in a cocoon, a velvet wrapping tended by mechs.

They had found an alternative to war: wealth. And simple human kindness. *Human* kindness.

Maybe that was all gone now.

And it was no tragedy, either. Not if it gave them back the world as it could be, a life of tangs and zests and the gritty rub of real things. He had dwelled in the crystal spaces of the mind while beneath such cool antiseptic entertainments his body yearned for the hot raw earth and its moist mysteries.

Nelson and Mercer were collecting mech insignia. "Want an AB? We found one over here. Musta got caught up and brought along by these worker mechs?" Nelson asked Bradley.

"I'll just take down the serial numbers," Bradley said automatically, not wanting to talk to Nelson more than necessary. Or to anyone. There had been so much talk.

He spent time getting the numbers logged into his comm and then with shoving mech carcasses off the road.

Dexter came over to him and said, "Sure you don't want one of these?" It was a laser one of the reb mechs had used. Black, ribbed, with a glossy sheen. "Angel's keeping one. She'll be telling the story of her wound and showing the laser that maybe did it, prob'ly for the rest of her life."

Bradley looked at the sleek, sensuous thing. It gleamed in the raw sunlight like a promise. "No."

"Sure?"

"Take the damned stuff away."

Dexter looked at him funny and walked off. Bradley stared at the mechs he was shoving off the road and tried to think how they were different from the boy, who probably was indeed less intelligent than they were, but it was all clouded over with the memory of how much he liked the rifle and the sweet grass and shooting at the targets when they came up to the crossfire point in the sharp sun. It was hard to think at all as the day got its full heat and after a while he did not try. It was easier that way.

THE NUMBER OF
THE SAND

George Zebrowski

*There are those who believe not only in
the infinity of number but in actual infinity, and others who deny it, yet claim that
the number of the sand cannot be said
because it is too large.*

—ARCHIMEDES

Hannibal dismounts and walks out into the center of the valley of Zama, followed only by his interpreter, a trusted veteran of the Italian campaign. Scipio also approaches with only an interpreter. At each general's back, unseen armies wait in the hot Tunisian afternoon. The two leaders stop half a dozen steps apart and regard each other in silence.

Hannibal is the taller and older figure, with a sunburned face half-covered with a cloth that hides his graying hair. He turns his head slightly to benefit his good eye.

Scipio seems tense as he stands bareheaded, holding his helmet, but his expression is that of a proud, handsome man. There is gold inlay on his breastplate, but no other mark of Roman military rank.

"Do you prefer Latin or Greek?" Hannibal asks in Greek. "I know of your interest in the Hellenes."

"It is one of your loves also," Scipio replies. "I've heard that you write in Greek."

Both men glance at their interpreters, then return their attention to each other.

"They will only witness our discussion," Scipio says. "Neither of us needs the delay of having our words repeated."

Hannibal nods at this sign of respect, then stands straighter and shifts his weight to his right leg. "Luck has been with you, Consul," he says, "but we both know that good fortune cannot continue unbroken."

Scipio draws a deep breath and says, "Fortune had little to do with the fact that you were compelled by obvious necessity, and your own honorable character, to leave Italy and come to the defense of your native city. All wars must aim at a truer peace."

Hannibal smiles. "Why be modest? The necessity was of your making, and might have been otherwise." He pauses and waits for a reply, but Scipio waits longer, and Hannibal at last says, "You and I seem to be the only ones who understand that war should be a way to a more lasting peace. Our peoples will only benefit if we end our conflict here and now."

"What do you offer?" Scipio asks.

"The islands," Hannibal says, "even the smaller ones, such as the Malta group, between Italy and Africa. Carthage will also give up Spain."

"But this is less," Scipio replies, "than the terms of the armistice already signed in Rome."

"Which you drafted," Hannibal says quickly, "whether signed by your government or not."

"You offer us our own terms," Scipio counters, "but without the surrender of war vessels or the return of deserters and fugitives in your ranks." The Roman general raises a hand. "I know that they make up the majority of the army with which you fled Italy, and I realize that you will not betray your veterans, but I cannot accept less than Rome's original terms."

Hannibal sighs and nods. "I knew there was no possibility of peace between us, but I wished to meet you, and I do not regret it. We will have to attempt to destroy each other's force. Neither of us can shirk that duty."

The two men gaze at each other for a long, frozen moment, then make gestures of salute and turn away. . . .

A sea of simmering noise swallowed the scene at Zama. The historian ended his first observation of the meeting between Scipio and Hannibal in North Africa, near Carthage, in the year 202 B.C., as the first step in his *New Study of History.* Any randomly selected coordinate of any linear history would have served as well.

As the Prolegomena to his study, he had sampled numerous studies of history, observing how oral narratives gave way to the art of writing down a connected chronicle from surviving documents. This crude form of history was constructed not from a continuous flow of events, but from available, discontinuous samples; from these moments, no one could reconstruct any one true past, and the result was always biased toward the concerns of the investigating present.

When the first linear history machines become operational, the interpretive art of the old historians collapsed, as the whole linear range of human time could now be observed at any desired speed. The old studies of history were replaced by a half-million-year literal record, which could be observed at any point along its meandering course.

After nearly a century, despite the efforts of interpretive observers, the past became the dead past, because nothing usable could be learned from it beyond curious fact. As the old problems of history were settled, the world rushed toward a future-event horizon of incomprehensibility, on the other side of which waited a culture so changed in its biology and goals that little of history would have any meaning for it.

Even when the cliometricon uncovered quantum history, access to the infinity of historical variants only continued to lessen the importance of history in human affairs. Everything had happened and was going to happen; no lesson that could be extracted from the past had any meaning to an accelerating history. All previously false histories of the past became true in some world. Lessons could be applied, imperfectly, to restricted sequences of human experience, in which the time of one generation and the next was essentially unchanged; but to be led by the past in a quickening time would shackle the future, if it could even be done. The universe was not a closed, self-consistent system; it was open, unfinished, and infinite in all directions, including time. Its true nature was mirrored in the incompleteness of both natural and mathematical languages, and in the failure of human law to keep up with emergent circumstances.

The cliometricon's ability to retrieve decaying, fading information from the cosmic background had extended the history machine's capabilities, but without any clear advantage for humanity beyond the satisfaction of scholarly curiosity. Meanwhile, the history machine's ability to show the past, even the immediate, fleeing past measured in seconds and minutes, made possible the emergence, after a stormy transition, of the first panoptic human culture. This transition included the so-called privacy wars, and led to the acceptance of peeping as the right of every human being. Since there was no way to blind the all-seeing eye, humankind had simply faced up to the fact of peeping with a new social stability based on informational nakedness, in which everyone was rewarded. The price of peeping was to be peeped. For the first time in its history, humankind revealed itself to itself in a systematic way, settling many questions of individuality and human nature. Past humanity had only glimpsed itself through its poetries, fictions, and visual dramas; but now all curiosities were satisfied, and the result was greater understanding and compassion for some, and boredom for others.

Cliometricians continued to pursue greater issues, even though they routinely used linear history machines to verify the priority of their colleagues' areas of interest, personal as well as professional, and avoided poaching on all staked claims. But the profession always avoided facing up to the question of its legitimacy, which seemed irresolvable.

There could be no complete history of histories. Events ran to infinity in all directions, diverging at every moment, at every fraction of a moment, at every point in each variant of space-time. Yet this process always meant something to the interiors that were intelligent entities; even when it seemed to make no sense, meaning was felt. The cliometrician watched the embarrassment of the old historians as they were confronted with the living past—and their denials as they drowned in the ocean of truth, claiming that it was all a simulation constructed from massed data by imaging programs. They could not accept that human history was one of the masks of chaos, behind which there was nothing.

In the first hour of horizon light, a sleepless Hannibal watches from a hillock as the elephants stir and begin to advance. Behind them are Mago's men—silent Ligurians, complaining Gauls, wild Moors, and a small group of Spaniards. Well drilled, heavily armed and battlewise, the men advance shoulder to shoulder. A second force of Carthaginian recruits, led by the aging Hanno, advances behind the elephants, followed by the third force, Hannibal's veterans, the army of Bruttium, which deliberately lags behind, and is all but invisible to the Romans in the gray morning light.

Only Hannibal and his waiting messengers know why this is not his usual long battle line. If all goes according to plan, three separate battles will be fought at Zama.

But despite the starlight start of his first force, Hannibal sees that the Roman force is already moving across the valley, its standards a slow moving fence, flanked by horsemen. Three ranks of machinelike infantry—front, spearmen, and supporting legions of *triarii*—come forward. There are puzzling breaks in the line, which are defended by only a few javelin-throwers.

As the armies collide in the same place where Scipio and Hannibal had met, the Roman horns and trumpets cry out, startling Hannibal's elephants. Many of the beasts panic and rush into the openings in the Roman lines, where they are greeted with swarms of missiles and herded through the lines to the rear. Confused, the remaining elephants turn and charge the Carthaginian cavalry. Scipio's mounted force scatters Hannibal's horsemen. They struggle to regroup and fight, but are too few for Laelius's and Masinissa's squadrons. The massed riders move off as a single storm, out of sight.

Hannibal watches as Mago's Gauls and Ligurians lock man to man with the first Roman line and bring it to a stop; but the *triarii* slip through the openings, and the Roman line surges forward again. The second wave, Carthaginian recruits from the city itself, fail to relieve Mago's force, because Hannibal has ordered his three forces to keep apart. The survivors of the first wave retreat and turn with rage on the Carthaginian recruits, who push them back as the Roman line drops its spears and javelins and advances with shields and swords, supported by second-rank spearmen.

Desperately, the Carthaginians hold back the legions, but by late morning the last of Hannibal's two forces breaks to the sides of the valley, leaving the ground strewn with the dead and dying.

On his hillock, Hannibal knows that he must now send in his third force, the ten thousand veterans of Italy, who stand waiting for the moment when Scipio can no longer retreat, while on either side the survivors of the first two waves regroup.

Trumpets command the Romans to remove their wounded, recover weapons, and clear away debris. The standards still fly as the men drink water and rest.

Then, in response to swift new orders from Scipio, the three lines reform. Spearmen move off to one flank of the front line; the *triarii* take the other. The Roman line lengthens far beyond Hannibal's, and closes it on the weak Carthaginian flanks. The armies are equally matched now, except that Hannibal's veterans are fresh, and they have never known defeat at the hands of the Romans.

Suddenly the Roman cavalry returns—and charges into the rear of Hannibal's veterans. There is no Carthaginian cavalry left to stop them. The army of Italy is caught between the infantry and horsemen. The Bruttians turn to defend their flanks and rear.

They fight and die across the afternoon, until nearly all are killed. Hannibal sends a message to Carthage, counseling acceptance of all surrender terms, and with a few survivors flees eastward.

The historian returned to the first meeting between Scipio and Hannibal, and listened again to their great-souled but hopeless words. Then he crossed the lines, watching the variations.

A servile Hannibal admitted his crimes against Rome to a pompous Scipio, mouthing the words of Livy's history, which was true here and a lie elsewhen. The Tunisian landscape seemed frozen. Grains of sand hung suspended in the air at Zama. Hannibal's headcloth disappeared. He wore a patch over one eye. He became stooped, then stood taller and lost an arm. Scipio appeared, now wearing his helmet. Insignias of rank appeared on his breastplate. The two leaders spoke only through their interpreters, who seemed changeless. The viewtank flashed as the historian paused. Scipio and Hannibal were conversing from horseback.

"They hate me back in Rome," Scipio says in Greek, "and that hate will only increase if I defeat you here. There are those who fear my success."

Hannibal smiles and says, "I too am disappointed with the city I left behind as a boy. The fat rich rule it for their sons and daughters. Honor is dead."

"You might restore it," Scipio answers, "if you became its just ruler."

Hannibal laughs. "Your Senate will not tolerate a Carthage with me at its head!"

"But it might not fear a Carthage without you," Scipio answers.

Hannibal considers, then says, "You and I will not fight, then. Will you give me your word that Carthage will not burn?"

Scipio nods. The two men clasp arms, then turn and ride away.

The historian cut across the variants and found Hannibal alone again, looking out across the empty valley of Zama, where there had been no battle. Was Hannibal thinking of how he could have won? Was this aging soldier still in love with the craft of battle as he rode away, hoping for peace?

But in this variant Rome betrays Scipio, replaces him as commander of its forces in Africa, and burns Carthage to the ground. Scipio commits suicide. In Bithynia, far to the east, Hannibal receives the double news with sorrow, and drinks poison in the garden of his house as Roman soldiers approach. A servant flees north with his memoirs, forgetting the last piece of parchment, which lies on the table before the dead Carthaginian. In this variant, the writing reads: "The anxiety of the Romans is at an end. I am the old man for whose death you have waited so long. There will be only one Rome, but it might have been Rome or Carthage..."

While at Zama, the three battles that became one defeat flare across infinity, and each of its three struggles is an infinity, changing through infinitesimal steps. The Roman horsemen do not return, having been ambushed by the sons of Syphax and their Numidian cavalry, leaving Hannibal to an honest test of his Bruttians against Scipio's weary infantry. A few variants earlier, the Roman cavalry had arrived, but too late to save Scipio; and before that only at half-strength; and before that...

The historian watched Carthage destroyed, then built up into a Roman city because the site was too good a center for commerce to be ignored. He watched Rome leveled and raised into a Carthaginian city, for the same reason. The variants ran through endless minor differences in these two outcomes, until he left these lines behind.

He could have of probability what he wanted—but what was it? An endless flickering structured out of nothing, differentiated into individual things by measurementlike interactions among components, copying itself endlessly, providing examples but no prescriptions. These could be studied definitively and forever, but to no end. There was no wall around past quantum-transitional time, so he could have of it what he wanted, even though he could not stand apart from its infinity and see it whole. Only the quantum future was forbidden, even to licensed historical observers, whose linear and quantum history machines were restricted by basic design. There had been a time when the study of history had called for a concern with the future, then with alternate futures, extending the study of the past toward the creation of desirable futures; but the quantum-transitional cliometricon had stifled that new history. Futurity's informational influx into the past was feared and prevented; and yet there had to be variants in which it was embraced, where cultures of past and future mingled informationally without fear, because they understood that the stuff of being was blossoming into 100^{100+N} directions, matter and living flesh metamorphosing toward distant, ever more tenuous and mysterious states, and that these conscious innards of time must huddle all their histories together....

He imagined history whole—as a writhing, boiling cloud. Cliometricians hurled themselves through the enigma but could not stand away from it, which was what it would take to penetrate its mystery. Objectivity was ruinously relative, after all; no one could have history as a separate object of study, even though it seemed that way in the viewtank, without remaining part of it....

In Spain, a year before crossing the Alps into Italy, Hannibal marries a princess of Castulo, a dark-tressed woman of the Olcades people, to help secure the frontier between the Silver Mountains, the Iberians, and Carpetanians, to strengthen the Carthaginian presence in Spain.

On their wedding night, Hannibal mounts Imilce from the rear, but after a few powerful strokes reveal her discomfort, he turns her over on her back. She receives him again and wraps her legs around his middle. Her long hair is at her sides down to her waist. Her lips and pale breasts swell as she nears completion. The dark-skinned Hannibal cries out, bringing joy to her face.

"Come with me!" she whispers as he relaxes and strokes her neck. "At Carthage we'll take passage to Greece, where you can take up the life of study that you have desired."

The Carthaginian shakes his head in denial. "War is coming. My city will perish without me."

"You flatter yourself," she says. "Others also understand what needs to be done. They will step into your place."

"But they don't love the craft of war as I do. They will never see what is possible, and fail."

"The Romans are not fools," she says, and closes her eyes.

A year later, high in a stone tower, Imilce gives birth to a son. Hannibal puts wife and child on a ship for Carthage and marches his army toward the Alps. All through the sixteen-year raid on the Roman peninsula, he carries with him his wife's parting gift—a small Greek statue of Hercules—and rejects the enjoyment of captive women....

But across the variants, Imilce prevails. Word by word, their discussion in the bridal chamber changes through a thousand small steps, until finally Hannibal travels with her and his son to Greece, where he perfects his use of the language and writes a series of dialogues encompassing the experience of Mediterranean peoples. Carthage withdraws from Spain. Rome is not roused from its republican state. The two cities prosper and make treaties of friendship, delaying the Punic Wars and the rise of imperial Rome by a century....

The historian asked himself, what could it all ever mean? The significance of these varying moments had peaked when they were happening. No one else could ever have them from the *inside* except the original players. All historians tacitly entered the minds of past figures and imagined direct knowledge of their thoughts and feelings. Cliometricians were the extreme of panoptic humankind, which observed itself endlessly, down to the smallest details of life, displaying itself to itself, but never able to become one....

Perhaps there should be walls around time, he told himself, and greater ones around individuals. The long-lived should practice periodic amnesia, following the way of the past's short-lived generations, because history is only important while it is being made...

... but there is never an empty moment. History is being made all the time, so it is always important, even though he could not say how. *Being* was adding to itself endlessly, an infinite growing thing, branching, probing through a greater infinity of probability, springing from no soil and obeying no tropism....

In the endless array of gossamer display tanks, each one an event horizon on quantum-transitional times that can be observed but not entered, the historian watches himself contemplating history from the center of an infinite web of information. Once in a while he glances over his shoulder at his unseen alternates, who see him turn his head; but he can only see into the regress of variants in front of him. Do all the cliometricians glance back simultaneously, as if the entire infinite set were one mind? He imagines that vast intelligence sitting at the privileged observer's point, where all regress stops, even though he knows there can be no such point. He could traverse billions of variants and still hope to reach the privileged point on the next try. Attempted passages across an infinity always generated the question: Is this an infinity, or only very large? Aristotle had denied infinity because it could only be defined, but never possessed.

The historian knows that he has lost his struggle with history. Infinities are tractable only when treated as wholes, but the mathematician's way could never encompass the complexities of human events. He sits in his cul-de-sac and yearns for the closure that would end the dismay of infinities, the final, firm place to stand, from which there is no one to glance back to, where all perspectives converge into the sleepless eternity of perfect knowing that would never belong to him. He would never awake from the dream of history in which he was embedded and see it whole.

In the twenty years of wandering exile after his defeat at Zama, Hannibal is told by a Greek oracle that he will be buried in African soil. Untroubled that he will die before returning home, he writes his brief study of history in the house given to him by the king of Bithynia.

Across a million variants he glances out the window and sees Roman soldiers closing their circle around the house. He hides his manuscript in the hollow doorstone, then swallows the poison in his ring. In the billionth variant he learns too late that there is a place in Bithynia called Africa, and that this house stands on it. He smiles as he sits back in his chair, perhaps at the cleverness of the Greek oracles, and his life slips away before the Romans reach the house . . . .

In the same year, across the sea, Scipio also dies, and is buried outside Roman territory, in compliance with his last wishes. . . .

The soldiers break into the house in Bithynia . . . at the thousandth variant they find the manuscript in the stone . . . in the trillionth the room is empty, but under the table there is an open door into a tunnel that runs through the hillside to the harbor. Quinctius Flamininus, the Roman commander, notices that there is a note on the table addressed to him. He picks it up and reads:

> You are hardly a worthy descendant of the men who warned Pyrrhus against the poison prepared for them.
>
> —HANNIBAL

He grimaces, peers into the hole under the table as if it were a tunnel out of history, then hurries outside to the cliff's edge and searches the sea. Hannibal's ship is halfway to the horizon, running with wind and tide to fulfill the Greek oracle's prophecy.

IF LEE HAD NOT WON THE BATTLE OF GETTYSBURG

The Right Honourable
Winston S. Churchill, M.P.

The quaint conceit of imagining what would have happened if some important or unimportant event had settled itself differently, has become so fashionable that I am encouraged to enter upon an absurd speculation. What would have happened if Lee had not won the Battle of Gettysburg? Once a great victory is won it dominates not only the future but the past. All the chains of consequence clink out as if they never could stop. The hopes that were shattered, the passions that were quelled, the sacrifices that were ineffectual are all swept out of the land of reality. Still it may amuse an idle hour, and perhaps serve as a corrective to undue complacency, if at this moment in the twentieth century—so rich in assurance and prosperity, so calm and buoyant—we meditate for a spell upon the debt we owe to those Confederate soldiers who by a deathless feat of arms broke the Union front at Gettysburg and laid open a fair future to the world.

It always amuses historians and philosophers to pick out the tiny things, the sharp agate points, on which the ponderous balance of destiny turns; and certainly the details of the famous Confederate victory of Gettysburg furnish a fertile theme. There can be at this date no conceivable doubt that Pickett's charge would have been defeated, if Stuart with his encircling cavalry had not arrived in the rear of the Union position at the supreme moment. Stuart might have been arrested in his decisive swoop if any one of twenty commonplace incidents had occurred. If, for instance, General Meade had organised his lines of communication with posts for defence against raids, or if he had used his cavalry to scout upon his flanks, he would have received a timely warning. If General Warren had only thought of sending a battalion to hold Little Round Top, the rapid advance of the masses of Confederate cavalry must have been detected. If only President Davis's letter to

General Lee, captured by Captain Dahlgren, revealing the Confederacy plans had reached Meade a few hours earlier, he might have escaped Lee's clutches.

Anything, we repeat, might have prevented Lee's magnificent combinations from synchronising, and if so Pickett's repulse was sure. Gettysburg would have been a great Northern victory. It might have well been a final victory. Lee might, indeed, have made a successful retreat from the field. The Confederacy with its skillful generals and fierce armies might have survived for another year, or even two, but once defeated decisively at Gettysburg, its doom was inevitable. The fall of Vicksburg, which happened only two days after Lee's immortal triumph, would in itself by opening the Mississippi to the river fleets of the Union, have cut the Secessionist States almost in half. Without wishing to dogmatise, we feel we are on solid ground in saying that the Southern States could not have survived the loss of a great battle in Pennsylvania, and the almost simultaneous bursting open of the Mississippi.

However, all went well. Once again by the narrowest of margins the compulsive pinch of military genius and soldierly valour produced a perfect result. The panic which engulfed the whole left of Meade's massive army has never been made a reproach against the Yankee troops. Every one knows they were stout fellows. But defeat is defeat, and rout is ruin. Three days only were required after the cannon at Gettysburg had ceased to thunder before General Lee fixed his headquarters in Washington. We need not here dwell upon the ludicrous features of the hurried flight to New York of all the politicians, place hunters, contractors, sentimentalists and their retinues, which was so successfully accomplished. It is more agreeable to remember how Lincoln, "greatly falling with a falling State," preserved the poise and dignity of a nation. Never did his rugged yet sublime common sense render a finer service to his countrymen. He was never greater than in the hour of fatal defeat.

But, of course, there is no doubt whatever that the mere military victory which Lee gained at Gettysburg would not by itself have altered the history of the world. The loss of Washington would not have affected the immense numerical preponderance of the Union States. The advanced situation of their capital and its fall would have exposed them to a grave injury, would no doubt have considerably prolonged the war; but standing by itself this military episode, dazzling though it may be, could not have prevented the ultimate victory of the North. It is in the political sphere that we have to look to find the explanation of the triumphs begun upon the battlefield.

Curiously enough, Lee furnishes an almost unique example of a regular and professional soldier who achieved the highest excellence both as a general and as a statesman. His ascendancy throughout the Confederate States on the morrow of his Gettysburg victory threw Jefferson Davis and his civil government irresistibly, indeed almost unconsciously, into the shade. The beloved and victorious commander, arriving in the capital of his mighty antagonists, found there the title deeds which enabled him to pronounce the grand decrees of peace. Thus it happened that the guns of Gettysburg fired virtually the last shots in the American Civil War.

The movement of events then shifted to the other side of the Atlantic Ocean. England—the name by which the British Empire was then commonly described—had been riven morally in twain by the drama of the American struggle. We have always admired the steadfastness with which the Lancashire cotton operatives, though starved of cotton by the Northern blockage—our most prosperous county reduced to penury, almost become dependent upon the charity of the rest of England— nevertheless adhered to the Northern cause. The British working classes on the whole judged the quarrel through the eyes of Disraeli and rested solidly upon the side of the abolition of slavery. Indeed, all Mr. Gladstone's democratic flair and noble eloquence would have failed, even upon the then restricted franchise, to carry England into the Confederate camp as a measure of policy. If Lee after his triumphal entry into Washington had merely been the soldier, his achievements would have ended on the battlefield. It was his august declaration that the victorious Confederacy would pursue no policy towards the African negroes, which was not in harmony with the moral conceptions of Western Europe, that opened the high roads along which we are now marching so prosperously.

But even this famous gesture might have failed if it had not been caught up and implemented by the practical genius and trained parliamentary aptitudes of Gladstone. There is practically no doubt at this stage that the basic principle upon which the colour question in the Southern States of America has been so happily settled, owed its origin mainly to Gladstonian ingenuity, and to the long statecraft of Britain in dealing with alien and more primitive populations. There was not only the need to declare the new fundamental relationship between master and servant, but the creation for the liberated slaves of institutions suited to their own cultural development and capable of affording them a different, yet honourable status in a commonwealth, destined eventually to become almost world-wide.

Let us only think what would have happened supposing the liberation of the slaves had been followed by some idiotic assertion of racial equality, and even by attempts to graft white democratic institutions upon the simple, docile, gifted African race belonging to a much earlier chapter in human history. We might have seen the whole of the Southern States invaded by gangs of carpet-bagging politicians exploiting the ignorant and untutored coloured vote against the white inhabitants and bringing the time-honoured forms of parliamentary government into unmerited disrepute. We might have seen the sorry face of black legislatures attempting to govern their former masters. Upon the rebound from this there must inevitably have been a strong reassertion of local white supremacy. By one device or another the franchises accorded to the negroes would have been taken from them. The constitutional principles of the Republic would have been proclaimed, only to be evaded or subverted; and many a warm-hearted philanthropist would have found his sojourn in the South no better than "A Fool's Errand."

But we must return to our main theme and to the procession of tremendous events which followed the Northern defeat at Gettysburg and the surrender of Washington. Lee's declaration abolishing slavery, coupled as it was with the inflexible resolve to secede from the American Union, opened the way for British intervention.

Within a month the formal treaty of alliance between the British Empire and the Confederacy had been signed. The terms of this alliance being both offensive and defensive, revolutionised the military and naval situation. The Northern blockade could not be maintained even for a day in the face of the immense naval power of Britain. The opening of the Southern ports released the pent-up cotton, restored the finances and replenished the arsenals of the Confederacy. The Northern forces at New Orleans were themselves immediately cut off and forced to capitulate. There could be no doubt of the power of the new allies to clear the Mississippi of Northern vessels throughout the whole of its course through the Confederate States. The prospect of a considerable British army embarking for Canada threatened the Union with a new military front.

But none of these formidable events in the sphere of arms and material force would have daunted the resolution of President Lincoln, or weakened the fidelity of the Northern States and armies. It was Lee's declaration abolishing slavery which by a single master stroke gained the Confederacy an all-powerful ally, and spread a moral paralysis far and wide through the ranks of their enemies. The North were waging war against Secession, but as the struggle had proceeded, the moral issue of slavery had first sustained and then dominated the political quarrel. Now that the moral issue was withdrawn, now that the noble cause which inspired the Union armies and the Governments behind them was gained, there was nothing left but a war of reconquest to be waged under circumstances infinitely more difficult and anxious than those which had already led to so much disappointment and defeat. Here was the South victorious, reinvigorated, reinforced, offering of her own free will to make a more complete abolition of the servile status on the American continent than even Lincoln had himself seen fit to demand. Was the war to continue against what soon must be heavy odds merely to assert the domination of one set of English-speaking people over another; was blood to flow indefinitely in an ever-broadening stream to gratify national pride or martial revenge?

It was this deprivation of the moral issue which undermined the obduracy of the Northern States. Lincoln no longer rejected the Southern appeal for independence. "If," he declared in his famous speech in Madison Square Gardens in New York, "our brothers in the South are willing faithfully to cleanse this continent of negro slavery, and if they will dwell beside us in neighbourly goodwill as an independent but friendly nation, it would not be right to prolong the slaughter on the question of sovereignty alone."

Thus peace came more swiftly than war had come. The Treaty of Harper's Ferry which was signed between the Union and Confederate States on the 6th September 1863 embodied the two fundamental propositions, that the South was independent, and the slaves were free. If the spirit of old John Brown had revisited the battle-scarred township which had been the scene of his life and death, it would have seen his cause victorious; but at a cost to the United States terrible indeed. Apart from the loss of blood and treasure, the American Union was riven in twain. Henceforth there would be two Americas in the same northern continent. One of them would have renewed in a modern and embattled form its old ties of kinship and affiliation with the Mother Country across the ocean. It was evident though peace might be signed and soldiers furl their flags, profound antagonisms, social, economic and military, underlay the life of the English-speaking world. Still slavery was abolished. As John Bright said, "At last after the smoke of the battlefield has cleared away, the horrid shape which had cast its shadow over the whole continent, had vanished and was gone for ever."

At this date when all seems as simple and clear, one has hardly the patience to chronicle the bitter and lamentable developments which occupied the two succeeding generations.

But we may turn aside in our speculation to note how strangely the careers of Mr. Gladstone and Mr. Disraeli would have been altered if Lee had not won the Battle of Gettysburg. Mr. Gladstone's threatened resignation from Lord Palmerston's Cabinet on the morrow of General

Lee's pronouncement in favour of abolition, induced a political crisis in England of the most intense character. Old friendships were severed, old rancours died, and new connections and resentments took their place. Lord Palmerston found himself at the parting of the ways. Having to choose between Mr. Gladstone and Lord John Russell, he did not hesitate. A Coalition Government was formed in which Lord Robert Cecil (afterwards the great Lord Salisbury) became Foreign Secretary, but of which Mr. Gladstone was henceforward the driving force. We remember how he had said at Newcastle on 7th October 1862, "We know quite well that the people of the Northern States have not yet drunk of the cup—they will try hard to hold it far from their lips—which all the rest of the world see they nevertheless must drink. We may have our own ideas about slavery; we may be for or against the South; but there is no doubt that Jefferson Davis and the other soldiers of the South have made an army; they are making, it appears, a navy; *and they have made what is more than either, they have made a nation.*" Now the slavery obstacle was out of the way and under the aegis of his aged chief, Lord Palmerston, who in Mr. Gladstone's words "desired the severance (of North and South) as the diminution of a dangerous power," and aided by the tempered incisiveness of Lord Robert Cecil, Mr. Gladstone achieved not merely the recognition but an abiding alliance between Great Britain and the Southern States. But this carried him far. In the main the friends of the Confederacy in England belonged to the aristocratic well-to-do and Tory classes of the nation; the democracy, as yet almost entirely unenfranchised and most of the Liberal elements, sympathised with the North. Lord Palmerston's new Government formed in September 1863, although nominally Coalition, almost entirely embodied the elements of Tory strength and inspiration. No one can say that Gladstone's reunion with the Tories would have been achieved apart from Gettysburg and Lee's declaration at Washington.

However, it was achieved, and henceforward the union of Mr. Gladstone and Lord Robert Cecil on all questions of Church, State, and Empire, became an accomplished and fruitful fact. Once again the "rising hope of the stern and unbending Tories" had come back to his old friends, and the combination, armed as it was with prodigious executive success, reigned for a decade irresistible.

It is strange, musing on Mr. Gladstone's career, how easily he might have drifted into radical and democratic courses. How easily he might have persuaded himself that he, a Tory and authoritarian to his fingertips, was fitted to be the popular and even populist, leader of the working classes. There might in this event have stood to his credit nothing but sentimental pap, pusillanimous surrenders of British inter-

ests, and the easy and relaxing cosmopolitanism which would in practice
have made him the friend of every country but his own. But the sabres
of Jeb Stuart's cavalry and the bayonets of Pickett's division had, on the
slopes of Gettysburg, embodied him forever in a revivified Tory party.
His career thus became a harmony instead of a discord; and he holds his
place in the series of great builders to whom the largest synthesis of the
world is due.

Precisely the reverse effect operated upon Mr. Disraeli. What had he
to do with the Tory aristocracy? In his early days he was prejudiced in
their eyes as a Jew by race. He had, indeed, only been saved from the
stigma of exclusion from public life before the repeal of the Jewish
disabilities by the fact of his having been baptized in infancy. He had
stood originally for Parliament as a Radical. His natural place was with
the left-out millions, with the dissenters, with the merchants of the
North, with the voteless proletariat. He might never have found his
place, if Lee had not won the Battle of Gettysburg. But for that he might
have continued leading the Conservative Party, educating them against
their will, dragging them into all sorts of social policies which they
resented, making them serve as agents for extensions of the franchise.
Always indispensable, always distrusted, but for Lee and Gettysburg he
might well have ended his life in the House of Lords with the exclama-
tion, "Power has come to me too late!"

But once he was united by the astonishing events of 1863 with the
democratic and Radical forces of the nation, the real power of the man
became apparent. He was in his native element. He had always es-
poused the cause of the North; and what he was pleased to describe as
"the selfish and flagitious intrigue (of the Palmerston-Gladstone Government) to split the American Union and to rebuild out of the miseries of a
valiant nation the vanished empire of George III," aroused passions in
England strong enough to cast him once and for all from Tory circles. He
went where his instinct and nature led him, to the Radical masses which
were yearly gathering strength. It is to this we owe his immense
contribution to our social services. If Disraeli had not been drawn out of
the Conservative Party, the whole of those great schemes of social and
industrial insurance which are forever associated with his name, which
followed so logically upon his speeches—"Health and the laws of health,"
"sanitas sanitatum omnia sanitas"—might never have been passed into
law in the nineteenth century. They might no doubt well have come
about in the twentieth. It might have been left to some sprout of the
new democracy or some upstart from Scotland, Ireland, or even Wales,
to give to England what her latest Socialist Prime Minister has de-

scribed as "our incomparable social services." But "Dizzy," "The people's Dizzy," would never have set these merciful triumphs in his record.

We must return to the main theme. We may, however, note, by the way, that if Lee had not won the Battle of Gettysburg, Gladstone would not have become the greatest of Conservative Empire and Commonwealth builders, nor would Disraeli have been the idol of the toiling masses. Such is Fate.

But we cannot occupy ourselves too long upon the fortunes of individuals. During the whole of the rest of the nineteenth century the United States of America, as the truncated Union continued to style itself, grew in wealth and population. An iron determination seemed to have taken hold of the entire people. By the 'eighties they were already cleared of their war debt, and indeed all traces of the war, except in the hearts of men, were entirely eradicated. But the hearts of men are strange things, and the hearts of nations are still stranger. Never could the American Union endure the ghastly amputation which had been forced upon it. Just as France after 1870 nursed for more than forty years her dream of *revanche*, so did the multiplying peoples of the American Union concentrate their thoughts upon another trial of arms.

And to tell the truth, the behaviour of the independent Confederacy helped but little in mitigating the ceaselessly fermenting wrath. The former Confederate States saw themselves possessed of a veteran army successful against numerous odds, and commanded by generals to whose military aptitude history has borne unquestioned tribute. To keep this army intact and—still more important—employed, became a high problem of state. To the south of the Confederacy lay Mexico, in perennial alternation between anarchy and dictatorship. Lee's early experiences in the former Mexican War familiarized him with the military aspects of the country and its problems, and we must admit that it was natural that he should wish to turn the bayonets of the army of northern Virginia upon this sporadically defended Eldorado. In spite of the pious protests of Mr. Disraeli's Liberal and pacifist Government of 1884, the Confederate States after three years' sanguinary guerrilla fighting conquered, subdued and reorganised the vast territories of Mexico. These proceedings involved a continuous accretion of Southern military forces. At the close of the Mexican War seven hundred thousand trained and well-tried soldiers were marshalled under what the North still called "the rebel flag." In the face of these potentially menacing armaments who can blame the Northern States for the precautions they took? Who can accuse them of provocation because they adopted the principle of compulsory military service? And when this was retorted by similar measures south of the Harper's Ferry Treaty line, can we be surprised that they increased the period of compulsory service from one year to two, and thereby turned their multitudinous militia into the cadres of an army "second to none." The Southern States, relying on their alliance with the supreme naval power of Britain, did not expend their money upon a salt-water navy. Their powerful ironclad fleet was designed solely for the Mississippi. Nevertheless, on land and water the process of armament and counter-armament proceeded ceaselessly over the whole expanse of the North American continent. Immense fortresses guarded the frontiers on either side and sought to canalise the lines of reciprocal invasion. The wealth of the Union States enabled them at enormous sacrifice at once to fortify their southern front and to maintain a strong fleet and heavy military garrison in the fortified harbours of the great lakes of the Canadian frontier. By the 'nineties North America bristled with armaments of every kind, and what with the ceaseless growth of the Confederate army—in which the reconciled negro population now formed a most important element—and the very large forces which England and Canada maintained in the North, it was computed that not less than two million armed men with trained reserves of six million were required to preserve the uneasy peace of the North American continent. Such a process could not go on without a climax of tragedy or remedy.

The climax which came in 1905 was perhaps induced by the agitation of war excitement arising from the Russo-Japanese conflict. The roar of Asiatic cannon reverberated around the globe, and everywhere found immense military organisations in an actively receptive state. Never has the atmosphere of the world been so loaded with explosive forces. Europe and North America were armed camps, and a war of first magnitude was actually raging in Manchuria. At any moment, as the Dogger Bank incident had shown, the British Empire might be involved in war with Russia. Indeed, we had been within the ace on that occasion. And apart from such accidents the British Treaty obligations towards Japan might automatically have drawn us in. The President of the United States had been formally advised by the powerful and highly competent American General Staff that the entry of Great Britain into such a war would offer in every way a favourable opportunity for settling once and for all with the Southern Republic. This fact was also obvious to most people. Thus at the same time throughout Europe and America precautionary measures of all kinds by land and sea were actively taken; and everywhere fleets and armies were assembled and arsenals clanged and flared by night and day.

Now that these awful perils have been finally warded off it seems to us almost incomprehensible that they could have existed. Nevertheless, it is horrible even to reflect that scarcely a quarter of a century ago

English-speaking people ranged on opposite sides, watched each other with ceaseless vigilance and drawn weapons. By the end of 1905 the tension was such that nothing could long avert a fratricidal struggle on a gigantic scale, except some great melting of hearts, some wave of inspiration which should lift the dull, deadly antagonisms of the hour to a level so high that—even as a mathematical quantity passing through infinity changes its sign—they would become actual unities.

We must not underrate the strength of the forces which on both sides of the Atlantic Ocean and on both sides of the American continental frontiers were labouring faithfully and dauntlessly to avert the hideous doom which kindred races seemed resolved to prepare for themselves. But these deep currents of sanity and goodwill would not have been effective unless the decisive moment had found simultaneously in England and the United States leaders great enough to dominate events and marvelously placed upon the summits of national power. In President Roosevelt and Mr. Arthur Balfour, the British Prime Minister, were present two diverse personalities which together embodied all the qualities necessary alike for profound negotiation and for supreme decision.

After all, when it happened it proved to be the easiest thing in the world. In fact, it seemed as if it could not help happening, and we who look back upon it take it so much for granted that we cannot understand how easily the most beneficent Covenant of which human records are witness might have been replaced by the most horrible conflict and world tragedy.

The Balfour-Roosevelt negotiations had advanced some distance before President Wilson, the enlightened Virginian chief of the Southern Republic, was involved in them. It must be remembered that whatever may be thought of Mr. Gladstone's cold-blooded *coup* in 1863, the policy of successive British Governments had always been to assuage the antagonism between North and South. At every stage the British had sought to promote goodwill and close association between her southern ally and the mighty northern power with whom she had so much in common. For instance, we should remember how in the Spanish-American War of 1895 the influence of Great Britain was used to the utmost and grave risks were run in order to limit the quarrel and to free the United States from any foreign menace. The restraining counsels of England on this occasion had led the Southern Republic to adopt a neutrality not only benevolent, but actively helpful. Indeed, in this war several veteran generals of the Confederate army had actually served as volunteers with the Union forces. So that one must understand that side by side with the piling up of armaments and the old antagonisms, there was an immense under-tide of mutual liking and respect. It is the glory of Balfour, Roosevelt and Wilson—this august triumvirate—that they were able so to direct these tides that every opposing circumstance or element was swept before them.

On Christmas Day 1905 was signed the Covenant of the English-speaking Association. The essence of this extraordinary measure was crystal clear. The doctrine of common citizenship for all the peoples involved in the agreement was proclaimed. There was not the slightest interference with the existing arrangements of any member. All that happened was that henceforward the peoples of the British Empire and of what were happily called in the language of the line "The Re-United States," deemed themselves to be members of one body and inheritors of one estate. The flexibility of the plan which invaded no national privacy, which left all particularisms entirely unchallenged, which altered no institutions and required no elaborate machinery, was its salvation. It was, in fact, a moral and psychological rather than political reaction. Hundreds of millions of people suddenly adopted a new point of view. Without prejudice to their existing loyalties and sentiments, they gave birth in themselves to a new higher loyalty and a wider sentiment. The autumn of 1905 had seen the English-speaking world on the verge of catastrophe. The year did not die before they were associated by indissoluble ties for the maintenance of peace between themselves, for the prevention of war among outside Powers and for the economic development of their measureless resources and possessions.

The Association had not been in existence for a decade before it was called upon to face an emergency not less grave than that which had called it into being. Every one remembers the European crisis of August 1914. The murder of the Archduke at Sarejevo, the disruption or decay of the Austrian and Turkish Empires, the old quarrel between Germany and France, and the increasing armaments of Russia—all taken together produced the most dangerous conjunction which Europe has ever known. Once the orders for Russian, Austrian, German, and French mobilisation had been given and twelve million soldiers were gathering upon the frontiers of their respective countries, it seemed that nothing could avert a war which might well have become Armageddon itself.

What the course and consequences of such a war would have been are matters upon which we can only speculate. M. Bloch in his thoughtful book published in 1909, indicated that such a war if fought with modern weapons would not be a short one. He predicted that field operations would quickly degenerate into long lines of fortifications, and that a devastating stalemate with siege warfare, or trench warfare, lasting for years, might well ensue. We know his opinions are not accepted by the leading military experts of most countries. But, at any rate, we cannot doubt that a war in which four or five of the greatest European Powers were engaged might well have led to the loss of many millions of lives, and to the destruction of capital that twenty years of toil, thrift, and privation could not have replaced. It is no exaggeration to say that had the crisis of general mobilisation of August 1914 been followed by war, we might to-day in this island see income tax at four or five shillings in the pound, and have two and a half million unemployed workmen on our hands. Even the United States far across the ocean, might against all its traditions have been dragged into a purely European quarrel.

But in the nick of time friendly though resolute hands intervened to save Europe from what might well have been her ruin. It was inherent in the Covenant of the English-speaking Association that the ideal of mutual disarmament to the lowest point compatible with their joint safety should be adopted by the signatory members. It was also settled that every third year a Conference of the whole Association should be held in such places as might be found convenient. It happened that the third disarmament conference of the English-speaking Association—the E.S.A. as it is called for short—was actually in session in July 1914. The Association had found itself hampered in its policy of disarmament by the immense military and naval establishments maintained in Europe. Their plenipotentiaries were actually assembled to consider this problem when the infinitely graver issue burst upon them. They acted as men accustomed to deal with the greatest events. They felt so sure of themselves that they were able to run risks for others. On the 1st August when the German armies were already approaching the frontiers of Belgium, when the Austrian armies had actually begun the bombardment of Belgrade, and when all along the Russian and French frontiers desultory picket firing had broken out, the E.S.A. tendered its friendly offices to all the mobilised Powers, counselling them to halt their armies within ten miles of their own frontiers, and to seek a solution of their differences by peaceful discussion. The memorable document added "that failing a peaceful outcome the Association must deem itself *ipso facto* at war with any Power in either combination whose troops invaded the territory of its neighbour."

Although this suave yet menacing communication was received with indignation in many quarters, it in fact secured for Europe the breathing space which was so desperately required. The French had already forbidden their troops to approach within ten miles of the German frontier, and they replied in this sense. The Czar eagerly embraced the opportunity offered to him. The secret wishes of the Kaiser and his emotions at this juncture have necessarily been much disputed. There are those who allege that carried away by the excitement of mobilisation and the clang and clatter of moving armies, he was not disposed to halt his troops already on the threshold of the Duchy of Luxembourg. Others avow that he received the message with a scream of joy and fell exhausted into a chair, exclaiming, "Saved! Saved! Saved!" Whatever may have been the nature of the Imperial convulsion, all we know is that the acceptance of Germany was the last to reach the Association. With its arrival, although there yet remained many weeks of anxious negotiation, the danger of a European war may be said to have passed away.

Most of us have been so much absorbed by the immense increases of prosperity and wealth, or by the commercial activity and scientific and territorial development and exploitation which have been the history of the English-speaking world since 1905, that we have been inclined to allow European affairs to fall into a twilight of interest. Once the perils of 1914 had been successfully averted and the disarmament of Europe had been brought into harmony with that already effected by the E.S.A., the idea of "An United States of Europe" was bound to occur continually. The glittering spectacle of the great English-speaking combination, its assured safety, its boundless power, the rapidity with which wealth was created and widely distributed within its bounds, the sense of buoyancy and hope which seemed to pervade the entire population; all this pointed to European eyes a moral which none but the dullest could ignore. Whether the Emperor Wilhelm II will be successful in carrying the project of European unity forward by another important stage at the forthcoming Pan-European Conference at Berlin in 1932, is still a matter of prophecy. Should he achieve his purpose he will have raised himself to a dazzling pinnacle of fame and honour, and no one will be more pleased than the members of the E.S.A. to witness the gradual formation of another great area of tranquillity and co-operation like that in which we ourselves have learned to dwell. If this prize should fall to his Imperial Majesty, he may perhaps reflect how easily his career might have been wrecked in 1914 by the outbreak of a war which might have cost him his throne, and have laid his country in the dust. If to-day he occupies in his old age the most splendid situation in Europe, let him not forget that he might well have found himself eating the bitter bread of exile, a dethroned sovereign and a broken man loaded with unutterable reproach. And this, we repeat, might well have been his fate, if Lee had not won the Battle of Gettysburg.

OVER THERE

Mike Resnick

I respectfully ask permission immediately to raise two divisions for immediate service at the front under the bill which has just become law, and hold myself ready to raise four divisions, if you so direct. I respectfully refer for details to my last letters to the Secretary of War.

—THEODORE ROOSEVELT
telegram to President Woodrow
Wilson, May 18, 1917

I very much regret that I cannot comply with the request in your telegram of yesterday. The reasons I have stated in a public statement made this morning, and I need not assure you that my conclusions were based upon imperative considerations of public policy and not upon personal or private choice.

—WOODROW WILSON,
telegram to Theodore Roosevelt,
May 19, 1917

The date was May 22, 1917.

Woodrow Wilson looked up at the burly man standing impatiently before his desk.

"This will necessarily have to be an extremely brief meeting, Mr. Roosevelt," he said wearily. "I have consented to it only out of respect for the fact that you formerly held the office that I am now privileged to hold."

"I appreciate that, Mr. President," said Theodore Roosevelt, shifting his weight anxiously from one leg to the other.

"Well, then?" said Wilson.

"You know why I'm here," said Roosevelt bluntly. "I want your permission to reassemble my Rough Riders and take them over to Europe."

"As I keep telling you, Mr. Roosevelt—that's out of the question."

"You haven't told *me* anything!" snapped Roosevelt. "And I have no interest in what you tell the press."

"Then I'm telling you now," said Wilson firmly. "I can't just let any man who wants to gather up a regiment go fight in the war. We have procedures, and chains of command, and—"

"I'm not just *any* man," said Roosevelt. "And I have every intention of honoring our procedures and chain of command." He glared at the president. "I created many of those procedures myself."

Wilson stared at his visitor for a long moment. "Why are you so anxious to go to war, Mr. Roosevelt? Does violence hold so much fascination for you?"

"I abhor violence and bloodshed," answered Roosevelt. "I believe that war should never be resorted to when it is honorably possible to avoid it. But once war has begun, then the only thing to do is win it as swiftly and decisively as possible. I believe that I can help to accomplish that end."

"Mr. Roosevelt, may I point out that you are fifty-eight years old, and according to my reports you have been in poor health ever since returning from Brazil three years ago?"

"Nonsense!" said Roosevelt defensively. "I feel as fit as a bull moose!"

"A one-eyed bull moose," replied Wilson dryly. Roosevelt seemed about to protest, but Wilson raised a hand to silence him. "Yes, Mr. Roosevelt, I know that you lost the vision in your left eye during a boxing match while you were president." He couldn't quite keep the distaste for such juvenile and adventurous escapades out of his voice.

"I'm not here to discuss my health," answered Roosevelt gruffly, "but the reactivation of my commission as a colonel in the United States Army."

Wilson shook his head. "You have my answer. You've told me nothing that might change my mind."

"I'm about to."

"Oh?"

"Let's be perfectly honest, Mr. President. The Republican nomination is mine for the asking, and however the war turns out, the Democrats will be sitting ducks. Half the people hate you for entering the war so late, and the other half hate you for entering it at all." Roosevelt paused. "If you will return me to active duty and allow me to organize my Rough Riders, I will give you my personal pledge that I will neither seek nor accept the Republican nomination in 1920."

"It means that much to you?" asked Wilson, arching a thin eyebrow.

"It does, sir."

"I'm impressed by your passion, and I don't doubt your sincerity, Mr. Roosevelt," said Wilson. "But my answer must still be no. I am serving my second term. I have no intention of running again in 1920, I do not need your political support, and I will not be a party to such a deal."

"Then you are a fool, Mr. President," said Roosevelt. "Because I am going anyway, and you have thrown away your only opportunity, slim as it may be, to keep the Republicans out of the White House."

"I will not reactivate your commission, Mr. Roosevelt."

Roosevelt pulled two neatly folded letters out of his lapel pocket and placed them on the president's desk.

"What are these?" asked Wilson, staring at them as if they might bite him at any moment.

"Letters from the British and the French, offering me commissions in *their* armies." Roosevelt paused. "I am first, foremost, and always an

American, Mr. President, and I had entertained no higher hopes than leading my men into battle under the Stars and Stripes—but I am going to participate in this war, and you are not going to stop me." And now, for the first time, he displayed the famed Roosevelt grin. "I have some thirty reporters waiting for me on the lawn of the White House. Shall I tell them that I am fighting for the country that I love, or shall I tell them that our European allies are more concerned with winning this damnable war than our own president?"

"This is blackmail, Mr. Roosevelt!" said Wilson, outraged.

"I believe that is the word for it," said Roosevelt, still grinning. "I would like you to direct Captain Frank McCoy to leave his current unit and report to me. I'll handle the rest of the details myself." He paused again. "The press is waiting, Mr. President. What shall I tell them?"

"Tell them anything you want," muttered Wilson furiously. "Only get out of this office."

"Thank you, sir," said Roosevelt, turning on his heel and marching out with an energetic bounce to his stride.

Wilson waited a moment, then spoke aloud. "You can come in now, Joseph."

Joseph Tummulty, his personal secretary, entered the Oval Office.

"Were you listening?" asked Wilson.

"Yes, sir."

"Is there any way out of it?"

"Not without getting a black eye in the press."

"That's what I was afraid of," said Wilson.

"He's got you over a barrel, Mr. President."

"I wonder what he's really after?" mused Wilson thoughtfully. "He's been a governor, an explorer, a war hero, a police commissioner, an author, a big-game hunter, and a president." He paused, mystified. "What more can he want from life?"

"Personally, sir," said Tummulty, making no attempt to hide the contempt in his voice, "I think that damned cowboy is looking to charge up one more San Juan Hill."

Roosevelt stood before his troops, as motley an assortment of warriors as had been assembled since the last incarnation of the Rough Riders. There were military men and cowboys, professional athletes and adventurers, hunters and ranchers, barroom brawlers and Indians, tennis players and wrestlers, even a trio of Maasai *elmoran* he had met on safari in Africa.

"Some of 'em look a little long in the tooth, Colonel," remarked Frank McCoy, his second-in-command.

"Some of *us* are a little long in the tooth, too, Frank," said Roosevelt with a smile.

"And some of 'em haven't started shaving yet," continued McCoy wryly.

"Well, there's nothing like a war to grow them up in a hurry."

Roosevelt turned away from McCoy and faced his men, waiting briefly until he had their attention. He paused for a moment to make sure that the journalists who were traveling with the regiment had their pencils and notebooks out, and then spoke.

"Gentlemen," he said, "we are about to embark upon a great adventure. We are privileged to be present at a crucial point in the history of the world. In the terrible whirlwind of war, all the great nations of the world are facing the supreme test of their courage and dedication. All the alluring but futile theories of the pacifists have vanished at the first sound of gunfire."

Roosevelt paused to clear his throat, then continued in his surprisingly high-pitched voice. "This war is the greatest the world has ever seen. The vast size of the armies, the tremendous slaughter, the loftiness of the heroism shown and the hideous horror of the brutalities committed, the valor of the fighting men and the extraordinary ingenuity of those who have designed and built the fighting machines, the burning patriotism of the peoples who defend their homelands and the far-reaching complexity of the plans of the leaders—all are on a scale so huge that nothing in history can compare with them.

"The issues at stake are fundamental. The free peoples of the world have banded together against tyrannous militarism, and it is not too much to say that the outcome will largely determine, for those of us who love liberty above all else, whether or not life remains worth living."

He paused again, and stared up and down the ranks of his men.

"Against such a vast and complex array of forces, it may seem to you that we will just be another cog in the military machine of the allies, that one regiment cannot possibly make a difference." Roosevelt's chin jutted forward pugnaciously. "I say to you that this is rubbish! We represent a society dedicated to the proposition that every free man makes a difference. And I give you my solemn pledge that the Rough Riders will make a difference in the fighting to come!"

It was possible that his speech wasn't finished, that he still had more to say... but if he did, it was drowned out beneath the wild and raucous cheering of his men.

One hour later they boarded the ship to Europe.

*   *   *

Roosevelt summoned a corporal and handed him a handwritten letter. The man saluted and left, and Roosevelt returned to his chair in front of his tent. He was about to pick up a book when McCoy approached him.

"Your daily dispatch to General Pershing?" he asked dryly.

"Yes," answered Roosevelt. "I can't understand what is wrong with the man. Here we are, primed and ready to fight, and he's kept us well behind the front for the better part of two months!"

"I know, Colonel."

"It just doesn't make any sense! Doesn't he know what the Rough Riders did at San Juan Hill?"

"That was a long time ago, sir," said McCoy.

"I tell you, Frank, these men are the elite—the cream of the crop! They weren't drafted by lottery. Every one of them volunteered, and every one was approved personally by you or by me. Why are we being wasted here? There's a war to be won!"

"Pershing's got a lot to consider, Colonel," said McCoy. "He's got half a million American troops to disperse, he's got to act in concert with the French and the British, he's got to consider his lines of supply, he's—"

"Don't patronize me, Frank!" snapped Roosevelt. "We've assembled a brilliant fighting machine here, and he's ignoring us. There *has* to be a reason. I want to know what it is!"

McCoy shrugged helplessly. "I have no answer, sir."

"Well, I'd better get one soon from Pershing!" muttered Roosevelt. "We didn't come all this way to help in some mopping-up operation after the battle's been won." He stared at the horizon. "There's a glorious crusade being fought in the name of liberty, and I plan to be a part of it."

He continued staring off into the distance long after McCoy had left him.

A private approached Roosevelt as the former president was eating lunch with his officers.

"Dispatch from General Pershing, sir," said the private, handing him an envelope with a snappy salute.

"Thank you," said Roosevelt. He opened the envelope, read the message, and frowned.

"Bad news, Colonel?" asked McCoy.

"He says to be patient," replied Roosevelt. "Patient?" he repeated furiously. "By God, I've been patient long enough! Jake—saddle my horse!"

"What are you going to do, Colonel?" asked one of his lieutenants.

"I'm going to go meet face-to-face with Pershing," said Roosevelt, getting to his feet. "This is intolerable!"

"We don't even know where he is, sir."

"I'll find him," replied Roosevelt confidently.

"You're more likely to get lost or shot," said McCoy, the only man who dared to speak to him so bluntly.

"Runs With Deer! Matupu!" shouted Roosevelt. "Saddle your horses!" A burly Indian and a tall Maasai immediately got to their feet and went to the stable area.

Roosevelt turned back to McCoy. "I'm taking the two best trackers in the regiment. Does that satisfy you, Mr. McCoy?"

"It does not," said McCoy. "I'm coming along, too."

Roosevelt shook his head. "You're in command of the regiment in my absence. You're staying here."

"But—"

"That's an order," said Roosevelt firmly.

"Will you at least take along a squad of sharpshooters, Colonel?" persisted McCoy.

"Frank, we're forty miles behind the front, and I'm just going to talk to Pershing, not shoot him."

"We don't even know where the front *is*," said McCoy.

"It's where we're *not*," said Roosevelt grimly. "And that's what I'm going to change."

He left the mess tent without another word.

The first four French villages they passed were deserted, and consisted of nothing but the burned skeletons of houses and shops. The fifth had two buildings still standing—a manor house and a church—and they had been turned into Allied hospitals. Soldiers with missing limbs, soldiers with faces swatched in filthy bandages, soldiers with gaping holes in their bodies lay on cots and floors, shivering in the cold damp air, while an undermanned and harassed medical team did their best to keep them alive.

Roosevelt stopped long enough to determine General Pershing's whereabouts, then walked among the wounded to offer words of encouragement while trying to ignore the unmistakable stench of gangrene and the stinging scent of disinfectant. Finally he remounted his horse and joined his two trackers.

They passed a number of corpses on their way to the front. Most had been plundered of their weapons, and one, lying upon its back, displayed a gruesome, toothless smile.

"Shameful!" muttered Roosevelt as he looked down at the grinning body.

"Why?" asked Runs With Deer.

"It's obvious that the man had gold teeth, and they have been removed."

"It is honorable to take trophies of the enemy," asserted the Indian.

"The Germans have never advanced this far south," said Roosevelt. "This man's teeth were taken by his companions." He shook his head. "Shameful!"

Matupu the Maasai merely shrugged. "Perhaps this is not an honorable war."

"We are fighting for an honorable principle," stated Roosevelt. "That makes it an honorable war."

"Then it is an honorable war being waged by dishonorable men," said Matupu.

"Do the Maasai not take trophies?" asked Runs With Deer.

"We take cows and goats and women," answered Matupu. "We do not plunder the dead." He paused. "We do not take scalps."

"There was a time when *we* did not, either," said Runs With Deer. "We were taught to, by the French."

"And we are in France now," said Matupu with some satisfaction, as if everything now made sense to him.

They dismounted after two more hours and walked their horses for the rest of the day, then spent the night in a bombed-out farmhouse. The next morning they were mounted and riding again, and they came to General Pershing's field headquarters just before noon. There were thousands of soldiers bustling about, couriers bringing in hourly reports from the trenches, weapons and tanks being dispatched, convoys of trucks filled with food and water slowly working their way into supply lines.

Roosevelt was stopped a few yards into the camp by a young lieutenant.

"May I ask your business here, sir?"

"I'm here to see General Pershing," answered Roosevelt.

"Just like that?" said the soldier with a smile.

"Son," said Roosevelt, taking off his hat and leaning over the lieutenant, "take a good look at my face." He paused for a moment. "Now go tell General Pershing that Teddy Roosevelt is here to see him."

The lieutenant's eyes widened. "By God, you *are* Teddy Roosevelt!" he exclaimed. Suddenly he reached his hand out. "May I shake your hand first, Mr. President? I just want to be able to tell my parents I did it."

Roosevelt grinned and took the young man's hand in his own, then waited astride his horse while the lieutenant went off to Pershing's quarters. He gazed around the camp: There were ramshackle buildings and ramshackle soldiers, each of which had seen too much action and too little glory. The men's faces were haggard, their eyes haunted, their bodies stooped with exhaustion. The main paths through the camp had turned to mud, and the constant drizzle brought rust, rot, and disease with an equal lack of cosmic concern.

The lieutenant approached Roosevelt, his feet sinking inches into the mud with each step.

"If you'll follow me, Mr. President, he'll see you immediately."

"Thank you," said Roosevelt.

"Watch yourself, Mr. President," said the lieutenant as Roosevelt dismounted. "I have a feeling he's not happy about meeting with you."

"He'll be a damned sight less happy when I'm through with him," said Roosevelt firmly. He turned to his companions. "See to the needs of the horses."

"Yes, sir," said Runs With Deer. "We'll be waiting for you right here."

"How is the battle going?" Roosevelt asked as he and the lieutenant began walking through the mud toward Pershing's quarters. "My Rough Riders have been practically incommunicado since we arrived."

The lieutenant shrugged. "Who knows? All we hear are rumors. The enemy is retreating, the enemy is advancing, we've killed thousands of them, they've killed thousands of us. Maybe the general will tell you; he certainly hasn't seen fit to tell *us*."

They reached the entrance to Pershing's quarters.

"I'll wait here for you, sir," said the lieutenant.

"You're sure you don't mind?" asked Roosevelt. "You can find some orderly to escort me back if it will be a problem."

"No, sir," said the young man earnestly. "It'll be an honor, Mr. President."

"Well, thank you, son," said Roosevelt. He shook the lieutenant's hand again, then walked through the doorway and found himself facing General John J. Pershing.

"Good afternoon, Jack," said Roosevelt, extending his hand.

Pershing looked at Roosevelt's outstretched hand for a moment, then took it.

"Have a seat, Mr. President," he said, indicating a chair.

"Thank you," said Roosevelt, pulling up a chair as Pershing seated himself behind a desk that was covered with maps.

"I mean no disrespect, Mr. President," said Pershing, "but exactly who gave you permission to leave your troops and come here?"

"No one," answered Roosevelt.

"Then why did you do it?" asked Pershing. "I'm told you were accompanied only by a red Indian and a black savage. That's hardly a safe way to travel in a war zone."

"I came here to find out why you have consistently refused my requests to have my Rough Riders moved to the front."

Pershing lit a cigar and offered one to Roosevelt, who refused it.

"There are proper channels for such a request," said the general at last. "You yourself helped create them."

"And I have been using them for almost two months, to no avail."

Pershing sighed. "I *have* been a little busy conducting this damned war."

"I'm sure you have," said Roosevelt. "And I have assembled a regiment of the finest fighting men to be found in America, which I am placing at your disposal."

"For which I thank you, Mr. President."

"I don't want you to thank me!" snapped Roosevelt. "I want you to unleash me!"

"When the time is right, your Rough Riders will be brought into the conflict," said Pershing.

"When the time is right?" repeated Roosevelt. "Your men are dying like flies! Every village I've passed has become a bombed-out ghost town! You needed us two months ago, Jack!"

"Mr. President, I've got half a million men to maneuver. I'll decide when and where I need your regiment."

"When?" persisted Roosevelt.

"You'll be the first to know."

"That's not good enough!"

"It will have to be."

"You listen to me, Jack Pershing!" said Roosevelt heatedly. "I *made* you a general! I think the very least you owe me is an answer. When will my men be brought into the conflict?"

Pershing stared at him from beneath shaggy black eyebrows for a long moment. "What the hell did you have to come here for, anyway?" he said at last.

"I told you: to get an answer."

"I don't mean to my headquarters," said Pershing. "I mean, what is a fifty-eight-year-old man with a blind eye and a game leg doing in the middle of a war?"

"This is the greatest conflict in history, and it's being fought over principles that every free man holds dear. How could I not take part in it?"

"You could have just stayed home and made speeches and raised funds."

"And you could have retired after Mexico and spent the rest of your life playing golf," Roosevelt shot back. "But you didn't, and I didn't, because neither of us is that kind of man. Damn it, Jack—I've assembled a regiment the likes of which hasn't been seen in almost twenty years, and if you've any sense at all, you'll make use of us. Our horses and our training give us an enormous advantage on this terrain. We can mobilize and strike at the enemy as easily as this fellow Lawrence seems to be doing in the Arabian desert."

Pershing stared at him for a long moment, then sighed deeply.

"I can't do it, Mr. President," said Pershing.

"Why not?" demanded Roosevelt.

"The truth? Because of you, sir."

"What are you talking about?"

"You've made my position damnably awkward," said Pershing bitterly. "You are an authentic American hero, possibly the first since Abraham Lincoln. You are as close to being worshiped as a man can be." He paused. "You're a goddamned icon, Mr. Roosevelt."

"What has *that* got to do with anything?"

"I am under direct orders not to allow you to participate in any action that might result in your death." He glared at Roosevelt across the desk. "*Now* do you understand? If I move you to the front, I'll have to surround you with at least three divisions to make sure nothing happens to you—and I'm in no position to spare that many men."

"Who issued that order, Jack?"

"My commander-in-chief."

"Woodrow Wilson?"

"That's right. And I'd no more disobey him than I would disobey you if you still held that office." He paused, then spoke again more gently. "You're an old man, sir. Not old by your standards, but too damned old to be leading charges against the Germans. You should be home writing your memoirs and giving speeches and rallying the people to our cause, Mr. President."

"I'm not ready to retire to Sagamore Hill and have my face carved on Mount Rushmore yet," said Roosevelt. "There are battles to be fought and a war to be won."

"Not by you, Mr President," answered Pershing. "When the enemy is beaten and on the run, I'll bring your regiment up. The press can go crazy photographing you chasing the few German stragglers back to Berlin. But I cannot and will not disobey a direct order from my commander-in-chief. Until I can guarantee your safety, you'll stay where you are."

"I see," said Roosevelt after a moment's silence. "And what if I relinquish my command? Will you utilize my Rough Riders then?"

Pershing shook his head. "I have no use for a bunch of tennis players and college professors who think they can storm across the trenches on their polo ponies," he said firmly. "The only men you have with battle experience are as old as you are." He paused. "Your regiment might be effective if the Apaches ever leave the reservation, but they are ill-prepared for a modern, mechanized war. I hate to be so blunt, but it's the truth, sir."

"You're making a huge mistake, Jack."

"You're the one who made the mistake, sir, by coming here. It's my job to see that you don't die because of it."

"Damn it, Jack, we could make a difference!"

Pershing paused and stared, not without sympathy, at Roosevelt. "War has changed, Mr. President," he said at last. "No one regiment can make a difference any longer. It's been a long time since Achilles fought Hector outside the walls of Troy."

An orderly entered with a dispatch, and Pershing immediately read and initialed it.

"I don't mean to rush you, sir," he said, getting to his feet, "but I have an urgent meeting to attend."

Roosevelt stood up. "I'm sorry to have bothered you, General."

"I'm still Jack to you, Mr. President," said Pershing. "And it's as your friend Jack that I want to give you one final word of advice."

"Yes?"

"Please, for your own sake and the sake of your men, don't do anything rash."

"Why would I do something rash?" asked Roosevelt innocently.

"Because you wouldn't be Teddy Roosevelt if the thought of ignoring your orders hadn't already crossed your mind," said Pershing.

Roosevelt fought back a grin, shook Pershing's hand, and left without saying another word. The young lieutenant was just outside the door, and escorted him back to where Runs with Deer and Matupu were waiting with the horses.

"Bad news?" asked Runs With Deer as he studied Roosevelt's face.

"No worse than I had expected."

"Where do we go now?" asked the Indian.

"Back to camp," said Roosevelt firmly. "There's a war to be won, and no college professor from New Jersey is going to keep me from helping to win it!"

"Well, that's the story," said Roosevelt to his assembled officers after he had laid out the situation to them in the large tent he had reserved for strategy sessions. "Even if I resign my commission and return to

America, there is no way that General Pershing will allow you to see any action."

"I knew Black Jack Pershing when he was just a captain," growled Buck O'Neill, one of the original Rough Riders. "Just who the hell does he think he is?"

"He's the supreme commander of the American forces," answered Roosevelt wryly.

"What are we going to do, sir?" asked McCoy. "Surely you don't plan just to sit back here and then let Pershing move us up when all the fighting's done with?"

"No, I don't," said Roosevelt.

"Let's hear what you got to say, Teddy," said O'Neill.

"The issues at stake in this war haven't changed since I went to see the general," answered Roosevelt. "I plan to harass and harry the enemy to the best of our ability. If need be we will live off the land while utilizing our superior mobility in a number of tactical strikes, and we will do our valiant best to bring this conflict to a successful conclusion."

He paused and looked around at his officers. "I realize that in doing this I am violating my orders, but there are greater principles at stake here. I am flattered that the president thinks I am indispensable to the American public, but our nation is based on the principle that no one man deserves any rights or privileges not offered to all men." He took a deep breath and cleared his throat. "However, since I *am* contravening a direct order, I believe that not only each one of you, but every one of the men as well, should be given the opportunity to withdraw from the Rough Riders. I will force no man to ride against his conscience and his beliefs. I would like you to go out now and put the question to the men; I will wait here for your answer."

To nobody's great surprise, the regiment voted unanimously to ride to glory with Teddy Roosevelt.

3 August, 1917
My Dearest Edith:
   As strange as this may seem to you (and it seems surpassingly strange to me), I will soon be a fugitive from justice, opposed not only by the German army but quite possibly by the U.S. military as well.
   My Rough Riders have embarked upon a bold adventure, contrary to both the wishes and the direct orders of the president of the United States. When I think back to the day he finally approved my request to reassemble the regiment, I cringe with chagrin at my innocence and naïveté; he sent us here only so that I would not have access to the press and he would no longer have to listen to my demands. Far from being

permitted to play a leading role in this noblest of battles, my men have been held far behind the front, and Jack Pershing was under orders from Wilson himself not to allow any harm to come to us.

When I learned of this, I put a proposition to my men, and I am extremely proud of their response. To a one, they voted to break camp and ride to the front so as to strike at the heart of the German military machine. By doing so, I am disobeying the orders of my commander-in-chief, and because of this somewhat peculiar situation, I doubt that I shall be able to send too many more letters to you until I have helped to end this war. At that time, I shall turn myself over to Pershing, or whoever is in charge, and argue my case before whatever tribunal is deemed proper.

However, before that moment occurs, we shall finally see action, bearing the glorious banner of the Stars and Stripes. My men are a finely-tuned fighting machine, and I daresay that they will give a splendid account of themselves before the conflict is over. We have not made contact with the enemy yet, nor can I guess where we shall finally meet, but we are primed and eager for our first taste of battle. Our spirit is high, and many of the old-timers spend their hours singing the old battle songs from Cuba. We are all looking forward to a bully battle, and we plan to teach the Hun a lesson he won't soon forget.

Give my love to the children, and when you write to Kermit and Quentin, tell them that their father has every intention of reaching Berlin before they do!

All my love,
Theodore

Roosevelt, who had been busily writing an article on ornithology, looked up from his desk as McCoy entered his tent.

"Well?"

"We think we've found what we've been looking for, Mr. President," said McCoy.

"Excellent!" said Roosevelt, carefully closing his notebook. "Tell me about it."

McCoy spread a map out on the desk.

"Well, the front lines, as you know, are *here*, about fifteen miles to the north of us. The Germans are entrenched *here*, and we haven't been able to move them for almost three weeks." McCoy paused. "The word I get from my old outfit is that the Americans are planning a major push on the German left, right about *here*."

"When?" demanded Roosevelt.

"At sunrise tomorrow morning."

"Bully!" said Roosevelt. He studied the map for a moment, then looked up. "Where is Jack Pershing?"

"Almost ten miles west and eight miles north of us," answered McCoy. "He's dug in, and from what I hear, he came under pretty heavy mortar fire today. He'll have his hands full without worrying about where an extra regiment of American troops came from."

"Better and better," said Roosevelt. "We not only get to fight, but we may even pull Jack's chestnuts out of the fire." He turned his attention back to the map. "All right," he said, "the Americans will advance along this line. What would you say will be their major obstacle?"

"You mean besides the mud and the Germans and the mustard gas?" asked McCoy wryly.

"You know what I mean, Frank."

"Well," said McCoy, "there's a small rise here—I'd hardly call it a hill, certainly not like the one we took in Cuba—but it's manned by four machine guns, and it gives the Germans an excellent view of the territory the Americans have got to cross."

"Then that's our objective," said Roosevelt decisively. "If we can capture that hill and knock out the machine guns, we'll have made a positive contribution to the battle that even Woodrow Wilson will be forced to acknowledge." The famed Roosevelt grin spread across his face. "We'll show him that the dodo may be dead, but the Rough Riders are very much alive." He paused. "Gather the men, Frank. I want to speak to them before we leave."

McCoy did as he was told, and Roosevelt emerged from his tent some ten minutes later to address the assembled Rough Riders.

"Gentlemen," he said, "tomorrow morning we will meet the enemy on the battlefield."

A cheer arose from the ranks.

"It has been suggested that modern warfare deals only in masses and logistics, that there is no room left for heroism, that the only glory remaining to men of action is upon the sporting fields. I tell you that this is a lie. *We matter!* Honor and courage are not outmoded virtues, but are the very ideals that make us great as individuals and as a nation. Tomorrow we will prove it in terms that our detractors and our enemies will both understand." He paused, then saluted them. "Saddle up—and may God be with us!"

They reached the outskirts of the battlefield, moving silently with hooves and harnesses muffled, just before sunrise. Even McCoy, who had seen action in Mexico, was unprepared for the sight that awaited them.

The mud was littered with corpses as far as the eye could see in the dim light of the false dawn. The odor of death and decay permeated the moist, cold morning air. Thousands of bodies lay there in the pouring rain, many of them grotesquely swollen. Here and there they had virtually exploded, either when punctured by bullets or when the walls of the abdominal cavities collapsed. Attempts had been made during the previous month to drag them back off the battlefield, but there was simply no place left to put them. There was almost total silence as the men in both trenches began preparing for another day of bloodletting.

Roosevelt reined his horse to a halt and surveyed the carnage. Still more corpses were hung up on barbed wire, and more than a handful of bodies attached to the wire still moved feebly. The rain pelted down, turning the plain between the enemy trenches into a brown, gooey slop.

"My God, Frank!" murmured Roosevelt.

"It's pretty awful," agreed McCoy.

"This is not what civilized men do to each other," said Roosevelt, stunned by the sight before his eyes. "This isn't war, Frank—it's butchery!"

"It's what war has become."

"How long have these two lines been facing each other?"

"More than a month, sir."

Roosevelt stared, transfixed, at the sea of mud.

"A month to cross a quarter mile of *this*?"

"That's correct, sir."

"How many lives have been lost trying to cross this strip of land?"

McCoy shrugged. "I don't know. Maybe eighty thousand, maybe a little more."

Roosevelt shook his head. "Why, in God's name? Who cares about it? What purpose does it serve?"

McCoy had no answer, and the two men sat in silence for another moment, surveying the battlefield.

"This is madness!" said Roosevelt at last. "Why doesn't Pershing simply march around it?"

"That's a question for a general to answer, Mr. President," said McCoy. "Me, I'm just a captain."

"We can't continue to lose American boys for *this*!" said Roosevelt furiously. "Where is that machine-gun encampment, Frank?"

McCoy pointed to a small rise about three hundred yards distant.

"And the main German lines?"

"Their first row of trenches are in line with the hill."

"Have we tried to take the hill before?"

"I can't imagine that we haven't, sir," said McCoy. "As long as they control it, they'll mow our men down like sitting ducks in a shooting gallery." He paused. "The problem is the mud. The average infantryman can't reach the hill in less than two minutes, probably closer to three—and until you've seen them in action, you can't believe the damage these guns can do in that amount of time."

"So as long as the hill remains in German hands, this is a war of attrition."

McCoy sighed. "It's been a war of attrition for three years, sir."

Roosevelt sat and stared at the hill for another few minutes, then turned back to McCoy.

"What are our chances, Frank?"

McCoy shrugged. "If it was dry, I'd say we had a chance to take them out—"

"But it's not."

"No, it's not," echoed McCoy.

"Can we do it?"

"I don't know, sir. Certainly not without heavy casualties."

"How heavy?"

"*Very* heavy."

"I need a number," said Roosevelt.

McCoy looked him in the eye. "Ninety percent—if we're lucky."

Roosevelt stared at the hill again. "They predicted fifty percent casualties at San Juan Hill," he said. "We had to charge up a much steeper slope in the face of enemy machine-gun fire. Nobody thought we had a chance—but I did it, Frank, and I did it alone. I charged up that hill and knocked out the machine-gun nest myself, and then the rest of my men followed me."

"The circumstances were different then, Mr. President," said McCoy. "The terrain offered cover and solid footing, and you were facing Cuban peasants who had been conscripted into service, not battle-hardened professional German soldiers."

"I know, I know," said Roosevelt. "But if we knock those machine guns out, how many American lives can we save today?"

"I don't know," admitted McCoy. "Maybe ten thousand, maybe none. It's possible that the Germans are dug in so securely that they can beat back any American charge even without the use of those machine guns."

"But at least it would prolong some American lives," persisted Roosevelt.

"By a couple of minutes."

"It would give them a *chance* to reach the German bunkers."

"I don't know."

"More of a chance than if they had to face machine-gun fire from the hill."

"What do you want me to say, Mr. President?" asked McCoy. "That if we throw away our lives charging the hill that we'll have done something glorious and affected the outcome of the battle? I just don't know!"

"We came here to help win a war, Frank. Before I send my men into battle, I have to know that it will make a difference."

"I can't give you any guarantees, sir. We came to fight a war, all right. But look around you, Mr. President—*this* isn't the war we came to fight. They've changed the rules on us."

"There are hundreds of thousands of American boys in the trenches who didn't come to fight this kind of war," answered Roosevelt. "In less than an hour, most of them are going to charge across the sea of mud into a barrage of machine-gun fire. If we can't shorten the war, then perhaps we can at least lengthen their lives."

"At the cost of our own."

"We are idealists and adventurers, Frank—perhaps the last this world will ever see. We knew what we were coming here to do." He paused. "Those boys are here because of speeches and decisions that politicians have made, myself included. Left to their own devices, they'd go home to be with their families. Left to ours, we'd find another cause to fight for."

"This isn't a cause, Mr. President," said McCoy. "It's a slaughter."

"Then maybe this is where men who want to prevent further slaughter belong," said Roosevelt. He looked up at the sky. "They'll be mobilizing in another half hour, Frank."

"I know, Mr. President."

"If we leave now, if we don't try to take that hill, then Wilson and Pershing were right and I was wrong. The time for heroes is past, and I *am* an anachronism who should be sitting at home in a rocking chair, writing memoirs and exhorting younger men to go to war." He paused, staring at the hill once more. "If we don't do what's required of us this day, we are agreeing with them that we don't matter, that men of courage and ideals can't make a difference. If that's true, there's no sense waiting for a more equitable battle, Frank—we might as well ride south and catch the first boat home."

"That's your decision, Mr. President?" asked McCoy.

"Was there really ever any other option?" replied Roosevelt wryly.

"No, sir," said McCoy. "Not for men like us."

"Thank you for your support, Frank," said Roosevelt, reaching out and laying a heavy hand on McCoy's shoulder. "Prepare the men."

"Yes, sir," said McCoy, saluting and riding back to the main body of the Rough Riders.

"Madness!" muttered Roosevelt, looking out at the bloated corpses. "Utter madness!"

McCoy returned a moment later.

"The men are awaiting your signal, sir," he said.

"Tell them to follow me," said Roosevelt.

"Sir . . ." said McCoy.

"Yes?"

"We would prefer you not lead the charge. The first ranks will face the heaviest bombardment, not only from the hill but also from the cannons behind the bunkers."

"I can't ask my men to do what I myself won't do," said Roosevelt.

"You are too valuable to lose, sir. We plan to attack in three waves. You belong at the back of the third wave, Mr. President."

Roosevelt shook his head. "There's nothing up ahead except bullets, Hank, and I've faced bullets before—in the Dakota Bad Lands, in Cuba, in Milwaukee. But if I hang back, if I send my men to do a job I was afraid to do, then I've have to face myself—and as any Democrat will tell you, I'm a lot tougher than any bullet ever made."

"You won't reconsider?" asked McCoy.

"Would you have left your unit and joined the Rough Riders if you thought I might?" asked Roosevelt with a smile.

"No, sir," admitted McCoy. "No, sir, I probably wouldn't have."

Roosevelt shook his hand. "You're a good man, Frank."

"Thank you, Mr. President."

"Are the men ready?"

"Yes, sir."

"Then," said Roosevelt, turning his horse toward the small rise, "let's do what must be done."

He pulled his rifle out, unlatched the safety catch, and dug his heels into his horse's sides.

Suddenly he was surrounded by the first wave of his own men, all screaming their various war cries in the face of the enemy.

For just a moment there was no response. Then the machine guns began their sweeping fire across the muddy plain. Buck O'Neill was the first to fall, his body riddled with bullets. An instant later Runs With Deer screamed in agony as his arm was blown away. Horses had their legs shot from under them, men were blown out of their saddles, limbs flew crazily through the wet morning air, and still the charge continued.

Roosevelt had crossed half the distance when Matupu fell directly in front of him, his head smashed to a pulp. He heard McCoy groan as half a dozen bullets thudded home in his chest, but looked neither right nor left as his horse leaped over the fallen Maasai's bloody body.

Bullets and cannonballs flew to the right and left of him, in front and behind, and yet miraculously he was unscathed as he reached the final hundred yards. He dared a quick glance around and saw that he was the sole survivor from the first wave, then heard the screams of the second wave as the machine guns turned on them.

Now he was seventy yards away, now fifty. He yelled a challenge to the Germans, and as he looked into the blinking eye of a machine gun, for one brief, final, glorious instant it was San Juan Hill all over again.

18 September 1917
Dispatch from General John J. Pershing to Commander-in-Chief, President Woodrow Wilson

Sir:
I regret to inform you that Theodore Roosevelt died last Tuesday of wounds received in battle. He had disobeyed his orders, and led his men in a futile charge against an entrenched German position. His entire regiment, the so-called Rough Riders, was lost. His death was almost certainly instantaneous, although it was two days before his body could be retrieved from the battlefield.

I shall keep the news of Mr. Roosevelt's death from the press until receiving instructions from you. It is true that he was an anachronism, that he belonged more to the nineteenth century than the twentieth, and yet it is entirely possible that he was the last authentic hero our country shall ever produce. The charge he led was ill-conceived and foolhardy in the extreme, nor did it diminish the length of the conflict by a single day, yet I cannot help but believe that if I had fifty thousand men with his courage and spirit, I could bring this war to a swift and satisfactory conclusion by the end of the year.

That Theodore Roosevelt died the death of a fool is beyond question, but I am certain in my heart that with his dying breath he felt he was dying the death of a hero. I await your instructions, and will release whatever version of his death you choose upon hearing from you.

—General John J. Pershing

22 September 1917
Dispatch from President Woodrow Wilson to General John J. Pershing, Commander of American Forces in Europe.

John:
That man continues to harass me from the grave.

Still, we have had more than enough fools in our history. Therefore, he died a hero.

Just between you and me, the time for heroes is past. I hope with all my heart that he was our last.

—Woodrow Wilson

And he was.

VOLUME 4

ALTERNATE AMERICAS

CONTENTS

INTRODUCTION   241
Gregory Benford
REPORT OF THE SPECIAL COMMITTEE   243
Harry Turtledove
INK FROM THE NEW MOON   248
A. A. Attanasio
VINLAND THE DREAM   261
Kim Stanley Robinson
IF THERE BE CAUSE   273
Sheila Finch
ISABELLA OF CASTILE ANSWERS
     HER MAIL   295
James Morrow
LET TIME SHAPE   308
George Zebrowski
RED ALERT   319
Jerry Oltion
SUCH A DEAL   330
Esther M. Friesner
LOOKING FOR THE FOUNTAIN   347
Robert Silverberg
THE ROUND-EYED BARBARIANS   368
L. Sprague de Camp
DESTINATION: INDIES   381
Brad Linaweaver

SHIP FULL OF JEWS   393
Barry Malzberg
THE KARAMAZOV CAPER   403
Gordon Eklund
THE SLEEPING SERPENT   419
Pamela Sargent

INTRODUCTION

Columbus was certainly not the first European to "discover" the New World as a reality. But he did discover—perhaps invent is a better word—the New World as an energetic metaphor.

Scholars have pretty well decided that the famous Leif Ericson landed as far south as Cape Cod around A.D. 1003. His brother Thorvald followed him, to the place they called Vinland, about 1007. (Naming the land for vines suggests they got fairly far south.) There is some evidence of later expeditions from Iceland and even settlements that struggled along for generations on the coast of Canada. They finally failed, probably from a chilling dip in the already harsh climate.

There have been dozens of other suggested sites. Stone ruins in New Hampshire that might be from the Bronze Age. Coins from Carthage turning up on mid-Atlantic islands. Phoenician inscriptions on rocks in Pennsylvania. Roman coins in Venezuela. Iron nails buried in Virginia. Legends like those about Quetzalcoatl, which may have sprung from a visit by Europeans in the century before Cortez.

All quite possible indeed. The New World was a huge place, consistently underestimated by map makers for centuries after 1492, and it was hard to make any impact on such vastness. Clearly the earlier adventurers didn't "take"—Europe did not rush to follow up these brave voyages.

Why not? Maybe the word didn't get to the right people, because the explorers were marginal types themselves, as far as most of Europe was concerned. Leif Ericson was a legend in Iceland, but nobody had heard of him in Spain. Then, too, the Little Ice Age made much of North America a tough place to start out for several centuries after the Icelanders ventured forth.

More generally historians mutter about the *Zeitgeist*, the spirit of the times. Europe wasn't prosperous and expansive enough, before 1492, to seize its opportunities. Perhaps that contributed to the curious inertia that earlier discoveries met.

Columbus was the right man at the right time. He was quite wrong about the size of the earth, but by determination and sailing skill he discovered what nobody anticipated—a paradigm of why we do research today. Others quickly followed up his epic voyages, wealth poured forth, vistas opened. Quite quickly, truly global trade began. Thus the Spanish hunger for gold, for that was just about all they could trade for the exotic treats of the Orient, such as silks and spices.

Columbus died moderately well off, though not rich. He did not know how great a change he had brought. Much recent talk has stressed the great damage done to native cultures by the Europeans, but it seems quite plausible that such destruction was inevitable, no matter how the Europeans behaved. (And indeed, many of them were quite awful.) Simple, low-level technologies crumble before advanced ones. Cultures built on stratification and order dissolve. Ideas worm their way in—and some native practices, such as human sacrifice, were forcefully ended.

That opening to fresh perspectives has brought the most far-reaching change possible. The Europeans exploded onto the world stage, and five hundred years later their curious scientific-technological culture, with its great stress on individual rights, stands astride all others.

But what if it had played a bit differently? History looks so inevitable in the hands of most historians. Few convey the fragile tissue of events, the way the past might have been altered. Indeed, the past keeps changing as we look at it, as Kim Stanley Robinson suggests in his story. Could the whole Vinland idea turn out to be shaky? It seems rock solid today. But imagine the changes in our attitudes if it proved wrong.

We have collected in this fourth volume of the *What Might Have Been* series a set of commissioned stories that look at ways the discovery and opening up of the New World might have been different. There are novel ideas here, both amusing and sobering, resulting in worlds that seem distinctly alien. Some are better, some worse. Settings range from our present, back to times shortly after the assumed changes have occurred. In sum they convey some sense of the many paths that grand human adventure might have followed.

—GREGORY BENFORD
3 DECEMBER 1991

REPORT OF THE SPECIAL COMMITTEE ON THE QUALITY OF LIFE

Harry Turtledove

30 November 1491

To: Their Hispanic Majesties Fernando II and Isabella
From: The Special Committee on the Quality of Life
Re: The environmental impact upon Spain of the proposed
        expedition of the Genoese navigator Cristóbal Colón,
        styled in his native Italian Cristoforo Colombo

The commission of learned men and mariners, established by Your Majesties under the chairmanship of Fr. Hernando de Talavera, during the period 1486–90 studied exhaustively the proposals set forth by the Genoese captain Colón and rejected them as being extravagant and impractical. In the present year a second commission, headed by the Grand Cardinal, Pedro González de Mendoza, has also seen fit to decline the services of Colón. The present Special Committee on the Quality of Life finds itself in complete accord with the actions of the previous two bodies of inquiry. It is our unanimous conclusion that the rash scheme advocated by this visionary would, if implemented, do serious damage to the finances and ecology of Spain; that this damage, if permitted, would set a precedent for future, more serious outrages of our environment; and, most important, that the proposed voyage would expose any sailors engaged thereon to unacceptable risk of permanent bodily illness and injury and even death.

Certain people may perhaps suggest that the sea program of this kingdom is essential to its future growth. To this uninformed view we may only offer our wholehearted opposition. The Atlantic sea program demands extremely high expenses and hazards in both men and matériel, for gains at best speculative but more likely nonexistent. Now more than ever, the kingdom's resources need to be concentrated at home, to bring the long war against the heathen Moors of Granada to a successful conclusion. At such a crucial time, we should waste no money on a program whose returns, if any, will not be manifest for some decades.

If funds must be committed to the sea program, they should be earmarked for national defense goals in the Mediterranean Sea, not spent on wild-eyed jaunts into the trackless and turbulent Atlantic. Until and unless we succeed in overcoming the corsair gap now existing, our southern coast will remain vulnerable to attacks from Algeria and Morocco even after the Moors of Granada are brought under our control. Moreover, if we fail to move against the heathen states of Africa, they shall surely fall under the aegis of the expansionist Ottoman sultanate, with potential profound consequences to the balance of power in the area, as strong infidel forces will then be enabled to strike at our routes to our Italian possessions.

It may be argued that shipbuilding will aid the economy of those areas near ports. This view is superficial and shortsighted. True, jobs may be provided for lumberjacks, carpenters, sailmakers, etc., but at what cost to the world in which they live? Barring reforestation projects, for which funding does not appear to be forthcoming, any extensive shipbuilding venture will inevitably result in the denuding of significant areas of the kingdom and the deformation of the long-established ecological patterns of the wildlife therein. In any case it is questionable whether shipbuilding represents the ideal utilization of our limited timber resources. The quantity of wood required to construct an oceangoing vessel could better be employed to provide low-income housing for whole villages of peasants, or to furnish even larger numbers of underprivileged citizens with firewood sufficient for an entire fiscal year.

Further, especially for long voyages such as that urged by Colón, ships must carry extensive stores (this point will again be alluded to later in the report). The question must be posed as to whether our agricultural industry is adequate even to care for the current needs of the population of Spain itself. Surely an affirmative answer to this question, such as cannot with assurance be given at present, is necessary before expansion can be contemplated and resources diverted for it. We must put a halt to these environmentally disadvantageous programs before they become so ingrained in our lifestyle that their removal presents difficulty.

There is yet another factor to be considered, one closely related to that referred to in the previous sentence. Even if Colón precisely fulfills his expectations, what will the consequences of this "success" be for

Spain? Many substances about which we know little, and which may well prove hazardous, will begin to enter the kingdom in large quantities, and control over their sale and distribution will be difficult to achieve. We run a substantial risk of seeing the nation filled with addicts to toxins now unknown. Nor is it possible to discount the dangers of ideological contamination, which is as much to be feared as is the physical. It is doubtful whether the inhabitants of the distant lands the Genoan plans to visit share our religious and cultural benefits. Yet it is also probable that certain of their number may settle on our soil and attempt to disseminate their inadequate but perhaps seductive doctrines among our populace. As we are now on the point of expelling the Jews from our state and have nearly overcome the Muslim Moors, why should we hazard the homogeneity we have at last achieved after almost eight centuries of sustained effort?

The sudden influx of new goods will also disrupt our traditional economic organization. There can be no doubt that there will be an increase in the monetary supply because of the profit made by reselling Eastern goods throughout Europe, but can a corresponding increase in the volume of goods and services be predicted? If the answer to this question is in the negative, as all current economic indicators would imply, then the "success" of Colón would seem to bring with it a concomitant inflationary pressure that would tend to eat into the profits derived from that success and would make life more difficult and expensive for the average Spaniard. Also, any substantial increase in the sea program would force the diversion of labor from its traditional concern to maritime activities. Such a shift could not help but further disjoint our economy, and cannot be anticipated with anything but trepidation. The dislocation could even be so severe as to cause emigration to the Eastern lands, which would of course entail a draining of the best of the kingdom's populace from its shores.

Finally, if the government of Spain is to approve, fund, and provide manpower for the Colón expedition, it must have some assurance that it is not dangerously imperiling the health and future well-being of the members of that expedition. The dangers of the seaman's trade are notorious and he performs his labors on a nutritionally inadequate diet of what can only be described as "junk food": hardtack, salt meat, and dried peas, with perhaps a bit of cheese. This regimen is manifestly unhealthful, and Colón and the men under his charge would be unable to supplement it except through fishing. They would not enjoy the advantage, as do sailors of the Mediterranean Sea and also the Portuguese in their journeys down the coast of Africa, of replenishing their supplies at relatively brief intervals, but would be compelled to make do once having departed the Canary Islands. Nor is the situation in regard to potables much better, these being restricted to casked water and wine. The probability is extremely high that at least some of the former will go bad; the latter faces not only this danger, but, if drunk to excess, has the potential of severely compromising the efficiency of ship's operations and thereby reducing an already low margin of safety. Ships are designed so that only the captain enjoys the luxury of a cabin with a bunk, and even this private space is scarcely more than might be found in a closet ashore. Sailors and underofficers are compelled to sleep wherever they are able to find room, in the same clothing they have worn during the day. Thus the life-support systems of any Atlantic sea expeditionary force at the current level of technology must be deemed inadequate.

Navigational instruments are also crude in the extreme. Quadrant and astrolabe are so cumbersome, and so likely to be grossly impacted by ship's motion, as to be little more useful than dead reckoning in the determination of latitude; dead reckoning alone serves in estimating longitude. For a voyage of the length anticipated by Colón, these factors, in combination with the stormy nature of the Atlantic and the likelihood of meeting unanticipated hazards with no support facilities upon which to fall back, give the Genoan's proposals a degree of risk so high that no merciful sovereign could in good conscience allow his subjects to endanger themselves in the pursuit thereof.

Therefore, it is the determination of the Special Committee on the Quality of Life, appointed by Your Hispanic Majesties as per the environmental protection regulations of the realm, that the proposals of Colón do in the several ways outlined above comprise a clear and present danger to the quality and security of life within the kingdom, and that they should for that reason be rejected once more. Respectfully in triplicate submitted by

Jaime Nosénada
Chairman of the Special Committee on the Quality of Life

INK FROM THE
NEW MOON

A. A. Attanasio

Here, at the farthest extreme of my journey, in the islands along the eastern shores of the Sandalwood Territories, with all of heaven and earth separating us—here at long last I have found enough strength to pen these words to you. Months of writing official reports, of recording endless observations of bamboo drill-derricks and cobblestone canals irrigating horizons of quilted fields, of interviewing sooty laborers in industrial barns and refineries roaring with steam engines and dazzling caldrons of molten metal, of scrutinizing prisoners toiling in salt-canyons, of listening to schoolchildren sing hymns in classrooms on hill-crowned woods and in cities agleam with gold-spired pavilions and towers of lacquered wood—all these tedious annotations had quite drained me of the sort of words one writes to one's wife; but, at last, I feel again the place where the world is breathing inside me.

Forgive my long silence, Heart Wing. I would have written sooner had not my journey across the Sandalwood Territories of the Dawn been an experience for me blacker than ink can show. Being so far from the homeland, so far from you, has dulled the heat of my life. Darkness occupies me. Yet this unremitting gloom brings with it a peculiar knowledge and wisdom all its own—the treasure that the snake guards—the so-called poison cure. Such is the blood's surprise, my precious one, that even in the serpent's grip of dire sorrow, I should find a clarity greater than any since my failures took me from you.

You, of course, will only remember me as you left me—a sour little man for whom being Third Assistant Secretarial Scribe at the Imperial Library was more punishment than privilege; the husband whittled away by shame and envy, whom you dutifully bid farewell from our farm's moon gate on the avenue of chestnuts in the cloud-shadowed bowl of the grasslands. All so long ago, it seems. What a humiliation that the only way I could support you was to leave you. And for such an ignoble task—to examine the social structure of rebel provinces that have repudiated our finest traditions. I was so embittered that for most of my journey I referred to the region as the Sandalwood Territories of the Dawn, as if their secession from the Kingdom had happened only in their minds, two hundred years of independence from us an illusion before the forty-five centuries of our written history. Even their name for themselves seemed sheer arrogance: the Unified Sandalwood Autocracies. As if there could be any true autocracy but the Emperor's. Still, I had been selected to regard them as if they were genuine, and I had to humble myself or face the ignominy of losing even this menial job.

I never said any of this to you then. I could barely admit it to myself. But I need to say it clearly now—all of it, the obvious and the obscure—to make sense of my life and yours. Yes, I do admit, I was ashamed, most especially in your eyes. Only you, Heart Wing, know me for who I truly am—a storyteller hooked on the bridebait of words, writing by the lamp of lightning. Yet my books, those poor, defenseless books written in the lyrical style of a far-gone time!—well, as you know too well, there was no livelihood for us on those printed pages. My only success as a writer was that my stories won you for me. After our blunderful attempt to farm in the Western Provinces, to live the lives of field-and-stream poet-recluses, which defiance of destiny and station cost us your health and the life of our one child, all my pride indeed soured to cynicism and self-pity. I felt obliged to accept the Imperial post because there seemed no other recourse.

From that day eighteen moons ago until now, the shadow of night has covered me. I was not there to console you in your grief when our second child fell from your womb before he was strong enough to carry his own breath. By then the big ship had already taken me to the Isles of the Palm Grove Vow in the middle of the World Sea. There I sat surrounded by tedious tomes of Imperial chronicles about the Sandalwood Territories, while you suffered alone.

Like you I never had a taste for the dry magisterial prose of diplomacy and the bitter punctuations of war that is history. What did it matter to me that five centuries ago, during the beginning of our modern era in the Sung Dynasty, the Buddhists, persecuted for adhering to a faith of foreign origin, set sail from the Middle Kingdom and, instead of being devoured by seven hundred dragons or plunging into the Maelstrom of the Great Inane, crossed nine thousand *li* of ocean and discovered a chain of sparsely populated tropical islands? Of what consequence was it to me that these islands, rich in palm, hardwoods, and the fragrant sandalwood beloved of the furniture makers, soon attracted merchants and the Emperor's soldiers? And that, once again, the Buddhists felt compelled to flee, swearing their famous Palm Grove Vow to sail east until they either faced death together or found a land of their own? And that after crossing another seven thousand *li* of ocean they arrived at the vast Land of Dawn, from whose easternmost extreme I am writing to you?

Surely you are pursing your lips now with impatience, wondering why I burden you with so much bothersome history, you, a musician's daughter, who always preferred the beauty of song to the tedium of facts. But stay with me yet, Heart Wing. My discovery, the hard-won clarity gained through my poison cure, will mean less to you without some sharing of what I have learned of this land's history.

We know from our school days that the merchants eventually followed the Buddhists to the Land of Dawn, where the gentle monks had already converted many of the aboriginal tribes. Typical of the Buddhists, they did not war with the merchants but retreated farther east, spreading their doctrine among the tribes and gradually opening the frontier to other settlers. Over time, as the Imperialists established cities and trade routes, the monks began preaching the foolishness of obeisance to a Kingdom far across the World Sea. "Here and now!" the monks chanted, the land of our ancestors being too far away and too entrenched in the veil of illusion to be taken seriously anymore. Though the Buddhists themselves never raised a weapon against the Emperor, the merchants and farmers eagerly fought for them, revolting against Imperial taxation. And out of the Sandalwood Territories of the Dawn, the settlers founded their own country: the Unified Sandalwood Autocracies.

There are numerous kingdoms here in the USA, each governed by an autocrat elected by the landowners of that kingdom. These separate kingdoms in turn are loosely governed by an overlord whom the autocrats and the landowners elect from among themselves to serve for an interval of no more than fifty moons. It is an alien system that the denizens here call Power of the People, and it is fraught with strife, as the conservative Confucians, liberal Buddhists, and radical Taoist-aboriginals continually struggle for dominance. Here, the Mandate of Heaven is not so much granted celestially as taken by wiles, wealth, or force, grasped and clawed for.

I will not trouble you with this nation's paradoxical politics: its abhorrence of monarchs, yet its glorification of leaders; its insistence on separation of government and religion, yet its reliance on oaths, prayers, and moralizing; its passionate patriotism, yet fervent espousal of individual endeavor. There are no slaves here as at home, and so there is no dignity for the upper classes, nor even for the lower classes, for all are slaves to money. The commonest street sweeper can invest his meager earnings to form his own road-maintenance company and after years of slavery to his enterprise become as wealthy as nobility. And, likewise, the rich can squander their resources and, without the protection of servants or class privilege, become street beggars. *Amitabha!* This land has lost entirely the sequence of divine order that regulates our serene sovereignty. And though there are those who profit by this increase of social and economic mobility, it is by and large a country mad with, and subverted by, its own countless ambitions. In many ways it is, I think, the Middle Kingdom turned upside down.

The rocky west coast, rife with numerous large cities, is the industrial spine of this nation, as the east coast is in our land. On the coast, as in our kingdom, refineries, paper mills, textile factories, and shipbuilding yards abound. Inland are the lush agricultural valleys—and then the mountains and beyond them the desert—just as in our country. Where to the north in our homeland the Great Wall marches across the mountains for over four thousand *li*, shutting out the Mongol hoards, here an equally immense wall crosses the desert to the south, fending off ferocious tribes of Aztecatl.

Heart Wing, there is even a village on the eastern prairie, beyond the mountains and the red sandstone arches of the desert, that looks very much like the village on the Yellow River where we had our ruinous farm. There, in a bee-filled orchard just like the cherry grove where we buried our daughter, my memory fetched back to when I held her bird-light body in my arms for the last time. I wept. I wanted to write you then, but there were irrigation networks to catalog and, on the horizons of amber wheat and millet, highways to map hundreds of *li* long, where land boats fly faster than horses, their colorful sails fat with wind.

Beyond the plains lies the Evil East, which is what the Dawn-Settlers call their frontier, because said hinterland is dense with ancient forests no ax has ever touched. Dawn legends claim that the hungry souls of the unhappy dead wander those dense woods. Also, tribes of hostile aboriginals who have fled the settled autocracies of the west shun the Doctrine of the Buddha and the Ethics of Confucius and reign there, as anarchic and wild as any Taoist could imagine.

When our delegation leader sought volunteers to continue the survey into that wilderness, I was among those who offered to go. I'm sorry, Heart Wing, that my love for you was not enough to overcome my shame at the failures that led to our child's death and that took me from you. Wild in my grief, I sought likeness in that primeval forest. I had hoped it would kill me and end my suffering.

It did not. I had somehow imagined or hoped that there might well be ghosts in the Evil East, or at least cannibalistic savages to whom I would be prey, but there were neither. So I survived despite myself, saddened to think that all our chances bleed from us, like wounds that never heal.

The vast expanse of forest was poignantly beautiful even in its darkest vales and fog-hung fens, haunted only with the natural dangers of serpents, bears, and wolves. As for the tribes, when they realized that we had come merely to observe and not to cut their trees or encroach on their land, they greeted us cordially enough, for barbarians. For their hospitality we traded them toys—bamboo dragonflies, kites, and firecrackers. I knew a simple joy with them, forgetting briefly the handful of chances that had already bled from me with my hope of fading from this world.

On the east coast are Buddhist missions and trading posts overlooking the Storm Sea. By the time we emerged from the wildwoods, a message for me from the west had already arrived at one of the posts by the river routes that the fur traders use. I recognized your father's calligraphy and knew before I read it—that you had left us to join the ancestors.

When the news came, I tried to throw myself from the monastery wall into the sea, but my companions stopped me. I could not hear beyond my heart. We who had once lived as one doubled being had become mysteries again to each other. I shall know no greater enigma.

For days I despaired. My failures had lost all my cherished chances, as a writer and a farmer, as a father and, now, as your mate. With that letter I became older than the slowest river.

It is likely I would have stayed at the monastery and accepted monkhood had not news come one day announcing the arrival of strangers from across the Storm Sea. Numb, indifferent, I sailed south with the delegation's other volunteers. Autumn had come to the forest. Disheveled oaks and maples mottled the undulant shores. But gradually the hoarfrost thinned from the air, and colossal domes of cumulus rose from the horizon. Shaggy cypress and palm trees tilted above the dunes.

Like a roving, masterless dog, I followed the others from one mission

to the next among lovely, verdant islands. Hunger abandoned me, and I
ate only when food was pressed on me, not tasting it. In the silence and
fire of night, while the others slept, my life seemed an endless web of
lies I had spun and you a bird I had caught and crippled. In the mirrors
of the sea I saw faces. Mostly they were your face. And always when I
saw you, you smiled at me with an untellable love. I grieved that I had
ever left you.

The morning we found the boats that had crossed the Storm Sea, I
greeted the strangers morosely. They were stout men with florid faces,
thick beards, and big noses. Their ships were clumsy, worm-riddled
boxes without watertight compartments and with ludicrous cloth sails set
squarely, leaving them at the mercy of the winds. At first they attempted
to impress us with their cheap merchandise, mostly painted tinware and
clay pots filled with sour wine. I do not blame them, for, not wishing to
slight the aboriginals, we had approached in a local raft with the tribal
leaders of that island.

Soon, however, beckoned by a blue smoke flare, our own ship
rounded the headland. The sight of her sleek hull and orange sails with
bamboo battens trimmed precisely for maximum speed rocked loose the
foreigners' arrogant jaws—for our ship, with her thwartwise staggered
masts fore-and-aft, approached *into* the wind. The Big Noses had never
seen the likes of it.

Ostensibly to salute us, though I'm sure with the intent of displaying
their might, the Big Noses fired their bulky cannon. The three awkward ships, entirely lacking leeboards, keeled drastically. Our vessel
replied with a volley of Bees' Nest rockets that splashed overhead in a
fiery display while our ship sailed figure-eights among the foreigners'
box-boats.

At that the Big Noses became effusively deferential. The captain, a
tall, beardless man with red hair and ghostly pale flesh, removed his hat,
bowed, and presented us with one of his treasures, a pathetically crude
book printed on coarse paper with a gold-leaf cross pressed into the
animal-hide binding. Our leader accepted it graciously.

Fortunately the Big Noses had on board a man who spoke Chaldean
and some Arabic, and two of the linguists in our delegation could
understand him slightly. He told us that his captain's name was Christ-
bearer the Colonizer and that they had come seeking the Emperor of
the Middle Kingdom in the hope of opening trade with him. They
actually believed that they were twenty-five thousand *li* to the west, in
the spice islands south of the Middle Kingdom! Their ignorance fairly
astounded us.

Upon learning their precise location, the Colonizer appeared dismayed and retreated to his cabin. From his second in command we eventually learned that the Colonizer had expected honor and wealth from his enterprise. Both would be greatly diminished now that it was evident he had discovered neither a route to the world's wealthiest kingdom nor a new world to be colonized by the Big Noses.

Among our delegation was much debate about the implications of the Colonizer's first name—Christ-bearer. For some centuries Christ-bearers have straggled into the Middle Kingdom, though always they were confined to select districts of coastal cities. Their gruesome religion, in which the flesh and blood of their maimed and tortured god is symbolically consumed, disgusted our Emperor, and their proselytizing zeal rightly concerned him. But here, in the USA, with the Dawn-Settlers' tolerance of diverse views, what will be the consequences when the Christ-bearers establish their missions?

I did not care. Let fat-hearted men scheme and plot in faraway temples and kingdoms. Heart Wing! I will never see the jewel of your face again. That thought—that truth—lies before me now, an unexplored wilderness I will spend the rest of my life crossing. But on that day when I first saw the Big Noses I had not yet grasped this truth. I still believed death was a doorway. I thought perhaps your ghost would cross back and succor my mourning. I had seen your face in the mirrors of the sea, a distraught girl both filled and exhausted with love. I had seen that, and I thought I could cross the threshold of this life and find you again, join with you again, united among the ancestors. I thought that.

For several more days I walked about in a daze, looking for your ghost, contemplating ways to die. I even prepared a sturdy noose from a silk sash and, one moon-long evening, wandered into the forest to hang myself. As I meandered through the dark avenues of a cypress dell seeking the appropriate bough from which to stretch my shameless neck, I heard voices. Three paces away, on the far side of a bracken screen, the Big Noses were whispering hotly. I dared to peek and spied them hurrying among the trees, crouched over, sabers and guns in hand and awkwardly hauling a longboat among them.

The evil I had wished upon myself had led me to a greater evil, and, without forethought, I followed the Big Noses. They swiftly made their way to the cove where the Imperial ship was moored. I knew then their intent. The entire delegation, along with most of the crew, were ashore at the mission interviewing the aboriginals who had first encountered the Big Noses and drafting a report for the Emperor and the local authorities about the arrival of the Christ-bearer in the USA. The Big Noses would meet little resistance in pirating our ship.

Clouds walked casually away from the moon, and the mission with its serpent pillars and curved roof shone gem-bright high on the bluff—too far away for me to race there in time or even for my cries to reach. Instead I ducked among the dunes and scurried through the switching salt grass to the water's edge even as the Big Noses pushed their longboat into the slick water and piled in. With a few hardy oar-strokes they reached the Imperial ship and began clambering aboard unseen by the watch, who was probably in the hold sampling the rice wine.

I stood staring at the ship perched atop the watery moon, knowing what I had to do but hardly believing I had such strength. I, who had iron enough in my blood to strangle my own life, wavered at the thought of defying other men, even the primitive Big Noses. Truly, what a coward I am! I would have stood rooted as a pine and watched the pirates sail our ship into the dark like a happy cloud scudding under the moon—but a scream and a splash jolted me.

The Big Noses had thrown the watch overboard. I saw him swimming hard for shore and imagined I saw fear in his face. His craven face galled me! The watch, flailing strenuously to save his own miserable life, would make no effort to stop barbarians from stealing the life of his own people! For I knew that we would lose nothing less if the Big Noses stole our ship and learned to build vessels that could challenge the USA and even the Middle Kingdom.

I dove into the glossed water and thrashed toward the ship. I am a weak swimmer, as you know, but there was not far to go, and the noise of the watch beating frantically to shore muted my advance. The moorings were cut, and the ship listed under the offshore breeze. The Big Noses, accustomed to climbing along yard-arms to adjust their sails, were unfamiliar with the windlasses and halyards that control from the deck the ribbed sails of our ship, and so there was time for me to clutch onto the hull before the sails unfurled.

After climbing the bulwark I slipped and fell to the deck right at the feet of the tall, ghost-faced captain! We stared at each other with moonbright eyes for a startled moment, and I swear I saw an avidity in his features as malefic as a temple demon's. I bolted upright even as he shouted. Blessedly the entire crew was busy trying to control the strange new ship, and I eluded the grasp of the Colonizer and darted across the deck to the gangway.

Death had been my intent from the first. When I plunged into the hold and collapsed among coils of hempen rope, I had but one thought: to reach the weapons bin and ignite the powder. I blundered in the dark, slammed into a bulkhead, tripped over bales of sorghum, and reached the powder bin in a gasping daze. Shouts boomed from the gangway, and the hulking shapes of the Big Noses filled the narrow corridor.

Wildly I grasped for the flintstriker I knew was somewhere near the bin. Or was it? Perhaps that was too dangerous to keep near the powder. The Big Noses closed in, and I desperately bounded atop the bin and shoved open the hatch that was there. Moonlight gushed over me, and I saw the horrid faces of the barbarians rushing toward me. And there, at my elbow, was a sheaf of matches.

I seized the fire-sticks and rattled them at the Big Noses, but they were not thwarted. The oafs had no idea what these were! They dragged me down, barking furiously. I gaped about in the moonglow, spotted a flintstriker hanging from a beam. Kicking like a madman, I twisted free just long enough to snatch the flintstriker. But I had inspired their fury, and heavy blows knocked me to the planks.

Stunned, I barely had the strength to squeeze the lever of the flintstriker. My feeble effort elicited only the tiniest spark, but that was enough to ignite a match. The sulfurous flare startled my assailants, and they fell back. Immediately I lurched about and held high the burning pine stick while gesturing at the powder bin behind me. The Big Noses pulled away.

With my free hand I grabbed a bamboo tube I recognized as a Beard-the-Moon rocket. I lit the fuse and pointed it at the open hatch. In a radiant whoosh sparks and flames sprayed into the night. The cries of the Big Noses sounded from the deck, and the men who had seized me fled. A laugh actually tore through me as I fired two more Beard-the-Moon rockets. I was going to die, but now death seemed a fate worthy of laughter.

Perhaps the longtime company of Buddhists and Taoists had affected me, for I had no desire to kill the Big Noses. I waited long enough for them to throw themselves into the sea before I ignited the fuses on several heaven-shaking Thunderclap bombs. My last thought, while waiting for the explosion to hurl me into the Great Inane, was of you, Heart Wing. Once I had committed myself to using death as a doorway, your ghost had actually come back for me, to lead me to the ancestors in a way that would serve the Kingdom. I thanked you, and the Thunderclap bombs exploded.

Yet I did not die—at least not in an obvious way. Later, when I could think clearly again, I realized that your ghost had not yet done with me. Who else but you could have placed me just where I was so that my body would be hurtled straight upward through the open hatch and into the lustrous night? I remember none of that, however, but the watch, who had made it to shore and been alerted by the showering of the Beard-the-Moon rockets, claims that when the Imperial ship burst into a fireball, he saw me flying, silhouetted against the moon.

He found me unconscious in the shallows, unscathed except that my beard and eyebrows were singed and my clothes torn. Like a meteor, I had fallen back to earth, back to life. I had fallen the way stars fall, from the remote darkness where they have shivered in the cold down into the warm, close darkness of earthly life. That night I fell from the gloom of my solitary grief into the dark of terrestrial life, where we all suffer together in our unknowing. Slapped alert by the watch, I sat up in the moon-dappled shallows and saw my forty summers fall away into emptiness. The ship was gone—just as you are gone, Heart Wing, and our daughter gone into that emptiness the Buddhists call *sunyata*, which is really the void of our unknowing, the mystery that bears everything that lives and dies.

How foolish to say all this to *you*, who dwells now in the heart of this emptiness. But I, I have been ignorant, asleep. I needed reminding that time and the things of falling shall not fall into darkness but into a new freedom we cannot name and so call emptiness. All of reality floats in that vacancy, like the spheres in the void of space, like these words floating in the emptiness of the page. Words try to capture reality, yet what they actually capture are only more words and deeper doubts. Mystery is the preeminent condition of human being—and yet it is also our freedom to be exactly who we are, free to choose the words our doubts require.

No one in the delegation understood this when I was taken back to the mission to account for myself. Grateful as they were for my stopping the theft of the Imperial ship, they were sure the explosion had addled me. I think the monks knew what I meant, but they are of the "just so" sect of Ch'an Buddhism, so they would be the last to let on.

Be that as it may, I sat there quite agog and amazed, awakened to the knowledge that the freedom to be who I am means, quite simply, that I am alone—without you. For now it is meant that this be so. For reasons I will never truly understand, death is denied me. So what am I to do with this life, then, and this loneliness? This freedom to *be*, this freedom whose chances bleed from us, creates new imperatives. In the place of my failure and shame waits a gaping emptiness wanting to be filled with what I might yet be.

As I meditated on this, the delegation wrote an official missive admonishing the Big Noses for their attempted thievery and threatening to report them to the Emperor. The Big Noses, all of whom had escaped the explosion and retreated to their ship, replied with a terse letter of halfhearted apology. With no other Imperial vessel anywhere in the vicinity and none of the Autocracies' forces nearby, our host, the monastery's abbot, urged us to accept the apology.

In an effort to both placate and hurry the Colonizer on his way, the delegation decided to load his ships with all the porcelain in the mission, several remarkable landscape paintings, a jade statue of Kwan Yin, goddess of serenity, as well as bales of crops he had never seen before, notably tobacco, peanuts, and potatoes. By then, inspired by my lack of family and career, I had decided to take the poison cure required by my sorrow: I have, dear wife, forsaken my return to the Middle Kingdom to go with the Colonizer on his return voyage across the Storm Sea to his homeland.

Do you admonish me for being foolish? Indeed, the decision was a difficult one, for I had hoped to return to our homeland and administer the rites myself at your gravesite. But if what I have learned of the emptiness is true, then you are no more there than here. The path of the Way is a roadlessness without departure or arrival. I have decided, Heart Wing, to follow that path, to fit the unaccomplished parts of my life to the future and embrace the unknown.

The delegation strove in vain to dissuade me. They fear that I have gone truly mad. But I don't care at all. I know you would understand, Heart Wing, you whom I first won with the bridebait of stories written by the lamp of lightning. So, as absurd as this may be, I sit here now, writing to you on the quarterdeck of a leaky vessel named *Santa María*.

I can tell from the way he looks at me that the Colonizer is still angry that I deprived him of his booty, and I know he has only taken me on board with the expectation of getting useful information from me. But for now our ignorance of each other's languages offers me a chance to win the Big Noses' respect by my deeds—and to watch and learn about these barbarians.

In time I will understand their language. I will inform their emperor of the wonders of the Middle Kingdom, of the achievements of the Unified Sandalwood Autocracies, of the glory of our people. And I will write again from the far side of the world, from so far east, it is the west where sun and moon meet. And from there I will send back to the Kingdom and to the USA stories everyone will read, stories of another world, written in ink from the new moon.

VINLAND THE DREAM

Kim Stanley Robinson

Abstract. It was sunset at L'Anse aux Meadows. The water of the bay was still, the boggy beach was dark in shadows. Flat arms of land pointed to flat islands offshore; beyond these a taller island stood like a loaf of stone in the sea, catching the last of the day's light. A stream gurgled gently as it cut through the beach bog. Above the bog, on a narrow grassy terrace, one could just make out a pattern of low mounds, all that remained of sod walls. Next to them were three or four sod buildings, and beyond the buildings, a number of tents.

A group of people—archeologists, graduate students, volunteer laborers, visitors—moved together onto a rocky ridge overlooking the site. Some of them worked at starting a campfire in a ring of blackened stones; others began to unpack bags of food, and cases of beer. Far across the water lay the dark bulk of Labrador. Kindling caught and their fire burned, a spark of yellow in the dusk's gloom.

Hot dogs and beer, around a campfire by the sea; and yet it was strangely quiet. Voices were subdued. The people on the hill glanced down often at the site, where the head of their dig, a lanky man in his early fifties, was giving a brief tour to their distinguished guest. The distinguished guest did not appear pleased.

Introduction. The head of the dig, an archeology professor from McGill University, was looking at the distinguished guest with the expression he wore when confronted by an aggressive undergraduate. The distinguished guest, Canada's Minister of Culture, was asking question after question. As she did, the professor took her to look for herself, at the forge, and the slag pit, and the little midden beside Building E. New trenches were cut across the mounds and depressions, perfect rectangular cuts in the black peat; they could tell the minister nothing of what they had revealed. But she had insisted on seeing them, and now she was asking questions that got right to the point, although they could have been asked and answered just as well in Ottawa. Yes, the professor explained, the fuel for the forge was wood charcoal, the temperature had gotten to around twelve hundred degrees Celsius, the process was direct reduction of bog ore, obtaining about one kilogram of iron for every five kilograms of slag. All was as it was in other Norse forges—except that the limonites in the bog ore had now been precisely identified by spectroscopic analysis; and that analysis had revealed that the bog iron smelted here had come from northern Quebec, near Chicoutimi. The Norse explorers, who had supposedly smelted the bog ore, could not have obtained it.

There was a similar situation in the midden; rust migrated in peat at a known rate, and so it could be determined that the many iron rivets in the midden had only been there a hundred and forty years, plus or minus fifty.

"So," the minister said, in English with a Francophone lilt. "You have proved your case, it appears?"

The professor nodded wordlessly. The minister watched him, and he couldn't help feeling that despite the nature of the news he was giving her, she was somewhat amused. By him? By his scientific terminology? By his obvious (and growing) depression? He couldn't tell.

The minister raised her eyebrows. "L'Anse aux Meadows, a hoax. Parcs Canada will not like it at all."

"No one will like it," the professor croaked.

"No," the minister said, looking at him. "I suppose not. Particularly as this is part of a larger pattern, yes?"

The professor did not reply.

"The entire concept of Vinland," she said. "A hoax!"

The professor nodded glumly.

"I would not have believed it possible."

"No," the professor said. "But—" He waved a hand at the low mounds around them—"So it appears." He shrugged. "The story has always rested on a very small body of evidence. Three sagas, this site, a few references in Scandinavian records, a few coins, a few cairns..." He shook his head. "Not much." He picked up a chunk of dried peat from the ground, crumbled it in his fingers.

Suddenly the minister laughed at him, then put her hand to his upper arm. Her fingers were warm. "You must remember, it is not your fault."

He smiled wanly. "I suppose not." He liked the look on her face; sympathetic as well as amused. She was about his age, perhaps a bit older. An attractive and sophisticated Quebeçois. "I need a drink," he confessed.

"There's beer on the hill."

"Something stronger. I have a bottle of cognac I haven't opened yet . . ."

"Let's get it and take it up there with us."

Experimental Methods. The graduate students and volunteer laborers were gathered around the fire, and the smell of roasting hot dogs filled the air. It was nearly eleven, the sun a half hour gone, and the last light of the summer dusk slowly leaked from the sky. The fire burned like a beacon. Beer had been flowing freely, and the party was beginning to get a little more boisterous.

The minister and the professor stood near the fire, drinking cognac out of plastic cups.

"How did you come to suspect the story of Vinland?" the minister asked as they watched the students cook hot dogs.

A couple of the volunteer laborers, who had paid good money to spend their summer digging trenches in a bog, heard the question and moved closer.

The professor shrugged. "I can't quite remember." He tried to laugh. "Here I am an archeologist, and I can't remember my own past."

The minister nodded as if that made sense. "I suppose it was a long time ago?"

"Yes." He concentrated. "Now what was it. Someone was following up the story of the Vinland map, to try and figure out who had done it. The map showed up in a bookstore in New Haven in the 1950s—as you may know?"

"No," the minister said. "I hardly know a thing about Vinland, I assure you. Just the basics that anyone in my position would have to know."

"Well, there was a map found in the 1950s called the Vinland map, and it was shown to be a hoax soon after its discovery. But when this investigator traced the map's history, she found that the book it had been in was accounted for all the way back to the 1820s, map and all. It meant the hoaxer had lived longer ago than I had expected." He refilled his cup of cognac, then the minister's. "There were a lot of Viking hoaxes in the nineteenth century, but this one was so early. It surprised me. It's generally thought that the whole phenomenon was stimulated by a book that a Danish scholar published in 1837, containing translations of the Vinland sagas and related material. The book was very popular among the Scandinavian settlers in America, and after that, you know . . . a kind of twisted patriotism, or the response of an ethnic group that had been made fun of too often. . . . So we got the Kensington stone, the halberds, the mooring holes, the coins. But if a hoax predated *Antiquitates Americanae* . . . it made me wonder."

"If the book itself were somehow involved?"

"Exactly," the professor said, regarding the minister with pleasure. "I wondered if the book might not incorporate, or have been inspired by, hoaxed material. Then one day I was reading a description of the field work here, and it occurred to me that this site was a bit too pristine. As if it had been built but never lived in. Best estimates for its occupation were as low as one summer, because they couldn't find any trash middens to speak of, or graves."

"It could have been occupied very briefly," the minister pointed out.

"Yes, I know. That's what I thought at the time. But then I heard from a colleague in Bergen that the *Gronlendinga Saga* was apparently a forgery, at least in the parts referring to the discovery of Vinland. Pages had been inserted that dated back to the 1820s. After that, I had a doubt that wouldn't go away."

"But there are more Vinland stories than that one, yes?"

"Yes. There are three main sources. The *Gronlendinga Saga*, *The Saga of Erik the Red*, and the part of *The Hauksbók* that tells about Thorfinn Karlsefni's expedition. But with one of those questioned, I began to doubt them all. And the story itself. Everything having to do with the idea of Vinland."

"Is that when you went to Bergen?" a graduate student asked.

The professor nodded. He drained his plastic cup, felt the alcohol rushing through him. "I joined Nielsen there and we went over *Erik the Red* and *The Hauksbók*, and damned if the pages in those concerning Vinland weren't forgeries too. The ink gave it away—not its composition, which was about right, but merely how long it had been on that paper. Which was thirteenth century paper, I might add! The forger had done a super job. But the sagas had been tampered with sometime in the early nineteenth century."

"But those are masterpieces of world literature," a volunteer laborer exclaimed, round-eyed; the ads for volunteer labor had not included a description of the primary investigator's hypothesis.

"I know," the professor said irritably, and shrugged.

He saw a chunk of peat on the ground, picked it up and threw it on the blaze. After a bit it flared up.

"It's like watching dirt burn," he said absently, staring into the flames.

Discussion. The burnt-garbage smell of peat wafted downwind, and offshore the calm water of the bay was riffled by the same gentle breeze. The minister warmed her hands at the blaze for a moment, then gestured at the bay. "It's hard to believe they were never here at all."

"I know," the professor said. "It looks like a Viking site, I'll give him that."

"Him," the minister repeated.

"I know, I know. This whole thing forces you to imagine a man in the eighteen twenties and thirties, traveling all over—Norway, Iceland, Canada, New England, Rome, Stockholm, Denmark, Greenland. . . . Crisscrossing the North Atlantic, to bury all these signs." He shook his head. "It's incredible."

He retrieved the cognac bottle and refilled. He was, he had to admit, beginning to feel drunk. "And so many parts of the hoax were well hidden! You can't assume we've found them all. This place had two butternuts buried in the midden, and butternuts only grow down below the St. Lawrence, so who's to say they aren't clues, indicating another site down there? That's where grapevines actually grow, which would justify the name Vinland. I tell you, the more I know about this hoaxer, the more certain I am that other sites exist. The tower in Newport, Rhode Island, for instance—the hoaxer didn't build that, because it's been around since the seventeenth century—but a little work out there at night, in the early nineteenth century . . . I bet if it were excavated completely you'd find a few Norse artifacts."

"Buried in all the right places," the minister said.

"Exactly." The professor nodded. "And up the coast of Labrador, at Cape Porcupine where the sagas say they repaired a ship. There too. Stuff scattered everywhere, left to be discovered or not."

The minister waved her plastic cup. "But surely this site must have been his masterpiece. He couldn't have done too many as extensive as this."

"I shouldn't think so." The professor drank deeply, smacked his numbed lips. "Maybe one more like this, down in New Brunswick. That's my guess. But this was surely one of his biggest projects."

"It was a time for that kind of thing," the volunteer laborer offered. "Atlantis, Mu, Lemuria. . . . "

The minister nodded. "It fulfills a certain desire."

"Theosophy, most of that," the professor muttered. "This was different."

The volunteer wandered off. The professor and the minister looked into the fire for a while.

"You are *sure?*" the minister asked.

The professor nodded. "Trace elements show the ore came from upper Quebec. Chemical changes in the peat weren't right. And nuclear resonance dating methods show that the bronze pin they found hadn't been buried long enough. Little things like that. Nothing obvious. He was amazingly meticulous, he really thought it out. But the nature of things tripped him up. Nothing more than that."

"But the effort!" the minister said. "This is what I find hard to believe. Surely it must have been more than one man! Burying these objects, building the walls—surely he would have been noticed!"

The professor stopped another swallow, nodded at her as he choked once or twice. A broad wave of the hand, a gasping recovery of breath:

"Fishing village, kilometer north of here. Boarding house in the early nineteenth century. A crew of ten rented rooms in the summer of 1842. Bills paid by a Mr. Carlsson."

The minister raised her eyebrows. "Ah."

One of the graduate students got out a guitar and began to play. The other students and the volunteers gathered around her.

"So," the minister said, "Mr. Carlsson. Does he show up elsewhere?"

"There was a Professor Ohman in Bergen. A Dr. Bergen in Reykjavik. In the right years, studying the sagas. I presume they were all him, but I don't know for sure."

"What do you know about him?"

"Nothing. No one paid much attention to him. I've got him on a couple transatlantic crossings, I think, but he used aliases, so I've probably missed most of them. A Scandinavian-American, apparently Norwegian by birth. Someone with some money—someone with patriotic feelings of some kind—someone with a grudge against a university— who knows? All I have are a few signatures, of aliases at that. A flowery handwriting. Nothing more. That's the most remarkable thing about him! You see, most hoaxers leave clues to their identities, because a part

of them wants to be caught. So their cleverness can be admired, or the
ones who fell for it embarrassed, or whatever. But this guy didn't want to
be discovered. And in those days, if you wanted to stay off the record . . ." He shook his head.

"A man of mystery."

"Yeah. But I don't know how to find out anything more about
him."

The professor's face was glum in the firelight as he reflected on this.
He polished off another cup of cognac. The minister watched him drink,
then said kindly, "There is nothing to be done about it, really. That is
the nature of the past."

"I know."

Conclusions. They threw the last big logs on the fire, and flames
roared up, yellow licks breaking free among the stars. The professor felt
numb all over, his heart was cold, the firelit faces were smeary primitive
masks, dancing in the light. The songs were harsh and raucous, he
couldn't understand the words. The wind was chilling, and the hot skin
of his arms and neck goosepimpled uncomfortably. He felt sick with alcohol,
and knew it would be a while before his body could overmaster it.

The minister led him away from the fire, then up the rocky ridge.
Getting him away from the students and laborers, no doubt, so he
wouldn't embarrass himself. Starlight illuminated the heather and broken granite under their feet. He stumbled. He tried to explain to her
what it meant, to be an archeologist whose most important work was the
discovery that a bit of their past was a falsehood.

"It's like a mosaic," he said, drunkenly trying to follow the fugitive
thought. "A puzzle with most of the pieces gone. A tapestry. And if you
pull a thread out . . . it's ruined. So little lasts! We need every bit we can
find!"

She seemed to understand. In her student days, she told him, she had
waitressed at a café in Montreal. Years later she had gone down the street
to have a look, just for nostalgia's sake. The café was gone. The street was
completely different. And she couldn't remember the names of any of
the people she had worked with. "This was my own past, not all that
many years ago!"

The professor nodded. Cognac was rushing through his veins, and as
he looked at the minister, so beautiful in the starlight, she seemed to
him a kind of muse, a spirit sent to comfort him, or frighten him, he
couldn't tell which. Cleo, he thought. The muse of history. Someone he
could talk to.

She laughed softly. "Sometimes it seems our lives are much longer than we usually think. So that we live through incarnations, and looking back later we have nothing but . . ." She waved a hand.

"Bronze pins," the professor said. "Iron rivets."

"Yes." She looked at him. Her eyes were bright in the starlight. "We need an archeology for our own lives."

Acknowledgments. Later he walked her back to the fire, now reduced to banked red coals. She put her hand to his upper arm as they walked, steadying herself, and he felt in the touch some kind of portent; but couldn't understand it. He had drunk so much! Why be so upset about it, why? It was his job to find the truth; having found it, he should be happy! Why had no one told him what he would feel?

The minister said good-night. She was off to bed; she suggested he do likewise. Her look was compassionate, her voice firm.

When she was gone he hunted down the bottle of cognac, and drank the rest of it. The fire was dying, the students and workers scattered—in the tents, or out in the night, in couples.

He walked by himself back down to the site.

Low mounds, of walls that had never been. Beyond the actual site were rounded buildings, models built by the park service, to show tourists what the "real" buildings had looked like. When Vikings had camped on the edge of the new world. Repairing their boats. Finding food. Fighting among themselves, mad with epic jealousies. Fighting the dangerous Indians. Getting killed, and then driven away from this land, so much lusher than Greenland.

A creak in the brush and he jumped, startled. It would have been like that: death in the night, creeping up on you—he turned with a jerk, and every starlit shadow bounced with hidden skraelings, their bows drawn taut, their arrows aimed at his heart. He quivered, hunched over.

But no. It hadn't been like that. Not at all. Instead, a man with spectacles and a bag full of old junk, directing some unemployed sailors as they dug. Nondescript, taciturn, nameless; one night he would have wandered back there into the forest, perhaps fallen or had a heart attack—become a skeleton wearing leathers and swordbelt, with spectacles over the skull's eyesockets, the anachronism that gave him away at last. . . . The professor staggered over the low mounds toward the trees, intent on finding that inadvertent grave. . . .

But no. It wouldn't be there. The taciturn figure hadn't been like that. He would have been far away when he died, nothing to show what he had spent years of his life doing. A man in a hospital for the poor, the bronze pin in his pocket overlooked by the doctor, stolen by an undertaker's assistant. An anonymous figure, to the grave and beyond. The creator of Vinland. Never to be found.

The professor looked around, confused and sick. There was a waist-high rock, a glacial erratic. He sat on it. Put his head in his hands. Really quite unprofessional. All those books he had read as a child. What would the minister think! Grant money. No reason to feel so bad!

At that latitude midsummer nights are short, and the party had lasted late. The sky to the east was already gray. He could see down onto the site, and its long sod roofs. On the beach, a trio of long narrow high-ended ships. Small figures in furs emerged from the longhouses and went down to the water, and he walked among them and heard their speech, a sort of dialect of Norwegian that he could mostly understand. They would leave that day, it was time to load the ships. They were going to take everything with them, they didn't plan to return. Too many skraelings in the forest, too many quick arrow deaths. He walked among them, helping them load stores. Then a little man in a black coat scurried behind the forge, and he roared and took off after him, scooping up a rock on the way, ready to deal out a skraeling death to that black intruder.

The minister woke him with a touch of her hand. He almost fell off the rock. He shook his head; he was still drunk. The hangover wouldn't begin for a couple more hours, though the sun was already up.

"I should have known all along," he said to her angrily. "They were stretched to the limit in Greenland, and the climate was worsening. It was amazing they got that far. Vinland. . . ." He waved a hand at the site—"was just some dreamer's story."

Regarding him calmly, the minister said, "I am not sure it matters."

He looked up at her. "What do you mean?"

"History is made of stories people tell. And fictions, dreams, hoaxes— they also are made of stories people tell. True or false, it's the stories that matter to us. Certain qualities in the stories themselves make them true or false."

He shook his head. "Some things really happened in the past. And some things didn't."

"But how can you know for sure which is which? You can't go back and see for yourself. Maybe Vinland was the invention of this mysterious stranger of yours; maybe the Vikings came here after all, and landed somewhere else. Either way it can never be anything more than a story to us."

"But . . ." He swallowed. "Surely it matters whether it is a true story or not!"

She paced before him. "A friend of mine once told me something he had read in a book," she said. "It was by a man who sailed the Red Sea, long ago. He told of a servant boy on one of the dhows, who could not remember ever having been cared for. The boy had become a sailor at age three—before that, he had been a beach-comber." She stopped pacing and looked at the beach below them. "Often I imagined that little boy's life. Surviving alone on a beach, at that age—it astonished me. It made me . . . happy."

She turned to look at him. "But later I told this story to an expert in child development, and he just shook his head. 'It probably wasn't true,' he said. Not a lie, exactly, but a . . ."

"A stretcher," the professor suggested.

"A stretcher, exactly. He supposed that the boy had been somewhat older, or had had some help. You know."

The professor nodded.

"But in the end," the minister said, "I found this judgment did not matter to me. In my mind I still saw that toddler, searching the tidepools for his daily food. And so for me the story lives. And that is all that matters. We judge all the stories from history like that—we value them according to how much they spur our imaginations."

The professor stared at her. He rubbed his jaw, looked around. Things had the sharp-edged clarity they sometimes get after a sleepless night, as if glowing with internal light. He said, "Someone with opinions like yours probably shouldn't have the job that you do."

"I didn't know I had them," the minister said. "I only just came upon them in the last couple of hours, thinking about it."

The professor was surprised. "You didn't sleep?"

She shook her head. "Who could sleep on a night like this?"

"My feeling exactly!" He almost smiled. "So. A *nuit blanche*, you call it?"

"Yes," she said. "A *nuit blanche* for two." And she looked down at him with that amused glance of hers, as if . . . as if she understood him.

She extended her arms toward him, grasped his hands, helped pull him to his feet. They began to walk back toward the tents, across the site of L'Anse aux Meadows. The grass was wet with dew, and very green. "I still think," he said as they walked together, "that we want more than stories from the past. We want something not easily found—something, in fact, that the past doesn't have. Something secret, some secret meaning... something that will give our lives a kind of sense."

She slipped a hand under his arm. "We want the Atlantis of childhood. But, failing that..." She laughed and kicked at a clump of grass; a spray of dew flashed ahead of them, containing, for just one moment, a bright little rainbow.

IF THERE BE CAUSE

Sheila Finch

*"Consider what a great voyage we are
like to make, the like was never made out
of England, for by the same the worst in
this fleet shall become a gentleman."*
—SIR FRANCIS DRAKE, 1578
The Inland Sea, 1776

Little Gull saw the men before I did.

A fine, early summer day, I remember, two days after we returned from the shores of Great Sea. We had just celebrated the coming of First Captain in the Big Canoes, swooping out of the setting sun.

I was gathering duck eggs when my brother came running to me, panting hard with excitement, abalone beads bouncing around his neck, berry basket bouncing on his back, spilling its purple fruit along the path. Five summers is not so many that a boy should remember berries and forget exciting news.

My pulse raced and I was filled with sudden hope. In spring I had met a young man here, not Miwok but yet one of The People. His name was White Cloud. We walked together beside the irrigation ditch, and he was full of questions. Why did our canoes have sails? Why did we bother to plant crops? Why were our fields so square and neat, each with its own hedge separating it from its neighbor? How did the windmills fill the ditch with water? I laughed at his childlike ignorance. The tribes farther south on the shores of Great Sea were not as rich and wise as we, but he did not even know a well when he saw one! Yet I thought him the most beautiful man I had ever seen. My heart shivered when he touched my hand. Someday, he promised, he would come back to claim me. I believed him utterly, as only those who love believe. In that blustery spring weather, I knew White Cloud was my destiny.

"Red Deer! Red Deer!" Little Gull called out breathlessly as he ran headlong into my arms. "There're men coming! Lots of men. Strange-looking men! Wearing very odd clothes!"

Hope that a moment before had made me light as thistledown vanished.

"Don't you want to see them, Red Deer? Come with me! Please? You can see them from the top of the hill."

I held Little Gull firmly by the arms. He had the light skin that often runs in our family, speckled all over with dark patches like the wings of a pheasant, and eyes the color of misty sky. But his hair was brown, the color of pine bark. My own hair had red light in it, as if a field of poppies grew there.

"Don't talk nonsense, Little Gull!" I said.

"A lot of hunters coming up the long valley," he insisted. "Some of them were—riding, it looked like. I couldn't tell what the beast was. And there were women with them. And children!"

I still did not want to give up my fantasy of White Cloud's return. "What kind of hunting party travels with its children?"

"I did see them, Red Deer," he said stubbornly. "I did!"

"Then we'd better tell Bear-With-One-Ear," I said.

My heart was heavy. White Cloud had vowed he would return, but the weeks went by, and my loneliness grew.

Holding hands, we ran down the hillside to the town, then up a street of very fine houses until we came to my uncle's house.

John Bear-With-One-Ear was sitting outside, where the overhanging thatch roof offered a shady spot to sit and enjoy the flower gardens. A sweet sound of music drifted on the fragrant air. My uncle's house was the largest and finest in the town, just as Nova Albion was the largest and most powerful of all the towns around the Inland Sea, which the old people called Lesser Sea. He was sharing a cane pipe of tobacco with his three brothers. Little Gull and I and our older brother, Francis Hawk Wing, were raised in his house, for our uncle had no children of his own.

(I tell you this at such length so that you should understand all things at last.)

We stood in front of the men, waiting for them to speak first, and I gripped Little Gull's arm to remind him to be polite, for he was shaking with excitement and would have blurted everything out before they asked him.

At last Bear-With-One-Ear laid down his pipe. He was an old man by then, but still handsome. The bright hair was only now fading to gray, but the locks that curled over the gray lace collar were just as thick as ever.

"Well, Little Gull," he said, "have you brought berries for our supper?"

Little Gull looked down at the basket and was much surprised to find it empty.

"My brother brings something better, Uncle," I said hastily, before Little Gull could cry. "He brings news. A large group of men approaching from the south."

Bear-With-One-Ear gazed at me. "And how is this unusual?"

"They're not Pomo or Miyakma or Yokuts. And they travel with their women and children!"

Bear-With-One-Ear frowned, and Edward Gray Seal, the youngest uncle, who had been playing the lute, said, "Not much to fear in that, I think."

"Still," one of the other uncles said (Walter Black Otter, I think it was, but my memory is not so clear now), "it *is* unusual."

Bear-With-One-Ear looked troubled. He was a strong leader, a peace-maker. Yet it was said of him that he was sometimes slower to anger than was good.

"We've heard of a gathering of strangers," he said. "Lookouts to the south sent word by the smoke towers. They seek land to grow food and raise children. The land is big enough to share a little with those who need it."

Black Otter set down his cup of fermented juice from apples I had helped harvest last autumn. "Where's my nephew, Hawk Wing?"

"My brother's hunting," Little Gull said proudly. "He's going to bring me an eagle feather for my cap!"

Bear-With-One-Ear smiled. "Your brother's skilled with a crossbow. But I doubt he hunts eagles with it!"

Little Gull pouted. "Someday I'm going to be *Big* Gull! And I'm going to kill enemies too."

Bear-With-One-Ear stopped smiling. "We have no enemies."

"Don't delude yourself, Brother," Black Otter said. "These strangers may be the very wolves of whom First Captain warned."

There was one uncle who had said nothing. I knew he was a shaman, although among the men it is done differently, and they did not seem to have the sight. I remember that his name was Henry Fog-On-Water.

Now Fog-On-Water said, "First Captain warned us of evil men who come from a land of abomination. They seek treasure and they kill all who oppose them."

"Then we must do something!" I said.

Black Otter smiled at me. "First Captain also gave us a strategy. Let the enemy advance into a fortified place until you have them surrounded!"

"These aren't matters a girl just turned woman should hear!" Fog-On-Water said sharply.

I started to protest, but Bear-With-One-Ear held up his hand.

"We won't begin by fighting in the family. Red Deer, take Little Gull to your grandmother. Little Gull, stay with your sister until I send for you. We'll need Lark Singing's wise counsel in this matter."

"There is now a very great gap opened very little
to the liking of the King of Spain. God work it all
to his glory."

"First Captain warned us to beware the coming of men who worshiped images, for they are wolves who would devour us," Elizabeth Lark Singing said. "He told us the leader of the wolf pack is called the *papa*. We must be vigilant against this man."

My grandmother had a fine house in town, next to the one of my uncle, Bear-With-One-Ear. But in spring she had built a hut of willow branches at the top of a little hill; it had three sides, the fourth open, facing away from the town to Lesser Sea. She said young men and girls might face the storms of Great Sea even as First Captain had, but Lesser Sea was kinder to the old. She liked to watch the fog creep in along the water, then slide up the hills till its cold fingers reached into her hut. She said she would not die inside four walls, or her spirit would not find its way out. Fog-On-Water scoffed at that, but Lark Singing quelled him with a glance, a hard look from eyes so blue I thought as a child a piece of the sky had fallen into them. My grandmother was a powerful medicine woman, and none of her sons could ever withstand that flinty look.

"Tell me what we must do," I asked her. But in my heart I did not want to *do* anything. I wanted White Cloud to come back. I wanted my life to go on as I had dreamed it would.

"Something is changing. My time is over. Yours is coming."

Little Gull played with a family of ducklings that had wandered into the hut while the mother bird watched from the open side. "How will we know if these are First Captain's enemies, Grandmother?" he asked.

Before she could answer, a shout rose outside, and I went quickly to look out, shielding my eyes against the sunset.

A small tribe of strangers was coming up the road along the stream toward Nova Albion. They were led by men in metal clothes that flashed in the sun, like the metal mirror in my uncle's house that had come from First Captain's canoe. Some of them rode on the backs of strange animals. They were warriors, for I saw their weapons—long knives that hung from their belts to their knees, and something else, like a metal pipe, that they handled lovingly as one touches a baby. They were followed by others on foot, some carrying banners, some dragging burdens on carts and sleds. Yet I saw also that Little Gull had spoken truly, for there were women and children and even tiny infants in their band.

Then I saw one man in a long gray robe, the top of whose head was hairless and shiny with sweat. He was holding a long stick in front of him, to which a shorter stick had been joined as a crosspiece. First Captain taught us also to hold that symbol sacred in our ceremonies, but there was something different here, something *wrong*.

"Grandmother," I began. "I must go back at once—"

But she cut my words off. "Tonight I will teach you many things, Red Deer. I will teach you to see, and to hear the truth."

Raising herself on one elbow, she told Little Gull to throw wood on the fire, and when the flames leaped up, she instructed me to take powder from her medicine pouch and pour it in a cup of water and give it to him. Then I wrapped him in a blanket and laid him on the sleeping mat at the back of the hut, and soon I could tell from his breathing he was asleep.

The valley outside filled with flooding dark, and a crescent moon rose, drawing stars with it like salmon on a fisherman's line. Somewhere in the distance I heard shouts, then laughter that suddenly ceased. Unease crawled over my skin as if I had sat by an anthill, and I wanted only to run to my uncle. But I, too, could not stand against my grandmother's fierce eyes.

She took out a small pipe, daubed with yellow and black paint on the bowl. She filled it with dried leaves of a plant I did not recognize and lit it from the embers. The smoke filled the hut with fragrance. I watched her face; it seemed small and gray, sharp as a bird's face.

After a while she opened her eyes and held the pipe out to me. I took it with both hands. She nodded at me, encouraging me to draw in a breath of smoke.

I think I must have known all my life that this moment would come, that I would someday learn the secrets of women's medicine. Only the women of our family had the sight. Now that the moment was here, I was afraid. It was a terrifying gift she would give me then. Once I received it, there would be no turning back. There might not even be room for my own life.

"You don't have a choice, Red Deer," she said to me. "The power chose you a long time ago, as it chooses us all."

But why must *she* choose now, I thought, when so much was happening!

I lifted the pipe to my lips and inhaled the sweet, dark smoke. My nose stung and my throat tightened, but nothing else happened for a moment, and I thought perhaps she was wrong about my being chosen.

Then the hut lurched, and outside an owl screeched, and my vision went black.

My inner eyes opened, and I saw the gray-robed man with the cross, but above him I now saw four frightening figures swooping down on the backs of eagles. I knew their names: Famine, Pestilence, War, and the pale rider who was Death. A voice said to me, *"There is no time to lose!"* I felt someone touch my hand, and I turned to see Elizabeth Lark Singing in a white deerskin robe trimmed with beads in the fashion of young brides. Her hair was braided, full and red, and her face was as young as mine. Then it seemed as if she were smoke drifting away, dissolving the shape of the young woman she had been. But before she was gone, she gave me my ceremonial name: Mary.

Mary Red Deer. The name echoed in my head.

I must have fallen down then in a faint, for when I woke again, it was early morning, and I was lying on the floor of my grandmother's hut. Little Gull was weeping.

"Don't cry, Little Gull, I'm alive," I said.

"I'm not crying for you, Red Deer!" my brother said indignantly. "I'm crying because Bear-With-One-Ear told me to stay here with you, so I can't go outside to see the strangers!"

The air was filled with the voices of men shouting in a language I had never heard before. I stood up and glanced at my grandmother to ask what to do, but Lark Singing slept soundly.

"If you're awake now, Red Deer," my little brother said hopefully. "Perhaps we could go out together?"

"Grandmother," I said, half afraid to disturb her, for she had been so sick.

"She's been asleep a long time," my brother said.

I looked again at Lark Singing, so still on the sleeping mat, and I knew she was dead. Her spirit had flown away over the water just as she had wished. Then I felt very lonely, for who would give us good counsel now? She had made me medicine woman in her place, but I knew how much I still had to learn.

Little Gull clutched at my skirt. "Please hurry, Red Deer!"

I made him help me gather sticks and kindling to make a funeral fire. When the hut and everything in it was burning well, smoke and sparks blowing over Lesser Sea, I took his hand and we stepped away. There was no time to mourn, nor would she have wanted us to. The ceremonies must come later. Now I must tell my uncle of Lark Singing's passing, but I would also let him know he would not be without a medicine woman!

In those days the town spread up from the banks of the little lake between Great Sea and Lesser Sea, to the top of the low hill where Lark Singing's hut was. The other side of the lake was empty, a water meadow where ducks nested and bees browsed among the flowers in summer. I saw at once that the field was not empty now. The strangers were setting up camp, and already bright banners fluttered over their heads, horns blew and bells rang. I saw women tending a cooking fire, and children racing about, their shrill voices coming toward me on the clear air. I heard their words, but I could not tell what they said.

Surely, I thought, the smoke-dream could not be right. Men who traveled with their women and infants must come in peace.

"Look! There's our uncle!" Little Gull said.

Bear-With-One-Ear had put on the tall hat of woven grass that Lark Singing made for him, its colors and patterns more beautiful than those she wove into seed or water baskets. He stood, head bowed and hands clasped before him, as Fog-On-Water asked Sky Father for a blessing, and the other captains stood with him. That done, he moved again toward the strangers, his brothers beside him, the men of the town following all in their finest deerskin and bear fur and lace collars. I thought how splendid they looked. If I had not grown up with the young men of our town, perhaps my heart would have been moved by them instead of by White Cloud.

But I had arrived too late to give him my news. I must be patient a little longer. Little Gull and I crowded at the back with the women and children.

"And there's Hawk Wing." Little Gull pointed. "How handsome he is!"

My older brother was not tall, but broad-shouldered, strong of limb, with a quantity of gleaming, red-brown curls spilling over his wide forehead. His eyes were blue and merry. He was bold enough when needed, and quick to take action. It was said of him that he carried the spirit of First Captain as well as the ceremonial name. Yet I knew that his impulsive ways did not always please Bear-With-One-Ear.

A family of ducks scurried hastily away as my uncles walked to this meeting, and the strangers fell silent.

I thought of the stories of the coming of the Big Canoes to the shore of Great Sea and the day my ancestors first saw First Captain. Everyone had put on their finest clothes and carried gifts, and First Captain, too, gave gifts, and there was feasting and speeches and singing. Even though the Big Canoes had come out of the sunset, we understood First Captain's home was far away in the direction of sunrise. He told us he was on a journey longer than we could imagine and needed to rest and repair the Big Canoes. Many good things happened between First

Captain and the Miwok before the Big Canoes rode out on Great Sea again. Even then some of his men stayed among us because they had taken wives. As the years went by, they taught us skills of planting and harvesting, building our town and governing it. This is why babies with light skin and eyes the color of sky or water are born so often among the Miwok, though red hair comes in our family alone.

Filled with these thoughts, I wondered, might not these strangers bring good gifts as First Captain had done? Yet the darkness that had touched me with Lark Singing's death and my first smoke-dream stole the joy from the scene, and I felt cold in the sunlight. We must be cautious, not giving our trust too quickly. I crept closer to my uncles so I could hear what was said and perhaps find a moment to whisper a warning.

The man with the ring of black hair surrounding his sweat-glazed crown and the shining one who had ridden in front stood apart from their group as Bear-With-One-Ear approached. The children hushed. Not even the larks sang in the sky then, and the breeze fell still.

My uncle raised his right hand to show he carried no weapon. "We greet you in peace, friends. I am called John Bear-With-One-Ear. Tell us now where you come from and what is your purpose in coming?"

The strangers looked at each other at that, and one of them said something I did not understand in a tongue that seemed to my ears to hiss and huff and slide about unpleasantly. One small, very dark man put a hand to his side where I saw a long knife like the one over the hearth that had belonged to First Captain himself.

Fog-On-Water, who was standing beside Bear-With-One-Ear, said quickly, "Don't trust these men! Remember what was taught!"

Bear-With-One-Ear turned a little toward him. "'We are English, who are well disposed if there be no cause to the contrary,'" he said mildly.

Though the language was that of First Captain and not of the Miwok, there was no child who had not learned the words by heart and what they meant. It was the rule by which we lived.

"Finish the saying, Brother!" Fog-On-Water urged.

I wanted to yell out to him that he *must* remember what came next! But Bear-With-One-Ear shook his head, his expression mild. "We are gentlemen, Brother, with a gentleman's honor."

In the silence that followed I could hear Little Gull's rasping breath, the lap of water on the shore, the soft beating of a butterfly's wings over my head. The strangers conferred in low tones.

Then there was a stir among them, and a young man about my own age stepped forward. My heart thundered in my breast and I thought I would faint again as I had after the smoke-dream. The young man wore a long robe like the stranger who carried the cross, so stained and dirty, I could not tell its right color, yet his skin was dark and he wore his hair in the fashion of the southerners. And when he spoke, he used the language of the Chumash tribe, which we understood with difficulty.

It could not be!

But it was White Cloud.

"God be with you," he said. "May the blood of Jesus Christ redeem you from your sins!"

Fog-On-Water growled in his throat. "What did I tell you?"

"I am called Angelito," White Cloud said.

"What kind of a name is that?" Hawk Wing muttered.

"My masters here—" White Cloud hesitated at that, for he knew The People recognized no masters. He pronounced more strange names: "*Lieutenant Moraga* and *Fra Palou* come to bring God's forgiveness to the heathen. We come in peace if you will accept the word of God. If not . . ."

White Cloud glanced quickly at the tall man he had identified as Lieutenant Moraga.

My thoughts whirled. I remembered walking with him along the hilltops. I remembered gray clouds blowing out on Great Sea, the harsh cry of gulls swooping through the sky, the faint spout of whales. I remembered the passion in his voice when he promised to return to me. I remembered how I had called upon Sky Father to give me my lover's seed that I might bear his children. I was so glad to see him again! And yet—what was he doing here with these strangers the smoke-dream had warned about?

"We know already of Sky Father," Fog-On-Water said with dignity, but under his words I could feel his anger rising. "Do you think—"

Bear-With-One-Ear put a hand on his brother's arm, silencing him. "If not?"

White Cloud said something. Lieutenant Moraga's fingers played over the handle of his own long knife, and his eyes glittered under heavy lids. There came a rustling as of impatience from among the warriors lined up behind him. The other stranger, who wore the gray robe and was called Fra Palou, spoke in a low voice to White Cloud, who bent his head reverently toward the man.

Then White Cloud turned to us again, translating. "We bring many gifts of beads and blankets and food. And the blessed salvation of God's love to all who will accept it."

My heart became a cold lump of clay.

"This makes my heart rejoice," Bear-With-One-Ear, the peacemaker, said. "Welcome, friends who also know of Sky Father! We'll light cooking fires and set fish to bake. We'll feast together this night."

White Cloud translated this, and I saw the strangers' faces soften into smiles, rigid muscles relaxed. Men wandered away from the gathering.

"'Beads and blankets?'" Gray Seal wondered.

I touched my uncle's sleeve.

"What is it, Red Deer?" he asked kindly, his expression showing his satisfaction.

"Lark Singing is dead, Uncle! But before she died, she made me—"

"What?" He stared at me, shock warring with the relief that had been in his face a moment ago.

"She died. I—I made the funeral pyre. I didn't think you had time right now."

"By what authority did you make this decision, Red Deer?"

His voice was calm, but I could hear anger in it, and I knew I must seize my own power at once or never have any in the tribe.

"I'm not a child anymore, Uncle. I'm a medicine woman. And I have warnings to give!"

All the uncles were staring at me, especially Fog-On-Water, who had never liked me. But Bear-With-One-Ear said, "I'm very glad to hear we won't be without counsel, Red Deer!"

Gray Seal laughed.

"I didn't mean—"

"We must mark Lark Singing's passing properly. But we'll talk about this later."

"That may be too late, Uncle! I've seen—"

"Our guests are waiting for a feast."

He turned away, deep in conversation with Fog-On-Water.

Little Gull tugged my arm. "That man who spoke for the strangers. He's looking at you, Red Deer!"

But I had failed my first task, and I could not bring myself to greet White Cloud.

> "I have taken that in hand that I know not in the world how to go through withal. It passeth my capacity. It hath even bereaved me of my wits to think on it."

"Fish," White Cloud said to me later as we sat in shadow at the edge of the feast. "Priests save the miserable creature for Lent or Friday penance!"

We had naturally come into each other's company, neither of us being important enough to sit with the captains after the first exchanges of pleasantries were over and the services of a translator were no longer needed, since the words both sides spoke no longer contained much of importance. My heart was pounding against my ribs. Something was different, something had changed. I felt full of dread.

"Tell me again, White Cloud," I said. "What're you doing in the company of these men? Why didn't you tell me of them before?"

"First of all," he said, "my name here is Angelito. Remember that. And there was nothing to tell before."

I thought about that. Among the adult Miwok, too, it was common to have a ceremonial name, just as my grandmother had given me mine, though we did not use it in everyday speech. So why did he turn his face away so I could not see his eyes?

"And now?" I asked when he had not said anything for a while.

"Don't make a fuss over trifles," he said. "Be happy we're together again, as I promised."

Though my mind flooded with doubt, my heart was happy to have me sit with him and listen to him explain the strangers. There were not many young men I could talk to with such pleasure. When a woman has grown up with her suitors, seen them as little boys, their hands dirty, noses unwiped, children who cannot yet control their bladders, it is hard to feel excitement in their presence. White Cloud—Angelito— whatever he wanted to be called—moved me in ways I had not known before.

"I'm still hungry," he complained after a while.

"Here's bread," Little Gull said. He had eaten his fill of clams and abalone and the silver fish that come up on the beach by moonlight and lay their eggs at this time of year. Now he was stuffing berry pies and honey cakes into his mouth, so that I was afraid he would soon be sick.

The noise was growing steadily as the feast ended. The strangers sat on one side of the fire, and the Miwok sat on the other. There was much gesturing and pointing and making faces from both groups, and both laughed a great deal and shouted out when a meaning jumped the barrier of language from one to the other. Bear-With-One-Ear had given orders that there be no shortage of cider for the feast, even though we seemed very nearly in danger of exhausting last season's apple harvest. When the eating was done, the tobacco pipes passed around.

Then the one called Lieutenant Moraga yelled something, and a man brought out a small wooden barrel from which he poured a liquid the color of pollen, and this he shared out both sides of the fire. It seemed the oftener this liquid went around the circle, the louder grew their voices, and the loudest ones belonged to my uncles, Bear-With-One-

Ear, Gray Seal, and Black Otter. They shouted and laughed and their faces were fiery red. Once, when the barrel came our way, Angelito offered me some. I tasted it—I remember still how it burned my tongue!—then I pushed it away. First Captain taught us to ferment the apples, and that was good, but this was liquid flame and dangerous.

"Sometimes we eat other things besides fish. Little birds or small game," Little Gull said. "What do you eat?"

I tugged playfully at his hair. A small boy's conversation is all out of time with that of his elders.

"Meat, of course!" Angelito said. "Buffalo or oxen. Or a tasty water fowl. You have plenty of them all over the place. Why didn't your chiefs serve them?"

"We never eat their flesh, only the eggs," I explained.

"You wouldn't kill the ducks?" Little Gull asked anxiously, and I hugged him to me.

Angelito's laughter, bubbling out like a spring of pure water melted my heart. "Why not?"

"Because we honor the First Captain," Little Gull said. He glanced at me to see if he had given the right answer, and I smiled at him.

But already the power my grandmother had passed to me began to shape my destiny, in spite of the wishes of my heart. I said, "Forgive me, Angelito, but I must ask again, and you must answer me this time. Why do you follow these strangers?"

"They aren't strangers to me," he said. "Have you heard of Junipero Serra? No, I suppose not. The good news has only just come to your poor towns! Fra Serra—a priest, like Fra Palou here—took me in when my father died, and taught me his language."

"'Priest,'" I said. "Shaman, do you mean?"

Angelito frowned. "Well, perhaps. But—different! It's Serra who's building all the missions up and down the shores of Great Sea. He sent me to assist de Anza on his quest—that was when I first saw you—and now I guide Moraga and Palou."

"What's a mission?" Little Gull asked.

"A place the good fathers build where The People can live and learn about the Lord Jesus Christ."

"Why is this good?" I asked. "Don't we have homes already?"

"Of course it's good!" Angelito said, and I heard irritation in his voice.

Then I asked, "And your mother, Angelito. What about her?"

Angelito hesitated. "She accepted the mercy of God." His right hand made an odd fluttering movement over his chest. "Now the Chumash live in the mission Fra Serra built, in the valley of the bears."

"And do you like it with the bears?" Little Gull asked. "What games do you play?"

Angelito made a face. "No time to play! Too much work to do. And prayer! A lot of that, to find salvation!"

His words made little sense to me. First Captain taught us to pray too. But among all The People, Miwok and Chumash and others up and down the shores of Great Sea, only shamans undertook a quest to find their spirit voices.

"But why have so many come on this quest?"

Angelito wiped fish grease off his fingers in the dust. "Fra Serra says Saint Francis needs his mission here. And de Anza thinks this inland sea will make a fine harbor for the tall canoes."

Confusion filled me then. Angelito had spoken the name of First Captain. Could it be these strangers revered First Captain? How fine that would be!

"Angelito, that name—Francis. Our First Captain was named Francis. What does this mean?"

He stared at me, frowning. "You're a strange woman, Red Deer. Yes, and the Miwok are different from The People to the south! I heard Lieutenant Moraga tell Fra Palou, such a pattern your square fields and hedges make—and the houses!—he hasn't seen the like since he visited England in his youth!"

England! The old people tell stories of their ancestors, First Captain's men who stayed behind, and the land they came from, so far away in the direction of sunrise.

"What do you know about England?" I asked, eager for fresh information.

"Not much. Only what I overhear. Some men from England may be building somewhere to the east—a long, long way from here, on the sunrise coast! It doesn't worry the holy fathers."

He knew about the people First Captain had come from! It seemed like a dream to be hearing about them. I was full of questions, but Angelito knew little more than I myself. I took a morsel of honey cake and thought about this. Something bothered me, like getting a thorn stuck in a tender part of the foot. I wanted so much to believe all was well. Yet I was still uneasy in my mind. There was a word I could not remember.

"This Fra Serra you speak of," I said. "He comes from the land south of the Chumash?"

"Holy Virgin, Mother of God!" Angelito did not look up from the dust, where his fingers were very busy. "How little you know!"

"You must promise not to harm the ducks," Little Gull said sleepily.

Angelito laughed. "Go to bed, little bird lover!"

Little Gull wandered away, rubbing his eyes.

My heart won its struggle against my mind, and I leaned over and kissed Angelito on the cheek. He held me close, his lips against my hair, and both of us paid little attention to the feast.

> "Our enemies are many but our Protector com-
> mandeth the whole world."

I awoke much later alone, screaming from a frightening dream.

The feasting had gone far into the night until there was no more wood to burn and no man who could stand upright long enough to fetch more. It seemed that the strangers' yellow drink softened the bones of the legs. Then Angelito and I lay down together in the darkness under the oak trees and became one. It was like fire and honey, violent as a storm on Great Sea and delicate as apple blossom. I gave up my soul to Angelito, and he his to me. As blood thundered through my veins, I thought it must be possible to serve both love and the power that had chosen me, for I did not see how I could ever give up my love.

In the next room I could hear Bear-With-One-Ear snoring. Even as the dream let go of my heart, I thought now that I was a medicine woman, I could not go on living in my uncle's house. I must soon build one for myself of oak wood and baked river mud colored white, with a thatched roof of tule reeds. Perhaps I would take Little Gull with me. For a while longer he could live with a woman. Then he must go to Hawk Wing's house to learn how to be a man.

At that I realized Little Gull was not asleep on his mat beside me.

I should have guessed he would become sick from eating so much! As I knew that, I also knew the sight had given me my answer in a dream. Death had entered our town, and I had remembered its name.

I scrambled up from the mat, my hands shaking with fear.

I found my brother outside his house, smoking a pipe, moonlight cloaking his bare shoulders like finest deerskin.

"Francis Hawk Wing!" I cried. "We're surrounded by enemies!"

He looked up, his expression ugly in the moonlight. "I saw you kiss the shaman's slave tonight. Have you come from his bed?"

I took in a quick gasp of cold night air. Then I raised my fist and hit my brother's cheek with all my strength. His hand flew up to touch the place, but he said nothing.

"Be silent, fool! Little Gull's gone. And I know the name of these strangers. They're Spaniards."

He stared at me. "First Captain fought Spaniards on land and sea! Burnt their ships. Took their treasure. Remember what he wrote?

'There was never anything that pleased me better than seeing the enemy flying with a southerly wind to the northwards!' "

"Yes, but do you know why he hated them?"

"The *papa*—and the lies he taught about Sky Father."

"More than that, Hawk Wing," I said. "Much more! Remember the stories from the long voyage of the Big Canoes?"

"He hated them for their cruelty to The People. He said every man had a right to be free, not a slave." Then he frowned. "How do you know this?"

"It came to me in a dream."

"A dream?" My brother's expression was incredulous. "Why should I take notice of such nonsense?"

"Because Lark Singing taught me to *see* before she died! I am the medicine woman of the tribe now. I tried to tell this to Bear-With-One-Ear—but we're wasting time!"

He gazed at me a moment longer while he thought it over. Then he jumped to his feet, his hand reaching for the crossbow that lay beside him. Hawk Wing ran fast, but I flew faster. Through the sleeping town we raced, to the place I had seen in my dream. Fires flickered where guards kept watch in the Spaniards' camp.

On the trampled grass where the feast had been held we found Little Gull, a clutch of duck feathers in his hand. His skull had been split open. Blood soaked into the earth around him.

I fell down on his small body, wailing. "Why? Why?"

Hawk Wing dragged me up again. "Later we'll find out why! Now we must avenge this Spanish killing!"

From across the lake, where the gray-robed priest camped under the oaks, came the smell of roasting flesh, and I gagged. Too much was happening, too quickly.

Inside my head the voice of Elizabeth Lark Singing said, "*My time is over. Yours is coming.*"

No! I said to the vision. I wanted only to live with my lover and raise children on the shores of Great Sea.

"What can we do?" I cried. "We're a peaceful people. We're not ready for war!"

Hawk Wing grabbed me by the arms and thrust his face close to mine. It was mottled red with his anger. "Do you remember the teaching First Captain gave us?"

"Yes." I looked down at Little Gull's small body. "But we don't know how to fight an enemy like this."

"I know how to fight Spaniards," Hawk Wing said. "First Captain taught that as the lore of men. He warned us one day Spaniards would come up the coast, even to our peaceful land, and we must be ready. This is why young men spend so much time learning the skills of killing that we need. And we've spread this teaching to the men of all the tribes around Lesser Sea. We're ready!"

"Do you think arrows will suffice against monsters who kill children?" I asked scornfully. "For that's all you have. Men who wear metal clothes will fight with stranger weapons than you can dream of!"

At that Hawk Wing smiled. "You think so because you're a woman! That long metal stick they carry? That's an harquebus. Oh, better perhaps than the two First Captain left with us so long ago. I can't make one, but I know how a gun works, and if I get one from the Spaniards, I'll use it against them! But, tell me, Red Deer. Do you truly know how to *see*? How to tell me where the advantage lies when I make war? Can you take Lark Singing's place? Will you do that?"

No one could take Lark Singing's place. I wept again, for Little Gull, for our people in the terrible days that the sight showed me would come, for the blood that would flow before we were rid of our enemies. And I wept for myself with the heavy burden of sight.

He was impatient with my tears. He shook me hard. "Well? Give me an answer!"

"I'll do it."

"Good." He released my arm. "Then I'll kill this Moraga before he knows what's happened! With him dead the Spaniards—"

"No!" I said sharply. "You don't know as much as you think about these enemies. First you must kill their shaman, Palou."

"Red Deer—"

"I have *seen* this, Hawk Wing! Listen to what I say. And when that's done, seek south for the shaman called Junipero Serra, and kill him too! Serra is the *papa's* wolf that would devour us as First Captain warned."

"I'll gather the men," my brother said. "We're ready. We'll kill all who travel under the Spaniards' banner!"

"Hawk Wing," I said as he turned to leave.

"Yes?"

"Spare Angelito."

"He's one of them!"

"Leave him for me."

"Done by English who are well disposed if there
be no cause to the contrary. If there be cause, we
will be devils rather than men."

Thus began the years of blood and fire that I had seen in the smoke-dream in my grandmother's hut. My memory quails before the task of retelling the death and the suffering of the Miwok during those years. (I tell it now only that you will understand that sometimes evil things must be done in order for good to come of them.)

The first arrow my brother shot took the priest Palou, and the second, the warrior Moraga. Then I learned the wisdom of my uncle Black Otter's remark, for we had the enemy surrounded. But even so the Spaniards were not easily killed, though there were few of them. They fought like demons. The battle lasted three days, and many of our own died too. I remember Bear-With-One-Ear was killed in that first battle, for he was old and slow-moving, and Black Otter with him. And when Hawk Wing and his warriors had finished in the river meadow outside our town, the dead lay in rows under the sun, their corpses crawling with flies, for there were too many to cremate all at once.

Angelito came to me, on the second day of the battle, begging shelter. I took him into the house that had been my uncle's but was mine now and I concealed him from my brother's warriors, hiding him under the blankets on my own bed. First Captain had told us Spaniards were our enemies, but I thought that The People must defend each other. Angelito did not argue when I gave him back his own name. I held him close to my breast while Death stalked outside with his fellow riders, Famine, Pestilence, and War. In spite of the danger outside we lay in each other's arms and were happy. We spoke of children we would have together, how the rivers of our blood would run together and create a tribe that would stand proudly against tall enemies. Miwok, Chumash, English—no mere Spaniard could frighten us!

When the battle was over at last and there was time to mourn the dead, I wrapped Little Gull's stiff body in his blanket and laid him on the funeral platform. I took First Captain's knife that had hung over the hearth to cut wood for the fire, and White Cloud went with me. It was a hot day, the valleys clotted with the odor of death, the sky full of smoke from the funeral fires.

"Little bird lover, I tried to warn you," White Cloud said, laying pine branches on my brother's body. "This wouldn't have happened if you'd stayed in bed."

Something stirred in me then, like a blind worm in the cold earth. I felt my destiny rising to confront me as I looked at my lover. "Why do you say that?"

"Because he tried to save a duck Lieutenant Moraga wanted. I told you these Spaniards were meat eaters." Then he laughed his easy laugh. "You should have served more than fish at your feast!"

"You saw this?" I said slowly. *No!* I said in my mind, *No! I will not accept this hard destiny!*

He nodded. "I had just gone back to camp."

"And did nothing?"

He gazed at me. "What could I do, Red Deer? I was only a priest's servant!" He turned back to heap more wood on the pyre.

Now I saw what it was First Captain had really warned us of. The real danger lay within us if we forgot ourselves, if we became slaves, smiling though we were bound. Even a man like White Cloud—so beautiful! so fine!—could become a slave in his heart.

I knew immediately what I must do, yet I fought it. The path of my life forked here, but I did not want to choose! *Why can I not have both?* I cried in my pain.

Once the power has taken a woman, her life is straight and clear, but very hard. And there is no going back.

So I closed my heart against my lover, and I filled my mind with the teachings of First Captain. While White Cloud's back was still turned, I drew out First Captain's knife. My hand trembled so much, I needed the other to steady it, but I stuck the knife deep into his ribs.

He gave a great, ragged gasp and half turned to me, dragging the knife out of my hands. "Red Deer!"

"You named yourself correctly, Angelito," I said. "You became one of them."

A stain as scarlet as the berries Little Deer had been picking when he first saw this man spread over his back where the knife still protruded.

"For the love of God—"

"For the love of The People, Angelito."

Blood bubbled at the corner of his mouth. He stared at me, his eyes already filming over. He stumbled, holding out his arms to me to steady him.

I stepped back and let him fall. *Enemy! Enemy!* I said over and over in my mind so that I would not cry.

I, too, could become a devil when there was cause.

After a few days Hawk Wing gathered men from many tribes along the coast of Great Sea and the inland valleys all around Lesser Sea and at my urging led them south to find Junipero Serra. Gray Seal went south with my brother, but Fog-On-Water remained here to hold the tribes together when they were gone, teaching them to trust no Spaniard, nor show mercy to gray-robed priests who would have given them none.

My brother's warriors found Serra a year later, with a party of Spaniards at the big mission he had built on the large bay where seals and sea otters played in the kelp and The People foraged for abalone. I had seen him there in a smoke-dream.

I was still in mourning for my uncles and for Little Gull, and I was nursing the infant when they brought Serra back to our town. I was surprised to see how small he was, and how frail. He walked with a limp, his shoulders bowed under the hot sun. I had thought this wolf must be a giant to have such power to harm us. It did not seem possible that such a weak man could create such havoc. The power of an evil shaman is such that he can make himself appear harmless, like a coiled snake waiting to strike. I knew he was the one who was truly guilty of my lover's death, for it was his teaching that had corrupted White Cloud so that I had been forced to kill him.

"See," I said to the infant. "This is your father's murderer!"

But it did not help the pain.

We kept little Serra for a while in a hut, because Fog-On-Water said we should see if these Spaniards would trade for him, to get him back. My uncle sent a message to the mission in the valley of the bears where White Cloud had been born, but there was no answer. We began to see that although the Spaniards were wolves, the pack might be small or too far from the den to have power if we attacked them. We knew now that we could win.

So when the apples ripened on the trees and the breeze off the inland sea cooled the evenings, I made Hawk Wing kill Serra too. The Miwok rejoiced with a feast. But I held my infant close to my breast and mourned for White Cloud in secret in my house.

Even that was not the end of it. All that year and the next and the one after, Spaniards came riding into Nova Albion with guns. But we had a few of the guns we had taken from Moraga's men in that first battle, though we soon ran out of powder for them.

I was wrong. The crossbow is strong and efficient, and arrows can kill as well as guns. And when that was not enough, I built fire and tipped the arrows with flame and gave them to my brother to shoot. Our warriors followed up each flight of arrows, racing yipping and yelping like coyotes into the midst of the Spaniards, who did not know whether to beat out the fires or beat off our warriors. So we held them off.

My brother was the boldest of the warriors, merry in the face of every danger, taking risks that made lesser men tremble, always attacking the fiercest of the enemy, never satisfied until he had killed the leader with his own hands. The Miwok said of him that he was First Captain himself, come back to us in our time of need.

One day Hawk Wing, too, was felled by the guns and lay on the ground, half his stomach gone. It took him a long time to die, and little I knew to ease the pain. But by then we had taken many of these weapons from the bodies of our enemies, and even the young women had learned how to use them. The Spaniards were already in flight when I laid my brother on his funeral pyre.

> "There must be a beginning of any great matter,
> but the continuing unto the end until it be thor-
> oughly finished yields the true glory."

Nova Albion, 1840

I tell this long tale of killing and being killed that you who have never known anything but peace should understand what it is you have dreamed this night.

Nova Albion is free from the threat of its enemies. Friendship and trust have spread among The People of a hundred towns around Lesser Sea. We have not forgotten to be vigilant, but until this night you have known nothing of war or bloodshed. We have lived in peace under the laws First Captain gave us, showing friendship to all who are friends to us, and punishing those who would harm us. Each year that passes brings more of The People up and down the coast and far inland to accept our laws, for they are just and wise. Our houses rise up the hills; our harvests prosper; our canoes sail far out over Great Sea for fish and across Lesser Sea to trade with our neighbors. Nova Albion thrives! And *Spaniard* has become only a name to make naughty children behave.

Look in this mirror. Do you see how the child gives way now to the young woman? I will braid your beautiful red hair while we talk of the vision the smoke gave you. Sky Father answered my prayer, though not as I had expected. Many bloodlines run in your veins, and you will need the wisdom of all of them.

That evil men should once again lust after our land is not surprising. This time they come from the east, but what of that? The descendants of the once-proud Spaniards in the south are weak and disorganized; we have nothing to fear from them! And though this metal you saw puzzles me—yellow as the sun, you say?—even that perhaps I have seen in flecks of sand on the beach at low tide by the river's mouth.

Travelers carry tales of strife and bloodshed across a great land that stretches from sunset to sunrise. Everywhere outside the boundaries of Nova Albion people fight to protect their land from invaders. They are not as strong as we are. Since those days I have spoken of, we built more smoke towers across the mountains and deserts to our east so that we might be warned when our enemies come. For as First Captain taught, he whose eyes be open to the horizon shall not be taken unaware by storm.

I have outlived my daughter, and I am glad my time is over and yours coming. The power has chosen you, and perhaps like me you will be called upon to sacrifice your desires and dreams. Yet I have learned something. Life itself is the answer, and a destiny larger than our petty wills drives us on, like the Big Canoes crossing Great Sea. We do what we do because of that.

I do not doubt there will be trouble. The smoke-dream does not lie. Your dream tells me we will continue to the end and take the victory once again.

Still, I am puzzled. This new pack of wolves, you say, speaks the tongue of First Captain. For his sake we will hold our fire until we determine whether they be honorable men, and perhaps we shall make a treaty among equals. Have no fear. First Captain taught us well that though our enemies be many, yet we shall defeat them if there be cause. We shall remain free!

Yet I wonder what he would think if we have to kill English?

ISABELLA OF CASTILE ANSWERS HER MAIL

James Morrow

To YOU, DON CRISTÓBAL COLÓN, our Admiral of the Ocean Sea, Viceroy and Governor of all the Islands to be found by you on your Great Voyage of Discovery, greetings and grace.

What a beautiful and welcome sight was your albatross messenger, swooping out of the skies like a new soul arriving in Heaven! How your letter raised my failing hopes and lifted my sagging spirits! O brave mariner, I feel confident that the seagoing gardens of which you spoke, those vast floating mats of sargasso weed, signify that your fleet has at last drawn near the Indies. By the time these words appear before your eyes, you will have walked the bejeweled streets of Cathay and toured the golden temples of Cipango.

Dear friend, I should like to know your opinion concerning a most troublesome matter. Do you hold any particular views on the Jewish Question? Predictably, my Edict of General Expulsion has proven highly controversial here at court. Our Keeper of the Privy Purse—I speak now of Santángel, perhaps the loudest of all those voices championing your expedition—became distressed to the point of tears, though as a *converso* he is doubtless biased by his blood. The clergy was divided, with Deza calling the measure vital to the future of the Church and Perez quoting the Sermon on the Mount. But it was my old confessor, Torquemada, who used the strongest words. As long as unbelievers live among us, the Inquisitor explained, there can be no racial purity, no *limpieza de sangre*, in Spain.

And yet, three nights ago a vivid and disquieting dream came to me. I no longer wore the Crown of Castile but the war helmet of Rameses II. Am I the new Pharaoh? In banishing Spain's Jews, have I thrust myself forever into God's disfavor? O Cristóbal, my heart feels like one of those great iron anchors you will soon be dropping into the waters off Asia.

Written in the City of Sante Fe on this twenty-seventh day of August, in the year of Our Lord Jesus Christ 1492.

I, THE QUEEN

TO YOU, ISABELLA, by the Grace of God Queen of Castile, León, Aragón, Granada, Sicily, Sardinia, and the Balearics, greetings and increase of good fortune.

Alas, we passed through the Sargasso Sea without sighting the Indies, a situation so dismaying to my officers and me that they begged me to turn back. I was comforting them as best I could, pointing out that we had not yet gone two thousand miles (though in truth we had gone twenty-eight hundred), when the Ocean Sea began suddenly to swell, arching like a mountain range in motion, pulling its slopes and valleys intact behind it. We rode those waves, my Queen, plummeting inexorably from crest to cavity and back again. Terror-struck at first, we soon realized that God Himself had sent this cataclysm to speed us toward the Moluccas. Such a miracle has not occurred since Egypt's chariots gave chase to the Children of Israel!

You spoke of Spain's own Jews. By curious coincidence, the same tide that bore the *Niña*, the *Pinta*, and the *Santa María* out of port also carried what I took to be a contingent of your General Expulsion, that Second Exodus that weighs so heavily on your heart. As we traveled down the Rio Saltés to the sea, our way was blocked by every sort of vessel imaginable, their holds jammed with refugees clutching kettles, crockery, toys, lanterns, and other meager possessions. Initially this scene aroused in your Admiral an unequivocal pity (the weeping, the wailing, the old ones jumping overboard and crawling onto the rocks to die, the rabbis beseeching Yahweh to part the waters of the Levant and lead the people dry-shod to a new Promised Land), but then Father Hojeda invited me to see it in a different light. "By driving the infidels from its cities, towns, and fields," Hojeda explained, "the Crown has made room for the pagan hordes we shall soon be ferrying to Spain from the Orient, thousands upon thousands of unbaptized souls yearning to embrace the Holy Faith." So do not despair, Sovereign Queen. Your edict has served a divine plan.

I must rest my pen. A cry of *"Tierra!"* has just gone up from the lookout stationed atop our mainmast. *Gloria in excelsis Deo*—the impossible is accomplished! We have sailed west and met the East!

Written aboard the caravel *Santa María* on this second day of September, in the year of Our Lord Jesus Christ 1492.

I, THE ADMIRAL

TO YOU, DON CRISTÓBAL COLÓN, our Admiral of the Ocean Sea, Viceroy and Governor of all the Islands to be found by you on your Great Voyage of Discovery, greetings and grace.

For five whole days I brooded upon the sobering news from North Africa—racking rumors of Jews cast naked into the sea by the captains we had hired to deport them, wrenching accounts of those very exiles starving on forgotten shores, grisly tales of these same refugees being eviscerated by Turkish mobs in quest of swallowed coins. Then came your letter of the second.

O noble navigator, you have surely delivered your Queen from madness! I now see that the true and final purpose of our expedition is not to plot a new route to the Indies, nor is it to forge an alliance with the Great Khan, nor is it to build a bastion from which we might attack the Turkish rear and win back Constantinople (though each of these aims is worthy). I now see that its true and final purpose is to lead all Asia to the Holy Faith. Not since my correspondence with Sixtus IV, through which he so kindly allayed my fears that in reducing the children of heretics to beggary the Inquisition had overstepped its mandate, has my conscience known such release. Is it blasphemous for a Queen to compare her Admiral with her Pope? Then may God forgive me.

So, courageous conquistador, you have found the Moluccas at last. In your subsequent missives you may, if so inclined, make mention of the following matters: gold, silver, rubies, sapphires, diamonds, emeralds, precious silks, rare spices. But speak to me first and foremost of the spiritual condition of the Indian people. Do they seem well disposed to receive the Gospel? Does Father Hojeda wish to perform all the baptisms himself, or shall I send a company of priests in your wake?

Written in our City of Sante Fe on this seventh day of September, in the year of Our Lord Jesus Christ 1492.

I, THE QUEEN

TO YOU, ISABELLA, by the Grace of God Queen of Castile, León, Aragón, etc., greetings and increase of good fortune.

How can mere words convey the miracle that is the Indies? How can I begin to describe the mysteries and marvels that have dazzled us in recent days? Vast, glittering palaces! Mighty minarets belching smoke and fire! Ships that sail without benefit of wind! Coaches that move without a single horse in harness! Carriages that fly through the air on featherless wings!

After slipping beneath the largest bridge I have ever seen, a mile-long passageway stretching over our heads like a bronze rainbow, our fleet sailed up a dark and oily strait and anchored off what we took to be one of the lesser Moluccas. Dominating the island was an iron idol rising a hundred and fifty feet at least, surmounting a pedestal of almost equal height. I forthwith gathered together an exploration party consisting of Father Hojeda, Captain Pinzón, and myself; plus our translator, Luis de Torres, and our master-at-arms, Diego de Harana. We came ashore in the dinghy of the *Santa María*, assembled in the shadow of the idol, and, thrusting the royal standard of Castile into the grassy soil, claimed the island for the Crown.

A most astonishing fact: there is no *limpieza de sangre* in Asia. Everywhere we turned, our eyes beheld a different fashion in flesh— dark, light, rough, coarse—and our ears rang with the greatest confusion of tongues since the Tower of Babel toppled. We saw Moors. We saw Nubians. Greeks. Jews. From amid the general cacophony Torres claimed he could discern not only Portuguese, Arabic, Yiddish, and Polish, but also the language of my native Genoa, though I caught no such syllables myself. Surprisingly, we soon encountered a sizable percentage of Indians for whom a peculiarly cadenced Castilian is the medium of choice. (I must confess, I was not aware that your Highness's overland mercantile endeavors had placed so many Spaniards in the Orient.) But the greatest shock, surely, was the omnipresence of English, not only in the mouths of the Indians but on the plethora of public signs, banners, mottoes, and decrees.

"Give me your weary, your indigent, your huddled multitudes seeking to breathe without hindrance, the miserable garbage of your crowded beaches . . ." So began Torres's rather diffident rendering of the incantation that accompanies the idol. (English is not his forte.) "Send these, the homeless, typhoon-buffeted to me," he continued. "I lift my lantern beside the portal of gold."

The idol's form is female, and she evidently embodies something called *libertad*—a difficult idea to explicate, but Torres has inferred it means "giving free rein to your worst instincts and basest impulses." No doubt the "huddled multitudes" are sacrificial victims. Some are probably burned to death—hence the firebrand in the idol's right hand. Others are impaled alive—hence the seven dreadful spikes decorating her crown.

With the setting of the sun I directed my party back to the caravels, dined alone on ham and beer, and began the present epistle. We are uncertain of our next move. From the Indians' chatter, Torres has surmised that other Moluccas lie in our vicinity—the Spice Island of Ellis to the north, the Spice Island of Governors to the east, the Spice Island of Manhattan to the northeast—and we are strongly inclined to explore them. But, O my Queen, this idol of *libertad* vexes us most sorely. The very sight of her looming over the fleet brings ice to our bowels. Might you perchance be willing to dispatch a regiment of soldiers to the Indies, so that we might undertake to baptize this cult without fear of immolation? Eagerly I await your reply.

Written aboard the caravel *Santa María* on this twelfth day of September, in the year of Our Lord Jesus Christ 1492.

I, THE ADMIRAL

TO YOU, DON CRISTÓBAL COLÓN, our Admiral of the Ocean Sea, Viceroy and Governor of all the Islands to be found by you on your Great Voyage of Discovery, greetings and grace.

Frankly, my Admiral, we don't quite know what to make of your Spice Islands and their polyglot aborigines. As with the Jewish Question, the court is of several minds. Santángel thinks you may have stumbled upon the Lost Tribes of Israel. The clergy believes you have sailed clear past the Indies and landed in one of these secret colonies set up by Europe's escaped convicts and fugitive mutineers.

In any event we cannot send you infantry support. Now that Granada is ours, we have demobilized the army, leaving in uniform only our border troops, our palace guards, and our Santa Hermandad. But even if an extra regiment did lie at our disposal, we would not send it across the Ocean Sea. Dearest Cristóbal, have you forgotten the sheer power of Scripture? Do you doubt the potency of Truth? Once Father Hojeda tells them the whole story, from the Virgin Birth to the Resurrection, this *libertad* cult will surely abandon its wicked, pagan, persecuting ways. So say friars Deza and Perez.

This is not a happy time for the Queen of Castile. My daughter still grieves for her husband, the Crown Prince Alfonso, killed last month in a riding accident, and she evinces no romantic interest in his successor. Day in, day out, the Infanta Isabella skulks about the castle, dressing in black, singing bawdy ballads, and, worst of all, threatening to join the Holy Sisters in Toledo. Let her marry our Lord Jesus Christ in the next life—at the moment her duty is to marry Portugal!

Yet another lady-in-waiting has acquiesced to Ferdinand's advances. As soon as her transgression became apparent, I hurried the harlot and her nascent baby off to the nearest convent, though in truth I would have preferred to hurry the king off to the nearest monastery. (It is quite enough to make me regret that you and I behaved so honorably last April in my Segovian rose garden.) If there were chastity belts for men, I would this very night slip one over my husband's lecherous loins, lock it up, and hide the key where I alone can find it.

I am bored, sir. Nothing amuses me. Yesterday I attended a bullfight—an unrelievedly gory and grotesque spectacle. I have half a mind to outlaw the entire sport. This morning's auto-da-fé was equally jejune. Of the nineteen heretics paraded through the streets in *sanbenitos*, eleven repented, seven went to the stake, and one dropped dead from fright. I left before the burnings, the weather having turned rainy and cold.

Cristóbal, you and you alone can relieve my tedium. You must visit these other Moluccas, teaching the Indians about eternal life, searching out *libertad's* golden portal, and having many beguiling adventures. And then, when you are finished, you must pick up your pen and excite me with your exploits.

Written in our City of Santa Fe on this seventeenth day of September, in the year of Our Lord Jesus Christ 1492.

I, THE QUEEN

TO YOU, ISABELLA, by the Grace of God Queen of Castile, León, Aragón, etc., greetings and increase of good fortune.

Following your directive of the seventeenth, we have spent the past fourteen hours in quest of souls and gold, and I must tell you at the outset that no man has ever endured a more perplexing day.

The *Niña* has always been my favorite of the fleet, and certainly the ship best designed for exploring coasts, so with dawn's first light I transferred my flag to her, leaving Pinzón and his brothers in charge of the *Santa María* and the *Pinta*. Once Torres, Harana, and Father Hojeda were aboard, we took off, eventually dropping our anchor perhaps sixty yards off Manhattan. Setting out in the dinghy, we disembarked at a place called Battery Park, unfurled our standard, and acquired the island for Spain.

We were immediately struck by the large number of beggars in our midst, men and women with dirty faces, torn clothing, hollow eyes, and vacant bellies. Poor as heretics' children, they carried all their earthly belongings about in sacks (rather like the Jews I noted traveling down the Saltees), and we quickly identified them as the "homeless, typhoon-buffeted" creatures named on the idol's plaque. An infinite remorse gripped me as I realized they were all destined to be skewered on the spikes of *libertad* and consumed by her flames.

Torres tried several times to start a conversation with these wretches, asking why they did not flee from Battery Park to whatever monasteries, convents, and sanctuaries might grace the interior. Their responses were invariably a crude idiomatic expression to the effect that Torres should forthwith become a hermaphrodite and experience self-contained sexual congress.

As if sensing our communication difficulties, a bold young Indian approached, offering his services as both interpreter and guide. Born Rodrigo Menendez, he said he was raised in the distant Spanish-speaking land of "Cuba-man." Though formidable in appearance, with a tiny gold ring through his right nostril, a dark blue kerchief tied around his forehead, and a shirt inscribed BEAM ME UP, SCOTTY, THERE'S NO INTELLIGENT LIFE DOWN HERE, he assured us he was of the Holy Faith, attending Mass regularly as well as something called "Cardinal O'Connor High School-man," situated on the Twenty-third Street. We offered to pay him in the various trinkets that appeal so profoundly to the African peoples with whom the Crown barters: red felt caps, glass necklaces, little brass bells. He was not interested. When we displayed the cask of vintage Marques de Cacares that Father Hojeda had so cleverly brought ashore, however, the youth's eyes lit up like votive candles, and for this good consideration he entered our employ.

A tour of "Lower Manhattan," Rodrigo assured us, typically begins with "the New York Stock Exchange." From his description, we surmised it was a principal meeting place of the *libertad* cult. Steeling ourselves, we followed the youth east along the "Wall" road, site of many grand citadels and lofty towers. The passing Indians fairly dripped of gold—gold bracelets, gold wedding bands, gold chains about their necks, gold pebbles in their teeth.

We entered the temple in question. Believe me, Your Highness, rarely has a faith excited such zeal. Those who attend the New York Stock Exchange celebrate with a frenzy I have never seen before. They run around like lunatics and shout like the Apostles at Pentecost. It did not take Father Hojeda long to decide that these stock exchangers are nowise ready to hear about Jesus Christ, so tenacious are their present beliefs. I am inclined to concur.

As we left the temple, the utter strangeness of the surrounding city prompted me to speculate we might have reached the fabled waterbound kingdom of which Marco Polo wrote. I asked Rodrigo if we could possibly be on one of the Cipango Islands.

He said, "The which?"

"Cipango Islands. You know—the Japans."

Whereupon the youth explained that Cipango indeed possessed many "holdings" on Manhattan, including treasuries, trading posts, and money-lending houses plus something called "Rockefeller Center-man." However, while these assorted enterprises evidently make Manhattan a kind of colony of Cipango, Rodrigo reckoned the actual Kingdom of Japan to be some considerable distance away.

"If we're not in Cipango, have we perhaps found Cathay?" asked Father Hojeda.

"Huh? Cathay?"

"Do you call it Quinsay? China, perhaps?"

"Ah—you want to see Chinatown!"

The youth guided us to an enclave consisting primarily of places to eat. It took us but a moment to realize that "Chinatown" is no more contiguous with Cathay than the money-lending houses are contiguous with Cipango. We did, however, enjoy an excellent lunch of pork, rice, and bamboo shoots. Rodrigo paid for this repast using the local currency, a debt we agreed to cover with a second cask of Marques de Cacares.

"Our fervent hope was to form an alliance with the Great Khan," I explained to the youth, making no effort to hide my disappointment over the disparity between Chinatown and Cathay. "We bear a royal letter of recommendation from the King and Queen of Spain."

"The closest we got to a khan is the mayor," the youth answered, "but I don't think he worries a whole lot about where he stands with the King and Queen of Spain."

Through further questioning of Rodrigo, we learned that this "mayor" claims an African heritage, whereupon Father Hojeda and I decided it was probably most accurate to regard him as a local chieftain. Rodrigo offered to take us to the ruler's headquarters, a "City Hall-man" lying perhaps a half mile south of Chinatown. We accepted. As we set out on our diplomatic mission, however, the youth casually mentioned that a previous such Chief of Manhattan had been of Jewish descent. Naturally I was not about to open negotiations with any realm whose throne has held the avaricious assassins of Christ—not without explicit orders from Your Highness.

"We would like to see the sources of the gold," I said to Rodrigo.

The youth replied, "Gold? Yeah, sure, I can show you some gold."

"We would also like to see the gems," added Harana.

"And the spices," added Torres.

"And the precious fabrics," added Father Hojeda.

"We go uptown-man," said the youth. "We take the subway, eh?"

These "subways" proved to be machines most terrible and terrifying: self-propelled coaches linked in serpentine configurations, racing through underground passageways at demonic speeds. All during the trip Rodrigo engaged in a long, rambling, unsolicited speech to the effect that while he doesn't question the sanctity of marriage, he is just as glad his parents got divorced, and while he admits the wrongfulness of thwarting semen on its journey, he would never leave home without a pocketful of penis sheaths, and while he understands that extracting fetuses from the womb is a sin, he doesn't know how he'd react if his girlfriend, Martina, ever became pregnant by him. O my dear Isabella, it would seem that,

before we attempt to convert this city's Indians to Catholicism, we must
first seek to convert its Catholics to Catholicism.

Reaching the "Pennsylvania" station via the "Seventh Avenue Local,"
we climbed back to the surface and followed our guide north to a place
where he promised we would see the precious fabrics. He spoke the
truth. All the way from the Thirty-fourth Street to the Fortieth, nimble
Indian peasants transported silks, satins, cashmere, velvet, gossamer,
chenille, damask, and a hundred other exotic cloths (including a
wrinkleproof material known as polyester), shuttling them about in the
form of both uncut bolts and finished suits. At the moment I cannot say
exactly what trading opportunities this bazaar may offer Spain. We saw
many Jews.

"What about the gold?" asked Harana.

"This way," said Rodrigo, pointing north. "Gold, silver, gems."

He took us to "the Jewelry District," on the Forty-seventh Street near
"the Avenue of the Americas." Again, the youth knew whereof he spoke.
Treasure lay everywhere, nearly all of it under the jurisdiction of Jews
wearing dreadlocks, grotesque hats, and long black coats. We must not
take anything, Rodrigo cautioned us. If we tried to remove the gold, the
policía would intervene, presumably cutting off our hands and feet in the
manner, my Queen, of your Santa Hermandad.

"Are the spices near?" asked Harana.

"Bit of a hike," said the youth. "You up for it?"

Our party traveled west, then north on the "Broadway" road to
"Columbus Circle," locus of an idol bearing a singularly pleasing countenance, then higher still to the Eighty-first Street, where we found
ourselves at the source of the spices. Even from the sidewalk we could
smell them: cloves, nutmeg, anise, cinnamon, thyme, ginger, basil—a
thousand and one Oriental delights, wafting into our nostrils like the
expirations of angels.

Then we saw the name.

Zabar's.

"Jews?" I inquired.

"Jews," the youth confirmed.

We did not go inside.

Dearest Isabella, could it possibly be that your Second Exodus beat us
across the Ocean Sea? Did your ministers by some strange quirk equip
the exiled infidels with ships faster even than the *Niña*, the *Pinta*, and
the *Santa María*?

I am back in my cabin now, scribbling by the light of a full moon, a
perfect sphere that sails the sky like a burning pomegranate. The tide is
rising in Upper New York Bay, lifting my flagship up and down on her

hawser like a ball riding atop the snout of a Bronx Zoo seal. The harbor air scrapes my throat, burns my chest, and brings tears to my eyes.

You must advise us, Sovereign Queen. These Spice Islands confound our minds and confuse our souls. Should we confiscate the gold? Lay claim to the silks and spices? Present our credences at City Hall-man? Attempt to convert the stock exchangers? What?

Written aboard the caravel *Santa María* on this twenty-second day of September, in the year of Our Lord Jesus Christ 1492.

I, THE ADMIRAL

TO YOU, DON CRISTÓBAL COLÓN, our Admiral of the Ocean Sea, Viceroy and Governor of all the Islands to be found by you on your Great Voyage of Discovery, greetings and grace.

Forgive my tardiness in answering, but we have recently uprooted our court, the food supplies in Sante Fe having become depleted and its latrines full, with the result that your communiqué of the twenty-second went momentarily astray.

What twisted wind, what perverted current has brought you to the city of which you speak? How are we to account for such a mad and upside-down dominion, this Manhattan where Jews prosper, prevail, and place themselves upon thrones? You are not in Asia, Cristóbal.

A consensus has emerged here. My King, my councillors, and my heart all agree. You must not linger another moment in that Satanic place. Leave, friend. We have no use for Manhattan's filthy gold. We do not seek its tarnished silver, tainted gems, rancid spices, rotten silks.

Predictably, Santángel offers a voice of dissent. He wants you to stay on Manhattan and learn how a city without *limpieza de sangre* has accomplished so many marvels. I believe it is the Jew in him talking. No matter. My wish, not his, is your command.

Take the next tide, Admiral. Pull up your anchor, sail south, and don't stop till you've found a world that makes some sense.

Written in our City of Barcelona on this first day of October, in the year of Our Lord Jesus Christ 1492.

I, THE QUEEN

TO YOU, ISABELLA, by the Grace of God Queen of Castile, León, Aragón, etc., greetings and increase of good fortune.

It is my supreme pleasure to report that your royal intuitions were correct. We quit New York within an hour of your letter's arrival, returning to the Ocean Sea and heading due south as you so wisely instructed. Once again the waves became like mountains, and once again we followed them to our destiny. On October twelfth, after a journey of six days, an exhilarating cry of *"Tierra!"* issued from my lookout.

The island we found that afternoon bore little resemblance to Manhattan. It had no citadels, subways, beggars, or Chinese inns. We came ashore on a pristine expanse of gleaming white coral, beyond which lay a jungle so lush and green we thought immediately of Eden before the Fall. When the natives appeared, at first peering out from among the trees, then walking down to the beach to greet us, we were further reminded of the Golden Age. They were gentle beyond telling, peaceful beyond belief, and naked as the day God made them. Unlike Rodrigo back on Manhattan, they eagerly accepted our gifts, placing the red felt caps on their heads, draping the glass necklaces atop their bare bosoms, and jangling the little brass bells like children. They call their world Guanahaní, but we forthwith named it San Salvador after Him whose infinite mercy brought us here.

Have we at least reached Asia? I cannot say. There are many beautiful islands in this part of creation. We have given them all Spanish names— Hispaniola, Santa María la Antigua, Puerto Rico, Trinidad, Santa Cruz—so God will know from which nation this Holy Endeavor proceeds. In every case the natives have proved as docile and prelapsarian as those on San Salvador. They are ignorant of horse and ox, innocent of wheel, plow, and musket. Beyond the occasional juju clutched in a brown fist or amulet slung about a sunbaked neck, we find no evidence of religion here. Say the word, and Father Hojeda will begin the baptisms.

At the moment I am on Hispaniola, watching a dozen maidens frolic in the clear blue waters of a bay called Acul. As the sun descends, it turns the girls' bare skin the very color of the bronze swords with which we shall keep these people in check. Have I arrived in Paradise, my Queen?

Written aboard the caravel *Santa María* on this seventeenth day of October, in the year of Our Lord Jesus Christ 1492.

I, THE ADMIRAL

TO YOU, DON CRISTÓBAL COLÓN our Admiral of the Ocean Sea, Viceroy and Governor of all the Islands to be found by you on your Great Voyage of Discovery, greetings and grace.

Friar Deza says Spain is now "on the threshold of a grand and glorious age." Father Torquemada thinks we stand "on the verge of a Thousand Year Empire such as the world has never known."

They may be right. Six days ago Emanuel I of Portugal asked for the Infanta Isabella's hand in marriage, and she dutifully accepted. The day after that the Islamic King Boabdil surrendered the keys to the Alhambra, and our victory over the Moors became complete. Then, twenty-four hours later, your missive arrived from Hispaniola.

O my Admiral, the belief here is that, if you are not in the Indies, you have come upon something no less valuable for Spain, a great pool of unclaimed souls both ripe for conversion and ready to relieve Castile of all strenuous and unseemly labor. When I read your letter to my councillors, a cheer resounded throughout the palace, and before long we were all drinking the same vintage of Marques de Cacares with which you bargained in Manhattan.

Santángel did not join our celebration. He says Torquemada's Thousand Year Empire will last no more than a few centuries. "In fleeing Manhattan, Spain has made a fatal mistake," he insists. "By running away to Hispaniola, Don Cristóbal has merely bought the Crown some time."

Last night a violent and frightening vision afflicted my sleep. Like the Golem of Jewish folklore, the idol of *libertad* had by some miracle come to life and had by no less a miracle betaken herself to Europe. So heavy were her footfalls that the very mountains of Spain commenced to tremble, then to crack apart, then to collapse upon themselves like ancient Atlantis sinking into the waters beyond the Pillars of Hercules.

What do you make of my dream, Cristóbal? Could it be that Santángel is right, and the best you can do for Spain is buy her some time? Very well. Amen. Empire is the art of the possible.

So baptize those brown natives, dear sailor. Put them to work. Punish those who cling to their fetishes and rites. And buy Spain some time, O my Admiral. Buy her some time.

Written in our City of Barcelona on this twenty-third day of October, in the year of Our Lord Jesus Christ 1492.

I, THE QUEEN

LET TIME SHAPE

George Zebrowski

"The ultimate aim of the historian is to resurrect all of history."

—HERODOTUS

As Carthage burned on the southeastern horizon, three ships slipped toward the Pillars of Hercules. In the lead vessel, Aeneas Oceanus, far-seeing engineer, explorer, and seer, took no pleasure in having been right; all his life he had known that the petty, jealous Romans would not be able to tolerate any prosperity but their own. Named Oceanus by his people because of his experience as a navigator, he had brought a plan of survival to his city.

At dawn the bonfire of the sun wiped away the glow of the dying city, and the refugees, a select group of shipbuilders, ironworkers, engineers, and young couples with children, turned their hopes westward. Oceanus looked backward with pity, still lamenting the loss that had been so long in coming. Hannibal had foretold it, warning that the decay of the city's inner life would only help the Romans.

In three days the ships escaped into the great ocean and turned south to the port of Lixus on the west coast of Africa, where they were met by two thousand refugees who had fled from Carthage by land during the last year, and were finishing the building of vessels large enough to challenge the western ocean.

In all, sixty ships fled the port of Lixus before the Roman legions seized it.

"Where are we going?" the commanders asked Oceanus, looking fearfully at the rough seas before them.

"Where are we going?" mothers cried from below, clutching their children in the dark holds.

"What we are doing," Oceanus said to calm his commanders, "will one day destroy Rome. But first we must survive."

His commanders pressed him for more of an answer, and he told them that he had sailed this course before, and had discovered new lands far to the west, on the other half of the world-sphere that circled the Sun with the other planets. There Carthage might live again.

Midway across the water he presented his plan to found New Carthage, where a scroll of rights would ensure that every citizen would be justly privileged. Let time shape what it will, he said, while a constitutional form of public power restrained the citizenry and prevented the drift into despotism so well described by Greek philosophers.

Although he grieved for the death of his city, Oceanus was confident that its passing was a chance for a new start. Hannibal's dream of a greater Carthage that would repudiate Rome's example and bring to fruition Athenian ideals would come to life. The new city would start with Hannibal's model for a senate, the one he had tried to create after the defeat at Zama, when he had stripped the merchant princes and landowners of their power and still brought them prosperity, and for that they had delivered his unconscious body into the hands of the Romans.

"But are not these lands in the west inhabited?" asked Hasdrubal, the son of Carthage's last commander.

"Yes, but there are few people. Large areas seem uninhabited."

"Where will we find slaves?" asked Gisco, the farmer, whose fields had fed the army.

"There will be no slaves in the new world," Oceanus replied. "I see our city growing outward, inviting other peoples into a cooperative system of states. And we will prosper because all will benefit, and we will be just!"

—and at this point the historian crouching inside Oceanus disengaged from the virtual figure and raced forward through the variants to see what had happened to the ideals of these Carthaginians, who shared experiences of persecution with the fleeing immigrants of other variants. He caught up with the *Niña, Pinta,* and *Santa María* as they sailed within sight of land, and slipped into the figure of Columbus as he stood on the deck of the largest vessel, looking excitedly at the small islands ahead, expecting the Asian shore, with all its riches, to slip into view from over the horizon.

But instead, on the starboard side, three smoking dragons climbed over the edge of the world. The crews of the Spanish ships cried out in fear and cursed their fate.

Columbus shouted, "Fear not, they are not what they seem!"

The men quieted and watched the approaching creatures, and soon saw that they were large metal vessels without sails.

The linear history machine begat the cliometricon, which simulated all that had been from a database so vast that no organic mind could traverse it. Every scrap of fact, speculation, audio and visual drama, as well as records of locales went into the burgeoning synthesis. Gaps were filled in, melding all documents and references for events and personalities into a tree of information that branched endlessly into probability. Everything became history, erasing all discontinuities, all distinctions between what was true and untrue. It made no difference, the cliometricians concluded, because so-called falsehoods canceled each other out in the cross-referencing mass of information, which was one with the very stuff of being that was the ground of every possible actuality. History's willful tree grew into infinity under an alien, unreachable light.

At first, only data that had been selected and shaped by licensed linear historians had been allowed to infect the cliometricon, before it taught them that everything was essential, no matter how false or trivial, because the cliometricon had the power to shape and reshape a large, incomplete database, and to present the otherwise unseeable to the historian. Like an optical telescope, it gathered and focused ancient light into a coherent image. The endless input of information was at first an indirect view of history, but this event horizon was pierced by capturing all unavailable information through simple brute enumeration—by running all possible variants of human history. The human genome was part of the cliometricon's database, so it simulated the past and present actions of all human beings who had ever lived and displayed their lives in dramatic form, even indicating their thoughts from observed behavior. Although the number of human variant histories was infinite, the number of significant past personalities was finite, and their actions capable of exhaustive representation.

Some historians dreamed of placing sensitive collectors a million or more light years beyond the solar system, with a cliometricon at the focus of the electromagnetic radiation cone, to extract all actual human history, as a check on the cliometricon. But other historians argued that this purely technical feat would only duplicate what the cliometricon had already done by the brute force of enumeration. No difference would be observed between history as it happened and what the cliometricon displayed in all possible variants. This had been demonstrated by blind comparisons of forced historical versions with well-documented events, which always turned out to be identical. An infinitely objective eye would see the same sum of histories displayed by the cliometricon.

It was observed that historians in every variant saw themselves as embedded in the *classical path*, but as use of the cliometricon spread through the variants, this idea was abandoned. All variants were real trajectories, even though some personalities were alive in one variant and not in another.

The deconstructing historians worked the variants like solitaire players uncovering cards, seeking related sets of differences, hoping to find variants that might mean something, whatever their significance. All finite bits of information available when someone died, the kind of data that had once been built up into a work of fiction, a drama for live players, or a film, was run through the probabilities and interpreted until the dead walked again in virtual embodiment. Detailed histories were observed and recorded, and the past lived and grew anew, resurrected in the cliometricon, developing in a secondary universe of information identical to all beings. . . .

Towed by three Carthaginian coast guard vessels, Columbus's ships entered the harbor of an impossible city. Towers of twenty and thirty stories rose above the water on the same site where New York stood in other variants. Large ships were loading and unloading at the docks. Well back from the harbor, towering above everything, sat a red pyramid. As the historian watched him in the guide monitor, Columbus, gripping the rail of the *Santa María*, astonished by the sight of such advanced commerce, wondered how he would ever be able to make his fortune here. This land was far greater than the China, India, and Japan that had glowed in his mind. No navy he had ever seen could stand against these ships. At best, Spain might hope to become this city's inferior trading partner, and the life he had spent in preparing for his voyage west would be lost in a world that was larger and richer than anyone he had ever known had imagined. The hundreds of crosses in his hold would not be planted in this land. There would be no gold to pay for the liberation of the Holy Land. His people would curse him for opening the way to humiliation.

Carthage lived in this variant, far from Rome, yet the two would conflict again, unless New Carthage had forgotten the death of the old. Or was vengeance coiled in all the variant hearts of this new city?

In another variant, a confederation of American States had broken with Great Britain, seeking refuge from European ways. They had sought to make the past count for less, but had failed by the third century. To escape the constraints of the past was the test of a civilization, and in the infinity of variants they all succeeded in one way or another, except the historian's own panoptic civilization, whose past could not yet be properly judged, since it had existed for less than a century. Observations of its own variants tended to be alike: endless series of observers processing information like sand through a sieve, seeking some significance beyond the peeping of one's neighbor.

Among the infinity of historians, there were those who chafed at the fact that Panoptica was locked in observational embrace with every

variant of its past, from which it could learn nothing, while access to the
future was forbidden. History seemed to be at an end.

Historians dreamed of looking ahead. Would the cliometricon escape
the infinitely variable fiction of its database? Or would it begin another
endless effort of capturing actual futures by sheer force of enumerating
the possible, as it did with the past, making the distinction between
reality and simulation meaningless? The resurrection of the past had
started from an initial database, but futures also rested on that base, so
brute force should not be overpowered in completing the empty spaces.
Past, present, and future would then be transformed into information,
completing panoptic civilization, and all consciousness would become a
sluggish cursor lost in the infinite ocean of data. . . .

The future was a constant temptation—greater than the compulsive
hours the historian spent examining the private lives of individuals,
varying sets of events, and details within details.

The romance of past time was hypnotic. The historian set the safeties
to break the virtual embodiment before addiction set in, and gazed at
the serrated skyline of New Carthage in the guide monitor. The program
eased him forward in the sequence, toward the great pyramid where
Columbus was now imprisoned, into—

—a windowless cell with a table, chair, and bed. An electric bulb
burned on the square ceiling. Columbus stood by the door, listening to
the silence, and the historian heard the explorer's doubts, as recorded
by Walt Whitman:

> What do I know of life?
>   what of myself?
> I know not even my own
>   work past or present;
> Dim ever-shifting guesses
>   of it spread before me,
> Of newer better worlds,
>   their mighty parturition,
> Mocking, perplexing me.

Finally the door opened, and a man entered. Columbus stepped back.
The man was dressed in a dark green suit of pants and jacket, buttoned
at the neck.

"Good evening," the man said in perfect Spanish, and gestured for
Columbus to sit down.

Columbus remained standing. "Who are you, Sir, and why am I a
prisoner?"

The man smiled and licked his thin lips. "Be patient."

"Who are you?" Columbus demanded.

"The Duke of Norfolk, and the English Ambassador to New Carthage, Captain Columbus. Please, do sit down."

"My rank is that of admiral," Columbus said as he obeyed.

"Forgive me." The Ambassador was silent for a moment, then said, "We've been in touch with the New Carthaginian States for some time, ever since Henry Tudor won the throne, with only His Majesty's Court and our allies knowing about it."

"States? Where then is China?"

The Ambassador shook his head in amusement. "These states extend as far as the river that divides this continent. There is another ocean to cross to reach China. The native peoples of this hemisphere and the Old Carthaginian settlers have made quite a confederation for themselves. My question to you is, where will your sympathies be? With Rome and the Spanish Court?"

"Where can they be?" Columbus said.

"With yourself, I would hope," the Ambassador said. "You know quite well that Roman Italy, together with its Spanish allies, intends to conquer Europe. Perhaps you would wish to help oppose the coming tyranny? You are without a doubt aware that we have only recently ended our civil strife."

Columbus nodded, irritated by the man's directness.

"And it was our good fortune," the Duke continued, "to find new allies across the sea. Our latest information tells us that Germany is gone, and much of Europe, right up to Moscow, is threatened. England will be next unless something is done."

Columbus stood up. "All of that is now happening?"

The Ambassador nodded.

"But how can you know that?" Columbus asked.

"We have long-range communications that can bring us messages almost instantly. We knew you were coming. Our observers are very thorough."

"But what could I do for you?"

"You're an educated man and a skilled seafarer. I think you would be happy to learn new ways. But the basic question is what do you want from your abilities as a navigator, captain, and adventurer? You may be completely candid with me."

"My greatest desire is to secure wealth, power, and glory for myself, my family in Spain, and my heirs."

"But don't you also love knowledge, seafaring, and exploration?"

Columbus nodded. "For myself—but I am by nature not a generous man. Why are you asking me such questions?"

"To learn whether you wish to be of service to us," the Ambassador replied. "I note that in your words you have left out any mention of Isabella's Castile and Ferdinand's Aragon, from which I conclude that they do not mean much to you, except as a means of support for your ventures. I can assure you that if you join us, you will have all that you want. We will remove your family to England, of course. Please understand that the New Carthaginians, and we English also, think it wise to control the coming contact with Europe, for the sake of all. Uncontrolled, it would be devastating, both physically and economically. You are quarantined here, for example, because of diseases you may be carrying. You seem fairly healthy, but medicines have been given to you with your food."

"But why do you ask me to join you?" Columbus asked.

"Do you think yourself unworthy?" the Ambassador replied. "Our agents in Europe have observed you long enough to know how familiar you are with the Spanish Court. And we know that you take a lively interest in world affairs, despite being vain, boastful, and a bit dishonest."

"Exactly what is it that you will ask of me?"

This Columbus had not been greeted by gentle natives, ripe for Christianity, welcoming him as a man from heaven. He had been the backward native, arriving in creaking ships. Here, as in other variants, he would not become admiral of the ocean sea and viceroy of all discovered lands. His voyages would not be a victory for Christianity, leading to the growth of Spanish power. The Papacy would not divide the new lands between Spain and Portugal and convert the natives, or cover the ceilings of European churches with stolen gold. Columbus would be spared the need to seize slaves for profit, and he would not be arrested by Spanish authorities for incompetence as governor of Hispaniola, where half a million natives would not perish within the four years of his rule. He would not die in disgrace and obscurity. There would be no disagreement over where his bones were buried. Europeans would not discover and claim other peoples' lands and start new countries within them and confine native cultures to museum displays and small tracts of land. Carthage and the natives would come together as a confederation of states, along ideals developed by the Iroquois and the Athenians, ruling as the metaphoric gods of Plato's Forms. The hemisphere that was called the New World in other variants would here evangelize the Old.

How simple were the old variants, the historian thought as he withdrew from Columbus and sat in the virtual chamber, listening to the ever-branching forest of the mariner's thoughts. Puzzles of power and rivalry—nothing like what his panoptic civilization faced. Columbus was eager to learn more, and the English needed puppets in Europe. The

Carthaginians still carried their hatred of Rome. The dream of Aeneas Oceanus would be fulfilled in this variant. Across a million variants it would not be otherwise.

Alone in his cell, despairing of his fate, Columbus prayed to his God and searched within himself for an answer to his predicament, fearful that the empire of the Carthaginians was perhaps the main course of history, the true descendent of Paradisio—and Europe a hell reserved for sinners, where he had suffered half a lifetime of delay, waiting to voyage west, and to which he could return only as a failure, if he returned at all.

He thought of Doña Beatriz, the widow who had been appointed Governor of Gomera in the Canary Islands because the women of the Spanish Court feared her beauty. Although she had provided the safe harbor needed to repair the *Pinta*'s steering system and replace the caravel's sails, and had expressed admiration and approval of his enterprise, she had turned away his love because he was, after all, only a sailor whose place in the *mappaemundi* was far from certain.

As he reentered the figure, the historian caught the Admiral transfixed by his own image in the full-length mirror on the wall, as only a man who had never seen good mirrors could be affected. The stocky, well-built figure, taller than average, stood perfectly still, pale eyes in a long face gazing into themselves in bewildered solitude. The aquiline nose remained confident, while the thoughts lamented the blond hair that had turned white at the age of thirty. Nevertheless, he told himself, historians might still find him impressive looking, if he amounted to anything.

What would become of him? The Carthaginians would imprison him for the rest of his life, he realized, if he refused to be their instrument; but if he agreed, they would give him everything he had ever wanted— position and wealth, and revenge on his enemies. The Holy Land might still be freed from the infidel, making way for the Second Coming. No other life would ever offer him more, he told himself. No nation in the world could ignore this great power, which sought to remake the world in its own image. Perhaps God had finally raised him up to act on the true stage of the world. He could cower in this cell and weep for himself, or he could embrace the true scale of the world, reach out and transform the world he had known, not with gold, silver, and slaves, but with the wealth that would grow from knowledge.

And Doña Beatriz de Peraza y Bobadilla, the most beautiful woman he had ever known, would certainly accept his justly won nobility.

Admiral Columbus shivered slightly as he stood on the open bridge of his iron whale and peered into the mists of the English Channel. A fleet of twelve submarines now hunted the Roman armada. He had spent a year improving his navigational skills and learning all he could about the Carthaginian continent. After the war he would be installed as governor of Spain, a role for which he was deemed well suited by his new patrons. His oldest son would become the governor of Italy. There would be time to write memoirs, especially now that the New Carthaginian physicians had so improved his health. He especially liked the new set of teeth they had given him.

A signal light flashed at his right. He went below and stood by his Captain at the periscope as the submarine submerged.

"Only a few minutes until dawn, Admiral." The Captain, a descendant of a northern forest people, spoke Carthaginian with an accent, forcing Columbus, who had so recently learned the tongue's rudiments, to listen carefully. "The sun will burn off this fog in an hour or two. They'll never know what hit them, even if there are survivors. They might even think it was sabotage of their powder stores, or a storm."

It still startled Columbus to think that he had slogged across the Atlantic in three slow, pitiably small ships, while these undersea vessels slipped over in three days or less, even though the globe was a quarter larger than he had calculated. A quarter larger! Steam and electricity were wonders to him despite his efforts to understand them, and would probably remain so for the rest of his life.

As soon as the Roman Armada was sunk, the English-Carthaginian invasion of the continent would begin. From the east would come the English Crown's Russian allies, and Roman power would be crushed forever. The world through which he had risen with so much pain would die. He now believed that Vatican Rome was not the true City of God, which still remained to be built. His love of the sea and sailing, his dreams of going beyond the walls of the world, had brought him to New Carthage, the true center of the globe.

"There they are!" the Captain shouted, then turned and made way for Columbus to look. "At least a hundred vessels."

Columbus peered through the periscope, saw the proud galleons bending with the wind, and felt sorry for them. They had no chance to escape these iron whales sent by the greatest commercial power in the world. No army in the world could stand against the mechanized force that was massing in England. Nevertheless, he worried at the resistance to Carthaginian rule that might grow in Europe. Given the ideals of government professed by the New Carthaginian States, he saw why its leaders preferred an alliance with the English to one with a Spanish-Italian empire, but would this special relationship endure?

"Admiral," the Captain said at his side. "The heirs of Aeneas Oceanus and the Peacemaker's Longhouse Nations would be pleased if you gave the command."

Columbus stepped back and waited for the Captain to aim and signal the rest of the fleet, so that all the blows would fall as one.

"All is ready, Admiral," the Captain said.

Columbus banished his doubts and nodded, determined to be grateful that God's providence had brought him here. Yes, God himself. "Fire all tubes!"

As he withdrew from the figure and sat in the black silence of the virtual chamber, the historian longed for the play of events that had given Columbus his fulfillment. The Columbian Exchange of peoples, animals, foodstuffs, diseases, and knowledge would take place with more control and vision in this variant; but as with all variants prior to Panoptica, this was a transition from one dynamic state to another, with no final state envisioned. Panoptic observation could offer nothing like this inner experience. Forbidden to peer beyond its own equilibrium of observers and information, it feared to learn from the quantum sea of futures or to take the past as any guide. Panoptica, unable to stand aside from history absolutely, had stood aside in a relative way. Development continued at a trivial pace, and the historians of future Panopticas could only look back at an infinity of observers identical to themselves.

He imagined world lines where history grew at a quantum pace, rather than creeping from state to state through an unrecordable infinity of steps. Surely, in all infinity, there had to be leaping, verbicular forms of history, where new things sprang from the unconscious soil of memory, where the brute force of deductive reason could not enumerate all joys. He wanted to throw himself into swift currents and be reshaped by time's rough stones. He longed to be involved, even to intervene in history.

Trembling as he leaned forward, he oriented himself in the guide monitor and reentered Columbus on the bridge of the submarine as it ran on the surface. Low clouds reflected the flames of the Roman armada burning on the horizon. Columbus felt the heat, and for an instant the pale, vicarious warmth of the flames also caressed the historian's face.

RED ALERT

Jerry Oltion

The scramble siren catapulted him out of a sound sleep. Red Cloud shuddered and sat up in bed, wincing a second time as the lights automatically switched on. In the next bunk Sitting Bull groaned and fumbled to free himself from his covers. The siren died just as the door between the two bunks opened and Brave Joseph stuck his head in.

"Look lively!" Joseph shouted. "Trouble on the Island."

"Where else?" Red Cloud muttered, but Joseph was already moving down the hallway, banging on doors and bellowing orders.

Sitting Bull staggered to his feet and began pulling flight gear from the rack. Red Cloud matched him action for action, donning G-suit, harness, survival vest, combat moccasins, and so on with practiced precision.

"Ready to fly?" he asked as he pulled the zipper on his flight jacket up to his neck. It would be cold outside, this late in the autumn.

For answer Sitting Bull grinned and howled a Sioux war cry at the ceiling.

Red Cloud took up the call, and together they ran whooping from their quarters out to the airfield where their Eagle-15s waited, ground crews swarming around them. The smell of JP-4, the sharp, bladelike silhouette of the jet against the morning sky, the sound of engines already howling up to speed, all mixed with a kick of adrenaline to send Red Cloud swarming up the ladder and leaping eagerly into the cockpit of his plane.

Helmet and shoulder straps took ten seconds. The checklist took another thirty; then he was rolling, Sitting Bull right beside him on the taxiway, less than five minutes from first alarm.

"Eagle One ready," he said into the helmet microphone.

"Eagle Two ready." Sitting Bull's voice was tight with excitement.

"Cleared for takeoff," the flight controller said.

Red Cloud rolled out onto the runway, turned, and pushed the throttles in a smooth slide all the way forward until the afterburners kicked in. Acceleration pushed him back into his seat. He watched his airspeed climb past 100, the needle a blur. At 150 he inched the stick back, and the Eagle leaped into the sky. He looked out to his left. Sitting Bull was still right beside him, half a wingspan away.

"Course zero eight three," the flight controller said.

"Zero . . . eight . . . three," Red Cloud grunted as the g-force pushed him deeper into the cushion. He centered the stick again at a forty-five-degree climb and said, "All right, we're on our way. What's the mission?"

"Photo recon," the controller said. "High-level overflight caught signs of heavy building activity in Central Park. We want you to check it out up close."

"How close?" Sitting Bull asked.

"Stay on our side of the line," control replied. "You do not have airspace-violation clearance."

"Damn."

"Be careful what you wish for," Red Cloud said, but he knew how Sitting Bull felt. In his four years as a pilot, Sitting Bull had never violated the palefaces' territory. In his seventeen years, Red Cloud had done it only once, in retaliation for the cowardly strafing of the airfield that had cost the life of Geronimo, his former wingman. It had been exhilarating, that flight into hostile territory, but that one raid had nearly started an all-out war. Never mind that the palefaces flew over Indian territory whenever they pleased, ignoring treaties and honor alike; they regarded any incursion into *their* territory as an act of aggression.

And they were always claiming more airspace than they actually owned.

Red Cloud eyed the banks of gauges and switches before him and said, "Double-check your weapons arming systems."

"Weapons arming systems check green," said Sitting Bull.

Red Cloud's own weapons were ready as well. One flip of a switch would arm the four *Tomahawk* heat-seeking missiles, the four *Warpath* radar-guided missiles, and the two machine guns slung under his wings.

He looked back out the windshield. The Island was coming up already. Red Cloud leveled out his Eagle at ten thousand feet and throttled back the engines to 50 percent—just enough to maintain cruising speed. He could see the skyscrapers silhouetted against the early-morning sky. Photography would be tricky in this light; shadows would be black pools that could hide anything.

"Let's make a sunwise circuit," he said. That would bring them close to Central Park first, maybe before the palefaces could scramble their own fighters into the air.

"Sounds good." Sitting Bull backed off to give them some maneuvering distance.

The two Eagles arrowed toward the Island. The palefaces called it Manhattan, but to the Indians it was simply the Island. Thirteen miles long, barely two miles wide, bought for all of twenty-four dollars' worth of beads and red cloth over two centuries ago; the paleface colony had been the tail that wagged the North American dog ever since. When Red Cloud had been a kid on the plains, he'd heard so many tales of the place that he'd mistaken Greenland for it when he'd first looked at a globe. He'd been insulted to learn its true size. Insulted and alarmed; he'd shuddered to think how much trouble the palefaces could have caused if his ancestors hadn't limited them to their one legitimate purchase, and he'd vowed that day to join the Iroquois Federation's intertribal peacekeeping force to help keep them in their place.

More than once he'd wondered why his people didn't just wipe them out once and for all, like they'd done to the other colonies, but he always came back to the same answer. The palefaces had stolen other land, but they'd bought the Island fair and square. It was *their* land, and if the Indians were going to insist that the rest of the continent was Indian land, then they had to honor the palefaces' right of ownership as well.

But no one had to like it.

The skyscrapers grew until the tallest—the Plymouth Building—disappeared below the Eagle's nose. Red Cloud knew from experience that he was less than a mile from the territorial boundary. "Begin circuit," he said, pushing his control stick to the left. The plane responded instantly with a hard left bank; he let it go to a full ninety degrees, then pulled back on the stick, the g's shoving him deep into his seat. He kept an eye on the Hackensack River, climbing upward out his left window, and when he was heading roughly parallel with it, he banked right until he was flying level again. A quick roll confirmed his position: The Hudson was directly below him, and the Island just to his right. The tallest skyscrapers were already receding behind.

"Start shooting," he said, triggering the high-resolution camera in his right wingtip.

"Rolling," Sitting Bull said.

Cameras whirring, they flew up the length of the Island, pulled more hard g's at the northern end, and flew back down over the East River. Red Cloud tried to spot the activity in Central Park that might be causing interest back at base, but he couldn't distinguish anything at this distance.

His earphones pinged. Two green dots glowed on the right edge of his radar screen.

"Bogeys at four," Sitting Bull warned.

"I see 'em."

"Do you have pictures, yet?" Control asked.

"One pass, both sides," Red Cloud answered.

"Then return to base immediately. Do not confront paleface fighters."

"Acknowledged."

"Damn," said Sitting Bull.

"Don't go looking for trouble," Red Cloud reminded him. "You'll get it soon enough in this business." They flew a few seconds in silence, then he said, "But at least let's let them know we were here." He reached forward and flipped a switch on the far right of the control console, a switch he'd installed himself. Just in back of the right engine, a pressurized canister sprayed dye into the hot exhaust. Red Cloud shoved the throttles all the way forward, and his Eagle leaped ahead, leaving a streak of red smoke behind. On the east side of the Island, with the sun rising behind it, it would be visible from every building.

Sitting Bull's signature—written in alternating dashes of white smoke from both engines—joined Red Cloud's as they punched through the sound barrier and left the frustrated paleface pilots behind.

Brave Joseph caught up with them at lunch. "Eat light," he told them, sitting down just as they began their meal. "You're going back to the Island, and this time you get what you've been asking for, kid." He punched Sitting Bull on the shoulder as the younger man's eyes lit up with excitement. "That's right, you're cleared for airspace violation. Straight over Central Park. One pass east to west, you first with Red Cloud covering your tail, then the both of you get the hell back to base. We'll have fifty planes scrambled the moment you cross the Island; let them take care of the palefaces. We want you two back here intact with photos."

"Photos of what?" Red Cloud asked. "What's going on in there?"

"Looks like the palefaces are building missile silos. We want to make sure before we scream treaty violation."

"Missile silos," Red Cloud said quietly. "There's no way they can call missiles defensive weapons."

"They can call 'em anything they want, once they get 'em in place," Joseph said. "If they get first-strike capability, they'll have us by the throats."

Red Cloud closed his eyes. The image of mushroom clouds rising all across the nation waited right there behind his eyelids. The palefaces had already used nuclear bombs in their war against the Turks; only a fool would suppose they wouldn't do the same to the Indians if given a chance.

He pushed his food away. It would be no trouble to eat light; he'd lost his appetite completely.

They came in over Long Island, only fifty feet off the deck, dodging treetops in their effort to stay below paleface radar. At the last moment they jinked northeast, popped up to two thousand feet, and arrowed straight for Central Park, cameras running.

Their own radar screens filled immediately with the ping of two contacts, one north of their target, one south.

"The bastards are already in the air," Sitting Bull muttered.

Red Cloud waited for a second sweep. Both dots moved; the northward one was headed away from the park, but the southward one toward it. They were evidently flying patrol around the Island.

"Looks like we'll only have to deal with one," Red Cloud said. He looked at the digital readout below his radar screen. "He's at five thousand. You stay low and go for the pictures; I'll keep him high."

"Got it."

Red Cloud pulled back on the stick and shouted his battle cry: "*Geronimo!*" Seconds later he crossed five thousand feet, rose to six thousand, and veered left on a course that would put him behind the paleface plane. He didn't expect that to last long, and it didn't; the paleface immediately rolled hard over and came straight for him.

Which was right where Red Cloud wanted him. As the two planes flew toward one another, Sitting Bull pushed his throttles into afterburner and sped on toward Central Park unhindered.

Red Cloud waited impatiently for the distance to close, his finger hovering over the Master Arm switch. He didn't want to go offensive unless the paleface did, but he knew a moment's hesitation could lose him the fight, if fight it would be, even though his weapons were better than the paleface's. The Indians had finally pulled ahead in the long technology race with their enemies, but superior armament didn't always win battles. The Aztecs had beaten Cortez with spears and bows, after all.

He waited, waited, waited, then luck or instinct or the Great Spirit Wakantanka told him to jink left and dive, just as the radar lock warning howled in his earphones and the paleface fired a missile. The missile arced downward after him, but the angle was too steep for it; Red Cloud shot past below it with a hundred yards to spare. He reversed his turn and jammed the throttles forward, itching to complete the loop and fire one of his own missiles at the paleface—or at least one of the miniature nonexplosive coup sticks—but he followed orders instead, turning back toward the park while the paleface frantically turned to pursue him. The missile, its radar lock lost, sped on toward the ground until the paleface pilot detonated it by remote.

"Camera rolling," Sitting Bull said. "Crossing Central Park."

"I'm right behind you." Red Cloud aimed for a spot a little to the south of Sitting Bull's path, started his cameras, and made his own pass over the park. He kept his eyes on the radar screen, but the paleface pilot who'd shot at him was just completing his turn, miles back, and the other pilot was flying an intercept that would put him well into Indian territory before he made contact.

It took the speeding planes only a few seconds to reach the Hudson. "Drop armament," Red Cloud said, pushing his panic button. His missiles, wing tanks, and belly tank dropped away, reducing the Eagle's air resistance. Sitting Bull did the same, and both planes shot toward home base at top speed, their smoke signatures streaming out behind them.

The palefaces pursued them, of course, but with loaded planes they had no hope of catching up, and within a few more miles an entire squadron of Eagles rose up out of the west and chased them back to the Island. Red Cloud grinned at the radio traffic:

"Hey, Red Cloud; you scared this guy's hair white!"

"It isn't white; it's blond."

"So it is. Hey, I bet this is that hotshot new guy we heard about. The one who—"

"Look out! Missile!"

"I'm clear."

"Trigger-happy bastard. Maybe we should teach him a lesson."

"Good idea."

"I'm on him. Arming the stick. Targeting . . . locked. Stick away."

"Look at 'im dodge! Forget it, buddy, you're outnumbered."

"Hah, hit 'im right on the canopy. I count coup, Yellow Hair."

"Yee-ha! My turn!"

A scant thirty minutes later Brave Joseph showed them the pictures. "They're missile silos, all right," he said, pointing at a half-dozen buildings clustered together near the middle of the park. "From the side they look like basic apartment complexes, but when you look down from above, you can see the launch tubes inside. We count ten per building. That means sixty missiles, and if they've figured how to build multiple warheads that could mean first-strike capability to as many as six hundred separate targets."

"So what're we going to do about it?" Sitting Bull asked.

"Tecumseh's arranging to meet with Lee right now. He'll threaten to blockade the Island if they don't dismantle the silos. Trouble is, we think they've already got this one operational." Joseph pointed at the southernmost "building."

"You think they'd actually launch?" Red Cloud asked. "We'd blow the Island off the map, and most of Europe, too, if they did."

"Who knows what those crazy palefaces would do? They don't fight like civilized people."

"I say we take 'em out before they try it," Sitting Bull said.

"That's not our decision. Tecumseh's the chief."

"Yeah, well, he's going to be chief of a bunch of radioactive braves if he decides wrong." Sitting Bull looked down at the photographs again. "I think we ought to scalp the bastards once and for all, and do it now."

Joseph shook his head. "We'll try diplomacy first."

"Diplomacy." Sitting Bull spat. "To a paleface *diplomacy* is just another word for a stab in the back."

The hours passed slowly. Red Cloud watched the ground crew rearming his Eagle and wondered if these missiles would wind up ditched in the Hudson like the others, or if they would find human targets this time instead. A slow anger had been building in him all afternoon, to the point where he wasn't sure which he preferred.

"We're going back," a voice said. It took him a moment to realize it was real. Red Cloud turned to see Sitting Bull grinning in anticipation, and Brave Joseph beside him wearing a more somber expression.

"I take it the meeting didn't go well," Red Cloud said.

Brave Joseph shook his head. "When Tecumseh told Lee we'd blockade the Island, all hell broke loose. Everybody in the meeting room started shouting at once, until Lee took off his shoe and banged it on the table and outshouted everyone."

"What'd he say?"

"He said, 'We will bury you.'"

"'We will bury you?'" Red Cloud could hardly believe his ears.

Joseph nodded. "That's right."

"Wonderful. So when are we making the raid?"

"As soon as your planes are ready. You two will make the actual run; we'll have a dozen other planes ahead of you for a lure."

Sitting Bull smacked fist into palm. "We'll get the bastards."

"*Just* the missile silos," Joseph cautioned him. "We don't want any unnecessary loss of life. We want to come out of this looking clean as spring water to the rest of the world, so think of this as a surgical strike, not a bombing run."

"Gotcha."

Red Cloud nodded, feeling adrenaline surge through his blood again. A "surgical strike" on the Island. He'd known this moment was coming, known it since the day he'd left the plains to join the peacekeeping forces. Standing, he reached out and slapped his wing man on the shoulder. "Let's do it," he said.

The Manhattan skyline once again loomed before them; this time higher than ever. They were approaching from the south, over the bay, but only a dozen feet or so above the water. Ahead of them flew the lure: an even dozen planes whose pilots would engage the palefaces and draw them away from the true action. It was an old trick, but the palefaces never seemed to learn; they were all too eager to get themselves an "Injun."

Sure enough, as the squadron approached the southern end of the Island, a swarm of paleface fighters swooped downriver toward them. The Indians accelerated to attack speed, banked hard right, and led the chase east over Long Island. Within a minute Red Cloud's radar screen was clear.

But just in case it wasn't as clear as it looked, they had another plan. . . .

The buildings drew closer. Red Cloud climbed a couple hundred feet, but he was still well below even the average-sized ones. "Drop behind and watch your wingtips," he said as the twin towers of the Roanoke Memorial reached out to swat them down. "*Geronimo!*" he shouted, nervously eyeing the gap between them, but just when he was sure the plane wouldn't fit, the buildings seemed to move aside, and he shot through like a spit watermelon seed. A jumble of older streets rushed by below, then Fifth Avenue stretched out before him, leading straight to the target. Red Cloud shoved the throttles forward and streaked toward it at Mach 1, windows no doubt shattering in his wake.

A loud ping in his headphones warned him of another aircraft. He glanced at the radar screen, saw that the trace was dead ahead, but when he looked up, he saw only the street and a stockade of buildings flashing by. The paleface had ducked down another street.

"Go evasive step one," Red Cloud said. "I think we're about to be surprised."

"Evasive one," said Sitting Bull.

Red Cloud pulled back on the stick, banked, and rolled over the top of the block to drop down into the Amerigo's Avenue canyon. Before the buildings separated them, he saw Sitting Bull doing the same in the opposite direction.

Seconds later a bloodcurdling yell came over the radio. "Yeow! I just about clipped his tail. The bastard's on Madison!"

"Evasive two," Red Cloud said, rolling left and high again, but this time he continued the bank and dropped down over an east-west street. His radar pinged again on the way over the top; the paleface was above the skyline, too, no doubt turning to follow.

Red Cloud flew a few blocks, then popped up and over and down to head north again, toward Central Park. His radar pinged at him again. For a moment he hesitated, wondering whether to try more evasive maneuvers, but at last he decided to stay low and hope the paleface would pick the wrong street. "Making my run," he said.

"Me too," said Sitting Bull. "Coming up behind you."

The last mile or so passed in a descending blur, the buildings growing shorter as he neared the park. Red Cloud set his targeting radar to its narrowest field and searched for the "apartment complex" housing the missiles, but when Sitting Bull shouted, "Look out! He's on you!" he abandoned the search and banked hard right. His headphones squealed with the enemy radar warning, but not with the intensity that would indicate a weapons lock-on.

"I'm on him," Sitting Bull said, and seconds later he shouted, "*Tomahawk* away!"

Red Cloud craned his neck to see if he could spot the paleface by eye, and saw him just as the missile hit. Paleface planes were tough, he'd give them that; the right engine erupted in flame, but the plane stayed in one piece, trailing thick smoke as it dropped out of the sky. The pilot even seemed to have some control over it.

"He's going for the lake," Sitting Bull said.

"Let him go. Let's take out the silos and go home." Red Cloud once again scanned for targets, locked onto the proper building, and fired a radar-guided *Warpath* at it. When the rocket hit, nothing happened for a second; then the explosion reached the missiles inside and the whole thing erupted in a ball of flame.

Sitting Bull's rocket took out the building next to it. Unfinished, it didn't hold any missiles, but the concussion brought it down just as effectively. Red Cloud retargeted and fired again at the next building in line, and at the next. Sitting Bull took out the last two.

They circled the paleface on their way out. He rocked back and forth beneath his parachute, long yellow hair spilling out from beneath his helmet. He held his right arm extended toward them, and Red Cloud could see tiny flashes from his service revolver.

Sitting Bull saw it, too. "Boy, that guy doesn't know when to give up, does he?"

Red Cloud laughed. "Palefaces never do." He banked away from the downed pilot and headed for home, triggering the switch that would draw his signature across the sky as he did so. Watching Sitting Bull draw his own signature beside him, he said, "Let me tell you, kid, we've borrowed a lot of things from the palefaces—their technology, some of their ways of life—but the sum total of what we've actually *learned* from them can be stated in one sentence." He paused, amusedly aware that they were flying directly into the autumn sunset.

"What? Shoot first, ask questions later?" Sitting Bull asked.

"Nope. Try again."

"Walk softly, but carry a big stick?"

"Closer." Red Cloud grinned, imagining the next step in the technology war. The palefaces would probably try longer-range missiles so they could launch from Europe. The Indians would have to develop them, too, as well as better surveillance techniques to watch over the situation on the other side of the world. That meant either strengthening the navy to provide a base of operations or using the improved missile technology in a new way: to go for the high ground. Red Cloud looked out the canopy, straight up. Was that where his future lay?

"So what's the line, O fount of wisdom?"

"Huh? Oh, that." Red Cloud quoted the Aztec, Montezuma, who'd first warned of the paleface threat: " 'The price of freedom is eternal vigilance.' "

SUCH A DEAL

Esther M. Friesner

Hisdai ibn Ezra, noted merchant of Granada (retired), did his best to conceal his amusement when his servant entered and announced, "There—there is a vis—a visitor to see you, *sidi*. A—a Castilian, he said to tell you."

*How you twist your face and stammer, Mahmoud!** the old Jew thought. *You are jumpy as a flea-ridden monkey. This unexpected guest of mine has you at a loss, I see. Well, you are young yet, and it is no common thing for foreigners to frequent this house since I left the trader's calling. I still recall what a hubbub we had when the Genoese navigator first arrived, and that was supposed to be a secret visit. Lord of Hosts, whatever has become of that one? And of Daud . . .*

He banished the thought, dreading the despair it must bring him. Better to study Mahmoud's confusion and hold back laughter instead of tears.

Mahmoud was obviously waiting for his master to summon guards, or send word to Sultan Muhammad's palace of the infidel interloper's presence. When Hisdai did neither—only turning another leaf in his *Maimonides*—the servant seemed ready to jig out of his skin.

The old Jew swallowed a chuckle. *You look as if you could do with a little reading from the "Guide for the Perplexed" yourself, boy. You did not expect this, did you? One of those cause-mad Christians in the house of a Jew who lives quite comfortably under the reign of an Islamic lord? Least of all when the armies of Ferdinand and Isabella are camped before our walls, laying siege to Granada. No, you have every right to wear that astonished expression. If only it were not so comical!*

He sighed and set aside his book. "Are there any refreshments in this house worthy of so exalted a caller, Mahmoud? A little spiced wine? A handful of dates not too wizened? Some other delicacies that Cook may have secreted away from happier times, may the Lord bless him for the prudent ant he so wisely emulates?"

Mahmoud knit his brows, his bewilderment mounting visibly. "Come, lad!" Hisdai said, trying to hearten his servant into action. "There is no mystery here. For me to expect Cook to have secret stores of exotic tidbits despite the passage of nearly a year and a half since the Christians have come before our gates—that is just my knowing Cook's character."

"Oh, it is not that, *sidi*; it is only. . ." Mahmoud paused, his tongue caught in a snare set by his discretion.

"Only what?" Hisdai ibn Ezra could not restrain a mildly cynical smile. "Fear nothing; I have heard all the whispering my servants do about me for more years than you have been alive." He stroked his silvery beard. "They call me master-merchant to my face, but behind my back I vow that more than one idle tongue wags that I have trafficked less with human clientele and more with *dijinn* and *Iblis*. Is this not so?"

Very reluctantly Mahmoud nodded. Hisdai laughed. "Therefore, why stand amazed at our unheralded visitor? Give thanks that he merely comes from our enemies' ranks and not from the fiery Pit itself!"

Mahmoud made it his business to say, "O *sidi*, I do not believe the tales. How can I, who behold you daily, give credence to such lies?"

Hisdai lifted one gray and shaggy brow. "Are you quite certain they *are* lies, Mahmoud?"

Like most new servants, Mahmoud took everything his master said at face value. "They must be lies, O *sidi*. For one thing, you do not even look like a wizard."

The boy spoke truth, and Hisdai ibn Ezra knew it. If he flattered himself that he resembled the dark magicians of legend, any good mirror would disabuse him at once. He knew himself to be a small, crinkle-faced cricket-chirp of a man. White hairs—sparse beneath his turban, lush upon his chin—held constant argument with brown eyes of a youthful sparkle. Long hours of study of the driest and most petrified of scholarly subjects, which drifted off into longer hours of heavy-headed sleep, painted him old. Then he would wake and speak with such lively insight and interest of current affairs near and far that he left younger men panting to follow the lightning path of his wit and insight.

True that Paradox had long made her scruffy nest beneath the roof of the onetime merchant prince, but for a Castilian to come a-calling in these times—! That was too much for even the most seasoned of servants to bear without dashing away at once to auction off the news to his comrades' eager ears.

Now that Mahmoud's initial startlement had faded, Hisdai could see that he was avid to have his duty done and be whisking this tale with him to the kitchens, and so the old Jew gently urged him on his way, saying, "Go now, haste. It does not do to keep demons *or* Castilians waiting."

Mahmoud departed. He returned not much later, followed by a gentleman whose decidedly simple European clothes were in startling contrast to the splendor of Hisdai ibn Ezra's flowing Moorish robes.

"Pelayo Fernández de Santa Fe, O *sidi*," Mahmoud announced, bowing. Hisdai recognized that the lad was a skilled-enough servitor to lower his eyes to the very stones while still observing absolutely everything around him. This time, as others, that talent would provide Mahmoud with a most instructive spectacle.

Then Hisdai ibn Ezra gazed from the clothes before him to the face above and turned to a lump of ice as solid as any to be found on the summit of snow-capped Mulhacé. He felt the color ebb from his face like a fleeing tide, felt for the first time the palsy of age cause his outstretched hands to tremble. The old man's breath rushed into his lungs with an audible rasping, a sound too near the final deathbed croak for any servant who valued his pay to remain unmoved.

Yet when Mahmoud rushed forward, a wail of paid loyalty on his lips, the strength gushed back into Hisdai's body. He stood straight as a poplar and sharply motioned Mahmoud away. "Unworthy servant, where are your manners? Our honored guest will think himself to be still among his own barbarous people. Go, fetch scented water and soft towels! Bread and salt! My finest wine! Why are you gawking? You'll gape less when one of King Ferdinand's men drives a pike through your gizzard. Go, I say!"

Mahmoud did not wait for further instructions. He had more than enough meat for meditation, and the other servants would treat him royally for it. Any diversion not connected with the infernal siege was worth its weight in gold, especially to folk who lacked anything more precious than copper.

Hisdai ibn Ezra watched Mahmoud scamper off, listening until he judged his servant's pattering footsteps had retreated a sufficient distance for his liking. Then and only then did he turn to give his visitor a proper welcome.

"You *idiot*!" He snatched the man's hat from his hands and flung it out the window into the courtyard below.

The visitor flew after his hat, but wisely halted his own flight short of the abyss. Leaning over the tiled sill, he remarked, "I see that you've kept the false awning in place down there. I thought that since you retired, you wouldn't need to maintain such emergency measures in case of dissatisfied royal customers."

"I may not deal with Sultan Muhammad anymore, nor need to provide for the possibility of—ahem!—expeditious departures, but only a fool dreams any peace is permanent," Hisdai growled. "Most definitely not in these times."

His guest was unmoved by the old man's peevishness. He was still admiring Hisdai's escape stratagem, with which he seemed to be disconcertingly familiar. "To be able to jump from this height and land safely—! Ah, one day I must try it, just to see how it feels. Unfortunately my hat missed the awning and the cushions under it and landed right in the fishpond. Was that necessary? I was rather attached to that hat."

"Would that your brain were as attached to the inside of your skull! Do you realize what you risked, coming here in the teeth of the siege like this?"

"Unless I misremember," Hisdai's guest drawled, "it was not ten months ago that I found you entertaining a certain Genoese in this very room. When I asked you how Master Columbus had managed to breach the siege, you only smiled and said, 'I have my ways. One key opens many gates, if that key be made of gold.'" He winked at Hisdai. "For once, I recalled your wisdom and used it well, particularly now that I have more of your precious keys than any locksmith."

"What is this blather of keys?" Hisdai snorted. "When Mahmoud informed me that there was a Castilian come calling—all Christians are Castilians to him—I expected to greet a common seaman bringing word from the admiral. That Genoese is no fool. He has more sense than to venture his neck for nothing!"

The young man murmured into his beard, "There you speak a greater truth than you know."

His words went unheard. As suddenly as it had erupted, Hisdai's burst of sour temper vanished altogether. He rushed to fling the silken wings of his sleeves around the "Castilian."

"Ah, Daud! Daud, my son, it is *I* who am the fool! If you are back, what else matters? My Daud—or shall I call you by that abominable Castilian name you bestowed upon yourself?"

Daud pretended to take umbrage. "I thought it a very good alias, and most handy for getting past the more officious of the Catholic Monarchs' sentries. Stop a man named for *don* Pelayo, he who began the reconquest of this land from the Moors? Most ill-omened at this juncture." He shook his head solemnly. "Now that Ferdinand and Isabella are about to retake the last Iberian foothold of our Moorish rulers, that would be most ill-omened indeed."

Hisdai beamed over his son's resourcefulness. "Still the clever rogue, my pride! Blessed be the Lord, the God of Israel, for bringing me to this season. My heart, my child, I never thought to see your face again."

The young man laughed out of a face that was a less-wrinkled version of his sire's. His beard was somewhat shorter, the hair on his head summer midnight to Hisdai's winter dawn, but the eyes held the same fire.

"Indeed, my father, there were moments in the voyage when I myself questioned whether the next face I saw would be yours or Elijah's!" He sighed. "May Heaven witness, our valiant admiral suffered celestial visions enough for us all. There must be truth in what they say, that madness is but a divinely given spark of genius that burns with the most peculiar flame. That man has a sufficiency of such embers to burn all *al-Andalus* to ashes." Laughter departed his lips as he added, "As he may yet do."

"What is this you say, my son?" Hisdai clapped his hands to his eldest's shoulders. "Do you mean that the voyage was—a failure? The homeland we seek, the refuge for our people once these accursed Catholic Monarchs destroy Granada, is only another of the admiral's insane fancies?"

Daud's travel-tattered moustache twisted itself into a wry expression. "O my father, if I hear *you* call the admiral mad, you'll have me thinking there's some truth to Mother's allegations. Why else would you commend me to a madman's care?"

Hisdai waved off his son's words impatiently. "Your mother, foremost of my wives, is a virtuous woman. As such, her price is above rubies, even if her love of gossip is beneath contempt. You are my heir, Daud! Would I entrust a diamond of untold price to a lunatic? But if the diamond is yet rough, I would select with utmost care the jeweler into whose hands I place it for proper cutting, polishing, setting, until the every refinement of his art had perfected it as it deserves to be."

"In other words, you sent me to fall off the edge of the earth for my own good," Daud concluded.

"Also to get you away from that Egyptian dancing-girl your worthless friend Barak spends all his money on," Hisdai grumbled under his breath.

Daud heard, and did his best not to choke on laughter. "Fear not, O my father! We encountered no such temptresses in the court of the Great Khan. As is well known, the almighty monarch of Cathay surrounds himself exclusively with the fairest daughters of Israel, the flowers of Judaea, the untouched virgins of Jerusalem-in-exile, the—"

"Is it so much for an old man to want his son wed to a nice Jewish girl?" Hisdai sulked into his beard.

"Ah, Father, you would not be satisfied until I wed a veritable princess!"

"And is that such a bad ambition?" Hisdai demanded.

"Not at all, not at all." Daud gazed at his father with real affection. "So it was my taste for forbidden delights that counted as one more rough spot for your Genoese jeweler to strike off? And here I thought it was the dream of establishing a new homeland for our people that drove you to pour my patrimony into those three rachitic ships you bought him."

Hisdai ibn Ezra was in no joking mood. "Daud, I see that at least one of my dreams has been in vain. You return as much the mocker as you departed."

"Oh no, my father." Daud dropped all pretense of jest. "Believe me, I return to your house a changed man. If I banter with you now, it is only to keep my heart from crumbling beneath the full weight of what I have to tell you."

Fear and consternation showed themselves boldly in the old Jew's eyes. "What news, then? Tell me! Not that the voyage failed, no, or else you could not be here, solid flesh beneath my hands. What then? The Great Khan denied our petition, rejected my gifts? Once there were many Jews in Cathay, respected, honored, permitted to dwell in peace, to follow the ways of our fathers. Did you remind the Great Khan of the prosperity we brought the land?"

Daud nodded. "I tried. Our translator did, at any rate. Moshe ibn Ahijah is a wonderful scholar. No one was more surprised than he when the Great Khan did not know Hebrew, Arabic, Aramaic, Castilian, Greek, or Latin."

"But surely you managed to communicate? By signs? By a show of gifts? In my day, when I accompanied the caravans, I always managed to make my intents clear—"

"We, too, managed. The gifts you sent to the Great Khan," Daud replied, "were very eloquent. Entertaining, I should say. They made him laugh."

"Laugh! At masterpieces of the goldsmith's art? Gems that were the finest I could call in from our people here in *al-Andalus*, in *Castilla*, in France, in Italy, even across the water in *Mamlakah al-Maghribiyah*—!" Hisdai began to pace the room. "When word first reached me of this man Columbus, I thought it to be the answer to my wildest prayers. Any half-educated man knows that the ancients proved the world to be round—that much of the Genoese's fancies needed no confirmation—but to apply that knowledge to the establishment of a westerly trade

route—!" He smacked a fist into his palm. "That was the prize I desired.
A way for us, for all Jews, to reach the haven of the East safely, there to
live unmolested by the periodic excesses of zeal that afflict our Christian
neighbors. Once there, we would prosper as never before."

"So you said, my father." Daud remained glum.

"So I said, and so it would be! The East has ever favored us, and with
new trade routes opened we would thrive. Oh, Daud, you will never
know how fervently I thanked the Lord when those purblind Catholic
Monarchs rejected Columbus's plan and sent him packing! You cannot
begin to imagine all I did, or how speedily, to bring him here so that I
might finance his scheme, and our future!"

"I recall it well. I did not spend *all* my time mooning over Barak's
dancing-girl."

In his distracted state Hisdai disregarded Daud's mordant comments.
"My son, the treasure I sent with you was to be the ransom of the Jews,
our payment for refuge in the lands of the distant East once that
vainglorious Genoese proved a safe sea route there possible. And you
say the Great Khan *laughed?*"

In silence Daud reached into the large leather pouch at his side. His
fist emerged overflowing with the glitter of pure gold and priceless
jewels. Chains and pendants, adornments for ears, breast, wrist, and
ankle, gorgeous enhancements for body parts beyond the old man's
imagining all spilled over the blue-and-green carpet.

While Hisdai gaped, Daud simply plunged his hand back into the
pouch and followed the first handful of gold with a second, then a third,
then a fourth, each scattered with the disinterested prodigality of a rich
man tossing crumbs to the birds.

"You see now why he laughed? Because next to the treasure hoard the
Great Khan already commands, our gifts were regarded as no better
than the pinched clay figurine one of his children might make him for a
present: charming, but hardly to be taken seriously. What you behold is
merely my share of the first gift the Great Khan made to us. The *first*,
mark me. It was a reward."

"A—reward?" Hisdai managed to wrench his gaze away from the heap
of wealth strewn so casually at his feet. "What for?"

"For making the admiral shut up about Christ." Daud shrugged. "His
harangues were putting the Great Khan's priests off their stride, and
they had such a lot of people to—to serve that day." An unpleasant
memory appeared to grip him. Fine sweat stood out on his forehead.

"Christ?" Hisdai echoed, overlooking his son's discomfort. "But I
thought he was over all that."

"My father, one does not *get over* one's faith as one does a fever," Daud commented tartly.

"Bah! Christianity was never truly the admiral's faith. It was a—a convenience, the path that seemed to him smoothest for getting on in the world, particularly as he desired royal backing for this unheard-of voyage of his." Hisdai spoke as one who knows such things too surely to debate them.

"You may be right," Daud admitted. "In all our time on board the *Tziporah*, I often thought that the admiral gave his prayers to God but his worship to himself."

"Of course I am right!" Hisdai snapped. "Christian just for show, he was, and to gain the ear of the powerful. Much good it did him! He had so many royal doors slammed in his face that he had the arms of *Castilla, León, y Aragón* impressed on his forehead."

He began to pace the floor, kicking aside the golden baubles. "He came to me fresh from long and profitless waiting upon Ferdinand and Isabella. In my presence he no longer needed to play the pious Catholic. He told me that his own folk back in Genoa were our kindred—as if I had not already secured that knowledge before sending for him!—exiles from the Christian kingdoms of Spain. I did not have to tell him what our fate would be if Granada falls. Ah, my son, if you could have but heard how wistfully he spoke of the faith of his ancestors!"

"Was this before or after you offered him the money for his expedition?" Daud's question was dust-dry.

"Now you say he preached Christ in the Great Khan's court?" Hisdai ibn Ezra wrung his hands. "Alas, what was he thinking of?"

"Probably the same thing he is acting on even now." Without warning, Daud seized Hisdai by the shoulders, fixing him with a terrible, burning glance. "Father, cease your wailing and pay heed. Your Genoese friend may be a visionary, but he could give the Evil One lessons in opportunism. Christopher Columbus has returned with two of your three ships intact. The *Tziporah* he ran aground off the coast of Cathay before we began our homeward sail. The *Bat-sheba* we brought safely to harbor in Tangier, where its—ah—cargo is presently being sent after me by our family connections in *Mamlakah al-Maghribiyah*, and as for the third—"

"Cargo?" Hisdai interrupted, the keen professional interest of a seasoned merchant lighting up his eyes.

"*Listen* to me, I said!" Daud came dangerously close to shaking his father soundly. "As for the *third* ship, the *Hadassah ha-Malkah*, as soon as we came within sight of Tangier, your precious admiral ordered it to veer away north. Yes—do not stare—I said north; north to the ports of the Catholic Monarchs! North with a hold filled with the later gifts of the

Great Khan, beside which what you see upon the carpet here is nothing. And even now, as we speak he has gone to present himself before Ferdinand and Isabella at their battle camp at Santa Fe. Don't you see? Now he has proof that will command the attention of royalty in a manner they cannot ignore. The paltry gold of Granada's Jews was insufficient to buy us refuge from the Castilian troops, or safety for the last city where our Moorish masters allowed us to follow our faith in peace. The endless gold of Cathay *will* buy your pet Genoese what he has always hungered for—a noble title, royal patronage, and his place as the honored favorite of our enemies!" His face was a mask of scorn as he added, "Once a snob, always a snob."

"But we must stop him!" Hisdai grabbed his son's arms in a grip that was the equal of the younger man's.

"Do you think we did not try, O my father? Too late. By the time we realized what he was about, he had gained too much time. After the wreck of the *Tziporah*, he made certain to crew the *Hadassah ha-Malkah* with men who would go along with his treachery."

"Impossible." Hisdai shook his head like one suddenly weary. "Everyone aboard those ships was of our own people. They knew our great purpose! How could they—?"

"Present promises of a greater share in a hold full of treasure weighs more with some men than dreams of a distant Jewish homeland," Daud said with neither pride nor shame.

Hisdai slumped in his son's grasp. "Even so. How can I blame them? The siege has lasted almost a year and a half. Granada is all that remains to our sultan." With faltering steps he turned from Daud and went to the window. "In the streets he is no longer called Abu Abd Allah Muhammad, but *al-zogoybi*, and in truth he is a poor devil. He will go down, and we shall fall with him. The taking of Granada is the death of our people's last truly safe haven. In the dark times to come many will fancy gold a better rock to cling to than Torah."

So rapt was Hisdai by his burden of hopelessness, he hardly noticed that when his son's shadow crept up behind him, a second shade—then a third, then a fourth—glided silently into the room and joined it. He only half heard Daud say, "O my father, you are wise to have kept faith."

"Faith?" Hisdai's laugh was brittle and hollow. He continued to gaze up at the steel-bright sky above Granada. "Of what use is faith? I have squandered our wealth to back the vision of a renegade! We need soldiers, Daud—not scholars, not visionaries—and soldiers will not fight for faith alone."

"Yet I hear these Catholic Monarchs call this battle for Granada a new Crusade."

"That shows all you know of Crusades, my son. If Granada were a poor mud-hut village, these Catholic Monarchs and their minions would not care if we worshiped the birds of the air or the snakes that crawl over the face of the earth, but because we have wealth—"

"Father," Daud cautioned. "Father, it would be wiser not to speak with mockery of snakes and birds."

"I mean no scorn. Who am I to mock the Lord's creation?" Hisdai leaned heavily against the side of the window. "I am just a poor man who put his faith in dreams. Dreams fly. Only death is certain."

Then Hisdai ibn Ezra turned from the window, and in that instant beheld a sight that convinced him that madness, too, is one of life's little certainties. "Blessed Lord," he murmured, and took one backward step that came near to toppling him out the window.

Daud sprang forward and seized Hisdai by the arm. "Have a care, O my father. It is not courtesy to leave your faithful so precipitously."

"Faithful?" Hisdai quavered.

"Well, so he has assured me. Although officially he is a priest of Huitzilopochtli, he has confided in me that his heart"—for some reason, Daud swallowed hard—"his heart is devoted to the worship of Quetzalcoatl, the Plumed Serpent. Uh . . . would you mind if he touched your beard? It would be an honor, and he has promised us so much—"

Giddy with trying to make sense of the gibberish Daud was spouting, Hisdai found himself face-to-face with a man unlike any he had ever encountered, even in the years of his widest mercantile wanderings. Straight black hair, deep copper skin marked with tattoos and other scars, wide nose ornamented with plugs of gold and jade, the apparition regarded him with an unreadable expression.

"He wants to . . . touch my beard?" Hisdai could not tear his eyes away. From the gilded and gemmed sandals on this creature's feet to the exquisite feathered mantle on his shoulders to the gorgeously plumed headdress crowning all, one thing about the new caller was certain: Not even Mahmoud would mistake him or the two burly fellows accompanying him for Castilians.

As if to confirm this, Mahmoud chose that moment to enter with the refreshments, a dish that was tribute to both Cook's frugality and his creativity. "Remember to tell *ya-sidi* Hisdai that the meat is for the Castilian only," he mumbled to himself, so intent on keeping the heavy tray level that at first he did not really notice the extra people now gathered in the room. "Remember to tell him, or Cook will have my head. Master is—*was*—so fond of Rover."

This apposite consumer warning now went flying out of Mahmoud's skull as he looked up from his burden and actually *saw* his master's additional guests. One wore what looked like a leopard's pelt, the head a fanged helmet, the other was sheathed in feathered armor with an eagle's beak overshadowing his keen eyes. Both were heavily armed with eccentric weapons that looked nonetheless mortally effective for all their strangeness.

Mahmoud screamed, dropped the canine *khus-khus*, and ran. The eagle-helmed warrior threw what looked like a primitive ax, which nailed the fleeing servant's sleeve to the doorpost.

Before Mahmoud could wrench free, he was laid hold of by both bizarrely armored men and thrust to the floor at Hisdai's feet, as if for the older man's approval.

Daud stepped in at once. "O my father," he said smoothly, "may it please you to welcome the beloved nephew of the Great Khan Ahuitzotl, the Lord Moctezuma?"

Without word or hint of their intentions, the three copper-skinned strangers fell to the carpet alongside Mahmoud and assumed positions of the utmost humble submission. Hisdai opened and closed his mouth, wet his lips numerous times, nibbled the ends of his snowy moustache, and in general made every visual preamble to speech without actually managing to utter an intelligible word. He looked as if he did not know whether to object to the display of obeisance at his feet, to demand an explanation, to offer the abused Mahmoud a raise in salary, or just to go to the window, leap for the padded awning below, and make a break for it. There was also the chance that he might miss the awning, but at the moment that did not seem like such a bad alternative to the irrationality besetting him. At the end of his reason, he searched his son's face and ultimately managed to choke out a hoarse yet eloquent plea:

"*Nu?*"

Daud looked sheepish. "Ah, yes, there was one small matter I forgot to mention about my new friend, O my father."

He reached once more into his pouch and pulled out a rolled parchment on which was a meticulously copied drawing of a venerable-looking gentleman—bearded, fair-skinned—whose preferred mode of transport was obviously a raft made out of live snakes. "I made the drawing myself, copying it from one of Lord Ahuitzotl's holiest manuscripts," he said, showing it to Hisdai. "This is Quetzalcoatl, the Plumed Serpent, the god who departed, sailing away to the East, but whose return has been foretold. Specifically foretold. Promised, I should say, for a few years from now. Of course, as I told Lord Moctezuma, who are we to quibble if a god shows up for his appointments a trifle early?"

He tilted the page so that the light might fall on it from a better angle, and hopefully prompted his father, "You *do* see the resemblance?"

Hisdai's reaction to this unsought Annunciation would remain one of Time's unfinished mysteries. From somewhere beyond the walls a long, blood-chilling ululation shivered the air and tore all attention from every matter save itself. It was a scream beautiful in its ghastly perfection. Not even the most ignorant of hearers could confound a sound that horripilating with the muezzin's common cry; not unless the muezzin had suddenly been seized with the urge to boil himself alive slowly, in a vat of vengeance-minded lobsters.

At the fearful outcry the primal instincts of every man in that small room asserted themselves. Mahmoud tendered his resignation and bolted. Hisdai clutched his grown son protectively to him as if Daud were still a child. Moctezuma and his entourage calmly lifted their heads and smiled: quaint, nostalgic smiles such as other folk might wear on hearing a dear, old, familiar cradle-tune.

"Oh, good," said Daud. The model of unflappability, he disengaged himself from his father's arms and brought a stub of charcoal and a much-folded document out his shirt bosom. The blood of generations of steel-nerved merchant princes never flowed more coolly through his veins as he consulted the parchment, checked off an item, and remarked to all concerned, "I see the rest of the cargo has arrived."

On the battleground before Granada the troops of the Catholic Monarchs knew that already.

In spite of Hisdai's protests that he had no place on the field of combat, his son, Daud, and his newfound retainers insisted that he accompany them to the city gate to view the proceedings. Shock did little to diffuse Hisdai's innate stubbornness, and he put teeth in his refusal by making that long-contemplated leap out the window.

To no avail. There were more of the eagle-helmed Cathayans in the patio below, the translator Moshe ibn Ahijah with them. They simply waited until he stopped bouncing, then (with ibn Ahijah's able intervention) hailed him as Lord Quetzalcoatl, All-Powerful Sovereign, Savior-Whose-Coming-Was-Foretold-For-A-Few-Years-Later-Than-This-But-Who's-Counting?, and hauled him off to see how well his loyal people served him.

So it was that Hisdai ibn Ezra came to witness the end of the siege of Granada and the grim finale to all the Catholic Monarchs' dreams of finishing the Reconquest. Instead the Reconquest finished them. As he stood upon the battlements of the city, Hisdai beheld a vast force of Cathayans sweep through the Christian ranks with astonishing zeal and ferocity.

"Incredible," he remarked to Daud. "And yet they make such delicate porcelains."

"I just hope Lord Tizoc and those jaguar knights of his find you a throne quickly," Daud replied, not really listening. "This is going to be over sooner than I thought."

"And why should I need a throne?" Hisdai inquired.

"Why, to receive the captives!"

"Captives?" The old Jew made a deprecating sound.

Twenty minutes later he was making it out of the other side of his mouth as he gazed down at his noble prisoners and felt distinctly uncomfortable. It was not the fault of his seat—the throne was the best Lord Tizoc's men could transport from the great Alhambra palace on such short notice—but of Hisdai ibn Ezra's new position. During his few previous interviews with royalty, he had been firmly entrenched on the giving end of any and all obeisances, grovels, and general gestures of submission. This was different, and would take some getting used to.

Not all of the captives were making the transition any easier for the former merchant. Queen Isabella of *Castilla y León* was the only woman who could kneel in the dirt at the foot of a god's throne and still make it look as if everyone present had come to pay homage to her. Her husband and consort, Ferdinand of *Aragón*, crouched beside her, eyes hermetically shut, whimpering, any pretense of royal pride long since abandoned. Unlike his mate, he had been in the thick of the last battle and seen too many sights that properly belonged in a sinner's nightmare of hell.

Ferdinand and Isabella were not alone. Sultan Muhammad and his mother were with them, the regal quartet linked at the necks with a single rope whose end was fast in the hand of Moctezuma's finest jaguar warrior.

Off to one side Christopher Columbus crouched within a ring of eagle knights—the "cargo" of that ship he had abandoned because he thought a shipment of gold had the greater worth than a shipment of heathen ambassadors. The error of his commercial instincts had just been proven beyond doubt on the battlefield.

Using care, so as not to upset the towering headdress his new subjects had insisted he wear, Lord Hisdai ibn Ezra y Quetzalcoatl beckoned Daud nearer. "This is wrong," he whispered.

"Try it for a time; you may like it," Daud suggested.

"But this is blasphemy!" Hisdai maintained, pounding on the arm of his throne. "*Thou shalt have no other gods before me*, says the Lord!"

"Well, *you* have no other gods before Him, do you, Father? And if your new subjects choose to worship a Jew, they won't be the first. Given time, they might even convert entirely. If Judaism is good enough for your Lord Quetzalcoatl, I will tell them, it should be good enough for you! It won't take long. Moshe ibn Ahijah only had to explain to them about horses *once* when we reached Tangier, and you saw how well they handled the Castilian cavalry."

"Yes, but to *eat* the poor beasts afterward—!"

"Well, they do have their little ways. . . ."

Hisdai considered this. Unfortunately his meditations were interrupted by Queen Isabella, who decided to make her royal displeasure known by spitting at his feet and calling him a name that showed her deep ignorance of Jewish family life. Two of the jaguar warriors sprang forward to treat her sacrilege by a method whose directness would have warmed the figurative heart of the Inquisition. Only a horrified shout from Hisdai made them lower their obsidian-toothed warclubs, still sticky with assorted bits of skullbone and brain-matter collected in the course of the recent fray.

Moctezuma himself came before his chosen Lord, bowing low. "O august Lord Quetzalcoatl, mighty Plumed Serpent, bringer of the arts of peace, what is your will that we do with the graceless devils who dared attack your chosen stronghold and those who so poorly defended it until now?" His bastard blend of Hebrew, Arabic, Aramaic, Castilian, Greek, and Latin was really quite good for one who had only picked up snatches of the tongues on board a sailing vessel.

"He means the kings," Daud whispered. "Both Catholic and Moorish. And Granada."

"I know who and what he means," Hisdai snapped back, sotto voce. "I still don't know why he has to mean me, with all those barbarous names. What have I to do with the kings anyway?"

"Well, you'll have to do *something* with them. Your new subjects expect—they expect. . ." Daud hesitated. Having witnessed the aftermath of more than one battle while visiting the Great Khan Ahuitzotl's court, he knew just what these people expected and how touchy they would be if they didn't get it. On the other hand, there was no way short of a new Creation that his father would consent to what Lord Moctezuma had in mind, even in the name of religious freedom.

Daud was pondering this dilemma when he heard his father exclaim, "Stop pestering me, Moctezuma! I tell you I don't know *what* I want done with them! Can't it wait?"

"Puissant lord, it cannot. If we do not feed the sun—"

"What? Feed what? Daud, you speak this man's tongue better than he speaks ours, see if you can understand him. What is he trying to say?"

Daud smiled as a second, figurative sun shed the lovely rays of revelation within his mind. "Never mind, Father," he said. "I'll take care of everything. You go ahead to the palace. You know they cannot start the banquet without you."

Reluctant as he was to leave loose ends behind him, Hisdai was still too flummoxed to do other than comply with his son's suggestion. Flanked by jaguar warriors and preceded by eagle knights, he allowed himself to be led up to the splendors of the Alhambra, where the promised victory feast awaited. Word of the bizarre conquest had spread rapidly through the Jewish population of Granada, and mad celebration followed. With the help of Moshe ibn Ahijah's linguistically talented family, Jews, Cathayans, and the always pragmatic Moors had cooperated to lay on a wondrous repast in very little time. Cook was in his glory. There was not an empty goblet nor an occupied kennel left in all the city.

Hisdai had barely taken his place in the feasting hall when Daud returned and whispered something in his ear.

"A job?" Hisdai echoed. "That renegade Genoese betrays us and you give him a job?"

"Why not?" Daud made a lazy, beckoning gesture, and one of Moctezuma's doe-eyed waiting-women hastened to fetch a tray of chilled melon slices. As part of the Great Khan's favorite nephew's entourage, these select highborn ladies had been definitely off-limits for the course of the voyage. Now, however, they were just another gift to Lord Quetzalcoatl's household. "You didn't want to be bothered."

Hisdai lowered his eyes. "I feared having my enemies in my power. Nothing reduces a man to his animal nature faster than the opportunity for exacting unlimited revenge."

"Most admirable. Which was precisely why I sent Christopher Columbus to deliver your will to our—I mean, your new subjects."

"My will? How, when I never stated it?"

"Not precisely, perhaps, but I assumed you wished the captives be shown mercy."

"True."

"You just couldn't trust yourself to say as much with Isabella addressing you so—unwisely."

"And shall I trust the Genoese to do as much? The Catholic Monarchs scorned him once. Has he the strength of character to resist paying them back now?"

"Perhaps not." Daud ogled the waiting-woman, and she returned a look of most exquisite promise. "Which was why I told him Moctezuma has already been advised that the fate of one captive is the fate of all."

Hisdai relaxed visibly. "My son, you are wise. But—you did tell him to request compassionate treatment? You are certain? Does Columbus know enough of the Cathayan tongue to make himself understood beyond doubt?"

Daud sighed. "Alas, no. Christopher Columbus is a man of vision, not linguistics. Which was why I took the precaution of having Moshe ibn Ahijah translate the *exact* words our once-admiral should relay to Lord Moctezuma."

The waiting-woman knelt beside him with seductive grace, offering her tray and more besides for Daud's inspection. Rumor had it that she and the others were ranked as princesses in their own land. Idly Daud wondered whether—the lady's eventual conversion permitting—such a match would satisfy Hisdai. So caught up was he in these pleasant musings that he did not hear his father's next question.

"Daud! Daud, wake up. I asked you something."

"Hmm? And what was that, O my fondle—father?"

"What he *said*. What you told the Genoese to *say*."

"Oh, that. I kept it simple. I told him to say—"

From somewhere outside a loud cheer from many throats assaulted heaven, loud enough certainly to cover the lesser cry of one man surprised by the religious practices of another.

"—have a heart."

LOOKING FOR THE FOUNTAIN

Robert Silverberg

My name is Francisco de Ortega and by the grace of God I am eighty-nine years old and I have seen many a strange thing in my time, but nothing so strange as the Indian folk of the island called Florida, whose great dream it is to free the Holy Land from the Saracen conquerors that profane it.

It was fifty years ago that I encountered these marvelous people, when I sailed with his excellency the illustrious Don Juan Ponce de León on his famous and disastrous voyage in quest of what is wrongly called the Fountain of Youth. It was not a Fountain of Youth at all that he sought, but a Fountain of Manly Strength, which is somewhat a different thing. Trust me: I was there, I saw and heard everything, I was by Don Juan Ponce's side when his fate overtook him. I know the complete truth of this endeavor and I mean to set it all down now so there will be no doubt; for I alone survive to tell the tale, and as God is my witness I will tell it truthfully now, here in my ninetieth year, all praises be to Him and to the Mother who bore Him.

The matter of the Fountain, first.

Commonly, I know, it is called the Fountain of Youth. You will read that in many places, such as in the book about the New World which that Italian wrote who lived at Seville, Peter Martyr of Anghiera, where he says, "The governor of the Island of Boriquena, Juan Ponce de León, sent forth two caravels to seek the Islands of Boyuca in which the Indians affirmed there to be a fountain or spring whose water is of such marvelous virtue, that when it is drunk it makes old men young again."

This is true, so far as it goes. But when Peter Martyr talks of "making old men young again," his words must be interpreted in a poetic way.

Perhaps long life is truly what that Fountain really provides, along with its other and more special virtue—who knows? For I have tasted of that Fountain's waters myself, and here I am nearly ninety years of age and still full of vigor, I who was born in the year of our Lord 1473, and how many others are still alive today who came into the world then, when Castile and Aragón still were separate kingdoms? But I tell you that what Don Juan Ponce was seeking was not strictly speaking a Fountain of Youth at all, but rather a Fountain that offered a benefit of a very much more intimate kind. For I was there, I saw and heard everything. And they have cowardly tongues, those who say it was a Fountain of Youth, for it would seem that out of shame they choose not to speak honestly of the actual nature of the powers that the Fountain which we sought was supposed to confer.

It was when we were in the island of Hispaniola that we first heard of this wonderful Fountain, Don Juan Ponce and I. This was, I think, in the year 1504. Don Juan Ponce, a true nobleman and a man of high and elegant thoughts, was governor then in the province of Higuey of that island, which was ruled at that time by Don Nicolas de Ovando, successor to the great Admiral Cristóbal Colón. There was in Higuey then a certain Indian cacique or chieftain of remarkable strength and force, who was reputed to keep seven wives and to satisfy each and every one of them each night of the week. Don Juan Ponce was curious about the great virility of this cacique, and one day he sent a certain Aurelio Herrera to visit him in his village.

"He does indeed have many wives," said Herrera, "though whether there were five or seven or fifty-nine I could not say, for there were women surrounding all the time I was there, coming and going in such multitudes that I was unable to make a clear count, and swarms of children also, and from the looks of it the women were his wives and the children were his children."

"And what sort of manner of man is this cacique?" asked Don Juan Ponce.

"Why," said Herrera, "he is a very ordinary man, narrow of shoulders and shallow of chest, whom you would never think capable of such marvels of manhood, and he is past middle age besides. I remarked on this to him, and he said that when he was young he was easily exhausted and found the manly exercises a heavy burden. But then he journeyed to Boyuca, which is an island to the north of Cuba that is also called Bimini, and there he drank of a spring that cures the debility of sex.

Since then, he asserts, he has been able to give pleasure to any number of women in a night without the slightest fatigue."

I was there. I saw and heard everything. *El enflaquecimiento del sexo* was the phrase that Aurelio Herrera used, "the debility of sex." The eyes of Don Juan Ponce de León opened wide at this tale, and he turned to me and said, "We must go in search of this miraculous fountain some day, Francisco, for there will be great profit in the selling of its waters."

Do you see? Not a word had been spoken about long life, but only about the curing of *el enflaquecimiento del sexo*. Nor was Don Juan Ponce in need of any such cure for himself, I assure you, for in the year 1504 he was just thirty years old, a lusty and aggressive man of fiery and restless spirit, and red-haired as well, and you know what is said about the virility of red-haired men. As for me, I will not boast, but I will say only that since the age of thirteen I have rarely gone a single night without a woman's company, and have been married four times, on the fourth occasion to a woman fifty years younger than myself. And if you find yourself in the province of Valladolid where I live and come to pay a call on me I can show you young Diego Antonio de Ortega whom you would think was my great-grandson, and little Juana Maria de Ortega who could be my great-granddaughter, for the boy is seven and the girl is five, but in truth they are my own children, conceived when I was past eighty years of age; and I have had many other sons and daughters too, some of whom are old people now and some are dead.

So it was not to heal our own debilities that Don Juan Ponce and I longed to find this wonderful Fountain, for of such shameful debilities we had none at all, he and I. No, we yearned for the Fountain purely for the sake of the riches we might derive from it: for each year saw hundreds or perhaps thousands of men come from Spain to the New World to seek their fortunes, and some of these were older men who no doubt suffered from a certain *enflaquecimiento*. In Spain I understand they used the powdered horn of the unicorn to cure this malady, or the crushed shells of a certain insect, though I have never had need of such things myself. But those commodities are not to be found in the New World, and it was Don Juan Ponce's hope that great profit might be made by taking possession of Bimini and selling the waters of the Fountain to those who had need of such a remedy. This is the truth, whatever others may claim.

But the pursuit of gold comes before everything, even the pursuit of miraculous Fountains of Manly Strength. We did not go at once in search of the Fountain because word came to Don Juan Ponce in Hispaniola that the neighboring island of Borinquen was rich in gold, and thereupon he applied to Governor Ovando for permission to go there and conquer it. Don Juan Ponce already somewhat knew that island, having seen its western coast briefly in 1493 when he was a gentleman volunteer in the fleet of Cristóbal Colón, and its beauty had so moved him that he had resolved someday to return and make himself master of the place.

With one hundred men, he sailed over to this Borinquen in a small caravel, landing there on Midsummer Day, 1506, at the same bay he had visited earlier aboard the ship of the great Admiral. Seeing us arrive with such force, the cacique of the region was wise enough to yield to the inevitable and we took possession with very little fighting.

So rich did the island prove to be that we put the marvelous Fountain of which we had previously heard completely out of our minds. Don Juan Ponce was made governor of Borinquen by royal appointment and for several years the natives remained peaceful and we were able to obtain a great quantity of gold indeed. This is the same island that Cristóbal Colón called San Juan Bautista and which people today call Puerto Rico.

All would have been well for us there but for the stupidity of a certain captain of our forces, Cristóbal de Sotomayor, who treated the natives so badly that they rose in rebellion against us. This was in the year of our Lord 1511. So we found ourselves at war; and Don Juan Ponce fought with all the great valor for which he was renowned, doing tremendous destruction against our pagan enemies. We had among us at that time a certain dog, called Bercerillo, of red pelt and black eyes, who could tell simply by smell alone whether an Indian was friendly to us or hostile, and could understand the native speech as well; and the Indians were more afraid of ten Spaniards with this dog, than of one hundred without him. Don Juan Ponce rewarded Bercerillo's bravery and cleverness by giving the dog a full share of all the gold and slaves we captured, as though he were a crossbowman; but in the end the Indians killed him. I understand that a valiant pup of this Bercerillo, Leoncillo by name, went with Nunxez de Balboa when he crossed the Isthmus of Panama and discovered the great ocean beyond.

During this time of our difficulties with the savages of Puerto Rico, Don Diego Colón, the son of the great Admiral, was able to take advantage of the trouble and make himself governor of the island in the place of Don Juan Ponce. Don Juan Ponce thereupon returned to Spain and presented himself before King Ferdinand and told him the tale of the fabulous Fountain that restores manly power. King Ferdinand, who was greatly impressed by Don Juan Ponce's lordly bearing and noble appearance, at once granted him a royal permit to seek and conquer the isle of Bimini where this Fountain was said to be. Whether this signifies that His Most Catholic Majesty was troubled by debilities of a sexual sort, I would not dare to say. But the king was at that time a man of sixty years and it would not be unimaginable that some difficulty of that kind had begun to perplex him.

Swiftly Don Juan Ponce returned to Puerto Rico with the good news of his royal appointment, and on the third day of March of the year of our Lord 1513 we set forth from the Port of San Germán in three caravels to search for Bimini and its extraordinary Fountain.

I should say at this point that it was a matter of course that Don Juan Ponce should have asked me to take part in the quest for this Fountain. I am a man of Tervás de San Campos in the province of Valladolid, where Don Juan Ponce de León also was born less than one year after I was, and he and I played together as children and were friends all through our youth. As I have said, he first went to the New World in 1493, when he was nineteen years of age, as a gentleman aboard the ship of Admiral Cristóbal Colón, and after settling in Hispaniola he wrote to me and told me of the great wealth of the New World and urged me to join him there. Which I did forthwith; and we were rarely separated from then until the day of his death.

Our flagship was the *Santiago*, with Diego Bermúdez as its master—the brother to the man who discovered the isle of Bermuda—and the famous Antón de Alaminos as its pilot. We had two Indian pilots too, who knew the islands of that sea. Our second ship was the *Santa María de Consolación*, with Juan Bono de Quexo as its captain, and the third was the *San Cristóbal*. All of these vessels were purchased by Don Juan Ponce himself out of the riches he had laid by in the time when he was governor of Puerto Rico.

I have to tell you that there was not one priest in our company, not that we were ungodly men but only that it was not our commander's purpose on this voyage to bring the word of Jesus to the natives of Bimini. We did have some few women among us, including my own wife Beatriz, who had come out from Spain to be with me, and grateful I was to have her by my side; and my wife's young sister Juana was aboard the ship also, that I could better look after her among these rough Spaniards of the New World.

Northward we went. After ten days we halted at the isle of San Salvador to scrape weeds from the bottom of one of our ships. Then we journeyed west-northwest, passing the isle of Ciguateo on Easter Sun-

day, and, continuing onward into waters that ran ever shallower, we
caught sight on the second day of April of a large delightful island of
great and surpassing beauty, all blooming and burgeoning with a great
host of wildflowers whose delectable odors came wafting to us on the
warm gentle breeze. We named this isle La Florida, because Easter is
the season when things flower and so we call that time of year in our
language *Pascua Florida*. And we said to one another at once, seeing so
beautiful a place, that this island of Florida must surely be the home of
the wondrous Fountain that restores men to their fleshly powers and
grants all their carnal desires to the fullest.

Of the loveliness of Florida I could speak for a day and a night and a
night and a day, and not exhaust its marvels. The shallowing green
waters give way to white crests of foam that fall upon beaches paved
hard with tiny shells; and when you look beyond the beach you see
dunes and marshes, and beyond those a land altogether level, not so
much as a hillock upon it, where glistening sluggish lagoons bordered
brilliantly with rushes and sedges show the way to the mysterious forests
of the interior.

Those forests! Palms and pines, and gnarled gray trees whose names
are known only to God! Trees covered with snowy beards! Trees whose
leaves are like swords! Flowers everywhere, dizzying us with their
perfume! We were stunned by the fragrance of jasmine and honeyflower.
We heard the enchanting songs of a myriad of birds. We stared in
wonder at the bright blooms. We doffed our helmets and dropped to our
knees to give thanks to God for having led us to this most beautiful of
shores.

Don Juan Ponce was the first of us to make his way to land, carrying
with him the banner of Castile and León. He thrust the royal standard
into the soft sandy soil and in the name of God and Spain took
possession of the place. This was at the mouth of a river which he named
in honor of his patron, the blessed San Juan. Then, since there were no
Indians thereabouts who might lead us to the Fountain, we returned to
our vessels and continued along the coast of that place.

Though the sea looked gentle we found the currents unexpectedly
strong, carrying us northward so swiftly that we feared we would never
see Puerto Rico again. Therefore did Don Juan Ponce give orders for us
to turn south; but although we had a fair following wind the current was
so strong against us that we could make no headway, and at last we were
compelled to anchor in a cove. Here we spent some days, with the ships
straining against their cables; and during that time the little *San
Cristóbal* was swept out to sea and we lost sight of her altogether,

though the day was bright and the weather fair. But within two days by God's grace she returned to us.

At this time we saw our first Indians, but they were far from friendly. Indeed they set upon us at once, and two of our men were wounded by their little darts and arrows, which were tipped with sharp points made of bone. When night came we were able to withdraw and sail on to another place that we called the Rio de la Cruz, where we collected wood and water; and here we were attacked again, by sixty Indians, but they were driven off. And so we continued for many days, until in latitude 28 degrees 15 minutes we did round a cape, which we called Cabo de los Corrientes on account of the powerful currents, which were stronger than the wind.

Here it was that we had the strangest part of our voyage, indeed the strangest thing I have ever seen in all my ninety years. Which is to say that we encountered at this time in this remote and hitherto unknown land the defenders of the Christian Faith, the sworn foes of the Saracens, the last sons of the Crusades, whose great dream it was, even now, to wrest the Holy Land of our Savior's birth from those infidel followers of Muhammad who seized it long ago and rule it today.

We suspected nothing of any of what awaited us when we dropped our anchors near an Indian town on the far side of Cabo de los Corrientes. Cautiously, for we had received such a hostile reception farther up the coast, we made our landfall a little way below the village and set about the task of filling our water casks and cutting firewood. While this work was being carried out we became aware that the Indians had left their village and had set out down the shore to encounter us, for we heard them singing and chanting even before we could see them; and we halted in our labors and made ourselves ready to deal with another attack.

After a short while the Indians appeared, still singing as they approached. Wonder of wonders, they were clothed, though all the previous natives that we had seen were naked, or nearly so, as these savages usually are. Even more marvelous was the nature of their clothing, which was of a kind not very different from that which Christians wear, jerkins and doublets and tunics, and such things. And—marvel of marvel—every man of them wore upon his chest a white garment that bore the holy cross of Jesus painted brightly in red! We could not believe our eyes. But if we had any doubt that these were Christian men, it was eradicated altogether when we saw that in the midst of the procession came certain men wearing the dark robes of priests, who carried great wooden crosses held high aloft.

Were these indeed Indians? Surely not! Surely they must be Spaniards like ourselves! We might almost have been in Toledo, or Madrid, or Seville, and not on the shore of some strange land of the Indies! But indeed we saw without doubt now that the marchers were men of the sort that is native to the New World, with the ruddy skins and black hair and sharp features of their kind, Christian though they might be in dress, and carrying the cross itself in their midst.

When they were close enough so that we could hear distinctly the words of their song, it sounded to some of us that they might be Latin words, though Latin of a somewhat barbarous kind. Could that be possible? We doubted the evidence of our ears. But then Pedro de Plasencia, who had studied for the priesthood before entering the military, crossed himself most vigorously and said to us in wonder, "Do you hear that? They are singing the *Gloria in excelsis Deo!*" And in truth we could tell that hymn was what they sang, now that Pedro de Plasencia had picked out the words of it for us. Does that sound strange to you, that Indians of an unknown isle should be singing in Latin? Yes, it is strange indeed. But doubt me at your peril. I was there; I saw and heard everything myself.

"Surely," said Diego Bermúdez, "there must have been Spaniards here before us, who have instructed these people in the way of God."

"That cannot be," said our pilot, Antón de Alaminos. "For I was with Cristóbal Colón on his second voyage and have been on every voyage since of any note that has been made in these waters, and I can tell you that no white man has set foot on this shore before us."

"Then how came these Indians by their crosses and their holy hymns?" asked Diego Bermúdez. "Is it a pure miracle of the saints, do you think?"

"Perhaps it is," said Don Juan Ponce de León, with some heat, for it looked as if there might be a quarrel between the master and the pilot. "Who can say? Be thankful that these folk are our Christian friends and not our enemy, and leave off your useless speculations."

And in the courageous way that was his nature, Don Juan Ponce went forward and raised his arms to the Indians, and made the sign of the cross in the air, and called out to them, saying, "I am Don Juan Ponce de León of Valladolid, in the land of Spain, and I greet you in the name of the Father, and of the Son, and of the Holy Ghost." All of which he said clearly and loudly in his fine and beautiful Castilian, which he spoke with the greatest purity. But the Indians, who by now had halted in a straight line before us, showed no understanding in their eyes. Don Juan Ponce spoke again, once more in Spanish, saying that he greeted them also in the name of His Most Catholic Majesty King Ferdinand of Aragón and Castile. This too produced no sign that it had been understood.

One of the Indians then spoke. He was a man of great presence and bearing, who wore chains of gold about his chest and carried a sword of strange design at his side, the first sword I had ever seen a native of these islands to have. From these indications it was apparent that he was the cacique.

He spoke long and eloquently in a language that I suppose was his own, for none of us had ever heard it before, not even the two Indian pilots we had brought with us. Then he said a few words that had the sound and the ring of French or perhaps Catalan, though we had a few men of Barcelona among us who leaned close toward him and put their hands to their ears and even they could make no sense out of what they heard.

But then finally this grand cacique spoke words which we all could understand plainly, garbled and thick-tongued though his speaking of them was: for what he said was, and there could be no doubt of it however barbarous his accent, "In nomine Patris, et Filii, et Spiritus Sancti," and he made the sign of the cross over his chest as any good Christian man would do. To which Don Juan replied, "Amen. Dominus vobiscum." Whereupon the cacique, exclaiming, "Et cum spiritu tuo," went forthrightly to the side of Don Juan Ponce, and they embraced with great love, likewise as any Christian men might do, here on this remote beach in this strange and lovely land of Florida.

They brought us then to their village and offered a great feast for us, with roasted fish and the meat of tortoises and sweet fruits of many mysterious kinds, and made us presents of the skins of animals. For our part we gave them such trinkets as we had carried with us, beads and bracelets and little copper daggers and the like, but of all the things we gave them they were most eager to receive the simple figurines of Jesus on the cross that we offered them, and passed them around amongst themselves in wonder, showing such love for them as if they were made of the finest gold and studded with emeralds and rubies. And we said privately to each other that we must be dreaming, to have met with Indians in this land who were of such great devotion to the faith.

We tried to speak with them again in Spanish, but it was useless, and so too was speaking in any of the native tongues of Hispaniola or Puerto Rico that we knew. In their turn they addressed us in their own language, which might just as well have been the language of the people of the Moon for all we comprehended it, and also in that tantalizing other tongue which seemed almost to be French or Catalan. We could not make anything of that, try though we did. But Pedro de Plasencia, who was the only one of us who could speak Latin out loud like a priest, sat down with the cacique after the meal and addressed him in that language. I mean not simply saying things like the Pater Noster and the Ave Maria, which any child can say, but speaking to him as if Latin was a real language with words and sentences of common meaning, the way it was long ago. To which the cacique answered, though he seemed to be framing his words with much difficulty; and Pedro answered him again, just as hesitatingly; and so they went on, talking to each other in a slow and halting way, far into the night, nodding and smiling most jubilantly whenever one of them reached some understanding of the other's words, while we looked on in astonishment, unable to fathom a word of what they were saying.

At last Pedro rose, looking pale and exhausted like a man who has carried a bull on his back for half a league, and came over to us where we were sitting in a circle.

"Well?" Don Juan Ponce demanded at once.

Pedro de Plasencia shook his head wearily. "It was all nonsense, what the cacique said. I understood nothing. Nothing at all! It was mere incomprehensible babble and no more than that." And he picked up a leather sack of wine that lay near his feet and drank from it as though he had a thirst that no amount of drinking ever could quench.

"You appeared to comprehend, at times," said Don Juan Ponce. "Or so it seemed to me as I watched you."

"Nothing. Not a word. Let me sleep on it, and perhaps it will come clear to me in the morning."

I thought Don Juan Ponce would pursue him on the matter. But Don Juan Ponce, though he was an impatient and high-tempered man, was also a man of great sagacity, and he knew better than to press Pedro further at a time when he seemed so troubled and fatigued. So he dismissed the company and we settled down in the huts that the Indians had given us for lodging, all except those of us who were posted as sentries during the night to guard against treachery.

I rose before dawn. But I saw that Don Juan Ponce and Pedro de Plasencia were already awake and had drawn apart from the rest of us and were talking most earnestly. After a time they returned, and Don Juan Ponce beckoned to me.

"Pedro has told me something of his conversation with the cacique," he said.

"And what is it that you have learned?"

"That these Indians are indeed Christians."

"Yes, that seems to be the plain truth, strange though it seems," I said. "For they do carry the cross about, and sing the *Gloria*, and honor the Father and the Son."

"There is more."

I waited.

He continued, "Unless Pedro much mistook what the cacique told him, the greatest hope in which these people live is that of wresting the Holy Land from the Saracen, and restoring it to good Christian pilgrims."

At that I burst out into such hearty laughter that Don Juan Ponce, for all his love of me, looked at me with eyes flashing with reproof. Yet I could not withhold my mirth, which poured from me like a river.

I said at last, when I had mastered myself, "But tell me, Don Juan, what would these savages know of the Holy Land, or of Saracens, or any such thing? The Holy Land is thousands of leagues away, and has never been spoken of so much as once in this New World by any man, I think; nor does anyone speak of the Crusade any longer in this age, neither here nor at home."

"It is very strange, I agree," replied Don Juan Ponce. "Nevertheless, so Pedro swears, the cacique spoke to him of *Terra Sancta*, *Terra Sancta*, and of infidels, and the liberation of the city of Jerusalem."

"And how does it come to pass," I asked, "that they can know of such things, in this remote isle, where no white man has ever visited before?"

"Ah," said Don Juan Ponce, "that is the great mystery, is it not?"

In time we came to understand the solution to this mystery, though the tale was muddled and confused, and emerged only after much travail, and long discussions between Pedro de Plasencia and the cacique of the Indians. I will tell you the essence of it, which was this:

Some three hundred years ago, or perhaps it was four hundred, while much of our beloved Spain still lay under the Moorish hand, a shipload of Frankish warriors set sail from the port of Genoa, or perhaps it was Marseilles, or some other city along the coast of Provence. This was in the time when men still went crusading, to make war for Jesus' sake in the Holy Land against the followers of Muhammad who occupied that place.

But the voyage of these Crusaders miscarried; for when they entered the great Mar Mediterraneo, thinking to go east they were forced west by terrible storms and contrary winds, and swept helpless past our Spanish shores, past Almería and Málaga and Tarifa, and through the narrow waist of the Estrecho de Gibraltar and out into the vastness of the Ocean Sea.

Here, having no sound knowledge as we in our time do of the size and shape of the African continent, they thought to turn south and then east below Egypt and make their voyage yet to the Holy Land. Of course this would be impossible, except by rounding the Buena Fortuna cape and traveling up past Arabia, a journey almost beyond our means to this day. But being unaware of that, these bold but hapless men made the attempt, coasting southerly and southerly and southerly, and the land of course not only not ending but indeed carrying them farther and farther outward into the Ocean Sea, until at last, no doubt weary and half dead of famine, they realized that they had traveled so far to the west that there was no hope of returning eastward again, nor of turning north and making their way back into the Mediterraneo. So they yielded to the westerly winds that prevail near the Canary Isles, and allowed themselves to be blown clear across the sea to the Indies. And so, after long arduous voyaging they made landfall in this isle we call Florida. Thus these men of three hundred years ago were the first discoverers of the New World, although I doubt very greatly that they comprehended what it was they had achieved.

You must understand that we received few of these details from our Indian hosts: only the tale that men bound to Terra Sancta departing from a land in the east were blown off course some hundreds of years previous and were brought after arduous sailing to the isle of Florida and to this very village where our three caravels had made their landfall. All the rest did we conclude for ourselves, that they were Crusaders and so forth, after much discussing of the matter and recourse to the scholarship that the finest men among us possessed.

And what befell these men of the Crusade, when they came to this Florida? Why, they offered themselves to the mercies of the villagers, who greeted them right honorably and took them to dwell amongst them, and married them to their daughters! And for their part the seafarers offered the word of Jesus to the people of the village and thereby gave them hope of Heaven; and taught these kindly savages the Latin tongue so well that it remained with them after a fashion hundreds of years afterward, and also some vestiges of the common speech that the seafaring men had had in their own native land.

But most of all did the strangers from the sea imbue in the villagers the holy desire to rid the birthplace of Jesus of the dread hand of the Mussulman; and ever, in years after, did the Christian Indians of this Florida village long to put to sea, and cross the great ocean, and wield their bows and spears valiantly amidst the paynim enemy in the defense of the True Faith. Truly, how strange are the workings of God Almighty, how far beyond our comprehension, that He should make Crusaders out of the naked Indians in this far-off place!

You may ask what became of those European men who landed there, and whether we saw anyone who plainly might mark his descent from them. And I will tell you that those ancient Crusaders, who intermarried with the native women since they had brought none of their own, were wholly swallowed up by such intermarrying and were engulfed by the fullness of time. For they were only forty or fifty men among hundreds, and the passing centuries so diluted the strain of their race that not the least trace of it remained, and we saw no pale skin or fair hair or blue eyes or other marks of European men here. But the ideas that they had fetched to this place did survive, that is, the practicing of the Catholic faith and the speaking of a debased and corrupt sort of Latin and the wearing of a kind of European clothes, and such. And I tell you it was passing strange to see these red savages in their surplices and cassocks, and in their white tunics bearing the great emblem of our creed, and other such ancient marks of our civilization, and to hear them chanting the *Kyrie eleison* and the *Confiteor* and the *Sanctus, Sanctus, Sanctus Dominus Deus Sabaoth* in that curious garbled way of theirs, like words spoken in a dream.

Nay, I have spoken untruthfully, for the men of that lost voyage did leave other remnants of themselves among the villagers beside our holy faith, which I have neglected to mention here, but which I will tell you of now.

For after we had been in that village several days, the cacique led us through the close humid forest along a tangled trail to a clearing nearby just to the north of the village, and here we saw certain tangible remains of the voyagers: a graveyard with grave markers of white limestone, and the rotting ribs and strakes and some of the keel of a seafaring vessel of an ancient design, and the foundation walls of a little wooden church. All of which things were as sad a sight as could be imagined, for the grave-stones were so weathered and worn that although we could see the faint marks of names we could not read the names themselves, and the vessel was but a mere sorry remnant, a few miserable decaying timbers, and the church was only a pitiful fragment of a thing.

We stood amidst these sorry ruins and our hearts were struck into pieces by pity and grief for these brave men, so far from home and lonely, who in this strange place had nevertheless contrived to plant the sacred tree of Christianity. And the noble Don Juan Ponce De León went down on his knees before the church and bowed his head and said,

"Let us pray, my friends, for the souls of these men, as we hope that someday people will pray for ours."

We spent some days amongst these people in feasting and prayer, and replenishing our stock of firewood and water. And then Don Juan Ponce gave new thought to the primary purpose of our voyage, which was, to find the miraculous Fountain that renews a man's energies. He called Pedro de Plasencia to his side and said, "Ask of the cacique, whether he knows such a Fountain."

"It will not be easy, describing such things in my poor Latin," answered Pedro. "I had my Latin from the Church, Don Juan, and what I learned there is of little use here, and it was all so very long ago."

"You must try, my friend. For only you of all our company has the power to speak with him and be understood."

Whereupon Pedro went to the cacique; but I could see even at a distance that he was having great difficulties. For he would speak a few halting words, and then he would act out his meaning with gestures, like a clown upon a stage, and then he would speak again. There would be silence; and then the cacique would reply, and I would see Pedro leaning forward most intently, trying to catch the meaning of the curious Latin that the cacique spoke. They did draw pictures for each other also in the sand, and point to the sky and sweep their arms to and fro, and do many another thing to convey to each other the sense of their words, and so it went, hour after hour.

At length Pedro de Plasencia returned to where we stood, and said, "There does appear to be a source of precious water that they cherish on this island, which they call the Blue Spring."

"And is this Blue Spring the Fountain for which we search?" Don Juan Ponce asked, all eagerness.

"Ah, of that I am not certain."

"Did you tell him that the water of it would allow a man to take his pleasure with women all day and all night, and never tire of it?"

"So I attempted to say."

"With many women, one after another?"

"These are Christian folk, Don Juan!"

"Yes, so they are. But they are Indians also. They would understand such a thing, just as any man of Estramadura or Galicia or Andalusia would understand such a thing, Christian though he be."

Pedro de Plasencia nodded. "I told him what I could, about the nature of the Fountain for which we search. And he listened very close, and he said, Yes, yes, you are speaking of the Blue Spring."

"So he understood you, then?"

"He understood something of what I said, Don Juan, so I do firmly believe. But whether he understood it all, that is only for God to know."

I saw the color rise in Don Juan Ponce's face, and I knew that restless choleric nature of his was coming to the fore, which had always been his great driving force and also his most perilous failing.

He said to Pedro de Plasencia, "And will he take us to this Blue Spring of his, do you think?"

"I think he will," said Pedro. "But first he wishes to enact a treaty with us, as the price of transporting us thither."

"A treaty."

"A treaty, yes. He wants our aid and assistance."

"Ah," said Don Juan Ponce. "And how can we be of help to these people, do you think?"

"They want us to show them how to build seafaring ships," said Pedro. "So that they can sail across the Ocean Sea, and go to the rescue of the Holy Land, and free it from the paynim hordes."

There was much more of back and forth, and forth and back, in these negotiations, until Pedro de Plasencia grew weary indeed, and there was not enough wine in our sacks to give him the rest he needed, so that we had to send a boat out to fetch more from one of our ships at anchor in the harbor. For it was a great burden upon him to conduct these conversations, he remembering only little patches of Church Latin from his boyhood, and the cacique speaking a language that could be called Latin only by great courtesy. I sat with them as they talked, on several occasions, and not for all my soul could I understand a thing that they said to each other. From time to time Pedro would lose his patience and speak out in Spanish, or the cacique would begin to speak in his savage tongue or else in that other language, somewhat like Provencal, which must have been what the seafaring Crusaders spoke amongst themselves. But none of that added to the understanding between the two men, which I think was a very poor understanding indeed.

It became apparent after a time that Pedro had misheard the cacique's terms of treaty: what he wished us to do was not to teach them how to build ships but to *give* them one of ours in which to undertake their Crusade.

"It cannot be," replied Don Juan Ponce, when he had heard. "But tell him this, that I will undertake to purchase ships for him with my own funds, in Spain. Which I will surely do, after we have received the proceeds from the sale of the water from the Fountain."

"He wishes to know how many ships you will provide," said Pedro de Plasencia, after another conference.

"Two," said Don Juan Ponce. "No: three. Three fine caravels."

Which Pedro duly told the cacique; but his way of telling him was to point to our three ships in the harbor, which led the cacique into thinking that Don Juan Ponce meant to give him those three actual ships then and now, and that required more hours of conferring to repair. But at length all was agreed on both sides, and our journey toward the Blue Spring was begun.

The cacique himself accompanied us, and the three priests of the tribe, carrying the heavy wooden crosses that were their staffs of office, and perhaps two dozen of the young men and girls of the village. In our party there were ten men, Don Juan Ponce and Pedro and I, and seven ordinary seamen carrying barrels in which we meant to store the waters of the Fountain. My wife Beatriz and her sister Juana accompanied us also, for I never would let them be far from me.

Some of the ordinary seamen among us were rough men of Estramadura, who spoke jestingly and with great licentiousness of how often they would embrace the girls of the native village after they had drunk of the Fountain. I had to silence them, reminding them that my wife and her sister could overhear their words. Yet I wondered privately what effects the waters would have on my own manhood: not that it had ever been lacking in any aspect, but I could not help asking myself if I would find it enhanced beyond its usual virtue, for such curiosity is but a natural thing to any man, as you must know.

We journeyed for two days, through hot, close terrain where insects of great size buzzed among the flowers and birds of a thousand colors astounded our eyes. And at last we came to a place of bare white stone, flat like all other places in this isle of Florida, where clear cool blue water gushed up out of the ground with wondrous force.

The cacique gestured grandly, with a great sweep of his arms.

"It is the Blue Spring," said Pedro de Plasencia.

Our men would have rushed forward at once to lap up its waters like greedy dogs at a pond; but the cacique cried out, and Don Juan Ponce also in that moment ordered them to halt. There would be no unseemly haste here, he said. And it was just as well he did, for we very soon came to see that this spring was a holy place to the people of the village, and it would have been profaned by such an assault on it, to our possible detriment and peril.

The cacique came forward, with his priests beside him, and gestured to Don Juan Ponce to kneel and remove his helmet. Don Juan Ponce obeyed; and the cacique took his helmet from him, and passed it to one of the priests, who filled it with water from the spring and poured it down over Don Juan Ponce's face and neck, so that Don Juan Ponce laughed out loud. The which laughter seemed to offend the Indians, for they showed looks of disapproval, and Don Juan Ponce at once grew silent.

The Indians spoke words which might almost have been Latin words, and there was much elevating of their crosses as the water was poured down over Don Juan Ponce, after which he was given the order to rise.

And then one by one we stepped forth, and the Indians did the same to each of us.

"It is very like a rite of holy baptism, is it not?" said Aurelio Herrera to me.

"Yes, very much like a baptism," I said to him.

And I began to wonder: How well have we been understood here? Is it a new access of manly strength that these Indians are conferring upon us, or rather the embrace of the Church? For surely there is nothing about this rite that speaks of anything else than a religious enterprise. But I kept silent, since it was not my place to speak.

When the villagers were done dousing us with water, and speaking words over us and elevating their crosses, which made me more sure than ever that we were being taken into the congregation of their faith, we were allowed to drink of the spring—they did the same—and to fill our barrels. Don Juan Ponce turned to me after we had drunk, and winked at me and said, "Well, old friend, this will serve us well in later years, will it not? For though we have no need of such invigoration now, you and I, nevertheless time will have its work with us as it does with all men."

"If it does," I said, "why, then, we are fortified against it now indeed."

But in truth I felt no change within. The water was pure and cool and good, but it had seemed merely to be water to me, with no great magical qualities about it; and when I turned and looked upon my wife Beatriz, she seemed pleasing to me as she always had, but no more than that. Well, so be it, I thought: this may be the true Fountain or maybe it is not, and only time will tell; and we began our return to the village, carrying the casks of water with us; and the day of our return, Pedro de Plasencia drew up a grand treaty on a piece of bark from a tree, in which we pledged our sacred honor and our souls to do all in our power to supply this village with good Spanish ships so that the villagers would be able to fulfill their pledge to liberate the Holy Land.

"Which we will surely do for them," said Don Juan Ponce with great conviction. "For I mean to come back to this place as soon as I am able, with many ships of our own as well as the vessels I have promised them from Spain; and we will fill our holds with cask upon cask of this virtuous water from the Fountain, and replenish our fortunes anew by selling that water to those who need its miraculous power. Moreover we ourselves will benefit from its use in our declining days. And also we will bring this cacique some priests, who will correct him in his manner of practicing our faith, and guide him in his journey to Jerusalem. All of which I will swear by a great oath upon the Cross itself, in the presence of the cacique, so that he may have no doubt whatsoever of our kindly Christian purposes."

And so we departed, filled with great joy and no little wonder at all that we had seen and heard.

Well, and none of the brave intentions of Don Juan Ponce were fulfilled, as you surely must know, inasmuch as the valiant Don Juan Ponce de León never saw Spain again, nor did he live to enjoy the rejuvenations of his body that he hoped the water of the Fountain would bring him in his later years. For when we left the village of the Indian Crusaders, we continued on our way along the coast of the isle of Florida a little further in a southerly direction, seeking to catch favorable winds and currents that would carry us swiftly back to Puerto Rico; and on the twenty-third of May we halted in a pleasing bay to gather wood and water—for we would not touch the water of our casks from the Fountain! —and to careen the *San Cristóbal,* the hull of which was fouled with barnacles. As we did our work there, a party of Indians came forth out of the woods.

"Hail, brothers in Christ!" Don Juan Ponce called to them with great cheer, for the cacique had told him that his people had done wonderful things in bringing their neighbors into the embrace of Jesus, and he thought now that surely all the Indians of this isle had been converted to the True Faith by those Crusading men of long ago.

But he was wrong in that; for these Indians were no Christians at all, but only pagan savages like most of their kind, and they replied instantly to Don Juan Ponce's halloos with a volley of darts and arrows that struck five of us dead then and there before we were able to drive them off. And among those who took his mortal wound that day was the valiant and noble Don Juan Ponce de León of Valladolid, in the thirty-ninth year of his life.

I knelt beside him on the beach in his last moments and said the last words with him. And he looked up at me and smiled—for death had never been frightening to him—and he said to me, almost with his last breath, "There is only one thing that I regret, Francisco. And that is that I will never know, now, what powers the water of that Fountain would have conferred upon me, when I was old and greatly stricken with the frailty of my years." With that he perished.

What more can I say? We made our doleful way back to Puerto Rico, and told our tale of Crusaders and Indians and cool blue waters. But we were met with laughter, and there were no purchasers for the contents of our casks, and our fortunes were greatly depleted. All praise be to God, I survived that dark time and went on afterward to join the magnificent Hernando Cortés in his conquest of the land of Mexico, which today is called New Spain, and in the fullness of time I returned to my native province of Valladolid with much gold in my possession, and here I live in health and vigor to this day.

Often do I think of the isle of Florida and those Christian Indians we found there. It is fifty years since that time. In those fifty years the cacique and his people have rendered most of Florida into Christians by now, as we now know, and I tell you what is not generally known, that this expansion of their nation was brought about the better to support their Crusade against the Mussulman once the ships that Don Juan Ponce promised them had arrived.

So there is a great warlike Christian kingdom in Florida today, filling all that land and spreading over into adjacent isles, against which we men of Spain so far have struggled in vain as we attempt to extend our sway to those regions. I think it was poor Don Juan Ponce de León, in his innocent quest for a miraculous Fountain, who without intending it caused them to become so fierce, by making them a promise which he could not fulfill, and leaving them thinking that they had been betrayed by false Christians. Better that they had remained forever in the isolation in which they lived when we found them, singing the *Gloria* and the *Credo* and the *Sanctus*, and waiting with Christian patience for the promised ships that are to take them to the reconquest of the Holy Land. But those ships did not come; and they see us now as traitors and enemies.

I often think also of the valiant Don Juan Ponce, and his quest for the wondrous Fountain. Was the Blue Spring indeed the Fountain of legend? I am not sure of that. It may be that those Indians misunderstood what Pedro de Plasencia was requesting of them, and that they were simply offering us baptism—us, good Christians all our lives! —when what we sought was something quite different from that.

But if the Fountain was truly the one we sought, I feel great sorrow and pity for Don Juan Ponce. For though he drank of its waters, he died too soon to know of its effects. Whereas here I am, soon to be ninety years old, and the father of a boy of seven and a girl of five.

Was it the Fountain's virtue that has given me so long and robust a life, or have I simply enjoyed the favor of God? How can I say? Whichever it is, I am grateful; and if ever there is peace between us and the people of the isle of Florida, and you should find yourself in the vicinity of that place, you could do worse, I think, than to drink of that Blue Spring, which will do you no harm and may perhaps bring you great benefit. If by chance you go to that place, seek out the Indians of the village nearby, and tell them that old Francisco de Ortega remembers them, and cherishes the memory, and more than once has said a Mass in their praise despite all the troubles they have caused his countrymen, for he knows that they are the last defenders of the Holy Land against the paynim infidels.

This is my story, and the story of Don Juan Ponce de León and the miraculous Fountain, which the ignorant call the Fountain of Youth, and of the Christian Indians of Florida who yearn to free the Holy Land. You may wonder about the veracity of these things, but I beg you, have no doubt on that score. All that I have told you is true. For I was there. I saw and heard everything.

THE ROUND-EYED BARBARIANS

L. Sprague de Camp

Ho Youwen, General of the Advanced Imperial Eastern Force, to the esteemed Li Ganjing, Director of the Eastern Continent Section of the Barbarian Relations Bureau of the External Affairs Department of the Overseas Branch of His Imperial Majesty's government. Health, prosperity, and many sons!

Dear old friend: This person thinks that, besides his formal report on the affair of the round-eyed barbarians, which will follow in the next dispatch, you would also like a personal letter to furnish background for this turn on events. It is all very well for officials of the Upper Mandarinate to sneer at barbarian thoughts and deeds as of no interest to representatives of mighty Zhongguo.* True, barbarians' customs are often strange and disgusting, their beliefs outlandish, their manners appalling, and their emotions childish. But to be realistic, barbarous tribes and nations also include many dangerously vigorous and ingenious people. It was just such a toplofty attitude that in the days of the Sung led to the Mongol plague and the subjection of civilization to the rule of barbarian hordes for a century.

The same shortsightedness threatened a century ago, when Zhengtung was the Son of Heaven. A cabal of scholars and soldiers sought to end the voyages of exploration and tribute gathering begun by the great Zheng Ho. These misguided persons sought to stop all foreign contacts. They held that, since the Middle Kingdom had everything needed by civilization, such contacts would only have adverse effects.

Luckily the cabal was defeated; the work of exploration and of

---

*In the Pinyin transcription of Chinese, zh stands for the sound of the j in journal.

scientific development initiated under the accursed Mongols was continued. Hence the exploration and conquest of this Eastern Continent has proceeded in an orderly manner. The red-skinned barbarians, realizing the futility of opposing the advance of civilization with weapons of wood and stone, have been offered the benefits of our superior culture. Many take advantage of this opportunity and, in another few centuries, may have raised themselves almost to the level of civilized human beings.

But to return to the round-eyed barbarians. One day this summer, this person was reconnoitering the eastern side of the Lower Mountains, in an area not yet brought under the benevolent sway of the Son of Heaven. I led a company of Hitchiti infantry, armed with our new breech-loading rifles. A scout reported the approach of a force of redskin warriors of the Ochuse tribe, who dwell on the shores of the great water to the south. Signal drums and gongs alerted my detachment.

A *shi* later this force debouched from the trail. First came a scattering of redskins, from their paint evidently the Ochuse. After them rode a horseman in a steel helmet, cuirass, and other pieces of plate armor. After him came hundreds of round-eyed men afoot, less impressively armored, in the garb of Yuropian barbarians, wherewith the voyages of Admiral Xing have familiarized us. Their loins were covered with short, bulging breeches, below which they either went bare-legged or wore a kind of skintight trouser on each leg. They bore pikes, crossbows, and firearms of primitive types, obsolete in the Celestial Empire for a century. My redskin spies had warned me of the incursions of such people along the coast of this continent, but these were the first such intruders whom I had personally seen.

Behind them, threading their way through the forest, I glimpsed many other redskins, men and women bowed beneath the weight of the burdens they bore. Farther back yet, barely visible amid the towering trees, came a troop of armored horsemen and other men leading unsaddled horses.

At the sight of my group, taking cover behind rocks, bushes, and hummocks, the newcomers halted. The armored man in the lead swung off his horse with a clank of armor and handed the reins to another round-eye, who led the animal to the rear. The armored round-eye was handed a pole, and another man afoot joined him in front of the array. This was a lean man in a long black robe; through my telescope I saw that he was clean-shaven.

The armored man drove the butt of his pole into the soil. From the upper end of this pole hung a flag; but since the day was still, there was no wind to flutter this banner. All I could see was that it bore a pattern of red and yellow.

The armored man then shouted in his native gibberish. Through my telescope I saw that he was of medium size, with a sun-browned skin, sharp, beak-nosed features, and a full black beard. This, I perceived, must be one of those round-eyed barbarians inhabiting the Far Western Peninsula, called Yuropa by its natives, of which Admiral Xing informed us on his return from those lands in the reign of Hung Wu. The other round-eyes crowded up behind him.

When the armored man finished his proclamation, the other round-eye, the black-robed one, raised his hands and uttered another unintelligible speech. I called to the scout Falaya nearby:

"O scout, you know the Ochuse tongue. Find out what this be all about!"

Falaya stood up and shouted in the tongue of the coastal redskins. Presently one of the Ochuse conferred with the armored man and shouted back. This translating back and forth, as you can imagine, proved a lengthy, tedious business. Mankind were better off if all men spake the tongue of Zhongguo, which is after all the speech of civilization. At length Falaya turned to me, saying in broken Zhongguo:

"O General, he say man in armor say he claim all this land in name of his king, Felipe of Espanya."

Somewhat astonished, I told Falaya: "Ask this bold fellow, who claims lands belonging to the Son of Heaven, who he be?"

After the usual pause for translation from Zhongguo to Ochuse and from Ochuse to the armored man's Yuropian dialect, the reply came back:

"He say he Captain Tristan de Luna y Arellano, and who be we?"

This person gave Falaya the needed information, adding: "And by whose leave, barbarian, do you trespass on the lands of the Son of Heaven and, moreover, claim parts of it in the name of some tribal chieftain in the Far Western Peninsula?"

I know not how literally my words were translated, but they seemed to arouse the armored round-eye to a frenzy. He began to shout a reply; but the black-robed one laid a hand on his arm. I could not hear what they said at that distance—not that I could have understood their blather anyway. But black-robe seemed to be urging negotiation.

At last the armored round-eye fell silent and signaled black-robe to speak. The result, translated sentence by sentence, was a lengthy homily. It reminded me of the endless sermons of that loquacious bonze, Brother Xiao-jin, whom we sent home last year. He could put a hungry tiger to sleep with his endless disquisitions on the wisdom of the compassionate Buddha.

This fellow, the black-robed one, advanced an astonishing claim: that his master, a Yuropian high priest called a *papa*, had divided the world between two Yuropian rulers, the kings of Espanya and Portugar; and this part had gone to the King of Espanya. There was more, about how the Yuropian god had commanded all men to love one another; and if we would but accept his theological doctrines, we were all assured of endless bliss in his Yuropian Heaven. If we refused to swallow these myths, we should all be slain by the Yuropians' weapons and then suffer eternal torment in the Yuropian Hell, a fearsome afterworld reminding me of the more eccentric afterlife concepts of the Tibetan Buddhists.

Although this person knows better than to laugh under such serious circumstances, I could not suppress a burst of mirth. I sent back the message that his *papa* seemed very free in giving away other peoples' countries and that in any case all men came naturally under the dominion of the Son of Heaven.

As for his theology, I was satisfied that I must have done something right in a previous incarnation to have earned my present rank as a reward. I would try by correct action and keeping my *karma* clean at least to maintain this status, compared to which round-eyed barbarians were less than worms beneath my feet. They must have committed grave offenses in previous lives to have been born into such a lowly estate.

At this the armored man altogether lost control of himself and screamed orders. His redskins spread out to the flanks, nocking their arrows, whilst a couple of hundred other round-eyes formed a double line facing us and readying their primitive firearms. These operated by means of lengths of cord, treated to burn slowly; I have seen specimens of similar weapons in the Imperial War Museum.

One round-eye passed down the line with a bucket of glowing coals, wherein each of the invaders dipped the end of his cord until it was alight. Then he clamped it to the mechanism of his gun. Meanwhile those armed with crossbows cocked them. The leader shouted some more, and my scout reported:

"He say we surrender or die, sir!"

I replied with a vulgarism expressing my disdain for such primitive insolence. The armored man shouted again, whereupon the other round-eyes discharged their weapons. After the first rank had fired and begun the lengthy business of reloading, the second rank stepped forth between them and fired in their turn. On their flanks, the redskins shot arrows.

The guns made loud reports and tremendous puffs of smoke, whilst their musket balls and crossbow bolts whistled past us. Since my people were well under cover, and those of the second rank had fired blindly because of the curtain of smoke before them, we sustained no casualties save a few flesh wounds among my Hitchiti from the arrows.

When the pall of smoke had somewhat dissipated, I said: "Fire!"

Our rifles opened up, and a number of trespassers, both round-eyed and red-skinned, fell.

"Reload!" I said, and then: "Fire!"

The round-eyes were still struggling to reload, which with firearms of that archaic type is a protracted process. As I later learned, such a gunner does well to get off twenty shots in one *ko*, whereas a well-trained soldier can fire one of our breech-loaders a hundred times in that interval, if he run not out of cartridges.

At our third volley, the intruders' redskins fled. Half the round-eyes were down; but the leader was still erect, shouting commands and defiance. I told the captain of my force:

"Choose a sharpshooter and order him to wound that armored man in the leg. I wish him alive, and also a redskin who can speak his language."

So it was done. At the fall of the leader, the other round-eyes joined the redskins in flight: first a few here and there, then all of them. Some dropped their guns to run faster. Behind them the redskin porters also dropped their loads and fled, while the horsemen cantered off with their armor jingling. I did not command a pursuit, knowing that in these forests of immense trees the pursued can easily slip away and the pursuer as easily get lost. My Hitchiti broke from cover and raced away to collect the scalps of the fallen foes.

Later, when I had donned my official robe instead of my filthy uniform, and my peacock-feather hat in place of the steel cap, I commanded that the wounded Yuropian leader be brought to my tent, along with his redskin interpreter and our own Ochuse-speaking scout. I also sent men to retrieve the baggage dropped by the fleeing porters.

This Tristan de Luna appeared at the entrance to my tent with a pair of my redskins gripping his arms. His armor had been shed, and his garb was ordinary Yuropian, with the puffed trunks and below them the skintight trousers of their kind. He sweated heavily in the heat, limped on his bandaged leg, and supported himself by a tree branch he had somehow obtained, whittled down to a walking stick.

Now that I had a closer look at the man, I saw that he was older than I had thought. His curly black hair and beard were, like mine, beginning to show gray. But his stance was still erect and his movements youthfully springy, save for his wounded leg.

As he neared, I became aware that the man had not bathed lately, if

ever. Not to put too fine a point on it, he stank. I then attributed this to
the exigencies of travel, but my redskin spies inform me that this is
usual with Yuropians. Not only have they a naturally stronger bodily
odor than normal folk; but also the Yuropian religion discourages cleanliness. Most adhere to Christianity, whereas the other major western
creeds, Islam and Judaism, value bathing and cleanliness. Christians
suspected of going over to either of these other faiths are burned alive,
as the more warlike redskin tribes do to captive foes. Therefore among
Christians cleanliness arouses suspicion of conversion to one of those
other cults, which are completely outlawed in Espanya.

At the entrance Captain Tristan wrenched loose an arm, placed his
hand over his heart, and made a low bow. This gesture, evidently meant
as a polite greeting, overbalanced him in his crippled state. He staggered
and would have fallen had not the two redskins caught him. He did not
go to his knees and touch his forehead to the carpet, but one must make
allowances for barbarians who have never been taught civilized manners;
the full *ko-tou* would have been difficult for him in any way.

At least this barbarian had evidently decided on a more urbane
approach. His translated words were:

"Sir, now that I perceive you more closely, it appears that you come
from the Great Khan of Cathay. Be this true?"

Yuropians had evidently not kept up with events in the Middle
Kingdom. I told Tristan: "Two centuries past, your impression might
have been apt. But we sons of Han expelled the Khans long ago and
restored the Celestial Empire to the proper Sons of Heaven, now
reigning as the glorious Ming. The Khans were but barbarian usurpers
from the Gobi. Whence came you?"

He said: "From the land that the deceased Captain Ponce discovered
and named *la Florida*. He thought it an island, but unbroken land
appears to extend far to the north thereof, and also to the west to
Mexico." After a pause he continued:

"Then be we in truth in the Indes? When that Italian Colón returned
from his voyages, half a century ago, he insisted that he had reached
them, or at least come to a chain of islands to the east of them, whence
another day's sail would have brought him to the Spice Islands.

"But a ship of that fellow Magallanes returned to Espanya thirty-odd
years ago. The captain thereof, Delcano, asserted that far to the west of
these lands lies an ocean so vast as to require three or four months to sail
across, and that the lands of the Great Khan lie beyond it. But this
Delcano was a Basque and therefore not to be implicitly trusted. If this
be the true Indes, that were greatly to the advantage of my sovran."

I told him: "Your Captain Delcano is quite correct. In any case, the

Eastern Continent whereon we now stand is wide enough to take a well-mounted man, with remounts, as long to ride across as your Magallanes found the Eastern Ocean. It has nought to do with the land of India, which is even farther than the Celestial Empire. And now, what is all this nonsense about claiming this land for some Yuropian chieftain?"

The man muttered: "So huge a world!" Then followed another harangue, essentially repeating what the black-robed man had said before the shooting began.

"I could better explain it," said Tristan, "if your men had not slain our holy father. I myself have small knowledge of letters and history. But what have you done with my woman?"

"Woman? We have no captive women. There were a couple of female bodies in the woods behind your battle line. I suppose they were struck by our fire before all your redskins fled. What woman claim you to have had?"

"The daughter of a chief of the Nanipacana," said he. "We fell in love and eloped."

To straighten this out took further questions, since there be nought in Zhongguo exactly corresponding to these concepts, save perhaps in Li Po's poetry. But, like Captain Tristan, I am no literary man, familiar with such things. Besides, the mating habits of barbarians afford endless amusement.

Tristan said that he and the woman had not only fled secretly, defying the wrath of the woman's father, but had also caused the black-robed one to conduct a rite over their union, according to his customs rendering it permanent and unbreakable. I later learned that Tristan already had a wife somewhere, notwithstanding that Yuropians are supposed to be monogamous. But that is no affair of ours.

"Sir," said Tristan, "could you let me have something to eat? We are all half-starved, for the Indians" (as the Espanyans ridiculously call the redskins, although these live halfway round the world from the true Indians) "along the route had fled, taking all their food supplies with them before we arrived. Those *cabrones*—"

Falaya could not translate that word, but questioning revealed that it meant a eunuch. Notwithstanding the high rank of the eunuchs of the Imperial Court, the term is a deadly insult among round-eyes.

Whilst this person was getting Captain Tristan's meaning straightened out, a Hitchiti of my personal guard thrust his head into the tent. "O General!" he cried. "Our scouts report a large force of Nanipacana approaching, in full war paint."

"Kwanyin save us!" I exclaimed, rising. "Sound the alarms!"

* * *

This time things went more smoothly despite the war paint. The new
force was led by Chief Imathla, with whom I had had dealings and so
knew personally. I had been trying to persuade him voluntarily to place
himself under the protection of the Son of Heaven, to save us the
necessity of conquering him. So, when Imathla thrust his spear into the
ground and laid his skull-cracker beside it, I signaled him to advance.

When he and I returned to my headquarters tent, the round-eye
Tristan still stood there, leaning on his walking stick and with his free
hand hungrily gnawing an ear of maize. At the sight of him, Chief
Imathla burst into a tirade. Had he had his weapons to hand, I would
not have wagered a brass cash on Tristan's life. The round-eye shouted
back. When the polemics ran down, I said to Falaya:

"Ask whether this speech refers to the chief's daughter."

At length Falaya reported: "He say aye, it does. This round-eye carry
off his daughter, delight of his age, and chief set out in pursuit. When
his war party near this place, they come upon daughter Mihilayo
wandering, lost, in forest, with some Piachi whom Espanyans enslave
and now flee back home. From her chief learn that round-eye and his
men fight great general and lose. He say he happy to see scoundrel
captive, and he know some excellent tortures to dispose of him."

Tristan, to whom his own interpreter had been feeding a translation,
visibly paled beneath his swarthy skin at the mention of torture. Then
he squared his shoulders, raised his chin, and assumed an attitude of
defiance, as captive redskin warriors are wont to do at the prospect of
being burned alive by their foes. I could not help a twinge of admiration
for his courage, barbarian though he was. He asked:

"Where be she now?"

Imathla replied: "Know that she is safe under her father's protection.
Where that be is no affair of yours."

"She is my lawful wedded wife! That is whose affair it be! Fetch her
here!"

I suggested: "That might be a sensible thought, O Chief, to unravel
this knot."

"Never!" said Imathla. "You know not, O General, the depths of evil
of these palefaces. Before they passed through our tribal lands, they had
descended upon the Piachi tribe, whom they enslaved to furnish porters
for their supplies. When some Piachi defied the palefaces' commands,
the invaders seized them, chopped off their hands and feet, and cast
them out to die. Others they strung up by the hands and affixed weights
to their feet until they expired, or forced water down their throats until
they burst inside."

"Why should they go to so much trouble? If one wishes to kill a man, it is quicker and easier to shoot him or chop off his head."

"They have a passion for that pretty yellow metal that we get in ornaments by trade from other tribes. They would not believe that there were no hidden stores of this metal, and they thought that by such treatment they could force the Piachi to reveal its whereabouts. Of course the Piachi are not Nanipacana and so not real human beings, or we should have felt obliged to avenge them.

"Twenty years ago the accursed Ernando de Soto came through, treating those who gainsaid him in this same ferocious manner. He also brought strange diseases amongst the tribes, whereof over half of us perished. Had our towns been still fully populated, O General, you would not have found it so easy to pass amongst us unscathed."

The round-eye was hopping up and down on his unwounded leg, indicating an eagerness to say his say. I told Falaya to give Tristan my permission. The barbarian shouted:

"These savages are too stupid and ignorant to appreciate the benefits we offer! They refuse to understand that by accepting our religion they may live to serve us, as is only right for such lowly folk, in return for the boons we bestow. Then, after death, they shall enjoy an eternity of pleasures in Heaven, praising the true God."

"Is that all you do in this Heaven?" I asked.

"What more is needed? We sit on clouds, play the *arpa*, and sing the praises of God."

"Forever?"

"Aye, forever."

This person commented: "Your Yuropian God must get bored with incessant flattery. Our gods are more rational; they are busy keeping records and otherwise carrying out their duties in the Heavenly bureaucracy."

When this had been translated, Tristan gave a contemptuous snort. But he forbore to argue theology, for which I doubt whether either of us had enough book knowledge. I regretted that the bonze Xiao-jin was no longer with us, having set out to return to his monastery in civilization. He would have argued spiritual matters with the barbarian all day and all the following night. Tristan said:

"I still demand my wife! I rescued her when two of my colonists would have raped her and then slain her for her golden earrings."

"All the demands in the world will not get the poor thing," said Chief Imathla. "She is well quit of you."

"Then fetch her here and let her choose her own fate!" cried Tristan.

"Ridiculous!" cried Imathla. Those twain began shouting again, until I roared them to silence. I said: "Come, honorable Chief, tell me: Is the woman where we can reach her?"

"She is under the protection of my personal guard," growled Imathla.

"Well, am I to understand that you wish her to be happy?"

"Aye, O General. That is my dearest wish, since her mother died of one of those diseases these accursed palefaces brought into our land."

"Then why not fetch her here, set the alternatives before her, and let her decide? If after that she be not happy, the fault will not be yours."

Imathla growled a bit, but after further argument I talked him round. The fact that he was alone in my tent, with rifle-bearing Hitchiti standing by, may have influenced his decision.

So Imathla put his head out the tent and called to one of his warriors. After some converse in Nanipacana, the warrior set off at a run. Whilst we waited, I caused tea to be brewed and offered to our guests. Imathla drank his, while Tristan took a mouthful, made a face, and returned the cup to the Hitchiti who had brought it.

At length the warrior returned, leading a young Nanipacana female. When she entered the tent, Tristan limped forward and seized her in an embrace. He performed that gesture of affection used by Yuropians and Arabs, of pressing the lips against the esteemed one.

Then Tristan placed his hands on the woman's shoulders and held her at arm's length. He said something sharply to her; she replied, and they argued. It sounded as if he were making some demand and she refusing. I asked Falaya for a translation.

"O General," he said, "he say she must cover self; she say no cover, too hot."

Mihilayo was clad in the normal garb of these southern redskins in hot weather, namely: naked save for a pair of golden earrings and reticular designs painted on her body and limbs. Yuropians, coming I suspect from a cooler climate, regard such exposure as improper.

A heated argument followed amongst the three: the woman Mihilayo, the round-eye Captain Tristan, and the Chieftain Imathla. Mihilayo and Imathla spake in Nanipacana, whilst Mihilayo and Tristan conversed in the tongue of Espanya, which she spake albeit somewhat brokenly. Tristan and Imathla, having no tongue in common, had to communicate through the interpreters.

At last Imathla said to me: "My daughter wishes to know if you, O General, need a wife."

The question so surprised me that for a few heartbeats I was unable to reply. At last I said:

"I have my Number One wife back at Fort Tai-ze. But she has long nagged me to take a second wife, to relieve her of some of the burdens of domesticity. Besides, she says that she is too old to enjoy the act of love any more, whereas I am still fully able. Suppose I did take Mihilayo as proposed; how would that sit with you?"

Imathla grinned. "I should deem it a splendid idea, giving me access to the General's ear, and high standing amongst the tribes."

"Does your daughter truly wish this?"

"She assures me that indeed she does."

"How about that previous indissoluble marriage to Captain Tristan?"

"Oh, she says that is easy. His Yuropian mumbo-jumbo means nought to her. If there be any doubt on that score, the answer is simple. Slay him and make her a widow, free to wed whom she likes under any nation's customs."

According to what I hear, she was not quite correct, since it is said that in India they burn widows alive. A wasteful custom, I should say. But I saw no point in correcting the woman.

When Tristan's interpreter had given him the gist of this dialogue, the round-eye uttered a scream of rage. Wrenching loose from his guards— for he was a powerful man—he limped forward, gripping his walking stick in both hands and raising it over his head. I know not whom he meant to bludgeon first: Mihilayo, Imathla, or me. Before he got within hitting distance, however, one of my guards fired his rifle at close range. With a howl of frustrated fury, Tristan fell back on my Tang-dynasty rug, writhed a little, and fell still. He was dead from a bullet that entered his ribs below the heart, came out his back, and punched a hole in the canvas behind him.

I questioned Imathla about Nanipacana marriage customs. He told me that when a man and a woman moved into the same hut, that was deemed a marriage. There were none of the processions, music, gifts, fireworks, and so forth that solemnize a wedding in civilization. Imathla said in Nanipacana that he gave Mihilayo to me, and that was that.

Later I asked my new bride why she had chosen me in lieu of her round-eye lover. That, she said, was simple. When she saw the power that Captain Tristan commanded by his thunder sticks and his armor and weapons of this Yuropian metal, she decided that he would make a suitable spouse and protector of her and their children. When she observed that I commanded even greater power, by my superior thunder sticks and my well-trained army, she decided that I should be an even more effective protector. Besides, the union would confer honor on her family, clan, and tribe. She added that Tristan stank; although redskins, as a result of smearing their bodies with animal fats to protect themselves against insect bites, are also fairly rank.

Such a foresightedly practical outlook makes me hopeful of eventually raising the redskins to our level of civilization. About the emotional Yuropians I am more doubtful.

Now I am back in Fort Tai-ze with two wives. My Number One carped about my taking a Number Two whom she had never seen, let alone chosen for me; but that died down. A more vexing problem is acting as judge when the two women daily disagree over some detail of household management. Although Mihilayo is fast becoming fluent in the language of civilization, I fear she does not fully accept her position as subordinate to the Number One. She also tries to elicit from me more frequent lovemaking than is easy for a man of middle age.

On the other hand, ere we parted, Chief Imathla declared his allegiance to the Son of Heaven and placed the Nanipacana beneath our benevolent protection.

With this letter I shall send samples of the guns and armor of the round-eyes, to see whether they have features that might usefully be copied and improved upon by our makers of armaments. I doubt that this be the case; for in these techniques the men of Espanya seem to be about where we of Zhongguo were a century and a half ago.

I regret the death of Captain Tristan de Luna, fool though he was. Had he lived, I should have brought him back to Tai-ze. I should have questioned him about conditions in Yuropa and amongst the men of Espanya who have landed along the coasts of the Eastern Continent and begun to subdue and enslave the redskins. If he proved reticent, I have ample means to loosen his tongue.

But how typically barbarian to make such an unseemly fracas over so trivial a matter as affection for a woman! As I said at the start, their customs are strange, their beliefs outlandish, and their emotions childish. Let us thank the divine bureaucrats that we, at least, are truly civilized!

DESTINATION: INDIES

Brad Linaweaver

WHAT HAS GONE BEFORE: *In the previous installments Captain Christopher Columbus (a.k.a. Cristoforo Colombo) studied quantum theology, advanced geographical theory, and the art of how to make friends and influence potentates. At the court of Ferdinand and Isabella he faced much treachery and intrigue. The Dark Duke tried to frame our stalwart hero as an agent of the Turks, sent to divert precious resources from military necessities into mad voyages. But Columbus saved the day by proving that the Dark Duke had financial interests in the Canary Islands that would be put in jeopardy should a westward route to the Indies be discovered. In his rage the Dark Duke kidnapped our hero's lovely girlfriend at court, but Columbus was able to rescue her with the aid of Poncho, his trusty sidekick, and a highly complicated bit of trickery involving five different kinds of cheeses and a ship's compass.*

Granted one last opportunity to make his case at court, Columbus eschewed his scientific and economic arguments for global access and the tendency of gold and spices to accumulate when traveling westerly along a particular latitude. This time he directed his appeal to the queen's heart, pointing out that the future promised greater things than temporary victories over the Moors, the burning of random heretics, and the expulsion or conversion of Jews. With a new route to Asia and storehouses bulging with gold, Spain could reclaim holy Jerusalem with a surprise attack from the east!

A final masterstroke was the manner in which Columbus forever destroyed the Dark Duke's credibility by suggesting the man might be a secret agent working for the French, the English, the Portuguese, the Moors, the Knights of Malta (but at least not the Knights of Columbus) . . . and that maybe the man was a practicing Satanist as well. The queen was so thrilled with this presentation that she offered to hock the royal jewels to help finance Columbus's mission, but he cannily suggested that liquidating the Dark Duke's holdings would produce a sufficiency of funds.

Meanwhile the Dark Duke had finished reporting to the French, the English, the Portuguese, the Moors, the Knights of Malta . . . and had used microdemonic engineering to create his own ship for the exploration of Water Space. Realizing that he must keep out of sight during the voyage, he decided to make his craft fully submersible so that he can follow his enemies without being sighted . . . until the time is right for him to strike!

The Santa María, Pinta, and Niña are launched from Palos on August 3, 1492. Admiral Columbus is aboard the Santa María. Identical twins, Martín Alonso Pinzón and Vincente Yáñez Pinzón, command the Pinta and Niña respectively. There is only one mishap on the voyage to the Canary Islands, the last outlying post of Spanish territory. A saboteur is found trying to damage the Pinta's rudder. Short work is made of him. Then it's on to the islands and last preparations before the dangerous part.

After a torrid affair with the island's female governor, the lovely Donna Beatrice (who bears a startling resemblance to the girlfriend he left behind in Spain), Columbus is ready for anything. Three ships and ninety men challenge the deepest, darkest depths of the Unknown.

Meanwhile the Dark Duke and his handpicked crew of cannibals, child molesters, and heretics rescued from the Inquisition follows in the wake of his enemies. We resume our tale with the log being kept by Poncho, the loyal sidekick.

Chapter CVII

"It is late in the day, and gray clouds sail across the sky, moving low, hazarding the reef that is the sturdy mast of our ship. After a sea of faces at court, bobbing up and down on the tidal movements of fear and greed, how our brave leader must prefer the real elements of sea and sky."

The admiral leaned over my shoulder and told me that the previous paragraph is all right, but not nearly purple enough. I imagined that he wanted me to more fully describe the multicolored hues that swirled about the prow of our good craft as we surged ever onward into the receptive waves that mark the shimmering surface of Water Space.

Ever since I graduated from Saint Pedro's Academy for Loyal Side-kicks, I've been driven to prove myself. That the admiral would choose me for such an important mission left me speechless... almost. I knew that he kept his own log; but his suggestion that someone else should keep a log so that there would be a more objective record of our adventures thrilled me more than words can say. Why, I worship the very planks that man trods upon and I wasn't about to let him down. If it's objectivity he wants, it's objectivity he'll get, by all the saints.

As Columbus faced the horizon, his jaw jutting ever westward, I knew that it would be no great matter to lay my life down for this man. But no sooner had these thoughts crossed my mind than we faced a great danger! I cursed myself if idle thoughts of my own destruction should bring harm down on the heads of my betters.

"Sea monster off the port bow," cried a salty seaman from Madrid. We all dropped what we were doing—even my quill pen fluttered down, where it tasted rough-hewn boards—and we gazed in astonishment at what was rising from the vasty depths. It was amazing. It was astounding. It was really big.

I had seen whales before, but at a distance where it was very difficult to estimate their true size. Once a dead whale washed ashore at my humble village. It had been as big as a felled tree, and the teeth were fearsome to behold. But that poor creature was as a minnow compared with the dimensions of this behemoth. I heard the ship's alchemist whisper one word, "Leviathan," and he spoke truly.

The wind was blowing at about ten knots. The rhythm of the sea was steady, the water lapping at our ships, all three of them bobbing like corks. The way our ships were laid out formed a kind of triangle, and the monster was rising in the dead center between us. Sea foam churned around its sleek, blue hide, while the water around it was a viridian shade of blue. It was as if the ocean had chosen this moment to manifest itself in a living form larger than all three of our ships put together. I shuddered to think what kind of teeth it might have, but it had a peculiar-looking mouth and it was not clear that it had teeth at all.

"It doesn't seem aggressive," said Columbus. "That is well, for I doubt that any of our weapons would hinder the monster."

There was a muttering of agreement, a medley of "ayes" and "ahrrrrs," but one old sailor lost his nerve. "It's a sign," he cried. "This mission's cursed. If yon monster doesn't make a dinner of us all, then we'll surely be pulled in the direction of the magnetic mountain that will draw all the nails from our craft, and we will fall into the sea of darkness before being swept off the edge of the earth."

The admiral looked at the poor, raving dolt with more sympathy than the man deserved. Then he summoned the ship's morale officer, who gently took the man by the shoulder, turned him around, and drove him through with two feet of fine steel. There were more "ayes" and "ahrrrrs" at this demonstration of permissive therapy.

"The monster doesn't seem to notice us," said Diago, the admiral's good right hand.

"Pray God it remains so," was the answer.

Suddenly there was another cry of "Monster off the starboard bow."

"Shiver me timbers," said the dying man through foaming lips. Sure enough the water was becoming agitated off to starboard. We turned and watched the surfacing of what appeared to be a considerably smaller whale, but a particularly mean-looking specimen, all black with oddly shaped fins sticking out all over its surface. The smaller whale headed straight for the leviathan.

"It's trying to drive off the larger beast," said the luckless man whose turn it was today to prepare our rancid meals.

"I don't think so," answered the admiral, his brow furrowed in thought. "The big one is placid. Now with this sudden attack . . . "

The small, black beast was headed straight for the flanks of the big one. We expected the leviathan to heave to, or dive, or do something. But it just waited, oblivious of the insect making a run for its side. And then the little one struck. There was no roar as we expected, just a soft thud. The smaller whale bounced off and then the larger one submerged. Unfortunately it began moving in our direction as it went beneath the waves.

"Make yourselves secure," shouted the admiral, grabbing ahold of my throat as the nearest object by which he could steady himself. We counted ourselves fortunate that the monster did not actually strike us, but the wake of its passing had our ship tossing and turning in the most frightful manner. Ironically several boxes of some mysterious objects called phyrecrackers (provided by the ship's alchemist) were set off, sending out their bright sparkles as we half fell and stumbled to one side of the ship, and then the other side, back and forth, monotonously back and forth, until I, for one, was sick to my stomach. I say it was ironic that a product of far-off Cathay should add to our distress as this was yet another market to be opened to us should our voyage prove a success.

"Well, that was close," said the admiral, releasing me as I slumped to the deck, my chest heaving as air rushed back into my tortured lungs; and then I threw up to make the perfect end to a perfect day.

"Aye," said his second, third, and fourth in command.

"Ahrrrr," said the sailors.

"Was a mighty fish indeed," agreed Snooty, the ship's expert on flotsam and jetsam.

"Perhaps you men noticed that the black beast was no sea creature at all," announced Columbus.

"Whatever was it, then?" I heard myself croak through a badly damaged windpipe.

"What sea beast carries on its flank the crest of the Dark Duke?" asked Columbus.

"You mean . . . " asked the sailor we were certain had been slain but, despite a tremendous loss of blood, sounded better than I did.

"Yes, you pathetic sea biscuit. We are being followed by the Dark Duke."

"How did he get himself inside a big fish like that?" asked the temporary chef, no doubt through professional interest.

"He must have constructed the thing as we build our ships to sail the surface. But being the work of the devil, his craft sails below."

More "ayes" and "ahrrrs" at this last revelation. Sailors always respect sound reasonings. When we had established that there were no casualties, and signaled the good news to the other ships, it was definitely time to break out a great flagon of grog for the men (or was it simply rum?). I was among the privileged few invited to sample wine from the admiral's table. At any moment rowboats would come alongside bearing the captains from the other two ships for a general rehashing of the events just passed; and they would be thirsty too. Normally we passed messages back and forth by bringing the ships close together (as we did every evening so that we wouldn't lose one another) and sending a little bag across by means of a rope. But something as dramatic as what had just occurred demanded more personal contact. Or, to put it more objectively, the admiral would be in a lecturing mood.

I was already on my second glass of the best Thunderous Vino (from a bottle put aside expressly for my use) when captains Pinzón and Pinzón arrived. They were not happy about this latest encounter. And there were other problems as well. The admiral sensed that the time had come to be frank with us.

"I'll tell you whatever you want to know," he said.

"When we venture into waters swarming with monsters, perhaps we should consider turning back," said one Pinzón.

"And I'm concerned that something is amiss with your figures, Admiral," added another. "I'm certain that we have traveled more leagues than you indicate in your log."

"Gentlemen," he said, in the sternest possible tones, "I thought we would sight land within three weeks. We've now been at sea for three and one-half weeks. And I admit that I have been underreporting the distance traveled. We've traveled sixteen hundred miles." Everyone in the room gasped, except for those who, far gone in wine, belched instead. I, too, was shocked that he had not given the distance in leagues.

"But why?" asked the Pinzóns as one.

"Because the world is a big place, and the ocean is big. When the priest gave us his blessing in Latin the day we sailed, I wished for ten times that blessing, for fear the world would be ten times greater in size than we imagine. All educated men know that we live on some kind of sphere, although I believe it is more pear-shaped than ball-shaped. The direction in which we travel must inevitably lead us to the Indies. But what lies between us and that final destination is a mystery. That our direction is correct I know to be absolutely true. It is at the very heart of my Theory. But the distances involved are another matter."

"But, Admiral," Diago piped in, "you have some idea of the distance. You said as much at court."

Admiral Christopher Columbus, the greatest navigator the world has ever known, smiled and spread his hands. "Look, guys, it took me years to get the approval and appropriations for this mission. And I'm not interested in some onetime stunt where we plant the flag of Spain on some rock in the middle of nowhere, find a plant or something to take home, and that's it. The race is on between the European powers, and we'd better win it because there is no defense against a nation that rules the waves."

When he got worked up like this, it was best to let him get around to the point without further prompting. We sat and waited. The gentle rocking of the ship and the good cheer provided by the wine had everyone in a receptive mood. It felt as if it was going to be downhill all the way from this point on. The admiral would tell us what we needed to know.

"This mission was sold on three things: mathematics, maps, and money. We sail on three hopes: God, gold, and..." He paused, but I had faith he would maintain his alliteration, "...guts. When I told the queen that it would be seven hundred and fifty leagues to India, it was a guess and nothing more."

"But the biblical basis!" said the ship's alchemist, demonstrating a knack for alliteration himself.

"That foundation remains sound," said the admiral. "When it is said that waters are gathered into the seven parts of the world, and there are six parts of land to one of water, the only conclusion we can draw is that there must be much more land yet to be discovered. But the Scriptures give us no idea of what the total volume might be! The point I'm trying to make is that I fully expect to find many strange new lands between us and our ultimate destination. I mentioned this in passing to the queen, but what is unknown is harder to sell than what is known. So I stressed the Indies in my presentation, and what we can ultimately achieve by finding a new route to the East." His eyes twinkled, and he smiled, showing off the whitest teeth I'd ever seen. And to think the Dark Duke had called him that little upstart from Genoa.

"I am concerned," he concluded, "that we have not encountered islands by now. But despite recent sightings of birds flying southwest, I am determined to remain on our current course due west."

"The ships cannot stand the strain," said Snooty, but no one paid him any heed.

Diago was more concerned about the men: "We may have more adventure than we want if provisions don't hold out. There are mutterings among the sailors already."

"What's a sea voyage without loose talk?" asked Columbus, laughing. "There's a long way between that and mutiny. I'm sure we'll find land very soon. Meanwhile let's keep our eyes on all the marlin pikes and meat hooks. And there are a few convicts who came along because of the queen's promise of a pardon. Let's watch them a bit more closely."

Diago nodded and said, "You've handled the sailors well so far. That business about the compass still being reliable when the position of the North Star shifted . . . I thought some of the men would go mad."

"Superstitious sailors," Columbus agreed. "That's when they first thought we'd left the natural waters God intends for us to sail and entered forbidden realms of Water Space." He laughed again, and the rest of us joined in, although I detected a certain nervousness on the part of some.

"The change is a sign of divine approval," said the ship's alchemist. "Before, the needle declined to the east; now it declines to the west. It is well."

Everyone toasted the mission. It was a good time to call the meeting to an end, which the admiral did. Except. . . .

"Wait," I said before the company broke up. "What about the Dark Duke?"

There was a sudden silence in the admiral's cabin, broken only by the creaking sounds of the ship, the lapping of the water, and a squeaking made by the lantern that swung above the table on which were scattered all the charts and a state-of-the-art quadrant. All eyes were turned on me, and they did not have a pleasing aspect.

"I didn't want that subject brought up, Poncho." I had forgotten that the Pinzón brothers had not been aboard when he made the observation about the black whale having his enemy's crest. I had forgotten, also, that the Pinzóns became terribly upset at the mere mention of their fiendish fellow countryman.

"We are doomed," suggested one.

"We'll never be famous now," added the other.

For the first time I could see that my hero was really angry with me. What tipped me off was the admiral's suggestion: "I think Poncho here needs to be taught a lesson."

I had a pretty good idea what that would mean. "I'm sorry, Admiral. Have mercy!" He paid no heed, but sent word that the sailors should gather to witness my punishment. In retrospect I realize that he made the right decision. What else could he do after I let him down? Of course I never liked it when he had me keelhauled. It made it difficult to write afterward. But if he let me get away with a serious mistake, that would set a bad example for the men.

So they tied me up and cast me in the salty brine. The underside of the *Santa María* was every bit as rough as I had remembered from the last time, and soon the water was full of my blood and everything went black.

When I came to, it was morning; but whether it was the next day or many days later I could not tell. The ship's boy was singing the traditional welcome to the dawn: "Blessed be the day, and He who sends the night away." For a moment I thought the song referred to our great leader until I remembered He whom even Columbus must honor.

Our Creator must have been in an interesting mood when he allowed to come into the world the myriad wonders that even now assaulted my senses (damaged though they were by stern correction). In the golden light of dawn I beheld a Brave New World that seemed to dwarf even the accomplishments of Spain.

"Astounding," said the man to my left.

"Amazing," said the man to my right.

"If. . ." I began but was interrupted by a strange constriction in my throat that I attributed to the keelhauling. Fortunately my vision was unimpaired, and I had an unobstructed view of the Miracle.

It was as if someone had taken a heavenly city from its place in the firmament and placed it in the middle of our earthly sea. We had laid to in the harbor of this golden metropolis. And golden was the right word! As the rosy fingers of the dawn touched each building, we could espy the glint of burnished gold. The edifices were huge pyramid shapes, except that they were flat on the top. Strange flying things traveled back and forth between these pyramids, and they, too, seemed made of gold!

"Are we off the coast of Asia?" I asked. "Perhaps we will meet the Great Khan."

"I don't think so," said the ship's alchemist. "Through a close study of ancient writings, and one in particular by a scribe named Plato, I conclude that we have found the lost continent of Atlantis."

A new word came to me, although I could not credit the source. "Goshwow! As soon as my hands heal, I will record all this. But look, even now here come some people to welcome us. I will call them Atlanteans."

Suddenly the strong arm of my commander was on my shoulder. As I gazed into his steel-gray eyes, I realized that he had forgiven me, thank the Virgin. "Good Poncho," he said, "I suggest we call them Indians, because that would show due respect to the Theory, without which you'd still be eating pig dung back in that hovel you call a home." Even as he spoke, his strong fingers dug into my lacerated shoulder.

"Oh yes," I gagged the words, "*Indians* is what they are!"

A sleek, metal craft pulled up alongside our ship. A remarkable personage stood at the prow of this boat wearing feathers, gold, some shiny white material, and having a dark-brown complexion that almost made him appear to be made out of wood. "Permission to come aboard," he said in a voice as cultivated as a member of the Castilian aristocracy.

As the man clambered over the wooden railing of the *Santa María*, Columbus asked him, "How is it that you speak our language?"

"From monitoring your church services," he answered. "We speak all the tongues of Europe." A few "ayes" and "ahrrrrs" could be heard in the background. "Well, almost all . . ." concluded this ambassador from a strange new world.

More metal craft were coming alongside to take our party ashore. We were astounded that these boats were not too heavy to float. I was selected to go with the admiral and was glad that I would not be needed to row. I was in considerable pain. These boats didn't seem to require rowing, but were propelled by some magical force that had our ship's alchemist so excited that he almost drooled.

I learned that quite a lot had happened while I was unconscious. The *Pinta* and *Niña* had been sunk by the black beast. "It almost got us, too," said one of the men, "but the admiral tricked it with an amazing subterfuge involving five cheeses and the ship's compass."

"By San Fernando," I exclaimed. I hadn't realized that we had any cheese aboard. The stench must have been terrible by this time, but I'd been spared any unpleasantness, having lost my nose during one of the keelhaulings.

A regal figure was waiting for us ashore. His attire was so bright that it hurt to look upon him. He wore a symbol of the sun on his massive chest. "The time of reckoning is at hand, Admiral," he said.

Columbus showed no fear. "You have the advantage, sir. You know more of me than I do of you."

"I've had a good tutor!" said our host. "I know of your previous voyages. I know how they turned you down in Portugal and how it took eight years to persuade the Spanish crown to finance this trip of yours."

"He just wouldn't give up," came a terribly familiar voice. We all turned around to behold none other than the Dark Duke!

"Saints preserve us," said a little redheaded sailor.

The duke was in a bragging mood: "After sinking your other ships, I got here ahead of you in plenty of time to warn these people about your mad dreams of conquest."

"A thought that never crosses *your* mind," said Columbus, his voice dripping with sarcasm.

The regal figure held up his hand, and all were silent. "Your petty squabbles are no concern of ours," said the Atlant... I mean, Indian. "So long as you restricted yourselves to your part of the world, we could afford to leave you alone. But now, with improved sailing methods, not to mention a submersible craft worthy of our own shipbuilding, you threaten to extend your violence to our peaceful shores. You leave us no choice."

He clapped his hands, and two European men appeared from behind a huge wall. They were very old, with beards down to their ankles, and they wore horned helmets. Each carried a strange weapon made of crystal and gold, with rotating blades.

"The two of you will fight a stupid, bloody duel to the death," said our host, inclining his head first to Columbus, and then to the duke. "We are pacifists, so we will derive much pleasure from watching the spectacle."

This seemed fair all around. Clearly these people were civilized. But the admiral's practical approach to life did not desert him now: "What will the winner claim as prize?"

The shining man held up a shining cup of water. "This liquid comes from a land to the west. We call it Floridated water, and it will make He who drinks it immortal. The survivor and his crew will be given this water and our most seaworthy submersible, the *Nautilus*. They may explore the rest of the world so long as they never return to bother us."

The admiral did not avail himself of this opportunity to hold forth on the demonic nature of boats that travel underwater. Diago had a practical question too: "What happens to the loser's crew?"

"They will be fed to a giant octopus of course," came the unemotional answer.

As the weapons were passed to the men from Europe, the Dark Duke made a surprisingly cryptic comment: "No matter how far we travel, we find ourselves there."

Suddenly a volcano erupted.

TO BE INDEFINITELY CONTINUED

SHIP FULL OF JEWS

Barry N. Malzberg

Cristoforo could hear the moaning from steerage, the Chassids were chanting again, moaning and raving in their strange and steeped tongue, the sounds of the Hebrew emerging cloudily from the deck of the *Pinta*, filling him with some mixture of dread and regard, religiosity and hope, the swells and pitching of the barren seas reminding him of the essential perilousness of his journey. Images of spices, fragrant bouquets from the sullen and mysterious East rose in his nostrils, taunting thoughts of the new and deadly continent opening up before him possessed him with a kind of graciousness. The sounds of the Chassids were overwhelming. Sometimes they would pray for hours, unstopping, one choir beginning when another paused, filling the moist air with imprecations and song, at other times they were silent, pitching and rolling in the deck, the queasiness of their condition doubtless the origin of this strange and necessary silence. Cristoforo did not understand any of it.

Of course the Chassids were not to understand, they were to transport. Isabella had pointed this out to him. "They are none of your concern," she had said, "they are being deported, will keep to themselves under guard, will pray and rave in their strange way, but have nothing to do with your journey." The excitable queen had gazed at him, her eyes full and penetrating in the darkness. There was something very special between she and Cristoforo; that had been his intimation from the start, but of course under Ferdinand's cruel gaze and with the happenstance of the Inquisition, it was impossible to bring this strange and stunned accord to any kind of realization. Cristoforo was a temporal man, his mind was seized by the fragrance of spices, but his imagination remained clear and pristine, somewhere to the side of fantasy. He had an assignment to commit, the Chassids were only the most marginal part. Standing on the deck, swaying, finding purchase on the thin and

decaying boards of this wretched ship that was, his great friend, the
queen, had insisted, the very best available to him, Cristoforo pondered
his fate, considered his condition, swung his keen and penetrating gaze
toward *el Norte*, the hidden land beyond the dip of the great horizon.
Santa María, Cristoforo murmured, and did not know if he was invoking
that mother of passage or merely repeating the name of that third and
most eccentric ship, filled with roustabouts and assassins, also deported
from Spain, a gang so cruel that he had taken Ferdinand's instruction
not to deal with that ship at all, even in his capacity as overseer of the
voyage. "You will really be much better, my son," Ferdinand had said,
"staying with your crew and examining the route with compass and
disjunction, allowing the guards to control that hostile ship." Cristoforo
had shrugged. Who was he to argue with Ferdinand? A king's reputation
stood between him and all desire. Cristoforo lusted hopelessly for the
queen, but all proportion was necessary within the arc of condition.
Sometimes his thoughts were metaphysical, sometimes they were practical, and at all times the three ships rolled and sculled their way toward
the New World. Abolish all desire, Cristoforo thought, and the spices of
desire may someday soon be yours.

"Excuse me, master," his yeoman said, approaching with downcast
gaze and suitable humility. Everyone knew of Cristoforo's special relationship with Isabella, also his terrible temper and the secret instructions from the queen, which reportedly granted him the right to scuttle
any who displeased him. Behind lay the specter of the Inquisition, only
for the Jews so far, but who could tell; ahead lay the equally impondera-
ble New World; but somewhere in the middle Cristoforo presided, and
his word was terrible, his authority absolute. "The rabbi has requested
permission to speak to you. He asked me to carry this message."

Rabbi? What Rabbi? Cristoforo could feel his consciousness swim as
he slowly reoriented himself to the possession of a steerage filled not
only with chanting but with hierarchy. There was a leader or several
leaders of the Chassids, yes, and they obtained not only the spiritual but
the temporal title *rebbe*, corrupted by the idiomatic language of his day
to this less forbidding form. Jesus had been *rebbe*, too, Cristoforo noted,
not a religious man, no longer possessed by any vision other than the
spicy and nefarious East toward which they so perilously cruised, he
recalled from his childhood pictures of the bearded Master, who had of
course emerged from the Pharisees of his day and had been put to
torture and death for daring to rival them in popularity. Or was that the
story? He was not sure; the Inquisition of course was a final settling of
accounts for this ancient injustice, but Cristoforo, concerned with matters of the sea as well as certain entanglements on shore, which even

before Isabella had made his life colorful and difficult, had not paid much attention to this. "Master," the yeoman said, "I have brought the Rabbi to the deck. He is instant over there; he is asking for appearances."

Cristoforo shrugged. A shrug seemed to possess him head to toe, front to back, through all the specious and yet solid aspects of his frame; he had been shrugging, he sometimes thought, all his life. Shrug for the mean-spirited Barcelona of his day, which seemed obsessed with questions of reparation that could not concern a simple master of the seas. A shrug for Isabella, who, after all, was beyond him for all of her flirtatiousness and desirability and would have made much trouble in the possession, a trouble that he suspected, she would have found no less titillating than the specter of his murder. Shrug for the *Santa María* and its decks full of felons who would be the first to grapple with the savages of the New Land if the savages were to show any hostile intention. Shrug for the jewels and fragrances that Ferdinand had promised him if he were successful on this difficult mission. Shrug for this and shrug for that, meet the temper of the world with a certain calculated indifference and ignore the screams and concerns of the Inquisition which, after all, had absolutely nothing to do with him and which would go on its tortuous way whether or not he was present. "So, bring him here," Cristoforo said. "Let me discuss with you later the proper way to deal below deck, do you hear me?"

"Whatever you say, master," the yeoman said, and gestured. The rabbi, a huge bearded man wrapped in the vestments of his calling—but they *all* seemed to wear this strange and elaborate garb—shuffled toward him downcast, his eyes seeking the deck, then his head tilting upward, the strange, luminous, Israelic eyes locking with Cristoforo's in a way that induced strange sensations, perhaps due to the odors of steerage wafting from the rabbi and the vague screams across the water, which might have been emanating from the *Niña*, just barely visible, or the more distant *Santa María*, which, *Jesus Christo*, he could not and would not want to see in these conditions. "Well, well," he said to the Jew as the yeoman backed away, submission in all of his posture—if nothing else he had established deference in this crew, he had the weight of royalty behind him, and there were rumored special and terrible arrangements that the king could visit even at a distance upon mutineers, spies among the crew. "Tell me what brings you above deck? Yes, what do you want?"

The Jew, still staring at him in that curious and affecting way, said, "My name is Solomon. *Schelemo*, I come to ask you a favor."

"I am not interested in your name," Cristoforo said. "Your names, frankly, mean nothing to me."

"Yes, but—"

"If I wanted to establish special relations with Jews," Cristoforo said, "it would not be through the medium of names. I would request your presence in other ways. You are here, below the decks, on sufferance, through the mercy of Isabella and Ferdinand, our king and queen. I have nothing whatsoever to do with any of this, I am simply under orders."

"That is understood," the Jew said. "The conditions below are impossible. There are five hundred and fifty two of us, and we are fainting. We are placed one upon another in tight racks and without fresh air, without even the possibility of air. There is much fainting and illness."

"This is not my account," Cristoforo said. "Conditions are difficult for all of us. This is a voyage of privation."

"I beg of you," Solomon said. "Permit us to come above decks. Not all together, but ten or twenty at a time, just to relieve ourselves of this torment, to take the air, to move—"

"Conditions are worse on the *Santa María*," Cristoforo said. "It is a slave ship, filled with the darkest felons of our time. But they do not complain. They drift upon the waters to the New World uncomplainingly, and they hold against the day."

"I know nothing of that," Solomon said. "I know only the conditions below deck. We are perishing. Soon the disease will begin, then the slow and terrible wasting of flesh. Even our most fervent prayers will go unanswered."

Cristoforo shrugged. Another shrug. Shrug at this, turn away from that, consider the Marins, who, it was rumored, had renounced their Judaism to live in secret and had thus evaded the eye of the Inquisition while seeking penalties in other ways. Shrug at the sea, shrug at the New World itself. If it had been left to him, he would have been a merchant at the port of Barcelona and would have left conditions such as these to the more intrepid. How did this happen to him? How had he become the master of such a rude voyage? It was all that Cristoforo could do not to reach out and shake the rabbi, explain that there were many in agony here and that agony was not now only a matter of steerage. But he said nothing of course. The loneliness and fervency of command.

"I am sorry," he said, "I cannot help you. You will have to do what you can down there. It is so decreed. The conditions were made quite explicit to me, surely the same was done for you."

"But how long," Solomon said. "How long will this voyage be?"

Another shrug. Shrug at distance, at lust, at all the complications of empire and design. "I can't answer that," Cristoforo said. "It could be

weeks, it could be a matter of days. We have been at sea for almost a
month and we are in uncharted waters. When the New World looms
over the horizon and not before, then the journey will end. The rest is
in hands we cannot understand. Surely you know of imponderables, of
fate."

"I know of nothing," Solomon said. "You misjudge us, all of us,
clearly. We are not cattle. We are as you, and we are suffering. Men,
women, and little children, some with pets smuggled aboard, all in pain,
all of them with special and necessary grace. Do you understand any of
this?"

"You are to return below deck at once," Cristoforo said, the dark lash
of anger trailing through his bowels. "Now, before this continues. You
are insolent and you are exceeding my patience. You were taken aboard
by measure of the queen's generosity and because she took a sudden and
unaccustomed pity upon you. I know of nothing else."

"They cry," Solomon said. "They pray, and in their prayers is their
spirit and their torment." He gestured. "Can't you hear?" Indeed, the
keening of the Jews to which Cristoforo had accommodated himself as he
had to the stunning curvature of the water struck him suddenly, rose up
within him now with the urgency if not the fragrance of those spices he
sought. Words seemed to emerge dimly from the groans of insistence,
then subsided. "*Adonai*," the Jews cried. "*Elohim. Brich hu omen.*" "O
countrymen," Solomon said, "my countrymen, my brother—"

"Enough," Cristoforo said. "I am the captain." He turned his back to
signal that the interview was over, that the petition had been reviewed
and denied, that, no less than Torquemada, he had been forced to
obduracy as a means of containing these people. Behind him he could
hear grunts, then whimpers as if Solomon were planning some desperate final assault. Cristoforo shook his head, folded his arm, stared grimly
at the sea, which heaved from its greenish depths the small mysteries of
flotsam, small pieces of debris that assumed vaguely organic shape, then
were swallowed by the water. "*V'yisgadal. Shmeh rabo.*" The small and
diminished sound of Solomon pattering away from him and then the
chants rising from the spaces of Neptune, mingling with the sounds of
the sea itself, swaddling Cristoforo in the dangerous and terrible sounds
that signaled the slow turning of the earth, the emergence of the New
World to the starboard. In the distance Cristoforo imagined that he
could see mountains, could glimpse the tread of elephant, could see the
bangles of princes as they contended with one another for the splendors
of their new estate, but he knew the signs of delirium when from a great
distance he let it signal him. He was a man of the sea. Cristoforo
shrugged again, shrug for the Jews, for Torquemada's insistence, for

Torquemada's descent. Shrug for the New World, shrug for the troubles and purchase of five hundred Jews below deck whom he would never see, could never grasp. More was to be done and later. He felt his body lighten as a sense of decision came upon him. This would only last to a certain point, then there would be another circumstance. He was sure of it. Shrug and step, step and shrug, a sudden disturbing intimation of Isabella's swollen and needful breast prodding at him as he signaled the yeoman to take over the helm, however momentarily.

On the *Santa María* Torquemada, enthused, gathered the desperadoes around him. Garbed as they, indistinguishable from them, far departed from the priestly robes of his magnificence, he had become their equal and therefore their superior. The plan was working. The cunning and ingenious plan—worked out in the most sacred places of the Church and then with the king and queen—was working. "O listen to me," Torquemada said. "O listen, friends and companions. They gathered around him, the most desperate men of Spain, men so desperate that on this voyage of desperadoes they had been segregated. Only Torquemada could control them, could understand and apprehend their spirit, and it was for this reason—*to test himself*—that he had embarked upon this exile. Behind him the Jews, who soon enough would be encountered. "The New World beckons," Torquemada said. "A place of justice, light, and peace. Attend to it! Can you not see it?" Unshaven and desperate heads turned, gleaning the new land through the spume of the sea. "Here we will begin afresh," Torquemada said. "That was the plan, the plan for all of us." They murmured in response. "Here," Torquemada said, "we will take the Jews and plant them, rid the world of Israel, depart then for new and better shores. But you must keep your courage up. Must not fail."

"Kill them," one of the men said. "We should go back to the master's ship and kill them now."

Torquemada smiled, thinking of how far he had taken them, how far all of them had come in this one sharp, difficult month of voyage. "Not just yet," he said. "It must be at the right time for the right purpose. Now it would be just slaughter. There was enough slaughter in Spain, here it will be of a different kind. We will seed the ground," Torquemada said. "We will expend their blood in the purposes of consecration, and it will be better."

"You talk like a priest," one of them said. "Are you a priest, then? Or are you one of us."

"I am one of this and one of the other," Torquemada said. "I make faith with you in these spaces as you make faith with me. Soon the

mountains, the tablelands of the New World will be upon us and we will
turn them holy under the gush of sacrificial blood. But for now," he said,
"for now we must once again pray, we must place our knives and
ordnance in protected places and pray for a good conclusion to this
voyage. Do you hear me? *Ave María*," Torquemada said, and continued
with the familiar litany. They settled in with him, attentive as scholars to
the rhythm of his words. *I had no choice*, Torquemada thought, looking
at the high plumes of the water, the sails glinting against the turbulence.
*It was difficult, but the only means to carry forth the Inquisition. One
must constantly move outward in order to move inward. We had
accomplished our sacred purposes in Madrid. Barcelona had become
ours as well. Soon it would have turned within, and by losing everything
we would have gone beyond risk. But here, here, by transporting the
Jews, by moving forth even as we move back, we have encountered and
made ripe the oldest possibilities of all.*

Or am I not sanctified? he thought, a man of doubt as well as of faith,
just as the honored Savior himself had been. *Is it this or that? Is it one
thing or the other? Is that shipful of Jews headed for the Jerusalem of
the spirit that we will erect or, aligned in the sign of the cross, will they
perish at the bottom of the seas?* In Cristoforo's hands, he thought, *but
fortunately I can attend to the matters of transcendence, leave the
temporal in the hands of Cristoforo.* "Thy will be done," Torquemada
said. They looked at him intently. He raised his hands in the gesture of
submission, feeling the terrible power of the water underneath.

In the racks Solomon said, "I did the best I could. I pleaded with
him. I asked for air and light."

"But he said no," the three Davids said. "He said no," the Israelites
said. "He would not have us," Judith and Rachel said, wiping the
foreheads of the children who clustered. "He refused."

"That is right," Solomon said. "He refused. He said that we were
steerage, garbage, at the behest of the queen but of no concern to him. I
told him that we would die, and he turned away. There is nothing to be
done."

"Cristoforo is not a man of mercy," Judith said. "He cares nothing for
any of us."

"That is not so," Solomon said. "He is doing what he must, just as we
are. He is in the control of larger forces. At least we are on the seas. We
have been spared the Inquisition. Maybe it will be different for those of
us who live. If they live. If we live. This damnable voyage..."

"Spared the Inquisition," Ruth said, taking Solomon's hand, "but not
the Inquisitor. The Inquisitor is always with us. He comes in the night,

he follows on the seas, he screams from the bowels of Neptune. I understand that now."

"Nothing to be done," Solomon said. "We are creatures of their mercy."

"I tell you," Rachel said, "that there is a judgment coming that is beyond all of us. They seek a New World, but it is eternally the old."

The steerage, silent when Solomon had returned, cast down to silence by hope or at least curiosity, resumed, broken fragments of prayers ascending only to the thin bulkheads that made them crouch against the racks, then dispersed. "It will not be long," Solomon said, "we cannot survive this. We are a shipful of Jews, not of mystics or explorers, and in our flight is our guilt and our culpability. Nevertheless—"

"Nevertheless," Judith said, as if she had taken his thought, pressing his hand, "nevertheless we have at least carried ourselves, carried a bit of testimony, moved to some different place through the designs of our own spirit. We are not Marins. We are not apostosaic. Our apostasy is of a different kind."

"All displacement is apostasy," Solomon said, the chanting murmuring about him, the disputation with Judith—*this woman*, to engage not only in prayers but Talmudic disputation with women was their peculiar but necessary fate in these conditions—continuing, all of their strange and strangely confluent anguish melding as the *Pinta* inexorably carried them toward a fate they could not determine, in all faith, in the faith of God, the one God of Israel whose Name was One and whose Oneness was indivisible in the heart of their exile.

Torquemada, seized by a sudden spirit of ecstasy and affirmation, struck as if by a bolt from the brow of the Holy Ghost, began to dance and heave upon the deck of the *Santa María*, incognizant of the stares of the felons, indifferent to the risks that this display of ecstasy might bring upon him, the steps of his dance, carrying him from one side of the ship to the next while on the bosom of the ocean the craft lurched and spilled not only its provisions but its prayers in the sullen light of this journey.

And so, and so they came upon the New World then, the slave ship and the master's ship and the ship between, the shipful of Jews and the ship of the Inquisitor, caught their first glimpse of the New World through the mist and fog of their combined prayers, and in that moment, as Torquemada leapt, as the Jews chanted, as a grim and compliant Cristoforo set sextant and compass and shrugged toward this newest part of his destiny, in that moment it was as if all the centuries had slipped by and this strange and mismatched concatenation of spirits and flesh, voyagers and prisoners, repelled and necessitous, were gathered

by that bolt that had struck Torquemada and that swept them from the
bosom of the ocean to the bowels of the ship, then expelled them to all
of the crevices of the twentieth century itself, myths of purgation and
collision hastening their way toward the apostasies to come. The shipful
of Jews, their captain, their keeper, and their inquisitor joined at last in
that voyage of transcendence. Cristoforo dreamed it, dreamed it all,
dreamed that he was in the enormous grasp of Isabella herself, her
capacious sex absorbing and expelling him as would all of the centuries
and scholars to come and the spray of his seed upon the ocean of the
queen the plume to drag him past myth and toward that first terrible
awareness of his destiny. Cristoforo the Jew. Cristoforo the keeper of
souls *V'ysh ka'dash. Shmeh rabbo.*
    Brich hu.
    Omen.

THE KARAMAZOV CAPER

Gordon Eklund

One: On the Pier

November 1917

A *foul bleak and forlorn country*, thinks Trotsky as he staggers, swaying, down the gangplank toward shore, hands gripping the ropes for balance. *The entire fucking land reeks of rotting gutted fish.* (Poor Trotsky dreams now constantly of vanquished Moscow nights when freedom and revolt rode the chill wintery air like a blast of Christ's omniscient breath.) (And lovely dark women slithering naked abed.) (The images are confused, interwoven. Trotsky groans. Sixteen dreadful days on the trans-Siberian train, five more aboard ship tossing in Arctic waves will do depraved things to a man's dreams.)

Yet what can any of it mean in this day and age with sad, brave Lenin tortured and dying in his cell and the Jew fool Zinoviev baying for mercy on bent knees, dawn light slashing through the bars of Lubianka Prison like the blades of knives. *And you alone, Trotsky, can save me.* (No, wrong, fool stupid Jew bastard. Wrong, wrong, wrong. It is I alone, Trotsky, who can kill you.) (And who did! And who fucking well did!)

A dense trickily drizzle of rain oozes down upon his head and shoulders as Trotsky steps upon the wooden pier, knees buckling at the shock of solid motionless terrain underfoot. *So where*, he thinks, *is my official welcoming delegation of police agents in black beards and stovepipe hats, all splendidly attired?* Instead there is only a lone, hugely fat, cigar-puffing native red man in a vast ankle-length fur coat and a ridiculously broad-brimmed cloth hat. A jagged scar like a lion's slash wound (Trotsky has only lately returned from an inspection tour of czarist East Africa) runs down the man's left cheek to the cleft of his jaw.

"Are you Trotsky, the investigator?" says the red man, approaching delicately on tiny feet, his gait like a dance. His words curl around the butt of his cigar.

"No, I am Czar Nicholas II, ruler of all of imperial Russia, including this blasted land. And you, native idiot, who the hell might you be?" (Trotsky's irritability remains simmering.)

"I am called Redburn, at your service." His smile reveals sharp yellow incisors like those of a cannibal. "I am the senior ranking police official for the township of Sealth."

"And what, pray tell, is this Sealth?"

"The name we natives prefer for what you Russians term Bering's City of the New Lands."

"This Sealth was the last acknowledged free chieftain of your tribe as I recall."

Redburn's face remains as blank as stone, his smile frozen, his eyes bleak as winter. "You are a knowledgeable man, Trotsky."

"I make the attempt to find things out."

"Then perhaps you should also know that Chief Sealth was both a drunkard and an imbecile. He kissed the butt cheeks of you Russians and came away with shit embedded between his teeth forever. Among my people his name is a badge of shame and degradation."

Trotsky has heard enough of this native self-pity. There are far worse fates for a man, he believes, than shame or degradation. "Take me to my inn. I am tired and wish to rest."

Redburn's brows rise quizzically. "Before interrogating the prisoner?"

"Yes. The fool will surely keep."

Redburn removes his cigar, blows smoke, shrugs. "As you wish."

They move along the pier. Meager waves slap the wooden seawall like gently clapping hands. There is a brackish scent in the air. Mounds of seaweed float on top of the water like clumps of discolored hair.

"You are one of the Jew race, are you not, friend Trotsky?" asks Redburn. They turn away from the pier, mount steep wooden steps. Somewhere above, a trolley bell jangles. The light oozing drizzle has dwindled to a mist, barely damp.

"I am. So?"

"So some would claim that makes you and I brothers in blood." Redburn's smile broadens around his cigar, showing molars as broad as tree stumps, as yellow as parchment.

"What do you mean by that?"

"The belief held by some that we natives of the New Lands are one of the lost tribes of your Israel."

"It is not my Israel. I am an atheist."

Redburn chuckles within his great fur coat. "An atheist in this universe only or in all universes everywhere?"

"What do you mean?"

"I refer to the theory held by some that there is more than one universe, that God still exists in some but has vanished from others."

"A peculiar theory, that."

Redburn shrugs. "No more peculiar than many I have heard enunciated in recent days. We live in a peculiar time, Trotsky, and this is a desperate land. The nearby forests are again rife with prophets and messiahs, some native, some Russian, some false, others not."

"One of whom has been charged with the crime I have been sent to investigate."

"A simple crime. A baby murdered, its heart removed and apparently eaten. The culprit has been apprehended." Redburn suddenly tosses a warm arm around his companion's gaunt shoulders. The fused odors of cigar smoke and dead animal skin overwhelm Trotsky's senses. "Hardly something to concern an investigator of your repute."

"The dead baby was that of the German ambassador," Trotsky implores, struggling to break free of the native's smothering grasp.

"Coincidence. Pure coincidence." Redburn lets go of Trotsky. Together they turn toward the township of Sealth (or Bering's City), which rises, heavenlike, upon hills to the east. Bonfires can be glimpsed flickering through the mist. It is the middle of the day but as dark as an hour before dawn.

Two: The Prisoner Speaks

The jail is a gray brick edifice perched upon a precipice's edge, the cells clustered in the basement floor. Few are currently occupied. The prisoner sits, stiffly erect, on a bloodstained cot in the last cell in the row. Redburn in his long coat slouches on his left. Trotsky, across the room in a chair, keeps notes in a pad. The toilet is a hole in the floor. The air reeks of piss, shit, and vomit, of sweat and blood and fear.

Trotsky: Your name is Mikhail Sergeiovitch Karamazov known as Mishka.

Prisoner (through swollen lips): That is correct, Investigator.

Trotsky: Your family first came to the New Lands in the year 1897.

Prisoner: That is also correct, Investigator.

Trotsky: In Russia your father was charged with the crime of murdering his own father.

Prisoner: That is true. But he was innocent.

Trotsky: Have you been beaten?

Prisoner: Yes, Investigator.

Trotsky: To make you confess?

Prisoner (glancing to his left): I do not know the reason.

Trotsky: I will see that it stops.

Prisoner: Thank you, Investigator.

Trotsky: But now you also have been charged with murder. Of a child. A baby.

Prisoner: I am innocent as well.

Trotsky: Blood was found upon your clothes. Recent blood. Great thick splashes of it. There was also a knife in your possession similarly coated in blood.

Prisoner: I may have killed a chicken that day. Or another animal. I am unsure.

Trotsky: You took a life but have no memory of the event?

Prisoner: I suffer at times from epileptic seizures. There are occasions when I remember nothing for days.

Trotsky: And you claim this was one such occasion?

Prisoner: It may have been, yes.

Redburn (intervening with a snort): He is lying, Investigator.

Trotsky: But if you say you remember nothing, Mishka, then you could as easily remember nothing of the murder of a baby as the killing of a chicken.

Prisoner: Oh, no. Impossible. That I could never forget. You must believe me, Investigator. I am not a murderer. I am a foul bleak sinner who reeks miserably of the putrid shit of my flesh. But I accept and follow all God's commandments. I seek in all manner of my life to become as one with my Lord who is Jesus Christ.

Redburn (muttering): There is no fucking God in this universe, you dumb shit.

Trotsky: You have some reputation as a prophet, friend Mishka.

Prisoner: I must deny that as well. Prophecy hints at some foreknowledge of God's master plan. I have none. I am a miserable desperate sinner. My flesh rots and mildews upon my bones as it does with all men, good and evil alike.

Redburn (softly): What good men?

Trotsky: But you have on occasion preached among the native tribes.

Prisoner: I have spoken to them of the ways of Christ, yes.

Trotsky: You have visited their villages, entered their lodgings.

Prisoner: Primitive heathen hovels in the bleak dank forests of this forsaken land. But I have gone there, yes. For the word of God must be spoken where the body and blood of Christ shall prevail.

Trotsky: An admirable sentiment, friend Mishka. But are you not unaware of where the body of the slain child was discovered to be lying?

Redburn (interrupting): What the Jew means is the baby who had its heart ripped out and its carcass buried in shit in the woods.

Prisoner: I know nothing of that, nothing.

Trotsky: But it was within less than half a kilometer of the village of the Skokomish chieftain Meekla, where you were known to have preached two days before.

Prisoner: And was driven away with sticks. (Twisting to reveal wounds on his back and shoulders.) Beaten and struck and made to bleed.

Trotsky: The same day the baby of the German ambassador vanished.

Prisoner: I know nothing of that, nothing.

Redburn (turning as he sits and grasping the prisoner by the shirt front): You pathetic fucking liar. You were seen at the ambassador's house that same day. You knocked on the goddamned door.

Prisoner: To ask for a simple begging for Christ, nothing more.

Redburn (yelling): To steal a baby. For a sacrifice. A blood sacrifice. To the village where you were driven away with sticks. A baby with its heart gouged out. While it was still alive. Still beating. Answer me, Karamazov. Did you eat the heart? (He slaps the prisoner.) Is that the kind of devil you are? A cannibal who eats the flesh of its own kind? (He slaps the prisoner again.)

Prisoner: No, no, I—I—!

Trotsky (rising to his feet to intervene): Redburn, let—

Redburn (slapping the prisoner repeatedly as Trotsky grasps his arm): You devil! You evil fucking devil!

Three: A Forest Journey

The motorcar jerks and sways precariously as it cuts a path through the deep mud of the mountain road. In the driver's seat Redburn sits

hunched at the wheel while Trotsky beside him grips the door handle,
struggling not to be thrown from his seat. It has been a journey of some
two hours thus far with, according to Redburn, at least as much
remaining before they reach the murder site. Twice already the car has
stuck fast in the mud and Trotsky has had to climb out and push. His
shoes, stockings, and trouser legs are wet and soaked. A light drizzle
continues to fall, windshield wipers whipping erratically at clots of mud
and rain. Trotsky cannot avoid wondering how the prisoner Karamazov
could have managed this same journey while carrying with him the
kidnapped baby of the German ambassador. But this and other unanswered
questions are why he has demanded that Redburn bring him to the
actual killing ground.

Redburn, who has remained silent throughout the journey, suddenly
clears his throat. He is sucking at one of his cigars, the fumes filling the
interior of the car like a cloud. "Are you familiar, friend Trotsky, with the
story of Anna Petrovna?"

Trotsky has to think for a moment. "The name sounds familiar,
yes."

"The first white woman to set foot in the New Lands. And a true
beauty to boot. Blond and blue-eyed and as lovely as a flower. Do you
admire women of beauty, friend Trotsky?"

He shrugs. "Doesn't everyone?"

"Not everyone, no. Our friend back in the jail cell, the murderer
Karamazov, he doesn't strike me as one to concern himself overly with
female beauty."

"He doubtlessly has other things on his mind."

"Of course. He is a philosopher. But you and I, we are men of the
world, correct? We do not resist the lures of flesh. Another cunt licked is
another cunt known, right? But about Anna Petrovna. She came to these
shores from New Archangel at age eighteen in the company of her
young husband the navigator Bulygin aboard the brig *Saint Nicholas* on
a trading expedition to the New Lands in the Christian year of 1808.
The voyage had proceeded without incident until one October night
when a sudden squall struck the moored vessel near Destruction Island,
driving it on the rocks and forcing its crew and passengers to land. The
survivors had not been ashore long when a group of curious natives
emerged from the forest. They were Quillayutes, a usually peaceable,
though primitive tribal group. Nevertheless an incident soon transpired.
Perhaps one of the Quillayutes grew too curious, perhaps concerning
Anna Petrovna herself. Shoves and pushes were exchanged. Someone
shouted out. A rock was thrown. Then a spear. There were musket

shots. It was raining. Three of the Quillayutes lay dead. The others quickly scattered to the forest.

"A conference was held among the Russians, and it was decided to press south along the coastline toward where another expedition was thought to be due to land. Unbeknownst to the Russians, however, their every step of the way was being dogged by several hundred natives hidden in the forest and bent upon avenging the Quillayutes. This revenge reached fruition on the banks of the River Hoh when the Russian party was forced to split itself into three groups in order to ford the river by canoe. The women—three Aleuts plus Anna Petrovna— rode in the first canoe. When it reached shore, the natives emerged from the forest and began hurling spears. The other two canoes were sunk. The women, including Anna Petrovna, were taken prisoner. The natives then vanished into the forest as swiftly and silently as they had emerged.

"One can only speculate upon the dread and horror experienced by the young groom Bulygin. What hideous thoughts of rape and degradation must surely have filled his head. In any event, in grief and shock he voluntarily relinquished command of the expedition to one Tarakanov, a soldier and adventurer, and it was Tarakanov who wisely rejected all immediate attempts by the natives to bargain for Anna Petrovna's freedom in return for the Russians' own muskets. It is recorded that on one occasion Anna Petrovna was actually produced in the flesh so that her husband could verify that she was not dead. Some say that Bulygin then broke down completely and went out of his mind for a while. Whatever the circumstances, Tarakanov soon ordered the expedition upriver away from the ocean and its winter storms. The surviving Russians did not reemerge for another ten weeks. By the time they did, Anna Petrovna had been sold as tribute to the chieftain of the Makahs, a tribe living on the shores of the strait to the north.

"At Bulygin's pleading, Tarakanov finally agreed to go north and parlay with the Makahs. Anna Petrovna soon appeared. She was clean, warmly garbed, and plainly well fed. It was obvious to all that she had become, with her blond hair and blue eyes, a particular favorite of the old Makah chieftain. Nevertheless her first words still deeply shocked all who heard them, most especially her young husband. For it was Anna Petrovna's strong desire to remain among the Makahs until rescue could be arranged. She further suggested that all of them, including her husband, give themselves over to the Makahs for safekeeping. In the end only four members of the expedition agreed, including both Tarakanov and poor Bulygin, who clearly would hesitate at no degradation in order to remain near his lovely and vital wife. The others turned back south, but within days their boat struck a rock and sank, and all of them were captured by Quillayutes and sold into slavery. A goodly number, in fact, soon ended up among the Makahs reunited with their former comrades.

"Time passed. Spring coursed into summer, summer into fall. No rescue ships were sighted. The Makahs grew bored with their white prisoners. Many were sold and some sold again. Even the old Makah chieftain grew weary of Anna Petrovna's charms and gave her over to a nearby tribe, where she was less well treated and often forced to eat rotten fish. According to one account, she was made to copulate publicly with two men at a time, one in her anus. Her husband may well have witnessed this. She grew forlorn. Her blond hair fell from her scalp in clumps. Her blue eyes misted over. She wept without restraint. It is known that Bulygin on several occasions threatened to kill her and once had to be physically subdued by Tarakanov. A sign appeared in the sky—a naked woman astride a stallion. On the night of November 1, 1809, of Christ's reign, Anna Petrovna took her own life. Five days later Bulygin died of apparently natural causes.

"It wasn't until the following spring, in fact, that a Russian trading vessel at last appeared like a beacon from heaven through the gray mists of the strait. The captain soon arranged for the rescue of the remaining prisoners by bartering with the natives. On June 9, 1810, the survivors reached New Archangel. Of the twenty who had originally sailed, seven were known to be dead, and one, a young student named Kotelnikov, could never be located."

"So why do you tell me all this?" Trotsky says.

"You did not find it an interesting tale?" Redburn asks.

"Interesting, yes, but pointless." Past the windshield rain pours effortlessly from the sky.

"Not if one also thinks of the man known as Colombo."

"Who?"

"The Genoan navigator who in 1492 first reached the eastern shores of these lands."

"Has this been verified? It is new information to me."

"The verification in the form of navigation charts and a travel diary is sufficient to satisfy most scholars."

"Then you are claiming that it is this Colombo, not Bering, who truly discovered the New Lands?"

"For factual purposes, yes. But since Colombo was tortured and killed shortly after his return and further such voyages prohibited by papal edict, his discovery had no practical effect."

"So why was he killed?"

"Like yourself, he was a Jew."

"You said he was Genoan."

"He was apparently a Genoan Jew. The minions of Pope Boniface did not torture and kill Genoans who were merely Genoans."

"And so, what is your point?" Trotsky asks. Outside, the storm has worsened. He can see nothing through the windshield but darkness. The landscape beyond is a hidden, unknown country.

"So if Colombo's voyage had been permitted to stand and others had followed, it would have been the westerners from Spain and Portugal and perhaps even the backward, primitive English before their papal conquest who would have colonized the New Lands."

"But they didn't."

"No, they didn't."

"And I still fail to understand the connection with your tale of Anna Petrovna."

Redburn at the wheel shrugs. "Because she was raped and degraded, friend Trotsky. By my own people. We natives of the New Lands. Had it been the other way, had it been Colombo with the weight of all civilized Europe behind him who first occupied these lands, it would have been my people who would have become intimate with rape and degradation."

"And the Germans now?" says Trotsky.

Redburn frowns, tight-lipped. He nods slowly. "Then you do comprehend my meaning, friend Trotsky."

"I do?"

He turns his head to the side window. "This is a land without pity or remorse."

The rain falls relentlessly.

Four: The Killing Ground

A clearing in the forest. Pine needles like a carpet on the ground. Cones scattered everywhere. Everything wet and soaked and damp and clammy. A pervasive mildew stink like an open grave. *This forest is a place where nothing seems to be wholly alive,* thinks Trotsky, *where everything seems to be either dead or dying. Redburn and his fucking smelly cigar. Blood caked on his knuckles too. (Does the man ever wash?)* And poor Trotsky, swallowing hard, shivering like a fallen angel, thinking again of warm Moscow nights when both life and youth burned with infernal heat.

He kneels in front of the three shallow graves, hand on chin, concentrating.

—Well, well, sez Redburn stepping up from behind, hovering like a huge fat bird, is there anything else ye wish to eyeball, friend Trotsky? For there below ye were first put to rest the sad rotting remnants of that frail innocent, struck down in the rawness of infancy by the man-beast Karamazov. Do ye not smell the smell of sin here as we stand, friend Trotsky? Does not the place reek of the foul deed done?

Trotsky comes to his feet, unconvinced. He shakes his head, spreads his arms, turning. —Thats still no proof, sez he, that Karamazov was the killer.

—Oh slugshit, sez Redburn. Thats no rub even if rub is what ye seek. (Nodding sagely to himself.) For who else, sweet friend? Tell me that if tell me something ye must. If not Karamazov, then who the fuck else? For to be a true killing the dreadful deed must also have its true killer, correct? And that, say I, is yon Karamazov. Him is the one that done the deed as surely as it makes no good sense to piss in a strong wind. So hang him by the tip of his prick, I say. Hang him till his balls pop out of their sack like peanuts from a shell.

A steady drizzle descends like a blanket. Trotsky draws his coat collar high around his throat but the wet oozes through. Again he has forgotten a hat. He feels as if he will never again in his life know dryness—or warmth. As a baby rocked in the arms of its mother. The smothering heat. The taste of breast milk sweet upon the lips and tongue. None of this ever again—never.

He meets Redburn's gaze firmly. —I need to visit the Skokomish village. This chieftain Meekla—I wish to meet and converse with him.

Redburn spits tobacco on the ground. —Ah, ye do, do ye? And concerning what matters, may I beg to inquire, me being the chief police official hereabouts and dont ye soon forget it?

—About Karamazov of course. What hes been up to hereabouts. And his preaching—its precise nature. I feel I need to know more about that.

—The ravings of a Christ-addled lunatic, Im certain. (Huffily.)

—That will be for me to decide. (Stiffly.)

Redburn spits again. —Then come along if come ye must, mere mortal fool.

Redburn leads the way along a twisting forest path. Long loping strides, great coat billowing and flapping around his legs. Beneath the sheltering umbrella of massed firs the rain eases to a gentle trickle. Trotsky, taking long deep, languorous draughts of air, follows at a more sedate pace. He is suddenly convinced of Karamazov's innocence, that the true solution to the mystery lies within the confines of the Skokomish village. He is reminded as he walks of what the world must have been like at the moment when life first burst upon the earth. Perhaps it's the all-encompassing wetness of everything, the pervasive dampness that turns his thoughts in such directions.

Ahead drumbeats reverberate. Trotsky hears a piercing animallike scream.

Redburn, oblivious of everything else, enunciates a theory of the cosmos: —I call it Christ-addled lunacy because you see friend Trotsky there is no God in this universe that you and I presently inhabit. Not a one. Oh there was once upon a time dont get me wrong Im no moronic atheist like yourself. But He aint here now brother. Hes done gone and been slain murdered killed snookered bumped off demised by a dagger in the hand of the devil driven through His once beating heart. How did it come to occur? you may well ask. I say it occurred when mankind distracted Him with a deed so foul and dreadful that He was set back rocking on His godly heels and the devil took advantage of the instant and plunged in the blade and that was the end of that. If I had to pick a time and place it would be papal Rome the late afternoon of November 15 1486 when good Pope Innocent VIII was assassinated poisoned by the lunatic pretender who became Boniface X and instituted the Reign of Ignorance and Dread the effects of which we still suffer today for example in the New Lands to our east where the Germans are said to be plying their own policy of mass extermination doing to my people what Boniface did to your Jews four hundred years previous when he ordered the slaughter of the heathen.

—None of this has been proved, Trotsky says. Not about the Germans anyway.

—What I need from you, Redburn persists, is to conceive of the universe in a different manner. (The drumbeats grow steadily louder. There is another piercing scream.) Let us harken back to the critical instant of which we spoke and alter history as to how it might have been had God not been murdered. There is no slaughter of the Jews, no edicts of ignorance. The voyages of exploration begun under Prince Henry are allowed to continue. We have already discussed your brother Colombo and his initial discovery. The New Lands will soon be occupied by white Christian Europeans. From shore to shore, sea to sea. There will be no mass slaughter of anyone except we poor native peoples. And all of this simply because your God in whom you say you do not believe lives instead of dies.

—For God's sake what are you talking about? Trotsky bursts out, his patience at an end.

—Karamazov's lunatic preaching, Redburn says. You wanted to hear it. Well, now you have.

He stops, parting the foliage. The Skokomish village. Movement among the trees. Bronzed, naked bodies. Chanting fills the air. Drumbeats. A scream. Banshee howls. The ground itself seems to quake.

Redburn plunges ahead: —So to me it all seems to come down to this one past instant in our shared history when everything of life was transformed into something reeking of death, when God Our Father...

Dread clings to Trotsky like an odor. Time stops and starts like a man's breathing. The natives gather in a wide circle. Faces bathed in red paint. Drumbeats. Chanting. A shape at the center of the circle. Redburn clutches Trotsky's shoulder to pull him back. He shouts something in his ear. Unhearing, Trotsky breaks free, lunging ahead. Into the circle of red men. Through it. And beyond. At the center a naked priest, a shaman. Legs parted. Face painted. Head flung back. Hair coated in something slick and oily. Glistening. In his hands there is a knife.

And the baby oh my God the baby at his feet on the ground oh my God who is dead who its with its with its...

Trotsky feels the earth rushing up to meet him. There is a gunshot. Redburn? Then a blow behind the ear. Then darkness.

(And the baby with its heart cut out and still beating in the hands of the priest who is smiling, laughing, smiling, eating....)

Five: German Lands

In his inn in Sealth Trotsky is visited by his fellow investigator, Chekhov, a former physician. It was Chekhov who controlled Trotsky's activities during the period when Trotsky infiltrated (and thus helped destroy) the nascent democratic movement of anticzarist Leninists. Chekhov is a man of sixty, with the sallow unlined complexion of a man thirty years younger. His hair is shoulder length and snow white, his thin hooded eyes albino pink. Chekhov has only lately returned from a surreptitious sojourn through the German occupied lands to the east. During most of this time he lived among the nomadic natives of the plains.

He smokes one brown-paper cigarette after another.

"I saw aeroplanes," Chekhov says in a hushed expressionless voice, "come sweeping across the landscape like a plague of locusts. Aeroplanes with two wings, one on top of the other, plowing furrows through the sky. The pilots would fly their ships down close above the heads of the native horsemen and then spray them with machine-gun bullets like a covering blanket. In this fashion I saw as many as one thousand brave men slaughtered in a single afternoon. And then the tanks like mechanized insects would come rolling across the plain. Perhaps fifty tanks all in a row driving unhindered across the featureless flatness of the land. And the women and children would rush from their lodgings, fleeing ahead of the tanks. But it was only a question of time. Between the aeroplanes and the tanks death was as inevitable as the air one breathes. For tanks and aeroplanes are machines made by the hand of man and a machine never needs to pause and rest, a machine never needs to eat or drink. A machine cannot feel or laugh or know sorrow or pity or dread or love. But a machine can kill without thought. And so it was in the German lands. I saw children of no more than six or seven crushed under the treads of the giant tanks. I saw beautiful maidens, their bronzed bodies ripped into ribbons by machine-gun fire. I saw men as old as the wind fall to their knees and die with their eyes open."

Trotsky, his mouth parched, lips dry, hands quivering, examines the photographs Chekhov has made. These photographs, many of them as clear and bright and beautiful as a lake, depict everything: there can be no doubt of the absolute verity of Chekhov's tale.

Chekhov plucks the photographs from Trotsky's hand and puts them away. "They will never, of course, leave the ministry," he says.

"No?" says Trotsky, his head cocked at an awkward angle.

"The Germans are our fellow Christians. We cannot aid the native heathen over them."

"But heathens are human too," Trotsky explodes.

"Perhaps. But that is not the point, Leon."

Trotsky crosses to the window, peering out. It has ceased raining, and the black, winding street below illuminated by the frail glow of gas lanterns lies silent and motionless like the body of a slumbering snake. He says, "A man told me something interesting today, Anton. A native heathen. He said to me, "What if our universe, this one that we all inhabit, what if it turned out to be a universe in which God had died years ago?'"

"A god cannot die."

"How can we be sure?"

"I thought you were an atheist."

"I am. But the suffering in this world, the agony... Who else can one blame if not God?"

"Try man."

"But we are God's creations."

Chekhov shrugs. "But tell me of your own case. I hear it is solved."

Trotsky turns from the window. "Who told you?"

"This native police official, the one with the theory of the cosmos. Redburn, I believe he said his name was. Why? Did he lie?"

"The murderer," says Trotsky, "was a man named Karamazov. He kidnapped the baby of the German ambassador and cut out its heart while it was still living. He may well have eaten the heart as well. He will be returned to Moscow and hanged there for the horrible crime he has committed."

"He has confessed, then?"

"Not yet, no. But he soon shall."

Six: An Epiphany in the Snow

After Chekhov has departed, Trotsky stands at the window, facing out. There is a rapping on the door behind. Without turning he bades the caller to enter.

It is Redburn. He stands in the open door, coat open, cigar in his teeth. "I have come at once, Investigator Trotsky, to report a great tragedy. Only moments ago at the township jail the prisoner Karamazov took his own life. Both wrists and his throat were slit open and the blood of life drained out. How he obtained the knife he used will be the subject of further investigation."

"And before?" says Trotsky.

"And before his dreadful act," Redburn continues, "Karamazov had written in his own hand a thorough and complete confession to all his crimes. A copy of this confession is available for your personal perusal if you wish."

"How convenient," says Trotsky.

"What?"

"I said thank you, Redburn." He is gazing out the window again. It has begun to snow, the flakes fluttering down from the heavens, twisting in the wind, catching the light and glowing. A sudden sense of peace overwhelms him. It is not Redburn's murder of poor Karamazov that has disturbed him. That he has anticipated since the incident in the Skokomish village. It is the murder of God that has caused him to fear and dread. But now that fear and dread are gone. He is serene. For in the murder of God there is only nothingness. And nothingness cannot be feared. It is only the void. "When I was a child," he says without turning, "my mother told me that when it first snowed, if you looked just right, if you half shut your eyes and stared until it hurt and your eyes watered, sometimes—but only sometimes—you would glimpse the actual face of God Himself."

"And did it work?" says Redburn.

Trotsky turns, smiling. "No, never," he says.

THE SLEEPING SERPENT

Pamela Sargent

Yesuntai Noyan arrived in Yeke Geren in early winter, stumbling from his ship with the unsteady gait and the pallor of a man who had recently crossed the ocean. Because Yesuntai was a son of our Khan, our commander Michel Bahadur welcomed the young prince with speeches and feasts. Words of gratitude for our hospitality fell from Yesuntai's lips during these ceremonies, but his restless gaze betrayed his impatience. His mother, I had heard, was Frankish, and he had a Frank's height, but his sharp-boned face, dark slits of eyes, and sturdy frame were a Mongol's.

At the last of the feasts, Michel Bahadur seated me next to the Khan's son, an honor I had not expected. The commander, I supposed, had told Yesuntai a little about me, and would expect me to divert the young man with tales of my earlier life in the northern woods. As the men around us sang and shouted to servants for more wine, Yesuntai leaned toward me.

"I hear," he murmured, "that I can learn much from you, Jirandai Bahadur. Michel tells me that no man knows this land better than you."

"I am flattered by such praise." I made the sign of the cross over my wine, as I had grown used to doing in Yeke Geren. Yesuntai dipped his fingers into his cup, then sprinkled a blessing to the spirits. Apparently he followed our old faith, and not the cross; I found myself thinking a little more highly of him.

"I am also told," Yesuntai went on, "that you can tell many tales of a northern people called the Hiroquois."

"That is only the name our Franks use for all the nations of the Long House." I gulped down more wine. "Once, I saw my knowledge of that people as something that might guide us in our dealings with them. Now it is only fodder on which men seeking a night's entertainment feed."

The Noyan lifted his brows. "I will not ask you to share your stories with me here."

I nodded, relieved. "Perhaps we might hunt together sometime, Noyan. Two peregrines I have trained need testing, and you might enjoy a day with them."

He smiled. "Tomorrow," he said, "and preferably by ourselves, Bahadur. There is much I wish to ask you."

Yesuntai was soon speaking more freely with the other men, and even joined them in their songs. Michel would be pleased that I had lifted the Noyan's spirits, but by then I cared little for what that Bahadur thought. I drank and thought of other feasts shared inside long houses with my brothers in the northern forests.

Yesuntai came to my dwelling before dawn. I had expected an entourage, despite his words about hunting by ourselves, but the Khan's son was alone. He gulped down the broth my wife Elgigetei offered, clearly impatient to ride out from the settlement.

We saddled our horses quickly. The sky was almost as gray as the slate-colored wings of the falcons we carried on our wrists, but the clouds told me that snow would not fall before dusk. I could forget Yeke Geren and the life I had chosen for one day, until the shadows of evening fell.

We rode east, skirting the horses grazing in the land our settlers had cleared, then moved north. A small bird was flying toward a grove of trees; Yesuntai loosed his falcon. The peregrine soared, a streak against the gray sky, her dark wings scimitars, then suddenly plummeted toward her prey. The Noyan laughed as her yellow talons caught the bird.

Yesuntai galloped after the peregrine. I spied a rabbit darting across the frost-covered ground, and slipped the tether from my falcon; he streaked toward his game. I followed, pondering what I knew about Yesuntai. He had grown up in the ordus and great cities of our Frankish Khanate, been tutored by the learned men of Paris, and would have passed the rest of his time in drinking, dicing, card playing, and claiming those women who struck his fancy. His father, Sukegei Khan, numbered two grandsons of Genghis Khan among his ancestors, but I did not expect Yesuntai to show the vigor of those great forefathers. He was the Khan's son by one of his minor wives, and I had seen such men before in Yeke Geren, minor sons of Ejens or generals who came to this new land for loot and glory, but who settled for hunting along the great river to the north, trading with the nearer tribes, and occasionally raiding an Inglistani farm. Yesuntai would be no different; so I thought then.

He was intent on his sport that day. By afternoon, the carcasses of several birds and rabbits hung from our saddles. He had said little to me, and was silent as we tethered our birds, but I had felt him watching me. Perhaps he would ask me to guide him and some of his men on a hunt beyond this small island, before the worst of the winter weather came. The people living in the regions nearby would not trouble hunters. Our treaty with the Ganeagaono, the Eastern Gatekeepers of the Long House, protected us, and they had long since subdued the tribes to the south of their lands.

We trotted south. Some of the men watching the horse herds were squatting around fires near their shelters of tree branches and hides. They greeted us as we passed, and congratulated us on our game. In the distance, the rounded bark houses of Yeke Geren were visible in the evening light, wooden bowls crowned by plumes of smoke rising from their roofs.

The Great Camp—the first of our people who had come to this land had given Yeke Geren its name. "We will build a great camp," Cheren Noyan had said when he stepped from his ship, and now circles of round wooden houses covered the southern part of the island the Long House people called Ganono, while our horses had pasturage in the north. Our dwellings were much like those of the Manhatan people who had lived here, who had greeted our ships, fed us, sheltered us, and then lost their island to us.

Yesuntai reined in his horse as we neared Yeke Geren; he seemed reluctant to return to the Great Camp. "This has been the most pleasant day I have passed here," he said.

"I have also enjoyed myself, Noyan." My horse halted at his side. "You would of course find better hunting away from this island. Perhaps—"

"I did not come here only to hunt, Bahadur. I have another purpose in mind. When I told Michel Bahadur of what I wish to do, he said that you were the man to advise me." He paused. "My father the Khan grows even more displeased with his enemies the Inglistanis. He fears that, weak as they are, they may grow stronger here. His spies in Inglistan tell him that more of them intend to cross the water and settle here."

I glanced at him. All of the Inglistani settlements, except for the port they called Plymouth, sat along the coast north of the long island that lay to the east of Yeke Geren. A few small towns, and some outlying farms—I could not see why our Khan would be so concerned with them. It was unfortunate that they were there, but our raids on their westernmost farms had kept them from encroaching on our territory, and if they tried to settle farther north, they would have to contend with the native peoples there.

"If more come," I said, "then more of the wretches will die during the winter. They would not have survived this long without the aid of the tribes around them." Some of those people had paid dearly for aiding the settlers, succumbing to the pestilences the Inglistanis had brought with them.

"They will come with more soldiers and muskets. They will pollute this land with their presence. The Khan my father will conquer their wretched island, and the people of Eire will aid us to rid themselves of the Inglistani yoke. My father's victory will be tarnished if too many of the island dogs find refuge here. They must be rooted out."

"So you wish to be rid of the Inglistani settlements." I fingered the tether hanging from my falcon. "We do not have the men for such a task."

"We do not," he admitted, "but the peoples of these lands do."

He interested me. Perhaps there was some iron in his soul after all. "Only the Hodenosaunee, the Long House nations, can help you," I said, "and I do not know if they will. The Inglistanis pose no threat to the power of the Long House."

"Michel told me we have a treaty with that people."

"We have an agreement with the Ganeagaono, who are one of their five nations. Once the Long House People fought among themselves, until their great chiefs Deganawida and Hayawatha united them. They are powerful enough now to ignore the Inglistanis."

Yesuntai gazed at the bird that clutched his gauntleted wrist. "What if they believed the Inglistanis might move against them?"

"They might act," I replied. "The Hodenosaunee have no treaties with that people. But they might think they have something to gain from the Inglistani presence. We have never given firearms to the people here, but the Inglistanis do so when they think it's to their advantage. By making war on the Inglistani settlements, you might only drive them into an alliance with the Long House and its subject tribes, one that might threaten us."

"We must strike hard and exterminate the lot," Yesuntai muttered. "Then we must make certain that no more of the wretches ever set foot on these shores."

"You will need the Long House People to do it."

"I must do it, one way or another. The Khan my father has made his will known. I have his orders, marked with his seal. He will take Inglistan, and we will destroy its outposts here. There can be no peace with those who have not submitted to us—the Yasa commands it. Inglistan has not submitted, so it will be forced to bow."

I was thinking that Sukegei Khan worried too much over that pack of island-dwellers. Surely Hispania, even with a brother Khan ruling there, was more of a threat to him than Inglistan. I had heard many tales of the splendor of Suleiman Khan's court, of slaves and gold that streamed to Granada and Córdoba from the continent to our south, of lands taken by the Hispanic Khan's conquistadors. The Hispanians were as fervent in spreading their faith as in seizing loot. In little more than sixty years, it was said that as many mosques stood in the Aztec capital of Tenochtitlan as in Córdoba itself. Suleiman Khan, with African kings as vassals and conquests in this new world, dreamed of being the greatest of the European Khans. How easy it had been for him to allow us settlements in the north while he claimed the richer lands to the south.

But I was a Bahadur of Yeke Geren, who knew only what others told me of Europe. My Khanate was a land I barely remembered, and our ancient Mongol homeland no more than a setting for legends and tales told by travelers. The Ejens of the Altan Uruk, the descendants of Genghis Khan, still sent their tribute to Karakorum, but the bonds of our Yasa, the laws the greatest of men had given us, rested more lightly on their shoulders. They might bow to the Kha-Khan of our homeland, but many of the Khans ruled lands greater than his. A time might come when the Khans of the west would break their remaining ties to the east.

"Europe!" I cleared my throat. "Sometimes I wonder what our Khans will do when all their enemies are vanquished."

Yesuntai shook his head. "I will say this—my ancestor Genghis Khan would have wondered at what we are now. I have known Noyans who go no farther to hunt than the parks around their dwellings, and others who prefer brocades and perfumed lace to a sheepskin coat and felt boots. Europe has weakened us. Some think as I do, that we should become what we were, but there is little chance of that there."

Snow was sifting from the sky. I urged my horse on; Yesuntai kept near me.

By the time we reached my circle of houses, the falling snow had become a curtain veiling all but the nearest dwellings from our sight. Courtesy required that I offer Yesuntai a meal, and a place to sleep if the snow continued to fall. He accepted my hospitality readily; I suspected there was more he wanted to ask me.

We halted at the dwelling next to mine. Except for a horse-drawn wagon carrying a wine merchant's barrels, the winding roads were empty. I shouted to my servants; two boys hurried outside to take the peregrines and our game from us. A shadowy form stirred near the dwelling. I squinted, then recognized one of my Manhatan servants. He lay in the snow, his hands around a bottle.

Anger welled inside me. I told one of the boys to get the Manhatan to his house, then went after the wagon. The driver slowed to a stop as I reached him. I seized his collar and dragged him from his seat.

He cursed as he sprawled in the snow. "I warned you before," I said. "You are not to bring your wine here."

He struggled to his feet, clutching his hat. "To your Manhatans, Bahadur—that's what you said. I was passing by, and thought others among your households might have need of some refreshment. Is it my fault if your natives entreat me for—"

I raised my whip. "You had one warning," I said. "This is the last I shall give you."

"You have no reason—"

"Come back to my circle, Gérard, and I'll take this whip to you. If you are fortunate enough to survive that beating—"

"You cannot stop their cravings, Bahadur." He glared up at me with his pale eyes. "You cannot keep them from seeking me out elsewhere."

"I will not make it easier for them to poison themselves." I flourished the whip; he backed away from me. "Leave."

He waded through the snow to his wagon. I rode back to my dwelling. Yesuntai had tied his horse to a post; he was silent as I unsaddled my mount.

I led him inside. Elgigetei greeted us; she was alone, and my wife's glazed eyes and slurred speech told me that she had been drinking. Yesuntai and I sat on a bench in the back of the house, just beyond the hearth fire. Elgigetei brought us wine and fish soup. I waited for her to take food for herself and to join us, but she settled on the floor near our son's cradle to work at a hide. Her mother had been a Manhatan woman, and Elgigetei's brown face and thick black braids had reminded me of Dasiyu, the wife I had left among the Ganeagaono. I had thought her beautiful once, but Elgigetei had the weaknesses of the Manhatan people, the laziness, the craving for drink that had wasted so many of them. She scraped at her hide listlessly, then leaned over Ajiragha's cradle to murmur to our son in the Manhatan tongue. I had never bothered to learn the language. It was useless to master the speech of a people who would soon not exist.

"You are welcome to stay here tonight," I said to the Noyan.

"I am grateful for this snowstorm," he murmured. "It will give us more time to talk. I have much to ask you still about the Hiroquois." He leaned back against the wall. "In Khanbalik, there are scholars in the Khitan Khan's court who believe that the forefathers of the people in these lands came here long ago from the regions north of Khitai, perhaps even from our ancestral grounds. These scholars claim that once a land bridge far to the north linked this land to Sibir. So I was told by travelers who spoke to those learned men."

"It is an intriguing notion, Noyan."

"If such people carry the seed of our ancestors, there may be greatness in them."

I sipped my wine. "But of course there can be no people as great as we Mongols."

"Greatness may slip from our grasp. Koko Mongke Tengri meant for us to rule the world, yet we may lose the strength to hold it."

I made a sign as he invoked the name of our ancient God, then bowed my head. Yesuntai lifted his brows. "I thought you were a Christian."

"I was baptized," I said. "I have prayed in other ways since then. The Long House People call God Hawenneyu, the Great Spirit, but He is Tengri by another name. It matters not how a man prays."

"That is true, but many who follow the cross or the crescent believe otherwise." Yesuntai sighed. "Long ago, my ancestor Genghis Khan thought of making the world our pasturage, but then learned that he could not rule it without mastering the ways of the lands he had won. Now those ways are mastering us." He gazed at me with his restless dark eyes. "When we have slaughtered the Inglistanis here, more of our people will come to settle these lands. In time, we may have to subdue those we call our friends. More will be claimed here for our Khanate and, if all goes well, my father's sons and grandsons will have more of the wealth this land offers. Our priests will come, itching to spread the word of Christ among the natives, and traders will bargain for what we do not take outright. Do you find this a pleasing prospect?"

"I must serve my Khan," I replied. His eyes narrowed, and I sensed that he saw my true thoughts. There were still times when I dreamed of abandoning what I had here and vanishing into the northern forests.

He said, "An ocean lies between us and Europe. It may become easier for those who are here to forget the Khanate."

"Perhaps."

"I am told," Yesuntai said then, "that you lived for some time among the Long House People."

My throat tightened. "I dwelled with the Ganeagaono, the Owners of the Flint. Perhaps Michel Bahadur told you the story."

"Only that you lived among them."

"It is a long tale, but I will try to make it shorter. My father and I came to these shores soon after we found this island—we were in one of the ships that followed the first expedition. Cheren Noyan had secured Yeke Geren by then. I was nine when we arrived, my father's youngest son. We came alone, without my mother or his second wife—he was hoping to return to Calais a richer man." I recalled little of that journey, only that the sight of the vast white-capped sea terrified me whenever I was well enough to go up on deck to help the men watch for Inglistani pirates. Perhaps Yesuntai had also trembled at being adrift on that watery plain, but I did not wish to speak of my fear to him.

"A year after we got here," I went on, "Cheren Noyan sent an expedition upriver. Hendrick, one of our Dutch sailors, captained the ship. He was to map the river and see how far it ran, whether it might offer us a passageway west. My father was ordered to join the expedition, and brought me along. I was grateful for the chance to be with the men."

Yesuntai nodded. "As any boy would be."

"We went north until we came to the region the Ganeagaono call Skanechtade—Beyond the Openings—and anchored there. We knew that the Flint People were fierce warriors. The people to the south of their lands lived in terror of them, and have given them the name of Mohawk, the Eaters of Men's Flesh, but we had been told the Owners of the Flint would welcome strangers who came to them in peace. Hendrick thought it wise to secure a treaty with them before going farther, and having an agreement with the Ganeagaono would also give us a bond with the other four nations of the Long House."

I swallowed more wine. Yesuntai was still, but his eyes kept searching me. He would want to know what sort of man I was before entrusting himself to me, but I still knew little about him. I felt somehow that he wanted more than allies in a campaign against the Inglistanis, but pushed that notion aside.

"Some of us," I said, "rowed to shore in our longboats. A few Ganeagaono warriors had spied us, and we made ourselves understood with hand gestures. They took us to their village. Everyone there greeted us warmly, and opened their houses to us. All might have gone well, but after we ate their food, our men offered them wine. We should have known better, after seeing what strong drink could do to the Manhatan. The Flint People have no head for wine, and our men would have done well to stay sober."

I stared at the earthen floor and was silent for a time. "I am not certain how it happened," I continued at last, "but our meeting ended in violence. A few of our men died with tomahawks in their heads. Most of the others fled to the boats. You may call them cowards for that, but to see a man of the Flint People in the throes of drunkenness would terrify the bravest of soldiers. They were wild—the wine is poison to them. They were not like the Manhatan, who grow sleepy and calmly trade even their own children for strong drink."

"Go on," Yesuntai said.

"My father and I were among those who did not escape. The Ganeagaono had lost men during the brawl, and now saw us as enemies. They began their tortures. They assailed my father and his comrades with fire and whips—they cut pieces of flesh from them, dining on them while their captives still lived, and tore the nails from their hands with hot pincers. My father bore his torment bravely, but the others did not behave as Mongols should, and their deaths were not glorious." I closed my eyes for a moment, remembering the sound of their shrieks when the children had thrown burning coals on their staked bodies. I had not known then whom I hated more, the men for losing their courage or the children for their cruelty.

"I am sorry to hear it," Yesuntai said.

"Only my father and I were left alive. They forced us to run through the village while rows of people struck at us with whips and heavy sticks. The men went at us first, then the women, and after them the children. I did not understand then that they were honoring us by doing this. My father's wounds robbed him of life, but I survived the beatings, and it was then that the Ganeagaono made me one of them. I was taken to a house, given to a woman who admired the courage my father had shown during the torture, and was made a member of their Deer Clan. My foster mother gave me the name of Senadondo."

"And after that?" he asked.

"Another ship came upriver not long after. We expected a war party, but Cheren Noyan was wise enough to send envoys out from the ship to seek peace. Because I knew the Ganeagaono tongue by then, I was useful as an interpreter. The envoys begged forgiveness, saying that their men were to blame for violating the hospitality of the Flint People, so all went well. In the years to follow, I often dealt with the traders who came to us offering cloth and iron for furs and beaver pelts—they did not make the mistake of bringing wine again. After a time, I saw that I might be of more use to both my own people and my adoptive brothers if I returned to Yeke Geren. The Ganeagaono said farewell to me and sent me back with many gifts."

Speaking of the past made me long for the northern woods, for the spirits that sang in the mountain pines, for the sight of long houses and fields of corn, for Dasiyu, who had refused to come with me or to let our son depart with me. The boy belonged to her Wolf Clan, not to mine;

his destiny was linked to hers. It had always been that way among the Long House People. I had promised to return, and she had called my promise a lie. Her last words to me were a curse.

"I might almost think," Yesuntai said, "that you wish you were among those people now."

"Is that so strange, Noyan?"

"They killed your father, and brought you much suffering."

"We brought that fate upon ourselves. If my father's spirit had not flown from him, they would have let him live, and honored him as one of their own. I lost everything I knew, but from the time the Ganeagaono adopted me, they treated me only with kindness and respect. Do you understand?"

"I think I do. The children of many who fought against us now serve us. Yet you chose to return here, Jirandai."

"We had a treaty. The Flint people do not forget their treaties—they are marked with the strings of beads they call wampum, which their wise men always have in their keeping." Even as I spoke, I wondered if, in the end, my exile would prove useless.

How full of pride and hope I had been, thinking that my efforts would preserve the peace between this outpost of the Khanate and the people I had come to love. I would be, so I believed, the voice of the Ganeagaono in the Mongol councils. But my voice was often ignored, and I had finally seen what lay behind Cheren Noyan's offer of peace. A treaty would give his men time to learn more about the Long House, and any weaknesses that could later be exploited. Eventually, more soldiers would come to wrest more of these lands from the natives. Our Khan's minions might eventually settle the lands to the north, and make the Long House People as wretched as the Manhatans.

"I came back," I continued, "so that our Noyans and Bahadurs would remember the promises recorded on the belts we exchanged with the Owners of the Flint. We swore peace, and I am the pledge of that peace, for the Ganeagaono promised that they would be bound to us in friendship for as long as I remained both their brother and the Khan's servant. That promise lives here." I struck my chest. "But some of our people are not so mindful of our promises."

Yesuntai nodded. "It is the European influence, Bahadur. Our ancestors kept the oaths they swore, and despised liars, but the Europeans twist words and often call lies the truth." He took a breath. "I will speak freely to you, Jirandai Bahadur. I have not come here only to rid this land of Inglistanis. Europe is filled with people who bow to the Khans and yet dream of escaping our yoke. I would hate to see them slip from their bonds on these shores. Destroying the Inglistani settlements will show others that they will find no refuge here."

"I can agree with such a mission," I said.

"And your forest brothers will be rid of a potential enemy."

"Yes."

"Will you lead me to them? Will you speak my words to them and ask them to join us in this war?"

"You may command me to do so, Noyan," I said.

He shifted his weight on the bench. "I would rather have your assent. I have always found that those who freely offer me their oaths serve me better than those pressed into service, and I imagine you have your own reasons for wishing to go north."

"I shall go with you, and willingly. You will need other men, Noyan. Some in Yeke Geren have lost their discipline and might not do well in the northern forests. They wallow in the few pleasures this place offers, and mutter that their Khan has forgotten them."

"Then I will leave it to you to find good men who lust for battle. I can trust those whom I brought with me."

I took out my pipe, tapped tobacco into it from my pouch, lit it, and held it out to Yesuntai. "Will you smoke a pipe with me? We should mark our coming expedition with some ceremony."

He accepted the pipe, drew in some smoke, then choked and gasped for air before composing himself. Outside, I heard a man, a sailor perhaps, and drunk from the sound of him, call out to another man in Frankish. What purpose could a man find here, waiting for yet another ship to arrive with news from the Khanate and baubles to trade with the natives for the pelts, birds, animals, and plants the Khan's court craved? I was not the only man who thought of deserting Yeke Geren.

"I look forward to our journey," Yesuntai said, "and to seeing what lies beyond this encampment." He smiled as he passed the pipe to me.

That spring, with forty of Yesuntai's soldiers and twenty more men I had chosen, we sailed upriver.

2

The Ganeagaono of Skanechtade welcomed us with food. They crowded around us as we went from house to house, never leaving us alone even when we went to relieve ourselves. Several men of my Deer Clan came to meet me, urging more of the game and dried fish their women had prepared upon me and my comrades. By the time we finished our feast, more people had arrived from the outlying houses of the village to listen to our words.

Yesuntai left it to me to urge the war we wanted. After I was empty of eloquence, we waited in the long house set aside for our men. If the men of Skanechtade chose the warpath, they would gather war parties and send runners to the other villages of the Ganeagaono to persuade more warriors to join us.

I had spoken the truth to the people of Skanechtade. Deceit was not possible with the Ganeagaono, and especially not for me. I was still their brother, even after all the years I thought of as my exile. The Ganeagaono would know I could not lie to them; this war would serve them as well as us. Whoever was not at peace with them was their enemy. In that, they were much like us. A people who might threaten their domain as well as ours would be banished from the shores of this land.

Yet my doubts had grown, not about our mission, but of what might come afterward. More of our people would cross the ocean, and the Bahadurs who followed us to Yeke Geren might dream of subduing the nations we now called our friends. There could be no peace with those who did not submit to us in the end, and I did not believe the Ganeagaono and the other nations of the Long House would ever swear an oath to our Khan.

I had dwelled on such thoughts as we sailed north, following the great river that led to Skanechtade. By the time we rowed away from the ship in our longboats, I had made my decision. I would do what I could to aid Yesuntai, but whatever the outcome of our mission, I would not return to Yeke Geren. My place was with the Ganeagaono, who had granted me my life.

"Jirandai," Yesuntai Noyan said softly. He sat in the back of the long house, his back against the wall, his face hidden in shadows; I had thought he was asleep. "What do you think they will do?"

"A few of the young chiefs want to join us. That I saw when I finished my speech." Some of our men glanced toward me; most were sleeping on the benches that lined the walls. "We will have a few bands, at least."

"A few bands are useless to me," Yesuntai muttered. "A raid would only provoke our enemies. I must have enough men to destroy them."

"I have done what I can," I replied. "We can only hope my words have moved them."

Among the Ganeagaono, those who wanted war had to convince others to follow them. The sachems who ruled their councils had no power to lead in war; I had explained that to Yesuntai. It was up to the chiefs and other warriors seeking glory to assemble war parties, but a sign that a sachem favored our enterprise might persuade many to join us. I had watched the sachems during my speech; my son was among them. His dark eyes had not betrayed any of his thoughts.

"I saw how you spoke, Jirandai," Yesuntai said, "and felt the power in your words, even if I did not understand them. I do not believe we will fail."

"May it be so, Noyan." I thought then of the time I had traveled west with my adoptive father along the great trail that runs to the lands of the Nundawaono. There, among the Western Gatekeepers of the Long House nations, I had first heard the tale of the great serpent brought down by the thunderbolts of Heno, spirit of storms and rain. In his death throes, the serpent had torn the land asunder and created the mighty falls into which the rapids of the Neahga River flowed. My foster father had doubts about the story's ending, although he did not say so to our hosts. He had stood on a cliff near the falls and seen a rainbow arching above the tumultuous waters; he had heard the steady sound of the torrent and felt the force of the wind that never died. He believed that the serpent was not dead, but only sleeping, and might rise to ravage the land again.

Something in Yesuntai made me think of that serpent. When he was still, his eyes darted restlessly, and when he slept, his body was tense, ready to rouse itself at the slightest disturbance. Something was coiled inside him, sleeping but ready to wake.

Voices murmured beyond the doorway to my right. Some of the Ganeagaono were still outside. A young man in a deerskin kilt and beaded belt entered, then gestured at me.

"You," he said, "he who is called Senadondo." I lifted my head at the sound of the name his people had given to me. "I ask you to come with me," he continued in his own tongue.

I got to my feet and turned to Yesuntai. "It seems someone wishes to speak to me."

He waved a hand. "Then you must go."

"Perhaps some of the men want to hear more of our plans."

"Or perhaps a family you left behind wishes to welcome you home."

I narrowed my eyes as I left. The Noyan had heard nothing from me about my wife and son, but he knew I had returned to Yeke Geren as a man. He might have guessed I had left a woman here.

The man who had come for me led me past clusters of houses. Although it was nearly midnight, with only a sliver of moon to light our way, people were still awake; I heard them murmuring beyond the open doors. A band of children trailed us. Whenever I slowed, they crowded around me to touch my long coat or to pull at my silk tunic.

We halted in front of a long house large enough for three families. The sign of the Wolf Clan was painted on the door. The man motioned to me to go inside, then led the children away.

At first, I thought the house was empty, then heard a whisper near the back. Three banked fires glowed in the central space between the house's bark partitions. I called out a greeting; as I passed the last partition, I turned to my right and saw who was waiting for me.

My son wore his headdress, a woven cap from which a single large eagle feather jutted from a cluster of smaller feathers. Braided bands with beads adorned his bare arms; rattles hung from his belt. My wife wore a deerskin cloak over a dress decorated with beads. Even in the shadows beyond the fire, I saw the strands of silver in her dark hair.

"Dasiyu," I whispered, then turned to my son. "Teyendanaga."

He shook his head slightly. "You forget—I am the sachem Sohaewahah now." He gestured at one of the blankets that covered the floor; I sat down.

"I hoped you would come back," Dasiyu said. "I wished for it, yet prayed that you would not."

"Mother," our son murmured. She pushed a bowl of hommony toward me, then sat back on her heels.

"I wanted to come to you right away," I said. "I did not know if you were here. When the men of my own clan greeted me, I feared what they might say if I asked about you, so kept silent. I searched the crowd for you when I was speaking."

"I was there," Dasiyu said, "sitting behind the sachems among the women. Your eyes are failing you."

I suspected that she had concealed herself behind others. "I thought you might have another husband by now."

"I have never divorced you." Her face was much the same, only lightly marked with lines. I thought of how I must look to her, leather-faced and broader in the belly, softened by the years in Yeke Geren. "I have never placed the few belongings you left with me outside my door. You are still my husband, Senadondo, but it is Sohaewahah who asked you to come to this house, not I."

My son held up his hand. "I knew you would return to us, my father. I saw it in my vision. It is of that vision that I wish to speak now."

That a vision might have come to him, I did not doubt. Many spirits lived in these lands, and the Ganeagaono, as do all wise men, trust their dreams. But evil spirits can deceive men, and even the wise can fail to understand what the spirits tell them.

"I would hear of your vision," I said.

"Two summers past, not long after I became sohaewahah, I fell ill with a fever. My body fought it, but even after it passed, I could not rise from my bed. It was then, after the fever was gone, that I had my vision and knew it to be truth." He gazed directly at me, his eyes steady. "Beyond my doorway, I saw a great light, and then three men entered my dwelling. One carried a branch, another a red tomahawk, and the third bore the shorter bow and the firestick that are your people's weapons. The man holding the branch spoke, and I knew that Hawenneyu was speaking to me through him. He told me of a storm gathering in the east, over the Ojikhadagega, the great ocean your people crossed, and said that it threatened all the nations of the Long House. He told me that some of those who might offer us peace would bring only the peace of death. Yet his words did not frighten me, for he went on to say that my father would return to me, and bring a brother to my side."

He glanced at his mother, then looked back at me. "My father and the brother he brought to me," he continued, "would help us stand against the coming storm—this was the Great Spirit's promise. When my vision passed, I was able to rise. I left my house and went through the village, telling everyone of what I had been shown. Now you are here, and the people remember what my vision foretold, and yet I see no brother."

"You have a brother," I said, thinking of Ajiragha. "I left him in Yeke Geren."

"But he is not here at my side, as my vision promised."

"He is only an infant, and the Inglistanis are the storm that threatens you. More of them will cross the Great Salt Water."

"A war against them would cost us many men. We might trade with them, as we do with you. Peace is what we have always desired—war is only our way to prove our courage and to bring that peace about. You should know that, having been one of us."

"The Inglistanis will make false promises, and when more of them come, even the Long House may fall before their soldiers. You have no treaties with the Inglistanis, so you are in a state of war with them now. Two of the spirits who came to you bore weapons—the Great Spirit means for you to make war."

"But against whom?" Dasiyu asked. She leaned forward and shook her fist. "Perhaps those who are on your island of Ganono are the storm that will come upon us, after we are weakened by battle with the pale-faced people you hate."

"Foolish woman," I muttered, "I am one of you. Would I come here to betray you?" Despite my words, she reminded me of my own doubts.

"You should not have come back," she said. "Whenever I dreamed of your return, I saw you alone, not with others seeking to use us for their own purposes. Look at you—there is nothing of the Ganeagaono left in you. You speak our words, but your garments and your companions show where your true loyalty lies."

"You are wrong." I stared at her; she did not look away. "I have never forgotten my brothers here."

"You come to spy on us. When you have fought with our warriors in this battle, you will see our weaknesses more clearly, the ways in which we might be defeated, and we will not be able to use your pale-faced enemies against you."

"Is this what you have been saying to the other women? Have you gone before the men to speak against this war?"

Dasiyu drew in her breath; our son clutched her wrist. "You've said enough, Mother," he whispered. "I believe what he says. My vision told me he would come, and the spirits held the weapons of war. Perhaps my brother is meant to join me later." He got to his feet. "I go now to add my voice to the councils. It may be that I can persuade those who waver. If we are to follow the warpath now, I will set aside my office to fight with you."

He left us before I could speak. "You'll have your war," Dasiyu said. "The other sachems will listen to my son, and ask him to speak for them to the people. The wise old women will heed his words, because they chose him for his position."

"This war will serve you."

She scowled, then pushed the bowl of hommony toward me. "You insult me by leaving my food untouched."

I ate some of the dried corn, then set the bowl down. "Dasiyu, I did not come here only to speak of war. I swore an oath to myself that, when this campaign ends, I will live among you again."

"And am I to rejoice over that?"

"Cursed woman, anything I do would stoke your rage. I went back to speak for the Long House in our councils. I asked you to come with me, and you refused."

"I would have had to abandon my clan. My son would never have been chosen as a sachem then. You would not be promising to stay with us unless you believed you have failed as our voice."

Even after the years apart, she saw what lay inside me. "Whatever comes," I said, "my place is here."

She said nothing for a long time. The warmth inside the long house was growing oppressive. I opened my coat, then took off my headband to mop my brow.

"Look at you," she said, leaning toward me to touch the braids coiled behind my ears. Her hand brushed the top of my shaven head lightly. "You had such a fine scalplock— how could you have given it up?" She poked at my mustache. "I do not understand why a man would want hair over his lip." She fingered the fabric of my tunic. "And this—a woman might wear such a garment. I used to admire you so when I watched you dance. You were the shortest of the men, but no man here had such strong arms and broad shoulders, and now you hide them under these clothes."

I drew her to me. She was not as she had been, nor was I; once, every moment in her arms had only fed the flames inside me. Our fires were banked now, the fever gone, but her welcoming warmth remained.

"You have changed in another way, Senadondo," she said afterward. "You are not so nasty as you were."

"I am no longer a young man, Dasiyu. I must make the most of what moments I am given."

She pulled a blanket over us. I held her until she was asleep; she nestled against me as she once had, her cheek against my shoulder, a leg looped around mine. I did not know how to keep my promise to stay with her. Yesuntai might want a spy among the Flint People when this campaign was concluded; he might believe I was his man for the task.

I slept uneasily. A war whoop awakened me at dawn. I slipped away from my wife, pulled on my trousers, and went to the door.

A young chief was running through the village. Rattles were bound to his knees with leather bands, and he held a red tomahawk; beads of black wampum dangled from his weapon. He halted in front of the war post, lifted his arm, and embedded the tomahawk in the painted wood. He began to dance, and other men raced toward him, until it seemed most of the village's warriors had enlisted in the war.

They danced, bodies bent from the waist, arms lifting as if to strike enemies, hands out to ward off attack. Their feet beat against the ground as drums throbbed. I saw Yesuntai then; he walked toward them, his head thrown back, a bow in one hand. I stepped from the doorway, felt my heels drumming against the earth, and joined the dancers.

3

Yesuntai, a Khan's son, was used to absolute obedience. The Ganeagaono, following the custom of all the Long House People, would obey any war chiefs in whom they had confidence. I had warned Yesuntai that no chief could command the Flint People to join in this war, and that even the women were free to offer their opinions of the venture.

"So be it," the young Noyan had said to that. "Our own women were fierce and brave before they were softened by other ways, and my ancestor Bortai Khatun often advised her husband Genghis Khan, although even that great lady would not have dared to address a war kuriltai. If these women are as formidable as you say, then they must have bred brave sons." I was grateful for his tolerance.

But the people of Skanechtade had agreed to join us, and soon their messengers returned from other villages with word that chiefs in every Ganeagaono settlement had agreed to go on the warpath. My son had advised us to follow the custom of the Hodenosaunee when all of their nations fought in a common war, and to choose two supreme commanders so that there would be unanimity in all decisions. Yesuntai, it was agreed, would command, since he had proposed this war, and Aroniateka, a cousin of my son's, would be Yesuntai's equal. Aroniateka, happily, was a man avid to learn a new way of warfare.

This was essential to our purpose, since to have any chance against the Inglistanis, the Ganeagaono could not fight in their usual fashion. The Long House People were still new to organized campaigns with many warriors, and most of their battles had been little more than raids by small parties. Their men were used to war, which, along with the hunt, was their favorite pursuit, but this war would be more than a ritual test of valor.

The Flint People had acquired horses from us in trade, but had never used them in warfare. Their warriors moved so rapidly on foot through the forests that mounts would only slow their progress. We would have to travel on foot, and take any horses we might need later from the Inglistania. The men I had chosen in Yeke Geren had hunted and traded with the Hodenosaunee, and were used to their ways. Those Yesuntai had brought were veterans of European campaigns, but willing to adapt.

The whoops of Skanechtade's warriors echoed through the village as they danced. The women busied themselves making moccasins and preparing provisions for their men. Runners moved between villages with the orders of our two commanders and returned with promises that the other war parties would follow them. Yesuntai would have preferred more time for planning, to send out more scouts before we left Ganeagaono territory, but we had little time. War had been declared, and our allies were impatient to fight. We needed a swift victory over our enemy. If we did not defeat the Inglistanis by late autumn, the Ganeagaono, their honor satisfied by whatever they had won by then, might abandon us.

A chill remained in the early spring air, but most of the Ganeagaono men had shed the cloaks and blankets that covered their upper bodies in winter. Our Mongols followed their example and stripped to the waist, and I advised Yesuntai's men to trade their felt boots for moccasins. Dasiyu gave me a kilt and a pair of deerskin moccasins; I easily gave up my Mongol tunic and trousers for the garb I had once worn.

Eight days after we had come to Skanechtade, the warriors performed their last war dance. Men streamed from the village toward the river; Dasiyu followed me to the high wall that surrounded the long houses and handed me dried meat and a pouch of corn flour mixed with maple sugar.

"I will come back," I said, "when this war is over."

"If you have victory, I shall welcome you." She gripped my arms for a moment, then let go. "If you suffer defeat, if you and your chief lead our men only to ruin, your belongings will be outside my door."

"We will win," I said.

The lines around her lids deepened as she narrowed her eyes. "See that you do, Senadondo."

We crossed to the eastern side of the great river, then moved south. Some of our scouts had explored these oak-covered hills, and Yesuntai had planned his campaign with the aid of Inglistani maps our soldiers had taken during a raid the year before. We would travel south, then move east through the Mahican lands, keeping to the north of the enemy settlements. Our forces would remain divided during the journey, so as not to alert the Inglistanis. Plymouth, the easternmost enemy settlement, overlooked an ocean bay. When Plymouth was taken, we would move south toward another great bay and the town called Newport. This settlement lay on an island at the mouth of the bay, and we would advance on it from the east. Any who escaped us would be forced to flee west toward Charlestown.

A wise commander always allows his enemy a retreat, since desperate defenders can cost a general many men, while a sweep by one wing of his force can pick off retreating soldiers. We would drive the Inglistanis west. When Charlestown fell, the survivors would have to run to the settlement they called New Haven. When New Haven was crushed, only New London, their westernmost town, would remain, and from there the Inglistanis could flee only to territory controlled by us.

At some point, the enemy was likely to sue for peace, but there could be no peace with the Inglistanis. Our allies and we were agreed; this would be a war of extermination.

These were our plans, but obstacles lay ahead. The Mahicans would present no problem; as payers of tribute to the Long House, they would allow us safe passage through their lands. But the Wampanoag people dwelled in the east, and the Pequots controlled the trails that would lead us south to Newport. Both groups feared the Flint People and had treaties with the Inglistanis. Our men would be more than a match for theirs if the Wampanoags and Pequots fought in defense of their pale-faced friends. But such a battle would cost us warriors, and a prolonged battle for Plymouth would endanger our entire strategy.

Our forces remained divided as we moved. Speed is one of a soldier's greatest allies, so we satisfied our hunger with our meager provisions and did not stop to hunt. At night, when we rested, Ganeagaono warriors marked the trees with a record of our numbers and movements, and we halted along the way to read the markings others had left for us. Yesuntai kept me at his side. I was teaching him the Ganeagaono tongue, but he still needed me to speak his words to his fellow commander Aroniateka.

In three days, we came to a Mahican settlement, and alerted the people there with war cries. Their chiefs welcomed us outside their stockade, met with us, and complained bitterly about the Inglistanis, who they believed had designs on their lands. They had refrained from raids, not wanting to provoke the settlers, but younger Mahicans had chided the chiefs for their caution. After we spoke of our intentions, several of their men offered to join us. We had expected safe passage, but to have warriors from among them lifted our spirits even higher.

We turned east, and markings on tree trunks told us of other Mahicans that had joined our forces. Yesuntai, with his bowcase, quiver, and sword hanging from his belt, and his musket over his shoulder, moved as easily through the woods as my son in his kilt and moccasins. A bond was forming between them, and often they communicated silently with looks and gestures, not needing my words. Wampanoag territory lay ahead, yet Yesuntai's confidence was not dampened, nor was my son's. The Great Spirit our Ganeagaono brethren called Hawenneyu, and that Yesuntai knew under the name of Tengri, would guide them; I saw their faith in their dark eyes when they lifted their heads to gaze through the arching tree limbs at the sky. God would give them victory.

4

God was with us. Our scouts went out, and returned with a Wampanoag boy, a wretched creature with a pinched face and tattered kilt. A Mahican with us knew the boy's tongue, and we soon heard of the grief that had come to his village. Inglistani soldiers had attacked without warning only a few days ago, striking in the night while his people slept. The boy guessed that nearly two hundred of his Wampanoag people had died, cut down by swords and firesticks. He did not know how many others had managed to escape.

We mourned with him. Inwardly, I rejoiced. Perhaps the Inglistanis would not have raided their allies if they had known we were coming against them, but their rash act served our purpose. The deed was proof of their evil intentions; they would slaughter even their friends to claim what they wanted. Wampanoags who might have fought against us now welcomed us as their deliverers. Yesuntai consulted with Aroniateka, then gave his orders. The left wing of our force would strike at Plymouth, using the Wampanoags as a shield as they advanced.

The Wampanoags had acquired muskets from the Inglistanis, and now turned those weapons against their false friends. By the time my companions and I heard the cries of gulls above Plymouth's rocky shore, the flames of the dying town lighted our way. Charred hulls and blackened masts were sinking beneath the gray waters; warriors had struck at the harbor first, approaching it during the night in canoes to burn the ships and cut off any escape to the sea. Women leaped from rocks and were swallowed by waves; other Inglistanis fled from the town's burning walls, only to be cut down by our forces. There was no need to issue a command to take no prisoners, for the betrayed Wampanoags were in no mood to show mercy. They drove their captives into houses and set the dwellings ablaze; children became targets for their arrows.

The Flint People do not leave the spirits of their dead to wander. We painted the bodies of our dead comrades, then buried them with their weapons and the food they would need for the long journey ahead. Above the burial mound, the Ganeagaono freed birds they had captured to help bear the spirits of the fallen to Heaven, and set a fire to light their way.

From the ruins of Plymouth, we salvaged provisions, bolts of cloth, and cannons. Much of the booty was given to the Wampanoags, since they had suffered most of the casualties. Having achieved the swift victory we needed, we loaded the cannons onto ox-drawn wagons, then moved south.

5

The center and left wings of our forces came together as we entered Pequot territory. The right wing would move toward Charlestown while we struck at Newport.

Parties of warriors fanned out to strike at the farms that lay in our path. We met little resistance from the Pequots, and they soon understood that our battle was with the Inglistanis, not with them. After hearing of how Inglistani soldiers had massacred helpless Wampanoags, many of their warriors joined us, and led us to the farms of those they had once called friends. The night was brightened by the fires of burning houses and crops, and the silence shattered by the screams of the dying. We took what we needed, and burned the rest.

A few farmers escaped us. The tracks of their horses ran south; Newport would be warned. The enemy was likely to think that only enraged Wampanoags and Pequots were moving against them, but would surely send a force to meet us. We were still four days' distance from the lowlands that surrounded Newport's great bay when we caught sight of Inglistani soldiers.

They were massed together along the trail that led through the forest, marching stiffly in rows, their muskets ready. The Wampanoags fired upon them from the trees, then swept toward them as the air was filled with the sharp cracks of muskets and the whistling of arrows. Volleys of our metal-tipped arrows and the flint-headed arrows of the Ganeagaono flew toward the Inglistanis; enemy soldiers fell, opening up breaks in their line. Men knelt to load their weapons as others fired at us from behind them, and soon the ground was covered with the bodies of Wampanoag and Pequot warriors.

The people of these lands had never faced such carnage in battle, but their courage did not fail them. They climbed over the bodies of dead and wounded comrades to fight the enemy hand-to-hand. The soldiers, unable to fire at such close range, used their muskets as clubs and slashed at our allies with swords; men drenched in blood shrieked as they swung their tomahawks. I expected the Inglistanis to retreat, but they held their ground until the last of their men had fallen.

We mourned our dead. The Wampanoags and the Pequots, who had lost so many men, might have withdrawn and let us fight on alone. Aroniateka consulted with their war chiefs, then gave us their answer. They would march with us against Newport, and share in that victory.

6

Swift, early successes hearten any warrior for the efforts that lie ahead. We advanced on Newport fueled by the victories we had already won.

Summer was upon us as we approached the southeast end of the great bay. The island on which Newport stood lay to the west, across a narrow channel; the enemy had retreated behind the wooden walls of the town's stockade.

By day, we concealed ourselves amid the trees bordering the shore's wetlands. At night, the Ganeagaono cut down trees and collected rope we had gathered from Inglistani farms. Several of Yesuntai's older officers had experience in siege warfare; under their guidance, our allies quickly erected five catapults. In the early days of our greatness, we had possessed as little knowledge of sieges as the Flint People, but they seemed more than willing to master this new art. We did not want a long siege, but would be prepared for one if necessary. If Newport held out, we would leave a force behind and move on to our next objective.

When the moon showed her dark side to the earth, we brought out our catapults under cover of darkness and launched cannonballs at the five ships anchored in Newport's harbor, following them with missiles of rock packed with burning dried grass. The sails of the ships became torches, and more missiles caught enemy sailors as they leaped from the decks. The ships were sinking by the time we turned the catapults against the town's walls. The Inglistanis would have no escape by sea, and had lost the ships they might have used to bombard us.

We assaulted Newport for three days, until the Inglistani cannons fell silent. From the western side of the island, Inglistanis were soon fleeing in longboats toward Charlestown. There were many breaches in the stockade's walls, and few defenders left in the doomed town when we began to cross the channel in our canoes, but those who remained fought to the last man. Even after our men were inside the walls, Inglistanis shot at us from windows and roofs, and for every enemy we took there, two or three of our warriors were lost. We stripped enemy bodies, looted the buildings, then burned the town. Those hiding on the western side of the bay in Charlestown would see the great bonfire that would warn them of their fate.

The Wampanoags returned to their lands in the north. We left the Pequots to guard the bay and to see that no more Inglistani ships landed there. Our right wing would be advancing on Charlestown. We returned to the bay's eastern shore and went north, then turned west. A party of men bearing the weapons of war met us along one woodland trail, and led us to their chiefs. By then, the Narragansett people of the region had decided to throw in their lot with us.

7

Terror has always been a powerful weapon against enemies. Put enough fear into an enemy's heart, and victories can be won even before one meets him in the field. Thus it was during that summer of war. Charlestown fell, ten days after Newport. In spite of the surrender, we expected some of the survivors to hide in their houses and take their revenge when we entered the town. Instead, they gave up their weapons and waited passively for execution. Those I beheaded whispered prayers as they knelt and stretched their necks, unable to rouse themselves even to curse me. A few gathered enough courage to beg for their children's lives.

Yesuntai was merciful. He spared some women and children, those who looked most fearful, led them and a few old men to a longboat, and gave them a message in Frankish to deliver to those in New Haven. The message was much like the traditional one sent by Mongol Khans to their enemies: God has annihilated many of you for daring to stand against us. Submit to us, and serve us. When you see us massed against you, surrender and open your gates to us, for if you do not, God alone knows what will happen to you.

It was easy to imagine the effect this message would have on New Haven's defenders, if the Inglistanis we had spared survived their journey along the coast to deliver it. I did not believe that the Inglistanis would surrender immediately, but some among them would want to submit, and dissension would sap their spirit.

Most of our forces moved west, toward New Haven, followed by Inglistanis we had spared to carry canoes and haul cannons. Yesuntai had mastered enough of the Flint People's language to speak with Aroniateka, and left me with the rear guard. We would travel to the north of the main force, paralleling its path, and take the outlying farms.

Most of the farms we found were abandoned. We salvaged what we could and burned the rest. Days of searching empty farmhouses gave me time to reflect on how this campaign would affect my Ganeagaono brothers.

Their past battles had been for glory, to show their courage, to bring enemies to submission, and to capture prisoners who might, in the end, became brothers of the Long House. They had seen that unity among their Five Nations would make them stronger. Now we were teaching them that a victory over certain enemies was not enough, that sometimes only the extermination of that enemy would end the conflict, that total war might be necessary. Perhaps they would have learned that lesson without us, but their knowledge of this new art would change them, as surely as the serpent who beguiled the first man and woman changed man's nature. They might turn what they had learned against us.

Victories can hearten any soldier, but a respite from battle can also cause him to let down his guard. With a small party led by my son, I followed a rutted road toward one farm. From the trees beyond the field, where the corn was still only tall enough to reach to a man's waist, we spied a log dwelling, with smoke rising from its chimney. A white flag attached to a stick stood outside the door.

"They wish to surrender," I murmured to my son.

He shook his head. "The corn will hide us. We can get close enough to—"

"They are willing to give themselves up. Your men will have captives when they return to their homes. The Inglistanis have lost. Yesuntai will not object if we spare people willing to surrender without a fight."

My son said, "You are only weary of killing. My people say that a man weary of war is also weary of life."

"The people whose seed I carry have the same saying." He had spoken the truth. I was tiring of the war I had helped to bring about, thinking of what might follow it. "I shall speak to them."

"And we will guard your back," my son replied.

I left the trees and circled the field as the others crept through the corn. When I was several paces from the door, I held out my hands, palms up. "Come outside," I shouted in Frankish, hoping my words would be understood. "Show yourselves." I tensed, ready to fling myself to the ground if my son and his men suddenly attacked.

The door opened. A man with a graying beard left the house, followed by a young girl. A white cap hid her hair, but bright golden strands curled over her forehead. She gazed at me steadily with her blue eyes; I saw sorrow in her look, but no fear. A brave spirit, I thought, and felt a heaviness over my heart that might have been pity.

The man's Frankish was broken, but I was able to grasp his words. Whatever his people had done, he had always dealt fairly with the natives. He asked only to be left on his farm, to have his life and his family's spared.

"It cannot be," I told him. "You must leave this place. My brothers will decide your fate. That is all I can offer you, a chance for life away from here."

The man threw up an arm. The girl was darting toward the doorway when I saw a glint of metal beyond a window. A blow knocked the wind from me and threw me onto my back. I clutched at my ribs and felt blood seep from me as the air was filled with the sound of war whoops.

They had been lying in wait for us. Perhaps they would not have fired at me if I had granted the man his request; perhaps they had intended an ambush all along. I cursed myself for my weakness and pity. I would have another scar to remind me of Inglistani treachery and the cost of a moment's lack of vigilance, if I lived.

When I came to myself, the cabin was burning. A man knelt beside me, tending my wounds. Pain stabbed at me along my right side as I struggled to breathe. Two bodies in the gray clothes of Inglistani farmers lay outside the door. The Ganeagaono warriors danced as the flames leaped before them.

My son strode toward me, a scalp of long, golden hair dangling from his belt. "You cost me two men," he said. I moved my head from side to side, unable to speak. "I am sorry, Father. I think this war will be your last."

"I will live," I said.

"Yes, you will live, but I do not think you will fight again." He sighed. "Yet I must forgive you, for leading us to what your people call greatness." He lifted his head and cried out, echoing the war whoops of his men.

8

I was carried west on a wagon, my ribs covered with healing herbs and bound tightly with Inglistani cloth. A few men remained with me while the rest moved on toward New Haven. Every morning I woke expecting to find that they had abandoned me, only to find them seated around the fire.

A man's pride can be good medicine, and the disdain of others a goad. I was able to walk when Yesuntai sent a Bahadur to me with news of New Haven's surrender. Few soldiers were left in New Haven; most had fled to make a stand in New London. The young Noyan expected a fierce battle there, where the valor of the Inglistanis would be fired by desperation. He wanted me at his side as soon as possible.

The Bahadur had brought a spare horse for me. As we rode, he muttered of the difficulties Yesuntai now faced. Our Narragansett allies had remained behind in their territory, as we had expected, but the Mahicans, sated by glory, were already talking of returning to their lands. They thought they could wait until spring to continue the war; they did not understand. I wondered if the Ganeagaono had the stomach for a siege that might last the winter. They would be thinking of the coming Green Corn festival, of the need to lay in game for the colder weather and of the families that waited for them.

The oaks and maples gave way to more fields the Inglistanis had cleared and then abandoned. I smelled the salt of the ocean when we caught sight of Mongol and Mahican sentries outside a makeshift stockade. Yesuntai was camped to the east of New London, amid rows of Ganeagaono bark shelters. In the distance, behind a fog rolling in from the sea, I glimpsed the walls of the town.

Yesuntai and Aroniateka were outside one shelter, sitting at a fire with four other men. I heaved myself from my horse and walked toward them.

"Greetings, Jirandai," Yesuntai said in Mongol. "I am pleased to see you have recovered enough to take part in our final triumph."

I squatted by the fire and stretched out my hands. My ribs still pained me; I suspected they always would. "This is likely to be our hardest battle," I said.

"Then our glory will be all the greater when we win it." Yesuntai accepted a pipe from Aroniateka and drew in the smoke. "We will take New London before the leaves begin to turn."

"You plan to take it by storm?" I asked. "That will cost us."

"I must have it, whatever it costs. My fellow commander Aroniateka is equally impatient for this campaign to end, as I suspect you are, Bahadur." His eyes held the same look I had seen in my son's outside the burning farmhouse, that expression of pity mingled with contempt for an old man tired of war.

I slept uneasily that night, plagued by aching muscles strained by my ride and the pain of my wounds. The sound of intermittent thunder over the ocean woke me before dawn. I crept from my shelter to find other men outside, shadows in the mists, and then knew what we were hearing. The sound was that of cannons being fired from ships. The Inglistanis would turn the weapons of their ships against us, whatever the risk to the town. They would drive us back from the shore and force us to withdraw.

Yesuntai had left his shelter. He paced, his arms swinging as if he longed to sweep the fog away. I went to him, knowing how difficult it would be to persuade him to give up now. A man shouted in the distance, and another answered him with a whoop. Yesuntai would have to order a retreat, or see men slaughtered to no purpose. I could still hear the sound of cannons over the water, and wondered why the Inglistanis had sailed no closer to us.

A Mongol and a Ganeagaono warrior were pushing their way through knots of men. "Noyan!" the Mongol called out to Yesuntai. "From the shore I saw three ships—they fly the blue and white banners of your father! They have turned their weapons against the Inglistanis!"

The men near us cheered. Yesuntai's face was taut, his eyes slits. He turned to me; his hands trembled as he clasped my shoulders.

"It seems," he said softly, "that we will have to share our triumph."

The ships had sailed to New London from Yeke Geren. They bombarded the town as we advanced from the north and east, driving our remaining Inglistani captives before us against the outer stockade. The sight of these wretches, crying out in Inglistani to their comrades and dying under the assault of their own people's weapons, soon brought New London's commander to send up white flags.

Michel Bahadur left his ship to accept the surrender. We learned from him that our Khan had at last begun his war against Inglistan that spring; a ship had brought Michel the news only recently. By now, he was certain, the Khanate's armies would be marching on London itself. Michel had quickly seen that his duty lay in aiding us, now that we were openly at war with the Inglistanis.

Michel Bahadur praised Yesuntai lavishly as they embraced in the square of the defeated town. He spoke of our courage, but in words that made it seem that only Michel could have given us this final triumph. I listened in silence, my mind filled with harsh thoughts about men who claimed the victories of others for their own.

We celebrated the fall of New London with a feast in the town hall. Several Inglistani women who had survived the ravages of Michel's men stood behind them to fill their cups. There were few beauties among those wan and narrow-faced creatures, but Michel had claimed a pretty dark-haired girl for himself.

He sat among his men, Yesuntai at his side, drinking to our victory. He offered only a grudging tribute to the Ganeagaono and the Mahicans and said, with the air of a man granting a great favor, that they would be given their share of captives. I had chosen to sit with the Ganeagaono chiefs, as did most of the Mongols who had fought with us. Michel's men laughed when three of the Mahican chiefs slid under tables, overcome by the wine and whiskey. My son, watching them, refused to drink from his cup.

"Comrades!" Michel bellowed in Frankish. I brooded over my wine, wondering what sort of speech he would make now. "Our enemies have been crushed! I say now that in this place, where we defeated the last of the Inglistani settlers, we will make a new outpost of our Khanate! New London will become another great camp!"

I stiffened in shock. The men around Michel fell silent as they watched us. Yesuntai glanced in my direction; his fingers tightened around his cup.

"New London was to burn," Yesuntai said at last. "It was to suffer the fate of the other settlements."

"It will stand," Michel said, "to serve your father our Khan. Surely you cannot object to that, Noyan."

Yesuntai seemed about to speak, then sank back in his seat. Our Narragansett and Wampanoag allies would feel betrayed when they learned of Michel's intentions. The Bahadur's round, crafty face reminded me of everything I despised in Europeans—their greed, their treachery, their lies.

My son motioned to me, obviously expecting me to translate Michel's words. I leaned toward him. "Listen to me," I said softly in the tongue of the Flint People, "and do nothing rash when you hear what I must say now. The war chief who sailed here to aid us means to camp in this place. His people will live in this town we have won."

His hand darted toward his tomahawk, then fell. "So this is why we fought. I should have listened to Mother when she first spoke against you."

"I did not know what Michel Bahadur meant to do, but what happens here will not trouble the Long House."

"Until your people choose to forget another promise."

"I am one of you," I said.

"You are only an old man who allowed himself to be deceived." He looked away from me. "I know where honor lies, even if your people do not. I will not shame you before your chief by showing what I think of him. I will not break our treaty in this place." He turned to Aroniateka and whispered to him. The chiefs near them were still; only their eyes revealed their rage.

I had fulfilled my duty to my Khan. All that remained was to keep my promise to myself, and to Dasiyu.

9

I walked along New London's main street, searching for Yesuntai. Warriors stumbled along the cobblestones, intoxicated by drink, blind to the contemptuous stares of our Frankish and Dutch sailors. The whiskey Michel's men had given them from the looted stores had made them forget their villages and the tasks that awaited them there.

I found Yesuntai with a party of Ganeagaono warriors and a few Inglistani captives. "These comrades are leaving us," Yesuntai said. "You must say an eloquent farewell for me. I still lack the words to do it properly."

One of the men pulled at his scalplock. "It is time for us to go," he said in his language. Five Mahicans clutching bottles of whiskey staggered past us. "To see brave men in such a state sickens me."

I nodded in agreement. "My chief Yesuntai will forever remember your valor. May Grandfather Heno water your fields, the Three Sisters give you a great harvest, and the winter be filled with tales of your victories."

The warriors led their captives away; two of the smaller children wept as they clung to their mothers' hands. They would forget their tears and learn to love the People of the Long House, as I had.

"The rest should go home as well," I said to Yesuntai. "There is nothing for them here now."

"Perhaps not."

"They will have stories to tell of this war for many generations. Perhaps the tales of their exploits can make them forget how they were treated here. I wish to speak to you, Noyan."

"Good. I have been hoping for a chance to speak to you."

I led him along a side street to the house where Aroniateka and my son were quartered with some of their men. All of them were inside, sitting on blankets near the fireplace. At least these men had resisted the lure of drink, and had refused the bright baubles Michel's men had thrown to our warriors while claiming the greater share of the booty for themselves. They greeted us with restraint, and did not ask us to join them.

We seated ourselves at a table in the back of the room. "I swore an oath to you, Yesuntai Noyan," I said, "and ask you to free me from it now." I rested my elbows on the table. "I wish to return to Skanechtade, to my Ganeagaono brothers."

He leaned forward. "I expected you to ask for that."

"As for my wife Elgigetei and my son Ajiragha, I ask only that you accept them into your household. My wife will not miss me greatly, and perhaps you can see that Ajiragha does not forget his father. You were my comrade in arms, and I will not sneak away from your side in the night. You do not need me now. Even my son will tell you that I am a man who has outlived his taste for battle. You will lose nothing by letting me go."

"And what will you do," he said, "if my people forsake their treaties?"

"I think you know the answer to that."

"You told me of the treaty's words, that we and the Flint People would be at peace for as long as you were both their brother and the Khan's servant. You will no longer be our servant if you go back to Skanechtade."

"So you are ready to seize on that. If the men of Yeke Geren fail to renew their promises, that will show their true intentions. I had hoped that you—"

"Listen to me." Yesuntai's fingers closed around my wrist. "I have found my brothers in your son and Aroniateka, and among the brave men who fought with us. They are my brothers, not the rabble who came here under Michel's command."

"Those men serve your father the Khan."

"They serve themselves," he whispered, "and forget what we once were."

I shook my arm free of his grasp. He was silent for a while, then said, "Koko Mongke Tengri, the Eternal Blue Sky that covers all the world, promised us dominion over Etugen, the Earth. I told you of the wise men in Khitai who believe that the ancestors of the peoples in these lands once roamed our ancient homeland. I know now that what those scholars say is true. The people here are our long-lost brothers—they are more truly Mongol than men whose blood has been thinned by the ways of Europe. For them to rule here is in keeping with our destiny. They could make an ulus here, a nation as great as any we have known, one that might someday be a match for our Khanates."

I said, "You are speaking treason."

"I am speaking the truth. I have had a vision, Jirandai. The spirits have spoken to me and shown me two arcs closing in a great circle, joining those who have been so long separated. When the peoples of this land are one ulus, when they achieve the unity our ancestors found under Genghis Khan, then perhaps they will be the ones to bring the rest of the world under their sway. If the Khans in our domains cannot accept them as brothers, they may be forced to bow to them as conquerors." Yesuntai paused. "Are we to sweep the Inglistanis from these lands only so that more of those we rule can flood these shores? They will forget the Khanate, as our people are forgetting their old homeland. They will use the peoples of this land against one another in their own disputes, when they have forgotten their Khan and fall to fighting among themselves. I see what must be done to prevent that. You see it, too. We have one more battle to fight before you go back to Skanechtade."

I knew what he wanted. "How do you plan to take Yeke Geren?" I asked.

"We must have Michel's ships. My Mongols can man them. We also need the Ganeagaono." He gazed past me at the men seated by the fire. "You will speak my words to your son and Aroniateka, and then we will act—and soon. Your brothers will be free of all their enemies."

Yesuntai spoke of warring tribes on the other side of the world, tribes that had wasted themselves in battles with one another until the greatest of men had united them under his standard. He talked of a time long before that, when other tribes had left the mountains, forests, and steppes of their ancient homeland to seek new herds and territories, and of the northern land bridge they had followed to a new world. He spoke of a great people's destiny, of how God meant them to rule the world, and of those who, in the aftermath of their glory, were forgetting their purpose. In the lands they had conquered, they would eventually fall out among themselves; the great ulus of the Mongols would fracture into warring states. God would forsake them. Their brothers in this new world could reach for the realm that rightly belonged to them.

Aroniateka was the first to speak after I translated the Noyan's speech. "We have a treaty with your people," he said. "Do you ask us to break it?"

"We ask that you serve the son of our Khan, who is our rightful leader here," I replied. "Those who came here to claim our victory will take the lands we freed for themselves, and their greed will drive them north to yours. Michel Bahadur and the men of Yeke Geren have already broken the treaty in their hearts."

"I am a sachem," my son said, "and will take up my duties again when I am home. I know what is recorded on the belts of wampum our wise men have in their keeping. Our treaty binds us as long as my father Senadondo is our brother and the servant of his former people, as long as he is our voice among them."

"I found that many grew deaf to my voice," I said. "I will not go back to live in Yeke Geren. I have told my chief Yesuntai that I will live among the Owners of the Flint until the end of my days."

My son met Yesuntai's gaze. How alike their eyes were, as cold and dark as those of a serpent. "My dream told me that my father would bring me a brother," my son said. "I see my brother now, sitting before me." I knew then that he would bring the other chiefs to agree to our plans.

We secured the ships easily. Yesuntai's soldiers rowed out to the vessels; the few sailors left on board, suspecting nothing, were quickly overcome. Most of Michel's men were quartered in the Inglistani commander's house and the three nearest it; they were sleepy with drink when we struck. Michel and his officers were given an honorable death by strangulation, and some of the Dutch and Frankish sailors hastily offered their oaths to Yesuntai. The others were given to the Ganeagaono, to be tortured and then burned at the stake as we set New London ablaze.

I sailed with Yesuntai and his men. The Ganeagaono and the Mahicans who had remained with us went west on foot with their Inglistani captives. When we reached the narrow strait that separated Yeke Geren from the long island of Gawanasegeh, people gathered along the cliffs and the shore to watch us sail south toward the harbor. The ships anchored there had no chance to mount a resistance, and we lost only one of our vessels in the battle. By then, the Ganeagaono and Mahicans had crossed to the northern end of Yeke Geren in canoes, under cover of night, and secured the pastures there.

They might have withstood our assault. They might have waited us out, until our allies tired of the siege and the icy winds of winter forced us to withdraw to provision our ships. But too many in Yeke Geren had lost their fighting spirit, and others thought it better to throw in their lot with Yesuntai. They surrendered fourteen days later.

About half of the Mongol officers offered their oaths to Yesuntai; the rest were beheaded. Some of the Mahicans would remain in what was left of Yeke Geren, secure treaties with the tribes of Gawanasegeh and the smaller island to our southwest, and see that no more ships landed there. The people of the settlement were herded into roped enclosures. They would be distributed among the Ganeagaono and taken north, where the Flint People would decide which of them were worthy of adoption.

I searched among the captives for Elgigetei and Ajiragha. At last an old man told me that they had been taken by a fever only a few days before we attacked the harbor. I mourned for them, but perhaps it was just as well. My son might not have survived the journey north, and Dasiyu would never have accepted a second wife. I had the consolation of knowing that my deeds had not carried their deaths to them.

Clouds of migrating birds were darkening the skies when I went with Yesuntai to our two remaining ships. A mound of heads, those of the officers we had executed, sat on the slope leading down to the harbor, a monument to our victory and a warning to any who tried to land there.

The Noyan's men were waiting by the shore with the surviving Frankish and Dutch sailors. The ships were provisioned with what we could spare, the sailors ready to board. Men of the sea would be useless in the northern forests, and men of uncertain loyalties who scorned the ways of the Flint People would not be welcome there.

Yesuntai beckoned to a gray-haired captain. "This is my decree," he said. "You will sail east, and carry this message to my father." He gestured with a scroll. "I shall recite the message for you now: I will make a Khanate of this land, but it will not be sullied by those who would bring the sins of Europe to its shores. When an ulus has risen here, it will be the mighty nation of our long-lost brothers. Only then will the circle close and all our brothers be joined, and only if all the Khans accept the men of this land as their equals. It is then that we will truly rule the world, and if my brother Khans do not willingly join this ulus of the world to come, only God knows what will befall them."

"We cannot go back with such a message," the captain said. "Those words will cost us our heads."

"You dishonor my father by saying that. You are my emissaries, and no Khan would stain his hands with the blood of ambassadors." Yesuntai handed the scroll to the old man. "These are my words, marked with my seal. My father the Khan will know that I have carried out his orders, that the people of Inglistan will not set foot here again. He will also know that there is no need for his men to come here, since it is I who will secure this new Khanate." He narrowed his eyes. "If you do not wish to claim the Khan's reward for this message, then sail where you will and find what refuge you can. The Khan my father, and those who follow him to his throne, will learn of my destiny in time."

We watched as the sailors boarded the longboats and rowed toward the ships. Yesuntai threw an arm over my shoulders as we turned away from the sea and climbed toward Yeke Geren. "Jirandai," he murmured, "or perhaps I should call you Senadondo now, as your Long House brothers do. You must guide me in my new life. You will show me what I must do to become a Khan among these people."

He would not be my Khan. I had served him for the sake of the Flint People, not to make him a Khan, but would allow him his dream for a little while. Part of his vision would come to pass; the Long House People would have a great realm, and Yesuntai might inspire them to even greater valor. But I did not believe that the Hodenosaunee, a people who allowed all to raise their voices in their councils, would ever bow to a Khan and offer him total obedience. My son would honor Yesuntai as a brother, but would never kneel to him. Yesuntai's sons would be Ganeagaono warriors, bound to their mother's clan, not a Mongol prince's heirs.

I did not say this to Yesuntai. He would learn it in time, or be forced to surrender his dream to other leaders who would make it their own. The serpent that had wakened to disturb the lands of the Long House would grow, and slip westward to meet his tail.

ABOUT THE EDITORS

GREGORY BENFORD is the author of several acclaimed novels, including *Tides of Light, Great Sky River, Heart of the Comet* (with David Brin), *In the Ocean of Night, Across the Sea of Suns,* and *Timescape,* which won the Nebula Award, the British Science Fiction Award, the John W. Campbell Memorial Award, and the Australian Ditmar Award. Dr. Benford, a Woodrow Wilson Fellow, is a professor of physics at the University of California, Irvine. He and his wife live in Laguna Beach.

MARTIN H. GREENBERG is the editor or author of over 300 books, the majority of them anthologies in the science fiction, fantasy, horror, mystery, and western fields. He has collaborated editorially with such authors as Isaac Asimov, Robert Silverberg, Gregory Benford, and Frederik Pohl. A professor of political science at the University of Wisconsin, he lives with his wife and baby daughter in Green Bay.